"What Are You Doing Here in the Middle of the Night?"

"Swimming," she tossed at him, brave despite the fact that he held her captive.

He shifted as she continued to struggle beneath him. "Swimming," he repeated. He'd watched her walk out of the sea—perhaps it was as innocent as that. Of all the ill-timed . . . "You're not Greek," he murmured.

His thoughts underwent a rapid readjustment. She was an American, out for a moonlight swim. He'd have to play this one carefully, or there'd be hell to pay.

NORA ROBERTS
lives in Maryland's Blue Ridge Mountains with her two sons. She tends to favor American settings, heroines with spirit, and heroes who are tender as well as strong. She stresses relationships—not just romance—and considers humor an important element because she can't imagine a life without it.

Dear Reader:

There is an electricity between two people in love that makes everything they do magic, larger than life. This is what we bring you in SILHOUETTE INTIMATE MOMENTS.

SILHOUETTE INTIMATE MOMENTS are longer, more sensuous romance novels filled with adventure, suspense, glamor or melodrama. These books have an element no one else has tapped: excitement.

We are proud to present the very best romance has to offer from the very best romance writers. In the coming months look for some of your favorite authors such as Elizabeth Lowell, Nora Roberts, Erin St. Claire and Brooke Hastings.

SILHOUETTE INTIMATE MOMENTS are for the woman who wants more than she has ever had before. These books are for you.

Karen Solem
Editor-in-Chief
Silhouette Books

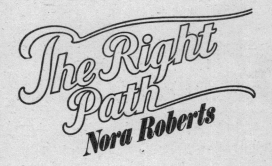

The Right Path

Nora Roberts

Silhouette Intimate Moments
Published by Silhouette Books New York
America's Publisher of Contemporary Romance

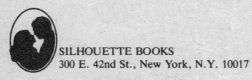
SILHOUETTE BOOKS
300 E. 42nd St., New York, N.Y. 10017

Copyright © 1985 by Nora Roberts

Distributed by Pocket Books

ISBN: 0-373-07085-3

First Silhouette Books printing March, 1985

10 9 8 7 6 5 4 3 2 1

America's Publisher of Contemporary Romance

Printed in the U.S.A.

Books by Nora Roberts

Silhouette Romance

Irish Thoroughbred #81
Blithe Images #127
Song of the West #143
Search for Love #163
Island of Flowers #180
From This Day #199
Her Mother's Keeper #215
Untamed #252
Storm Warning #274
Sullivan's Woman #280
Less of a Stranger #299

Silhouette Special Edition

The Heart's Victory #59
Reflections #100
Dance of Dreams #116
First Impressions #162
The Law Is a Lady #175
Opposites Attract #199

Silhouette Intimate Moments

Once More With Feeling #2
Tonight and Always #12
This Magic Moment #25
Endings and Beginnings #33
A Matter of Choice #49
Rules of the Game #70
The Right Path #85

Pocket Books

Promise Me Tomorrow

To Isabel, who understands me.

Chapter 1

THE SKY WAS CLOUDLESS—THE HARD, PERFECT BLUE of a summer painting. A breeze whispered through the roses in the garden. Mountains were misted by distance. A scent—flowers, sea, new grass—drifted on the air. With a sigh of pure pleasure, Morgan leaned farther over the balcony rail and just looked.

Had it really only been yesterday morning that she had looked out on New York's steel and concrete? Had she run through a chill April drizzle to catch a taxi to the airport? One day. It seemed impossible to go from one world to another in only a day.

But she was here, standing on the balcony of a villa on the Isle of Lesbos. There was no gray drizzle at all, but strong Greek sunlight. There was quiet, a deep blanketing stillness that contrasted completely with the fits and starts of New York traffic. If I could paint, Morgan mused, I'd paint this view and call it *Silence*.

"Come in," she called when there was a knock on the door. After one last deep breath, she turned, reluctantly.

"So, you're up and dressed." Liz swept in, a small, golden fairy with a tray-bearing maid in her wake.

"Room service." Morgan grinned as the maid placed the tray on a glass-topped table. "I'll begin to wallow in luxury from this moment." She took an appreciative sniff of the platters the maid uncovered. "Are you joining me?"

"Just for coffee." Liz settled in a chair, smoothing the skirts of her silk and lace robe, then took a long survey of the woman who sat opposite her.

Long loose curls in shades from ash blond to honey brown fell to tease pale shoulders. Almond-shaped eyes, almost too large for the slender face, were a nearly transparent blue. There was a straight, sharp nose and prominent cheekbones, a long, narrow mouth and a subtly pointed chin. It was a face of angles and contours that many a model starved herself for. It would photograph like a dream had Morgan ever been inclined to sit long enough to be captured on film.

What you'd get, Liz mused, would be a blur of color as Morgan dashed away to see what was around the next corner.

"Oh, Morgan, you look fabulous! I'm so glad you're here at last."

"Now that I'm here," Morgan returned, shifting her eyes back to the view, "I can't understand why I put off coming for so long. *Efxaristo,*" she added as the maid poured her coffee.

"Show-off," Liz said with mock scorn. "Do you know how long it took me to master a simple Greek hello, how are you? No, never mind." She waved her hand before Morgan could speak. The symphony of diamonds and sapphires in her wedding ring caught the flash of sunlight. "Three years married to Alex and living in Athens and Lesbos, and I still stumble over the language. Thank you, Zena," she added in English, dismissing the maid with a smile.

"You're simply determined not to learn." Morgan bit enthusiastically into a piece of toast. She wasn't hungry, she discovered. She was ravenous. "If you'd open your mind, the words would seep in."

"Listen to you." Liz wrinkled her nose. "Just because you speak a dozen languages."

"Five."

"Five is four more than a rational person requires."

"Not a rational interpreter," Morgan reminded her and dug wholeheartedly into her eggs. "And if I hadn't spoken Greek, I wouldn't have met Alex and you wouldn't be *Kryios* Elizabeth Theoharis. Fate," she announced with a full mouth, "is a strange and wonderful phenomenon."

"Philosophy at breakfast," Liz murmured into her coffee. "That's one of the things I've missed about you. Actually, I'd hate to think what might have happened if I hadn't been home on layover when Alex popped up. You wouldn't have introduced us." She commandeered a piece of toast, adding a miserly dab of plum jelly. "I'd still be serving miniature bottles of bourbon at thirty thousand feet."

"Liz, my love, when something's meant, it's meant." Morgan cut into a fat sausage. "I'd love to take credit for your marital bliss, but one brief introduction wasn't responsible for the fireworks that followed." She glanced up at the cool blond beauty and smiled. "Little did I know I'd lose my roommate in less than three weeks. I've never seen two people move so fast."

"We decided we'd get acquainted after we were married." A grin warmed Liz's face. "And we have."

"Where is Alex this morning?"

"Downstairs in his office." Liz moved her shoulders absently and left half her toast untouched. "He's building another ship or something."

Morgan laughed outright. "You say that in the same tone you'd use if he were building a model train. Don't you know you're supposed to become spoiled and disdainful when you marry a millionaire—especially a foreign millionaire?"

"Is that so? Well, I'll see what I can do." She topped off her coffee. "He'll probably be horribly busy for the next few weeks, which is one more reason I'm glad you're here."

"You need a cribbage partner."

"Hardly," Liz corrected as she struggled with a smile. "You're the worst cribbage player I know."

"Oh, I don't know," Morgan began as her brows drew together.

"Perhaps you've improved. Anyway," Liz went on, concealing with her coffee cup what was now a grin, "not to be disloyal to my adopted country, but it's just so good to have my best friend, and an honest-to-God American, around."

"*Spasibo.*"

"English at all times," Liz insisted. "And I know that wasn't even Greek. You aren't translating government hyperbole at the U.N. for the next four weeks.'' She leaned forward to rest her elbows on the table. ''Tell me the truth, Morgan, aren't you ever terrified you'll interpret some nuance incorrectly and cause World War III?''

''Who me?'' Morgan opened her eyes wide. ''Not a chance. Anyway, the trick is to think in the language you're interpreting. It's that easy.''

''Sure it is.'' Liz leaned back. ''Well, you're on vacation, so you only have to think in English. Unless you want to argue with the cook.''

''Absolutely not,'' Morgan assured her as she polished off her eggs.

''How's your father?''

''Marvelous, as always.'' Relaxed, content, Morgan poured more coffee. When was the last time she had taken the time for a second cup in the morning? Vacation, Liz had said. Well, she was damn well going to learn how to enjoy one. ''He sends you his love and wants me to smuggle some ouzo back to New York.''

''I'm not going to think about you going back.'' Liz rose and swirled around the balcony. The lace border at the hem of her robe swept over the tile. ''I'm going to find a suitable mate for you and establish you in Greece.''

''I can't tell you how much I appreciate your handling things for me,'' Morgan returned dryly.

''It's all right. What are friends for?'' Ignoring the sarcasm, Liz leaned back on the balcony. ''Dorian's a likely candidate. He's one of Alex's top men and really attractive. Blond and bronzed with a profile that belongs on a coin. You'll meet him tomorrow.''

"Should I tell Dad to arrange my dowry?"

"I'm serious." Folding her arms, Liz glared at Morgan's grin. "I'm not letting you go back without a fight. I'm going to fill your days with sun and sea, and dangle hordes of gorgeous men in front of your nose. You'll forget that New York and the U.N. exist."

"They're already wiped out of my mind . . . for the next four weeks." Morgan tossed her hair back over her shoulders. "So, satiate and dangle. I'm at your mercy. Are you going to drag me to the beach this morning? Force me to lie on the sand and soak up rays until I have a fabulous golden tan?"

"Exactly." With a brisk nod, Liz headed for the door. "Change. I'll meet you downstairs."

Thirty minutes later, Morgan decided she was going to like Liz's brand of brainwashing. White sand, blue water. She let herself drift on the gentle waves. *Too wrapped up in your work.* Isn't that what Dad said? *You're letting the job run you instead of the other way around.* Closing her eyes, Morgan rolled to float on her back. Between job pressure and the nasty breakup with Jack, she mused, I need a peace transfusion.

Jack was part of the past. Morgan was forced to admit that he had been more a habit than a passion. They'd suited each other's requirements. She had wanted an intelligent male companion; he an attractive woman whose manners would be advantageous to his political career.

If she'd loved him, Morgan reflected, she could hardly think of him so objectively, so . . . well, coldly. There was no ache, no loneliness. What there was, she admitted, was relief. But with the relief had come the odd feeling of being at loose ends. A feeling Morgan was neither used to nor enjoyed.

Liz's invitation had been perfectly timed. And this, she thought, opening her eyes to study that perfect sweep of sky, was paradise. Sun, sand, rock, flowers —the whispering memory of ancient gods and goddesses. Mysterious Turkey was close, separated only by the narrow Gulf of Edremit. She closed her eyes again and would have dozed if Liz's voice hadn't disturbed her.

"Morgan! Some of us have to eat at regular intervals."

"Always thinking of your stomach."

"And *your* skin," Liz countered from the edge of the water. "You're going to fry. You can overlook lunch, but not sunburn."

"All right, Mommy." Morgan swam in, then stood on shore and shook like a wet dog. "How come you can swim and lie in the sun and still look ready to walk into a ballroom?"

"Breeding," Liz told her and handed over the short robe. "Come on, Alex usually tears himself away from his ships for lunch."

I could get used to eating on terraces, Morgan thought after lunch was finished. They relaxed over iced coffee and fruit. She noted that Alexander Theoharis was still as fascinated with his small, golden wife as he had been three years before in New York.

Though she'd brushed off Liz's words that morning, Morgan felt a certain pride at having brought them together. A perfect match, she mused. Alex had an old world charm—dark aquiline looks made dashing by a thin white scar above his eyebrow. He was only slightly above average height but with a leanness that was more aristocratic than rangy. It was the ideal complement for Liz's dainty blond beauty.

"I don't see how you ever drag yourself away from here," Morgan told him. "If this were all mine, nothing would induce me to leave."

Alex followed her gaze across the glimpse of sea to the mountains. "But when one returns, it's all the more magnificent. Like a woman," he continued, lifting Liz's hand to kiss, "paradise demands constant appreciation."

"It's got mine," Morgan stated.

"I'm working on her, Alex." Liz laced her fingers with his. "I'm going to make a list of all the eligible men within a hundred miles."

"You don't have a brother, do you, Alex?" Morgan asked, sending him a smile.

"Sisters only. My apologies."

"Forget it, Liz."

"If we can't entice you into matrimony, Alex will have to offer you a job in the Athens office."

"I'd steal Morgan from the U.N. in a moment," Alex reminded her with a move of his shoulders. "I couldn't lure her away three years ago. I tried."

"We have a month to wear her down this time." She shot Alex a quick glance. "Let's take her out on the yacht tomorrow."

"Of course." He agreed immediately. "We'll make a day of it. Would you like that, Morgan?"

"Oh, well, I'm constantly spending the day on a yacht on the Aegean, but"—her lake-blue eyes lit with laughter—"since Liz wants to, I'll try not to be too bored."

"She's such a good sport," Liz confided to Alex.

It was just past midnight when Morgan made her way down to the beach again. Sleep had refused to come. Morgan welcomed the insomnia, seeing it as an excuse to walk out into the warm spring night.

The light was liquid. The moon was sliced in half but held a white, gleaming brightness. Cypresses which flanked the steps down to the beach were silvered with it. The scent of blossoms, hot and pungent during the day, seemed more mysterious, more exotic, by moonlight.

From somewhere in the distance, she heard the low rumble of a motor. A late-night fisherman, she thought, and smiled. It would be quite an adventure to fish under the moon.

The beach spread in a wide half circle. Morgan dropped both her towel and wrap on a rock, then ran into the water. Against her skin it was so cool and silky that she toyed with the idea of discarding even the brief bikini. Better not, she thought with a low laugh. No use tempting the ghosts of the gods.

Though the thought of adventure appealed to her, she kept to the open bay and suppressed the urge to explore the inlets. They'd still be there in the daylight, she reminded herself. She swam lazily, giving her strokes just enough power to keep her afloat. She hadn't come for the exercise.

Even when her body began to feel the chill, she lingered. There were stars glistening on the water, and silence. Such silence. Strange, that until she had found it, she hadn't known she was looking for it.

New York seemed more than a continent away, it seemed centuries away. For the moment, she was content that it be so. Here she could indulge in the fantasies that never seemed appropriate in the rush of day-to-day living. Here she could let herself believe in ancient gods, in shining knights and bold pirates. A laugh bubbled from her as she submerged and rose again. Gods, knights, and pirates . . . well, she supposed she'd take the pirate if she had her pick. Gods were too bloodthirsty, knights too chivalrous, but a pirate . . .

Shaking her head, Morgan wondered how her thoughts had taken that peculiar turn. It must be Liz's influence, she decided. Morgan reminded herself she didn't want a pirate or any other man. What she wanted was peace.

With a sigh, she stood knee-deep in the water, letting the drops stream down her hair and skin. She was cold now, but the cold was exhilarating. Ignoring her wrap, she sat on the rock and pulled a comb from its pocket and idly ran it through her hair. Moon, sand, water. What more could there be? She was, for one brief moment, in total harmony with her own spirit and with nature's.

Shock gripped her as a hand clamped hard over her mouth. She struggled, instinctively, but an arm was banded around her waist—rough cloth scraping her naked skin. Dragged from the rock, Morgan found herself molded against a solid, muscular chest.

Rape? It was the first clear thought before the panic. She kicked out blindly as she was pulled into the cover of trees. The shadows were deep there. Fighting wildly, she raked with her nails wherever she could reach, feeling only a brief satisfaction at the hiss of an undrawn breath near her ear.

"Don't make a sound." The order was in quick, harsh Greek. About to strike out again, Morgan felt her blood freeze. A glimmer of a knife caught the moonlight just before she was thrust to the ground under the length of the man's body. "Wildcat," he muttered. "Keep still and I won't have to hurt you. Do you understand?"

Numb with terror, Morgan nodded. With her eyes glued to his knife, she lay perfectly still. I can't fight him now, she thought grimly. Not now, but somehow, somehow I'll find out who he is. He'll pay.

The first panic was gone, but her body still trembled as she waited. It seemed an eternity, but he made no move, no sound. It was so quiet, she could hear the waves lapping gently against the sand only a few feet away. Over her head, through the spaces in the leaves, stars still shone. It must be a nightmare, she told herself. It can't be real. But when she tried to shift under him, the pressure of his body on hers proved that it was very, very real.

The hand over her mouth choked her breath until vague colors began to dance before her eyes. Morgan squeezed them tight for a moment to fight the faintness. Then she heard him speak again to a companion she couldn't see.

"What do you hear?"

"Nothing yet—in a moment." The voice that answered was rough and brisk. "Who the devil is she?"

"It doesn't matter. She'll be dealt with."

The roaring in her ears made it difficult to translate the Greek. Dealt with? she thought, dizzy again from fear and the lack of air.

The second man said something low and furious about women, then spat into the dirt.

"Just keep your ears open," Morgan's captor ordered. "And leave the woman to me."

"Now."

She felt him stiffen, but her eyes never left the knife. He was gripping it tighter now, she saw the tensing of his fingers on the handle.

Footsteps. They echoed on the rock steps of the beach. Hearing them, Morgan began to struggle again with the fierce strength of panic and of hope. With a whispered oath, he put more of his weight on her. He smelt faintly of the sea. As he shifted she caught a brief glimpse of his face in a patchy stream of moonlight. She saw dark, angular features, a grim mouth, and narrowed jet eyes. They were hard and cold and ruthless. It was the face of a man prepared to kill.

Why? She thought as her mind began to float. I don't even know him.

"Follow him," he ordered his companion. Morgan heard a slight stirring in the leaves. "I'll take care of the woman."

Morgan's eyes widened at the sharp glimmer of the blade. She tasted something—bitter, copper—in her throat, but didn't recognize it as terror. The world spun to the point of a pin, then vanished.

The sky was full of stars, silver against black. The sea whispered. Against her back, the sand was rough. Morgan rose on her elbow and tried to clear her head. Fainted? Good God, had she actually fainted? Had she simply fallen asleep and dreamed it all? Rubbing her fingers against her temple, she wondered if her fantasies about pirates had caused her to hallucinate.

A small sound brought her swiftly to her feet. No, it had been real, and he was back. Morgan hurled herself at the shadow as it approached. She'd accepted the inevitability of death once without a struggle. This time, he was going to have a hell of a fight on his hands.

The shadow grunted softly as she struck, then Morgan found herself captured again, under him with the sand scraping her back.

"*Diabolos!* Be still!" he ordered in furious Greek as she tried to rip at his face.

"The hell I will!" Morgan tossed back in equally furious English. She fought with every ounce of strength until he pinned her, spread eagle beneath him. Breathless, fearless in her rage, she stared up at him.

Looking down, he studied her with frown. "You're not Greek." The statement, uttered in surprised and impatient English, stopped her struggles. "Who are you?"

"None of your business." She tried, and failed, to jerk her wrists free of his hold.

"Stop squirming," he ordered roughly, as his fingers clamped down harder. He wasn't thinking of his strength or her fragility, but that she wasn't simply a native who had been in the wrong place at the wrong time. His profession had taught him to get answers and adjust for complications. "What were you doing on the beach in the middle of the night?"

"Swimming," she tossed back. "Any idiot should be able to figure that out."

He swore, then shifted as she continued to struggle beneath him. "Damn it, be still!" His brows were lowered, not in anger now but concentration. "Swimming," he repeated as his eyes narrowed again. He'd watched her walk out of the sea—perhaps it was as innocent as that. "American," he mused, ignoring Morgan's thrashing. Weren't the Theoharises expecting an American woman? Of all the ill-timed . . . "You're not Greek," he murmured again.

"Neither are you," Morgan said between clenched teeth.

"Half." His thoughts underwent some rapid readjustments. The Theoharises' American houseguest, out for a moonlight swim—he'd have to play this one carefully or there'd be hell to pay. Quite suddenly, he flashed her a smile. "You had me fooled. I thought you could understand me."

"I understood perfectly," she retorted. "And you won't find it an easy rape now that you don't have your knife out."

"Rape?" Apparently astonished, he stared at her. His laughter was as sudden as the smile. "I hadn't given that much thought. In any case, Aphrodite, the knife was never intended for you."

"Then what do you mean by dragging me around like that? Flashing a knife in my face and nearly suffocating me?" Fury was much more satisfying than fear, and Morgan went with it. "Let me go!" She pushed at him with her body, but couldn't nudge him.

"In a moment," he said pleasantly. The moonlight played on her skin, and he enjoyed it. A fabulous face, he mused, now that he had time to study it. She'd be a woman accustomed to male admiration. Perhaps charm would distract her from the rather unique aspect of their meeting. "I can only say that what I did was for your own protection."

"Protection!" she flung back at him and tried to wrench her arms free.

"There wasn't time for amenities, fair lady. My apologies if my . . . technique was unrefined." His tone seemed to take it for granted that she would understand. "Tell me, why were you out alone, sitting like Lorelei on the rock and combing your hair?"

"That's none of your business." His voice had dropped, becoming low and seductive. The dark eyes had softened and appeared depthless. She could almost believe she had imagined the ruthlessness she'd glimpsed in the shadows. But she felt the light throbbing where his fingers had gripped her flesh. "I'm going to scream if you don't let me go."

Her body was tempting now that he had time to appreciate it, but he rose with a shrug. There was still work to be done that night. "My apologies for your inconvenience."

"Oh, is that right?" Struggling to her feet, Morgan began to brush at the sand that clung to her skin. "You have your nerve, dragging me off into the bushes, smothering me, brandishing a knife in my face, then apologizing like you've just stepped on my toe." Suddenly cold, she wrapped her arms around herself. "Just who are you and what was this all about?"

"Here." Stooping, he picked up the wrap he had dropped in order to hold her off. "I was bringing this to you when you launched your attack." He grinned as she shrugged into the wrap. It was a pity to cover that lengthy, intriguing body. "Who I am at the moment isn't relevant. As for the rest"—again the smooth, easy shrug—"I can't tell you."

"Just like that?" With a quick nod, Morgan turned and stalked to the beach steps. "We'll see what the police have to say about it."

"I wouldn't if I were you."

The advice was quiet, but vibrated with command. Hesitating, Morgan turned at the base of the steps to study him. He wasn't threatening now. What she felt wasn't fear, but his authority. He was quite tall, she noticed suddenly. And the moonlight played tricks with his face, making it almost cruel one moment, charming the next. Now it held all the confidence of Lucifer regrouping after the Fall.

Looking at him, she remembered the feel of hard, wiry muscles. He was standing easily, hands thrust into the pockets of jeans. The aura of command fit him perfectly. His smile didn't disguise it, nor did his casual stance. Damn pirates, she thought, feeling a quick twinge. Only lunatics find them attractive. Because she felt vulnerable, Morgan countered with bravado.

"Wouldn't you?" She lifted her chin and walked back to him.

"No," he answered mildly. "But perhaps, unlike me, you look for complications. I'm a simple man." He took a long, searching look of her face. *This is not,* he decided instantly, *a simple woman.* Though in his mind he cursed her, he went on conversationally. "Questions, reports to fill out, hours wasted on red tape. And then, even if you had my name''—he shrugged and flashed the grin again—''no one would believe you, Aphrodite. No one.''

She didn't trust that grin—or the sultry way he called her by the goddess's name. She didn't trust the sudden warmth in her blood. ''I wouldn't be so sure,'' Morgan began, but he cut her off, closing the slight distance between them.

''And I didn't rape you.'' Slowly, he ran his hands down her hair until they rested on her shoulders. His fingers didn't bite into her flesh now, but skimmed lazily. She had the eyes of a witch, he thought, and the face of a goddess. His time was short, but the moment was not to be missed. ''Until now, I haven't even given into the urge to do this.''

His mouth closed over hers, hot and stunningly sweet. She hadn't been prepared for it. She pushed against him, but it was strictly out of reflex and lacked strength. He was a man who knew a woman's weakness. Deliberately, he brought her close, using style rather than force.

The scent of the sea rose to surround her, and heat—such a furnace heat that seemed to come from within and without at the same time. Almost leisurely, he explored her mouth until her heart thudded wildly against the quick, steady beat of his. His hands were clever, sliding beneath the wide sleeves of her robe to tease and caress the length of her arms, the slope of her shoulders.

When her struggles ceased, he nibbled at her lips as if he would draw out more taste. Slow, easy. His tongue tempted hers then retreated, then slipped through her parted lips again to torment and savor. For a moment, Morgan feared she would faint for a second time in his arms.

"One kiss," he murmured against her lips, "is hardly a criminal offense." She was sweeter than he had imagined and, he realized as desire stirred hotly, deadlier. "I could take another with little more risk."

"No." Coming abruptly to her senses, Morgan pushed away from him. "You're mad. And you're madder still if you think I'm going to let this go. I'm going—" She broke off as her hand lifted to her throat in a nervous gesture. The chain which always hung there was missing. Morgan glanced down, then brought her eyes back to his, furious, glowing.

"What have you done with my medal?" she demanded. "Give it back to me."

"I'm afraid I don't have it, Aphrodite."

"I want it back." Bravado wasn't a pose this time; she was livid. She stepped closer until they were toe to toe. "It's not worth anything to you. You won't be able to get more than a few drachmas for it."

His eyes narrowed. "I didn't take your medal. I'm not a thief." The temper in his voice was cold, coated with control. "If I were going to steal something from you, I would have found something more interesting than a medal."

Her eyes filled in a rush, and she swung out her hand to slap him. He caught her wrist, adding frustration to fury.

"It appears the medal is important," he said softly, but his hand was no longer gentle. "A token from a lover?"

"A gift from someone I love," Morgan countered.

"I wouldn't expect a man like you to understand its value." With a jerk, she pulled her wrist from his hold. "I won't forget you," she promised, then turned and flew up the stairs.

He watched her until she was swallowed by the darkness. After a moment he turned back to the beach.

Chapter 2

THE SUN WAS A WHITE FLASH OF LIGHT. ITS DIA-
monds skimmed the water's surface. With the gentle
movement of the yacht, Morgan found herself half-
dozing.

Could the moonlit beach and the man have been a
dream? she wondered hazily. Knives and rough hands
and sudden draining kisses from strangers had no place
in the real world. They belonged in one of those
strange, half remembered dreams she had when the
rush and demands of work and the city threatened to
become too much for her. She'd always considered
them her personal release valve. Harmless, but absolutely secret—something she'd never considered telling
Jack or any of her co-workers.

If it hadn't been for the absence of her medal, and
the light trail of bruises on her arms, Morgan could

have believed the entire incident had been the product of an overworked imagination.

Sighing, she shifted her back to the sun, pillowing her head on her hands. Her skin, slick with oil, glistened. Why was she keeping the whole crazy business from Liz and Alex? Grimacing, she flexed her shoulders. They'd be horrified if she told them she'd been assaulted. Morgan could all but see Alex placing her under armed guard for the rest of her stay on Lesbos. He'd make certain there was an investigation —complicated, time-consuming, and in all probability fruitless. Morgan could work up a strong hate for the dark man for being right.

And what, if she decided to pursue it, could she tell the police? She hadn't been hurt or sexually assaulted. There'd been no verbal threat she could pin down, not even the slimmest motivation for what had happened. And what had happened? she demanded of herself. A man had dragged her into the bushes, held her there for no clear reason, then had let her go without harming her.

The Greek police wouldn't see the kiss as a criminal offense. She hadn't been robbed. There was no way on earth to prove the man had taken her medal. And damn it, she added with a sigh, as much as she'd like to assign all sorts of evil attributes to him, he just didn't fit the role of a petty thief. Petty anything, she thought grudgingly. Whatever he did, she was certain he did big . . . and did well.

So what was she going to do about it? True, he'd frightened and infuriated her—the second was probably a direct result of the first—but what else was there?

If and when they caught him, it would be his word against hers. Somehow, Morgan thought his word would carry more weight.

So I was frightened—my pride took a lump. She shrugged and shifted her head on her hands. It's not worth upsetting Liz and Alex. Midnight madness, she mused. Another strange adventure in the life and times of Morgan James. File it and forget it.

Hearing Alex mount the steps to the sun deck, Morgan rested her chin on her hands and smiled at him. On the lounger beside her, Liz stirred and slept on.

"So, the sun has put her to sleep." Alex mounted the last of the steps, then settled into the chair beside his wife.

"I nearly dozed off myself." With a yawn, Morgan stretched luxuriously before she rolled over to adjust the lounger to a sitting position. "But I didn't want to miss anything." Gazing over the water, she studied the clump of land in the distance. The island seemed to float, as insubstantial as a mist.

"Chios," Alex told her, following her gaze. "And"—he gestured, waiting for her eyes to shift in the direction of his—"The coast of Turkey."

"So close," Morgan mused. "It seems as though I could swim to it."

"At sea, the distance can be deceiving." He flicked a lighter at the end of a black cigarette. The fragrance that rose from it was faintly sweet and exotic. "You'd have to be a hardy swimmer. Easy enough with a boat, though. There are some who find the proximity profitable." At Morgan's blank expression, Alex laughed. "Smuggling, innocence. It's still popular even though the punishment is severe."

"Smuggling," she murmured, intrigued. Then the word put her in mind of pirates again and her curious expression turned into a frown. A nasty business, she reminded herself, and not romantic at all.

"The coast," Alex made another gesture, sweeping, with the elegant cigarette held between two long fingers. "The many bays and peninsulas, offshore islands, inlets. There's simple access from the sea to the interior."

She nodded. Yes, a nasty business—they weren't talking about French brandy or Spanish lace. "Opium?"

"Among other things."

"But Alex." His careless acceptance caused her frown to deepen. Once she'd sorted it through, Morgan's own sense of right and wrong had little middle ground. "Doesn't it bother you?"

"Bother me?" he repeated, taking a long, slow drag on the cigarette. "Why?"

Flustered with the question, she sat up straighter. "Aren't you concerned about that sort of thing going on so close to your own home?"

"Morgan." Alex spread his hands in an acceptance of fate. The thick chunk of gold on his left pinky gleamed dully in the sunlight. "My concern would hardly stop what's been going on for centuries."

"But still, with crime practically in your own backyard . . ." She broke off, thinking about the streets of Manhattan. Perhaps she was the pot calling the kettle black. "I supposed I'd think you'd be annoyed," she finished.

His eyes lit with a touch of amusement before he shrugged. "I leave the matter—and the annoyance—to the patrols and authorities. Tell me, are you enjoying your stay so far?''

Morgan started to speak again, then consciously smoothed away the frown. Alex was old world enough not to want to discuss unpleasantries with a guest. ''It's wonderful here, Alex. I can see why Liz loves it.''

He flashed her a grin before he drew in strong tobacco. ''You know Liz wants you to stay. She's missed you. At times, I feel very guilty because we don't get to America to see you often enough.''

''You don't have to feel guilty, Alex.'' Morgan pushed on sunglasses and relaxed again. After all, she reflected, smuggling had nothing to do with her. ''Liz is happy.''

''She'd be happier with you here.''

''Alex,'' Morgan began with a smile for his indulgence of his wife. ''I can't simply move in as a companion, no matter how much both of us love Liz.''

''You're still dedicated to your job at the U.N.?'' His tone had altered slightly, but Morgan sensed the change. It was business now.

''I like my work. I'm good at it, and I need the challenge.''

''I'm a generous employer, Morgan, particularly to one with your capabilities.'' He took another long, slow drag, studying her through the mist of smoke. ''I asked you to come work for me three years ago. If I hadn't been''—he glanced down at Liz's sleeping figure—''distracted''—he decided with a mild smile—''I would have taken more time to convince you to accept.''

''Distracted?'' Liz pushed her sunglasses up to her forehead and peered at him from under them.

"Eavesdropping," Morgan said with a sniff. A uniformed steward set three iced drinks on the table. She lifted one and drank. "Your manners always were appalling."

"You have a few weeks yet to think it over, Morgan." Tenacity beneath a smooth delivery was one of Alex's most successful business tactics. "But I warn you, Liz will be more persistent with her other solution." He shrugged, reaching for his own drink. "And I must agree—a woman needs a husband and security."

"How very Greek of you," Morgan commented dryly.

His grin flashed without apology. "I'm afraid one of Liz's candidates will be delayed. Dorian won't join us until tomorrow. He's bringing my cousin Iona with him."

"Marvelous." Liz's response was drenched in sarcasm. Alex sent her a frown.

"Liz isn't fond of Iona, but she's family." The quiet look he sent his wife told Morgan the subject had been discussed before. "I have a responsibility."

Liz took the last glass with a sigh of acceptance. Briefly she touched her hand to his. "We have a responsibility," she corrected. "Iona's welcome."

Alex's frown turned into a look of love so quickly, Morgan gave a mock groan. "Don't you two ever fight? I mean, don't you realize it isn't healthy to be so well balanced?"

Liz's eyes danced over the rim of her glass. "We have our moments, I suppose. A week ago I was furious with him for at least—ah, fifteen minutes."

"That," Morgan said positively, "is disgusting."

"So," Alex mused, "you think a man and woman must fight to be . . . healthy?"

Shaking back her hair, Morgan laughed. "*I* have to fight to be healthy."

"Morgan, you haven't mentioned Jack at all. Is there a problem?"

"Liz." Alex's disapproval was clear in the single syllable.

"No, it's all right, Alex." Taking her glass, Morgan rose and moved to the rail. "It's not a problem," she said slowly. "At least I hope it's not." She stared into her drink, frowning, as if she wasn't quite sure what the glass contained. "I've been running on this path— this very straight, very defined path. I could run it blindfolded." With a quick laugh, Morgan leaned out on the rail to let the wind grab at her hair. "Suddenly, I discovered it wasn't a path, but a rut and it kept getting deeper. I decided to change course before it became a pit."

"You always did prefer an obstacle course," Liz murmured. But she was pleased with Jack's disposal, and took little trouble to hide it.

The sea churned in a white froth behind the boat. Morgan turned from her study of it. "I don't intend to fall at Dorian's feet, Liz—or anyone else you might have in mind—just because Jack and I are no longer involved."

"I should hope not," Liz returned with some spirit. "That would take all the fun out of it."

With a sigh of exasperated affection, Morgan turned back to the rail.

The stark mountains of Lesbos rose from the sea. Jagged, harsh, timeless. Morgan could make out the pure white lines of Alex's villa. She thought it looked like a virgin offering to the gods—cool, classic, certainly feminine. Higher still was a rambling gray structure which seemed hewn from the rock itself. It faced the sea; indeed, it loomed over it. As if challenging Poseidon to claim it, it clung to the cliff. Morgan saw it as arrogant, rough, masculine. The flowering vines which grew all around it didn't soften the appearance, but added a haunted kind of beauty.

There were other buildings—a white-washed village, snuggled cottages, one or two other houses on more sophisticated lines, but the two larger structures hovered over the rest. One was elegant; one was savage.

"Who does that belong to?" Morgan called over her shoulder. "It's incredible."

Following her gaze, Liz grinned and rose to join her. "I should have known that would appeal to you. Sometimes I'd swear it's alive. Nicholas Gregoras, olive oil, and more recently, import-export." She glanced at her friend's profile. "Maybe I'll include him for dinner tomorrow if he's free, though I don't think he's your type."

Morgan gave her a dry look. "Oh? And what is my type?"

"Someone who'll give you plenty to fight about. Who'll give you that obstacle course."

"*Hmm.* You know me too well."

"As for Nick, he's rather smooth and certainly a charmer." Liz tapped a fingernail against the rail as she considered. "Not as blatantly handsome as Dorian, but he has a rather basic sort of sex appeal. Earthier, and yet . . ." She trailed off, narrowing her eyes as she tried to pigeonhole him. "Well, he's an odd one. I suppose he'd have to be to live in a house like that. He's in his early thirties, inherited the olive oil empire almost ten years ago. Then he branched into import-export. He seems to have a flair for it. Alex is very fond of him because they go back to short pants together."

"Liz, I only wanted to know who owned the house. I didn't ask for a biography."

"These facts are part of the service." She cupped her hands around her lighter and lit a cigarette. "I want to give you a clear picture of your options."

"Haven't you got a goatherd up your sleeve?" Morgan demanded. "I rather like the idea of a small, white-washed cottage and baking black bread."

"I'll see what I can do."

"I don't suppose it occurs to you or Alex that I'm content to be single—the modern, capable woman on her own? I know how to use a screwdriver, how to change a flat tire . . ."

"'Methinks she doth protest too much,'" Liz quoted mildly.

"Liz—"

"I love you, Morgan."

On a frustrated sigh, Morgan lifted her drink again. "Damn it, Liz," she murmured.

"Come on, let me have my fun," she coaxed, giving Morgan a friendly pat on the cheek. "As you said yourself, it's all up to fate anyway."

"Hoist by my own petard. All right, bring on your Dorians and your Nicks and your Lysanders."

"Lysander?"

"It's a good name for a goatherd."

With a chuckle, Liz flicked her cigarette into the churning water. "Just wait and see if I don't find one."

"Liz . . ." Morgan hesitated for a moment, then asked casually, "Do many people use the beach where we swam yesterday?"

"Hmm? Oh." She tucked a pale blond strand behind her ear. "Not really. It's used by us and the Gregoras villa for the most part. I'd have to ask Alex who owns it, I've never given it any thought. The bay's secluded and only easily accessible by the beach steps which run between the properties. Oh, yes, there's a cottage Nick owns which he rents out occasionally," she remembered. "It's occupied now by an American. Stevens . . . no," she corrected herself. "Stevenson. Andrew Stevenson, a poet or a painter or something. I haven't met him yet." She gave Morgan a frank stare. "Why? Did you plan for an allover tan?"

"Just curious." Morgan rearranged her thoughts. If she was going to file it and forget it, she had to stop letting the incident play back in her mind. "I'd love to get a close look at that place." She gestured toward the gray villa. "I think the architect must have been just a little mad. It's fabulous."

"Use some charm on Nick and get yourself an invitation," Liz suggested.

"I might just do that." Morgan studied the villa consideringly. She wondered if Nick Gregoros was the man whose footsteps she had heard when she had been held in the bushes. "Yes, I might just."

That evening, Morgan left the balcony doors wide. She wanted the warmth and scents of the night. The house was quiet but for the single stroke of a clock that signaled the hour. For the second night in a row she was wide awake. Did people really sleep on vacations? she wondered. What a waste of time.

She sat at the small rosewood desk in her room, writing a letter. From somewhere between the house and the sea, an owl cried out twice. She paused to listen, hoping it would call again, but there was only silence. How could she describe how it felt to see Mount Olympus rising from the sea? Was it possible to describe the timelessness, the strength, the almost frightening beauty?

She shrugged, and did what she could to explain the sensation to her father on paper. He'd understand, she mused as she folded the stationery. Who understood better her sometimes whimsical streaks of fancy than the man she'd inherited them from? And, she thought with a lurking smile, he'd get a good chuckle at Liz's determination to marry her off and keep her in Greece.

She rose, stretched once, then turned and collided with a hard chest. The hand that covered her mouth used more gentleness this time, and the jet eyes laughed into hers. Her heart rose, then fell like an elevator with its cable clipped.

"*Kalespera*, Aphrodite. Your word that you won't scream, and you have your freedom."

Instinctively she tried to jerk away, but he held her still without effort, only lifting an ironic brow. He was a man who knew whose word to accept and whose word to doubt.

Morgan struggled for another moment, then finding herself outmatched, reluctantly nodded. He released her immediately.

She drew in the breath to shout, then let it out in a frustrated huff. A promise was a promise, even if it was to a devil. "How did you get in here?" she demanded.

"The vines to your balcony are sturdy."

"You climbed?" Her incredulity was laced with helpless admiration. The walls were sheer, the height was dizzying. "You must be mad."

"That's a possibility," he said with a careless smile.

He seemed none the worse for wear after the climb. His hair was disheveled, but then she'd never seen it otherwise. There was a shadow of beard on his chin. His eyes held no strain or fatigue, but rather a light of adventure that drew her no matter how hard she tried to resist. In the lamplight she could see him more clearly than she had the night before. His features weren't as harsh as she had thought and his mouth wasn't grim. It was really quite beautiful, she realized with a flood of annoyance.

"What do you want?"

He smiled again, letting his gaze roam down her leisurely with an insolence she knew wasn't contrived but inherent. She wore only a brief cinnamon-colored teddy that dipped low at the breast and rose high at the thighs. Morgan noted the look, and that he stood squarely between her and the closet where she had left her robe. Rather than acknowledge the disadvantage, she tilted her chin.

"How did you know where to find me?"

"It's my business to find things out," he answered. Silently, he approved more than her form, but her courage as well. "Morgan James," he began. "Visiting friend of Elizabeth Theoharis. American, living in New York. Unmarried. Employed at the U.N. as interpreter. You speak Greek, English, French, Italian, and Russian.''

She tried not to let her mouth fall open at his careless rundown on her life. ''That's a very tidy summary,'' she said tightly.

''Thank you. I try to be succinct.''

''What does any of that have to do with you?''

''That's yet to be decided.'' He studied her, thinking again. It might be that he could employ her talents and position for his own uses. The package was good, very good. And so, more important at the moment, was the mind.

''You're enjoying your stay on Lesbos?''

Morgan stared at him, then slowly shook her head. No, he wasn't a ruffian or a rapist. That much she was sure of. If he were a thief, which she still reserved judgment on, he was no ordinary one. He spoke too well, moved too well. What he had was a certain amount of odd charm, a flair that was hard to resist, and an amazing amount of arrogance. Under different circumstances, she might even have liked him.

''You have incredible gall,'' she decided.

''You continue to flatter me.''

''All right.'' Tight-lipped, Morgan strode over to the open balcony doors and gestured meaningfully. ''I gave you my word I wouldn't scream, and I didn't. But I have no intention of standing here making idle conversation with a lunatic. Out!''

With his lips still curved in a smile, he sat on the edge of the bed and studied her. ''I admire a woman of her word.'' He stretched out jean-clad legs and crossed his feet. ''I find a great deal to admire about you,

Morgan. Last night you showed good sense and courage—rare traits to find together.''

"Forgive me if I'm not overwhelmed.''

He caught the sarcasm, but more important, noted the change in her eyes. She wasn't as angry as she tried to be. "I did apologize,'' he reminded her and smiled.

Her breath came out in a long-suffering sigh. She could detest him for making her want to laugh when she should be furious. Just who the devil was he? He wasn't the mad rapist she had first thought—he wasn't a common thief. So just what was he? Morgan stopped herself before she asked—she was better off in ignorance.

"It didn't seem like much of an apology to me.''

"If I make a more . . . honest attempt,'' he began with a bland sincerity that made her lips twitch, "would you accept?''

Firmly, she banked down on the urge to return his smile. "If I accept it, will you go away?''

"But I find your company so pleasant.''

An irrepressible light of humor flickered in her eyes. "The hell you do.''

"Aphrodite, you wound me.''

"I'd like to draw and quarter you. Are you going to go away?''

"Soon.'' Smiling, he rose again. What was that scent that drifted from her? he wondered. It was not quite sweet, not quite tame. Jasmine—wild jasmine. It suited her. He moved to the dresser to toy with her hand mirror. "You'll meet Dorian Zoulas and Iona Theoharis tomorrow,'' he said casually. This time Morgan's mouth did drop. "There's little on the island I'm not aware of,'' he said mildly.

"Apparently," she agreed.

Now he noted a hint of curiosity in her tone. It was what he had hoped for. "Perhaps, another time, you'll give me your impression of them."

Morgan shook her head more from bafflement than offense. "I have no intention of there being another time, or of gossiping with you. I hardly see why—"

"Why not?" he countered.

"I don't *know* you," she said in frustration. "I don't know this Dorian or Iona either. And I don't understand how you could possibly—"

"True," he agreed with a slight nod. "How well do you know Alex?"

Morgan ran a hand through her hair. *Here I am, wearing little more than my dignity, exchanging small talk with a maniac who climbed in the third-story window.* "Look, I'm not discussing Alex with you. I'm not discussing anyone or anything with you. Go away."

"We'll leave that for later too, then," he said mildly as he crossed back to her. "I have something for you." He reached into his pocket, then opened his hand and dangled a small silver medal by its chain.

"Oh, you did have it!" Morgan grabbed, only to have him whip it out of her reach. His eyes hardened with fury.

"I told you once, I'm no thief." The change in his voice and face had been swift and potent. Involuntarily, she took a step away. His mouth tightened at the movement before he went on in a more controlled tone. "I went back and found it in the grove. The chain had to be repaired, I'm afraid."

With his eyes on hers, he held it out again. Taking it,

Morgan began to fasten it around her neck. "You're a very considerate assailant."

"Do you think I enjoyed hurting you?"

Her hands froze at the nape of her neck. There was no teasing banter in his tone now, no insolent light of amusement in his eyes. This was the man she recognized from the shadows. Waves of temper came from him, hardening his voice, burning in his jet eyes. With her hands still lifted, Morgan stared at him.

"Do you think I enjoyed frightening you into fainting, having you think I would murder you? Do you think it gives me pleasure to see there are bruises on you and know that I put them there?" He whirled away, stalking the room. "I'm not a man who makes a habit of misusing women."

"I wouldn't know about that," she said steadily.

He stopped, and his eyes came back to hers. Damn, she was cool, he thought. And beautiful. Beautiful enough to be a distraction when he couldn't afford one.

"I don't know who you are or what you're mixed up in," she continued. Her fingers trembled a bit as she finished fastening the chain, but her voice was calm and unhurried. "Frankly, I don't care as long as you leave me alone. Under different circumstances, I'd thank you for the return of my property, but I don't feel it applies in this case. You can leave the same way you came in."

He had to bank down on an urge to throttle her. It wasn't often he was in the position of having a half-naked woman order him from her bedroom three times in one evening. He might have found it amusing if he hadn't been fighting an overwhelming flood of pure and simple desire.

The hell with fighting it, he thought. A woman who kept her chin lifted in challenge deserved to be taken up on it.

"Courage becomes you, Morgan," he said coolly. "We might do very well together." Reaching out, he fingered the medal at her throat and frowned at it. With a silent oath, he tightened his grip on the chain and brought his eyes back to hers.

There was no fear in those clear blue pools now, but a light, maddening disdain. A woman like this, he thought, could make a man mad, make him suffer and ache. And by God, a woman like this would be worth it.

"I told you to go," she said icily, ignoring the sudden quick thud of her pulse. It wasn't fear—Morgan told herself she was through with fear. But neither was it the anger she falsely named it.

"And so I will," he murmured and let the chain drop. "In the meantime, since you don't offer, I take."

Once again she found herself in his arms. It wasn't the teasing, seductive kiss of the night before. Now he devoured her. No one had kissed her like this before— as if he knew every secret she horded. He would know, somehow, where she needed to be touched.

The hot, insistent flow of desire that ran through her left her too stunned to struggle, too hungry to reason. How could she want him? her mind demanded. How could she want a man like this to touch her? But her mouth was moving under his, she couldn't deny it. Her tongue met his. Her hands gripped his shoulders, but didn't push him away.

"There's honey on your lips, Morgan," he murmured. ''Enough to drive a man mad for another taste.''

He took his hand on a slow journey down her back, pressing silk against her skin before he came to the hem. His fingers were strong, calloused, and as clever as a musician's. Without knowing, without caring what she did, Morgan framed his face with her hands for a moment before they dove into his hair. The muttered Greek she heard from him wasn't a love word but an oath as he dragged her closer.

How well she knew that body now. Long and lean and wiry with muscle. She could smell the sea on it, almost taste it beneath that hot demand as his mouth continued to savage hers.

The kiss grew deeper, until she moaned, half in fear of the unexplored, half in delight of the exploration. She'd forgotten who she was, who he was. There was only pleasure, a dark, heavy pleasure. Through her dazed senses she felt a struggle—a storm, a fury. Then he drew her away to study her face.

He wasn't pleased that his heartbeat was unsteady. Or that the thoughts whirling in his head were clouded with passion. This was no time for complications. And this was no woman to take risks with. With an effort, he slid his hands gently down her arms. ''More satisfying than a thank you,'' he said lightly, then glanced with a grin toward the bed. ''Are you going to ask me to stay?''

Morgan pulled herself back with a jolt. He must have hypnotized her, she decided. There was no other rational explanation. ''Some other time, perhaps,'' she managed, as carelessly as he.

Amusement lightened his features. Capturing her hand, he kissed it formally. "I'll look forward to it, Aphrodite."

He moved to the balcony, throwing her a quick grin before he started his descent. Unable to prevent herself, Morgan ran over to watch him climb down.

He moved like a cat, confident, fearless, a shadow clinging to the stark white walls. Her heart stayed lodged in her throat as she watched him. He sprang to the ground and melted into the cover of trees without looking back. Whirling, Morgan shut the doors to the balcony. And locked them.

Chapter 3

MORGAN SWIRLED HER GLASS OF LOCAL WINE BUT drank little. Though its light, fruity flavor was appealing, she was too preoccupied to appreciate it. The terrace overlooked the gulf with its hard blue water and scattering of tiny islands. Small dots that were boats skimmed the surface, but she took little notice of them. Most of her mind was occupied in trying to sort out the cryptic comments of her late-night visitor. The rest was involved with following the conversation around her.

Dorian Zoulas was all that Liz had said—classically handsome, bronzed, and sophisticated. In the pale cream suit, he was a twentieth-century Adonis. He had intelligence and breeding, tempered with a golden beauty that was essentially masculine. Liz's maneuvers might have caused Morgan to treat him with a polite aloofness if she hadn't seen the flashes of humor in his eyes. Morgan had realized immediately that he not only knew the way his hostess's mind worked, but had decided to play the game. The teasing challenge in his eyes relaxed her. Now she could enjoy a harmless flirtation without embarrassment.

Iona, Alex's cousin, was to Morgan's mind less appealing. Her dark, sultry looks were both stunning and disturbing. The gloss of beauty and wealth didn't quite polish over an edge that might have come from poor temperament or nerves. There was no humor in the exotic sloe eyes or pouting mouth. Iona was, Morgan mused, like a volcano waiting to erupt. Hot, smoky, and alarming.

The adjectives brought her night visitor back to her mind. They fit him just as neatly as they fit Iona Theoharis, and yet . . . oddly, Morgan found she admired them in the man and found them disturbing in the woman. Double standard? she wondered, then shook her head. No, the energy in Iona seemed destructive. The energy in the man was compelling. Annoyed with herself, Morgan turned from her study of the gulf and pushed aside her disturbing thoughts.

She gave Dorian her full attention. "You must find it very peaceful here after Athens."

He turned in his chair to face her. With only a smile, he intimated that there was no woman but she on the terrace—a trick Morgan found pleasant. "The island's a marvelous place . . . tranquil. But I thrive on chaos. As you live in New York, I'm sure you understand."

"Yes, but at the moment, tranquility is very appealing." Leaning against the rail, she let the sun play warm on her back. "I've been nothing but lazy so far. I haven't even whipped up the energy to explore."

"There's quite a bit of local color, if that's what you have in mind." Dorian slipped a thin gold case from his pocket, and opening it, offered Morgan a cigarette. At the shake of her head, he lit one for himself, then leaned back in a manner that was both relaxed and alert. "Caves and inlets, olive groves, a few small farms and flocks," he continued. "The village is very quaint and unspoiled."

"Exactly what I want." Morgan nodded and sipped her drink. "But I'm going to take it very slow. I'll collect shells and find a farmer who'll let me milk his goat."

"Terrifying aspirations," Dorian commented with a quick smile.

"Liz will tell you, I've always been intrepid."

"I'd be happy to help you with your shells." He continued to smile as his eyes skimmed her face with an approval she couldn't have missed. "But as to the goat . . ."

"I'm surprised you're content with so little entertainment." Iona's husky voice broke into the exchange.

Morgan shifted her gaze to her and found it took more of an effort to smile. "The island itself is entertainment enough for me. Remember, I'm a tourist. I've always thought vacations where you rush from one activity to the next aren't vacations at all."

"Morgan's been lazy for two full days," Liz put in with a grin. "A new record."

Morgan cast her a look, thinking of her nighttime activities. "I'm shooting for two weeks of peaceful sloth," Morgan murmured. *Starting today,* she added silently.

"Lesbos is the perfect spot for idleness." Dorian blew out a slow, fragrant stream of smoke. "Rustic, quiet."

"But perhaps this bit of island isn't as quiet as it appears." Iona ran a manicured nail around the rim of her glass.

Morgan saw Dorian's brows lift as if in puzzlement while Alex's drew together in disapproval.

"We'll do our best to keep it quiet during Morgan's visit," Liz said smoothly. "She rarely stays still for long, and since she'd determined to this time, we'll see that she has a nice, uneventful vacation."

Morgan made some sound of agreement and managed not to choke over her drink. Uneventful! If Liz only knew.

"More wine, Morgan?" Dorian rose, bringing the bottle to her.

Iona began to tap her fingers on the arm of her wrought iron chair. "I suppose there are people who find boredom appealing."

"Relaxation," Alex said with a slight edge in his voice, "comes in many forms."

"And of course," Liz went on, skimming her hand lightly over the back of her husband's, "Morgan's job is very demanding. All those foreign dignitaries and protocol and politics."

Dorian sent Morgan an appreciative smile as he poured more wine into her glass. "I'm sure someone with Morgan's talents would have many fascinating stories to tell."

Morgan cocked a brow. It had been a long time since she had been given a purely admiring male smile—undemanding, warm without being appraising. She

could learn to enjoy it. "I might have a few," she
returned.

The sun was sinking into the sea. The rosy light
streamed through the open balcony doors and washed
the room. Red sky at night, Morgan mused. Wasn't
that supposed to mean clear sailing? She decided to
take it as an omen.

Her first two days on Lesbos had been a far cry from
the uneventful vacation Liz had boasted of, but that
was behind her now. With luck, and a little care, she
wouldn't run into that attractive lunatic again.

Morgan caught a glimpse of her own smile in the
mirror and hastily rearranged her expression. Perhaps
when she got back to New York, she'd see a psychia-
trist. When you started to find lunatics appealing, you
were fast becoming one yourself. Forget it, she ordered
herself firmly as she went to the closet. There were
more important things to think about—like what she
was going to wear to dinner.

After a quick debate, Morgan chose a drifting white
dress—thin layers of crepe de chine, full-sleeved,
full-skirted. Dorian had inspired her to flaunt her
femininity a bit. Jack, she recalled, had preferred the
tailored look. He had often offered a stern and unsolicited opinion on her wardrobe, finding her taste both
inconsistent and flighty. There might be a multicolored
gypsy-style skirt hanging next to a prim business suit.
He'd never understood that both had suited who she
was. Just another basic difference, Morgan mused as
she hooked the line of tiny pearl buttons.

Tonight she was going to have fun. It had been a
long while since she'd flirted with a man. Her thoughts

swung back to a dark man with tousled hair and a shadowed chin. Hold on, Morgan, she warned herself. *That* was hardly in the same league as a flirtation. Moving over, she closed the balcony doors and gave a satisfied nod as she heard the click of the lock. And that, she decided, takes care of that.

Liz glided around the salon. It pleased her that Morgan hadn't come down yet. Now she could make an entrance. For all her blond fragility, Liz was a determined woman. Loyalty was her strongest trait; where she loved, it was unbendable. She wanted Morgan to be happy. Her own marriage had given her nothing but happiness. Morgan would have the same if Liz had any say in it.

With a satisfied smile, she glanced around the salon. The light was low and flattering. The scent of night blossoms drifting in through the open windows was the perfect touch. The wines she'd ordered for dinner would add the final prop for romance. Now, if Morgan would cooperate . . .

"Nick, I'm so glad you could join us." Liz went to him, holding out both hands. "It's so nice that we're all on the island at the same time for a change."

"It's always a pleasure to see you, Liz," he returned with a warm, charming smile. "And a relief to be out of the crowds in Athens for a few weeks." He gave her hands a light squeeze, then lifted one to his lips. His dark eyes skimmed her face. "I swear, you're lovelier every time I see you."

With a laugh, Liz tucked her arm through his. "We'll have to invite you to dinner more often. Did I ever thank you properly for that marvelous Indian chest you found me?'' Smiling, she guided him toward the bar. ''I adore it.''

''Yes, you did.'' He gave her hand a quick pat. ''I'm glad I was able to find what you had in mind.''

''You never fail to find the perfect piece. I'm afraid Alex wouldn't know an Indian chest from a Hepplewhite.''

Nick laughed. ''We all have our talents, I suppose.''

''But your work must be fascinating.'' Liz glanced up at him with her wide-eyed smile as she began to fix him a drink. ''All those treasures and all the exotic places you travel to.''

''There are times it's more exciting just to be home.''

She shot him a look. ''You make that hard to believe, since you're so seldom here. Where was it last month? Venice?''

''A beautiful city,'' he said smoothly.

''I'd love to see it. If I could drag Alex away from his ships . . .'' Liz's eyes focused across the room. ''Oh dear, it looks like Iona is annoying Alex again.'' On a long breath, she lifted her eyes to Nick's. Seeing the quick understanding, she gave a rueful smile. ''I'm going to have to play diplomat.''

''You do it charmingly, Liz. Alex is a lucky man.''

''Remind him of that from time to time,'' she suggested. ''I'd hate for him to take me for granted. Oh, here comes Morgan. She'll keep you entertained while I do my duty.''

Following Liz's gaze, Nick watched as Morgan entered the room. ''I'm sure she will,'' was his murmured reply. He liked the dress she wore, the floating white that was at once alluring and innocent.

She'd left her hair loose so that it fell over her
shoulders almost as if it had come off a pillow. Quite
beautiful, he thought as he felt the stir. He'd always
had a weakness for beauty.

"Morgan." Before Morgan could do anymore than
smile her hello at Dorian, Liz took her arm. "You'll
keep Nick happy for a moment, I have a job to do.
Morgan James, Nicholas Gregoras." With the quick
introduction, Liz was halfway across the room.

Morgan stared in stunned silence. Nick lifted her
limp hand to his lips. "You," she managed in a choked
whisper.

"Aphrodite, you're exquisite. Even fully dressed."

With his lips lingering over her knuckles, he met her
eyes. His were dark and pleased. Regaining her senses,
Morgan tried to wrench her hand free. Without changing expression, Nick tightened his grip and held her
still.

"Careful, Morgan," he said mildly. "Liz and her
guests will wonder at your behavior. And explanations
would"—he grinned, exactly as she remembered—
"cause them to wonder about your mental health."

"Let go of my hand," she said quietly and smiled
with her lips only. "Or I swear, I'll deck you."

"You're magnificent." Making a small bow, he
released her. "Did you know your eyes literally throw
darts when you're annoyed?"

"Then I've the pleasure of knowing you're riddled
with tiny holes," she returned. "Let me know when
one hits the heart, *Mr*. Gregoras."

"Nick, please," he said in a polished tone. "We
could hardly start formalities now after all we've . . .
been through together."

Morgan gave him a brilliant smile. "Very well, Nick, you odious swine. What a pity this isn't the proper time to go into how detestable you are."

He inclined his head. "We'll arrange for a more appropriate opportunity. Soon," he added with the faintest hint of steel. "Now, let me get you a drink."

Liz breezed up, pleased with the smiles she had seen exchanged. "You two seem to be getting along like old friends."

"I was just telling Mr. Gregoras how enchanting his home looks from the sea." Morgan sent him a quick but lethal glance.

"Yes, Morgan was fascinated by it," Liz told him. "She's always preferred things that didn't quite fit a mold, if you know what I mean."

"Exactly." Nick let his eyes sweep over Morgan's face. A man could get lost in those eyes, he thought, if he wasn't careful. Very careful. "Miss James has agreed to a personal tour tomorrow afternoon." He smiled, watching her expression go from astonishment to fury before she controlled it.

"Marvelous!" Pleased, Liz beamed at both of them. "Nick has so many treasures from all over the world. His house is just like Aladdin's cave."

Smiling, Morgan thought of three particularly gruesome wishes, all involving her intended host. "I can't wait to see it."

Through dinner, Morgan watched, confused, then intrigued by Nick's manner. This was not the man she knew. This man was smooth, polished. Gone was the intensity, the ruthlessness, replaced by an easy warmth and charm.

Nicholas Gregoras, olive oil, import-export. Yes, she could see the touches of wealth and success—and the authority she'd understood from the first. But command sat differently on him now, with none of the undertones of violence.

He could sit at the elegant table, laughing with Liz and Alex over some island story with the gleam of cut crystal in his hand. The smoky-gray suit was perfectly tailored and fit him with the same ease as the dark sweatshirt and jeans she'd first seen him in. His arrogance had a more sophisticated tone now. All the rough edges were smoothed.

He seemed relaxed, at home—with none of that vital, dangerous energy. How could this be the same man who had flourished a knife, or climbed the sheer wall to her balcony?

Nick handed her a glass of wine and she frowned. But he was the same man, she reminded herself. And just what game was he playing? Lifting her eyes, Morgan met his. Her fingers tightened on the stem of the glass. The look was brief and quickly veiled, but she saw the inner man. The force was vital. If he was playing games, she thought, sipping her wine to calm suddenly tight nerves, it wasn't a pleasant one. And she wanted no part of it—or of him.

Turning to Dorian, Morgan left Nick to Iona. Intelligent, witty, and with no frustrating mysteries, Dorian was a more comfortable dinner companion. Morgan fell into the easy exchange and tried to relax.

"Tell me, Morgan, don't you find the words of so many languages a bit crowded in the mind?"

She toyed with her moussaka, finding her stomach too jittery to accept the rich sauce. Damn the man for interfering even with her appetite. "I do my thinking in one at a time," she countered.

"You take it too lightly," Dorian insisted. "It's an accomplishment to be proud of. Even a power."

"A power?" Her brows drew together for a moment, then cleared as she smiled. "I suppose it is, though I'd never really thought about it. It just seemed too limiting to only be able to communicate and think in one language, then once I got started, I couldn't seem to stop."

"Having the language, you'd be at home in many countries."

"Yes, I guess that's why I feel so—well, easy here."

"Alex tells me he's trying to entice you into his company." With a smile, Dorian toasted her. "I've drafted myself as promoter. Working with you would add to the company benefits."

Iona's rich laughter floated across the table. "Oh, Nicky, you say the most ridiculous things."

Nicky, Morgan thought with a sniff. I'll be ill any minute. "I think I might enjoy your campaign," Morgan told Dorian with her best smile.

"Take me out on your boat tomorrow, Nicky. I simply must have some fun."

"I'm sorry, Iona, not tomorrow. Perhaps later in the week." Nick softened the refusal with the trace of a finger down her hand.

Iona's mouth formed a pout. "I might die of boredom by later in the week."

Morgan heard Dorian give a quiet sigh. Glancing over, she noted the quick look of exasperation he sent Iona. "Iona tells me she ran into Maria Popagos in

Athens last week." The look of exasperation was gone, and his voice was gentle. "She has what—four children now, Iona?"

They treat her like a child, Morgan thought with distaste. And she behaves like one—a spoiled, willful, not quite healthy child.

Through the rest of the meal, and during coffee in the salon, Morgan watched Iona's moods go from sullen to frantic. Apparently used to it, or too good mannered to notice, Dorian ignored the fluctuations. And though she hated to give him the credit for it, so did Nick. But Morgan noted, with a flutter of sympathy, that Alex grew more distracted as the evening wore on. He spoke to his cousin in undertones as she added more brandy to her glass. Her response was a dramatic toss of her head before she swallowed the liquor and turned her back on him.

When Nick rose to leave, Iona insisted on walking with him to his car. She cast a look of triumph over her shoulder as they left the salon arm-in-arm. Now who, Morgan mused, was that aimed at? Shrugging, she turned back to Dorian and let the evening wind down naturally. There would be time enough to think things through when she was alone in her room again.

Morgan floated with the dream. The wine had brought sleep quickly. Though she had left the balcony doors securely locked, the night breeze drifted through the windows. She sighed, and shifted with its gentle caress on her skin. It was a soft stroking, like a butterfly's wing. It teased across her lips then came back to warm them. She stirred with pleasure. Her body was pliant, receptive. As the phantom kiss increased in pressure, she parted her lips. She drew the dream lover closer.

Excitement was sleepy. The tastes that seeped into her were as sweet and as potent as the wine that still misted her brain. With a sigh of lazy, languid pleasure, she floated with it. In the dream, her arms wrapped around the faceless lover—the pirate, the phantom. He whispered her name and deepened the kiss as his hands drew down the sheet that separated them. Rough fingers, familiar fingers, traced over her skin. A body, too hard, too muscular for a dream, pressed against hers. The lazy images became more tangible, and the phantom took on form. Dark hair, dark eyes, and a mouth that was grimly beautiful and oh, so clever.

Warmth became heat. With a moan, she let passion take her. The stroking along her body became more insistent at her response. Her mouth grew hungry, demanding. Then she heard the breathy whisper of a Greek endearment against her ear.

Suddenly, the filmy curtain of sleep lifted. The weight on her body was real, achingly real—and achingly familiar. Morgan began a confused struggle.

"The goddess awakes. More's the pity."

She saw him in the shaft of moonlight. Her body was alive with needs, her mind baffled with the knowledge that he had induced them. "What are you doing!" she demanded, and found her breathing was quick and ragged. His mouth had been on hers, she knew. She could still taste him. And his hands . . . "This is the limit! If you think for one minute I'm going to sit still for you crawling into my bed while I'm sleeping—"

"You were very agreeable a moment ago."

"Oh! What a despicable thing to do."

"You're very responsive," Nick murmured, and traced her ear with his fingertip. Beneath his hand he could feel the thunder of her heartbeat. He knew, though he fought to slow it, that his own beat as quickly. "It seemed to please you to be touched. It pleased me to touch you."

His voice had lowered again, as she knew it could—dark, seductive. The muscles in her thighs loosened. "Get off of me," she ordered in quick defense.

"Sweet Morgan." He nipped her bottom lip—felt her tremble, felt a swift rush of power. It would be so easy to persuade her . . . and so risky. With an effort, he gave her a friendly smile. "You only postpone the inevitable."

She kept her eyes level as she tried to steady her breathing. Something told her that if all else he had said had been lies, his last statement was all too true. "I didn't promise not to scream this time."

He lifted a brow as though the possibility intrigued him. "It might be interesting to explain this . . . situation to Alex and Liz. I could claim I was overcome with your beauty. It has a ring of truth. But you won't scream in any case."

"Just what makes you so sure?"

"You'd have given me away—or tried to by now—if you were going to." Nick rolled aside.

Sitting up, Morgan pushed at her hair. Did he always have to be right? she wondered grimly. "What do you want now? And how the hell did you get in this time? I locked . . ." Her voice trailed off as she saw the balcony doors were wide open.

"Did you think a lock would keep me out?" With a

laugh, Nick ran a finger down her nose. "You have a lot to learn."

"Now, you listen to me—"

"No, save the recriminations for later. They're understood in any case." Absently, he rubbed a lock of her hair between his thumb and forefinger. "I came back to make certain you didn't develop a convenient headache that would keep you from coming to the house tomorrow. There are one or two things I want to discuss with you."

"I've got a crateful of things to discuss with you," Morgan hissed furiously. "Just what were you doing that night on the beach? And who—"

"Later, Aphrodite. I'm distracted at the moment. That scent you wear, for instance. It's very . . ." He lifted his eyes to hers. "Alluring."

"Stop it." She didn't trust him when his voice dropped to that tone. She didn't trust him at all, she reminded herself and gave him a level look. "What's the purpose behind that ridiculous game you were playing tonight?"

"Game?" His eyes widened effectively. "Morgan, my love, I don't know what you're talking about. I was quite natural."

"Natural be damned."

"No need to swear at me," he said mildly.

"There's every need," she countered. How could he manage to be charming under such ridiculous circumstances? "You were the perfect guest this evening," Morgan went on, knocking his hand aside as he began to toy with the thin strap of her chemise. "Charming—"

"Thank you."

"And false," she added, narrowing her eyes.

"Not false," Nick disagreed. "Simply suitable, considering the occasion."

"I suppose it would have looked a bit odd if you'd pulled a knife out of your pocket."

His fingers tightened briefly, then relaxed. She wasn't going to let him forget that—and he wasn't having an easy time blanking out that moment she had gone limp with terror beneath him. "Few people have seen me other than I was tonight," he murmured, and began to give the texture of her hair his attention. "Perhaps it's your misfortune to count yourself among them."

"I don't want to see you *any* way, from now on."

Humor touched his eyes again as they shifted to hers. "Liar. I'll pick you up tomorrow at one."

Morgan tossed out a phrase commonly heard in the less elite portions of Italy. Nick responded with a pleased laugh.

"*Agapetike,* I should warn you, in my business I've had occasion to visit some Italian gutters."

"Good, then you won't need a translation."

"Just be ready." He let his gaze sweep down her then up again. "You might find it easier to deal with me in the daylight—and when you're more adequately attired."

"I have no intention of dealing with you at all," Morgan began in a furious undertone. "Or of continuing this ridiculous charade by going with you tomorrow."

"Oh, I think you will." Nick's smile was confident

and infuriating. "You'd find yourself having a difficult time explaining to Liz why you won't come when you've already expressed an interest in my home. Tell me, what was it that appealed to you about it?"

"The insanity of the architecture."

He laughed again and took her hand. "More compliments. I adore you, Aphrodite. Come, kiss me good night."

Morgan drew back and scowled. "I certainly will not."

"You certainly will." In a swift movement he had her pinned under him again. When she cursed him, he laughed and the insolence was back. "Witch," he murmured. "What mortal can resist one?"

His mouth came down quickly, lingering until she had stopped squirming beneath him. Gradually, the force went out of the kiss, but not the power. It seeped into her, so that she couldn't be sure if it was hers or his. Then it was only passion—clean and hot and senseless. On a moan, Morgan accepted it, and him.

Feeling the change in her, Nick relaxed a moment and simply let himself enjoy.

She had a taste that stayed with him long after he left her. Each time he touched her he knew, eventually, he would have to have it all. But not now. Now there was too much at stake. She was a risk, and he had already taken too many chances with her. But that taste . . .

He gave himself over to the kiss knowing the danger of letting himself become vulnerable, even for a moment, by losing himself in her. If she hadn't been on the beach that night. If he hadn't had to reveal himself to her. Would things have been different than they were now? he wondered as desire began to claw at him. Would he have been able to coax her into his arms, into his bed, with a bit of flair and a few clever words? If they had met for the first time tonight, would he have wanted her this badly, this quickly?

Her hands were in his hair. He found his mouth had roamed to her throat. Her scent seemed to concentrate there, and the taste was wild and dangerous. He lived with danger and enjoyed it—lived by his wits and won. But this woman, this feeling she stirred in him, was a risk he couldn't calculate. Yet it was done. There was no changing the course he had to take. And no changing the fact that she was involved.

He wanted to touch her, to tear off that swatch of silk she wore and feel her skin warm under his hand. He dared not. He was a man who knew his own limitations, his own weaknesses. Nick didn't appreciate the fact that Morgan James had become a weakness at a time when he could least afford one.

Murmuring his name, Morgan slid her hands beneath the loose sweatshirt, to run them over the range of muscle. Nick felt need shoot like a spear, white-tipped, to the pit of his stomach. Using every ounce of will, he banked down on it until it was a dull ache he could control. He lifted his head and waited for those pale, clouded blue eyes to open. Something dug into his palm, and he saw that he had gripped her medal in his hand without realizing it. Nick had to quell the urge to swear, then give himself a moment until he knew he could speak lightly. "Sleep well, Aphrodite," he told her with a grin. "Until tomorrow."

"You—" She broke off, struggling for the breath and the wit to hurl abuse at him.

"Tomorrow," Nick repeated as he brought her hand to his lips.

Morgan watched him stride to the balcony, then lower himself out of sight. Lying perfectly still, she stared at the empty space and wondered what she had gotten herself into.

Chapter 4

THE HOUSE WAS COOL AND QUIET IN THE MID-MORN-
ing hush. Gratefully, Morgan accepted Liz's order to
enjoy the beach. She wanted to avoid Iona's company,
and though she hated to admit it, she didn't think she
could handle Liz's carefree chatter about the dinner
party. Liz would have expected her to make some witty
observations about Nick that Morgan just didn't feel up
to. Relieved that Dorian had business with Alex, and
wouldn't feel obliged to keep her company, she set out
alone.

Morgan wanted the solitude—she did her best thinking when she was alone. In the past few days she had
accumulated quite a bit to think about. Now she
decided to work it through one step at a time.

What had Nicholas Gregoras been doing that night
on the beach? He'd had the scent of the sea on him, so
it followed that he had been out on the water. She

remembered the sound of a motor. She'd assumed it belonged to a fisherman but Nick was no fisherman. He'd been desperate not to be seen by someone . . . desperate enough to have been carrying a knife. She could still see the look on his face as she had lain beneath him in the shadows of the cypress. He'd been prepared to use the knife.

Somehow the knowledge that this was true disturbed her more now than it had when he'd been a stranger. Kicking bad-temperedly at a stone, she started down the beach steps.

And who had been with him? Morgan fretted. Someone had followed his orders without any question. Who had used the beach steps while Nick had held her prisoner in the shadows? Alex? The man who rented Nick's cottage? Frustrated, Morgan slipped out of her shoes and began to cross the warm sand. Why would Nick be ready to kill either one of them rather than be discovered by them? By anyone, she corrected. It could have been a servant of one of the villas, a villager trespassing.

One question at a time, Morgan cautioned herself as she kicked idly at the sand. First, was it logical to assume that the footsteps she had heard were from someone who had also come from the sea? Morgan thought it was. And second, she decided that the person must have been headed to one of the villas or a nearby cottage. Why else would they have used that particular strip of beach? Logical, she concluded, walking aimlessly. So why was Nick so violently determined to go unseen?

Smuggling. It was so obvious. So logical. But she had continued to push the word aside. She didn't want to think of him involved in such a dirty business. Somewhere, beneath the anger and resentment she felt for him, Morgan had experienced a totally different sensation. There was something about him—something she couldn't really pinpoint in words. Strength, perhaps. He was the kind of man you could depend on when no one else could—or would—help. She wanted to trust him. There was no logic to it, it simply was.

But was he a smuggler? Had he thought she'd seen something incriminating? Did the footsteps she'd heard belong to a patrol? Another smuggler? A rival? If he'd believed her to be a threat, why hadn't he simply used the knife on her? If he were a cold-blooded killer . . . no. Morgan shook her head at the description. While she could almost accept that Nick would kill, she couldn't agree with the adjective. And that led to hundreds of other problems.

Questions and answers sped through her mind. Stubborn questions, disturbing answers. Morgan shut her eyes on them. I'm going to get some straight answers from him this afternoon, she promised herself. It was his fault she was involved. Morgan dropped to the sand and brought her knees to her chest. She had been minding her own business when he had literally dragged her into it. All she had wanted was a nice, quiet vacation.

"Men!"

"I refuse to take that personally."

Morgan spun her head around and found herself staring into a wide, friendly smile.

"Hello. You seem to be angry with my entire gender." He rose from a rock and walked to her. He was tall and very slender, with dark gold curls appealingly disarrayed around a tanned face that held both youth and strength. "But I think it's worth the risk. I'm Andrew Stevenson." Still smiling, he dropped to the sand beside her.

"Oh." Recovering, Morgan returned the smile. "The poet or the painter? Liz wasn't sure."

"Poet," he said with a grimace. "Or so I tell myself."

Glancing down, she saw the pad he held. It was dog-eared and covered with a fine, looping scribble. "I've interrupted your work. I'm sorry."

"On the contrary, you've given me a shot of inspiration. You have a remarkable face."

"I think," Morgan considered, "that's a compliment."

"Dear lady, yours is a face a poet dreams of." He let his eyes roam it for a moment. "Do you have a name, or are you going to vanish in a mist and leave me bewitched?"

"Morgan." The fussy compliment, delivered with bland sincerity made her laugh. "Morgan James, and are you a good poet, Andrew Stevenson?"

"I can't say no." Andrew continued to study her candidly. "Modesty isn't one of my virtues. You said Liz. I assume that's Mrs. Theoharis. You're staying with them?"

"Yes, for a few weeks." A new thought crossed her mind. "You're renting Nicholas Gregoras's cottage?"

"That's right. Actually, it's a free ride." Though he set down the pad, he began to trace patterns in the sand as if he couldn't keep his hands quite still. "We're cousins.'' Andrew noted the surprise on her face. His smile deepened. ''Not the Greek side. Our mothers are related.''

''Oh, so his mother's American.'' This at least explained his ease with the language.

''A Norling of San Francisco,'' he stated with a grin for the title. ''She remarried after Nick's father died. She's living in France.''

''So, you're visiting Lesbos and your cousin at the same time.''

''Actually, Nick offered me the retreat when he learned I was working on an epic poem—a bit Homeric, you see.'' His eyes were blue, darker than hers, and very direct on her face. Morgan could see nothing in the open, ingenuous look to link him with Nick. ''I wanted to stay on Lesbos awhile, so it worked out nicely. The home of Sappho. The poetry and legend have always fascinated me.''

''Sappho,'' Morgan repeated, turning her thoughts from Nick. ''Oh, yes, the poetess.''

''The Tenth Muse. She lived here, in Mitilini.'' His gaze, suddenly dreamy, swept down the stretch of beach. ''I like to think Nick's house is on the cliff where she hurled herself into the sea, desperate for Phaon's love.''

''An interesting thought.'' Morgan looked up to where a portion of a gray stone wall was visible. ''And I suppose her spirit floats over the house searching for her love.'' Somehow, she liked the idea and smiled. ''Lord knows, it's the perfect house for a poetic haunting.''

''Have you been inside?'' Andrew asked her, his tone as dreamy as his eyes now. ''It's fantastic.''

"No, but I'm getting a personal tour this afternoon." Morgan kept her voice light as she swore silently in several languages.

"A personal tour?" Abruptly direct again, Andrew tilted his head, with brows lifted in speculation. "You must have made quite an impression on Nick. But then," he added with a nod, "you would. He sets great store by beauty."

Morgan gave him a noncommittal smile. He could hardly know that it wasn't her looks or charm that had secured the invitation. "Do you often write on the beach? I can't keep away from it myself." Morgan hesitated briefly, then plunged. "I came down here a couple of nights ago and swam by moonlight."

There was no shock or anxiety in his eyes at this information. Andrew grinned. "I'm sorry I missed that. You'll find me all over this part of the island. Here, up on the cliffs, in the olive groves. I go where the mood strikes me."

"I'm going to do some exploring myself." She thought wistfully of a carefree hour in the inlets.

"I'm available if you'd like a guide." His gaze skimmed over her face again, warm and friendly. "By now, I know this part of the island as well as a native. If you find you want company, you can usually find me wandering around or in the cottage. It isn't far."

"I'd like that." A gleam of amusement lit her eyes. "You don't happen to keep a goat, do you?"

"Ah—no."

Laughing at his expression, Morgan patted his hand. "Don't try to understand," she advised. "And now I'd better go change for my tour."

Andrew rose with her and captured her hand. "I'll

see you again." It was a statement, not a question. Morgan responded to the gentle pressure.

"I'm sure you will; the island's very small."

Andrew smiled as he released her hand. "I'd rather call it Kismet." He watched Morgan walk away before he settled back on his rock, facing the sea.

Nicholas Gregoras was very prompt. By five minutes past one, Morgan found herself being shoved out the door by an enthusiastic Liz. "Have fun, darling, and don't hurry back. Nick, Morgan will adore your house; all those winding passages and the terrifying view of the sea. She's very courageous, aren't you, Morgan?"

"I'm practically stalwart," she muttered while Nick grinned.

"Well, run along and have fun." Liz shooed them out the door as if they were two reluctant children being sent to school.

"You should be warned," Morgan stated as she slid into Nick's car, "Liz considers you a suitable candidate for my hand. I think she's getting desperate picturing me as her unborn child's maiden aunt."

"Aphrodite." Nick settled beside her and took her hand. "There isn't a male alive who could picture you as anyone's maiden aunt."

Refusing to be charmed, Morgan removed her hand from his, then studied the view out the side window. "I met your poet in residence this morning on the beach."

"Andrew? He's a nice boy. How did you find him?"

"Not like a boy." Turning back to Nick, Morgan frowned. "He's a very charming man."

Nick lifted a brow fractionally. "Yes, I suppose he is. Somehow, I always think of him as a boy, though there's barely five years between us." He moved his shoulders. "He does have talent. Did you charm him?"

" 'Inspire' was his word," she returned, annoyed.

Nick flashed her a quick grin. "Naturally. One romantic should inspire another."

"I'm not a romantic." The conversation forced her to give him a great deal more of her attention than she had planned. "I'm very practical."

"Morgan, you're an insatiable romantic." Her annoyance apparently amused him, because a smile continued to hover on his mouth. "A woman who combs her hair on a moonlit beach, wears filmy white, and treasures a valueless memento thrives on romance."

Uncomfortable with the description, Morgan spoke coolly. "I also clip coupons and watch my cholesterol."

"Admirable."

She swallowed what might have been a chuckle. "You, Nicholas Gregoras, are a first-rate bastard."

"Yes. I hate to be second-rate at anything."

Morgan flounced back in her seat, but lost all resentment as the house came into full view. "Oh, Lord," she murmured. "It's wonderful!"

It looked stark and primitive and invulnerable. The second story lashed out over the sea like an outstretched arm—not offering payment, but demanding it. None of the power she had felt out at sea was diminished at close range. The flowering shrubs and

vines which trailed and tangled were placed to disguise
the care of their planting. The result was an illusion of
wild abandon. Sleeping Beauty's castle, she thought, a
century after she pricked her finger.

"What a marvelous place." Morgan turned to him
as he stopped the car at the entrance. "I've never seen
anything like it."

"That's the first time you've smiled at me and meant
it." He wasn't smiling now, but looking at her with a
trace of annoyance. He hadn't realized just how much
he'd wanted to see that spontaneous warmth in her
eyes—directed at him. And now that he had, he wasn't
certain what to do about it. With a quick mental oath,
Nick slid from the car.

Ignoring him, Morgan climbed out and tried to take
in the entire structure at once. "You know what it looks
like," she said, half to herself. "It looks like Zeus
hurled a lightning bolt into the mountain and the house
exploded into existence."

"An interesting theory." Nick took her hand and
started up the stone steps. "If you'd known my
grandfather, you'd realize how close that is to the
truth."

Morgan had primed herself to begin hurling questions and demanding explanations as soon as they had
arrived. When she stepped into the entrance hall, she
forgot everything.

Wide and speckled in aged white, the hall was
sporadically slashed with stark colors from wall hang-
ings and primitive paintings. On one wall, long spears
were crossed—weapons for killing, certainly, but with
an ancient dignity she had to admire. The staircase

leading to the upper floors arched in a half circle with a banister of dark, unvarnished wood. The result was one of earthy magnificence. It was far from elegant, but there was a sense of balance and savage charm.

"Nicholas." Turning a full circle, Morgan sighed. "It's really wonderful. I expect a cyclops to come stalking down the stairs. Are there centaurs in the courtyard?"

"I'll take you through, and we'll see what we can do." She was making it difficult for him to stick to his plan. She wasn't supposed to charm him. That wasn't in the script. Still, he kept her hand in his as he led her through the house.

Liz's comparison to Aladdin's cave was completely apt. Room after room abounded with treasures— Venetian glass, Fabergé boxes, African masks, American Indian pottery, Ming vases. All were set together in a hodgepodge of cultures. What might have seemed like a museum was instead a glorious clutter of wonders. As the house twisted and turned, revealing surprise after surprise, Morgan became more fascinated. Elegant Waterford crystal was juxtaposed with a deadly-looking seventeenth-century crossbow. She saw exquisite French porcelain and a shrunken head from Ecuador.

Yes, the architect was mad, she decided, noting lintels with wolves' heads or grinning elves carved into them. Wonderfully mad. The house was a fairy tale— not the tame children's version, but with all the whispering shadows and hints of gremlins.

A huge curved window on the top floor gave her the sensation of standing suspended on the edge of the cliff. It jutted out, arrogantly, then fell in a sheer drop into the sea. Morgan stared down, equally exhilarated and terrified.

Nick watched her. There was a need to spin her around and seize, to possess while that look of dazzled courage was still on her face. He was a man accustomed to taking what he wanted without a second thought. She was something he wanted.

Morgan turned to him. Her eyes were still alive with the fascination of the sea and hints of excited fear. "Andrew said he hoped this was the cliff where Sappho hurled herself into the sea. I'm ready to believe it."

"Andrew's imaginative."

"So are you," she countered. "You live here."

"Your eyes are like some mythological lake," he murmured. "Translucent and ethereal. I should call you Circe rather than Aphrodite." Abruptly, he gripped her hair in his hand, tugging it until her face was lifted to his. "I swear you're more witch than goddess."

Morgan stared at him. There was no teasing in his eyes this time, no arrogance. What she saw was longing. And the longing, more than passion, seduced her. "I'm only a woman, Nicholas," she heard herself say.

His fingers tightened. His expression darkened. Then even as she watched, his mood seemed to shift. This time, he took her arm rather than her hand. "Come, we'll go down and have a drink."

As they entered the salon, Morgan reasserted her priorities. She had to get answers—she *would* get answers. She couldn't let a few soft words and a pair of dark eyes make her forget why she'd come. Before she could speak, however, a man slipped into the doorway.

He was small, with creased, leathered skin. His hair was gray with age, but thick. So were his arms—thick and muscled. He made her think of a small-scaled, very efficient tank. His moustache was a masterpiece. It spread under his nose to droop free along the sides of his mouth, reaching his chin in two flowing arches. He smiled, showing several gaps in lieu of teeth.

"Good afternoon." He spoke in respectful Greek, but his eyes were dancing.

Intrigued, Morgan gave him an unsmiling stare. *"Yiasou."*

"Stephanos, Miss James. Stephanos is my, ah, caretaker."

The checkerboard grin widened at the term. "Your servant, my lady." He bowed, but there was nothing deferential in the gesture. "The matter we discussed has been seen to, Mr. Gregoras." Turning to Nick, the old man spoke with exaggerated respect. "You have messages from Athens."

"I'll tend to them later."

"As you wish." The small man melted away. Morgan frowned. There had been something in the exchange that wasn't quite what it should be. Shaking her head, she watched Nick mix drinks. It wasn't Nick's relationship with his servants that she was interested in.

Deciding that plunging headfirst was the most direct route, Morgan leaped. "What were you doing on the beach the other night?"

"I rather thought we'd concluded I was assaulting you." His voice was very mild.

"That was only part of the evening's entertainment." She swallowed and took another dive. "Had you been smuggling?"

To his credit, Nick hesitated only briefly. As his back was to her, Morgan didn't see his expression range from surprise to consideration. A very sharp lady, he mused. Too damn sharp.

"And how did you come by such an astonishing conclusion?" He turned to hand her a delicate glass.

"Don't start that charade with me," Morgan fumed, snatching the glass. "I've seen you stripped." She sat down and aimed a level stare.

Nick's mouth twitched. "What a fascinating way you have of putting things."

"I asked if you were a smuggler."

Nick sat across from her, taking a long study of her face as he ticked off possibilities. "First, tell me why you think I might be."

"You'd been out on the water that night. I could smell the sea on you."

Nick gazed down into the liquid in his glass, then sipped. "It's fanciful, to say the least, that my being out on the water equals smuggling."

Morgan ground her teeth at the cool sarcasm and continued. "If you'd been out on a little fishing trip, you'd hardly have dragged me into the trees waving a knife."

"One might argue," he murmured, "that fishing was precisely my occupation."

"The coast of Turkey is very convenient from this part of the island. Alex told me smuggling was a problem."

"Alex?" Nick repeated. There was a quick, almost imperceptible change in his expression. "What was Alex's attitude toward smuggling?"

Morgan hesitated. The question had broken into her well-thought-out interrogation. "He was . . . resigned, like one accepts the weather."

"I see." Nick swirled his drink as he leaned back. "And did you and Alex discuss the intricacies of the procedure?"

"Of course not!" she snapped, infuriated that he had cleverly turned the interrogation around on her. "Alex would hardly be intimate with such matters. But," she continued, "I think you are."

"Yes, I can see that."

"Well?"

He sent her a mildly amused smile that didn't quite reach his eyes. "Well what?"

"Are you going to deny it?" She wanted him to, Morgan realized with something like a jolt. She very, very badly wanted him to deny it.

Nick considered her for another moment. "If I deny it, you won't believe me. It's easy to see you've already made up your mind." He tilted his head, and now the amusement crept into his eyes. "What will you do if I admit it?"

"I'll turn you over to the police." Morgan took a bold sip of her drink. Nick exploded with laughter.

"Morgan, what a sweet, brave child you are." He leaned over to take her hand before she could retort. "You don't know my reputation, but I assure you, the police would think you mad."

"I could prove—"

"What?" he demanded. His eyes were steady on hers, probing. The polished veneer was slowly fading. "You can't prove what you don't know."

"I know that you're not what you pretend to be." Morgan tried to pull her hand from his, but he held it firm. "Or maybe it's more accurate to say you're something you pretend not to be."

Nick watched her in silence, torn between annoyance and admiration. "Whatever I am, whatever I'm not, has nothing to do with you."

"No one wishes more than I that that was the truth."

Battling a new emotion, he sat back and studied her over the rim of his glass. "So your conclusions that I might be involved in smuggling would prompt you to go to the police. That wouldn't be wise."

"It's a matter of what's right." Morgan swallowed, then blurted out what was torturing her mind. "The knife—would you have used it?"

"On you?" he asked, his eyes as expressionless as his voice.

"On anyone."

"A general question can't be given a specific answer."

"Nicholas, for God's sake—"

Nick set down his drink, then steepled his fingers. His expression changed, and his eyes were suddenly dangerous. "If I were everything you seem to think, you're incredibly brave or incredibly foolish to be sitting here discussing it with me."

"I think I'm safe enough," she countered and straightened her shoulders. "Everyone knows where I am."

"I could always dispose of you another time if I

considered you an obstacle." Morgan's eyes flickered with momentary fear, quickly controlled. It was one more thing he could admire her for.

"I can take care of myself."

"Can you?" he murmured, then shrugged as his mood shifted again. "Well, in any case, I have no intention of wasting beauty, especially when I intend to enjoy its benefits. Your talents could be useful to me."

Her chin shot up. "I have no intention of being your tool. Smuggling opium is a filthy way to make money. It's a far cry from crossing the English Channel with French silks and brandy."

"With mists curling and eye-patched buccaneers?" Nick countered with a smile. "Is that how your practical mind sees it, Morgan?"

She opened her mouth to retort, but found herself smiling. "I refuse to like you, Nicholas."

"You don't have to like me, Morgan. Like is too tame for my tastes in any case." Outwardly relaxed, he picked up his glass again. "Don't you like your drink?"

Without taking her eyes from his, Morgan set it down. "Nicholas, I only want a straight answer—I deserve one. You're perfectly right that I can't go to the police, no matter what you tell me. You really have nothing to fear from me."

Something flashed in his eyes at her final statement, then was quickly banked. He considered his options before he spoke. "I'll tell you this much, I am—concerned with smuggling. I'd be interested to know of any conversations you might hear on the subject."

Frowning, Morgan rose to wander the room. He was making it difficult for her to remember the straight and narrow path of right and wrong. The path took some confusing twists and turns when emotions were involved. Emotions! She brought herself up short. No, no emotions here. She had no feelings toward him.

"Who was with you that night?" Keep to the plan, she told herself. Questions and answers. Save the introspection for later. "You were giving someone orders."

"I thought you were too frightened to notice." Nick sipped at his drink.

"You were speaking to someone," Morgan went on doggedly. "Someone who did precisely what you told him without question. Who?"

Nick weighed the pros and cons before he answered. With her mind she'd figure it out for herself soon enough. "Stephanos."

"That little old man?" Morgan stopped in front of Nick and stared down. Stephanos was not Morgan's image of a ruthless smuggler.

"That little old man knows the sea like a gardener knows a rose bush." He smiled at her incredulous expression. "He also has the advantage of being loyal. He's been with me since I was a boy."

"How convenient all this is for you." Depressed, Morgan wandered to a window. She was getting her answers, but she discovered they weren't the ones she wanted. "A home on a convenient island, a convenient servant, a convenient business to ease distribution. Who passed by the grove that night whom you wanted to avoid?"

Frightened or not, he thought angrily, she'd been far too observant. "That needn't concern you."

Morgan whirled. "You got me into this, Nicholas. I have a right to know."

"Your rights end where I say they do." He rose as his temper threatened. "Don't push me too far, Morgan. You wouldn't like the results. I've told you all I intend to for now. Be content with it."

She backed away a step, furious with herself for being frightened. He swore at the movement, then gripped her shoulders.

"I have no intention of harming you, damn it. If I had, there's already been ample opportunity. What do you picture?" he demanded, shaking her. "Me cutting your throat or tossing you off a cliff?"

Her eyes were dry and direct, more angry now than frightened. "I don't know what I picture."

Abruptly, he realized he was hurting her. Cursing himself, he eased the grip to a caress. He couldn't keep letting her get under his skin this way. He couldn't let it matter what she thought of him. "I don't expect you to trust me," he said calmly. "But use common sense. Your involvement was a matter of circumstance, not design. I don't want to see you hurt, Morgan. That much you can take as the truth."

And that much she believed. Intrigued, she studied his face. "You're a strange man, Nicholas. Somehow, I can't quite see you doing something as base as smuggling opium."

"Intuition, Morgan?" Smiling, Nick tangled his fingers in her hair. It was soft, as he remembered, and tempting. "Are you a woman who believes in her intuition, or in her reason?"

"Nicholas—"

"No. No more questions or I'll have to divert you. I'm very"—a frown hovered, then flashed into a grin—"very susceptible to beauty. You have a remarkable supply. Coupled with a very good mind, the combination is hard to resist." Nick lifted the medal at her throat, examined it, then let it fall before he moved back from her. "Tell me, what do you think of Dorian and Iona?"

"I resent this. I resent all of this." Morgan spun away from him. He shouldn't be allowed to affect her so deeply, so easily, then switch off like a light. "I came to Lesbos to get away from pressures and complications."

"What sort of pressures and complications?"

She turned back to him, eyes hot. "They're my business. I had a life before I went down to that damned beach and ran into you."

"Yes," he murmured and picked up his drink. "I'm sure you did."

"Now, I find myself tossed into the middle of some grade-B thriller. I don't like it."

"It's a pity you didn't stay in bed that night, Morgan." Nick drank deeply, then twirled his glass by the stem. "Maybe I'm Greek enough to say the gods didn't will it so. For the moment your fate's linked with mine and there's nothing either of us can do about it."

She surprised him by laying a hand on his chest. He didn't like the way his heart reacted to the touch. Needs . . . he couldn't need. Wants were easily satisfied or ignored, but needs ate at a man.

"If you feel that way, why won't you give me a straight answer?"

"I don't choose to." His eyes locked on hers, cementing her to the spot. In them she saw desires—his and a mirror of her own. "Take me for what I am, Morgan."

She dropped her hand. Frightened not of him now, but of herself. "I don't want to take you at all."

"No?" He pulled her close, perversely enjoying her resistance. "Let's see just how quickly I can make a liar of you."

She could taste anger on his mouth, and just as clearly she could taste need. Morgan stopped resisting. The path of right and wrong took a few more confusing twists when she was in his arms. Whoever, whatever he was, she wanted to be held by him.

Her arms wound around his neck to draw him closer. She heard him murmur something against her mouth; the kiss held a savageness, a demand she was answering with equal abandon.

Had this passion always been there, sleeping inside her? It wasn't asleep any longer. The force of it had her clinging to him, had her mouth urgent and hungry against his. Something had opened inside her, letting him pour through. His hands were in her hair, then running down her back in a swift stroke of possession. She arched against him as if daring him to claim her—taunting him to try.

Somehow she knew, as her body fit truly to his, that they would come back to each other, again and again, against their will, against all reason. She might fight it from moment to moment, but there would be a time. . . . The knowledge filled her with hunger and fear.

"Morgan." Her name wrenched from him on a sigh

of need. "I want you—by the gods, I want you. Come, stay here with me tonight. Here, where we can be alone."

His mouth was roaming her face. She wanted to agree. Her body was aching to agree to anything—to everything. Yet, she found herself drawing back. "No."

Nick lifted his face. His expression was amused and confident. "Afraid?"

"Yes."

His brows rose at the unexpected honesty, then drew together in frustration. The look in her eyes made it impossible for him to press his advantage. *"Diabolos,* you're an exasperating woman." He strode away and poured more liquor into his glass. "I could toss you over my shoulder, haul you up to the bedroom, and be done with it."

Though her legs were watery, Morgan forced herself to remain standing. "Why don't you?"

He whirled back, furious. She watched as he slowly pulled out the control. "You're more accustomed to a wine and candlelight seduction, I imagine. Soft promises. Soft lies." Nick drank deep, then set down his glass with a bang. "Is that what you want from me?"

"No." Morgan met his fury steadily while her hand reached instinctively for the medal at her throat. "I don't want you to make love to me."

"Don't take me for a fool!" He took a step toward her, then stopped himself. Another step and neither of them would have a choice. "Your body betrays you every time I touch you."

"That has nothing to do with it," she said calmly. "I don't want you to make love to me."

He waited a beat until the desire and frustration could be tamed a bit. "Because you believe I'm an opium smuggler?"

"No," she said, surprising both of them. She felt her strength waver a moment, then told him the truth. "Because I don't want to be one of your amusements."

"I see." Carefully, Nick dipped his hands into his pockets. "I'd better take you back before you discover I find nothing amusing in lovemaking."

A half-hour later, Nick slammed back into the house. His temper was foul. He stalked into the salon, poured himself another drink, and slumped into a chair. Damn the woman, he didn't have the time or patience to deal with her. The need for her was still churning inside him like a pain, sharp and insistent. He took a long swallow of liquor to dull it. Just physical, he told himself. He'd have to find another woman—any other woman—and release some of the tension.

"Ah, you're back." Stephanos entered. He noted the black temper and accepted it without comment. He'd seen it often enough in the past. "The lady is more beautiful than I remembered." Nick's lack of response left him unperturbed. He moved to the bar and poured himself a drink. "How much did you tell her?"

"Only what was necessary. She's sharp and remarkably bold." Nick eyed the liquid in his glass with a scowl. "She accused me flat out of smuggling." At Stephanos's cackle of laughter, Nick drained more liquor. "Your sense of humor eludes me at the moment, old man."

Stephanos only grinned. "Her eyes are sharp—they linger on you." Though Nick made no response,

Stephanos's grin remained. "Did you speak to her of Alex?"

"Not at length."

"Is she loyal?"

"To Alex?" Nick frowned into his drink. "Yes, she would be. Where she cares, she'd be loyal." He set down the glass, refusing to give in to the urge to hurl it across the room. "Getting information out of her won't be easy."

"You'll get it nonetheless."

"I wish to hell she'd stayed in bed that night," Nick said savagely.

The gap-toothed grin appeared before Stephanos tossed back the drink in one long swallow. He let out a wheezy sigh of appreciation. "She lingers in your mind. That makes you uncomfortable." He laughed loud and long at Nick's scowl, then sighed again with the effort of it. "Athens is waiting for your call."

"Athens can fry in hell."

Chapter 5

MORGAN'S FRAME OF MIND WAS AS POOR AS NICK'S when she entered the Theoharis villa. Somewhere on the drive back from Nick's she had discovered that what she was feeling wasn't anger. It wasn't fear or even resentment. In a few days Nick had managed to do something Jack hadn't done in all the months she had known him. He'd hurt her.

It had nothing to do with the bruises that were already fading on her arms. This hurt went deeper, and had begun before she had even met him. It had begun when he had chosen the life he was leading.

Nothing to do with me. Nothing to do with me, Morgan told herself again and again. But she slammed the front door as she swept into the cool white hall. Her plans to go immediately to her room before she could snarl at anyone were tossed to the winds by a call and a wave from Dorian.

"Morgan, come join us."

Fixing on a smile, Morgan strolled out to the terrace. Iona was with him, sprawled on a lounge in a hot-pink playsuit that revealed long, shapely legs but covered her arms with white lace cuffs at the wrists. She sent Morgan a languid greeting, then went back to her sulky study of the gulf. Morgan felt the tension hovering in the air and wondered if it had been there before or if she had brought it with her.

"Alex is on a transatlantic call," Dorian told her as he held out a chair. "And Liz is dealing with some domestic crisis in the kitchen."

"Without an interpreter?" Morgan asked. She smiled, telling herself Nick wasn't going to ruin her mood and make her as sulky as Alex's cousin.

"It's ridiculous." Iona gestured for Dorian to light her cigarette. "Liz should simply fire the man. Americans are habitually casual with servants."

"Are they?" Morgan felt her back go up at the slur on her friend and her nationality. "I wouldn't know."

Iona's dark eyes flicked over her briefly. "I don't imagine you've had many dealings with servants."

Before Morgan could retort, Dorian stepped in calmly. "Tell me, Morgan, what did you think of Nick's treasure trove?"

The expression in his eyes asked her to overlook Iona's bad manners, and told her something she'd begun to suspect the night before. He's in love with her, she mused, and felt a stab of pity. With an effort, Morgan relaxed her spine. "It's a wonderful place, like a museum without being regimented or stiff. It must have taken him years to collect all those things."

"Nick's quite a businessman," Dorian commented. Another look passed between him and Morgan. This time she saw it was gratitude. "And, of course, he uses his knowledge and position to secure the best pieces for himself."

"There was a Swiss music box," she remembered. "He said it was over a hundred years old. It played *Für Elise*." Morgan sighed, at ease again. "I'd kill for it."

"Nick's a generous man—when approached in the proper manner." Iona's smile was sharp as a knife. Morgan turned her head and met it.

"I wouldn't know anything about that either," she said coolly. Deliberately, she turned back to Dorian. "I met Nick's cousin earlier this morning."

"Ah, yes, the young poet from America."

"He said he wanders all over this part of the island. I'm thinking of doing the same myself. It's such a simple, peaceful place. I suppose that's why I was so stunned when Alex said there was a problem with smuggling."

Dorian merely smiled as if amused. Iona stiffened. As Morgan watched, the color drained from her face, leaving it strained and cold and anything but beautiful. Surprised by the reaction, Morgan studied her carefully. Why, she's afraid, she realized. Now why would that be?

"A dangerous business," Dorian commented conversationally. Since his eyes were on Morgan, Iona's reaction went unnoticed by him. "But common enough —traditional in fact."

"An odd tradition," Morgan murmured.

"The network of patrols is very large, I'm told, and

closely knotted. As I recall, five men were killed last year, gunned down off the Turkish coast." He lit a cigarette of his own. "The authorities confiscated quite a cache of opium."

"How terrible." Morgan noticed that Iona's pallor increased.

"Just peasants and fishermen," he explained with a shrug. "Not enough intelligence between them to have organized a large smuggling ring. It's rumored the leader is brilliant and ruthless. From the stories passed around in the village, he goes along on runs now and then, but wears a mask. Apparently, not even his cohorts know who he is. It might even be a woman." He flashed a grin at the idea. "I suppose that adds an element of romance to the whole business."

Iona rose and dashed from the terrace.

"You must forgive her." Dorian sighed as his eyes followed her. "She's a moody creature."

"She seemed upset."

"Iona's easily upset," he murmured. "Her nerves . . ."

"You care for her quite a lot."

His gaze came back to lock on Morgan's before he rose and strode to the railing.

"I'm sorry, Dorian," Morgan began immediately. "I didn't mean to pry."

"No, forgive me." He turned back and the sun streamed over his face, gleaming off the bronzed skin, combing through his burnished gold hair. Adonis, Morgan thought again, and for the second time since she had come to Lesbos wished she could paint. "My feelings for Iona are . . . difficult and, I had thought, more cleverly concealed.''

"I'm sorry," Morgan said again, helplessly.

"She's spoiled, willful." With a laugh, Dorian shook his head. "What is it that makes one person lose his heart to another?"

Morgan looked away at the question. "I don't know. I wish I did."

"Now I've made you sad." Dorian sat back down beside Morgan and took her hands. "Don't pity me. Sooner or later, what's between Iona and me will be resolved. I'm a patient man." He smiled then, his eyes gleaming with confidence. "For now, we'll talk of something else. I have to confess, I'm fascinated by the smuggling legends."

"Yes. It is interesting. You said the rumor is that no one, not even the men who work for him, know who the leader is."

"That's the story. Whenever I'm on Lesbos, I keep hoping to stumble across some clue that would unmask him."

Morgan murmured something as her thoughts turned uncomfortably to Nick. "Yet you don't seem terribly concerned about the smuggling itself."

"Ah, the smuggling." Dorian moved his shoulders. "That's something for the authorities to worry about. But the thrill of the hunt, Morgan." His eyes gleamed as they moved past her. "The thrill of the hunt."

"You wouldn't believe it!" Liz bustled out and plopped into a chair. "A half-hour with a temperamental Greek cook. I'd rather face a firing squad. Give me a cigarette, Dorian." Her smile and everyday complaint made the subject of smuggling absurd. "So tell me, Morgan, how did you like Nick's house?"

Pink streaks joined sky and sea as dawn bloomed. The air was warm and moist. After a restless night, it was the best of beginnings.

Morgan strolled along the water's edge and listened to the first serenading of birds. This was the way she had planned to spend her vacation—strolling along the beach, watching sunrises, relaxing. Isn't that what her father and Liz had drummed into her head?

Relax, Morgan. Get off the treadmill for a while. You never give yourself any slack.

She could almost laugh at the absurdity. But then, neither Liz nor her father had counted on Nicholas Gregoras.

He was an enigma, and she couldn't find the key. His involvement in smuggling was like a piece of a jigsaw puzzle that wouldn't quite fit. Morgan had never been able to tolerate half-finished puzzles. She scuffed her sandals in the sand. He was simply not a man she could categorize, and she wanted badly to shake the need to try.

On the other hand, there was Iona. Morgan saw the puzzle there as well. Alex's sulky cousin was more than a woman with an annoying personality. There was some inner agitation—something deep and firmly rooted. And Alex knows something of it, she mused. Dorian, too, unless she missed her guess. But what? And how much? Iona's reaction to talk of smuggling had been a sharp contrast to both Alex's and Dorian's. They'd been resigned—even amused. Iona had been terrified. Terrified of discovery? Morgan wondered. But that was absurd.

Shaking her head, Morgan pushed the thought aside. This morning she was going to do what she had come to Greece to do. Nothing. At least, nothing strenuous. She was going to look for shells, she decided, and after rolling up the hem of her jeans, splashed into a shallow inlet.

They were everywhere. The bank of sand and the shallow water were glistening with them. Some had been crushed underfoot or beaten smooth by the slow current. Crouching, she stuffed the pockets of her jacket with the best of them.

She noticed the stub of a black cigarette half-buried in the sand. So, Alex comes this way, she thought with a smile. Morgan could see Liz and her husband strolling hand in hand through the shallows.

As the sun grew higher, Morgan became more engrossed. If only I'd brought a tote, she thought, then shrugged and began to pile shells in a heap to retrieve later. She'd have them in a bowl on her windowsill at home. Then, whenever she was trapped indoors on a cold, rainy afternoon, she could look at them and remember Greek sunshine.

There were dozens of gulls. They flapped around her, circled, and called out. Morgan found the high, piercing sound the perfect company for a solitary morning. As the time passed, she began to find that inner peace she had experienced so briefly on the moonlit beach.

The hunt had taken her a good distance from the beach. Glancing up, she saw, with pleasure, a mouth of a cave. It wasn't large and was nearly hidden from view, but she thought it was entitled to an exploration. With a frown for her white jeans, Morgan decided to take a peek inside the entrance and come back when she was more suitably dressed. She moved to it with the water sloshing up to her calves. Bending down, she tugged another shell from its bed of sand. As her gaze swept over toward the cave, her hand froze.

The face glistened white in the clear water. Dark eyes stared back at her. Her scream froze in her throat, locked there by terror. She had never seen death before—not unpampered, staring death. Morgan stepped back jerkily, nearly slipping on a rock. As she struggled to regain her balance, her stomach heaved up behind the scream so that she could only gag. Even through the horror, she could feel the pressure of dizziness. She couldn't faint, not here, not with that only a foot away. She turned and fled.

She scrambled and spilled over rocks and sand. The only clear thought in her head was to get away. On a dead run, breath ragged, she broke from the conceal-ment of the inlet out to the sickle of beach.

Hands gripped her. Blindly, Morgan fought against them with the primitive fear that the thing in the inlet had risen up and come after her.

"Stop it! Damn it, I'll end up hurting you again. Morgan, stop this. What's wrong with you?"

She was being shaken roughly. The voice pierced the first layer of shock. She stared and saw Nick's face. "Nicholas?" The dizziness was back and she went limp against him as waves of fear and nausea wracked her. Trembling, she couldn't stop the trembling, but knew she'd be safe now. He was there. "Nicholas," she managed again as though his name alone was enough to shield her.

Nick caught her tighter and shook her again. Her face was deathly pale, her skin clammy. He'd seen enough of horror to recognize it in her eyes. In a moment, he knew, she'd faint or be hysterical. He couldn't allow either.

"What happened?" he demanded in a voice that commanded an answer.

Morgan opened her mouth, but found she could only shake her head. She buried her face against his chest in an attempt to block out what she had seen. Her breath was still ragged, coming in dry sobs that wouldn't allow for words. She'd be safe now, she told herself as she fought the panic. He'd keep her safe.

"Pull yourself together, Morgan," Nick ordered curtly, "and tell me what happened."

"Can't . . ." She tried to burrow herself into him.

In one quick move he jerked her away, shaking her. "I said tell me." His voice was cold, emotionless. He knew only one way to deal with hysteria, and her breath was still rising in gasps.

Dazed by the tone of his voice, she tried again, then jolted, clinging to him when she heard the sound of footsteps.

"Hello. Am I intruding?" Andrew's cheerful voice came from behind her, but she didn't look back. The trembling wouldn't stop.

Why was he angry with her? Why wasn't he helping her? The questions whirled in her head as she tried to catch her breath. Oh, God, she needed him to help her.

"Is something wrong?" Andrew's tone mirrored both concern and curiosity as he noted Nick's black expression and Morgan's shaking form.

"I'm not sure." Nick forced himself not to curse his cousin and spoke briefly. "Morgan was running across the beach. I haven't been able to get anything out of her yet." He drew her away, his fingers digging roughly in her skin as she tried to hold firm. She saw nothing in his face but cool curiosity. "Now, Morgan"—there was an edge of steel now—"tell me."

"Over there." Her teeth began to chatter as the next stage of reaction set in. Swallowing, she clamped them together while her eyes pleaded with him. His remained hard and relentless on hers. "Near the cove." The effort of the two short sentences swam in her head. She leaned toward him again. "Nicholas, please."

"I'll have a look." He grabbed her arms, dragging them away from him, wishing he didn't see what she was asking of him—knowing he couldn't give it to her.

"Don't leave, please!" Desperate, she grabbed for him again only to be shoved roughly into Andrew's arms.

"Damn it, get her calmed down," Nick bit off, tasting his own fury. She had no right—no right to ask for things he couldn't give. He had no right—no right to want to give them to her. He swore again, low and pungent under his breath as he turned away.

"Nicholas!" Morgan struggled out of Andrew's arms, but Nick was already walking away. She pressed a hand to her mouth to stop herself from calling him again. He never looked back.

Arms encircled her. Not Nick's. She could feel the

gentle comfort of Andrew as he drew her against his chest. Her fingers gripped his sweater. Not Nick. "Here now." Andrew brought a hand to her hair. "I had hoped to entice you into this position under different circumstances."

"Oh, Andrew." The soft words and tender stroking had the ice of shock breaking into tears. "Andrew, it was so horrible."

"Tell me what happened, Morgan. Say it fast. It'll be easier then." His tone was quiet and coaxing as he stroked her hair. Morgan gave a shuddering sigh.

"There's a body at the mouth of the cave."

"A body!" He drew her back to stare into her face. "Good God! Are you sure?"

"Yes, yes, I saw—I was . . ." She covered her face with her hands a moment until she thought she could speak.

"Easy, take it easy," he murmured. "And let it come out."

"I was collecting shells in the inlet. I saw the cave. I was going to peek inside, then I . . ." She shuddered once, then continued. "Then I saw the face—under the water."

"Oh, Morgan." He drew her into his arms again and held her tight. He didn't say any more, but in silence gave her everything she had needed. When the tears stopped, he kept her close.

Nick moved rapidly across the sand. His frown deepened as he saw Morgan molded in his cousin's arms. As he watched, Andrew bent down to kiss her hair. A small fire leaped inside him that he smothered quickly.

"Andrew, take Morgan up to the Theoharis villa and phone the authorities. One of the villagers has had a fatal accident."

Nodding, Andrew continued to stroke Morgan's hair. "Yes, she told me. Terrible that she had to find it." He swallowed what seemed to be his own revulsion. "Are you coming?"

Nick looked down as Morgan turned her face to his. He hated the look in her eyes as she stared at him—the blankness, the hurt. She wouldn't forgive him easily for this. "No, I'll stay and make sure no one else happens across it. Morgan . . ." He touched her shoulder, detesting himself. There was no response, her eyes were dry now, and empty. "You'll be all right. Andrew will take you home."

Without a word, Morgan turned her face away again.

His control slipped a bit as Nick shot Andrew a hard glance. "Take care of her."

"Of course," Andrew murmured, puzzled by the tone. "Come on, Morgan, lean on me."

Nick watched them mount the beach steps. When they were out of sight, he went back to search the body.

Seated in the salon, her horror dulled with Alex's best brandy, Morgan studied Captain Tripolos of Mitilini's police department. He was short, with his build spreading into comfortable lines that stopped just short of fat. His gray hair was carefully slicked to conceal its sparseness. His eyes were dark and sharp. Through the haze of brandy and shock, Morgan recognized a man with the tenacity of a bulldog.

"Miss James." The captain spoke in quick, staccato

English. "I hope you understand, I must ask you some questions. It is routine."

"Couldn't it wait?" Andrew was stationed next to Morgan on the sofa. As he spoke he slipped an arm around her shoulders. "Miss James has had a nasty shock."

"No, Andrew, it's all right." Morgan laid her hand over his. "I'd rather be done with it. I understand, Captain." She gave him a straight look which he admired. "I'll tell you whatever I can."

"Efxaristo." He licked the end of his pencil, settled himself in his chair, and smiled with his mouth only. "Perhaps you could start by telling me exactly what happened this morning, from the time you arose."

Morgan began to recount the morning as concisely as she could. She spoke mechanically, with her hands limp and still in her lap. Though her voice trembled once or twice, Tripolos noted that her eyes stayed on his. She was a strong one, he decided, relieved that she wasn't putting him to the inconvenience of tears or jumbled hysterics.

"Then I saw him under the water." Morgan accepted Andrew's hand with gratitude. "I ran."

Tripolos nodded. "You were up very early. Is this your habit?"

"No. But I woke up and had an impulse to walk on the beach."

"Did you see anyone?"

"No." A shudder escaped, but her gaze didn't falter. She went up another notch in Tripolos's admiration. "Not until Nicholas and Andrew."

"Nicholas? Ah, Mr. Gregoras." He shifted his eyes

to where Nick sprawled on a sofa across the room with Alex and Liz. "Had you ever seen the . . . deceased before?"

"No." Her hand tightened convulsively on Andrew's as the white face floated in front of her eyes. With a desperate effort of will, she forced the image away. "I've only been here a few days and I haven't been far from the villa yet."

"You're visiting from America?"

"Yes."

He made a quiet cluck of sympathy. "What a pity a murder had to blight your vacation."

"Murder?" Morgan repeated. The word echoed in her head as she stared into Tripolos's calm eyes. "But I thought . . . wasn't it an accident?"

"No." Tripolos glanced idly down at his note pad. "No, the victim was stabbed—in the back," he added with distaste. It was as if he considered murder one matter and back-stabbing another. "I hope I won't have to disturb you again." He rose and bowed over her hand. "Did you find many shells this morning, Miss James?"

"Yes I—I gathered quite a few." She felt compelled to reach in her jacket pocket and produce some. "I thought they were . . . lovely."

"Yes." He smiled, then turned to the others. "I regret we will have to question everyone on their whereabouts from last evening to this morning. Of course," he continued with a shrug, "we will no doubt find the murder was a result of a village quarrel, but with the body found so close to both villas . . ." He trailed off as he pocketed his pad and pencil. "One of you might recall some small incident that will help settle the matter.''

Settle the matter? Morgan thought on a wave of hysteria. Settle the matter. But a man's dead. I'm dreaming. I must be dreaming.

"Easy, Morgan," Andrew whispered in her ear. "Have another sip." Gently, he urged the brandy back to her lips.

"You have our complete cooperation, Captain," Alex stated, and rose. "It isn't pleasant for any of us to have such a thing happen so near our homes. It's particularly upsetting that a guest of mine should have found the man."

"I understand, of course." Tripolos nodded wearily, rubbing a hand over his square chin. "It would be less confusing if I spoke with you one at a time. Perhaps we could use your office?"

"I'll show you where it is." Alex gestured to the door. "You can speak to me first if you like."

"Thank you." Tripolos gave the room a general bow before retreating behind Alex. Morgan watched his slow, measured steps. He'd haunt a man to the grave, she thought, and shakily swallowed the rest of the brandy.

"I need a drink," Liz announced, moving toward the liquor cabinet. "A double. Anyone else?"

Nick's eyes skimmed briefly over Morgan. "Whatever you're having." He gestured with his hand, signaling Liz to refill Morgan's glass.

"I don't see why he has to question us." Iona moved to the bar, too impatient to wait for Liz to pour. "It's absurd. Alex should have refused. He has enough influence to avoid all of this." She poured something potent into a tall glass and drank half of it down.

"There's no reason for Alex to avoid anything." Liz handed Nick his drink before splashing another generous portion of brandy into Morgan's glass. "We have nothing to hide. What can I fix you, Dorian?"

"Hide? I said nothing about hiding," Iona retorted as she swirled around the room. "I don't want to answer that policeman's silly questions just because *she* was foolish enough to stumble over some villager's body," she said, gesturing toward Morgan.

"A glass of ouzo will be fine, Liz," Dorian stated before Liz could fire a retort. His gaze lit on Iona. "I hardly think we can blame Morgan, Iona. We'd have been questioned in any case. As it is, she's had to deal with finding the man as well as the questions. Thank you, Liz," he added as she placed a glass in his hand and shot him a grim smile.

"I cannot stay in this house today." Iona prowled the room, her movements as jerky as a nervous finger on a trigger. "Nicky, let's go out in your boat." She stopped and dropped to the arm of his chair.

"The timing's bad, Iona. When I'm finished here, I have paperwork to clear up at home." He sipped his drink and patted her hand. His eyes met Morgan's briefly, but long enough to recognize condemnation. Damn you, he thought furiously, you have no right to make me feel guilty for doing what I have to do.

"Oh, Nicky." Iona's hand ran up his arm. "I'll go mad if I stay here today. Please, a few hours on the sea?"

Nick sighed in capitulation while inside he fretted

against a leash that was too long, and too strong, for him to break. He had reason to agree, and couldn't let Morgan's blank stare change the course he'd already taken. "All right, later this afternoon." ·

Iona smiled into her drink.

The endless questioning continued. Liz slipped out as Alex came back in. And the waiting went on. Conversation came in fits and starts, conducted in undertones. As Andrew left the room for his conference, Nick wandered to Morgan's new station by the window.

"I want to talk to you." His tone was quiet, with the steel under it. When he put his hand over hers, she jerked it away.

"I don't want to talk to you."

Deliberately, he slipped his hands into his pockets. She was still pale. The brandy had steadied her but hadn't brought the color back to her cheeks. "It's necessary, Morgan. At the moment, I haven't the opportunity to argue about it."

"That's your problem."

"We'll go for a drive when the captain's finished. You need to get away from here for a while."

"I'm not going anywhere with you. Don't tell me what I need now." She kept her teeth clamped and spoke without emotion. "I needed you then."

"Damn it, Morgan." His muttered oath had all the power of a shout. She kept her eyes firmly on Liz's garden. Some of the roses, she thought dispassionately, were overblown now. The hands in his pockets were fists, straining impotently. "Don't you think I know that? Don't you think I—" He cut himself off before he lost control. "I couldn't give you what you needed—not then. Don't make this any more impossible for me than it is."

She turned to him now, meeting his fury with frost. "I have no intention of doing that." Her voice was as low as his but with none of his vibrating emotion. "The simple fact is I don't want anything from you now. I don't want anything to do with you."

"Morgan . . ." There was something in his eyes now that threatened to crack her resolve. Apology, regret, a plea for understanding where she'd never expected to see one. "Please, I need—"

"I don't care what you need," she said quickly, before he could weaken her again. "Just stay away from me. Stay completely away from me."

"Tonight," he began, but the cold fury in her eyes stopped him.

"Stay away," Morgan repeated.

She turned her back on him and walked across the room to join Dorian. Nick was left with black thoughts and the inability to carry them out.

Chapter 6

MORGAN WAS SURPRISED SHE'D SLEPT. SHE HADN'T been tired when Liz and Alex had insisted she lie down, but had obeyed simply because her last words with Nick had sapped all of her resistance. Now as she woke she saw it was past noon. She'd slept for two hours.

Groggy, heavy-eyed, Morgan walked into the bath to splash cool water on her face. The shock had passed, but the nap had brought her a lingering weariness instead of refreshment. Beneath it all was a deep shame—shame that she had run, terrified, from a dead man. Shame that she had clung helplessly to Nick and been turned away. She could feel even now that sensation of utter dependence—and utter rejection.

Never again, Morgan promised herself. She should have trusted her head instead of her heart. She should have known better than to ask or expect anything from a man like him. A man like him had nothing to give. You'd always find hell if you looked to a devil. And yet . . .

And yet it had been Nick she had needed, and trusted—him she had felt safe with the moment his arms had come around her. My mistake, Morgan thought grimly, and studied herself in the mirror over the basin. There were still some lingering signs of shock—the pale cheeks and too wide eyes, but she felt the strength returning.

"I don't need him," she said aloud, wanting to hear the words. "He doesn't mean anything to me."

But he's hurt you. Someone who doesn't matter can't hurt you.

I won't let him hurt me again, Morgan promised herself. Because I won't ever go to him again, I won't ever ask him again, no matter what.

She turned away from her reflection and went downstairs.

Even as she entered the main hall, Morgan heard the sound of a door closing and footsteps. Glancing behind her, she saw Dorian.

"So, you've rested." He came to her and took her hand. In the gesture was all the comfort and concern she could have asked for.

"Yes. I feel like a fool." At his lifted brow, Morgan moved her shoulders restlessly. "Andrew all but carried me back up here."

With a low laugh, he slipped an arm around her shoulders and led her into the salon. "You American women—do you always have to be strong and self-reliant?"

"I always have been." She remembered weeping in

Nick's arms—clinging, pleading—and straightened her spine. "I have to depend on myself."

"I admire you for it. But then, you don't make a habit of stumbling over dead bodies." He cast a look at her pale cheeks and gentled his tone. "There, it was foolish of me to remind you. Shall I fix you another drink?"

"No—no, I've enough brandy in me as it is." Morgan managed a thin smile and moved away from him.

Why was it she was offered a supporting arm by everyone but the one who mattered? No, Nick couldn't matter, she reminded herself. She couldn't let him matter, and she didn't need a supporting arm from anyone.

"You seem restless, Morgan. Would you rather be alone?"

"No." She shook her head as she looked up. His eyes were calm. She'd never seen them otherwise. There'd be strength in him, she thought, and wished bleakly it had been Dorian she had run to that morning. Going to the piano, she ran a finger over the keys. "I'm glad the captain's gone. He made me nervous."

"Tripolos?" Dorian drew out his cigarette case. "I doubt he's anything to worry about. I doubt even the killer need worry," he added with a short laugh. "The Mitilini police force isn't known for its energy or brilliance."

"You sound as if you don't care if the person who killed that man is caught."

"Village quarrels mean nothing to me," he countered. "I'm concerned more with the people I know. I don't like to think you're worried about Tripolos."

"He doesn't worry me," she corrected, frowning as he lit a cigarette. Something was nagging at the back of her mind, struggling to get through. "He just has a way of looking at you while he sits there, comfortable and not quite tidy." She watched the column of smoke curl up from the tip of the long, black cigarette. With an effort, Morgan shook off the feeling of something important, half remembered. "Where is everyone?"

"Liz is with Alex in his office. Iona's gone on her boat ride."

"Oh, yes, with Nicholas." Morgan looked down at her hands, surprised that they had balled into fists. Deliberately, she opened them. "It must be difficult for you."

"She needed to escape. The atmosphere of death is hard on her nerves."

"You're very understanding." Disturbed and suddenly headachy, Morgan wandered to the window. "I don't think I would be—if I were in love."

"I'm patient, and I know that Nick means less than nothing to her. A means to an end." He paused for a moment, before he spoke again, thoughtfully. "Some people have no capacity for emotion—love or hate."

"How empty that would be," Morgan murmured.

"Do you think so?" He gave her an odd smile. "Somehow, I think it would be comfortable."

"Yes, comfortable perhaps but . . ." Morgan trailed off as she turned back. Dorian was just lifting the cigarette to his lips. As Morgan's eyes focused on it, she remembered, with perfect clarity, seeing the stub of one of those expensive brands in the sand, only a few yards from the body. A chill shot through her as she continued to stare.

"Morgan, is something wrong?" Dorian's voice broke through so that she blinked and focused on him again.

"No, I—I suppose I'm not myself yet. Maybe I'll have that drink after all."

She didn't want it, but needed a moment to pull her thoughts together. The stub of a cigarette didn't have to mean anything, she told herself as Dorian went to the bar. Anyone from the villa could have wandered through that inlet a dozen times.

But the stub had been fresh, Morgan remembered— half in, half out of the sand, unweathered. The birds hadn't picked at it. Surely if someone had been that close to the body, they would have seen. They would have seen, and they would have gone to the police. Unless . . .

No, that was a ridiculous thought, she told herself as she felt a quick tremor. It was absurd to think that Dorian might have had anything to do with a villager's murder. Dorian or Alex, she thought as that sweet, foreign smoke drifted over her.

They were both civilized men—civilized men didn't stab other men in the back. Both of them had such beautiful, manicured hands and careful manners. Didn't it take something evil, something cold and hard to kill? She thought of Nick and shook her head. No, she wouldn't think of him now. She'd concentrate on this one small point and work it through to the end.

It didn't make any sense to consider Dorian or Alex as killers. They were businessmen, cultured. What possible dealings could they have had with some local fisherman? It was an absurd thought, Morgan told herself, but couldn't quite shake the unease that was creeping into her. There'd be a logical explanation, she insisted. There was always a logical explanation. She was still upset, that was all. Blowing some minor detail out of proportion.

Whose footsteps were on the beach steps that first night? a small voice insisted. Who was Nick hiding from? Or waiting for? That man hadn't been killed in a village quarrel, her thoughts ran on. She hadn't believed it for a moment, any more than she'd really believed the man had died accidentally. Murder . . . smuggling. Morgan closed her eyes and shuddered.

Who was coming in from the sea when Nick had held her in the shadow of the cypress? Nick had ordered Stephanos to follow him. Alex? Dorian? The dead man perhaps? She jolted when Dorian offered her the snifter.

"Morgan, you're still so pale. You should sit."

"No . . . I guess I'm still a little jumpy, that's all." Morgan cupped the snifter in both hands but didn't drink. She would ask him, that was all. She would simply ask him if he'd been to the inlet. But when her eyes met his, so calm, so concerned, she felt an icy tremor of fear. "The inlet—" Morgan hesitated, then continued before her courage failed her. "The inlet was so beautiful. It seemed so undisturbed." But so many shells had been crushed underfoot, she remembered abruptly. Why hadn't she thought of that before? "Do you—do a lot of people go there?"

"I can't speak for the villagers," Dorian began, watching as she perched on the arm of a divan. "But I'd think most of them would be too busy with their fishing or in the olive groves to spend much time gathering shells."

"Yes." She moistened dry lips. "But still, it's a lovely spot, isn't it?"

Morgan kept her eyes on his. Was it her imagination, or had his eyes narrowed? A trick of the smoke that wafted between them? Her own nerves?

"I've never been there," Dorian said lightly. "I suppose it's a bit like a native New Yorker never going to the top of the Empire State Building." Morgan's gaze followed his fingers as he crushed out the cigarette in a cut-glass ashtray. "Is there something else, Morgan?"

"Something—no." Hastily, she looked back up to meet his eyes. "No, nothing. I suppose like Iona, the atmosphere's getting to me, that's all."

"Small wonder." Sympathetic, he crossed to her. "You've been through too much today, Morgan. Too much talk of death. Come out in the garden," he suggested. "We'll talk of something else."

Refusal was on the tip of her tongue. She didn't know why, only that she didn't want to be with him. Not then. Not alone. Even as she cast around for a reasonable excuse, Liz joined them.

"Morgan, I'd hoped you were still resting."

Grateful for the interruption, Morgan set down her untouched brandy and rose. "I rested long enough." A quick scan of Liz's face showed subtle signs of strain. "You look like you should lie down awhile."

"No, but I could use some air."

"I was just taking Morgan out to the garden." Dorian touched a hand to Liz's shoulder. "You two go out and relax. Alex and I have some business we should clear up."

"Yes." Liz lifted her hand to his. "Thank you,

Dorian. I don't know what Alex or I would have done without you today.''

"Nonsense.'' He brushed her cheek with his lips. "Go, take your mind off this business.''

"I will. See if you can get Alex to do the same.'' The plea was light, but unmistakable before Liz hooked her arm through Morgan's.

"Dorian.'' Morgan felt a flush of shame. He'd been nothing but kind to her, and she'd let her imagination run wild. "Thank you.''

He lifted a brow at the gratitude, then smiled and kissed her cheek in turn. He smelt of citrus groves and sunshine. "Sit with the flowers for a while, and enjoy.''

As he walked into the hall, Liz turned and headed toward the garden doors. "Should I order us some tea?''

"Not for me. And stop treating me like a guest.''

"Good Lord, was I doing that?''

"Yes, ever since—''

Liz shot Morgan a quick look as she broke off, then grimaced. "This whole business really stinks,'' Liz stated inelegantly, and plopped down on a marble bench.

Surrounded by the colors and scents of the garden, isolated from the house and the outside world by vines, Morgan and Liz frowned at each other.

"Damn, Morgan, I'm so sorry that you had to be the one. No, don't shrug and try to look casual,'' she ordered as Morgan did just that. "We've known each other too long and too well. I know what it must have been like for you this morning. And I know how you must be feeling right now.''

"I'm all right, Liz." She chose a small padded glider and curled her legs under her. "Though I'll admit I won't be admiring seashells for a while. Please," she continued as Liz's frown deepened. "Don't do this. I can see that you and Alex are blaming yourself. It was just—just a horrible coincidence that I happened to take a tour of that inlet this morning. A man was killed; someone had to find him."

"It didn't have to be you."

"You and Alex aren't responsible."

Liz sighed. "My practical American side knows that, but . . ." She shrugged, then managed to smile. "But I think I'm becoming a bit Greek. You're staying in my house." Liz lit a cigarette resignedly as she rose to pace the tiny courtyard.

A black cigarette, Morgan noticed with a tremor of anxiety—slim and black. She'd forgotten Liz had picked up the habit of occasionally smoking one of Alex's brand.

She stared up into Liz's oval, classic face, then shut her eyes. She must be going mad if she could conceive, even for an instant, that Liz was mixed up in smuggling and back-stabbing. This was a woman she'd known for years—lived with. Certainly if there was one person she knew as well as she knew herself, it was Liz.

But how far—how far would Liz go to protect the man she loved?

"And I have to admit," Liz went on as she continued to pace, "though it sticks me in the same category as Iona, that policeman made me nervous. He was just too"—she searched for an adjective—"respectful," she decided. "Give me a good old American grilling."

"I know what you mean," Morgan murmured. She

had to stop thinking, she told herself. If she could just stop thinking, everything would be all right again.

"I don't know what he expected to find out, questioning us that way." Liz took a quick, jerky puff, making her wedding ring flash with cold, dazzling light.

"It was just routine, I suppose." Morgan couldn't take her eyes from the ring—the light, the stones. Love, honor, and obey—forsaking all others.

"And creepy," Liz added. "Besides, none of us even knew this Anthony Stevos."

"The captain said he was a fisherman."

"So is every second man in the village."

Morgan allowed the silence to hang. Carefully, she reconstructed the earlier scene in the salon. What were the reactions? If she hadn't been so dimmed with brandy and shock, would she have noticed something? There was one more person she'd seen lighting one of the expensive cigarettes. "Liz," she began slowly, "don't you think Iona went a little overboard? Didn't she get a bit melodramatic about a few routine questions?"

"Iona thrives on melodrama," Liz returned with grim relish. "Did you see the way she fawned all over Nick? I don't see how he could bear it."

"He didn't seem to mind," Morgan muttered. No, not yet, she warned herself. You're not ready to deal with that yet. "She's a strange woman," Morgan continued. "But this morning . . ." And yesterday, she remembered. Yesterday when I spoke of smuggling . . . "I think she was really afraid."

"I don't think Iona has any genuine feelings," Liz

said stubbornly. "I wish Alex would just cross her off as a bad bet and be done with it. He's so infuriatingly conscientious."

"Strange, Dorian said almost the same thing." Morgan plucked absently at an overblown rose. It was Iona she should concentrate on. If anyone could do something deadly and vile, it was Iona. "I don't see her that way."

"What do you mean?"

"Iona." Morgan stopped plucking at the rose and gave Liz her attention. "I see her as a woman of too many feelings rather than none at all. Not all healthy certainly, perhaps even destructive—but strong, very strong emotions."

"I can't abide her," Liz said with such unexpected venom, Morgan stared. "She upsets Alex constantly. I can't tell you how much time and trouble and money he's put into that woman. And he gets nothing back but ingratitude, rudeness."

"Alex has very strong family feelings," Morgan began. "You can't protect him from—"

"I'd protect him from anything," Liz interrupted passionately. "Anything and anyone." Whirling, she hurled her cigarette into the bushes where it lay smoldering. Morgan found herself staring at it with dread. "Damn," Liz said in a calmer tone. "I'm letting all this get to me."

"We all are." Morgan shook off the sensation of unease and rose. "It hasn't been an easy morning."

"I'm sorry, Morgan, it's just that Alex is so upset by all this. And as much as he loves me, he just isn't the kind of man to share certain areas with me. His trouble—his business. He's too damn Greek." With a quick laugh, she shook her head. "Come on, sit down. I've vented my spleen."

"Liz, if there were something wrong—I mean, something really troubling you, you'd tell me, wouldn't you?"

"Oh, don't start worrying about me now." Liz nudged Morgan back down on the glider. "It's just frustrating when you love someone to distraction and they won't let you help. Sometimes it drives me crazy that Alex insists on trying to keep the less-pleasant aspects of his life away from me."

"He loves you," Morgan murmured and found she was gripping her hands together.

"And I love him."

"Liz . . ." Morgan took a deep breath and plunged. "Do you and Alex walk through the inlet often?"

"Hmmm?" Obviously distracted, Liz looked back over her shoulder as she walked toward her bench. "Oh, no, actually, we usually walk on the cliffs—if I can drag him away from his office. I can't think when's the last time I've been near there. I only wish," she added in a gentler tone, "I'd been with you this morning."

Abruptly and acutely ashamed at the direction her thoughts had taken, Morgan looked away. "I'm glad you weren't. Alex had his hands full enough with one hysterical female."

"You weren't hysterical," Liz corrected in a quiet voice. "You were almost too calm by the time Andrew brought you in."

"I never even thanked him." Morgan forced herself to push doubts and suspicions aside. They were as ugly as they were ridiculous. "What did you think of Andrew?"

"He's a very sweet man." Sensing Morgan's changing mood, Liz adjusted her own thoughts. "He appeared to put himself in the role of your champion today." She smiled, deliberately looking wise and matronly. "I'd say he was in the first stages of infatuation."

"How smug one becomes after three years of marriage."

"He'd be a nice diversion for you," Liz mused, unscathed. "But he's from the genteel-poor side of Nick's family. I rather fancy seeing you set up in style. Then again," she continued as Morgan sighed, "he'd be nice company for you . . . for a while."

Dead on cue, Andrew strolled into the courtyard. "Hello. I hope I'm not intruding."

"Why, no!" Liz gave him a delighted smile. "Neighboring poets are always welcome."

He grinned, a flash of boyishness. With that, he went up several notches on Liz's list. "Actually, I was worried about Morgan." Bending over, he cupped her chin and studied her. "It was such an awful morning, I wanted to see how you were doing. I hope you don't mind." His eyes were dark blue, like the water in the bay—and with the same serenity.

"I don't." She touched the back of his hand. "At all. I'm really fine. I was just telling Liz I hadn't even thanked you for everything you did."

"You're still pale."

His concern made her smile. "A New York winter has something to do with that."

"Determined to be courageous?" he asked with a tilted smile.

"Determined to do a better job of it than I did this morning."

"I kind of liked the way you held on to me." He gave her hand a light squeeze. "I want to steal her for an evening," he told Liz, shifting his gaze from Morgan's face. "Can you help me convince her a diversion is what she needs?"

"You have my full support."

"Come have dinner with me in the village." He bent down to Morgan again. "Some local color, a bottle of ouzo, and a witty companion. What more could you ask for?"

"What a marvelous idea!" Liz warmed to Andrew and the scheme. "It's just what you need, Morgan."

Amused, Morgan wondered if she should just let them pat each other on the back for a while. But it was what she needed—to get away from the house and the doubts. She smiled at Andrew. "What time should I be ready?"

His grin flashed again. "How about six? I'll give you a tour of the village. Nick gave me carte blanche with his Fiat while I'm here, so you won't have to ride on an ass."

Because her teeth were tight again, Morgan relaxed her jaw. "I'll be ready."

The sun was high over the water when Nick set his boat toward the open sea. He gave it plenty of throttle, wanting the speed and the slap of the wind.

Damn the woman! he thought on a new surge of

frustration. Seething, he tossed the butt of a slender black cigarette into the churning waves. If she'd stay in bed instead of wandering on beaches at ridiculous hours, all of this could have been avoided. The memory of the plea in her voice, the horror in her eyes flashed over him. He could still feel the way she had clung to him, needing him.

He cursed her savagely and urged more speed from the motor.

Shifting his thoughts, Nick concentrated on the dead man. Anthony Stevos, he mused, scowling into the sun. He knew the fisherman well enough—what he had occasionally fished for—and the Athens phone number he had found deep inside Stevos's pants pocket.

Stevos had been a stupid, greedy man, Nick thought dispassionately. Now he was a dead one. How long would it take Tripolos to rule out the village brawl and hit on the truth? Not long enough, Nick decided. He was going to have to bring matters to a head a bit sooner than he had planned.

"Nicky, why are you looking so mean?" Iona called to him over the motor's roar. Automatically, he smoothed his features.

"I was thinking about that pile of paperwork on my desk." Nick cut the motor off and let the boat drift in its own wake. "I shouldn't have let you talk me into taking the afternoon off."

Iona moved to where he sat. Her skin glistened, oiled slick, against a very brief bikini. Her bosom spilled over in invitation. She had a ripe body, rounded and full and arousing. Nick felt no stir as she swung her hips moving toward him.

"Agapetikos, we'll have to take your mind off business matters.'' She wound herself into his lap and pressed against him.

He kissed her mechanically, knowing that, after the bottle of champagne she'd drunk, she'd never know the difference. But her taste lingered unpleasantly on his lips. He thought of Morgan, and with a silent, furious oath, crushed his mouth against Iona's.

"Mmm.'' She preened like a stroked cat. ''Your mind isn't on your paperwork now, Nicky. Tell me you want me. I need a man who wants me.''

''Is there a man alive who wouldn't want a woman such as you?'' He ran a hand down her back as her mouth searched greedily for his.

''A devil,'' she muttered with a slurred laugh. ''Only a devil. Take me, Nicky.'' Her head fell back, revealing eyes half closed and dulled by wine. ''Make love to me here, in the open, in the sun.''

And he might have to, he thought with a grinding disgust in his stomach. To get what he needed. But first, he would coax what he could from her while she was vulnerable.

''Tell me, *matia mou,''* he murmured, tasting the curve of her neck while she busily undid the buttons of his shirt. ''What do you know of this smuggling between Lesbos and Turkey?''

Nick felt her stiffen, but her response—and, he knew, her wits—were dulled by the champagne. In her state of mind, he thought, it wouldn't take much more to loosen her tongue. She'd been ready to snap for days. Deliberately, he traced his tongue across her skin and felt her sigh.

''Nothing,'' she said quickly and fumbled more

desperately at his buttons. "I know nothing of such things."

"Come, Iona." He murmured seductively. She was a completely physical woman, one who ran on sensations alone. Between wine and sex and her own nerves, she'd talk to him. "You know a great deal. As a businessman"—he nipped at her earlobe—"I'm interested in greater profit. You won't deny me a few extra drachmas, will you?"

"A few million," she murmured, and put her hand on his to show him what she wanted. "Yes, there's much I know."

"And much you'll tell me?" he asked. "Come, Iona. You and the thought of millions excite me."

"I know the man that stupid woman found this morning was murdered because he was greedy."

Nick forced himself not to tense. "But greed is so difficult to resist." He went with her as she stretched full length on the bench. "Do you know who murdered him, Iona?" She was slipping away from him, losing herself to the excess of champagne. On a silent oath, Nick nipped at her skin to bring her back.

"I don't like murder, Nicky," she mumbled, "and I don't like talking to the police even more." She reached for him, but her hands fumbled. "I'm tired of being used," she said pettishly, then added, "Perhaps it's time to change allegiance. You're rich, Nicky. I like money. I need money."

"Doesn't everyone?" Nick asked dryly.

"Later, we'll talk later. I'll tell you." Her mouth was greedy on his. Forcing everything from his mind, Nick struggled to find some passion, even the pretense of passion, in return. God, he needed a woman; his body ached for one. And he needed Iona. But as he felt her sliding toward unconsciousness, he did nothing to revive her.

Later, as Iona slept in the sun, Nick leaned over the opposite rail and lit a cigarette from the butt of another. The clinging distaste both infuriated and depressed him. He knew that he would have to use Iona, be used by her—if not this time, then eventually. He had to tap her knowledge to learn what he wanted to know. It was a matter of his own safety—and his success. The second had always been more important to him than the first.

If he had to be Iona's lover to gain his own end, then he'd be her lover. It meant nothing. Swearing, he drew deeply on the cigarette. It meant nothing, he repeated. It was business.

He found he wanted a shower, a long one, something to cleanse himself of the dirt which wouldn't wash away. Years of dirt, years of lies. Why had he never felt imprisoned by them until now?

Morgan's face slipped into his mind. Her eyes were cold. Flinging the cigarette out to sea, he went back to the wheel and started the engine.

Chapter 7

DURING A LEISURELY DRINK AFTER A LEISURELY TOUR, Morgan decided the village was perfect. White-washed houses huddled close together, some with pillars, some with arches, still others with tiny wooden balconies. The tidiness, the freshness of white should have lent an air of newness. Instead, the village seemed old and timeless and permanent.

She sat with Andrew at a waterfront *kafenion*, watching the fishing boats sway at the docks, and the men who spread their nets to dry.

The fishermen ranged from young boys to old veterans. All were bronzed, all worked together. There were twelve to each net—twenty-four hands, some wrinkled and gnarled, some smooth with youth. All strong. As they worked they shouted and laughed in routine companionship.

"Must have been a good catch," Andrew commented. He watched Morgan's absorption with the small army of men near the water's edge.

"You know, I've been thinking." She ran a finger down the side of her glass. "They all seem so fit and sturdy. Some of those men are well past what we consider retirement age in the States. I suppose they'll sail until they die. A life on the water must be a very satisfying existence." Pirates . . . would she ever stop thinking of pirates?

"I don't know if any of these people think much about satisfaction. It's simply what they do. They fish or work in Nick's olive groves. They've been doing one or the other for generations." Toying with his own drink, Andrew studied them too. "I do think there's a contentment here. The people know what's expected of them. If their lives are simple, perhaps it's an enviable simplicity."

"Still, there's the smuggling," Morgan murmured.

Andrew shrugged. "It's all part of the same mold, isn't it? They do what's expected of them and earn a bit of adventure and a few extra drachmas."

She shot him a look of annoyed surprise. "I didn't expect that attitude from you."

Andrew looked back at her, both brows raised. "What attitude?"

"This—this nonchalance over crime."

"Oh, come on, Morgan, it's—"

"Wrong," she interrupted. "It should be stopped," Morgan swallowed the innocently clear but potent ouzo.

"How do you stop something that's been going on for centuries in one form or another?"

"It's current form is ugly. I should think that men of influence like Alex and . . . Nicholas, with homes on the island, would put pressure on whoever should be pressured."

"I don't know Alex well enough to comment," Andrew mused, filling her glass again. "But I can't imagine Nick getting involved in anything that didn't concern himself or his business."

"Can't you?" Morgan murmured.

"If that sounds like criticism, it's not." He noted he had Morgan's full attention, but that her eyes were strangely veiled. "Nick's been very good to me, lending me the cottage and the money for my passage. Lord knows when I'll be able to pay him back. And it irks quite a bit to have to borrow, but poetry isn't the most financially secure career."

"I think I read somewhere that T.S. Eliot was a bank teller."

Andrew returned her understanding smile with a wry grimace. "I could work out of Nick's California office." He shrugged and drank. "His offer wasn't condescending, just absentminded. It's rough on the ego." He looked past her, toward the docks. "Maybe my ship will come in."

"I'm sure it will, Andrew. Some of us are meant to follow dreams."

His gaze came back to her. "And artists are meant to suffer a bit, rise beyond the more base needs at money and power?" His smile was brittle, his eyes cool. "Let's order." Morgan watched him shake off the mood and smile with his usual warmth. "I'm starved."

The evening sky was muted as they finished their

meal. There were soft, dying colors flowing into the western sea. In the east, it was a calm, deep violet waiting for the first stars. Morgan was content with the vague glow brought on by spiced food and Greek ouzo. There was intermittent music from a mandolin. Packets of people shuffled in and out of the café, some of them breaking into song.

Their waiter cum proprietor was a wide man with a thin moustache and watery eyes. Morgan figured the eyes could be attributed to the spices and cook smoke hanging in the air. American tourists lifted his status. Because he was impressed with Morgan's easily flowing Greek, he found opportunities to question and gossip as he hovered around their table.

Morgan toyed with a bit of *psomaki* and relaxed with the atmosphere and easy company. She'd found nothing but comfort and good will in the Theoharis villa, but this was something different. There was an earthier ambience she had missed in Liz's elegant home. Here there would be lusty laughter and spilled wine. As strong as Morgan's feelings were for both Liz and Alex, she would never have been content with the lives they led. She'd have rusted inside the perpetual manners.

For the first time since that morning, Morgan felt the nagging ache at the base of her skull begin to ease.

"Oh, Andrew, look! They're dancing." Cupping her chin on her hands, Morgan watched the line of men hook arms.

As he finished up the last of a spicy sausage, Andrew glanced over. "Want to join in?"

Laughing, she shook her head. "No, I'd spoil it—but you could," she added with a grin.

"You have," Andrew began as he filled her glass again, "a wonderful laugh. It's rich and unaffected and trails off into something sensuous."

"What extraordinary things you say, Andrew." Morgan smiled at him, amused. "You're an easy man to be with. We could be friends."

Andrew lifted his brows. Morgan was surprised to find her mouth briefly captured. There was a faint taste of the island on him—spicy and foreign. "For starters." At her stunned expression, he leaned back and grinned. "That face you're wearing doesn't do great things for my ego, either." He pulled a pack of cigarettes out of his jacket pocket, then dug for a match. Morgan stopped staring at him to stare at the thin black box.

"I didn't know you smoked," she managed after a moment.

"Oh, not often." He found a match. The tiny flame flared, flickering over his face a moment, casting shadows, mysteries, suspicions. "Especially since my taste runs to these. Nick takes pity on me and leaves some at my cottage whenever he happens by. Otherwise, I suppose I'd do without altogether." When he noticed Morgan's steady stare, he gave her a puzzled smile. "Something wrong?"

"No." She lifted her glass and hoped she sounded casual. "I was just thinking—you'd said you roam all over this part of the island. You must have been in that inlet before."

"It's a beautiful little spot." He reached over for her hand. "Or it was. I guess I haven't been there in over a week. It might be quite a while before I go back now."

"A week," Morgan murmured.

"Don't dwell on it, Morgan."

She lifted her eyes to his. They were so clear, so concerned. She was being a fool. None of them—Alex, Dorian, Andrew—none of them were capable of what was burning into her thoughts. How was she to know that some maniac from the village hadn't had a taste for expensive tobacco and back-stabbing? It made more sense, a great deal more sense than her ugly suspicions.

"You're right." She smiled again and leaned toward him. "Tell me about your epic poem."

"Good evening, Miss James, Mr. Stevenson."

Morgan twisted her head and felt the sky cloud over. She looked up into Tripolos's pudgy face. "Hello, Captain."

If her greeting lacked enthusiasm, Tripolos seemed unperturbed. "I see you're enjoying a bit of village life. Do you come often?"

"This is Morgan's first trip," Andrew told him. "I convinced her to come out to dinner. She needed something after this morning's shock."

Tripolos clucked sympathetically. Morgan noted the music and laughter had stilled. The atmosphere in the café was hushed and wary.

"Very sensible," the captain decided. "A young lady must not dwell on such matters. I, unfortunately, must think of little else at the moment." He sighed and looked wistfully at the ouzo. "Enjoy your evening."

"Damn, damn, *damn*!" she muttered when he walked away. "Why does he affect me this way? Every time I see him, I feel like I've got the Hope diamond in my pocket."

"I know what you mean." Andrew watched people

fall back to create a path for Tripolos. "He almost makes you wish you had something to confess."

"Thank God, it's not just me." Morgan lifted her glass again, noticed her hands were trembling, and drained it. "Andrew," she began in calm tones, "unless you have some moral objection, I'm going to get very drunk."

Sometime later, after learning Andrew's views on drinking were flexible, Morgan floated on a numbing cloud of ouzo. The thin light of the moon had replaced the colors of sunset. As the hour grew later, the café crowd grew larger, both in size and volume. Music was all strings and bells. If the interlude held a sheen of unreality, she no longer cared. She'd had enough of reality.

The waiter materialized with yet another bottle. He set it on the table with the air of distributing a rare wine.

"Busy night," Morgan commented, giving him a wide if misty, smile.

"It is Saturday," he returned, explaining everything.

"So, I've chosen my night well." She glanced about, seeing a fuzzy crush of people. "Your customers seem happy."

He followed her survey with a smug smile, wiping a hand on his apron. "I feared when the Mitilini captain came, my business would suffer, but all is well."

"The police don't add to an atmosphere of enjoyment. I suppose," she added slowly, "he's investigating the death of that fisherman."

He gave Morgan a quick nod. "Stevos came here

often, but he was a man with few companions. He was not one for dancing or games. He found other uses for his time." The waiter narrowed his eyes. "My customers do not like to answer questions." He muttered something uncomplimentary, but Morgan wasn't sure if it was directed at Stevos or Tripolos.

"He was a fisherman," she commented, struggling to concentrate on the Greek's eyes. "But it appears his comrades don't mourn him."

The waiter moved his shoulders eloquently, but she saw her answer. There were fishermen, and fishermen. "Enjoy your evening, *kyrios*. It is an honor to serve you."

"You know," Andrew stated when the waiter drifted to another table, "it's very intimidating listening to all that Greek. I couldn't pick up on it. What was he saying?"

Not wanting to dwell on the murder again, Morgan merely smiled. "Greek males are very red-blooded, Andrew, but I explained that I was otherwise engaged for this evening." She locked her hands behind her head and looked up at the stars. "Oh, I'm glad I came. It's so lovely. No murders—no smuggling tonight. I feel marvelous, Andrew. When can I read some of your poetry?"

"When your brain's functioning at a normal level." Smiling, he tilted more ouzo into her glass. "I think your opinion might be important."

"You're a nice man." Morgan lifted her glass and studied him as intensely as possible. "You're not at all like Nicholas."

"What brought that on?" Andrew frowned, setting the bottle back down again.

"You're just not." She held out her glass. "To Americans," she told him. "One hundred percent pure."

After tapping her glass with his, Andrew drank and shook his head. "I have a feeling we weren't toasting the same thing."

She felt Nick begin to push into her thoughts and she thrust him away. "What does it matter? It's a beautiful night."

"So it is." His finger traced lightly over the back of her hand. "Have I told you how lovely you are?"

"Oh, Andrew, are you going to flatter me?" With a warm laugh, she leaned closer. "Go ahead, I love it."

With a wry grin, he tugged her hair. "You're spoiling my delivery."

"Oh, dear . . . how's this?" Morgan cupped her chin on her hands again and gave him a very serious stare.

On a laugh, Andrew shook his head. "Let's walk for a while. I might find a dark corner where I can kiss you properly."

Rising, he helped Morgan to her feet. She exchanged a formal and involved good night with the proprietor before Andrew could navigate her away from the crowd.

Those not gathered in the *kafenion* were long since in bed. The white houses were closed and settled for the night. Now and then a dog barked, and another answered. Morgan could hear her own footsteps echo down the street.

"It's so quiet," she murmured. "All you can really hear is the water and the night itself. Ever since that first morning when I woke up on Lesbos, I've felt as if

I belonged. Nothing that's happened since has spoiled that for me. Andrew." She whirled herself around in his arms and laughed. "I don't believe I'm *ever* going home again. How can I face New York and the traffic and the snow again? Rushing to work, rushing home. Maybe I'll become a fisherman, or give into Liz and marry a goatherd."

"I don't think you should marry a goatherd," Andrew said practically, and drew her closer. Her scent was tangling his senses. Her face, in the moonlight, was an ageless mystery. "Why don't you give the fishing a try? We could set up housekeeping in Nick's cottage."

It would serve him right, her mind muttered. Lifting her mouth, Morgan waited for the kiss.

It was warm and complete. Morgan neither knew nor cared if the glow was a result of the kiss or the liquor. Andrew's lips weren't demanding, weren't urgent and possessive. They were comforting, requesting. She gave him what she could.

There was no rocketing passion—but she told herself she didn't want it. Passion clouded the mind more successfully than an ocean of ouzo. She'd had enough of hunger and passions. They brought pain with disillusionment. Andrew was kind, uncomplicated. He wouldn't turn away when she needed him. He wouldn't give her sleepless nights. He wouldn't make her doubt her own strict code of right and wrong. He was the knight—a woman was safe with a knight.

"Morgan," he murmured, then rested his cheek on her hair. "You're exquisite. Isn't there some man I should consider dueling with?"

Morgan tried to think of Jack, but could form no

clear picture. There was, however, a sudden, atrociously sharp image of Nick as he dragged her close for one of his draining kisses.

"No," she said too emphatically. "There's no one. Absolutely no one."

Andrew drew her away and tilted her chin with his finger. He could see her eyes in the dim glow of moonlight. "From the strength of your denial, I'd say my competition's pretty formidable. No."—he laid a finger over her lips as she started to protest—"I don't want to have my suspicions confirmed tonight. I'm selfish." He kissed her again, lingering over it. "Damn it, Morgan, you could be habit forming. I'd better take you home while I remember I'm a gentleman and you're a very drunk lady."

The villa shimmered white under the night sky. A pale light glowed in a first-floor window for her return.

"Everyone's asleep," Morgan stated unnecessarily as she let herself out of the car. Andrew rounded the hood. "I'll have to be very quiet." She muffled irrepressible giggles with a hand over her mouth. "Oh, I'm going to feel like an idiot tomorrow if I remember any of this."

"I don't think you'll remember too much," Andrew told her as he took her arm.

Morgan managed the stairs with the careful dignity of someone who no longer feels the ground under his feet. "It would never do to disgrace Alex by landing on my face in the foyer. He and Dorian are *so* dignified."

"And I," Andrew returned, "will have to resume my drive with the utmost caution. Nick wouldn't approve if I ran his Fiat off a cliff."

"Why, Andrew." Morgan stood back and studied him owlishly. "You're almost as sloshed as I am."

"Not quite, but close enough. However"—he let out a long breath and wished he could lie down—"I conducted myself with the utmost restraint."

"Very nicely done." She went off into a muffled peal of giggles again. "Oh, Andrew." She leaned against him so heavily that he had to shift his balance to support her. "I did have a good time—a wonderful time. I needed it more than I realized. Thank you."

"In you go." He opened the door and gave her a nudge inside. "Be careful on the stairs," he whispered. "Should I wait and listen for the sounds of an undignified tumble?"

"Just be on your way and don't take the Fiat for a swim." She stood on her toes and managed to brush his chin with her lips. "Maybe I should make you some coffee."

"You'd never find the kitchen. Don't worry, I can always park the car and walk if worse comes to worse. Go to bed, Morgan, you're weaving."

"That's you," she retorted before she closed the door.

Morgan took the stairs with painful caution. The last thing she wanted to do was wake someone up and have to carry on any sort of reasonable conversation. She stopped once and pressed her hands to her mouth to stop a fresh bout of giggles. Oh, it felt so good, so good not to be able to think. But this has to stop, she told herself firmly. No more of this, Morgan, straighten up and get upstairs before all is discovered.

She managed to pull herself to the top landing, then had to think carefully to remember in which direction her room lay. To the left, of course, she told herself with a shake of the head. But which way is left, for God's sake? She spent another moment working it out before she crept down the hall. She gripped the doorknob, then waited for the door to stop swaying before she pushed it open.

"Ah, success," she murmured, then nearly spoiled it by stumbling over the rug. Quietly, she shut the door and leaned back against it. Now, if she could just find the bed. A light switched on, as if by magic. She smiled absently at Nick.

"*Yaisou*, you seem to be a permanent fixture."

The fury in his eyes rolled off the fog as she stepped unsteadily out of her shoes.

"What the hell have you been up to?" he demanded. "It's nearly three o'clock in the morning!"

"Oh, how rude of me not to have phoned to tell you I'd be late."

"Don't get cute, damn it, I'm not in the mood." He stalked over to her and grabbed her arms. "I've been waiting for you half the night, Morgan, I . . . " His voice trailed off as he studied her. His expression altered from fury to consideration then reluctant amusement. "You're totally bombed."

"Completely," she agreed, and had to take a deep breath to keep from giggling again. "You're so observant, Nicholas."

Amusement faded as her hand crept up his shirt front. "How the hell am I supposed to have a rational conversation with a woman who's seeing two of everything?"

"Three," she told him with some pride. "Andrew's only up to two. I quite surpassed him." Her other hand slid up to toy with one of his buttons. "Did you know you have wonderful eyes. I've never seen eyes so dark. Andrew's are blue. He doesn't kiss anything like you do. Why don't you kiss me now?"

He tightened his grip for a moment, then carefully released her. "So, you've been out with young Andrew." He wandered the room while Morgan swayed and watched him.

"*Young* Andrew and I would have asked you to join us, but it just slipped our minds. Besides, you can be really boring when you're proper and charming." She had a great deal of trouble with the last word and yawned over it. "Do we have to talk much longer? My tongue's getting thick."

"I've had about enough of being proper and charming myself," he muttered, picking up a bottle of her scent and setting it down again. "It serves its purpose."

"You do it very well," she told him and struggled with her zipper. "In fact, you're nearly perfect at it."

"Nearly?" His attention caught, he turned in time to see her win the battle with the zipper. "Morgan, for God's sake, don't do that now. I—"

"Yes, except you do slip up from time to time. A look in your eyes—the way you move. I suppose it's convincing all around if I'm the only one who's noticed. Then again, it might be because everyone else knows you and expects the inconsistency. Are you going to kiss me or not?" She dropped the dress to the floor and stepped out of it.

He felt his mouth go dry as she stood, clad only in a flimsy chemise, watching him mistily. Desire thudded inside him, hot, strong, and he forced himself back to what she was saying.

"Noticed what?"

Morgan made two attempts to pick up the dress. Each time she bent, the top of the chemise drifted out to show the swell of her breasts. Nick felt the thud lower to his stomach. "Noticed what?" she repeated as she left the dress where it was. "Oh, we're back to that. It's definitely the way you move."

"Move?" He struggled to keep his eyes on her face and away from her body. But her scent was already clouding his brain, and her smile—her smile challenged him to do something about it.

"It's like a panther," Morgan told him, "who knows he's being hunted and plans to turn the attack to his advantage when he's ready."

"I see." He frowned, not certain he liked her analogy. "I'll have to be more careful."

"Your problem," Morgan said cheerfully. "Well, since you don't want to kiss me, I'll say good night, Nicholas. I'm going to bed. I'd see you down your vine, but I'm afraid I'd fall off the balcony."

"Morgan, I need to talk to you." He moved quickly and took her arm before she could sink onto the bed. That, he knew, would be too much pressure for any man. But she lost her already uncertain balance and tumbled into his arms. Warm and pliant, she leaned against him, making no objection as he molded her closer.

"Have you changed your mind?" she murmured, giving him a slow, sleepy-eyed smile. "I thought of you when Andrew kissed me tonight. It was very rude of me—or of you, I'm not sure which. Perhaps I'll think of Andrew if you kiss me now."

"The hell you will." He dragged her against him, teetering on the edge. Morgan let her head fall back.

"Try me," she invited.

"Morgan—the hell with all of it!"

Helplessly, he devoured her mouth. She was quickly and totally boneless, arousing him to desperation by simple surrender. Desire was a fire inside him, spreading dangerously.

For the first time, he let himself go. He could think of nothing, nothing but her and the way her body flowed in his hands. She was softer than anything he'd ever hoped to know. So soft, she threatened to seep into him, become a part of him before he could do anything to prevent it. The need was raging, overpowering, taking over the control he'd been master of for as long as he could remember. But now, he burned to forfeit it.

With her, everything could be different. With her, he'd be clean again. Could she turn back the clock?

He could feel the brush of the bedspread against his thigh and knew, in one movement, he could be on it with her. Then nothing would matter but that he had her—a woman. But it wasn't any woman he wanted. It had been her since the first night she had challenged him on that deserted beach. It had been her since the first time those light, clear eyes had dared him. He was afraid—and he feared little—that it would always be her.

Mixed with the desire came a quick twist of pain. With a soft oath, he pulled her away, keeping his grip firm on her arms.

"Pay attention, will you?" His voice was rough and unsteady, but she didn't seem to notice. She smiled up at him and touched his cheek with her palm.

"Wasn't I?"

He checked the urge to shake her and spoke calmly. "I need to talk to you."

"Talk?" She smiled again. "Do we have to talk?"

"There are things I need to tell you—this morning . . ." He fumbled with the words, no longer certain what he wanted to say, what he wanted to do. How could her scent be stronger than it had been a moment ago? He was drowning in it.

"Nicholas." Morgan sighed sleepily. "I drank an incredible amount of ouzo. If I don't sleep it off, I may very well die. I'm sure the body only tolerates a certain amount of abuse. I've stretched my luck tonight."

"Morgan." His breath was coming too quickly. His own pulse like thunder in his ears. He should let her go, he knew. He should simply let her go—for both their sakes. But his arms stayed around her. "Straighten up and listen to me," he demanded.

"I'm through listening." She gave a sleepy, sultry laugh. "Through listening. Make love with me or go."

Her eyes were only slits, but the clear, mystical blue pulled him in. No struggle, no force would drag him out again. "Damn you," he breathed as they fell onto the bed. "Damn you for a witch."

It was all hell smoke and thunder. He couldn't resist it. Her body was as fluid as wine—as sweet and as potent. Now he could touch her wherever he chose and she only sighed. As his mouth crushed possessively on hers, she yielded, but in yielding held him prisoner. Even knowing it, he was helpless. There'd be a payment—a price in pain—for succumbing to the temptation. He no longer cared for tomorrows. Now, this moment, he had her. It was enough.

He tore the filmy chemise from her, too anxious, too desperate, but she made no protest as the material ripped away. On a groan of need, he devoured her.

Tastes—she had such tastes. They lingered on his tongue, spun in his head. The crushed wild honey of her mouth, the rose-petal sweetness of her skin, drove him to search for more, and to find everything. He wasn't gentle—he was long past gentleness, but the quiet moans that came from her spoke of pleasure.

Words, low and harsh with desire, tumbled from him. He wasn't certain if he cursed her again or made her hundreds of mad promises. For the moment, it was all the same. Needs ripped through him—needs he understood, needs he'd felt before. But there was something else, something stronger, greedier. Then his flesh was against her flesh, and everything was lost. Fires and flames, a furnace of passion engulfed him, driving him beyond control, beyond reason. She was melting into him. He felt it as a tangible ache but had no will to resist.

Her hands were hot on his skin, her body molten. He could no longer be certain who led and who followed. Beneath his, her mouth was soft and willing, but he tasted her strength. Under him, her body was pliant, unresisting, but he felt her demand. Her skin would be white, barely touched by the sun. He burned to see it, but saw only the glimmer of her eyes in the darkness.

Then she pulled his mouth back to hers and he saw nothing, nothing but the blur of raging colors that were passion. The wild, sweet scent of jasmine seeped into him, arousing, never soothing, until he thought he'd never smell anything else.

With a last force of will, he struggled for sanity. He wouldn't lose himself in her—to her. He couldn't. Without self-preservation he was nothing, vulnerable. Dead.

Even as he took her in a near violent rage, he surrendered.

Chapter 8

THE SUNLIGHT THAT POURED THROUGH THE WIN-
dows, through the open balcony doors, throbbed and
pulsed in Morgan's head. With a groan she rolled over,
hoping oblivion would be quick and painless. The
thudding only increased. Morgan shifted cautiously
and tried for a sitting position. Warily, she opened her
eyes then groaned at the flash of white morning sun.
She closed them again in self-preservation. Slowly,
gritting her teeth for courage, she allowed her lids to
open again.

The spinning and whirling which had been enjoyable
the night before, now brought on moans and mutters.
With queasy stomach and aching eyes, she sat in the
center of the bed until she thought she had the strength
to move. Trying to keep her head perfectly still, she
eased herself onto the floor.

144

Carelessly, she stepped over her discarded dress and found a robe in the closet. All she could think of were ice packs and coffee. Lots of coffee.

Then she remembered. Abruptly, blindingly. Morgan whirled from the closet to stare at the bed. It was empty—maybe she'd dreamed it. Imagined it. In useless defense she pressed her hands to her face. No dream. He had been there, and everything she remembered was real. And she remembered . . . the anger in his eyes, her own misty, taunting invitation. The way his mouth had pressed bruisingly to hers, her own unthinking, abandoned response.

The passion—it had been all she had thought it would be. Unbearable, wonderful, consuming. He'd cursed her. She could remember his words. Then he had taken her places she'd never even glimpsed before. She'd given him everything, then mindlessly challenged him to take more. She could still feel those taut, tensing muscles in his back, hear that ragged, desperate breathing at her ear.

He had taken her in fury, and it hadn't mattered to her. Then he had been silent. She had fallen asleep with her arms still around him. And now he was gone.

On a moan, Morgan dropped her hands to her sides. Of course he was gone. What else did she expect? The night had meant nothing to him—less than nothing. If she hadn't had so much to drink . . .

Oh, convenient excuse, Morgan thought on a wave of disgust. She still had too much pride to fall back on it. No, she wouldn't blame the ouzo. Walking to the bed, she picked up the torn remains of her chemise. She'd wanted him. God help her, she cared for him—

too much. No, she wouldn't blame the ouzo. Balling the chemise in her fist, Morgan hurled it into the bottom of the closet. She had only herself to blame.

With a snap, Morgan closed the closet door. It was over, she told herself firmly. It was done. It didn't have to mean any more to her than it had to Nick. For a moment, she leaned her forehead against the smooth wooden panel and fought the urge to weep. No, she wouldn't cry over him. She'd never cry over him. Straightening, Morgan told herself it was the headache that was making her feel so weak and weepy. She was a grown woman, free to give herself, to take a man, when and where she chose. Once she'd gone down and had some coffee, she'd be able to put everything in perspective.

She swallowed the threatening tears and walked to the door.

"Good morning, *kyrios*." The tiny maid greeted Morgan with a smile she could have done without. "Would you like your breakfast in your room now?"

"No, just coffee." The scent of food didn't agree with her stomach or her disposition. "I'll go down for it."

"It's a beautiful day."

"Yes, beautiful." With her teeth clenched, Morgan moved down the hall.

The sound of crashing dishes and a high-pitched scream had Morgan gripping the wall for support. She pressed her hand to her head and moaned. Did the girl have to choose this morning to be clumsy!

But when the screaming continued, Morgan turned back. The girl knelt just inside the doorway. Scattered plates and cups lay shattered over the rug where the food had splattered.

"Stop it!" Leaning down, Morgan grabbed her shoulders and shook Zena out of self-defense. "No one's going to fire you for breaking a few dishes."

The girl shook her head as her eyes rolled. She pointed a trembling finger toward the bed before she wrenched herself from Morgan's hold and fled.

Turning, Morgan felt the room dip and sway. A new nightmare crept in to join the old. With her hand gripping the doorknob, she stared.

A shaft of sunlight spread over Iona as she lay on her back, flung sideways across the bed. Her head hung over the edge, her hair streaming nearly to the floor. Morgan shook off the first shock and dizziness and raced forward. Though her fingers trembled, she pressed them to Iona's throat. She felt a flutter, faint, but she felt it. The breath she hadn't been aware she'd held came out in a rush of relief. Moving on instinct, she pulled Iona's unconscious form until she lay back on the bed.

It was then she saw the syringe laying on the tumbled sheets.

"Oh, my God."

It explained so much. Iona's moodiness, those tight, jerky nerves. She'd been a fool not to suspect drugs before. She's overdosed, Morgan thought in quick panic. What do I do? There must be something I'm supposed to do.

"Morgan—dear God!"

Turning her head only, Morgan looked at Dorian standing pale and stiff in the doorway. "She's not

dead,'' Morgan said quickly. ''I think she's overdosed
—get a doctor—an ambulance.''

''Not dead?''

She heard the flat tone of his voice, heard him start
to come toward her. There was no time to pamper his
feelings. ''Do it quickly!'' she ordered. ''There's a
pulse, but it's faint.''

''What's Iona done now?'' Alex demanded in a tone
of strained patience. ''The maid's hysterical, and—oh,
sweet Lord!''

''An ambulance!'' Morgan demanded as she kept her
fingers on Iona's pulse. Perhaps if she kept them
there, it would continue to beat. ''In the name of God,
hurry!'' She turned then in time to see Alex rush from
the room as Dorian remained frozen. ''There's a
syringe,'' she began with studied calm. She didn't
want to hurt him, but continued as his gaze shifted to
her. His eyes were blank. ''She must have o.d.'d. Did
you know she used drugs, Dorian?''

''Heroin.'' And a shudder seemed to pass through
him. ''I thought it had stopped. Are you sure she's—''

''She's alive.'' Morgan gripped his hand as he came
to the bed. A wave of pity washed over her—for Iona,
for the man who's hand she held in her own. ''She's
alive, Dorian. We'll get help for her.''

His hand tightened on hers for a moment so that
Morgan had to choke back a protest. ''Iona,'' he
murmured. ''So beautiful—so lost.''

''She's not lost, not yet!'' Morgan said fiercely. ''If
you know how to pray, pray that we found her in
time.''

His eyes came back to Morgan's, clear, expressionless. She thought as she looked at him she'd never seen anything so empty. "Pray," he said quietly. "Yes, there's nothing else to be done."

It seemed to take hours, but when Morgan watched the helicopter veer off to the west, the morning was still young. Iona, still unconscious, was being rushed to Athens. Dorian rode with her and the doctor while Alex and Liz began hurried preparations for their own flight.

Still barefoot and in her robe, Morgan watched the helicopter until it was out of sight. As long as she lived, she thought, she'd never forget that pale, stony look on Dorian's face—or the lifeless beauty on Iona's. With a shudder, she turned away and saw Alex just inside the doorway.

"Tripolos," he said quietly. "He's in the salon."

"Oh, not now, Alex." Overcome with pity, she held out both hands as she went to him. "How much more can you stand?"

"It's necessary." His voice was tight with control and he held her hands limply. "I apologize for putting you through all this, Morgan—"

"No." She interrupted him and squeezed his hands. "Don't treat me that way, Alex. I thought we were friends."

"*Diabolos*," he murmured. "Such friends you have. Forgive me."

"Only if you stop treating me as though I were a stranger."

On a sigh, he slipped his arm around her shoulder. "Come, we'll face the captain."

Morgan wondered if she would ever enter the salon

without seeing Captain Tripolos seated in the wide, high-back chair. She sat on the sofa as before, faced him, and waited for the questions.

"This is difficult for you," Tripolos said at length. "For all of you." His gaze roamed over the occupants of the room, from Morgan to Alex to Liz. "We will be as discreet as is possible, Mr. Theoharis. I will do what I can to avoid the press, but an attempted suicide in a family as well known as yours . . ." He let the rest trail off.

"Suicide," Alex repeated softly. His eyes were blank, as if the words hadn't penetrated.

"It would seem, from the preliminary report, that your cousin took a self-induced overdose. Heroin. But I hesitate to be more specific until the investigation is closed. Procedure, you understand."

"Procedure."

"You found Miss Theoharis, Miss James?"

Morgan gave a quick, nervous jolt at the sound of her name, then settled. "No, actually, the maid found her. I went in to see what was wrong. Zena had dropped the tray and was carrying on . . . when I went in I saw Iona."

"And you called for an ambulance?"

"No." She shook her head, annoyed. He knew Alex had called, but wanted to drag the story from her piece by piece. Resigned, Morgan decided to accommodate him. "I thought at first she was dead—then I felt a pulse. I got her back into bed."

"Back into bed?"

Tripolos's tone had sharpened, ever so faintly, but Morgan caught it. "Yes, she was half out of it, almost on the floor. I wanted to lay her down." She lifted her hands helplessly. "I honestly don't know what I wanted to do, it just seemed like the right thing."

"I see. Then you found this?" He held up the syringe, now in a clear plastic bag.

"Yes."

"Did you know your cousin was a user of heroin, Mr. Theoharis?"

Alex stiffened at the question. Morgan saw Liz reach out to take his hand. "I knew Iona had a problem— with drugs. Two years ago she went to a clinic for help. I thought she had found it. If I had believed she was still . . . ill," he managed. "I wouldn't have brought her into my home with my wife and my friend."

"Mrs. Theoharis, were you unaware of Miss Theoharis's problem?"

Morgan heard the breath hiss out between Alex's teeth, but Liz spoke quickly. "I was perfectly aware of it." Alex's head whipped around but she continued calmly. "That is, I was aware that my husband arranged for her to have treatment two years ago, though he tried to shield me." Without looking at him, Liz covered their joined hands with her free one.

"Would you, Mr. Theoharis, have any notion where your cousin received her supply?"

"None."

"I see. Well, since your cousin lives in Athens, perhaps it would be best if I worked with the police there, in order to contact her close friends."

"Do what you must," Alex said flatly. "I only ask that you spare my family as much as possible."

"Of course. I will leave you now. My apologies for the intrusion, yet again."

"I must phone my family," Alex said dully when

the door closed behind Tripolos. As if seeking comfort, his hand went to his wife's hair. Then he rose and left without another word.

"Liz," Morgan began. "I know it's a useless phrase, but if there's anything I can do . . ."

Liz shook her head. She shifted her eyes from the doorway back to her friends. "It's all so unbelievable. That she's lying there, so near death. What's worse, I never liked her. I made no secret of it, but now . . ." She rose and walked to the window. "She's Alex's family, and he feels that deeply. Now, in his heart, he's responsible for whatever happens to her. And all I can think of is how cold I was to her."

"Alex is going to need you." Morgan rose and walked over to put a hand on her shoulder. "You can't help not liking her, Liz. Iona isn't an easy person to like."

"You're right, of course." With a deep breath Liz turned and managed a weak smile. "It's been a hell of a vacation so far, hasn't it? No, don't say anything." She squeezed Morgan's hand. "I'm going to see if Alex needs me. There'll be arrangements to be made."

The villa was silent as Morgan went up to change. As she buttoned her shirt, she stood by the terrace doors, staring out at the view of garden, sea, and mountain. How could it be that so much ugliness had intruded in such a short time? she wondered. Death and near death. This wasn't the place for it. But even Paradise named its price, she thought, and turned away.

The knock on her door was quiet. "Yes, come in."

"Morgan, am I disturbing you?"

"Oh, Alex." As she looked up, Morgan's heart welled with sympathy. The lines of strain and grief seemed etched into his face. "I know how horrible all this is for you, and I don't want to add to your problems. Perhaps I should go back to New York."

"Morgan." He hesitated for a moment. "I know it's a lot to ask, but I don't do it for myself. For Liz. Will you stay for Liz? Your company is all I can give her for a time." He released Morgan's hands and moved restlessly around the room. "We'll have to fly to Athens. I can't say how long—until Iona is well or—" He broke off as if he wasn't yet prepared for the word. "I'll have to stay with my family for a few days. My aunt will need me. If I could send Liz back knowing you'd be here with her, it would make it so much easier."

"Of course, Alex. You know I will."

He turned and gave her a phantom of a smile. "You're a good friend, Morgan. We'll have to leave you for at least a day and a night. After that, I'll send Liz back. I can be sure she'll leave Athens if you're here." With a sigh, he took her hand absently. "Dorian might choose to stay in Athens as well. I believe he . . . has feelings for Iona I didn't realize before. I'll ask Nick to look after you while we're gone."

"No." She bit her tongue on the hurried protest. "No, really, Alex, I'll be fine. I'm hardly alone, with the servants in the house. When will you leave?"

"Within the hour."

"Alex, I'm sure it was an accident."

"I'll have to convince my aunt of that." He held out his hands, searching his own palms for a moment.

"Though as to what I believe . . ." His look had hardened when he lifted his eyes again. "Iona courts disaster. She feeds on misery. I'll tell you now, because I won't ever be able to speak freely to anyone else. Not even Liz." His face was a grim mask now. Cold. "I detest her." He spit the words out as if they were poison. "Her death would be nothing but a blessing to everyone who loves her."

When Alex, Liz, and Dorian were gone, Morgan left the villa. She needed to walk—needed the air. This time she avoided her habit of heading for the beach. She was far from ready for that. Instead, she struck out for the cliffs, drawn to their jagged, daring beauty.

How clean the air was! Morgan wanted no floral scents now, just the crisp tang of the sea. She walked without destination. Up, only up, as if she could escape from everything if she could only get higher. If the gods had walked here, she thought, they would have come to the cliffs, to hear the water beat against rock, to breathe the thin, pure air.

She saw, to her pleasure, a scruffy, straggly goat with sharp black eyes. He stared at her a moment as he gnawed on a bit of wild grass he'd managed to find growing in between the rocks. But when she tried to get closer, he scrambled up, lightly, and disappeared over the other side of the cliff.

With a sigh, Morgan sat down on a rock perched high above the water. With some surprise, she saw tiny blue-headed flowers struggling toward the sun out of a crevice hardly wider than a thumbnail. She touched them, but couldn't bring herself to pluck any. Life's everywhere, she realized, if you only know where to look.

"Morgan."

Her hand closed over the blooms convulsively at the sound of his voice. She opened it slowly and turned her head. Nick was standing only a short distance away, his hair caught by the breeze that just stirred the air. In jeans and a T-shirt, his face unshaven, he looked more like the man she had first encountered. Undisciplined. Unprincipled. Her heart gave a quick, bounding leap before she controlled it.

Without a word, Morgan rose and started down the slope.

"Morgan." He caught her quickly, then turned her around with a gentleness she hadn't expected from him. Her eyes were cool, but beneath the frost, he saw they were troubled. "I heard about Iona."

"Yes, you once told me there was little that happened on the island you didn't know."

Her toneless voice slashed at him, but he kept his hands easy on her arms. "You found her."

She wouldn't let that uncharacteristic caring tone cut through her defenses. She could be—would be—as hard and cold as he had been. "You're well informed, Nicholas."

Her face was unyielding, and he didn't know how to begin. If she would come into his arms, he could show her. But the woman who faced him would lean on no one. "It must have been very difficult for you."

She lifted a brow, as though she were almost amused. "It was easier to find someone alive than to find someone dead."

He winced at that—a quick jerk of facial muscles, then dropped his hands. She'd asked him for comfort once, and now that he wanted to give it, needed to give it, it was too late. "Will you sit down?"

"No, it's not as peaceful here as it was."

"Stop slashing at me!" he exploded, grabbing her arms again.

"Let me go."

But the faint quaver in her voice told him something her words hadn't. She was closer to her own threshold than perhaps even she knew. "Very well, if you'll come back to the house with me."

"No."

"Yes." Keeping a hand on her arm, Nick started up the rough path. "We'll talk."

Morgan jerked her arm but his grip was firm. He propelled her up the rough path without looking at her. "What do you want, Nicholas? More details?"

His mouth thinned as he pulled her along beside him. "All right. You can tell me about Iona if you like."

"I don't like," she tossed back. They were already approaching the steps to his house. Morgan hadn't realized they were so close. What devil had prompted her to walk that way? "I don't want to go with you."

"Since when have I cared what you want?" he asked bitterly and propelled her through the front door. "Coffee," he demanded as Stephanos appeared in the hall.

"All right, I'll give you the details," Morgan raged as she whirled inside the door of the salon. "And then, by God, you'll leave me be! I found Iona unconscious, hardly alive. There was a syringe in bed with her. It seems she was an addict." She paused, unaware that her breath was starting to heave. "But you knew that, didn't you, Nicholas? You know all manner of things."

She'd lost all color, just as she had when she'd run across the beach and into his arms. He felt a twinge, an ache, and reached out for her.

"Don't touch me!" Nick's head jerked back as if she'd slapped him. Morgan pressed her hands against her mouth and turned away. "Don't touch me."

"I won't put my hands on you," Nick managed as they balled into fists. "Sit down, Morgan, before you keel over."

"Don't tell me what to do." Her voice quavered, and she detested it. Making herself turn back, she faced him again. "You have no right to tell me what to do."

Stephanos entered, silent, watchful. As he set the coffee tray down, he glanced over at Morgan. He saw, as Nick couldn't, her heart in her eyes. "You'll have coffee, miss," he said in a soft voice.

"No, I—"

"You should sit." Before Morgan could protest, Stephanos nudged her into a chair. "The coffee's strong."

Nick stood, raging at his impotence as Stephanos clucked around her like a mother hen.

"You'll have it black," he told her. "It puts color in your cheeks."

Morgan accepted the cup, then stared at it. "Thank you."

Stephanos gave Nick one long, enigmatic look, then left them.

"Well, drink it," Nick ordered, furious that the old man had been able to hack through her defenses when he felt useless. "It won't do you any good in the cup."

Because she needed to find strength somewhere, Morgan drank it down quickly. "What else do you want?"

"Damn it, Morgan, I didn't bring you here to grill you about Iona."

"No? You surprise me." Steadier, she set the cup aside and rose again. "Though why anything you do should surprise me, I don't know."

"There's nothing too vile you wouldn't attribute to me, is there?" Ignoring the coffee, Nick strode to the bar. "Perhaps you think I killed Stevos and left the body for you to find."

"No," she said calmly, because she could speak with perfect truth. "He was stabbed in the back."

"So?"

"You'd face a man when you killed him."

Nick turned away from the bar, the glass still empty in his hand. His eyes were black now, as black as she'd ever seen them. There was passion in them barely, just barely, suppressed. "Morgan, last night—"

"I won't discuss last night with you." Her voice was cold and final, cutting through him more accurately than any blade.

"All right, we'll forget it." This time he filled the glass. He'd known there would be a price to pay; somehow he hadn't thought it would be quite so high. "Would you like an apology?"

"For what?"

He gave a short laugh as his hand tightened on the glass. He tossed back the liquor. "God, woman, you've a streak of ice through you I hadn't seen."

"Don't talk to me of ice, Nicholas." Her voice rose with a passion she'd promised herself she wouldn't feel. "You sit here in your ancestral home, playing your dirty chess games with lives. I won't be one of your pawns. There's a woman barely alive in an Athens hospital. You make your money feeding her illness. Do you think you're remote from the blame because you cross the strait in the dead of night like some swashbuckling pirate?"

Very carefully, he set down the glass and turned. "I know what I am."

She stared at him until her eyes began to fill again. "So do I," she whispered. "God help me."

Turning, she fled. He didn't go after her.

Moments later, Stephanos came back into the room. "The lady's upset," he said mildly.

Nick turned his back to fill his glass again. "I know what the lady is."

"The past two days have been difficult for her." He clucked his tongue. "She came to you for comfort?"

Nick whirled but managed to bite back the words. Stephanos watched him calmly. "No, she didn't come to me. She'd go to the devil himself before she came to me again." With an effort, he controlled the rage and his tone. "And it's for the best, I can't let her interfere now. As things stand, she'll be in the way."

Stephanos caressed his outrageous moustache and whistled through his teeth. "Perhaps she'll go back to America."

"The sooner the better," Nick muttered and drained his glass. At the knock on the door, he swore. "See who the hell it is and get rid of them if you can."

"Captain Tripolos," Stephanos announced a few moments later. There was a gleam in his eye as he melted out of sight.

"Captain." Nick fought off the need to swear again. "You'll join me for coffee?"

"Thank you." Tripolos settled into a chair with a few wheezes and sighs. "Was that Miss James I just saw going down the cliff path?"

"Yes." With some effort, Nick prevented his knuckles from whitening against the handle of the pot. "She was just here."

Both men watched each other with what seemed casual interest. One was Morgan's panther—the other a crafty bear.

"Then she told you about Miss Theoharis."

"Yes." Nick offered the cream. "A nasty business, Captain. I intend to call Athens later this morning to see what news there is. Is Iona's condition why you're here?"

"Yes. It's kind of you to see me, Mr. Gregoras. I know you are a very busy man."

"It's my duty to cooperate with the police, Captain," Nick countered as he sat back with his coffee. "But I don't know how I can help you in this case."

"As you were with Miss Theoharis all of yesterday afternoon, I hoped you could shed some light on her frame of mind."

"Oh, I see." Nick sipped his coffee while his mind raced with possibilities. "Captain, I don't know if I can help you. Naturally, Iona was distressed that the man's murder was practically on her doorstep. She was edgy—but then, she often is. I can't say I saw anything different in her."

"Perhaps you could tell me what you did on your boat trip?" Tripolos suggested. "If Miss Theoharis

said anything which seemed to indicate she was thinking of suicide?''

Nick lifted a brow. "We weren't overly engaged in
conversation.''

"Of course.''

Nick wondered how long they would continue to
fence. He decided to execute a few flourishes of his
own. "I will say that Iona seemed a trifle nervous. That
is, as I said, however, a habitual trait. You'll find that
the people who know her will describe Iona as a . . .
restive woman. I can say with complete honesty that it
never entered my mind that she was contemplating
suicide. Even now, to be candid, I find the idea
impossible.''

Tripolos settled back comfortably. "Why?''

Generalities, Nick concluded, would suffice.
"Iona's too fond of herself to seek death. A beautiful
woman, Captain, and one greedy for life's pleasures.
It's merely an opinion, you understand. You know
much more about this sort of thing.'' He shrugged.
"My opinion is that it was an accident.''

"An accident, Mr. Gregoras, is unlikely.'' He was
fishing for a reaction, and Nick gave him another
curious lift of brow. "There was too much heroin in
her system for any but an amateur to take by mistake.
And Miss Theoharis is no stranger to heroin. The
marks of the needle tell a sad story.''

"Yes, I see.''

"Were you aware that Miss Theoharis was an
addict?''

"I didn't know Iona very well, Captain. Socially, of
course, but basically, she's a cousin of a friend—a

beautiful woman who isn't always comfortable to be around.''

"Yet you spent the day with her yesterday."

"A beautiful woman," Nick said again, and smiled. "I'm sorry I can't help you."

"Perhaps you'd be interested in a theory of mine."

Nick didn't trust those bland eyes but continued to smile. "Of course."

"You see, Mr. Gregoras," Tripolos went on. "If it was not an accident, and if your instincts are correct, there is only one answer."

"One answer?" Nick repeated, then allowed his expression to change slowly. "Do you mean you think someone attempted to . . . murder Iona?"

"I'm a simple policeman, Mr. Gregoras." Tripolos looked plumply humble. "It is my nature to look at such matters from a suspicious point of view. May I be frank?"

"By all means," Nick told him, admiring the captain's plodding shrewdness. Frank be damned, Nick mused, he's going to try to give me enough rope to hang myself.

"I am puzzled, and as a man who knows the Theoharis family well, I would like your opinion."

"Whatever I can do."

Tripolos nodded. "I will tell you first—and of course, you understand this cannot leave this room?"

Nick merely inclined his head and sipped his coffee.

"I will tell you Anthony Stevos was part of a smuggling ring operating on Lesbos."

"I must admit, the thought had crossed my mind." Amused, Nick took out a box of cigarettes, offering one to Tripolos.

"It's no secret that a group has been using this island's nearness to Turkey to smuggle opium across the strait." Tripolos admired the thin whisp of elegant tobacco before he bent closer to Nick for a light.

"You think this Stevos was murdered by one of his cohorts?"

"That is my theory." Tripolos drew in the expensive smoke appreciatively. "It is the leader of this group that is my main concern. A brilliant man, I am forced to admit." Reluctant respect crossed his face. "He is very clever and has so far eluded any nets spread for his capture. It is rumored he rarely joins in the boat trips. When he does, he is masked."

"I've heard the rumors, naturally," Nick mused behind a mist of smoke. "I put a great deal of it down to village gossip and romance. A masked man, smuggling—the stuff of fiction."

"He is real, Mr. Gregoras, and there is nothing romantic about back-stabbing."

"No, you're quite right."

"Stevos was not a smart man. He was being watched in hopes he would lead us to the one we want. But . . ." As was his habit, Tripolos let the sentence trail off.

"I might ask, Captain, why you're telling me what must be police business."

"As an important man in our community," Tripolos said smoothly, "I feel I can take you into my confidence."

The old fox, Nick thought, and smiled. "I appreciate that. Do you think this masked smuggler is a local man?"

"I believe he is a man who knows the island."

Tripolos gave a grim smile in return. "But I do not believe he is a fisherman."

"One of my olive pickers?" Nick suggested blandly, blowing out a stream of smoke. "No, I suppose not."

"I believe," Tripolos continued, "from the reports I have received on Miss Theoharis's activities in Athens, that she is aware of the identity of the man we seek."

Nick came to attention. "Iona?"

"I am of the opinion that Miss Theoharis is very involved in the smuggling operation. Too involved for her own safety. If . . . when," he amended, "she comes out of her coma, she'll be questioned."

"It's hard for me to believe that Alex's cousin would be a part of something like that." *He's getting entirely too close,* Nick realized, and swore silently at the lack of time. "Iona's a bit untamed," he went on, "but smuggling and murder. I can't believe it."

"I am very much afraid someone tried to murder Miss Theoharis because she knew too much. I will ask you, Mr. Gregoras, as one who is acquainted with her, how far would Miss Theoharis have gone for love—or for money?"

Nick paused as if considering carefully while his mind raced at readjustments to plans already formed. "For love, Captain, I think Iona would do little. But for money"—he looked up—"for money, Iona could justify anything."

"You are frank," Tripolos nodded. "I am grateful. Perhaps you would permit me to speak with you again on this matter. I must confess"—Tripolos's smile was sheepish, but his eyes remained direct—"it is a great help to discuss my problems with a man like yourself. It allows me to put things in order.''

"Captain, I'm glad to give you any help I can, of course.'' Nick gave him an easy smile.

For some time after Tripolos left, Nick remained in his chair. He scowled at the Rodin sculpture across the room as he calculated his choices.

"We move tonight,'' he announced as Stephanos entered.

"It's too soon. Things are not yet safe.''

"Tonight,'' Nick repeated and shifted his gaze. "Call Athens and let them know about the change in plan. See if they can't rig something up to keep this Tripolos off my back for a few hours.'' He laced his fingers together and frowned. "He's dangled his bait, and he's damn well expecting me to bite.''

"It's too dangerous tonight,'' Stephanos insisted. "There's another shipment in a few days.''

"In a few days, Tripolos will be that much closer. We can't afford to have things complicated with the local police now. And I have to be sure.'' Jet eyes narrowed, and his mouth became a grim line. "I haven't gone through all this to make a mistake at this point. I have to speed things up before Tripolos starts breathing down the wrong necks.''

Chapter 9

THE COVE WAS BLANKETED IN GLOOM. ROCKS GLIS-
tened, protecting it from winds—and from view.
There was a scent—lush wet leaves, wild blossoms that
flourished in the sun and hung heavy at night. But
somehow it wasn't a pleasant fragrance. It smelt of
secrets and half-named fears.

Lovers didn't hold trysts there. Legend said it was
haunted. At times, when a man walked near enough on
a dark, still night, the voices of spirits murmured
behind the rocks. Most men took another route home
and said nothing at all.

The moon shed a thin, hollow light over the face of
the water, adding to rather than detracting from the
sense of whispering stillness, of mystic darkness. The
water itself sighed gently over the rocks and sand. It
was a passive sound, barely stirring the air.

The men who gathered near the boat were like so

many shadows—dark, faceless in the gloom. But they were men, flesh and blood and muscle. They didn't fear the spirits in the cove.

They spoke little, and only in undertones. A laugh might be heard from time to time, quick and harsh in a place of secrets, but for the most part they moved silently, competently. They knew what had to be done. The time was nearly right.

One saw the approach of a new shadow and grunted to his companion. Stealthily, he drew a knife from his belt, gripping its crude handle in a strong, work-worn hand. The blade glittered dangerously through the darkness. Work stopped; men waited.

As the shadow drew closer, he sheathed the knife and swallowed the salty taste of fear. He wouldn't have been afraid to murder, but he was afraid of this man.

The thick, sturdy fingers trembled as they released the knife. "We weren't expecting you."

"I do not like to always do the expected." The answer was in brisk Greek as a pale finger of moonlight fell over him. He wore black—all black, from lean black slacks to a sweater and leather jacket. Lean and tall, he might have been god or devil.

A hood concealed both his head and face. Only the gleam of dark eyes remained visible—and deadly.

"You join us tonight?"

"I am here," he returned. He wasn't a man who answered questions, and no more were asked. He stepped aboard as one used to the life and sway of boats.

It was a typical fishing vessel. Its lines were simple. The decks were clean but rough, the paint fresh and black. Only the expense and power of its motor separated it from its companions.

Without a word, he crossed the deck, ignoring the men who fell back to let him pass. They were hefty, muscled men with thick wrists and strong hands. They moved away from the lean man as if he could crush them to bone with one sweep of his narrow hand. Each prayed the slitted eyes would not seek him out.

He placed himself at the helm, then gazed casually over his shoulder. At the look, the lines were cast off. They would row until they were out to sea and the roar of the motor would go unnoticed.

The boat moved at an easy pace, a lone speck in a dark sea. The motor purred. There was little talk among the men. They were a silent group in any case, but when the man was with them, no one wanted to speak. To speak was to bring attention to yourself—not many dared to do so.

He stared out into the water and ignored the wary glances thrown his way. He was remote, a figure of the night. His hood rippled in the salt-sprayed wind—a carefree, almost adventurous movement. But he was still as a stone.

Time passed; the boat listed with the movement of the sea. He might have been a figurehead. Or a demon.

"We are short-handed." The man who had greeted him merged with his shadow. His voice was low and coarse. His stomach trembled. "Do you wish me to find a replacement for Stevos?"

The hooded head turned—a slow, deliberate motion.

The man took an instinctive step in retreat and swallowed the copper taste that had risen to his throat.

"I will find my own replacement. You would all do well to remember Stevos." He lifted his voice on the warning as his eyes swept the men on deck. "There is no one who cannot be . . . replaced." He used a faint emphasis on the final word, watching the dropping of eyes with satisfaction. He needed their fear, and he had it. He could smell it on them. Smiling beneath the hood, he turned back to the sea.

The journey continued, and no one else spoke to him—or about him. Now and then a sailor might cast his eyes toward the man at the helm. The more superstitious crossed themselves or made the ancient sign against evil. When the devil was with them, they knew the full power of fear. He ignored them, treated them as though he were alone on the boat. They thanked God for it.

Midway between Lesbos and Turkey, the motor was shut off. The sudden silence resounded like a thunderclap. No one spoke as they would have done if the figure hadn't been at the helm. There were no crude jokes or games of dice.

The boat shifted easily in its own wake. They waited, all but one sweating in the cool sea breeze. The moon winked behind a cloud, then was clear again.

The motor of an approaching boat was heard as a distant cough, but the sound grew steadier, closer. A light signaled twice, then once again before the glow was shut off. The second motor, too, gave way to silence as another fishing vessel drifted alongside the first. The two boats merged into one shadow.

The night was glorious—almost still and silvered by the moon. Men waited, watching that dark, silent figure at the helm.

"The catch is good tonight," a voice called out from the second boat. The sound drifted, disembodied over the water.

"The fish are easily caught while sleeping."

There was a short laugh as two men leaned over the side and hauled a dripping net, pregnant with fish, onto the deck. The vessel swayed with the movement, then steadied.

The hooded man watched the exchange without word or gesture. His eyes shifted from the second vessel to the pile of fish lying scattered and lifeless on the deck. Both motors roared into life again and separated; one to the east, one to the west. The moon glimmered white. The breeze picked up. The boat was again a lone speck on a dark sea.

"Cut them open."

The men looked up sharply into the slitted eyes. "Now?" one of them dared to ask. "Don't you want them taken to the usual place?"

"Cut them open," he repeated. His voice sent a chill through the quiet night. "I take the cache with me."

Three men knelt beside the fish. Their knives worked swiftly and with skill while the scent of blood and sweat and fear prickled the air. A small pile of white packets grew as they were torn from the bellies of fish. The mutilated corpses were tossed back into the sea. No one would bring that catch to their table.

He moved quickly but without any sense of hurry, slipping packets into the pockets of his jacket. To a man they scrambled back from him, as if his touch might bring death—or worse. Satisfied, he gave them a brief survey before he resumed his position at the helm.

Their fear brought him a grim pleasure. And the cache was his for the taking. For the first time, he laughed—a long, cold sound that had nothing to do with humor. No one spoke, in even a whisper, on the journey back.

Later, a shadow among shadows, he moved away from the cove. He was wary that the trip had gone so easily, exhilarated that it was done. There had been no one to question him, no one with the courage to follow, though he was one man and they were many. Still, as he crossed the strip of beach, he moved with caution, for he wasn't a fool. He had more than just a few frightened fishermen to consider. And he would have more to deal with before he was done.

The walk was long, and steep, but he took it at an easy pace. The hollow call of an owl caused him to pause only briefly to scan the trees and rocks through the slits in the mask. From his position, he could see the cool white lines of the Theoharis villa. He stood where he was a moment—watching, thinking. Then he spun away to continue his climb.

He moved over rocks as easily as a goat—walking with a sure, confident stride in the darkness. He'd covered that route a hundred times without a light. And he kept clear of the path—a path meant men. He stepped around the rock where Morgan had sat that morning, but he didn't see the flowers. Without pausing, he continued.

There was a light in the window. He'd left it burning

himself before he had set out. Now for the first time he thought of comfort—and a drink to wash the taste of other men's fear from his throat.

Entering the house, he strode down the corridor and entered a room. Carelessly, he dumped the contents of his pockets on an elegant Louis XVI table, then removed his hood with a flourish.

"Well, Stephanos." Nick's teeth flashed in a grin. "The fishing was rich tonight."

Stephanos acknowledged the packets with a nod. "No trouble?"

"One has little trouble with men who fear the air you breath. The trip was as smooth as a whore's kiss." Moving away, he poured two drinks and handed one to his companion. The sense of exhilaration was still on him—the power that comes from risking death and winning. He drained his drink in one swallow. "A seedy crew, Stephanos, but they do their job. They're greedy, and"—he lifted the hood, then let it fall on the cache of opium, black on white—"terrified."

"A terrified crew is a cooperative one," Stephanos commented. He poked a stubby finger at the cache of opium. "Rich fishing indeed. Enough to make a man comfortable for a long time."

"Enough to make him want more," Nick stated with a grin. "And more. *Diabolos*, the smell of fish clings to me." He wrinkled his nose in disgust. "Send our cache to Athens, and see they send a report to me of its purity. I'm going to wash off this stink and go to bed."

"There's a matter you might be interested in."

"Not tonight." Nick didn't bother to turn around. "Save your gossip for tomorrow."

"The woman, Nicholas." Stephanos saw him stiffen and pause. There was no need to tell him which woman. "I learned she doesn't go back to America. She stays here while Alex is in Athens."

"*Diabolos*!" Nick swore and turned back into the room. "I can't be worried about a woman."

"She stays alone until Alex sends his lady back."

"The woman is not my concern," he said between his teeth.

As was his habit, Stephanos sniffed the liquor to add to his appreciation. "Athens was interested," he said mildly. "Perhaps she could still be of use."

"No." Nick took an agitated turn around the room. Nerves that had been cold as ice began to thaw. Damn her, he thought, she'll make me careless even thinking of her. "That woman is more trouble than use. No," he repeated as Stephanos lifted his brows. "We'll keep her out of it."

"Difficult, considering—"

"We'll keep her out of it," Nick repeated in a tone that made Stephanos stroke his moustache.

"As you wish, *kyrios*."

"Go to the devil." Annoyed with the mock respectful tone, Nick picked up his glass, then set it down again. "She's no use to us," he said with more calm. "More of a stumbling block. We'll hope she keeps her elegant nose inside the villa for a few days."

"And if she pokes her elegant nose out?" Stephanos inquired, enjoying his liquor.

Nick's mouth was a grim line. "Then I'll deal with her."

"I think perhaps," he murmured as Nick strode

from the room, "she has already dealt with you, old friend." He laughed and poured himself another drink. "Indeed, the lady's dealt you a killing blow."

After he had bathed, Nick couldn't settle. He told himself it was the excess energy from the night, and his success. But he found himself standing at his window, staring down at the Theoharis villa.

So she was alone, he thought, asleep in that big soft bed. It meant nothing to him. He'd climbed that damn wall to her room for the last time. He'd gone there the night before on impulse, something he'd known better than to do. He'd gone to see her, with some mad idea of justifying his actions to her.

Fool, he called himself as his hands curled tight around the stone railing. Only a fool justifies what he does. He'd gone to her and she'd taunted him, driven him to give up something he had no business giving up. His heart. Damn her, she'd wrenched it out of him.

His grip tightened as he remembered what it had been like to have her—to taste her and fill himself with her. It had been a mistake, perhaps the most crucial one he'd ever made. It was one matter to risk your life, another to risk your soul.

He shouldn't have touched her, Nick thought on yet another wave of anger. He'd known it even as his hands had reached for her. She hadn't known what she was doing, drunk on the ouzo Andrew had bought her. Andrew—he felt a moment's rage and banked it. There'd been moments when he hated Andrew, knowing he'd kissed her. Hated Dorian because Morgan had smiled at him. And Alex because he could touch her in friendship.

And, he knew, Morgan would hate him for what had

passed between them that night. Hadn't he heard it in the icy words she'd flung at him? He'd rather have handed her his own knife than to have the words of a woman slash at him that way. She would hate him for taking her when she was vulnerable—while that damn medal hung around her neck. And she would hate him for what he was.

On a rising wave of temper, Nick whirled away from the window. Why should it concern him? Morgan James would slip out of his life like a dream in only a few weeks in any case. He'd chosen his path before, long before he'd seen her. It was his way. If she hated him for what he was, then so be it. He wouldn't allow her to make him feel dirty and soiled.

If she'd touched his heart, he could deal with it. Sprawling into a chair, Nick scowled into the darkness. He would deal with it, he promised himself. After all he'd done, and all he'd faced, no blue-eyed witch would take him under.

Morgan felt completely alone. The solitude and silence she had so prized only a few days before now weighed down on her. The house was full of servants, but that brought her no comfort, no company. Alex and Liz and Dorian were gone. She wandered listlessly through the morning as she had wandered restlessly through the night. The house felt like a prison—clean and white and empty. Trapped inside it, she was too vulnerable to her own thoughts.

And because her thoughts centered too often on Nick, she found the idea of lying in the bed they had shared too painful. How could she sleep in peace in a place where she could still feel his hands on her, his lips ruthlessly pressing on hers? How could she sleep in a room that seemed to carry that faint sea-smell that so often drifted from him?

So she couldn't sleep, and her thoughts—and needs —haunted her. What could have happened to her to cause her to love such a man? And how long could she fight it? If she surrendered to it, she'd suffer for the rest of her life.

Knowing she was only adding to her own depression, Morgan changed into a bathing suit and headed for the beach.

It was ridiculous to be afraid of the beach, afraid of the house, she told herself. She was here to enjoy both for the next three weeks. Locking herself in her room wouldn't change anything that had happened.

The sand glistened, white and brilliant. Morgan found that on facing it again, the horror didn't materialize. Tossing aside her wrap, she ran into the sea. The water would ease the weariness, the tension. And maybe, just maybe, she would sleep tonight.

Why should she be keeping herself in a constant state of nerves over the death of a man she didn't even know? Why should she allow the harmless stub of a cigarette to haunt her? It was time to accept the simple explanations and keep her distance. The man had been killed as a result of a village brawl, and that was that. It had nothing to do with her, or anyone she knew. It was tragic, but it wasn't personal.

She wouldn't think about Iona, she told herself. She wouldn't think about smuggling or murders or—here she hesitated a moment and dived under a wave— Nicholas. For now, she wouldn't think at all.

Morgan escaped. In a world of water and sun, she

thought only of pleasures. She drifted, letting the tension sink beneath the waves. She'd forgotten, in her own misery, just how clean and alive the water made her feel. For a few moments she would go back to that first day, to that feeling of peace she'd found without even trying.

Liz was going to need her in the next day or two. And Morgan wouldn't be any help at all if she were haggard and tense. Yes, tonight she'd sleep—she'd had enough of nightmares.

More relaxed than she had been in days, Morgan swam back toward shore. The sand shifted under her feet with the gentle current. Shells dotted the shoreline, clean and glistening. She stood and stretched as the water lapped around her knees. The sun felt glorious.

"So Helen rises from the sea."

Lifting her hand, Morgan shielded her eyes and saw Andrew. He sat on the beach by her towel, watching her.

"It's easy to understand how she set kingdoms at odds." He stood and moved to the water's verge to join her. "How are you, Morgan?"

"I'm fine." She accepted the towel he handed her and rubbed it briskly over her hair.

"Your eyes are shadowed. A blue sea surrounded by clouds." He traced her cheek with a fingertip. "Nick told me about Iona Theoharis." He took her hand and led her back to the white sand. Dropping the towel, Morgan sat beside him. "It's a bit soon for you to have to handle something like that, Morgan I'm sorry you had to be the one to find her."

"It seems to be a talent of mine." She shook her head. "I'm much better today, really." Smiling, she touched his cheek. "Yesterday I felt . . . actually I don't think I felt much of anything yesterday. It was like I was watching everything through a fisheye lens. Everything was distorted and unreal. Today it's real, but I can cope with it."

"I suppose that's nature's way of cushioning the senses."

"I feel this incredible sorrow for Alex and Liz—and for Dorian." She leaned back on her elbows, wanting to feel the sun as it dried the water on her skin. "It's so hard on them, Andrew. It leaves me feeling helpless." She turned her face to his, pushing at her streaming hair. "I hope this doesn't sound hard, but I feel, after these past two days, I think I've just realized how glad I am to be alive."

"I'd say that's a very healthy, very normal reaction." He, too, leaned back on his elbows, narrowing his eyes against the sun as he studied her.

"Oh, I hope so. I've been feeling guilty about it."

"You can't be guilty about wanting to live, Morgan."

"No. Suddenly I realized how much I want to do. How much I want to see. Do you know, I'm twenty-six, and this is the first time I've been anywhere? My mother died when I was a baby and my father and I moved to New York from Philadelphia. I've never seen anything else." As drops of water trickled down her skin, she shook her damp hair back. "I can speak five languages, and this is the first time I've been in a country where English isn't needed. I want to go to Italy and France." She turned to face him more directly. Her eyes, though still shadowed, were huge with adventure. "I want to see Venice and ride in a gondola. I want to walk on the Cornish moors and on the Champs d'Élysées.'' She laughed and it felt marvelous. "I want to climb mountains."

"And be a fisherman?" He smiled and laid a hand over hers.

"Oh, I did say that, didn't I?" She laughed again. "I'll do that, too. Jack always said my taste was rather eclectic."

"Jack?"

"He's a man I knew back home." Morgan found the ease with which she put him in the past satisfying. "He was in politics. I think he wanted to be king."

"Were you in love with him?"

"No, I was used to him." She rolled her eyes and grinned. "Isn't that a terrible thing to say?"

"I don't know—you tell me."

"No," she decided. "Because it's the truth. He was very cautious, very conventional, and, I'm sorry to say, very boring. Not at all like . . ." Her voice trailed off.

Andrew followed her gaze and spotted Nick at the top of the cliff. He stood, legs apart, hands thrust in his pockets, staring down at them. His expression was unreadable in the distance. He turned, without a wave or a sign of greeting, and disappeared behind the rocks.

Andrew shifted his gaze back to Morgan. Her expression was totally readable.

"You're in love with Nick."

Morgan brought herself back sharply. "Oh, no. No, of course not. I hardly know him. He's a very disagreeable man. He has a brutal temper, and he's arrogant and bossy and without any decent feelings. He shouts."

Andrew took in this impassioned description with a lifted brow. "We seem to be talking about two different people."

Morgan turned away, running sand through her fingers. "Maybe. I don't like either one of them."

Andrew let the silence hang a moment as he watched her busy fingers. "But you're in love with him."

"Andrew—"

"And you don't want to be," he finished, looking thoughtfully out to sea. "Morgan, I'd been wondering, if I asked you to marry me, would it spoil our friendship?"

"What?" Astonished, she spun her head back around. "Are you joking?"

Calmly, he searched her face. "No, I'm not joking. I decided that asking you to bed would put a strain on our friendship. I wondered if marriage would. Though I didn't realize you were in love with Nick."

"Andrew," she began, uncertain how to react. "Is this a question or a proposal?"

"Let's take the question first."

Morgan took a deep breath. "An offer of marriage, especially from someone you care for, is always flattering to the ego. But egos are unstable and friendships don't require flattery." Leaning over, she brushed his mouth with hers. "I'm very glad you're my friend, Andrew."

"Somehow I thought that would be your reaction. I'm a romantic at heart." Shrugging, he gave her a rueful smile. "An island, a beautiful woman with a laugh like a night wind. I could see us setting up house in the cottage. Fires in the winter, flowers in the spring."

"You're not in love with me, Andrew."

"I could be." Taking her hand, he turned it palm up and studied it. "It isn't your destiny to fall in love with a struggling poet."

"Andrew—"

"And it isn't mine to have you." Smiling again, he kissed her hand. "Still, it's a warm thought."

"And a lovely one. Thank you for it."

He nodded before he rose. "I might decide Venice offers inspiration." Andrew studied the protruding section of the gray stone wall before turning back to her. "Maybe we'll see each other there." He smiled, the flashing boyish smile, and Morgan felt a twinge of regret. "Timing, Morgan, is such an essential factor in romance."

She watched him cross the sand and mount the steps before she turned back to the sea.

Chapter 10

THE VILLA WHISPERED AND TREMBLED LIKE AN OLD woman. Even after all her promises to herself that morning, Morgan couldn't sleep. She rolled and tossed in her bed, frantically bringing herself back from dreams each time she started to drift off. It was too easy for Nick to slip into her mind in a dream. Through sheer force of will, Morgan had blocked him out for most of the day. She wouldn't surrender to him now, for only a few hours sleep.

Yet awake and alone, she found herself remembering the inlet—the face under the water, the slim black stub of a cigarette. And Iona, pale and barely alive, with her thick mane of hair streaming nearly to the floor.

Why was it she couldn't rid herself of the thought that one had something to do with the other?

There was too much space, too much quiet in the villa to be tolerated in solitude. Even the air seemed hot and oppressive. As fatigue began to take over, Morgan found herself caught between sleep and wakefulness, that vulnerable land where thoughts can drift and tease.

She could hear Alex's voice, cold and hard, telling her that Iona would be better off dead. There were Dorian's eyes, so calm, so cool, as he lifted a thin black cigarette to his lips. Andrew smiling grimly as he waited for his ship to come in. Liz vowing passionately that she would protect her husband from anyone and anything. And the knife blade, so sharp and deadly. She knew without seeing that Nick's hand gripped the handle.

On a half scream, Morgan sat up and willed herself awake. No, she wouldn't sleep, not alone. She didn't dare.

Before giving herself time to think, she rose and slipped on jeans and a shirt. The beach had given her peace that afternoon. Maybe it would do the same for her tonight.

Outside, she found the openness comforting. There were no walls here or empty rooms. There were stars and the scent of blossoms. She could hear the cypress leaves whisper. The feeling of dread slid from her with every step. She headed for the beach.

The moon was nearly full now, and white as bone. The breeze off the water was degrees cooler than the air had been in her room. She followed the path without hesitation, without fear. Some instinct told her nothing would harm her that night.

After rolling up her pants legs, she stood, letting the water lap over her ankles, warm and silky. Gratefully, she breathed in the moist sea air and felt it soothe her. She stretched her arms toward the stars.

"Will you never learn to stay in bed?"

Morgan spun around to find herself face to face with Nick. Had he already been there? she wondered. She hadn't heard him walk behind her. Straightening, she eyed him coolly. Like her, he wore jeans and no shoes. His shirt hung unbuttoned over his bare chest. What madness was it, she wondered, that made her long to go to him. Whatever madness drew her to him, she suppressed.

"That's not your concern." Morgan turned her back on him.

Nick barely prevented himself from yanking her back around. He'd been standing sleepless at his window when he'd seen her leave the house. Almost before he had known what he was doing, he was coming down the beach steps to find her. And it was ice, that same ice, she greeted him with.

"Have you forgotten what happens to women who wander night beaches alone?" The words rang with mockery as he tangled his fingers in her hair. He'd touch her if he chose, he thought furiously. No one would stop him.

"If you plan to drag me around this time, Nicholas, I warn you, I'll bite and scratch."

"That should make it interesting." His fingers tightened as she tossed her head to dislodge his grip. "I'd think you'd have had your fill of beaches today, Aphrodite. Or are you expecting Andrew again?"

She ignored the taunt and the peculiar thrill that came whenever he called her by that name. "I'm not expecting anyone. I came here to be alone. If you'd go away, I could enjoy myself."

Hurting, wanting, Nick spun her around. His fingers

bruised her skin so that she made a surprised sound of pain before she could clamp it down. "Damn you, Morgan, don't push me any more. You'll find me a different breed from young Andrew."

"Take your hands off me." She managed to control her voice to a hard, cold steadiness. Her eyes glimmered with frost as they stared into his. She wouldn't cower before him again, and she wouldn't yield. "You'd do well to take lessons from Andrew"— deliberately, she tossed her head and smiled—"or Dorian on how to treat a woman."

Nick swore with quick Greek expertise. Unable to do otherwise, he gripped her tighter, but this time she made no sound. Morgan watched as the dark fury took total command of his face. He was half devil now, violent, with barely a trace of the man others knew. It gave her a perverse enjoyment to know she had driven him to it.

"So you offer yourself to Dorian as well?" He bit off the words as he fought to find some hold on his control. "How many men do you need?"

A flood of fury rose, but she stamped it down. "Isn't it strange, Nicholas," she said calmly, "how your Greek half seems to take over when you're angry? I simply can't see how you and Andrew can be related, however remotely."

"You enjoy leading him on, don't you?" The comparison stoked his fury higher. Morgan found she was gritting her teeth to prevent a whimper at the pain. She wouldn't give him the satisfaction. "Heartless bitch," he hissed at her. "How long do you intend to dangle and tease?"

"How dare you!" Morgan pushed against him.

Anger, unreasonable and full, welled up in her for all the sleepless hours he'd given her, and all the pain. "How dare you criticize me for anything! You, with the filthy games you play, and the lies. You care about *no one*—no one but yourself. I detest you and everything you are!" Wrenching free, Morgan fled into the sea, blind and senseless with rage.

"Stupid woman!" Nick tore through two sentences of furious Greek before he caught her and pulled her around. The water lapped around her hips as he shook her. When her feet slipped on the bottom, he dragged her back up. He couldn't think now, couldn't reason. His voice whipped out with the violence of his thoughts. "I'll be damned if you'll make me crawl. Damned if I'll beg for your good feelings. I do what I have to do, it's a matter of necessity. Do you think I enjoy it?"

"I don't care about your necessities or your smuggling or your murders! I don't care about anything that has to do with you. I hate you!" She took a swing at his chest and nearly submerged again. "I hate everything about you. I hate myself for ever letting you touch me!"

The words cut at him, deeper than he wanted them to. He fought not to remember what it had felt like to hold her, to press his mouth against her and feel her melt against him. "That's fine. Just keep your distance and we'll get along perfectly."

"There's nothing I want more than to keep away from you." Her eyes glittered as the words brought her a slash of pain. "Nothing I want more than to never see your face again or hear your name."

He controlled himself with an effort—for there was

nothing he wanted more at that moment than to crush her against him and beg, as he'd never begged anyone, for whatever she'd give him. "Then that's what you'll have, Aphrodite. Play your games with Dorian if you like, but tread carefully with Andrew. Tread carefully, or I'll break your beautiful neck."

"Don't you threaten me. I'll see Andrew just as often as I like." Morgan pushed at her dripping hair and glared at him. "I don't think he'd appreciate your protection. He asked me to marry him."

In one swift move, Nick lifted her off her feet and dragged her against his chest. Morgan kicked out, succeeding only in drenching both of them. "What did you tell him?"

"It's none of your business." She struggled, and though she was slick as an eel in the water, his hold remained firm. "Put me *down!* You can't treat me this way."

Fury was raging in him, uncontrollable, savage. No, he wouldn't stand by and watch her with another man. "Damn you, I said what did you tell him!"

"No!" she shouted, more in anger than in fear. "I told him *no.*"

Nick relaxed his grip. Morgan's feet met the sea bottom again as he formed a brittle smile. Her face was white as chalk and he cursed himself. God, would he do nothing but hurt her? Would she do nothing but hurt him? If there weren't so many walls in his way . . . if he could break down even one of them, he'd have her.

"That's fine." His voice was far from steady, but she had no way of knowing it was from panic rather than temper. "I won't stand by and watch you lead Andrew along. He's an innocent yet." He released her, knowing it might be the last time he'd ever touch her. "I don't suppose you chose to tell him about the lover you left behind."

"Lover?" Morgan pushed at her hair as she took a step back. "What lover?"

Nick lifted the medallion at her neck, then let it fall before he gave into the need to rip it from her. "The one who gave you the trinket you treasure so much. When a woman carries another man's brand, it's difficult to overlook it."

Morgan closed her hand over the small piece of silver. She had thought nothing could make her more angry than she already was. She was blind and trembling with it. "Another man's brand," she repeated in a whisper. "How typical of you. No one brands me, Nicholas. No one, no matter how I love."

"Your pardon, Aphrodite," he returned coolly. "An expression only."

"My father gave me this," she tossed at him. "He gave it to me when I was eight years old and broke my arm falling out of a tree. He's the kindest and most loving person I've ever known. You, Nicholas Gregoras, are a stupid man."

She turned and darted toward the beach, but he caught her again while the water was still around her ankles. Ignoring her curses and struggles, Nick turned her to face him. His eyes bored into hers. His breath was coming in gasps, but not from rage. He needed an answer, and quickly, before he exploded.

"You don't have a lover in America?"

"I said let me *go*!" She was glorious in fury—eyes

glittering, skin white as the moonlight. With her head thrown back, she dared him to defy her. In that moment he thought he would have died for her.

"Do you have a lover in America?" Nick demanded again, but his voice was quiet now.

Morgan threw up her chin. "I haven't a lover *anywhere*."

On an oath that sounded more like a prayer, Nick drew her close. The heat from his body fused through the soaked shirts as if they had been naked. Morgan's breath caught at the pressure and the sudden gleam of triumph in his eyes.

"You do now."

Capturing her mouth, he pulled her to the sand.

His lips were urgent, burning. His talk of branding raced through her head, but Morgan accepted the fire eagerly. And already he was stripping off her shirt as if he couldn't bear even the thin separation between them.

Morgan knew he would always love like this. Intensely, without thought, without reason. She gloried in it. Desire this strong took no denial. Her own fingers were busy with his shirt, ripping at the seam in her hurry to be flesh to flesh. She heard him laugh with his mouth pressed against her throat.

There was no longer any right or wrong. Needs were too great. And love. Even as passion drove her higher, Morgan knew and recognized her love. She had waited for it all of her life. With the heat building, there was no time to question how it could be Nick. She only knew it was, whatever, whoever, he was. Nothing else mattered.

When his hands found her naked breasts, he groaned and crushed his lips to hers again. She was so soft, so slender. He struggled not to bruise her, not again, but desire was wild and free in him. He'd never wanted a woman like this. Not like this. Even when he had taken her the first time, he hadn't felt this clean silver streak of power.

She was consuming him, pouring inside his mind. And the taste. Dear God, would he never get enough of the taste of her? He found her breast with his mouth and filled himself.

Morgan arched and dove her fingers into his hair. He was murmuring something, but his breathing was as ragged as hers and she couldn't understand. When his mouth was back on hers, there was no need to. She felt him tugging her jeans over her hips, but was too delirious to realize she had pulled at his first. She felt the skin stretched tight over his bones, the surprising narrowness of his body.

Then his lips and hands were racing over her—not in the angry desperation she remembered from the night before, but in unquestionable possession. There was no gentleness, but neither was there a fierceness. He took and took as though no one had a better right. Those strong lean fingers stroked down her, making her gasp out loud in pleasure, then moan in torment when they lay still.

His mouth was always busy, tongue lightly torturing, teeth taking her to the edge of control. There seemed to be no part of her, no inch he couldn't exploit for pleasure. And the speed never slacked.

Cool sand, cool water, and his hot, clever mouth—she was trapped between them. There was moonlight, rippling white, but she was a willing prisoner of the darkness. In the grove of cypresses a night bird called out—one long, haunting note. It might have been her own sigh. She tasted the sea on his skin, knew he would taste it on hers as well. Somehow, that small intimacy made her hold him tighter.

They might have been the only ones, washed ashore, destined to be lovers throughout their lives without the need for anyone else. The scent of the night wafted over her—his scent. They would always be the same to her.

Then she heard nothing, knew nothing, as he drove her beyond reason with his mouth alone.

She was grasping at him, demanding and pleading in the same breathless whispers for him to give her that final, delirious relief. But he held her off, pleasing himself, and pleasing her until she thought her body would simply implode at the pressure that was building.

With a wild, hungry kiss he silenced her while leading her closer to the edge. Though she could feel his heart racing against hers, he seemed determined to hold them there—an instant, an hour—hovering between heaven and hell.

When he drove them over, Morgan wasn't certain on which side they had fallen—only that they had fallen together.

Morgan lay quiet, cushioned against Nick's bare shoulder. The waves gently caressed her legs. In the aftermath of the demands of passion she was light and cool and stunned. She could feel the blood still pounding in his chest and knew no one, no one had ever wanted her like this. The sense of power it might have given her came as an ache. She closed her eyes on it.

She hadn't even struggled, she thought. Not even a token protest. She had given herself without thought—not in submission to his strength, but in submission to her own desires. Now, as the heat of passion ebbed, she felt the hard edge of shame.

He was a criminal—a hard, self-seeking man who trafficked in misery for profit. And she had given him her body and her heart. Perhaps she had no control over her heart, but Morgan was honest enough to know she ruled her own body. Shivering, she drew away from him.

"No, stay." Nick nuzzled in her hair as he held her against his side.

"I have to go in," she murmured. Morgan drew her body away as far as his arm would permit. "Please, let me go."

Nick shifted until his face hovered over hers. His lips were curved in amusement; his face was relaxed and satisfied. "No," he said simply. "You won't walk away from me again."

"Nicholas, please." Morgan turned her head aside. "It's late. I have to go."

He became still for a moment, then took her face firmly in his hand and turned it back to his. He saw the gleam of tears, tightly controlled, and swore. "It occurs to you suddenly that you've just given yourself to a criminal and enjoyed it."

"Don't!" Morgan shut her eyes. "Just let me go in. Whatever I've done, I've done because I wanted to."

Nick stared down at her. She was dry-eyed now, but her eyes were bleak. Swearing again, he reached for his partially dry shirt and pulled Morgan into a sitting position. Athens, he thought again, could fry in hell.

"Put this on," he ordered, swinging it over her shoulders. "We'll talk."

"I don't want to talk. There's no need to talk."

"I said we'll talk, Morgan." Nick pushed her arm into a sleeve. "I won't have you feeling guilty over what just happened." She could feel the simmering anger pulsing from him as he pulled his shirt over her breasts. "I won't have that," he muttered. "It's too much. I can't explain everything now . . . there are some things I won't ever explain."

"I'm not asking for explanations."

His eyes locked on hers. "You ask every time you look at me." Nick pulled a cigarette from the pocket of the shirt, then lit it. "My business in import-export has made me quite a number of contacts over the years. Some of whom, I imagine, you wouldn't approve of." He mused over this for a moment as he blew out a hazy stream of smoke.

"Nicholas, I don't—"

"Shut up, Morgan. When a man's decided to bare his soul, a woman shouldn't interrupt. God knows how dark you'll find it," he added as he drew in smoke again. "When I was in my early, impressionable twenties, I met a man who considered me suitable for a certain type of work. I found the work itself fascinating. Danger can become addicting, like any other drug."

Yes, she thought as she stared out over the water. If nothing else, she could understand that.

"I began to—free-lance." He smiled at the term, but it had little to do with humor. "For his organization.

For the most part I enjoyed it. In any case, I was content with it. It's amazing that a way of life, ten years of my life, should become a prison in a week's time.''

Morgan had drawn her knees close to her chest while she stared out over the water. Nick laid a hand on her hair, but she still didn't look at him. He was finding it more difficult to tell her than he had imagined. Even after he'd finished, she might turn away from him. He'd be left with nothing—less than nothing. He drew hard on his cigarette, then stared at the red glow at the tip.

"Morgan, there are things I've done . . ." He swore briefly under his breath. "There are things I've done I wouldn't tell you about even if I were free to. You wouldn't find them pleasant.''

Now she lifted her face. "You've killed people.''

He found it difficult to answer when she was looking at him with tired despair in her eyes. But his voice was cool with control. "When it was necessary.''

Morgan lowered her head again. She hadn't wanted to think him a murderer. If he had denied it, she would have tried to have taken him at his word. She hadn't wanted to believe he was capable of what she considered the ultimate sin. The taking of a life.

Nick scowled at the cigarette and hurled it into the sea. I could have lied to her, he thought furiously. Why the hell didn't I just lie—I'm an expert at it. Because I can't lie to her, he realized with a tired sigh. Not anymore. "I did what I had to do, Morgan,'' he said flatly. "I can't erase the way I've lived for ten years. Right or wrong, it was my choice. I can't apologize for it.''

"No, I'm not asking you to. I'm sorry if it seems

that way." She drew herself up again and faced him. "Please, Nicholas, let's leave it at this. Your life's your own. You don't have to justify it to me."

"Morgan—" If she had hurled abuse at him, stabbed him with ice, he might have been able to keep silent. But he couldn't be silent while she struggled to understand. He would tell her, and the decision he'd been struggling with for days would be made. "For the last six months, I've been working on breaking the smuggling ring that runs between Turkey and Lesbos."

Morgan stared at him as though she'd never seen him before. "Breaking it? But I thought . . . you told me—"

"I've never told you much of anything," he said curtly. "I let you assume. It was better that way. It was necessary."

For a moment she sat quietly, trying to sort out her thoughts. "Nicholas, I don't understand. Are you telling me you're a policeman?"

He laughed at the thought, and part of his anger drained. "No, Aphrodite, spare me that."

Morgan frowned. "A spy then?"

The rest of his anger vanished. He cupped her face in his hands. She was so unbearably sweet. "You will romanticize it, Morgan. I'm a man who travels and follows orders. Be content with that, it's all I can give you."

"That first night on the beach . . ." At last the puzzle pieces were taking a shape she could understand. "You were watching for the man who runs the smuggling ring. That was who Stephanos followed."

Nick frowned and dropped his hands. She believed him without question or hesitation. Already she'd forgotten that he'd killed—and worse. Why, when she was making it so easy for him did he find it so hard to go on? "I had to get you out of the way. I knew he'd cross that section of beach on his way to Stevos's cottage. Stevos was eliminated because he knew, as I don't yet, the man's exact position in the organization. I think he asked for a raise and got a knife in the back."

"Who is he, Nicholas?"

"No." His eyes came back to hers. His face was hard again, unreachable. "Even if I were sure, I wouldn't tell you. Don't ask me questions I can't answer, Morgan. The more I tell you, the more dangerous your position becomes." His eyes grew darker. "I was ready to use you once, and my organization is very interested in your talent with languages, but I'm a selfish man. You're not going to be involved." His tone was final and just a little furious. "I told my associate you weren't interested."

"That's a bit presumptuous," Morgan began. She frowned until he twisted his head and looked at her again. "I'm capable of making my own decisions."

"You haven't one to make," Nick countered coolly. "And once I know for certain the identity of the head of the ring, my job's finished. Athens will have to learn how to function without me."

"You're not going to do this . . ." She gestured vaguely, not knowing what title to give his work. "This sort of thing anymore?"

"No." Nick stared back out to sea. "I've been in it long enough."

"When did you decide to stop?"

When I first made love with you, he thought, and nearly said it. But it wasn't quite true. There was one more thing he would have to tell her. "The day I took Iona on the boat." Nick let out an angry breath and turned to her. He had his doubts that she would forgive him for what he was going to say. "Iona's in this, Morgan, deeply."

"In the smuggling? But—"

"I can only tell you that she is, and that part of my job was to get information out of her. I took her out on the boat, fully intending to make love to her to help loosen her tongue." Morgan kept her eyes steady and he continued, growing angrier. "She was cracking under pressure. I was there to help her along. That's why someone tried to kill her."

"Kill her?" Morgan tried to keep her voice level as she dealt with what he was telling her. "But Captain Tripolos said it was attempted suicide."

"Iona would no more have committed suicide than she would have tended goats."

"No," she said slowly. "No, of course you're right."

"If I could have worked on her a little longer, I would have had all that I needed."

"Poor Alex," she murmured. "He'll be crushed if it comes out that she was mixed up in this. And Dorian . . ." She remembered his empty eyes and his words. *Poor Iona—so beautiful—so lost.* Perhaps he already suspected. "Isn't there something you can do?" She looked up at Nick, this time with trust. "Do the police know? Captain Tripolos?"

"Tripolos knows a great deal and suspects more." Nick took her hand now. He wanted the link badly. "I don't work directly with the police, it slows things down. At the moment," he added cheerfully, "Tripolos has me pegged as the prime suspect in a murder, an attempted murder, and sees me in the role of the masked smuggler. Lord, I'd have given him a thrill last night."

"You enjoy your work, don't you?" Morgan studied him, recognizing the light of adventure in his eyes. "Why are you stopping?"

His smile faded. "I told you I was with Iona. It wasn't the first time I used that method. Sex can be a weapon or a tool, it's a fact of life." Morgan dropped her gaze to the sand. "She'd had too much champagne to be cooperative, but there would have been another time. Since that day, I haven't felt clean." He slid his hand under her chin and lifted it. "Not until tonight."

She was studying him closely, searching. In his eyes she saw something she had only seen once before— regret, and a plea for understanding. Lifting her arms, she brought his mouth down to hers. She felt more than his lips—the heady wave of his relief.

"Morgan." He pressed her back to the sand again. "If I could turn back the clock and have this past week to live over . . ." he hesitated, then buried his face in her hair. "I probably wouldn't do anything differently."

"You apologize beautifully, Nicholas."

He couldn't keep his hands off her. They were roaming again, arousing them both. "This thing should come to a head tomorrow night, then I'll be at loose ends. Come away somewhere with me for a few days. Anywhere."

"Tomorrow?" She struggled to keep her mind on his words while her body heated. "Why tomorrow?"

"A little complication I caused last night. Come, we're covered with sand. Let's take a swim."

"Complication?" Morgan repeated as he hauled her to her feet. "What kind of complication?"

"I don't think our man will tolerate the loss of a shipment," he murmured as he slipped his shirt from her shoulders.

"You stole it!"

He was pulling her into the water. His blood was already pounding for her as he saw the moonlight glow white over her body. "With incredible ease." When she was past her waist, he drew her against him. The water lapped around them as he began to explore her again. "Stephanos and I watched the connection from a safe distance on several runs." His mouth brushed over hers, then traced down to her throat. "We'd just come back from one the night I found you on the beach. Now, about those few days."

"What will you do tomorrow night?" Morgan drew back enough to stop his roaming hands and mouth. A hint of fear had worked its way in. "Nicholas, what's going to happen?"

"I'm waiting for some conclusive information from Athens. When it comes, I'll know better how to move. At any rate, I'll be there when the boat docks with its cache tomorrow night."

"Not alone?" She gripped his shoulders. "He's already killed a man."

Nick rubbed his nose against hers. "Do you worry for me, Aphrodite?"

"Don't joke!"

He heard the very real panic in her voice and spoke

soothingly. "By late tomorrow afternoon, Tripolos will be brought up to date. If everything goes as planned, I can brief him personally." He smiled down at the frown on her face. "He'll gain all official credit for whatever arrests are made."

"But that's unfair!" Morgan exclaimed. "After all your work, and the time, why shouldn't you—"

"Shut up, Morgan, I can't make love to a woman who's constantly complaining."

"Nicholas, I'm trying to understand."

"Understand this." Impatience shimmered in his voice as he pulled her close again. "I've wanted you from the minute I saw you sitting on that damn rock, and I haven't begun to have enough. You've driven me mad for days. Not anymore, Aphrodite. Not anymore."

He lowered his mouth, and all else was lost.

Chapter 11

HER JEANS WERE STILL DAMP AS MORGAN STRUGGLED into them, laughing. "You would make me so furious I'd run into the water fully dressed."

Nick fastened the snap on his own. "The feeling was mutual."

Turning her head, she looked at him as he stood, naked to the waist, shaking what sand he could from his shirt. A gleam of mischief lit her eyes. "Oh?" Taking a step closer, Morgan ran her palms up his chest—taking her time—enjoying the hard, firm feel of it before she linked them around his neck. "Did it make you furious thinking I was wearing a token from a lover waiting for me back home?"

"No," he lied with a careless smile. Gripping his shirt in both hands, Nick hooked it around her waist to draw her closer. "Why should that concern me?"

"Oh." Morgan nipped lightly at his bottom lip. "Then perhaps you'd like to hear about Jack."

"I damn well wouldn't," he muttered before his mouth crushed down on hers. Even as her lips answered his, Nick heard the low sound of her muffled laughter. "Witch." Then he took her deeper, deeper, until her laughter was only a sigh. "Maybe you prefer me when I'm angry."

"I prefer you," she said simply, and rested her head on his shoulder.

His arms tightened, strong, possessive. Yet somehow he knew strength alone would never keep her. "Dangerous woman," Nick murmured. "I knew it the first time I held you."

With a laugh, Morgan tossed back her head. "The first time you held me, you cursed me."

"And I continue to do so." But his lips sought hers again without an oath.

"I wish there was only tonight." Suddenly, she was clinging to him with her heart racing. "No tomorrows, only now. I don't want the sun to come up."

Nick buried his face in her hair as the guilt swamped him. He'd brought her fear from the first instant. Even loving her, he could bring her nothing else. He had no right to tell her now that his heart was hers for the asking. Once he told her, she might beg him to abandon his responsibility, leave his job half finished. And he would do just as she asked, he realized . . . and never feel like a man again.

"Don't wish your days away, Morgan," he told her lightly. "The sun comes up tomorrow, then goes down. And when it comes up again, we'll have nothing but time."

She had to trust him, had to believe that he would be safe—that the danger he lived with would be over in little more than twenty-four hours.

"Come back with me now." Lifting her head again, Morgan gave him a smile. Her worry and fears wouldn't help him. "Come back to the villa and make love with me again."

"You tempt me, Aphrodite." Bending, he kissed both her cheeks in a gesture she found unbearably gentle and sweet. "But you're asleep on your feet. There'll be other nights. I'll take you back."

She allowed him to turn her toward the beach steps. "You might not find it as easy to leave me there alone as you think," she commented with another smile.

With a quiet laugh, he drew her closer to his side. "Not easy perhaps, but—" His head whipped up abruptly, as if he were scenting the air. Narrowed and cold, his eyes swept the darkness of the cliffs above them.

"Nicholas, what—"

But his hand clamped over her mouth as he pulled her, once again, into the shadows of the cypress. Her heart leaped to her throat as it had before, but this time Morgan didn't struggle.

"Be still and don't speak," Nick whispered. Removing his hand, he pushed her back against the trunk of a tree. "Not a sound, Morgan."

She nodded, but he wasn't looking at her. His eyes were trained on the cliffs. Standing at the edge of the covering, Nick watched and waited. Then he heard it again—the quiet scrape of boot on rock. Tensing, he strained his eyes and at last saw the shadow. So, he thought with a grim smile as he watched the black form move swiftly over the rocks, he's come for his cache. But you won't find it, Nick told the shadow silently. And I'll be like a hound on your tail.

Soundlessly, he moved back to Morgan. "Go back to the villa and stay there." All warmth had dropped away from him. His voice was as cold as his eyes.

"What did you see?" she demanded. "What are you going to do?"

"Do as I say." Taking her arm, he pulled her toward the beach steps. "Go quickly, I haven't got time to waste. I'll lose him."

Him. Morgan felt a flutter of fear. She swallowed it. "I'm going with you."

"Don't be a fool." Impatient, Nick dragged her along. "Go back to the villa, I'll speak to you in the morning."

"No." Morgan pulled out of his hold. "I said I'm going with you. You can't stop me."

She was standing straight as an arrow, eyes blazing with a combination of fear and determination. Nick swore at her, knowing every second he stayed meant his man was farther away. "I don't have time—"

"Then you'd better stop wasting it," Morgan said calmly. "I'm coming."

"Then come," he said under his breath as he turned away from her. She won't last five minutes on the cliffs without shoes, he thought. She'd limp her way back to the villa in ten. He moved quickly up the beach steps without waiting for her. Gritting her teeth, Morgan raced after him.

As he left the steps to start his scramble up the cliff, Nick paid little attention to her. He cast his eyes to the sky and wished the night were not so clear. A cloud over the moon would allow him to risk getting closer to the man he followed. He gripped a rock and hauled himself up farther—a few pebbles loosened and skidded down. When he glanced back, he was surprised to see Morgan keeping pace with him.

Damn the woman, he thought with a twinge of reluctant admiration. Without a word, he held out his hand and pulled her up beside him. "Idiot," he hissed, wanting to shake her and kiss her all at once. "Will you go back? You don't have any shoes."

"Neither do you," Morgan gritted.

"Stubborn fool."

"Yes."

Cursing silently, Nick continued the climb. He couldn't risk the open path in the moonlight, so kept to the rocks. Though it wouldn't be possible to keep his quarry in sight, Nick knew where he was going.

Morgan clamped her teeth shut as the ball of her foot scraped against a rock. With a quick hiss of breath, she kept going. She wasn't going to whimper and be snapped at. She wasn't going to let him go without her.

On a rough ledge, Nick paused briefly to consider his options. Circling around would take time. If he'd been alone—and armed, he would have taken his chances with the narrow path now. Odds were that the man he followed was far enough ahead and confident enough to continue his journey without looking over his shoulder. But he wasn't alone, he thought on a flare of annoyance. And he had no more than his hands to protect Morgan if they were spotted.

"Listen to me," he whispered, hoping to frighten

her as he grabbed her by the shoulders. "The man's killed—and killed more than once, I promise you. When he finds his cache isn't where it should be, he'll know he's being hunted. Go back to the villa."

"Do you want me to call the police?" Morgan asked calmly, though he'd succeeded very well in frightening her.

"No!" The word whipped out, no louder than a breath. "I can't afford to give up the chance to see who he is." Frustrated, he glared at her. "Morgan, I don't have a weapon, if he—"

"I'm not leaving you, Nicholas. You're wasting time arguing about it."

He swore again, then slowly controlled his temper. "All right, damn you. But you'll do exactly as I say or I promise you, I'll knock you unconscious and shove you behind a rock."

She didn't doubt it. Morgan lifted her chin. "Let's go."

Agilely, Nick pulled himself over the ridge and onto the path. Before he could reach back to assist her, Morgan was kneeling on the hard ground beside him. He thought, as he looked into her eyes, that she was a woman men dreamed of. Strong, beautiful, loyal. Taking her hand, he dashed up the path, anxious to make up the time he'd wasted arguing with her. When he felt they'd been in the open long enough, he left the path for the rocks again.

"You know where he's going," Morgan whispered, breathing quickly. "Where?"

"A small cave near Stevos's cottage. He thinks to pick up last night's cache." He grinned suddenly. Morgan heard it in his voice. "He won't find it, and then, by God, he'll sweat. Keep low now—no more talk.''

She could see the beauty of the night clearly in the moonlight. The sky was velvet, pierced with stars, flooded by the moon. Even the thin, scruffy bushes working their way through rock held an ethereal allure. The sound of the sea rose from below them, soft with distance. An owl sent up a quiet hooting music of lazy contentment. Morgan thought, if she could look, she might find more blue-headed flowers. Then Nick was pulling her over the next ridge and pressing her to the ground.

''It's just up ahead. Stay here.''

''No, I—''

''Don't argue,'' he said roughly. ''I can move faster without you. Don't move and don't make a sound.''

Before she could speak, he was scrambling away, silently, half on his belly, half on his knees. Morgan watched him until he was concealed by another huddle of rocks. Then, for the first time since they had begun, she started to pray.

Nick couldn't move quickly now. If he had misjudged the timing, he'd find himself face to face with his quarry. He needed to save that pleasure for the following night. But to know—to know who he had been hounding for six months was a bonus Nick couldn't resist.

There were more rocks and a few trees for cover, and he used them as he skirted the dead man's rough cottage. An attempt had been made to clear the ground for a vegetable garden, but the soil had never been worked. Nick wondered idly what had become of the woman who had sometimes shared Stevos's bed and washed his shirts. Then he heard the quiet scrape of boot on rock again. Less than a hundred yards away, Nick estimated. Eyes gleaming in the darkness, he crept toward the mouth of the cave.

He could hear the movements inside, quiet, confident. Slipping behind a rock, he waited, patient, listening. The furious oath that echoed inside the cave brought Nick a rich thrill of pleasure.

Taste the betrayal, he told the man inside. And choke on it.

The movements inside the cave became louder. Nick's smile spread. He'd be searching now, Nick concluded. Looking for signs to tell him if his hiding place had been looted. But no, you haven't been robbed, Nick thought. Your little white bags were lifted from right under your nose.

He saw him then, striding out of the cave—all in black, still masked. Take it off, Nick ordered him silently. Take it off and let me see your face.

The figure stood in the shadows of the mouth of the cave. Fury flowed from him in waves. His head turned from side to side as if he were searching for something . . . or someone.

They heard the sound at the same instant. The shifting of pebbles underfoot, the rustling of bushes. Dear God, Morgan! Nick thought and half rose from his concealment. As he tensed, he saw the black-clad figure draw a gun and melt back into the shadows.

With his heart beating in his throat, Nick gripped the rock and prepared to lunge. He could catch the man off-guard, he thought rapidly, gain enough time to shout a warning to Morgan so that she could get away.

Fear licked at him—not for himself, but at the thought that she might not run fast enough.

The bush directly across the path trembled with movement. Nick sucked in his breath to lunge.

Bony, and with more greed than wit, a dusty goat stepped forward to find a more succulent branch.

Nick sunk down behind the rock, furious that he was trembling. Though she had done nothing more than what he had told her, he cursed Morgan fiercely.

With a furious oath, the man in black stuck the gun back in his belt as he strode down the path. As he passed Nick, he whipped off his mask.

Nick saw the face, the eyes, and knew.

Morgan huddled behind the rock where Nick had shoved her, her arms wrapped around her knees. It seemed she'd already waited an eternity. She strained to hear every sound—the whisper of the wind, the sigh of leaves. Her heart hadn't stopped its painful thudding since he'd left her.

Never again, Morgan promised herself. Never again would she sit and wait. Never again would she sit helpless and trembling, on the verge of hot, useless tears. If anything happened—she clamped down on the incomplete thought. Nothing was going to happen to Nick. He'd be back any moment. But the moments dragged on.

When he dropped down beside her, she had to stifle a scream. Morgan had thought her ears were tuned to hear even the dust blow on the wind, but she hadn't heard his approach. She didn't even say his name, just went into his arms.

"He's gone," Nick told her.

The memory of that one shuddering moment of terror washed over him. He crushed his mouth to hers as though he were starving. All of her fears whipped out, one by one, until there was nothing in her but a well of love.

"Oh, Nicholas, I was so frightened for you. What happened?"

"He wasn't pleased." With a grin that was both ruthless and daring, he pulled her to her feet. "No, he wasn't pleased. He'll be on the boat tomorrow."

"But did you see who—"

"No questions." He silenced her again with his mouth, roughly, as though the adventure were only beginning. "I don't want to have to lie to you again." With a laugh, Nick drew her toward the path and the moonlight. "Now, my stubborn, courageous witch, I'll take you back. Tomorrow when your feet are too sore to stand, you'll curse me."

He wouldn't tell her any more, Morgan thought. And for now, perhaps it was best. "Share my bed tonight." She smiled as she hooked her arm around his waist. "Stay another hour with me, and I won't curse you."

Laughing, he ran a hand down her hair. "What man could resist such an ultimatum?"

Morgan awoke as a soft knock sounded at her door. The small maid peeked inside.

"Your pardon, *kyrios*, a phone call from Athens."

"Oh . . . thank you, Zena, I'll be right there." Rising quickly, Morgan hurried to the phone in Liz's sitting room, belting her robe as she went. "Hello?"

"Morgan, did I wake you? It's past ten."

"Liz?" Morgan tried to shake away the cobwebs. It had been dawn before she had slept.

"Do you know anyone else in Athens?"

"I'm a bit groggy." Morgan yawned, then smiled with memories. "I went for a late-night swim. It was wonderful."

"You sound very smug," Liz mused. "We'll have to discuss it later. Morgan, I feel terrible about it, but I'm going to have to stay here until tomorrow. The doctors are hopeful, but Iona's still in a coma. I can't leave Alex to cope with his family and everything else alone."

"Please, don't worry about me. I'm sorry, Liz. I know it's difficult for both of you." She thought of Iona's involvement in the smuggling and felt a fresh wave of pity. "How is Alex holding up? He seemed so devastated when he left here."

"It would be easier if the whole family didn't look to him for answers. Oh, Morgan, it's so ugly." Strain tightened her voice and Morgan heard her take a deep breath to control it. "I don't know how Iona's mother will handle it if she dies. And suicide—it just makes it harder."

Morgan swallowed the words she wanted to say. Nick had spoken to her in confidence; she couldn't betray it even for Liz. "You said the doctors are hopeful."

"Yes, her vital signs are leveling, but—"

"What about Dorian, Liz? Is he all right?"

"Barely." Morgan heard Liz sigh again. "I don't know how I could have been so blind not to see how he felt about her. He's hardly left her bedside. If Alex hadn't bullied him, I think he might have slept in the

chair beside her last night instead of going home. From
the way he looks this morning, I don't think he got any
sleep anyway.''

''Please give him my best—and Alex, too.'' On a
long frustrated breath she sat down. ''Liz, I feel so
helpless.'' She thought of smuggling, attempted murder and shut her eyes. ''I wish there were something I
could do for you.''

''Just be there when I get back.'' Though her tone
lightened, Morgan recognized the effort. ''Enjoy the
beach for me, look for your goatherd. If you're going to
take moonlight swims, you should have some company
for them.'' When Morgan was silent, Liz continued
slowly. ''Or did you?''

''Well, actually . . .'' Smiling, Morgan trailed off.

''Tell me, have you settled on a goatherd or a poet?''

''Neither.''

''It must be Nick then,'' Liz concluded. ''Imagine
that—all I had to do was invite him to dinner.''

Morgan lifted a brow and found herself grinning. ''I
don't know what you're talking about.'' Life was
everywhere, she remembered, if you only knew where
to look.

''*Mmm-hmmm*. We'll talk about it tomorrow. Have
fun. The number's there if you need me for anything.
Oh, there's some marvelous wine in the cellar,'' she
added, and for the first time, the smile in her voice
seemed genuine. ''If you feel like a cozy evening—
help yourself.''

''I appreciate it, Liz, but—''

''And don't worry about me or any of us. Everything's going to be fine. I just know it. Give Nick my
love.''

"I will," Morgan heard herself saying.

"I thought so. See you tomorrow."

Smiling, Morgan replaced the receiver.

"And so," Stephanos finished, lovingly stroking his moustache, "after several glasses of ouzo, Mikal became more expansive. The last two dates he gave me when our man joined the fishing expedition were the last week in February and the second week in March. That doesn't include the evening we encountered Morgan James, or when you took the trip in his stead."

Smiling, Nick flipped through the reports on his desk. "And from the end of February to the first week of April, he was in Rome. Even without my stroke of luck last night, that would have ruled him out. With the phone call I just got from Athens, I'd say we've eliminated him altogether from having any part in this. Now we know our man works alone. We move."

"And you move with an easy heart?" Stephanos noted. "What did Athens say?"

"The investigation on that end is complete. He's clean. His books, his records, his phone calls and correspondence. From this end, we know he hasn't been on the island to take part in any of the runs." Nick leaned back in his chair. "I have no doubt that since our man learned of the loss of his last shipment, he'll make the trip tonight. He won't want another to slip through his fingers." He tapped idly on the papers which littered his desk. "Now that I have the information I've been waiting for, we won't keep Athens waiting any longer. We'll have him tonight."

"You were out very late last night," Stephanos commented, taking out an ugly pipe and filling it.

"Keeping tabs on me, Stephanos?" Nick inquired with a lift of brow. "I haven't been twelve for a very long time."

"You are in very good humor this morning." He continued to fill his pipe, tapping the tobacco with patient care. "You haven't been so for many days."

"You should be glad my mood's broken. But then, you're used to my moods, aren't you, old man?"

Stephanos shrugged in agreement or acceptance. "The American lady is fond of walking on the beach. Perhaps you encountered her last night?"

"You're becoming entirely too wise in your old age, Stephanos." Nick struck a match and held it over the bowl of the pipe.

"Not too old to recognize the look of a man satisfied with a night of pleasure," Stephanos commented mildly and sucked to get flame. "A very beautiful lady. Very strong."

Lighting a cigarette, Nick smiled at him. "So you've mentioned before. I'd noticed myself. Tell me, Stephanos, are you also not too old to have ideas about strong, beautiful ladies?"

Stephanos cackled. "Only the dead have no ideas about strong, beautiful ladies, Nicholas. I'm a long way from dead."

Nick flashed him a grin. "Keep your distance, old man. She's mine."

"She is in love with you."

The cigarette halted on its journey to Nick's lips. His smile faded. Stephanos stood grinning broadly as he was pierced with one of his friend's lancing looks. "Why do you say that?"

"Because it is true, I've seen it." He puffed enjoyably on his pipe. "It is often difficult to see what is standing before your eyes. How much longer is she alone?"

Nick brought his thoughts back and scowled at the papers on his desk. "I'm not certain. Another day or so at least, depending on Iona's condition. In love with me," he murmured and looked back at Stephanos.

He knew she was attracted, that she cared—perhaps too much for her own good. But in love with him. . . . He'd never allowed himself to consider the possibility.

"She will be alone tonight," Stephanos continued blandly, appreciating Nick's stunned look. "It wouldn't do for her to wander from the villa." He puffed a few moments in silence. "If all does not go smoothly, you would want her safely behind locked doors."

"I've already spoken to her. She understands enough to listen and take care." Nick shook his head. Today of all days he had to think clearly. "It's time we invited Captain Tripolos in. Call Mitilini."

Morgan enjoyed a late breakfast on the terrace and toyed with the idea of walking to the beach. He might come, she thought. I could phone and ask him to come. No, she decided, nibbling on her lip as she remembered all he had told her. If tonight is as important as he thinks, he needs to be left alone. I wish I knew more. I wish I knew what he was going to do. What if he gets hurt or . . . Morgan clamped down on the thought and wished it were tomorrow.

"Kyrios." At the maid's quiet summons, Morgan gasped and spun. "The captain from Mitilini is here to speak with you."

"What?" Panic rose and Morgan swallowed it. If Nick had spoken to him, Tripolos would hardly be waiting to see her, she thought frantically. Perhaps Nick wasn't ready yet. What could Tripolos possibly want with her?

"Tell him I'm out," she decided quickly. "Tell him I've gone to the beach or the village."

"Very good, *kyrios*." The maid accepted her order without question, then watched as Morgan streaked from the terrace.

For the second time, Morgan climbed the steep cliff path. This time, she knew where she was going. She could see Tripolos's official car parked at the villa's entrance as she rounded the first bend. She increased her pace, running until she was certain she herself was out of view.

Her approach had been noticed, however. The wide doors of Nick's villa opened before she reached the top step. Nick came out to meet her.

"*Yiasou*. You must be in amazing shape to take the hill at that speed."

"Very funny," she panted as she ran into his arms.

"Is it that you couldn't keep away from me or is something wrong?" He held her close a moment, then drew her back just far enough to see her face. It was flushed with the run, but there was no fear in her eyes.

"Tripolos is at the villa." Morgan pressed her hand to her heart and tried to catch her breath. "I slipped out the back because I didn't know what I should say to him. Nicholas, I have to sit down. That's a very steep hill."

He was searching her face silently. Still struggling for her breath, Morgan tilted her head and returned the survey. She laughed and pushed the hair from her eyes. "Nicholas, why are you staring at me like that?"

"I'm trying to see what's standing in front of my eyes."

She laughed again. "Well, I am, you fool, but I'm going to collapse from exhaustion any minute."

With a sudden grin, Nick swept her off her feet and into his arms. She circled his neck as his mouth came down on hers.

"What are you doing?" she asked when he let her breathe again.

"Taking what's mine."

His lips came back to hers and lingered. Slowly, almost lazily, he began to tease her tongue with his until he felt her breath start to shudder into his mouth. He promised himself that when everything was over, he would kiss her again, just like this—luxuriously with the heat of the sun warming her skin. When the night's work was finally over, he thought, and for a moment his lips were rough and urgent. Needs rushed through him almost painfully before he banked them.

"So . . ." He strolled into the house, still carrying her. "The captain came to see you. He's very tenacious."

Morgan took a deep breath to bring herself back from the power of the kiss. "You said you were going to speak with him today, but I didn't know if you were ready. If you'd gotten the information you needed. And to confess and humiliate myself, I'm a coward. I didn't want to face him again."

"Coward, Aphrodite? No, that's something you're not." He laid his cheek against hers a moment, making her wonder what was going on in his head. "I called

Mitilini,'' he continued, ''I left a message for Tripolos. After our talk, he should lose all interest in you.''

''I'll be devastated.'' He grinned and took her lips again. ''Would you put me down? I can't talk to you this way.''

''I'm enjoying it.'' Ignoring her request, he continued into the salon. ''Stephanos, I believe Morgan might like something cool. She had quite a run.''

''No, nothing really. *Efxaristo.*'' Faintly embarrassed, she met Stephanos's checkerboard grin. When he backed out of sight, she turned her head back to Nick. ''If you know who the man is who's running the smuggling, can't you just tell Captain Tripolos and have him arrested?''

''It's not that simple. We want to catch him when the cache is in his possession. There's also the matter of cleaning up the place in the hills where he keeps his goods stored before he ships them on. That part,'' he added with an absent interest, ''I'll leave to Tripolos.''

''Nicholas, what will you do?''

''What has to be done.''

''Nicholas—''

''Morgan,'' he interrupted. Standing her on feet, he placed his hands on her shoulders. ''You don't want a step-by-step description. Let me finish this without bringing you in anymore than I already have.''

He lowered his mouth, taking hers with uncharacteristic gentleness. He brought her close, but softly, as if he held something precious. Morgan felt her bones turn to water.

''You have a knack for changing the subject,'' she murmured.

"After tonight, it's the only subject that's going to interest me. Morgan—"

"A thousand pardons." Stephanos hovered in the doorway. Nick looked up impatiently.

"Go away, old man."

"Nicholas!" Morgan drew out of his arms, sending him a look of reproof. "Has he always been rude, Stephanos?"

"Alas, my lady, since he took his thumb out of his mouth."

"Stephanos," Nick began in warning, but Morgan gave a peal of laughter and kissed him.

"Captain Tripolos requests a few moments of your time, Mr. Gregoras," Stephanos said respectfully and grinned.

"Give me a moment, then send him in, and bring the files from the office."

"Nicholas." Morgan clung to his arm. "Let me stay with you. I won't get in the way."

"No." His refusal was short and harsh. He saw the hurt flicker in her eyes and sighed. "Morgan, I can't allow it even if I wanted to. This isn't going to touch you. I can't let it touch you. That's important to me."

"You're not going to send me away," she began heatedly.

He arched a brow and looked very cool. "I'm not under the same pressure I was last night, Morgan. And I will send you away."

"I won't go."

His eyes narrowed. "You'll do precisely what I say."

"Like hell."

Fury flickered, smoldered, then vanished in a laugh. "You're an exasperating woman, Aphrodite. If I had the time, I'd beat you." To prove his point, he drew her close and touched his lips to her. "Since I don't I'll ask you to wait upstairs."

"Since you *ask*."

"Mr. Gregoras. Ah, Miss James." Tripolos lumbered into the room. "How convenient. I was inquiring for Miss James at the Theoharis villa when your message reached me."

"Miss James is leaving," Nick told him. "I'm sure you'll agree her presence isn't necessary. Mr. Adonti from Athens has asked me to speak with you on a certain matter."

"Adonti?" Tripolos repeated. Nick watched surprise and interest move across the pudgy face before his eyes became direct. "So, you are acquainted with Mr. Adonti's organization?"

"Well acquainted," Nick returned mildly. "We've had dealings over the years."

"I see." He studied Nick with a thoughtful purse of his lips. "And Miss James?"

"Miss James chose an inopportune time to visit friends," Nick said and took her arm. "That's all. If you'll excuse me, I'll just see her out. Perhaps you'd care for a drink while you're waiting." With a gesture toward the bar, Nick drew Morgan out into the hall.

"He looked impressed with the name you just dropped."

"Forget the name," Nick told her briefly. "You've never heard it."

"All right," she said without hesitation.

"What have I done to deserve this trust you give

me?'' he demanded suddenly. ''I've hurt you again and again. I couldn't make up for it in a lifetime.''

''Nicholas—''

''No.'' He cut her off with a shake of his head. In an uncharacteristic gesture of nerves or frustration, he dragged a hand through his hair. ''There's no time. Stephanos will show you upstairs.''

''As you wish,'' Stephanos agreed from behind them. Handing Nick a folder, he turned to the stairs. ''This way, my lady.''

Because Nick had already turned back to the salon, Morgan followed the old man without a word. She'd been given more time with him, she told herself. She couldn't ask for any more than that.

Stephanos took her into a small sitting room off the master bedroom. ''You'll be comfortable here,'' he told her. ''I'll bring you coffee.''

''No. No, thank you, Stephanos.'' She stared at him, and for the second time he saw her heart in her eyes. ''He'll be all right, won't he?''

He grinned at her so that his moustache quivered. ''Can you doubt it?'' he countered before he closed the door behind him.

Chapter 12

THERE WAS NOTHING MORE FRUSTRATING THAN WAIT-
ing, Morgan decided after the first thirty minutes.
Especially for someone who simply wasn't made for
sitting still.

The little room was shaped like a cozy box and done
in warm, earthy colors with lots of polished wood that
gleamed in the early afternoon light. It was filled with
small treasures. Morgan sat down and scowled at a
Dresden shepherdess. At another time she might have
admired the flowing grace of the lines, the fragility.
Now she could only think that she was of no more
practical use than that pale piece of porcelain. She had,
in a matter of speaking, been put on the shelf.

It was ridiculous for Nick to constantly try to . . .
shield her. Morgan's sigh was quick and impatient.
Hadn't that been Liz's word when she had spoken of
Alex's actions? After all, Morgan thought as she rose

again, she was hardly some trembling, fainting scatter-brain who couldn't deal with whatever there was to face. She remembered trembling *and* fainting dead away in his arms. With a rueful smile, she paced to the window. Well, it wasn't as though she made a habit of it.

In any case, her thoughts ran on, he should know that she would, and could, face anything now that they were together. If he understood how she felt about him, then . . . but did he? she thought abruptly. She'd shown him, certainly she'd shown him in every possible way open to her, but she hadn't told him.

How can I? Morgan asked herself as she sunk into another chair. When a man had lived ten years of his life following his own rules, courting danger, looking for adventures, did he want to tie himself to a woman and accept the responsibilities of love?

He cared for her, Morgan reflected. Perhaps more than he was comfortable with. And he wanted her—more than any man had ever wanted her. But love . . . love wouldn't come easily to a man like Nicholas. No, she wouldn't pressure him with hers now. Even the unselfish offer of it would be pressure, she thought, when he had so much on his mind. She was only free to go on showing him, trusting him.

Even that seemed to throw him off-balance a bit, she mused, smiling a little. It was as if he couldn't quite accept that someone could see him as he was, know the way he had lived and still give him trust. Morgan wondered if he would have been more comfortable if she had pulled back from him a little after the things he had told her. He would have understood her condemnations more readily than her acceptance. Well, he'll just have to get used to it, she decided. He'll just have to get used to it because I'm not going to make it easy for him to back away.

Restless, she walked to the window. Here was a different view, Morgan thought, from the one she so often looked out on from her bedroom window. Higher, more dangerous. More compelling, she thought with a quick thrill. The rocks seemed more jagged, the sea less tame. How it suited the man she'd given her heart to.

There was no terrace there, and suddenly wanting the air and sun, Morgan went through to his bedroom and opened his balcony doors. She could hear the sea hissing before she reached the rail. With a laugh, she leaned farther out.

Oh, she could live with the challenge of such a view every day, she thought, and never tire of it. She could watch the sea change colors with the sky, watch the gulls swoop over the water and back to the nests they'd built in the cliff walls. She could look down on the Theoharis villa and appreciate its refined elegance, but she would choose the rough gray stone and dizzying height.

Morgan tossed back her head and wished for a storm. Thunder, lightning, wild wind. Was there a better spot on earth to enjoy it? Laughing, she dared the sky to boil and spew out its worst.

"My God, how beautiful you are."

The light of challenge still in her eyes, Morgan turned. Leaning against the open balcony door, Nick stared at her. His face was very still, his gaze like a lance. The passion was on him, simmering, bubbling, just beneath the surface. It suited him, Morgan thought, suited those long, sharp bones in his face, those black eyes and the mouth that could be beautiful or cruel.

As she leaned back on the railing, the breeze caught at the ends of her hair. Her eyes took on the color of the sky. Power swept over her, and a touch of madness. "You want me, I can see it. Come and show me."

It hurt, Nick discovered. He'd never known, until Morgan, that desire could hurt. Perhaps it was only when you loved that your needs ached in you. How many times had he loved her last night? he wondered. And each time, it had been like a tempest in him. Now, he promised himself, this time, he would show her a different way.

Slowly, he went to her. Taking both of her hands, he lifted them, then pressed his lips to the palms. When he brought his gaze to hers, Nick saw that her eyes were wide and moved, her lips parted in surprise. Something stirred in him—love, guilt, a need to give.

"Have I shown you so little tenderness, Morgan?" he murmured.

"Nicholas . . ." She could only whisper his name as her pulses raged and her heart melted.

"Have I given you no soft words, no sweetness?" He kissed her hands again, one finger at a time. She didn't move, only stared at him. "And still you come to me. I'm in your debt," he said quietly in Greek. "What price would you ask me?"

"No, Nicholas, I . . ." Morgan shook her head, unable to speak, nearly swaying with the weakness this gentle, quiet man brought her.

"You asked me to show you how I wanted you." He put his hands to her face as if she were indeed made of Dresden porcelain, then touched his lips almost reverently to hers. A sound came from her, shaky and small. "Come and I will."

He lifted her, not with a flourish as he had on the porch, but as a man lifts something he cherishes. "Now . . ." He laid her down with care. "In the daylight, in my bed."

Again, he took her hand, tracing kisses over the back and palm, then to the wrist where her pulse hammered. All the while he watched her as she lay back, staring at him with something like astonished wonder.

How young she looks, Nick thought as he gently drew her finger into his mouth. And how fragile. Not a witch now, or a goddess, but only a woman. His woman. And her eyes were already clouding, her breath already trembling. He'd shown her the fire and the storm, he thought, but not once—not once had he given her spring.

Bending, he nibbled lightly at her lips, allowing his hands to touch no more than her hair.

It might have been a dream, so weak and weightless did she feel. Nick kissed her eyes closed so that Morgan saw no more than a pale red glow. Then his lips continued, over her forehead, her temples, down the line of her cheekbones—always soft, always warm. The words he whispered against her skin flowed like scented oil over her. She would have moved to bring him closer if her arms had not been too heavy to lift. Instead, she lay in the flood of his tenderness.

His mouth was at her ear, gently torturing with a

trace of tongue, a murmured promise. Even as she moaned in surrender, he moved lower to taste and tease the curve of her neck. With kisses like whispers, and whispers like wine, he took her deeper. Gentleness was a drug for both of them.

Hardly touching her, he loosened the buttons of her blouse and slipped it from her. Though he felt the firm pressure of her breasts against him, he took his mouth to the slope of her shoulder instead. He could feel the strength there, the grace, and he tarried.

Morgan's eyes were closed, weighed down with gold-tipped lashes. Her breath rushed out between her lips. He knew he could watch those flickers of pleasure move over her face forever. With his hands once more buried in her hair, Nick kissed her. He felt the yielding and the hunger before he moved on.

Slowly, savoring, he took his lips down to the soft swell—circling, nibbling until he came to the tender underside of her breast. On a moan, Morgan fretted under him as if she were struggling to wake from a dream. But he kept the pace slow and soothed her with words and soft, soft kisses.

With aching gentleness he stroked his tongue over the peak, fighting a surge of desperation when he found it hot and ready. Her movements beneath him took on a rhythmic sinuousness that had the blood pounding in his brain. Her scent was there, always there on the verge of his senses even when she wasn't with him. Now he wallowed in it. As he suckled, he allowed his hands to touch her for the first time.

Morgan felt the long stroke of his hands, the quick scrape of those strong rough fingers that now seemed

sensitive enough to tune violins. They caressed lightly,
like a breeze. They made her ache.

Soft, slow, gentle, his mouth traveled down the
center of her body, lingering here, exploring there until
he paused where her slacks hugged across her stomach.
When she felt him unfasten them, she trembled. She
arched to help him, but Nick drew them down inch by
inch, covering the newly exposed flesh with moist
kisses so that she could only lie steeped in a pool of
pleasure.

And when she was naked, he continued to worship
her with his lips, with his suddenly gentle hands. She
thought she could hear her own skin hum. The muscles
in her thighs quivered as he passed over them, and her
desire leaped from passive to urgent.

"Nicholas," she breathed. "Now."

"You've scratched your feet on the rocks," he
murmured, pressing his lips against the ball of her foot.
"It's a sin to mar such skin, my love." Watching her
face, he ran his tongue over the arch. Her eyes flew
open, dazed with passion. "I've longed to see you like
this." His voice grew thick as his control began to slip.
"With sunlight streaming over you, your hair flowing
over my pillow, your body trembling for me."

As he spoke, he began the slow, aching journey
back, gradually back to her lips. Needs pressed at him
and demanded he hurry, but he wouldn't be rushed. He
told himself he could linger over the taste and the feel
of her for days.

Her arms weren't heavy now, but strong as they
curled around him. Every nerve, every pore of her
body seemed tuned to him. The harmony seemed

impossible, yet it sung through her. His flesh was as hot and damp as hers, his breath as unsteady.

"You ask how I want you," he murmured, thrilling to her moan as he slipped into her. "Look at me and see."

His control hung by a thread. Morgan pulled his mouth to hers and snapped it.

Nick held Morgan close, gently stroking her back while her trembles eased. She clung to him, almost as much in wonder as in love. How was she to have known he had such tenderness in him? How was she to have known she would be so moved by it? Blinking back tears, she pressed her lips to his throat.

"You've made me feel beautiful," she murmured.

"You are beautiful." Tilting her head back, Nick smiled at her. "And tired," he added, tracing a thumb over the mauve smudges under her eyes. "You should sleep, Morgan, I won't have you ill."

"I won't be ill." She snuggled against him, fitting herself neatly against the curve of his body. "And there'll be time for sleeping later. We'll go away for a few days, like you said."

Twining a lock of her hair around his finger, Nick gazed up at the ceiling. A few days with her would never be enough, but he still had the night to get through. "Where would you like to go?"

Morgan thought of her dreams of Venice and Cornish moors. With a sigh, she closed her eyes and drew in Nick's scent. "Anywhere. Right here." Laughing, she propped herself on his chest. "Wherever it is, I intend to keep you in bed a good deal of the time."

"Is that so?" His mouth twitched as he tugged on her hair. "I might begin to think you have designs only on my body."

"It is a rather nice one." In a long stroke, she ran her hands down his shoulders, enjoying the feel of firm flesh and strong bone. "Lean and muscled . . ." She trailed off when she spotted a small scar high on his chest. A frown creased her brow as she stared at it. It seemed out of place on that smooth brown skin. "Where did you get this?"

Nick tilted his head, shifting his gaze down. "Ah, an old battle scar," he said lightly.

From a bullet, Morgan realized all at once. Horror ripped through her and mirrored in her eyes. Seeing it, Nick cursed his loose tongue.

"Morgan—"

"No, please." She buried her face against his chest and held tight. "Don't say anything. Just give me a minute."

She'd forgotten. Somehow the gentleness and beauty of their lovemaking had driven all the ugliness out of her mind. It had been easy to pretend for a little while that there was no threat. Pretending's for children, she reminded herself. He didn't need to cope with a child now. If she could give him nothing else, she would give him what was left of her strength. Swallowing fear, she pressed her lips to his chest then rolled beside him again.

"Did everything go as you wanted with Captain Tripolos?"

A strong woman, Nick thought, linking his hand with hers. An extraordinary woman. "He's satisfied with the information I've given him. A shrewd man for all his plodding technique.''

''Yes, I thought he was like a bulldog the first time I encountered him.''

Chuckling, Nick drew her closer. ''An apt description, Aphrodite.'' He shifted then, reaching to the table beside him for a cigarette. ''I think he's one of the few policemen I find it agreeable to work with.''

''Why do you—'' She broke off as she looked up and focused on the slim black cigarette. ''I'd forgotten,'' Morgan murmured. ''How could I have forgotten?''

Nick blew out a stream of smoke. ''Forgotten what?''

''The cigarette.'' Morgan sat up, pushing at her tumbled hair. ''The stub of the cigarette near the body.''

He lifted a brow, but found himself distracted by the firm white breasts easily within reach. ''So?''

''It was fresh, from one of those expensive brands like you're smoking.'' She let out an impatient breath. ''I should have told you before, but it hardly makes any difference at this point. You already know who killed Stevos—who runs the smuggling.''

''I never told you I did.''

''You didn't have to.'' Annoyed with herself, Morgan frowned and missed Nick's considering look.

''Why didn't I?''

''You'd have told me if you hadn't seen his face. When you wouldn't answer me at all, I knew you had.''

He shook his head as a reluctant smile touched his

lips. "*Diabolos*, it's a good thing I didn't cross you earlier in my career. I'm afraid it would have been over quickly. As it happens," he added, "I saw the cigarette myself."

"I should have known you would," she muttered.

"I can assure you Tripolos didn't miss it either."

"That damn cigarette has driven me to distraction." Morgan gave an exasperated sigh. "There were moments I suspected everyone I knew—Dorian, Alex, Iona, even Liz and Andrew. I nearly made myself sick over it."

"You don't name me." Nick studied the cigarette in his hand.

"No, I already told you why."

"Yes," he murmured, "with an odd sort of compliment I haven't forgotten. I should have eased your mind sooner, Morgan, about what I do. You might have slept better."

Leaning over, she kissed him. "Stop worrying about my sleep. I'm going to start thinking I look like a tired hag."

He slid a hand behind her neck to keep her close. "Will you rest if I tell you that you do?"

"No, but I'll hit you."

"Ah, then I'll lie and tell you you're exquisite."

She hit him anyway, a quick jab in the ribs.

"So, now you want to play rough." Crushing out his cigarette, Nick rolled her beneath him. She struggled for a moment, then eyed him narrowly.

"Do you know how many times you've pinned me down like this?" Morgan demanded.

"No, how many?"

"I'm not sure." Her smile spread slowly. "I think I'm beginning to like it."

"Perhaps I can make you like it better." He muffled her laugh with his lips.

He didn't love her gently now, but fiercely. As desperate as he, Morgan let the passion rule her. Fear that it might be the last time caused her response and demands to be urgent. She lit a fire in him.

Now, where his hands had trailed slowly, they raced. Where his mouth had whispered, it savaged. Morgan threw herself into the flames without a second thought. Her mouth was greedy, searching for his taste everywhere while her hands rushed to touch and arouse.

Her body had never felt so agile. It could melt into his one moment, then slither away to drive him to madness. She could hear his desire in the short, harsh breath, feel it in the tensing and quivering of his muscles as she roamed over them, taste it in the dampness that sheened his skin. It matched her own, and again they were in harmony.

She arched against him as his mouth rushed low— but it was more a demand than an invitation. Delirious with her own strength and power, Morgan dug her fingers into his hair and urged him to take her to that first giddy peak. Even as she cried out with it, she hungered for more. And he gave more, while he took.

But she wasn't satisfied with her own pleasure. Ruthlessly she sought to undermine whatever claim he still held to sanity. Her hands had never been so clever, or so quick. Her teeth nipped at his skin before she soothed the tiny pains with a flick of her tongue. She heard him groan and a low, sultry laugh flowed from her. His breath caught when she reached for him, then came out in an oath. Morgan felt the sunlight explode into fragments as he plunged into her.

Later, much later, when he knew his time with her was nearly up, Nick kissed her with lingering tenderness.

"You're going," Morgan said, struggling not to cling to him.

"Soon. I'll have to take you back to the villa in a little while." Sitting up, he drew her with him. "You'll stay inside. Lock the doors, tell the servants to let no one in. No one."

Morgan tried to promise, and found she couldn't form the words. "When you're finished, you'll come?"

Smiling, he tucked her hair behind her ear. "I suppose I can handle your window vines again."

"I'll wait up for you and let you in the front door."

"Aphrodite." Nick pressed a kiss to her wrist. "Where's your romance?"

"Oh, God!" Morgan threw her arms around his neck and clung. "I wasn't going to say it—I promised myself I wouldn't. Be careful." Biting back tears, she pressed her face against his throat. "Please, please be careful. I'm terrified for you."

"No, don't." Feeling the dampness against his skin, he held her tighter. "Don't cry for me."

"I'm sorry." With a desperate effort, she forced back the tears. "I'm not helping you."

Nick drew her away and looked at the damp cheeks

and shimmering eyes. "Don't ask me not to go, Morgan."

"No." She swallowed again. "I won't. Don't ask me not to worry."

"It's the last time," he said fiercely.

The words made her shudder, but she kept her eyes on his. "Yes, I know."

"Just wait for me." He pulled her back against him. "Wait for me."

"With a bottle of Alex's best champagne," she promised in a stronger voice.

He pressed a kiss to her temple. "We'll have some of mine now, before I take you back. A toast," he told her as he drew her away again. "To tomorrow."

"Yes." She smiled. It almost reached her eyes. "I'll drink with you to tomorrow."

"Rest a moment." With another kiss, he laid her back against the pillow. "I'll go bring some up."

Morgan waited until the door had closed behind him before she buried her face in the pillow.

Chapter 13

IT WAS DARK WHEN SHE WOKE. CONFUSED, DISORI-
ented, Morgan struggled to see where she was. The
room was all shifting shadows and silence. There was a
cover over her—something soft and light with a fringe
of silk. Beneath it, she was warm and naked.

Nicholas, she thought in quick panic. She'd fallen
asleep and he'd gone. On a moan, she sat up, drawing
her knees to her chest. How could she have wasted
those last precious moments together? How long? she
thought abruptly. How long had he been gone? With
trembling fingers, she reached for the lamp beside the
bed.

The light eased some of her fears, but before she
could climb out of bed to find a clock, she saw the note
propped against the lamp. Taking it, Morgan studied
the bold, strong writing. *Go back to sleep* was all it
said.

How like him, she thought, and nearly laughed. Morgan kept the note in her hand, as if to keep Nick close, as she rose to look for her clothes. It didn't take her long to discover they were gone.

"The louse!" Morgan said aloud, forgetting the tender thoughts she had only moments before. So, he wasn't taking any chances making certain she stayed put. Naked, hands on her hips, she scowled around the room. Where the devil does he think I'd go? she asked herself. I have no way of knowing where he is . . . or what he's doing, she thought on a fresh flood of worry.

Wait. Suddenly cold, Morgan pulled the cover from the bed and wrapped herself in it. All I can do is wait.

The time dripped by, minute by endless minute. She paced, then forced herself to sit, then paced again. It would be morning in only a few more hours, she told herself. In the morning, the wait would be over. For all of them.

She couldn't bear it, she thought in despair one moment. She had to bear it, she told herself the next. Would he never get back? Would morning never come? On a sound of fury, she tossed the cover aside. She might have to wait, Morgan thought grimly as she marched to Nick's closet. But she'd be damned if she'd wait naked.

Nick shifted the muscles in his shoulders and blocked out the need for a cigarette. Even the small light would be dangerous now. The cove was bathed in milky moonlight and silence. There would be a murmur now and then from behind a rock. Not from a spirit, but from a man in uniform. The cove still held secrets. Lifting his binoculars, Nick again scanned the sea.

"Any sign?" Tripolos seemed remarkably comfortable in his squat position behind a rock. He popped a tiny mint into his mouth and crunched quietly. Nick merely shook his head and handed the glasses to Stephanos.

"Thirty minutes," Stephanos stated, chewing on the stem of his dead pipe. "The wind carries the sound of the motor."

"I hear nothing." Tripolos gave the old man a doubtful frown.

Nick chuckled as the familiar feeling of excitement rose. "Stephanos hears what others don't. Just tell your men to be ready."

"My men are ready." His gaze flicked over Nick's profile. "You enjoy your work, Mr. Gregoras."

"At times," Nick muttered, then grinned. "This time, by God."

"And soon it's over," Stephanos said from beside him.

Nick turned his head to meet the old man's eyes. He knew the statement covered more than this one job, but the whole of what had been Nick's career. He hadn't told him, but Stephanos knew. "Yes," he said simply, then turned his eyes to the sea again.

He thought of Morgan and hoped she was still asleep. She'd looked so beautiful—and so exhausted when he'd come back into the room. Her cheeks had been damp. Damn, he couldn't bear the thought of her tears. But he'd felt a wave of relief that she'd been asleep. He didn't have to see her eyes when he left her.

She's safer there than if I'd taken her back, Nick told

himself. With luck, she'd still be asleep when he got back and then he'd have spared her hours of worry. Stashing her clothes had been an impulse that had eased his mind. Even Morgan wouldn't go wandering around without a stitch on her back.

His grin flashed again. If she woke and looked for them, she'd curse him. The idea gave him a moment's pleasure. He could see her, standing in the center of his room with only the moonlight covering her as she raged.

He felt the low aching need in the pit of his stomach, and promised himself he'd keep her just that way—naked fire—until the sun went down again.

Lifting the binoculars, he scanned the dark sea. "They're coming."

The moon threw the boat into silhouette. A dozen men watched her approach from clumps of rock and shadows. She came in silence, under the power of oars.

She was secured with little conversation and a few deft movements of rope. There was a scent Nick recognized. The scent of fear. A fresh bubble of excitement rose, though his face was deadly calm. He's there, Nick thought. And we have him.

The crew left the boat to gather in the shadows of the beach. A hooded figure moved to join them. At Nick's signal, the cove was flooded with light. The rocks became men.

"In the King's name," Tripolos stated grandly, "this vessel will be searched for illegal contraband. Put up your weapons and surrender."

Shouts and the scrambling of men shattered the glasslike quiet of the cove. Men seeking to escape, and men seeking to capture tangled in the sudden chaos of sound and light. Gunfire shocked the balmy air. There were cries of pain and fury.

The smugglers would fight with fist and blade. The battle would be short, but grim. The sounds of violence bounced hollowly off the rocks and drifted out on the air.

Nick saw the hooded figure melt away from the confusion and streak from the cove. Swearing, he raced after it, thrusting his gun back in his belt. A burly form collided with him as another man sought escape. Each swore at the obstacle, knowing the only choice was to remove it.

Together, they rolled over the rocks, away from the noise and the light. Thrown into darkness, they tumbled helplessly until the ground leveled. A blade glistened, and Nick grasped the thick wrist with both hands to halt its plunge to his throat.

The crack of shots had Morgan springing up from her chair. Had she heard, or just imagined? she wondered as her heart began to thud. Could they be so close? As she stared into the darkness, she heard another shot, and the echo. Fear froze her.

He's all right, she told herself. He'll be here soon, and it'll be over. I know he's all right.

Before the sentence had finished racing through her mind, she was running down the steps and out of the villa.

Telling herself she was only being logical, Morgan headed for the beach. She was just going to meet him. He'd be coming along any minute, and she would see for herself that he wasn't hurt. Nick's jeans hung loosely at her hips as she streaked down the cliff path. Her breath was gasping now, the only sound as her feet padded on the hard dirt. Morgan thought it would almost be a relief to hear the guns again. If she heard them, she might be able to judge the direction. She could find him.

Then, from the top of the beach steps, she saw him walking across the sand. With a sob of shuddering relief, she flew down them to meet him.

He continued, too intent on his own thoughts to note her approach. Morgan started to shout his name, but the word strangled in her throat. She stopped running. Not Nicholas, she realized as she stared at the hooded figure. The moves were wrong, the walk. And he'd have no reason to wear the mask. Even as her thoughts began to race, he reached up and tore off the hood. Moonlight fell on golden hair.

Oh God, had she been a fool not to see it? Those calm, calm eyes—too calm, she thought frantically. Had she ever seen any real emotion in him? Morgan took a step in retreat, looking around desperately for some cover. But he turned. His face hardened as he saw her.

"Morgan, what are you doing out here?"

"I-I wanted to walk." She struggled to sound casual. There was no place for her to run. "It's a lovely night. Almost morning, really." As he advanced on her she moistened her lips and kept talking. "I didn't expect to see you. You surprised me. I thought—"

"You thought I was in Athens," Dorian finished with a smile. "But as you see, I'm not. And, I'm afraid, Morgan, you've seen too much." He held up the hood, dangling it a moment before he dropped it to the sand.

"Yes." There was no use dissembling. "I have."

"It's a pity." His smile vanished as though it had never been. "Still, you could be useful. An American hostage," he said thoughtfully as he scanned her face. "Yes, and a woman." Grabbing her arm, Dorian began to pull her across the sand.

She jerked and struggled against his hold. "I won't go with you."

"You have no choice"—he touched the handle of his knife—"unless you prefer to end up as Stevos did."

Morgan swallowed as she stumbled across the beach. He said it so casually. *Some people have no capacity for emotion—love, hate.* He hadn't been speaking of Iona, Morgan realized, but himself. He was as dangerous as any animal on the run.

"You tried to kill Iona too."

"She'd become a nuisance. Greedy not only for money, but to hold me. She thought to blackmail me into marriage." He gave a quick laugh. "I had only to tempt her with the heroin. I had thought the dose I gave her was enough."

Purposely, Morgan fell to her knees as though she'd tripped. "You would have finished her that morning if I hadn't found her first."

"You have a habit of being in the wrong place." Roughly, Dorian hauled her to her feet. "I had to play the worried lover for a time—dashing back and forth between Lesbos and Athens. A nuisance. Still, if I'd been allowed one moment alone with her in the hospital . . ." Then he shrugged, as if the life or the death of a woman meant nothing. "So, she'll live and she'll talk. It was time to move in any case."

"You lost your last shipment," Morgan blurted out, desperate to distract him from his hurried pace toward the beach steps. If he got her up there—up there in the rocks and the dark.

Dorian froze and turned to her. "How do you know this?"

"I helped steal it," she said impulsively. "Your place in the hills, the cave—"

The words choked off as his hand gripped her throat. "So, you've taken what's mine. Where is it?"

Morgan shook her head.

"Where?" Dorian demanded as his fingers tightened.

A god, she thought staring into his face as the moonlight streamed over it. He had the face of a god. Why hadn't she remembered her own thoughts that gods were bloodthirsty? Morgan put a hand to his wrist as if in surrender. His fingers eased slightly.

"Go to hell."

Swiftly, he swept the back of his hand across her face, knocking her to the sand. His eyes were a calm empty blue as he looked down at her. "You'll tell me before I'm through with you. You'll beg to tell me. There'll be time," he continued as he walked toward her, "when we're off the island."

"I'll tell you nothing." With the blood singing in her ears, Morgan inched away from him. "The police know who you are, there isn't a hole big enough for you to hide in."

Reaching down, he grabbed her by the hair and hauled her painfully to her feet. "If you prefer to die—"

Then she was free, going down to her knees again as Dorian stumbled back and fell onto the sand.

"Nick." Dorian rubbed the blood from his mouth as

his gaze traveled up. "This is a surprise." It dropped again to the revolver Nick held in his hand. "Quite a surprise."

"Nicholas!" Scrambling up, Morgan ran to him. He never looked at her. His arm was rigid as iron when she gripped it. "I thought—I was afraid you were dead."

"Get up," he told Dorian with a quick gesture of the gun. "Or I'll put a bullet in your head while you lie there."

"Were you hurt?" Morgan shook his arm, wanting some sign. She'd seen that cold hard look before. "When I heard the shots—"

"Only detained." Nick pushed her aside, his gaze fixed on Dorian. "Get rid of the gun. Toss it over there." He jerked his head and leveled his own revolver. "Two fingers. If you breathe wrong, you won't breathe again."

Dorian lifted out his gun in a slow, steady motion and tossed it aside. "I have to admit you amaze me, Nick. It's been you who's been hounding me for months."

"My pleasure."

"And I would have sworn you were a man concerned only with collecting his trinkets and making money. I've always admired your ruthlessness in business—but it seems I wasn't aware of *all* of your business." One graceful brow rose. "A policeman?"

Nick gave him a thin smile. "I answer to one man only," he said quietly. "Adonti." The momentary flash of fear in Dorian's eyes gave him great pleasure. "You and I might have come to this sooner. We nearly did last night."

A shadow touched Dorian's face briefly, then was gone. "Last night?"

"Did you think it was only a goat who watched you?" Nick asked with a brittle laugh.

"No." Dorian gave a brief nod. "I smelled something more—foolish of me not to have pursued it."

"You've gotten careless, Dorian. I took your place on your last run and made your men tremble."

"You," Dorian breathed.

"A rich cache," Nick added, "according to my associates in Athens. It might have been over for you then, but I waited until I was certain Alex wasn't involved. It was worth the wait."

"Alex?" Dorian laughed with the first sign of true pleasure. "Alex wouldn't have the stomach for it. He thinks only of his wife and his ships and his honor." He gave Nick a thoughtful glance. "But it seems I misjudged you. I thought you a rich, rather single-minded fool, a bit of a nuisance with Iona this trip, but hardly worth a passing thought. My congratulations on your talent for deceit, and"—he let his gaze travel and rest on Morgan—"your taste."

"Efxaristo."

Morgan watched in confusion, then in terror, as Nick tossed his gun down to join Dorian's. They lay side by side, black and ugly, on the white sand.

"It's my duty to turn you over to Captain Tripolos and the Greek authorities." Calmly, slowly, Nick drew out a knife. "But it will be my pleasure to cut out your heart for putting your hands on my woman."

"No! Nicholas, don't!"

Nick stopped Morgan's panicked rush toward him

with a terse command. "Go back to the villa and stay there."

"Please," Dorian interrupted with a smile as he got to his feet. "Morgan must stay. Such an interesting development." He pulled out his own knife with a flourish. "She'll be quite a prize for the one who lives."

"Go," Nick ordered again. His hand tensed on the knife. He was half Greek, and Greek enough to have tasted blood when he had seen Dorian strike her. Morgan saw the look in his eyes.

"Nicholas, you can't. He didn't hurt me."

"He left his mark on your face," he said softly, and turned the knife in his hand. "Stay out of the way."

Touching her hand to her cheek, she stumbled back.

They crouched and circled. As she watched, the knives caught the moonlight and held it. Glittering silver, dazzling and beautiful.

At Dorian's first thrust, Morgan covered her mouth to hold back a scream. There was none of the graceful choreography of a staged fight. This was real and deadly. There were no adventurous grins or bold laughs with the thrusts and parries. Both men had death in their eyes. Morgan could smell the sweat and the sweet scent of blood from both of them.

Starlight dappled over their faces, giving them both a ghostly pallor. All she could hear was the sound of their breathing, the sound of the sea, the sound of steel whistling through the air. Nick was leading him closer to the surf—away from Morgan. Emotion was frozen in him. Anger, such anger, but he knew too much to let it escape. Dorian fought coldly. An empty heart was its own skill.

"I'll pleasure myself with your woman before the night's over," Dorian told him as blade met blade. His lips curved as he saw the quick, naked fury in Nick's eyes.

Morgan watched with horror as a bright stain spread down Nick's sleeve where Dorian had slipped through his guard. She would have screamed, but there was no breath in her. She would have prayed, but even her thoughts were frozen.

The speed with which they came together left her stunned. One moment they were separate, and the next they were locked together as one tangled form. They rolled to the sand, a confusion of limbs and knives. She could hear the labored breathing and grunted curses. Then Dorian was on top of him. Morgan watched, numb with terror, as he plunged his knife. It struck the sand, a whisper away from Nick's face. Without thought, Morgan fell on the guns.

Once, the revolver slipped through her wet hands, back onto the sand. Gritting her teeth, she gripped it again. As she knelt, she aimed toward the entwined bodies. Coldly, willing herself to do what she had always despised, she prepared to kill.

A cry split the air, animal and primitive. Not knowing which one of them it had been torn from, Morgan clutched the gun with both hands and kept it aimed on the now motionless heap in the sand. She could still hear breathing—but only from one. If Dorian stood up, she swore to herself, and to Nick, that she would pull the trigger.

A shadow moved. She heard the labored breathing and pressed her lips together. Against the trigger, her finger shook lightly.

"Put that damn thing down, Morgan, before you kill me."

"Nicholas." The gun slipped from her nerveless hand.

He moved to her, limping a little. Reaching down, he drew her to her feet. "What were you doing with the gun, Aphrodite?" he said softly, when he felt her tremble under his hands. "You couldn't have pulled the trigger."

"Yes." Her eyes met his. "I could."

He stared at her for a moment and saw she was speaking nothing less than the truth. With an oath, he pulled her against him. "Damn it, Morgan, why didn't you stay in the villa? I didn't want this for you."

"I couldn't stay in the house, not after I heard the shooting."

"Yes, you hear shooting, so naturally you run outside."

"What else could I do?"

Nick opened his mouth to swear, then shut it again. "You've stolen my clothes," he said mildly. He wouldn't be angry with her now, he promised himself as he stroked her hair. Not while she was shaking like a leaf. But later, by God, later . . .

"You took mine first." He couldn't tell if the sound she made was a laugh or a sob. "I thought . . ." Suddenly, she felt the warm stickiness against her palm. Looking down, she saw his blood on her hand. "Oh, God, Nicholas, you're hurt!"

"No, it's nothing, I—"

"Oh, damn you for being macho and stupid. You're *bleeding!*"

He laughed and crushed her to him again. "I'm not

being macho and stupid, Aphrodite, but if it makes you happy, you can nurse all of my scratches later. Now, I need a different sort of medicine.'' He kissed her before she could argue.

Her fingers gripped at his shirt as she poured everything she had into that one meeting of lips. Fear drained from her, and with it, whatever force had driven her. She went limp against him as his energy poured over her.

''I'm going to need a lot of care for a very long time,'' he murmured against her mouth. ''I might be hurt a great deal more seriously than I thought. No, don't.'' Nick drew her away as he felt her tears on his cheeks. ''Morgan, don't cry. It's the one thing I don't think I can face tonight.''

''No, I won't cry,'' she insisted as the tears continued to fall. ''I won't cry. Just don't stop kissing me. Don't stop.'' She pressed her mouth to his. As she felt him, warm and real against her, the tears and trembling stopped.

''Well, Mr. Gregoras, it seems you intercepted Mr. Zoulas after all.''

Nick swore quickly, but without heat. Keeping Morgan close, he looked over her head at Tripolos. ''Your men have the crew?''

''Yes.'' Lumbering over, he examined the body briefly. He noted, without comment that there was a broken arm as well as the knife wound. With a gesture, he signaled one of his men to take over. ''Your man is seeing to their transportation,'' he went on.

Nick kept Morgan's back to the body and met Tripolos's speculative look calmly. ''It seems you had a bit of trouble here,'' the captain commented. His gaze drifted to the guns laying on the sand. He drew his own conclusions. "A pity he won't stand trial."

"A pity," Nick agreed.

"You dropped your gun in the struggle to apprehend him, I see."

"It would seem so."

Tripolos stooped with a wheeze and handed it back to him. "Your job is finished?"

"Yes, my job is finished."

Tripolos made a small bow. "My gratitude, Mr. Gregoras." He smiled at the back of Morgan's head. "And my congratulations."

Nick lifted a brow in acknowledgment. "I'll take Miss James home now. You can reach me tomorrow if necessary. Good night, Captain."

"Good night," Tripolos murmured and watched them move away.

Morgan leaned her head against his shoulder as they walked toward the beach steps. Only a few moments before she had fought to keep from reaching them. Now they seemed like the path to the rest of her life.

"Oh, look, the stars are going out." She sighed. There was nothing left, no fear, no anxiety. No more doubts. "I feel as if I've waited for this sunrise all my life."

"I'm told you want to go to Venice and ride on a gondola."

Morgan glanced up in surprise, then laughed. "Andrew told you."

"He mentioned Cornwall and the Champs d'Élysées as well."

"I have to learn how to bait a hook, too," she

murmured. Content, she watched as day struggled with night.

"I'm not an easy man, Morgan."

"*Hmm?* No," she agreed fervently. "No, you're not."

He paused at the foot of the steps and turned her to face him. The words weren't easy for him now. He wondered why he had thought they would be. "You know the worst of me already. I'm not often gentle, and I'm demanding. I'm prone to black, unreasonable moods."

Morgan smothered a yawn and smiled at him. "I'd be the last one to disagree."

He felt foolish. And, he discovered, afraid. Would a woman accept words of love when she had seen a man kill? Did he have any right to offer them? Looking down, he saw her, slim and straight in his clothes—jeans that hung over her hips—a shirt that billowed and hid small, firm breasts and a waist he could nearly span with his hands. Right or wrong, he couldn't go on without her.

"Morgan . . ."

"Nicholas?" Her smile became puzzled as she fought off a wave of weariness. "What is it?"

His gaze swept back to hers, dark, intense, perhaps a little desperate.

"Your arm," she began and reached for him.

"No! *Diabolos.*" Gripping her by the shoulders, he shook her. "It's not my arm, listen to me."

"I am listening," she tossed back with a trace of heat. "What's wrong with you?"

"This." He covered her mouth with his. He needed

the taste of her, the strength. When he drew her away, his hands had gentled, but his eyes gleamed.

With a sleepy laugh, she shook her head. "Nicholas, if you'll let me get you home and see to your arm—"

"My arm's a small matter, Aphrodite."

"Not to me."

"Morgan." Nick stopped her before she could turn toward the steps again. "I'll make a difficult and exasperating husband, but you won't be bored." Taking her hands, he kissed them as he had on his balcony. "I love you enough to let you climb your mountains, Morgan. Enough to climb them with you if that's what you want."

She wasn't tired now, but stunned into full alertness. Morgan opened her mouth, but found herself stupidly unable to form a word.

"Damn it, Morgan, don't just stare at me." Frustration and temper edged his voice. "Say yes, for God's sake!" Fury flared in his eyes. "I won't let you say no!"

His hands were no longer in hers, but gripping her arms again. She knew, any moment, he would start shaking her. But there was more in his eyes than anger. She saw the doubts, the fears, the fatigue. Love swept into her, overwhelmingly.

"Won't you?" she murmured.

"No." His fingers tightened. "No, I won't. You've taken my heart. You won't leave with it."

Lifting a hand, she touched his cheek, letting her finger trace over the tense jaw. "Do you think I could climb mountains without you, Nicholas?" She drew him against her and felt his shudder of relief. "Let's go home."

EYE OF THE STORM

MAURA SEGER

A powerful
portrayal of
the events of
World War II in the
Pacific, *Eye of the Storm* is a riveting story of how love
triumphs over hatred. In this, the first of a three-book
chronicle, Army nurse Maggie Lawrence meets Marine
Sgt. Anthony Gargano. Despite military regulations
against fraternization, they resolve to face together
whatever lies ahead.... Author Maura Seger, also known
to her fans as Laurel Winslow, Sara Jennings, Anne
MacNeil and Jenny Bates, was named 1984's
most Versatile Romance Author by *The Romantic Times*.

At your favorite bookstore in March or send your name, address and zip or
postal code, along with a check or money order for $4.25 (includes 75¢ for
postage and handling) payable to Harlequin Reader Service to:

HARLEQUIN READER SERVICE

In the U.S.
Box 52040
Phoenix, AZ 85072-2040

In Canada
5170 Yonge Street
P.O. Box 2800
Postal Station A
Willowdale, Ont. M2N 6J3

EYE-C-1

If you enjoyed this book...

Thrill to 4 more
Silhouette Intimate Moments
novels (a $9.00 value)—
ABSOLUTELY FREE!

If you want more passionate sensual romance, then Silhouette Intimate Moments novels are for you!

In every 256-page book, you'll find romance that's electrifying...involving... and intense. And now, these larger-than-life romances can come into your home every month!

4 FREE books as your introduction.

Act now and we'll send you four thrilling Silhouette Intimate Moments novels. They're our gift to introduce you to our convenient home subscription service. Every month, we'll send you four new Silhouette Intimate Moments books. Look them over for 15 days. If you keep them, pay just $9.00 for all four. Or return them at no charge.

We'll mail your books to you *as soon as they are published.* Plus, with every shipment, you'll receive the Silhouette Books Newsletter absolutely free. *And Silhouette Intimate Moments is delivered free.*

Mail the coupon today and start receiving Silhouette Intimate Moments. Romance novels for women...not girls.

Silhouette Intimate Moments

MAIL THIS COUPON
and get 4 thrilling

Silhouette Desire®

novels <u>FREE</u> (a $7.80 value)

Silhouette Desire books may not be for everyone. They *are* for readers who want a sensual, provocative romance. These are modern love stories that are charged with emotion from the first page to the thrilling happy ending—about women who discover the extremes of fiery passion. Confident women who face the challenge of today's world and overcome all obstacles to attain their dreams—*and their desires.*

We believe you'll be so delighted with Silhouette Desire romance novels that you'll want to receive them regularly through our home subscription service. Your books will be *shipped to you two months before they're available anywhere else*—so you'll never miss a new title. Each month we'll send you 6 new books to look over for 15 days, without obligation. If not delighted, simply return them and owe nothing. Or keep them and pay only $1.95 each. There's no charge for postage or handling. And there's no obligation to buy anything at any time. You'll also receive a subscription to the Silhouette Books Newsletter *absolutely free!*

So don't wait. To receive your four FREE books, fill out and mail the coupon below *today!*

SILHOUETTE DESIRE and colophon are registered trademarks and a service mark.

Sometimes a woman must risk it all . . .
to claim what is rightfully hers

THE CRITICS RAVE ABOUT
RIGHTFULLY MINE!

"A love story with as many characters as there are figures in the elaborate set of Brussels wedding tapestries that is central to the plot. . . . The sport for those who know the antiques trade is to figure out which dealers, which collectors and which auctioneers were Mortman's models. She catches the suspense of the salesroom, the thrill of the hunt and the lavishness of the parties that accompany major sales and shows, as well as the rivalries, rumors and risks that abound in the business. In addition, she constructs a complex plot that involves Interpol and the F.B.I., smugglers and purveyors of fakes. All these elements . . . make *Rightfully Mine* great fun to read."

—*The New York Times Book Review*

MEET GABY . . . AND THE UNFORGETTABLE
CHARACTERS OF HER WORLD

GABY . . . Suddenly alone, without money or love, she forges for herself a completely new identity, creating a sparkling forgery in a world that prides itself on authenticity. Her new life is based on a secret . . . and Gaby will soon learn that even small secrets can take on a life of their own.

MAXIMILIAN . . . Handsome, wealthy, he moves with graceful ease in the highest international circles. Maximilian's past is shrouded in secrecy. Does he—like Gaby herself—harbor a secret deep in his soul?

TURN THE PAGE FOR MORE RAVE REVIEWS OF
RIGHTFULLY MINE . . .

THE REMARKABLE PEOPLE
IN GABY'S WORLD

ARMAND . . . The mysteriously blacklisted partner in the prestigious dealership Lafitte et Fils U.S.A., he lives to restore his good name—and to exact his revenge.

CHELSEA . . . Blond, voluptuous, hers is a glamorous life of money and men. But behind the glittering facade, the real Chelsea yearns for something more.

MORE CAPTIVATING PEOPLE
FROM GABY'S WORLD

GARRETT . . . Heir to the great auction house Castleton's, he is embroiled in a vicious struggle for control of the family business . . . and in a desperate battle for Gaby's love.

BRIAN . . . Gaby's ex-husband, he abandoned her for another woman, never dreaming of the glamorous sophisticate Gaby would become. Now he wants her back . . . at any cost.

Bantam Books by Doris Mortman
Ask your bookseller for the books you have missed

CIRCLES
FIRST BORN
RIGHTFULLY MINE

RIGHTFULLY MINE

MINE

Doris Mortman

BANTAM BOOKS
NEW YORK · TORONTO · LONDON · SYDNEY · AUCKLAND

This novel is a work of fiction. Any references to real people, events, establishments, organizations or locales are intended only to give the fiction a sense of reality and authenticity. All of the main characters, organizations, events and incidents in this novel are creations of the author's imagination, and their resemblance, if any, to actual events or persons, living or dead, is entirely coincidental.

RIGHTFULLY MINE

A Bantam Book
Bantam hardcover edition / July 1989
Bantam paperback edition / August 1990

Jacket photo antiques and tapestries courtesy of Newel Art Galleries, Inc.,
New York, New York; shirt courtesy of Hanae Mori, New York, New York.

Bantam Books are published by Bantam Books, a division of Bantam
Doubleday Dell Publishing Group, Inc. Its trademark, consisting of the
words "Bantam Books" and the portrayal of a rooster, is Registered in U.S.
Patent and Trademark Office and in other countries. Marca Registrada.
Bantam Books, 666 Fifth Avenue, New York, New York 10103.

PRINTED IN THE UNITED STATES OF AMERICA

OPM   0 9 8 7 6 5 4 3 2 1

To Anne and Mike,
Andy and Karen, Judy and Michael.
Put them all together, they spell family.

ACKNOWLEDGMENTS

One of the joys of writing is the joy of learning. While researching the setting for my characters in this novel, not only was I introduced to a fascinating new world, but I was privileged to meet people whose love of antiques was evidenced by their enthusiasm for the subject and their willingness to pass it on to a novice. For their time, their generosity, and their patience, I thank them. In particular, Nicole Chevalier and Stan Olshefski, Patricia Curtin, Dominique and Pierre Chevalier, Phillipe Farley, and Anthony Victoria. Also, John Del Guidice, William Ketchum, Jr., whose class "The Antiques Business" at the New School added to my education, and Lloyd Bell, whose "Introduction to Antiques" at New York University filled so many of my Tuesday nights with unexpected pleasure. I'm grateful I have an agent like Peter Lampack and an editor like Linda Grey, because when the going gets tough, they make it easier. And of course, I'm eternally grateful to David, Lisa, and Alex, because they make it all worthwhile.

PROLOGUE

JANUARY 1987

"I *don't love you anymore!"*

As the silver Bentley turned left off Fifth Avenue and proceeded eastward on Fifty-seventh Street, Gabrielle Didier wondered when those five horrible words would stop haunting her.

"I don't love you anymore!"

Most of the time, she tried to forbid them from invading her consciousness, blocking them out along with the events that had preceded and followed their utterance. Often, she succeeded, but tonight, feeling as insecure as she did, they seemed to play over and over again, as if an old phonograph needle was rutted in a deep groove.

"I don't love you anymore!"

Though the windows of the limousine were closed, she pulled her fur coat closer, warding off a chill she knew was coming from within. On the seat beside her lay a creamy vellum card, the invitation to attend tonight's party. Like the Literary Lions' dinner or the reception to mark a new exhibit at the Met's Costume Institute, the Castleton gala heralding the opening of the January Antiques Fair—the largest and most prestigious antiques show in the United States—was a plum.

The Castletons, *père et fils*, were the owners of a venerable auction house with a history and reputation that rivaled both Sotheby's and Christie's. Established in 1743, a year before Sotheby's first auction, Castleton's had evolved from a modest family concern dealing predominantly in coins and prints into an international source of fine art and prized antiques. What differentiated this house from its competitors was not the respect its longevity inspired or the awe that its repeated successes engendered, but its unbroken continuity of ownership. For unlike the other houses, whose leadership resulted from partnership struggles, buyouts, and takeovers, for more than two hundred years a bloodline descendant of one of the four original Castleton brothers had managed the business. Tonight, Madame Gabrielle Didier was the personal guest of Garrett Castleton, Jr., the host of this evening's festivities.

Tonight, she told herself as the chauffeur came around to open the door and help her out of the car, Madame Gabrielle Didier had to forget the past. She had to concentrate on the present, the here and now. She had to quell the nervousness in her stomach and swallow the self-doubt that clogged her throat. Whatever had gone before was over. Whatever was going to be her future had already begun.

The Castleton town house was a rarity in New York. Situated on the corner of Fifty-eighth Street and Sutton Place, it boasted not only a two-car garage, but a private cul-de-sac as well. Five stories of sienna-tinted stucco, skylights peeking out from a tiled roof, large French windows underscored with stone planters, and thick bronze doors sculpted by a disciple of Lorenzo Ghiberti marked it as one of the jewels in the city's crown.

Inside, wherever one looked, there was something to excite the senses, something to see, to touch, to marvel at. Gray suede walls, a sixteenth-century Herat rug, and two large English globes—one terrestrial, one celestial, both signed in the early 1800s—graced the foyer. The space was small, but the mood, one of softness and intimacy, was totally in keeping with its function as a place of welcome.

In comparison, the central hall appeared stark. White walls and a white marble floor glistened like arctic ice beneath a grand Baccarat chandelier. Moonlight streamed in through a tall, uncovered window, bathing the space with a pearlescent glow.

Only the toasted richness of a Biedermeier tall case clock, the matte black of the wrought-iron banister, and the golden flamboyance of a Louis XV giltwood mirror intruded upon the unrelenting whiteness. The look was spartan, but the splendor of the pieces displayed transmitted exactly the message the owners desired: this was a home distinguished by excellence.

Though the entire residence was open for viewing, and clusters of people could be found everywhere, most of the guests had gathered in the living room, where white-jacketed waiters served hors d'oeuvres and champagne on silver trays to Vincent Prado, chairman of the January Antiques Fair, William Doyle of Doyle Galleries, Mark Hampton, Lee Radziwill, Lady Keith, Alfred Taubman, owner of Sotheby's, Charlotte Ford, Oscar de la Renta, Chessy Rayner, Mario Buatta, and the Buckleys, Pat and Bill. While the more ardent collectors examined the latest Castleton addition—a spectacular, neoclassical Steinway & Sons baby grand piano—most of the conversation centered on how much money the preview party would net and how well this year's show would do. Since almost everyone had participated in one way or another—as exhibitor, patron, or committee member—and since no one there was even vaguely acquainted with anything resembling failure, there was a joyous atmosphere born of assured success and shared applause.

Only once during the cocktail hour did the incessant babble still even slightly, and that was when Gabrielle appeared in the doorway. Heads turned. Whatever self-confidence she had mustered, wavered. Although she possessed an enviable mane of chestnut hair, deep-set cornflower-blue eyes, and a narrow, gently sloped nose, she blushed when she heard someone nearby refer to her as "exquisite." Her blush would have deepened had she heard the discussion about the small mole on her left cheek and the softly puffed, delicately puckered look of her lips, or the suggestion from several women that perhaps her near-mannequin reediness made her too thin to do justice to bare evening clothes. Obviously, every man in the room approved, since most of them continued to gaze at her long after their wives had returned to their conversations. Instead of being flattered, the intense scrutiny made Gabrielle feel exposed and extremely uncomfortable. Sensing a bubble of panic rising, she searched the room for her escort. When her eye caught his face, she was unsettled by what she saw. The man was not simply staring, he appeared utterly entranced.

What Gabrielle couldn't know was that Garrett Castleton had been watching for her, his nerves tightening as each minute ticked away. He had greeted his guests, participated in conversations, answered questions, laughed at punchlines, but never had he moved out of sight of the entry; never had he allowed himself to be maneuvered into a position where his back faced the door. Like a cat waiting for an unsuspecting bird to light, he had stood poised on the balls of his feet. The instant she arrived, he felt as if a pressure valve had been released and the tension exited his body in one long sigh of relief.

After greeting her with a hasty, self-conscious peck on the cheek, he took her hand, led her inside, and made the appropriate introductions, his attenuated face broadened by a huge smile, his clear blue eyes aglow with triumph. Though she was clearly the center of attention, Gabrielle appeared to take it all in stride, gliding through the room gracefully, nodding, shaking hands, exchanging pleasantries. When she met the Parisian contingent of *antiquaires*, she shifted easily into French, her speech softer and more lyrical.

Now and then, as they passed a cluster of people, however, Gabrielle noticed a few sidelong looks and overheard several catty remarks. Garrett, sensing her embarrassment, steered her in another direction.

"Though I despise idle chatter," he said, "I have to admit that, in this case, I can understand the need to fabricate information."

"I beg your pardon," Gabrielle said, defensively.

"You, my dear, are considered a mystery. Unlike so many of our set who gladly dispense their credentials and bank balances at the drop of a hat, you're exceptionally closemouthed."

"I'm a very private person," Gabrielle explained, her initial response softened. "I'm also rather shy. I don't like talking about myself."

"That's too bad," Garrett said, leaning closer. "I'd like nothing better than to talk to you about you."

She nodded and smiled politely, but he knew that she wouldn't. Rarely had he heard her volunteer any personal data. Never, as far as he knew, had she confided in anyone. In fact, when he thought about it, and lately Garrett thought about Gabrielle a lot, he realized that he knew very little about her.

He knew that she was thirty-nine, unmarried, and, from what he could gather, remarkably unattached. He knew that she spoke fluent French, carried herself with aristocratic grace, possessed both an incisive intellect and a droll wit, and dressed with individualistic chic, adding her own distinctive stamp to the styles declared *de rigueur* by the fashion bibles.

Garrett had met Gabrielle when Giles Deffand, the head of Castleton's European furniture department, had engaged her as his assistant. Their paths might have crossed only rarely, except that within a very short time stories about Gabrielle Didier's tireless dedication had filtered well beyond the doors of Deffand's domain. When Garrett investigated Castleton's new phenom, he discovered a woman of unlimited enthusiasm. It was not uncommon to find Gabrielle in the storeroom with her silk sleeves rolled up, uncrating and checking the condition of new arrivals, or helping catalogue items for auction, or hunched over research material attempting to verify provenances. He began to notice that she was the first to arrive and the last to leave, often with a stack of books she planned to study at home. But even more than by her boundless energy, he was impressed by her infinite supply of fresh ideas.

She had first caught his attention with a proposal that Castleton's initiate a lecture series aimed at the beginning collector, in which the heads of each major department would give an overview of their areas of expertise as well as advice about buying art and antiques. Then there was the recommendation that Castleton's cosponsor an auction to benefit a trendy cause. Then there was the suggestion that perhaps the gallery itself might be made available for worthwhile —translation: having great publicity value—charity dinner dances. And the idea that the catalogues for special auctions be bound in hardcover as if they themselves were collector's items. Initially, Garrett had been intrigued, but little beyond that, until, goaded by Deffand to implement some of her ideas and watching them meet with almost instantaneous success, his respect for, and interest in, Madame Didier increased.

Several times he asked her to join him for lunch or to have a drink after the gallery closed. Once or twice he had even tried to wangle an invitation to her apartment, claiming professional curiosity. But if he thought she was a woman committed to her work, he quickly found she was even more committed to maintaining her privacy. It was said that she lived on Fifth Avenue in a co-op rumored to be exquisite. One woman told him she heard it had taken three years to complete. Another said she understood the lighting alone was a triumph. A third claimed the flat was a small museum. Yet as far as Garrett knew, no one had ever actually seen it.

None of that seemed important now. She was here at his side and he was undeniably bewitched. Tonight, Gabrielle surpassed mere beauty. Tonight, sheathed in a black jersey gown with a single stripe of jet sequins snaking from a bow on her left shoulder to the curve of her right hip, she was breathtaking. Onyx and diamond deco earrings peeked out from behind a chestnut wave, while a matching bracelet adorned a pale white wrist. Her cheeks were barely blushed, her eyes only slightly shadowed, her scent delicately floral. Except for the Venetian red that rouged her lips, she was the personification of a whisper— soft, subtle, civilized.

Taking her arm and linking it through his, he escorted her out of the living room and up the stairs to the third-floor parlor.

"I thought you might enjoy a quiet drink before dinner," he said, offering her a seat on a velvet settee.

As he poured their champagne, he wished he could control the unexpected sensations she had aroused in him. From the moment he had seen her standing beneath the living room portal, an indelible smile had taken possession of his lips. He felt like a schoolboy experiencing his first crush. He fought it. He tried to maintain his dignity, but the effervescent feeling overrode his normal reserve, making him lightheaded.

"I'm delighted you're here," he said, marveling at his own understatement. "For a while, I was afraid I was going to have to suffer the pangs of rejection. And I don't suffer well."

"Neither do I," she said, raising her glass to his, touched that he seemed so oblivious to the fact that many employers would have viewed her appearance as a command performance. "Thank you for inviting me. It's a marvelous party."

"It is marvelous, isn't it?" he said, pleased with himself. "I wouldn't be terribly distressed, however, if in twenty minutes they all went home and you and I were left completely alone.''

He inched forward on his chair, taking her hand in his.

"But we wouldn't be alone," she said, smiling so he wasn't insulted when she slid her hand away. "There would be at least forty policemen running around investigating the suicide of your caterer. Think of the mess! Think of the publicity!"

He laughed and held up his hands in mock horror. "I'd rather not."

As he sipped his champagne, Gabrielle shifted her attention to her surroundings. Though she had not yet toured the entire house, the other rooms she had seen had combined modern-day sleekness with eighteenth-century splendor. But this room was pure Victorian bravado—dark-patterned walls, dark-stained woods, thick velvet portieres, glossy brocades, tufted slenderwaisted chairs and settees shawled with crocheted antimacassars, pots of ferns, tabletop vignettes, a profusion of Oriental rugs and tasseled throw pillows. Marble busts sat beside milk-white globe lamps, silver picture frames alongside feather-filled vases. Even the fireplace seemed out of character with the rest of the house. A monumental construction of extravagantly carved rosewood, it refused to confine itself merely to hearth and mantel. Swirling, curling rococo carvings asserted themselves up and around a towering mirror that reflected the exuberance of the Victorian era in its grandiloquent style.

"This room is my mother's pride and joy," Garrett said, watching as Gabrielle picked up a tortoiseshell and ivory cigarette case, noting her approval. "She wanted to recreate a turn-of-the-century drawing room with all the feminine shapes and symbols and fancies that dominated nineteenth-century homes."

"She has exquisite taste," Gabrielle said, replacing the case and smiling at Garrett.

"She also has impeccable manners, and I know she would not approve of this obvious dereliction of my hosting duties." Garrett stood and offered Gabrielle his hand. "Much as I would love to spend the entire evening here with you, I think I must return to my guests."

As they stepped into the hall, an outburst of laughter rose above the din. Gabrielle turned. In the doorway of an adjacent bedroom, a group of men crowded around a tall, slim blonde in a clingy, red Charmeuse gown. As the woman spoke, lively gestures punctuated her words. Her wrists glittered with a mass of diamond bracelets, her fingernails glowed like bright red coals against ash-white skin. Though the woman's back was to Gabrielle, something about her was terribly familiar: the voice, the stance, the way she talked with her hands. Gabrielle was certain she knew her, even more certain that this was neither the time nor the place for a reunion. She was debating what to do when one of the men, his mouth still curled in an amused smile, happened to look over the blonde's shoulder and catch Gabrielle's eye. He was incredibly handsome, with dark, near-black hair and deep blue eyes the color of delft. His stare was penetrating, and for a moment Gabrielle felt unnerved, as if he had willed her to remain fixed within his line of vision. When Garrett took her arm and led her down to the dining room, an odd mix of regret and relief joined the swirl of emotions the dark blue stare had evoked.

Gabrielle was not accustomed to grand entrances. Though she was doing her best to appear nonchalant and self-assured, she had been affected by all the whispered asides and judgmental looks. She was beginning to feel as if she were an item on display. Even the blue-eyed man's innocent glance had been an assessment, making her uncomfortable, edgy. She tried to tell herself that every late arrival was subjected to that kind of scrutiny; that any woman on the arm of Garrett Castleton, Jr., would inspire jealousy or, at the very least, curiosity. She was a newcomer to this elevated circle, and until she had been tested and proven she would remain an outsider. But she was not a woman easily deluded, even by her own carefully constructed rationalizations. She knew that, bottom line, in the minds of many, Gabrielle Didier simply didn't belong, and never would. Worse, she knew they were right.

During the short time Garrett and Gabrielle had been upstairs, the caterers had prepared the two lower floors for dinner, furnishing the library, the dining room, a sitting room, and another parlor with round tables skirted in richly swirled, white moiré that had been splashed with lavish bows of gold ribbon-striped silk. Ornate vermeil flatwear framed settings of Limoges china, each table dressed with a different floral design, each met hers, he smiled and something inside her quivered, trembling like the first, hesitant notes of a song.

"Next thing we know, Max, you'll have us on our feet doing the Belgian national anthem," Vincent said, raising his glass with a waggish smile.

Gabrielle raised her glass also, nodding first at Prado and then at Garrett, who said, "I drink to the depth of your beauty, the wealth of your knowledge, and the height of your courage."

"Courage?"

Garrett leaned closer and whispered in her ear. "There are few who take on the formidable Mr. Prado and live to tell about it."

Gabrielle tried to smile, but her mouth was tight. She knew all too well what happened to those who challenged Vincent Prado.

By the time coffee was served, many of the guests had started to move about, shifting positions and dinner companions. Gabrielle and Vincent Prado were two of the few who had remained in their original seats. Though Garrett had excused himself once again to attend to his hosting duties, Prado had stayed, diluting his attentiveness only when one of his loyal subjects came to pay obeisance. He had shifted his chair away from the table so that those who wished to stand before him could. And many did, chatting, bobbing, weaving, prompting Gabrielle to expect that at any moment, one of the faithful would feel compelled to fall to the floor and genuflect. Several times, someone sat in Garrett's empty chair and spoke over, around, or through Gabrielle, whichever they found most effective. This time, however, the person in Garrett's seat was the handsome blue-eyed man and he wasn't at all interested in Vincent Prado.

"I'm Maximilian Richard," he said, pronouncing his name in the French manner. "Otherwise known as 'Max.'" He took her hand and brushed it with his lips, his deep baritone enhanced by the uneven cadence of one whose native language was Flemish. "What a pleasure to meet someone so beautiful and so knowledgeable about the woven arts."

"Tapestries are one of my passions," Gabrielle explained, acknowledging his compliments with a nod of her head.

"What else are you passionate about?"

Gabrielle feigned deep thought. "Eighteenth-century antiques, old Fred Astaire movies, caramel candy, Ted Koppel, and baseball."

Max laughed. "All of that and tapestries too. I think I have found the only true living Renaissance woman."

"She is that and more." Garrett returned to the table and placed a proprietary hand on Gabrielle's shoulder. He looked down at Max, waiting for him to stand and relinquish his place. When he didn't, Garrett took the vacant seat next to Prado. "Ever since Gabrielle joined Castleton's, she has been a godsend." He smiled affectionately at Gabrielle. "I'd be lost without her."

"I can understand why," Prado said. The edge in his voice made it clear that in his opinion, Garrett needed all the help he could get. "I know you try, dear man, but you should have availed yourself of your sister Irina's party-planning skills. Sometimes your dinner table constructions are sorely lacking in imagination. If not for Madame Didier, I think that immediately after the soup, I might have expired due to extreme boredom."

Garrett swallowed his anger and curled his mouth into a plastic smile.

"You didn't look bored when Gabrielle called you on your Franco-Flemish faux pas. Did you think he looked bored, Richard?"

"Not exactly," Max said, enjoying Prado's momentary discomfort. "But then again, more than one expert has confused the origins of tapestries from that era."

"Speaking of which," Vincent said, eagerly changing the subject, "the grapevine has it that you've sent out the hounds looking for the missing Dinant tapestry. Is that so?"

"It's no secret that I'm an avid collector. I would love to own it. Who wouldn't? It's a true masterpiece."

"Have you had any luck tracking it down?"

Max shook his head. "I'm afraid not."

Prado turned to Garrett. "How about Castleton's? Have your sources unearthed anything?"

"No. And we've had people looking for it all over Europe."

"Well, I too have organized a search party," Prado announced, delighting in the immediate look of shock that flushed the faces of both Garrett and Max Richard. "Not only do I have at least twenty clients who would pay a king's ransom for that piece, but when I think of the publicity I could attract exhibiting it at the Antiques Fair, my body just thrills with excitement!''

"That tapestry belongs in a museum in Brussels. Nowhere else!''

The intensity in Max's voice piqued Gabrielle's interest.

"With all due respect," she said, "there were many splendid tapestries woven in Flanders during the Renaissance. Just because it might have been loomed in Brussels doesn't mean it has to reside there.''

"Do you know anything about the Dinant tapestries?''

Though it sounded like a simple question, Max's eyes had darkened. Obviously, this was one of his passions.

"Only that they were a series of seven tapestries woven around the end of the fifteenth century and that the jewel of the collection is missing.''

"There's more to it than that," Max said, his tone more modulated, his manner more relaxed. "This particular series is unique. It was commissioned by a Flemish lord as a wedding gift to his bride, a French-speaking Walloon, and depicts the trials and tribulations of the two young lovers. That in itself is not unusual. As I'm sure you know, many tapestries of the time commemorated marriages, but this one, called *The Marriage of Brussels,* is the only one that commemorates the unification of Belgium. Naturally, as a Belgian, I'd like to see it housed at either the Hôtel de Ville in the Grande Place or in the Royal Palace.''

"I don't mean to be a wet blanket," Garrett said, "but there are plenty of museums outside of Belgium which might be more than willing to fight for the Dinant piece. The Met, the Louvre, the Getty, the Cleveland Museum of Art, the Tate, the Victoria and Albert, just to name a few.''

"It's worth fighting for," Max countered, in a way that said he not only anticipated a battle, but was fully prepared to do whatever he had to in order to get his way.

Prado lifted a brandy snifter to his lips and sipped the amber liquid without taking his eyes off the other two men. While the conversation had started as pleasant after-dinner banter, the atmosphere was suddenly charged with an undercurrent of competition.

"I thought most of the Dinant tapestries had been sold at auction," he said to Garrett, continuing his reconnoitering.

"Only three—*The Meeting, The Battle of the Lion and the Unicorn,* and *The Contract.*"

Gabrielle heard the names and, immediately, jumbles of colors and shapes teased her brain. She begged her memory to recall the pictures that went with the titles, but before this evening, the Dinant tapestries had been nothing more than a group of color plates in a dusty reference book. She remembered studying them briefly, remembered hearing them mentioned once or twice in passing, but for now, no matter how hard she tried to bring them into focus, they remained hazy images.

"Who owns them now?" she asked.

"They were bought by collectors who preferred to remain anonymous."

"Could one person own all three?"

"Possibly. Each time one came up for auction, the bids were placed over the phone by a broker representing the actual buyer. Since the purchasers' names were never revealed, and since there was a different person brokering each sale, there's no way to know for sure. They weren't sold together, or even through the same auction house, so my guess is that three different people bought the three separate pieces."

"I thought Castleton's owned two," Prado said.

"We do, but they were acquired through private transactions."

"That's six, counting the one that's lost," Gabrielle said, growing more and more intrigued. "Where is the seventh?"

"It was called *The Triumph of Chastity,* and it used to hang in a small convent in Dinant, Le Couvent des Soeurs de la Croix. When the Germans razed the town during the First World War, it disappeared. Since the convent was burned to the ground, the assumption is that the tapestry burned with it."

"I thought I read that a descendant of the original family had rescued it and hidden it away," Max said.

Garrett shrugged. "I've heard that theory also, but since no one has been able to locate any surviving members of the de Rosier clan, and since no one has seen or heard of *The Triumph of Chastity* since 1914, it doesn't matter whether it was burned or lost in some other way. The fact is, it's gone."

"How do you know that *The Marriage of Brussels* wasn't destroyed also?" Gabrielle asked.

"Because until forty years ago, it had been seen."

"Where?"

"To be honest, Gabrielle, I don't recall."

Garrett's voice hinted at impatience, convincing Gabrielle that he knew exactly where the tapestry had been seen, when, how often, and by whom. She realized at once that Garrett would not answer her question and thus answer the unasked questions of his adversaries.

"Why all this sudden interest in the Dinant tapestries?" she said, willing to shift gears but unwilling to get off the subject entirely. "And that one in particular?"

"Because it's worth a bloody fortune!" Prado exclaimed, his eyes glossed with greed.

"Is that true?" Gabrielle turned to Garrett for confirmation.

Garrett nodded and then proceeded with a reluctant explanation.

"Among cognoscenti, the Dinant tapestries are considered one of the great art treasures of the late Middle Ages, on a par with the Unicorn tapestries at the Cloisters and the Lady with the Unicorn set at the Cluny Museum in Paris. *The Marriage of Brussels* is reputed to be the most spectacular of them all. To many, it's the finest tapestry ever loomed."

"And," Prado added, "because it's been missing for about forty years, its cachet has been greatly enhanced by that ever-popular intangible known as 'mystique.' " He paused, waiting as an actor might for his audience to absorb his words. Then he continued. "Everybody wants what he can't have, whether he deserves it or not. Isn't that so, Garrett?"

Garrett bristled, but held his tongue. The others might not have understood, but he knew that Prado was referring to the chairmanship of Castleton's International. It was no secret that Prado was *simpático* with Garrett's sister Irina and therefore opposed to Garrett's taking over the reins of the business. For all he knew, Prado's search was on behalf of his elder sister. In fact, the more he thought about it, the more sense it made. Irina probably hoped to use *The Marriage of Brussels* the same way Garrett planned to use it—as a *coup de théâtre* to dazzle and impress their father. Irina had probably solicited Prado's help in exchange for a major position with Castleton's or for stock in the firm. The thought turned Garrett's stomach.

"It's difficult to debate that point with you," he said, looking squarely at Prado, "when, clearly, the underlying philosophy of an auction house is, if you want something badly enough, keep at it until you get it."

Like a Roman gladiator facing a snarling but unarmed foe, Prado smiled with the confidence of expected victory, his thin lips pressed together.

"I quite agree," he said, with lightly disguised disdain. "After all, what is an auction if not another of life's civilized battles. One person wins and everyone else loses. What a pity that the spoils can't be shared." Then, as if he had fired a killing shot, Prado turned his sights from Garrett to Max. The man had never afforded Prado the respect he thought he deserved. "But I suppose it's the basic nature of any soldier to be selfish. One fights for something, and subsequently feels he owns it. Isn't that right, Richard? Didn't you acquire your substantial fortune by playing winner take all on the fields of corporate combat?"

If Prado was looking to antagonize Max Richard, he had succeeded. If he was looking to draw him into a three-way contretemps with Castleton, he was going to be disappointed. Max stood and faced the two men.

"I make it a habit never to discuss business, either mine or yours, outside the office," he said flatly. "Especially in the company of a lady. Now, judging by the sounds filtering in from the hallway, I would guess that Bobby Short is about to play. If you gentlemen would like to finish your conversation in private, I'd be honored to escort Madame Didier to the living room for the evening's entertainment."

With a gallant bow of his head, he extended his hand to Gabrielle, who, grateful for the chance to make a graceful exit, eagerly rose to her feet. She looked at Garrett and said quietly, "I'll see you inside."

As Max guided Gabrielle out of the dining room, Garrett glared at Prado.

"I don't know what you were trying to pull with your double entendres and your steady stream of innuendo, but as far as I'm concerned, Vincent, you and I are finished." With that, he turned and headed toward the kitchen.

Neither he nor Max nor Gabrielle looked back. If they had, they might have noticed the satisfied smile licking the lips of the woman who had come to stand at Prado's side—Garrett's sister, Irina Stoddard.

Standing in the corner of the massive living room, surrounded by a court of male admirers, Chelsea Reynolds, the blonde in the red Charmeuse gown, watched as Maximilian Richard led a stunning brunette to a seat near the piano. She recalled the hubbub when the woman had first arrived. Garrett Castleton's date, someone had told her. Madame Gabrielle Didier. New in town. Not very well known. Private. Almost too private, someone had said. Chelsea might have indulged her curiosity, but at the time, she was being flattered by an extremely handsome, young Milanese gentleman whose undisguised lust had promised more excitement than anything Madame Didier's dossier could offer. Even now, as he vied for her affection, taking advantage of the darkness to press himself against her thigh, she wondered why she felt herself drawn to a woman she had never heard of until tonight.

As Bobby Short played and the young romeo reached for her hand, Chelsea observed. Madame Didier's bearing was regal, but carriage had little to do with credentials, and nothing to do with class or character. Any acting coach could provide carriage. She was magnificently groomed and beautifully gowned, but so was everyone else in the room. No. It wasn't the obvious that compelled Chelsea to train her jade-green eyes on the woman's back. It was a feeling that they had seen each other before, known each other perhaps. Like a reporter writing a lead paragraph, she asked herself the pertinent questions. What? Where? When? At first, Chelsea had no answers, until the woman turned and they faced each other. Then Chelsea knew *who*. What she didn't know was *why*.

The crowd had thinned. Small groups mingled on the stairs and in the hallways, saying their good nights, as they waited for their limousines to pull into the cul-de-sac. Gabrielle had been standing off to the side, allowing Garrett to bid his guests farewell, but now that the last few couples had retrieved their coats, she deliberately moved into the throng, motioning to the butler that she was ready to leave.

"If you'll wait just a little longer, Gabrielle, I'll be happy to see you home," Garrett whispered, drawing her close and sliding his arm around her waist.

She kissed his cheek and smiled.

"You have a thousand details to attend to. I don't have to be one of them." She squeezed his arm and then broke away. "I'll be fine."

As she turned to go, she bumped into Maximilian Richard.

"I was just looking for you," he said, obviously pleased to have found her. "I wanted to tell you how very glad I was that I had the chance to meet you. Perhaps we'll get to see each other again soon." With all the savoir faire of a European prince, he bussed her hand and tipped his head in a gesture of respect. They might have spoken more, but someone behind Gabrielle had distracted Max. He smiled and stepped aside, allowing the blonde in the brilliant red dress to join them.

"Chelsea, do you know Gabrielle Didier?" The blonde shook her head. "Gabrielle, Chelsea Reynolds."

"I noticed you earlier," the woman said, noting Gabrielle's barely polite nod and dismissing it. "All evening, I've been trying to figure out why you look so familiar. Haven't we met before?"

"I don't believe so."

"I'm usually so good at faces and names. You're certain we don't know each other?"

"Yes. Quite certain."

Gabrielle looked away, suddenly very preoccupied with a bothersome speck of dust on her gown. The dazzling blonde with the high cheekbones and the ripe, red lips moved closer. As she did, Gabrielle reached up and began to rub her temples.

"Are you all right?" Max asked.

"I have a splitting headache. I really must go."

She did look ill. Her color had drained. The smile had left her face. And now that he thought about it, she had seemed a bit edgy the past few minutes.

"Do you have a car?"

She nodded, but kept her eyes down.

"Garrett was kind enough to let me use his car."

"I'll get it for you. Wait here."

She smiled wanly and continued to massage the sides of her head. Chelsea was undaunted.

"Don't you think it's odd that I'm so sure we've met and you're so sure we haven't?" Her voice was soft, but her tone was unmistakably menacing.

"I'm sorry if you feel insulted, Miss Reynolds, but I don't remember ever seeing you before tonight. Now, if you don't mind, I have a terrible headache."

"I think I'm more amused than insulted," she said, her mouth beginning to draw upward in a devious grin, "because you see, despite your protestations to the contrary, we have met before."

Gabrielle tried to step past her, but the other woman shifted, stretched out an arm, and blocked her path.

"I know exactly who you are and *what* you are."

Max signaled that the Castleton limousine had arrived. Gabrielle practically ran toward the waiting car. As the Bentley pulled away, she looked back.

In the doorway, Chelsea Reynolds stood with her arms crossed and a huge smile on her face.

"I don't know what you're up to," she muttered, more to herself than to the departing car. "But I do know that *you*, Madame Gabrielle Didier, are an outrageous fake!"

PART
ONE

1

In Europe in 1944, even the most romantic souls no longer believed in Cupid's fateful dart. War was the only matchmaker. It ripped couples apart and brought couples together. Then, it wasn't being in the right place at the right time that mattered, only being in the same place at the same time. Bill Cocroft had come to Paris with the American First Army. He was a flag-waving, rifle-toting GI Joe, a twenty-two-year-old first sergeant who wore his uniform proudly and took the liberation of France as his personal responsibility. Delphine Didier was in Paris working as a sous chef in a small restaurant in the fourteenth *arrondissement* and as a sometime courier for the Resistance. She was the youngest of five children. Her parents and one of her sisters had been killed during a German air raid on the Loire Valley; one of her brothers had died fighting in North Africa; her other brother, Bernard, had suffered a permanent leg injury trying to stave off the attacks on the Maginot Line; and her older sister, Simone, had been widowed. To Delphine, the liberation of France was also a personal matter.

Bill and Delphine met at an out-of-the-way wine bar on the Avenue du Maine. Because Chez Matelot was a haven for young people low on funds but high on commitment, the casual drinker in search of a cheap drunk or a quick pickup quickly discovered that he was better served elsewhere. Often, French soldiers who had grown up in the neighborhood brought their American comrades to the bistro for its good wine, hearty provincial fare, and most of all, lively discussions on everything from the price of beef to the fate of Pétain. Though there were Gamays, Saumurs, Champignys, and Muscadets to choose from, there was only one political vintage allowed at the oaken bar—de Gaulle loyalism.

One night, while yet another political argument raged, Bill and Delphine were introduced. For each of them, it was a *coup de foudre*. They fell in love and consummated their relationship quickly. When Bill was sent to Cologne, they vowed to write and to remain faithful and to continue to love each other no matter what. Many wartime lovers promised the same things, but only a few were able to keep those promises. Bill and Delphine were one of those couples. Three months after Bill's return to Paris, they were married. Bill was honorably discharged and sent home to Wadsworth, Ohio, courtesy of Uncle Sam. Delphine followed soon after, courtesy of her older sister, Simone.

Two years later, after months of trying to conceive, Delphine became pregnant. The delivery was difficult, and after, Delphine was told that she could bear no more children. Gabrielle was to be the Cocrofts' only offspring.

Everyone was agreed that Gaby was a delightful child. She was bright and outgoing, kind and compassionate. Early on, it became apparent that she had a photographic memory which enabled her to recite a poem after one reading, become fluent in French by the age of three, and get top grades in school with a minimum of dedicated study time and a maximum of night-before-a-test cramming.

She had a vivid imagination, which expressed itself most often in the privacy of her room. There, without siblings to play with, or argue with, or whisper with in the night, she created her own special world, a place where she wasn't as skinny as she really was, a place where her hair was sleek and straight like her friend Amy Ann's instead of thick and wavy, a place where she was as stylish as her mother and as smart as her father, a place where she had brothers and sisters and, eventually, a husband and nine children. She loved making things up and pretending and inventing situations and characters and often, especially after she had come home from a really terrific movie or had finished a really good book, she fancied herself an actress, doing the same things she did in her room in front of an adoring audience.

Gaby was also extremely observant. She had a penchant for spotting details normally overlooked by others. It wasn't unusual for Gaby to be the only one who noticed slight tics or mismatched socks, a missing button or a too-tight seam; or for her to pick up on subtle mood changes and emotional swings, even when she was too young to understand what they meant. Her antennae seemed to home in on peculiar quirks or odd habit shifts. Gaby always knew when her father was worried or her mother was fretting, when a person was nervous or shy or feeling guilty about a misdeed. It wasn't that she was clairvoyant, it was simply that her instincts were finely tuned. It followed that she was an inveterate people watcher, and thanks to the convivial spirit that pervaded the Cocroft household, as well as the almost constant flow of visitors, she had plenty of opportunity to indulge her favorite pastime.

Bill was an architect slowly establishing a name for himself in Cleveland. He was also a man with a passion for politics. He had been elected to the local city council before he was thirty, and at thirty-five he had become Wadsworth's youngest mayor. He was always conducting meetings at home, always inviting unexpected guests for dinner. As if that didn't create enough living room traffic, when Bill decided to leave the large architectural firm he had started with and go out on his own, Delphine had opened a cooking school to help bring in extra money. At the time, it had seemed like the natural thing to do. Her culinary talents had become well-known in the neighborhood, and so it was not uncommon to find two or three women sitting around Delphine's table learning to debone a chicken breast or to mince garlic with a knife instead of crushing it with a press. The moment her announcement appeared in the newspaper, her classes were filled, including a his-and-hers class she conducted on Friday nights for couples—with Bill as her assistant—and a mommy-and-me class she held on Wednesdays after school for mothers and children over five—with Gaby by her side.

The older she got, the more Gaby loved being the daughter of Bill and Delphine. She thought her father was the most wonderful man in the world. He was handsome and clever and popular and important and always treated her as if she were someone very special. He kissed her good night every single night, wrote her poems, sent her flowers even when it wasn't Valentine's Day or her birthday, took her to his office and let her help him draw buildings, discussed serious issues with her as if she were an adult and then made her giggle by tickling her or telling silly jokes.

If her father was her ideal, her mother was her idol. Delphine was beautiful, with lustrous, dark brown hair and silky, spun-sugar skin. Her café noir eyes were large, deep set, and full of life. Her mouth was wide, her upper lip slightly larger than the lower, her smile broad and winsome. Except for her eyes, Gaby looked just like Delphine, but she was too young to see the resemblance, too self-conscious to understand that even the most dazzling bird starts out as an awkward, scrawny chick. She recognized the fact that Delphine was thin, but on her, Gaby thought it an enviable trait, instead of a defect to be hidden beneath bulky sweaters and two-sizes-too-big shirts. Gaby tried endlessly to emulate her mother's look, but she always felt shapeless next to Delphine, who could don the simplest frock and transform it into something near haute couture.

Part of Delphine's secret was that she sewed like a professional seamstress, often copying dresses right from the pages of *Vogue* and *Harper's Bazaar*. Because she sought to pass on to her child whatever knowledge she possessed, Delphine taught Gaby not only the finer points of sewing—how to make French seams and add lace to hems and alter patterns—but also the elements of *le style français,* that innate ability, on which French women seem to have a monopoly, to add pizzazz to something plain, to make inexpensive department store separates look like boutique ensembles, to put this with that and arrive at something unique and modish, even if the "this and that" were five-and-dime items. Though Gaby wouldn't see the results of Delphine's teachings until much later, and though it was frustrating constantly to try and constantly appear to fail, Gaby loved the lessons, because she loved the closeness.

Yet no matter how wonderful Gaby thought her parents were, no matter how exciting and worldly they seemed to be, Gaby was not the child of reigning monarchs or the scion of a great ancestral line. She was a commoner, a middle-class girl living a middle-class life, an existence so normal and uneventful, it was charmed.

Until one memorable Wednesday in March 1959, when Gaby was twelve.

The first hint Gaby had of anything unusual, was that her mother was not waiting for her when she arrived home after school. Normally, Delphine was at the door, smiling, waving, calling out *bienvenue* while Gaby was still halfway down the block. That day, the door was closed and locked. Gaby rang the bell several times. Finally, assuming that her mother was out shopping for last-minute items for that afternoon's mommy-and-me session, she went around the back, reached down under the milkbox, found the key, and let herself in.

The large kitchen, which had been remodeled two years before to accommodate Delphine's burgeoning business, was all set up for a class. Instruction sheets printed with Delphine's signature fleur-de-lis were stacked in a neat pile on the table. Plastic aprons were folded and waiting on a chair. Two huge pots sat ready on the stove. On the work counter, wire baskets held freshly scrubbed potatoes, carrots, celery, turnips, and onions. In the refrigerator, Gaby found two large briskets which she knew would·be cut into cubes of beef, several small balls of noodle dough, and twelve peeled and cored apples she guessed were for *pommes à la Delphine*.

She ran upstairs, quickly changed into her assistant's clothes— white slacks and a white T-shirt with a blue fleur-de-lis and a red "Delphine's"—and started her homework. By four-thirty, though she had thought it odd for her mother to be so late, Gaby still entertained no premonitions, no sense of foreboding. When the doorbell rang, her first thought was that one of Delphine's students had come early. Her second thought was that Delphine had returned and misplaced her key. But that couldn't be. Her mother wasn't the careless type. Besides, she could have come in the back, the way Gaby had.

She ran down the steps, taking them two at a time, and opened the door. Standing before her were Reverend Clarke, the pastor of her church, Amy Ann Holbrook's mother, and a high-way patrolman introduced as Officer West. Reverend Clarke's face was somber and unsmiling, but since he wasn't a particularly humorous man, his attitude was not alarming. Mrs. Holbrook's eyes were bloodshot and watery, but she was known to be highly emotional and hopelessly addicted to soap operas. The only truly disturbing presence was that of the policeman. His face was expressionless.

Gaby's young mind raced. She couldn't remember doing anything so awful that it would demand the attention of the police, or her minister for that matter. Think, she told herself. If Mrs. Holbrook was there, whatever it was obviously involved Amy Ann. Okay, Gaby and Amy Ann had pulled off more than a few mischievous pranks lately, but nothing that was worth this kind of visit. Maybe Amy Ann had been caught smoking again. She had been caught twice by the principal in school, but had skillfully manipulated her way out of anything more than a week's detention. Had Reverend Clarke caught her last Sunday in the ladies' room? Was it against the law to smoke in or near the church? Had they found out that Amy Ann had cheated on her algebra midterm? Were they here to get Gaby to swear that she knew about her friend's crib sheets?

Suddenly, Gaby was very nervous. She invited the trio inside, chatting as they entered, explaining that her father was still at work, that her mother was late getting home, that she had been upstairs doing her homework, that the onion smell was because of the cooking class which would begin in half an hour. Their silence was even more disturbing than the fact that she felt compelled to keep talking. If she stopped, they would tell her why they had come, and instinct warned she wasn't going to like what they had to say.

After asking if she could get any of them something to drink, she sat on the sofa. Reverend Clarke sat on one side of her, Mrs. Holbrook on the other, Officer West in the chair across from them. Gaby kept her hands folded neatly on her lap. Considering the circumstances, she tried to appear every inch the well-mannered, obedient child. The last thing she wanted was to give Mrs. Holbrook the opportunity to tell Delphine that Gaby had been impolite or improper. Then she would have to listen to another lecture on what it meant to be a young lady and . . .

"Something has happened, Gabrielle."

Reverend Clarke's voice broke through the protective barrier of frivolous thought and admitted a chill that began to seep into Gaby's bloodstream and spread throughout her body.

"There was an accident."

He took Gaby's hand. Mrs. Holbrook began to weep.

"Your father and mother were driving on the interstate when another car hit them. The driver was drunk."

Dread clung to her like a plastic wrap, cutting off her air, making her dizzy from lack of oxygen. Again and again, she breathed deeply, unable to fill her lungs completely.

"They were killed instantly."

Silence descended on the room as three adults waited for a young girl to absorb the horrible, irreversible fact that she no longer had a mother and a father. They expected her to scream, to cry, to collapse. Instead, she shook her head.

"You've made a mistake," Gaby said quietly. "My father's at work. My mother's running errands. They'll both be home soon." She looked down at her wrist, wanting to check the time, hoping to verify her story. She wasn't wearing a watch. She looked up again, her eyes glossed with fear. "They'll be here. Any minute now."

Reverend Clarke patted her hand, as if that small gesture could lessen the impact of the news he had just delivered. Mrs. Holbrook put her arm around Gaby's shoulder. Officer West leaned forward, crossed his arms, rested them on his knees, and spoke to her softly, but distinctly, knowing how difficult this was for her, also knowing how important it was that she understand what he was saying.

"I wish it was a mistake, Gaby, but it isn't. Both your mom and dad had identification on them." He glanced at a page in a black notebook. "William and Delphine Cocroft."

Again, Gaby shook her head. She removed her hand from Reverend Clarke's. She shrugged off Mrs. Holbrook's arm. Taking another deep breath, she looked at the policeman. Her face was pinched with a desperate calm.

"My father never takes off from work. Ask anyone. They'll tell you. You're wrong. Those people in that car must be someone else."

"We found a receipt from a doctor in Cleveland in your father's wallet. According to the information on it, he visited an orthopedist at Lakeside Hospital and had X rays taken of his left leg.''

Gaby's eyes clouded. Her control weakened.

''He got hurt in the war,'' she said quietly, almost to herself. ''He was in the army. He and my mother met in Paris. They fell in love and got married there.''

The policeman smiled briefly, gently. He had performed this gruesome task often enough to know that this recitation of facts was the child's way of denying the truth, of forestalling the inevitable reality of what she had just been told.

''I called your mother's sister, Simone, in Antibes,'' Reverend Clarke said. ''She and your Uncle Bernard will be here as soon as they can. Until they arrive, however, I thought it might be best if you stayed next door with the Holbrooks.''

Mrs. Holbrook stood immediately, clearly relieved to have something to do, some purpose that would remove her from this terrible scene.

''I'll go upstairs and pack a few things, all right, Gaby darling?''

Gaby turned to Officer West. She didn't want to speak to the others. She didn't want to hear what they thought was best. She didn't want to agree to anything until this man said it was okay. The others were trying to be helpful and solicitous, but Gaby felt smothered by a pity she wasn't prepared to accept, surrounded by a grief she wasn't ready to give in to. The police officer represented an unfeeling, unemotional sanity. She still had so many questions. He would give her answers.

''Where are my parents now?''

''They're in Cleveland, at Lakeside.'' Her face brightened momentarily, as if mentioning the hospital meant there was still hope. ''Once the funeral arrangements are made, we'll bring them back here to Wadsworth.''

Funeral. Arrangements. Like a ship disappearing behind the horizon, hope faded, and once again Gaby's face paled.

''Will you take care of them?''

''Yes, if you'd like.''

She nodded. Somehow, it seemed very important to her that he escort her parents home.

''Can I see them?''

''I wouldn't, Gaby. Not now.''

She looked into his eyes. They were brown, she noticed, with flecks of orange, kind and honest. If he had thought it would have helped to see her parents, he would have allowed it. But he was saying no. He was telling her that Bill and Delphine had been bloodied and battered and mangled. Gaby felt her stomach lurch and a huge lump pushed its way into her throat.

"Can't I stay here? Do I have to go to Amy Ann's? Can't I sleep in my own house?"

He heard the panic, the strangled voice. He saw the fear and the uncertainty, the need to cling to that which she knew, that which was familiar.

"I don't think it's a good idea for you to be alone," he said.

She was trying to be brave, but being a father himself, he knew that most children took their strength from their parents, from knowing that there was always someone there to back them up, to catch them when they fell, to kiss their wounds and make the hurt go away. This child's loss was enormous, and it would take more than simple courage to cope. It would take love and caring and unbelievable amounts of attention from someone close. He turned to Reverend Clarke.

"Does she have any family nearby?"

"No. Bill had no family to speak of, and all of Delphine's people are in France."

"Is there anyone who could spend the night with her here?"

Reverend Clarke shook his head.

"I don't think so." He stroked Gaby's hair, wishing he had the power to reverse this terrible chain of events and return Gaby's life to the peaceful, happy existence it had been only hours before. "It's just for tonight, my dear. Tomorrow, your Aunt Simone will be here and everything will be all right."

Gaby responded with a blank stare. Did he expect her to take comfort in those words? To look forward to the arrival of an aunt and uncle she barely knew? Was everything really going to be all right tomorrow? The only people she wanted to see were her parents, and according to him and Mrs. Holbrook and Officer West, they were dead. They were never coming home. Nothing would ever be all right again.

That night, she lay quietly in Amy Ann's room, listening to her friend's steady breathing in the next bed. She tried to sleep, but each time she closed her eyes, all she saw were crashing cars and bent metal and orange flames and mutilated flesh. With wide, tear-filled eyes, she stared into the darkness, fighting off the frightening images that insisted upon flashing before her, the terrifying thoughts that insisted upon invading her brain.

Where would she live? What would she do for clothes? for food? Who would take care of her? What would happen to her house? What would happen to her? Reverend Clarke was right. Her father had no family. Her mother's family lived in France. Would she have to go to an orphanage? a foster home? Would they make her move away? Would she have to go to another school? Would she have to leave her friends? Suddenly, she looked over at Amy Ann. They had been best friends all their lives. Only Amy Ann knew Gaby still needed her baby blankies to fall asleep. Only Gaby knew that, until recently, Amy Ann had been a bed wetter. They told each other their most intimate secrets, shared their most intimate dreams. What would they do without each other?

She turned on her side and pulled her legs up under her chin, trying to find a friendly spot in which to rest. She had slept in this bed hundreds of times, yet now, this night, this familiar bed felt strange and alien. Probably because she herself felt strange and alien, as if she were suddenly terribly out of place. But she was. She wasn't there as a guest. She was there because she was out of place in her own house.

God! How could this have happened?

Despite her flannel pajamas and the down comforter Mrs. Holbrook had covered her with, Gaby felt cold. Her body trembled and her teeth chattered. She pulled the blanket closer, trying to muffle her shivering so she wouldn't wake Amy Ann, but nothing could warm her, nothing could snap the arctic cold that had wrapped around her soul.

By three in the morning, sleeplessness, panic, and heartache had anesthetized her, numbing some but not all of her pain. Her head throbbed, but somewhere in the back of her mind a faint voice urged her to go home, hinting that perhaps that afternoon had been a cruel nightmare, that her imagination had simply been working overtime, that for some perverse reason she had concocted the entire story herself, but that now she was awake and if she went home, everything would be fine, everything would have returned to normal. As if in a trance, she rose from

the bed, searched around in the dark until she found her keys, and tiptoed down the stairs, out of the Holbrooks' house, next door to her house. Quietly, she let herself in.

Without thinking, she went upstairs, opened the door to her parents' room and found her way to their bed. By habit, she scooted into the middle, in between two fluffy, floral-shammed pillows. From the time she had been a toddler, she had crawled into this bed on Sunday mornings, dragging her stuffed animals and blankies with her, her menagerie as much a part of the weekend routine as the funny papers and the croissants and jam and tea that Delphine always brought upstairs on the breakfast tray.

Gaby smiled, remembering how, just recently, her father had teased her about how hard it was going to be to try to find a wedding gown with a blankie pouch. She had laughed then and she laughed now. Even tonight, she had brought her treasured security blankets with her. Holding them close, her mind lost in another time, she slid her feet under the covers, expecting to find warmth and comfort. Instead, the sheets were cold and stiff, the blankets tight and unyielding. She closed her eyes, forcing herself to visualize Bill and Delphine on either side of her. Still clutching her blankies, she reached out and touched the space next to her. Nothing. She reached over and touched the other side. Nothing. The bed was empty. Suddenly, the facts she had been fighting off came crashing down on her. The bed was empty because some bastard had had too much to drink and had hit her parents' car. The bed was empty because her parents were dead, gone, never to return, never to be anything more than memories or visions or faces in a photograph.

Gaby climbed out from under the covers and threw her timeworn blankets across the floor. They were supposed to have given her security. They were supposed to have kept her safe and happy and to have ensured that nothing awful would ever happen to her. Her mother had always said they were for babies. Well, she wasn't a baby anymore. She couldn't be. Babies had mommies and daddies. She didn't. She was alone. She was an orphan.

For the first time since Reverend Clarke had rung her door-bell, she cried, sobbing, screaming, allowing her tears to flow unchecked. For the first time, she acknowledged her grief and allowed her heart to vent its pain. And for the first time in her life, she fell asleep alone, with no one to tuck her in or kiss her good night.

She awoke to the harsh sound of a freezing rain pelting against the windows and the comforting feel of a woman's arms holding her close. Disoriented, Gaby's eyelids fluttered, taking in quick views of her bedside companion. The arms belonged to a familiar face, framed by dark hair and distinguished by deep-set eyes and a wide mouth. The scent was different. The body didn't feel quite right, but Gaby knew who it was.

See, she told the evil spirits that had tormented her throughout the night. See! It isn't true. My parents haven't died!

Her eyes snapped open and for an instant, just an instant, her heart lifted. But then, a tender hand brushed a lock of hair off Gaby's face and a soft voice spoke to her in French.

"Ma chère, Gabrielle. C'est tante Simone."

"I thought you were . . ." Her eyes flooded with tears as once again she was forced to deal with reality instead of being able to find comfort in her fantasies.

"Je sais, ma petite. I know. It's all so terrible." Simone pulled a handkerchief out from under her cuff and dabbed at Gaby's eyes. "Oncle Bernárd and I love you very much. We loved your mother and father very much, and we too are devastated by their loss. But if we hold each other very close, mon enfant, if we share our tears as well as our memories, maybe we can find a way to cope with what's happened."

Simone had lost her parents also, and on the long plane flight she had tried to reach deep into her memory and recall exactly how she had felt. She had felt vacant, empty, eviscerated, as if someone had opened her body and removed all her vital organs, everything that made it possible for her to think and breathe and feel. But she had been an adult. She had been married, living away from home. It had been wartime. There had been death all around, so much death that it had become almost as routine an occurrence as birth. But this was not Europe during the war and Gaby was not an adult. She was twelve, on the threshold of young womanhood. Her entire existence had revolved around Bill and Delphine. Her entire self-image was tied up in them as role models, in the standards they had established, in achieving their approval.

Partly because of her young niece's distress and partly because of her own shaky confidence, Simone reached out, hoping to cradle Gaby, to shelter her, to let her know that she was not without family, that she was not completely alone. But as she brought Gaby to her, the child stiffened and pulled away.

The next few days ran together in a mindless blur. Gaby barely functioned. She simply reacted to whatever went on around her. She submitted to unwanted hugs, unsolicited advice, and insensitive repetitions of the details of the car accident that had taken her parents' lives. She supposed that having Simone and Bernard there made things a little easier—they did insist that her privacy be respected and they did run interference with curious strangers and meddlesome neighbors and they did make sure she ate—but because they didn't know anyone and because Uncle Bernard's English was halting and because they, too, were wrestling with their own grief, sometimes, without meaning to, they became more a part of the problem than of the solution.

Almost every year, Gaby and her parents had summered with Simone and Bernard at Simone's house in Antibes, so her aunt and uncle were not complete strangers, but neither were they familiar. Many of their living habits upset Gaby—the thick, stinging odor of Bernard's Gauloises, the bitter aroma of Simone's French roast coffee, the uneven footsteps caused by the stiffness in Bernard's leg and his limp, the constant jangling of Simone's gold chains and bracelets. She disliked the spicy Provençal bent of Simone's cooking, the ever-present wine bottle at dinner, the necessity to speak more French than English. But what disturbed Gaby most was Simone's striking resemblance to Delphine. Simone was fuller faced and fuller figured, she was a bit taller, her hair was a shade darker, but the features were the same, the laugh was the same, the eyes were the same. Gaby tried to keep the two women separate, but each time she looked at her aunt, instead of being consoled by the presence of a close family member, she felt confronted by a cruel reminder of what she had lost.

The day of the funeral, Gaby didn't know whether it was cold or hot, rainy or sunny, windy or calm. She felt as if someone had lifted her up and was dangling her by her ankles. Everything appeared enshrouded by a thick, gray fog. There were no rainbows, no flowers, no birds, no puffy clouds, no beaming sun. There were only harsh whites and opaque blacks, two gaping holes in the ground, two polished mahogany boxes, and a bottomless, sorrowful void.

While the mourners gathered, Gaby's eyes remained locked on those big boxes. As if she had been ordered to watch them without blinking, she focused on only them. For reasons she couldn't explain, even to herself, it was important to her that she maintain her dignity, that she not cry like a baby or throw herself on the ground. Valiantly, she suppressed her emotions by fixing her mind on what it had been like when her parents were alive—the stories her father used to invent to get her to laugh when she was sad or sick, the bawdy ditties her mother used as a way of teaching her colloquial French, the way her mother's hair smelled after a bath, the way her father's arms felt when he hugged her, the way her mother's lips puckered when she called her *mon chou,* the way her father's voice softened when he called her petunia.

She felt Bernard move closer to her and Simone take her hand. She heard Reverend Clarke's voice begin to intone the eulogy. He seemed to be speaking directly to her, just as he had in church. He mourned the passing of her parents and prayed that they would find eternal peace. He asked the Lord's forgiveness for their earthly sins, and he entreated those who had come to bid farewell to William and Delphine Cocroft to remember God's mercy, to remember that sometimes mere mortals were incapable of understanding God's wisdom, to remember that even the most painful experiences had a purpose. He looked at Gaby and asked that she and others struggling with the pain of this double loss maintain their faith and continue to trust in the power of the Lord.

Gaby wanted to obey, but inside her gut, down deep, beyond the numbness, beyond the fear, beyond the anguish, anger seethed. No matter what Reverend Clarke said, she would never forgive God for what He had done. She had no mother, no father, and as hard as she tried, she could find no purpose in that. Once, she had accepted the notion of faith as something noble and glorious, as something that good people had and bad people lost. Now it seemed little more than a replacement for a logical explanation of God's ways. Until someone could present Gaby with a reason for her parents' being cut down long before their alloted biblical three-score and ten, she would not set foot inside a church. How could God expect her to find solace inside His house when He had taken from her house the very people who had made it a home?

"A foster home is out of the question," Simone said. It was the evening after the funeral, and Gaby had gone to bed.

Bernard agreed, but to Simone, his suggestion that they take Gaby back to France, that Simone give up her house in Antibes and the two of them move in with him in Paris, was just as unthinkable. While it was conceivable that Simone might learn to enjoy living in the city and, perhaps, at forty-five might find motherhood a pleasurable experience, under no circumstances could she imagine living with Bernard.

"I think you must return to Paris. You have a shop there and friends and, frankly, my dear brother, you know less about caring for a teenage girl than I do." She smiled, especially when Bernard nodded his head in agreement and, she suspected, with a small amount of relief. Gaby had descended into a horrible blackness, and coaxing her out of it would be no easy task, especially for a bachelor with no experience in such matters. "I will remain here in Wadsworth and raise Gabrielle. I think it's what Delphine would have wanted."

"What about money?" Bernard asked. "Though Bill made a good salary, most of Bill and Delphine's savings went to buy their house and then to renovate the kitchen for Delphine's school and even to fund their annual trips to visit us in France."

"What about life insurance?"

"He had only the barest minimum."

Of course, Simone thought. Bill was a young man who had thought he would live forever. He hadn't, and now Simone and Bernard were left to figure out how to support Gaby, the Cocrofts' mortgage, and the not-so-distant prospect of a college education.

"I have the solution," Simone said. "You'll sell my house and my antiques shop as quickly as you can. You'll ship my inventory to me here, I'll open another shop, and *voilà*, Gaby and I will have an income. We'll have you to turn to if we need, and we will make a go of it."

Bernard looked at his older sister, noting how handsome she was, despite the dark circles etched under her eyes by grief and concern. He wanted to meet her enthusiasm with conviction of his own, but he was worried.

"Simone, you have a life in Antibes. You're used to the world of the Riviera, the ways of the French, the ways of Provence. How are you going to get along here in this strange place?"

"I'll be fine. Just fine."

"You have friends in Antibes, lovers. You will be alone here."

"I won't be alone. I'll have Gabrielle."

"I know that what I'm about to say is going to sound callous, but will that be enough?"

Simone looked at Bernard. He was too loving, too compassionate ever to be callous. He was simply thinking of his sister and her needs. But Simone's needs were secondary, and both of them understood that.

"It will have to be enough, won't it?"

"I'll do whatever is best, Simone. You know that. If you want me to stay here with you, I will."

"No. Just sell my house and my shop."

Bernard rose from the chair, went to where Simone was sitting, wrapped his arms around her, and then sat next to her.

"I'll sell the shop, but we'll keep the house so that you and Gaby and I can be together during August, the way it used to be. I want to be part of this family too, you know."

Simone patted his cheek and tried to look encouraging, but all she could think about was whether or not she could persuade an orphaned twelve-year-old to want to be part of this family.

In the beginning, Gaby's relationship with Simone fell just short of an armed truce. Gaby didn't want Simone living in her parents' house. She didn't want Simone sleeping in the guest room. She didn't want Simone cooking at her mother's stove or eating at her father's table. She viewed her aunt's presence as an intrusion and wasn't at all shy about making her feelings known. She never smiled, hardly uttered more than three words at a time, and when she did, it was with an undertone of hostility and repressed rage.

Though many well-meaning neighbors clucked about Gaby's shaky emotional state, Simone waved away their concerns. Having been widowed as well as orphaned by the war, Simone had had more than one experience with unexpected death and its aftershock. Simone understood all too well what Gaby was going through. Gaby didn't want anything to do with Simone. She wanted her parents. The longer Simone stayed, the more she reinforced the reality that Bill and Delphine were never coming home. Fortunately for both of them, Simone was as patient as she was understanding.

When, finally, she had stocked her store, which she named Tante Simone after the reason for her move to Ohio, and hung out her Open for Business sign, Simone beseeched Gaby to help her. After all, she said, her English was still faulty, she was unfamiliar with local customs, and she had a terrible memory for names. If only Gaby would sit with her after school and on weekends until she settled in, she would be most grateful. Gaby wanted to refuse, but despair had dulled the edge of her resistance.

For weeks, Gaby appeared promptly at three-thirty with the fresh pastries Simone requested for their afternoon *goûter*. Every day, the two of them sat silently across from each other at a little table which Simone had dressed with a linen cloth, a silver tea set, and delicate china. At first, though she made her daily appearances, Gaby tried to make their after-school snack two separate experiences they had together instead of one experience they shared. Simone ignored her silences, chattering away in French and English, as if she had a responsive companion. She refused to concede defeat. Someday, somehow, she knew she would reach this sad, silent child. She just had to keep trying.

One of the ways she diverted her niece's attention was by introducing her to the wonder of antiques. Each day, she imparted a snippet of information on one piece or another. One afternoon, Simone appeared transfixed by the dishes she had set out for their small repast. She expounded at length on the beauty of eighteenth-century Chinese Export porcelain, wondering aloud at how glorious their own everyday china must have been, if the porcelain they exported was merchandise the Chinese considered unworthy.

Another time, she made a fuss over the little table on which she served their cakes and tea.

"Can you imagine," she exclaimed. "This piece of furniture

was named for a dwarf! Not just any dwarf, mind you, but a servant to Louis XIV.''

She paused, as if waiting for Gaby to say, ''Tell me more, Tante Simone.'' Gaby said nothing. She remained rigid in her seat, sullen, stone faced, but Simone thought she noticed a glimmer of interest in her sad, puppy-dog eyes.

''His name was Guéridon,'' she continued, ''and it was his job to bring the king small cakes like these on a tray. Because of his size, he didn't place the tray on a table, but instead stood alongside the king and held the tray until the king was finished with his snack. From that time on, small round tray tables like this were forever called gueridons, in honor of Louis's loyal servant. Isn't that fascinating?''

Gaby didn't answer, but Simone sensed that, like sweet syrup poured into a fine sieve, droplets were slowly filtering through.

In time, as the thick veil of her oppressive grief began to lift, Gaby's natural inquisitiveness reasserted itself. She began to look forward to afternoons with her aunt. She began to ask questions and listen to the answers. She began to tell Simone about her school day and to speak to the customers who came into the store. She began to help Simone around the house. And then, one day, she came to the shop, called out to Simone and was greeted with a strange, metallic echo. She looked around, but her aunt was nowhere to be found. She called again and this time heard the sound of someone humming a tune. A sound that seemed very far away. A tiny smirk insinuated itself on Gaby's mouth. Slowly, playfully, she searched the shop, enticing the odd voice to sing louder so that she could track it. After extending the game as long as she could, Gaby approached a lumbering suit of armor that held court in a back corner. When she lifted the grated visor and Simone poked her head out, Gaby laughed for the first time in a year. Simone laughed too, a grateful burst of joy and relief. Her beloved Gabrielle was finally ready to live again.

That night, they talked. Gaby had been so lost in her own anguish, that she had forgotten how much Simone had loved her sister and brother-in-law. The depth of Simone's feelings surprised her and touched off a spasm of guilt over the way she had treated her aunt.

"I'm sorry," she said. "I haven't been very nice to you."

"Don't be sorry, *ma chérie*. Life wasn't very nice to you. You had to take your anger out on someone. Why not Tante Simone?"

"I think I was too angry for too long."

It wasn't a statement. It was a question. One Simone was more than willing to answer.

"When you are hurt like that, anger is good. It's what makes you strong. It's what makes you a survivor. Those who have no anger at injustice are weak. They are the ones who ultimately fail."

Gaby just stared. She had never thought of herself as being strong. Willful, yes. Stubborn, sometimes. But strong?

"I don't feel much like a survivor."

"Ah, but you are. And do you know why?"

Gaby shook her head.

"Because the Didiers are blessed with the spirit of the phoenix. Do you know about the phoenix?"

Again, Gaby shook her head.

"The phoenix was a beautiful, magical bird. Legend says it burned itself on a funeral pyre at the end of its five-hundred-year life cycle. Then, when it had been reduced to nothing but a pile of dull gray ash, miraculously, it rose from those very ashes to live again." Simone smiled, enjoying her story. "We Didiers have had many tragedies, but each time, my pet, we've risen from the ashes of defeat. We've fanned those painful embers of loneliness and loss until they flamed into roaring fires of determination and will. And because we did, we survived."

Simone's enthusiasm was contagious. Gaby's face grew brighter, her back straighter. Still, Simone spotted uncertainty.

"But merely surviving is not enough, is it?"

"I feel alone," Gaby confessed. "Kind of unconnected."

"And wobbly and unsure of yourself?"

Gaby nodded.

"I feel that way, too. That's because we're both trying to get used to life without your mother and father and at the same time, trying to understand who we are without them. It's very difficult, *ma chérie*, very difficult indeed." Simone took Gaby's hand and squeezed it. "Do you know what I think? I think that if we make a pact here and now to tell each other whenever we're feeling shaky and alone, we can help each other. What do you say?''

Gaby heard the love in her aunt's voice. She saw the extended hand, sensed the open heart. She hadn't felt loved in so long that she was overwhelmed. Unable to speak, she threw her arms around Simone's neck. The two of them clung to each other. That said it all.

From that day on, Gaby and Tante Simone grew exceedingly close. Simone Boyer became mother, sister, guardian, confidante, advisor, disciplinarian (although Simone wasn't very good at saying no to Gaby), tutor, and friend to her young niece. She was the fulcrum on which Gaby's life was balanced. She provided warmth and love and strong roots from which Gaby could grow into adulthood. Yet there were some who felt that if not for Brian Thayer, Gaby never would have blossomed into womanhood.

Gaby had known Brian all her life, and for most of that time, although she had been too young to define her feelings, she had had a crush on him. He was only a year older than she, brutishly handsome and extremely popular. He was confident and gregarious and adventurous and all the things Gaby was not. She thought about him and dreamed about him, fantasizing that one day he would notice her. He gave her no encouragement except for an occasional smile as they passed each other in the hall at school, but still, she thought he was wonderful. The night of their junior year Valentine Cotillion, he proved how wonderful he was.

The student council had decided that parents would be invited so that fathers and daughters and mothers and sons could dance the sweethearts' dance together. When the invitation came, Gaby threw it out. Simone found it.

"I'm not going," Gaby said when Simone questioned her.

"Why not?"

"Because I don't want to."

"Don't you know how to dance?"

"Of course I do," Gaby said, annoyed that Simone was pretending she didn't understand. "That's not the reason and you know it."

Simone shrugged her shoulders. "Proms and cotillions are supposed to be fun."

"This one's different. I'll be out of place."

"Not every dance is going to be for fathers and daughters. Only one, and during that one, *ma chérie*, you and I will be wallflowers. We'll watch them, and then after, when it's boys and girls, I'll watch you. *C'est bien?*"

Gaby was reluctant. She argued, she fought, but Simone wore her down. For weeks before the event, Simone and Gaby shopped Cleveland's department stores, looking for the perfect dress. Whatever Gaby liked, Simone didn't. Whatever Simone liked, Gaby hated. Whatever they both liked was too expensive. When they had exhausted every possibility, Simone recalled that one of her admirers had given her a lace shawl from an antique clothing store in a suburban mall. It took them two hours to find the place, but when they did, they decided the trek had been worth it.

The night of the dance, Gaby looked like a finely carved Victorian cameo. The dress was pure Alençon lace, a delicate web of floral sprays and lush spirals that had aged to an eggshell white with just a hint of pink. It was high necked and long sleeved, with a gentle trumpet skirt that began to flare just below the curve of Gaby's hip. She wore ecru satin pumps that Simone decorated with mother-of-pearl ear clips, a silver and rose-diamond Sévigné brooch from the Tante Simone private-customers-only stock of fine antique jewelry, and, dangling from her wrist, a small lace fan that had once belonged to Queen Victoria herself.

When they walked into the gymnasium and every eye locked on Gaby, Simone beamed. Gaby blanched. All the other girls were wearing strapless froths of tulle with lacquered bouffant hairdos, Cleopatra eyes, and candy-pink lips. Gaby's mouth was glossed tea rose. Her face was delicately powdered and pale. And her hair was piled into a soft, turn-of-the-century topknot graced with loose tendrils that gently kissed her neck.

"I'm dressed all wrong," she said, turning to leave. "I look like a fool."

Simone stopped her. "You look like an angel. They all look alike. Come. Let's go over to the punch bowl where everyone can see how beautiful you are."

Suddenly, the lights lowered and the band began to play "Daddy's Little Girl." All around, fathers escorted their daughters onto the dance floor. Grown men and young girls glided about in time to the music. Gaby felt horribly conspicuous. Though no one was looking at her, she felt as if everyone were staring at her, talking about her, pitying her. Bill had been dead for three years and in that time she had suffered countless moments of longing for her father. But those moments had been private. Her loss had been private. Suddenly, it felt public and she hated it.

Simone saw the pain and embarrassment etched on Gaby's young face and understood. She had noticed the occasional stare, the whisper, the pointed finger. How could I have been so cruel, she asked herself? Gently, she took Gaby's arm and started for the door.

"May I have this dance?"

Gaby and Simone turned at the same time. Brian Thayer, looking rakishly handsome in a navy-blue suit and crisp white shirt, bowed gallantly and held out his hand, inviting Gaby to join him on the floor.

"It's for fathers and daughters," Gaby mumbled, too tongue-tied to think of anything else to say.

"I don't have a daughter and I hate dancing with my father," he said. "But I would enjoy dancing with you. What do you say?"

For the rest of their junior year, they dated as often as schoolwork and Simone permitted. That summer, when Gaby walked off with the Miss Wadsworth title and reigned as queen of the annual Blue Tip Festival, Brian gave her his class ring. They went steady throughout Gaby's senior year and the following summer, but when she went off to Skidmore and he returned to the University of Michigan, they decided it might be better if they saw other people. Brian dated anything in a skirt. Gaby went out now and then, but never really found anyone interesting enough to dilute her feelings for Brian.

During the summers, their courtship continued. Brian worked as a lifeguard at a Lake Erie country club. During the week, Gaby worked as a waitress in a local diner. Weekends, she and Simone traveled to auctions looking for items for Tante Simone. But at night—except for the two weeks Gaby and Simone spent vacationing with Bernard in Antibes—Gaby and Brian were inseparable. They held hands wherever they went, necked in the movie theater, fogged the windows of Brian's '63 Bonneville, and swore undying love for each other on the couch in Gaby's living room. But once summer was over and Brian returned to Michigan, his passions seemed to redirect themselves toward any coed willing to receive his pass.

Gaby might not have noticed that the intensity of Brian's attentions coincided with the university calendar, but Simone did. She began to suspect the degree of honor in Brian's intentions. Also, she was not unaware of the objections being raised by Brian's parents to his constant pursuit of someone as socially and financially limited as Gaby. Every chance she got, Simone encouraged Gaby to see other young men.

"You're young. Get out there and enjoy life," she'd say. "There'll be plenty of time to sit around and watch the grass grow when you're old. Now you must have fun! You must experience things! You must experience men!"

Gaby tried, but Brian had a peculiar hold on her. It was so strong, it was almost mystical. Perhaps it was because he had been the first boy ever to pay any attention to her. Perhaps it was because his courtly manners always made her feel pretty and special and like a somebody. Perhaps it was because she had allowed him to explore private parts of her body and was experiencing virgin's guilt. Perhaps it was because it was his nature to be domineering and her nature to be obedient. For whatever reason, Gaby was devoted to Brian, and when he asked her to marry him, she never hesitated before saying yes.

Though Simone tried to stall the nuptials, Brian negated all of her excuses by explaining that he and Gaby had to be married as quickly as possible so that he could avoid the draft.

"I love Gaby and she loves me. We're going to get married eventually. Why should I take the chance of getting shot in some stinking jungle in Vietnam when, if we got married now, I wouldn't have to go?"

For the first time in years, Simone thought of Alain Boyer, the handsome, virile husband she had lost to a German howitzer. Standing there, looking at Brian bathed in the yellow light of his unashamed cowardice, she felt an ancient anger rise up and sting her throat. She wanted to lecture him on bravery and courage and the obligation to do what your country asked you to do. She wanted to preach about honor and selflessness and the notion of giving being more blessed than receiving. But then she looked at

Gaby, so in love, so trusting. She willed herself to remember the horror of being handed Alain's Croix de Guerre, a cold piece of metal that was supposed to replace the warm flesh of the man she loved. And she forced herself to acknowledge the constant, inner ache that had become a part of her being, the immutable loneliness that had become a fact of her life.

"Whatever makes Gaby happy," she said.

Gaby threw her arms around Simone, hugging her and thanking her. Simone smiled at the two of them, but in her heart, she knew she didn't deserve Gaby's thanks. In her heart, she knew that Brian Thayer could never make Gaby truly happy.

2

Gaby was not a woman prone to philosophizing, but to her, it seemed as if life's catastrophes always occurred on ordinary days. On the day her parents had been killed, there had been no nuclear accident, no hurricane, no earthquake, no assassination, no declaration of war. It had been an ordinary day.

The day Gaby's marriage died was just as ordinary. The events of September 28, 1984, produced no banner headlines, prompted no news bulletins, merited no mention in history books. Gaby had awakened at seven, fixed breakfast for herself and Brian, sent him off to work, dressed, straightened up the house, wrote a letter to her son, Steven, at boarding school, played two sets of doubles, went food shopping, showered, changed, prepared dinner, and waited for Brian to come home.

Some women might have been apprehensive when their husbands were four hours late for dinner and hadn't bothered to call. Some women might have been furious. Gaby thought nothing of it. For much of their sixteen-year marriage, Brian had been a salesman for the Wadsworth Match Company, on the road every few months, away for a week, sometimes two. When Brian had been made a vice-president the year before, the traveling had stopped, but he had been working late very often trying to prove himself worthy of his promotion.

To Gaby, that night appeared no different from dozens of other nights. Except that on that night, when Brian entered their bedroom at eleven o'clock, instead of saying "hello" or "I'm sorry I'm late" or "it's good to be home," he said, "I'm leaving."

At first, Gaby thought Brian was playing a cruel joke on her, but then, as she watched him empty his drawers into a suitcase, she realized he was quite serious. He was leaving her, and she had no idea why.

"Where are you going?" She dropped her needlepoint and climbed off the bed, panic racing throughout her body with the effect of an amphetamine, shortening her breath, flushing her face. "What are you doing?"

"What does it look like I'm doing? I'm packing."

He never broke his stride, never turned to look at her. He just continued to throw his belongings into the luggage she had bought him for their twelfth anniversary.

"But why? What have I done?"

Months later, when the shock had numbed, Gaby would remember that her first thought had been that *she* was guilty of some wrongdoing, that *she* was the one responsible for the breakup of their marriage. Later, she would judge with an open mind the circumstances that had unraveled the fabric of their lives. Then, she had judged only herself.

"What have I done?" she shouted again, grabbing the back of his coat, tugging at him, demanding that he face her. "Tell me. I'll make it right. Whatever it is, just tell me."

"It's not something you've done." His voice was low, but the hostility she heard assaulted her eardrums like crashing cymbals.

"Then why?" Tears crowded her eyes, blinding her to the futility of her entreaties, just as habit and complacency must have blinded her to the symptoms of a decaying marriage.

"I don't love you anymore. I haven't loved you for a very long time. Maybe I never loved you."

"You don't mean that!"

He turned and stared at her. In the instant before he spoke, Gaby's emotions rollercoastered wildly. Please, she prayed. Drop the suitcases. Take me in your arms. Hold me. But then she remembered. He hadn't held her in months.

"I'm in love with someone else," he said, as if he were telling her the sky was blue and the grass was green.

"Who is she? Do I know her? How long have you been seeing her?" Gaby could hear the shrillness in her voice, but she was helpless to control it. She had known Brian all her life. If she pushed herself, she might be able to imagine not loving him, but she could never imagine being without him.

"I've been seeing her for almost a year," he said as he walked into the bathroom and began to fill his kitbag. "And no, you don't know her."

"Well, thank you for that." She glared at him, overwhelmed by disbelief. Did he expect her to compliment him for keeping this a secret for so long? Did he expect her to be grateful for sparing her the indignity of sleeping with one of her friends? Outrage flooded her being, making her feel as if she wanted to move about, to pace, to do something other than stand riveted to the floor, but at the first step, a wave of nausea washed over her and her knees buckled. "Who is she?" she demanded again.

"Pamela Frost."

"And what is a Pamela Frost?" Her sarcasm provoked an immediate frown.

"She's an account executive for Hampton and Rowe Advertising."

His obvious pride sliced through Gaby's heart.

"It's only an affair," she said suddenly, shocked by her own words, saying them anyway. "You did it. It's finished. You don't have to leave. We'll work it out."

"There's nothing to work out." He brushed her arm off his, snapped the last suitcase shut and started for the door. "I don't want to live with you. I want to live with Pamela. She's young and exciting, and she makes me feel young and exciting."

"And I don't."

"No. You definitely don't."

"What about Steven?"

"I'll take care of him. And I'll take care of you. You won't have to worry about a thing. All you have to do is let me go."

"All you have to do . . ." It sounded simple, and for Brian

it was. The changes in Brian's life were barely noticeable. The fact that he and Gaby had separated was almost incidental. It didn't affect his job or his regular squash game or his Thursday night poker game. He still ran every morning at seven, still worked out at the gym three times a week, still had three-minute eggs, coffee light, and whole wheat toast for breakfast. The same men he had palled around with before, he buddied with now. The same woman he had slept with before, he slept with now. The only difference was that he no longer lived with his wife.

For Gaby, everything was different. For sixteen years, she had thought of herself as Mrs. Brian Thayer. She had been half of a couple, part of a pair, one out of two. Now she was only one, and suddenly a life which had been structured on comfortable routine was thrown into chaos. Not knowing what else to do, she hid, seeing no one, speaking to no one, behaving as if she had been sent on retreat to contemplate her sins. By day, she wandered about the house, circling, trying to find a place to nest, a place where she might feel safe and secure. It was all so familiar, yet at the same time, so very strange. She tried to reorder the present by rearranging the furniture. She tried to blot out the past by destroying mementos. Nothing helped. She felt like a foreigner in her own home. She couldn't cook in her kitchen. She couldn't eat in her dining room. The couch was suddenly uncomfortable. No chair seemed to fit her needs. At night, she stayed awake until she was almost unconscious, and when she finally allowed herself to sleep it was not in her bed, but rather in the guest bedroom, where there were fewer ghosts.

She was angry, but her anger faded in and out, often coming in explosive spurts. She was sad, but the weight of her depression wavered between being burdensome one day, bearable the next. There were moments when she felt vengeful. There were moments when she felt guilty. There were moments when she didn't feel anything at all.

The first time Brian returned to the house, Gaby shook. He spoke, but her head filled with a bristling static. She saw his mouth move and tried to concentrate, but her ears clogged and her eyes blurred. When he suggested that they work out some sort of financial arrangement, she was too distraught to participate in a discussion about money, so she simply left it to him, just as she had always left budgetary concerns to him. He promised to pay for all of Steven's expenses—boarding school, clothes, allowance, travel—as well as whatever she needed to run the house. Each week, he would give her a check for two hundred and fifty dollars and two hundred and fifty dollars in cash. Though she thought this procedure was odd, she never questioned him. She was too busy questioning herself.

"Do you know how many times I said I wanted to go to work?" Gaby asked Simone, racing around the store, propelled by gallons of resentment. "Dozens of times. Especially after Steven went away to school last year. Brian always said no. My wife doesn't have to work, he said. My wife belongs at home. So I stayed home. I took care of the house and Steven and filled my days as best I could, just the way he wanted. Now I'm boring, and some postadolescent advertising whiz is the most exciting thing to happen to him since he had his braces off!"

Gaby had been rambling for more than an hour, her perspective shifting from rage to fear to self-doubt with the speed of a butterfly's wings.

"I should have insisted. I just should have gone out and gotten a job. What would he have done? Left me?" Gaby laughed, a sad, mocking sound that sounded more like a sob.

Simone sat and sipped a cup of hot tea, wishing Gaby would do the same. For weeks, ever since Brian had moved out, Gaby had been withdrawn and sullen. Despite Simone's encouragement, Gaby had steadfastly refused to discuss what had happened, as if talking made her situation fact, silence kept it fictional. She didn't know what had detonated the bomb, but since Simone believed in the cathartic benefits of anger, she had been delighted when Gaby had stormed into the store that morning and exploded.

"And what do I do now? Where do I go? I don't know how to start looking for work. What's worse, I don't know what I'm capable of doing." Her voice broke and she covered her face with her hands, so completely disgraced by her current circumstances that even in front of Tante Simone she felt embarrassed. "I've never worked anywhere except here. I'm thirty-seven years old and I've never held a real job. Since I've been twenty-two, all I've ever been is a wife and a mother."

"There's nothing wrong with that, *ma petite*," Simone said, incensed that Brian had walked out on her niece, outraged that in the process he had managed to vanquish all Gaby's sense of pride and self-worth. "You're a wonderful mother and you were always a caring, loving wife. Don't let Brian's failings distort your thinking. Doubt him, not yourself."

Gaby heard Simone's voice, but she never really heard what Simone was saying. The words brushed against her ears, but nothing penetrated.

Once again, she began to pace. Back and forth, from the front of the store to the rear, her steps aggressive but unsteady. On one of her tours, she paused in front of a huge bull's-eye mirror. She looked at her reflection and drew back, shocked at what she saw. Her eyes were rimmed with black. Her hair hung limp, and her skin had gone sallow from lack of sleep.

"No wonder he went to another woman!"

She grabbed a clump of hair and combed it with her fingers, stopping when she noticed several strands of gray. She stared at them as if seeing them for the first time, horrified, as if they had been introduced as evidence in a trial.

"I should have restyled my hair. I should have colored it. No matter how much he said he liked it," she said, looking at Simone through watery eyes. "That's the problem. I never changed. I never grew. If things were good, I left them that way, thinking that if I did, they would always be good. I was a fool!"

"I will not allow you to speak like this," Simone snapped. "Brian didn't leave you because you didn't dye your hair or paint your cheeks. He didn't leave you because you were a housewife instead of a business executive. He left because his libido itched and he was too immature to control his urge to scratch!"

Gaby began to shake. Her eyes teared and she pounded a table with her fist.

"The thought of him coming home and getting into bed with me after sleeping with her makes me sick!"

Simone watched Gaby cry and wondered whether or not she could have spared her niece some of this pain. Certainly, she could have predicted the breakup of this marriage. Long before this, long before Pamela Frost, Simone had suspected that Brian had violated his wedding vows. She had been the other woman too often not to recognize the signs of a philandering man. But what should she have done? Warned Gaby of her suspicions? Never. Brian would have denied it. She would have looked like a meddling old woman. And Gaby would have been furious. Rather than risk losing Gaby or her grand-nephew, Steven, she had held her tongue.

When Gaby calmed, Simone motioned for her to come sit beside her. Too exhausted to resist, Gaby allowed Simone to pamper her with hot tea and croissants.

"I thought we'd always be together," she said softly.

"Sometimes people grow apart."

"Is that what happened, Tante Simone?"

"I think so."

"I should have tried harder. I should have paid closer attention."

Simone stroked Gaby's cheek, wiping away the tears that seemed to have become an endless stream.

"Don't torture youself with might-have-beens or should-have-dones. Just work on healing these awful wounds and getting on with your life."

Gaby leaned back and closed her eyes for a few seconds. When she spoke, her voice was weak.

"Steven is so confused and so angry. He acts as if it's all my fault."

"He's a child and he's away from home. He'll be all right."

"Maybe, but he's my child and I feel as if I've let him down."

"Total blame is much too heavy a burden for anyone to carry."

"I have to make things right for him."

"First, make things right for yourself."

Gaby sighed. "Easier said than done."

"True," Simone said, taking Gaby's hand, "but you can do it. I know you can."

Gaby leaned forward and hugged her aunt, holding onto her as she had when she was a child.

"What would I do without you?" she asked.

"The same thing you're going to do with me," Simone said,

taking Gaby's face in her hands and staring into her eyes. "The same thing you've always done. You're going to fight back!"

As the days and weeks passed, Gaby struggled to adjust to the unfamiliar rhythms of her new life—the sudden need to budget, the need to find a job, the constant loneliness, the steady ache of humbled pride. Slowly, she began to make progress, forcing herself forward, forcing herself to heal. Then Thanksgiving came.

Steven was coming home. Ever since she had called and told him of the separation, his attitude had not softened. Even over the phone, Gaby could feel a barrier springing up between them, growing like a thick-leafed shrub preventing her from reaching him. They needed this vacation. They needed to be alone, she thought, so they might retrace familiar paths and resurrect the unique camaraderie that had always existed between them.

Steven had problems. When he was in the first grade, his teacher had called Gaby and Brian to school for a conference. She said she thought she noticed a problem. It wasn't something that threatened to keep Steven from achieving any of his goals, the woman had said, but it was a learning disability and it did require attention. Brian's reaction was immediate and, Gaby realized now, predictable. It was her excuse for being a rotten teacher, Brian had said. How dare she insult his son? Who did she think she was, implying that there was something wrong, that Steven was lacking in any way? Despite the endless, frustrating hours Gaby had spent trying to convince Brian that it wasn't a deformity or an embarrassment, that with proper tutoring and special instruction Steven could learn to overcome his disability, Brian insisted there was no disability and therefore no need for further discussion.

Gaby had reacted in a way that, she realized now, had also been predictable: she had done whatever had to be done on her own. She found an educational therapist in Cleveland, arranged for Steven to be tested, and tutored him herself. A year ago, just before Steven was to enter his freshman year in high school, she had finally succeeded in convincing Brian to send Steven to a special boarding school rather than insist that he suffer the humiliation of repeated failure. At the time, she had been certain it was the right thing to do. Now, though she still believed

Steven was better off there than in a public school, she regretted the distance.

Thanksgiving would bridge that distance, she told herself. She would prepare the same feast she always had, scaled down. She would make all of Steven's favorite dishes. She would set the table with her best china. She would carve out a pumpkin and sit it on a bed of autumnal leaves. They would work side by side in the kitchen, just like they used to, cooking, talking, maybe even laughing. Tante Simone would be there and amuse them with funny stories about Oncle Bernard's latest caper or some of her more eccentric customers. It was going to be wonderful. Gaby was certain of it.

Buoyant at the prospect of a reconciliation with her son, she went to the market the Wednesday morning before Thanksgiving. As she toured the aisles with her shopping list, she couldn't help noticing that everyone else's wagon overflowed with fruits and vegetables and pie preparations and jugs of cider. Everyone else's cart boasted a huge, great-bellied turkey, while her small hand basket held only a small bird, a few sweet potatoes, a bag of apples, and a head of cauliflower. Refusing to surrender to a wave of depression, she remembered how much Steven loved pepperoni and headed for the deli counter. While she was waiting her turn, someone tapped her on the shoulder.

"Gaby, my dear. What a coincidence. I was going to call you this afternoon."

It took Gaby a moment to recover from the shock of running into her mother-in-law, but in that moment she bit down on a sarcastic reply. Ethel Thayer hadn't called her more than three dozen times in her marriage. She hadn't called at all since the separation.

"I wanted to speak to you about tomorrow," Ethel whispered, steering Gaby into a corner away from the crowd. Her eyes narrowed with concern and her mouth pursed, the skin above her upper lip shirring like the top of a curtain. "I know this is uncomfortable for all of us, but I'm having the entire family for Thanksgiving dinner and I'd like Steven to be there."

The entire family. Gaby cringed. Her signature had not yet been inked onto divorce papers, but Ethel was making it quite clear that Gaby was no longer considered a Thayer. Was she ever, she wondered? Brian had two sisters, and for as long as

Gaby could remember, Gaby had been the odd one out. The older sister, Helen, lived in Florida. Helen was nice enough and she and Gaby got along, but because Helen visited Ohio so rarely and because when she did Ethel occupied almost every minute of her daughter's time, their relationship had never progressed beyond acquaintanceship.

The younger sister, Enid, had followed in Ethel's social-climbing footsteps by marrying up and moving out of Wadsworth, into Shaker Heights. In her case, familiarity had definitely bred contempt. Enid had never forgiven Gaby for marrying her older brother. The night before their wedding, Gaby had been forced to sit in the Thayers' living room while Enid had held Brian captive in her bedroom, wailing and sobbing and wondering why he was leaving her for Gaby. The fact that Enid was engaged at the time was irrelevant. For sixteen years, Gaby had suffered the younger woman's hostility, constantly being made to feel as if Enid expected her to apologize for the duration of the marriage. The thought that this divorce was giving Enid immense satisfaction upset Gaby almost more than the idea of being excluded from Ethel Thayer's party.

"I was planning on making dinner for Steven, Simone, and myself," Gaby said.

Ethel glanced at Gaby's half-empty basket and then at Gaby, her expression registering unmistakable disapproval.

"He can have dinner with you Friday or Saturday," she said, her words clipped and impatient. "I know you wouldn't want to keep him from his aunts and uncles and cousins. After all, at a time like this, a boy needs to feel connected to something strong and stable. He needs to be part of a large family."

Gaby wanted to protest, but Ethel had struck a chord. Apart from Tante Simone and Oncle Bernard, Gaby had no family for Steven to feel connected to. There were no young aunts and uncles, no cousins, no grandparents. With her father's death, the Cocroft line had been erased. The Thayer line, however, continued. Ethel's logic—self-serving though it may have been—made Gaby's plans for a mother-son reunion seem like a selfish indulgence. Reluctantly, she acquiesced.

After her encounter with Ethel, Gaby steeled herself to the idea that she and Simone would celebrate Thanksgiving without Steven, but she was completely unprepared for the fact that she remained alone throughout Steven's stay. He slept in his old room but was up and out of the house early each morning, having barely exchanged a word with his mother over hurriedly consumed breakfasts. Occasionally, he came home to change his clothes, but Brian and his family had manipulated Steven's schedule in such a way that every moment was taken up with some activity far more pleasant than babysitting his mother. When Brian and Pamela brought Steven home from the football game Sunday afternoon and then waited outside in the driveway to take him to the airport, denying Gaby even that small privacy, something inside her snapped. She kissed her son good-bye, walked back into the house, packed a suitcase, shut the lights, locked the doors, got into the car, and drove away.

Like most runaways, Gaby didn't care which place she was going to. The only thing that mattered was the place she was running from. For hours, she drove like an automaton, blindly, with no thought of a possible destination. One highway merged with another. Road signs passed in an hypnotic blur. Faster and faster she went, further and further away.

I did my best, she said, taking a hand off the wheel to wipe her eyes. *But my best wasn't good enough for either of them.*

Steven's face insinuated itself on the windshield—smiling at Brian, talking to Pamela Frost. The image faded, just as Steven's smile had faded when she had tried to steal a few moments with him to explain, to tell him what had happened.

So many signs. So many clues.

Suddenly, a blinking orange light caught her eye. At first she ignored it, just as she had ignored all the other distress signals in her life. But this one continued to blink, insisting that she notice that the needle on the gas gauge was tipped perilously close to E. How apt! she thought as she pulled off into the next roadside gas station-cum-restaurant to refuel and get something to eat. E for empty, just like her life.

What went wrong? When did it start? When Brian had been on the road, she had refused to worry that he might be unfaithful to her. It had seemed so stereotyped to assume he was hopping from bed to bed, just because he was traveling from city to city; so much like a stale bad joke. Had she been too trusting? too stupid? too naive? Or had she simply been protecting the status quo? Keeping her home intact, safe and secure for herself and her son? What had she been trying to prove? That she was some kind of saint? That no matter what the symptoms, she could cure whatever ailed her marriage?

The coffee was bitter, but Gaby drank it anyway. She was cold and tired, and if nothing else, the brew was hot and a source of much-needed caffeine.

"I should have known," she mumbled to no one in particular. "I should have done something."

She could feel their eyes on her. She could sense them talking about her. Quickly, she looked away, making a show of finding her wallet so she could pay her bill and leave.

Once inside the dark, sheltered privacy of her car, Gaby began to shake. Her eyes teared and she pounded the steering wheel with her fists.

An icy rain began to fall. The road slicked. Driving grew treacherous. Gaby should have pulled over. She should have found a place to sleep, a place to stay until the weather cleared. But instead, she continued on. The windshield wipers beat back and forth with a thumping rhythm that seemed to fill the car with a strange, tribal music. Mile after mile she went, listening to the sounds of the road, shutting off her brain, allowing the highway to anesthetize her, to numb her against the sting of resentments.

Hours passed. Five. Six. Eight. She was still fighting the elements when she crossed the Pennsylvania border into New Jersey and realized she was headed for New York.

Why not? she said to the darkness.

New York. Chicago. Cincinnati. What did it matter? As long as it was a big city with crowded streets and nameless places and easy access to the one thing she desperately craved—anonymity.

An hour and a half later, she crossed the George Washington Bridge, cut onto the West Side Highway, and headed south, toward midtown. Before her, a colossal field of concrete stalagmites shot skyward, towering over her, making her feel small and insignificant. Suddenly, the realization of where she was and what she had done balled into a lump of fear that stuck in her throat.

Okay, she said to herself. *Now what?*

Not knowing where else to go or what else to do, Gaby checked into the nearest Hilton Hotel, on Sixth Avenue and

Fifty-third Street. After a huge dinner and a long, luxurious bath, she climbed into bed, but sleep was difficult. Her eyelids were heavy, but her mind refused to shut down. Random thoughts scrambled about, bumped against each other, then broke apart, changing pattern and focus like chips in a kaleidoscope. She had behaved like a child. No one knew where she was. Probably, no one knew she was gone. Did anyone care that she was gone? Other than Tante Simone, no. Isn't that why she left? But what was here for her?

It took hours, but finally, too weak to continue debating, she made a decision. She would stay in New York for a few days and use the time to get herself together. When she was ready, when she felt stronger, she would start home.

The first two days, she allowed herself to follow in the hurried footsteps of the other tourists who flooded New York between Thanksgiving and Christmas. She went to the top of the Empire State Building, ogled the holiday displays in the department store windows, wandered around Rockefeller Center, ate dinner in Chinatown, and spent an afternoon strolling around the South Street Seaport. Though she might have preferred a companion, she found it easy to be alone. She moved at her own pace, fulfilled her own wishes. She looked at everything, but spoke to no one. She lingered in museums and hurried her meals. She rose early in the morning and read till late at night.

By the third evening, she was exhausted from the rigors of her sightseeing and introspection. She needed to rest. But she couldn't rest. Something insisted on holding her attention, something that nagged at her.

It was late. The remnants of Gaby's dinner sat in a corner on a room service tray. The coffee was cold, but she held onto the cup as she walked over to the window and looked out at the bright lights below her. Her own reflection caught her eye and brought a wry smile to her lips. She had watched countless movies in which men and women had done exactly the same thing. They stood at hotel windows studying the New York nightscape. What did they see? What were they looking for? Were they hoping to find inspiration in the never-ending energy of this city? Were they searching for bits of themselves in the moving minutiae on the streets below? Were they avoiding the future and ignoring the past by hiding in an impersonal present?

Gaby had no answers, for them or for herself. All she had was the notion that perhaps she had been brought here by fate, because here she would find what she was looking for—a new beginning.

The next morning, she called Simone.

"Tante Simone. Did I wake you?" Simone sounded groggy. She was usually awake long before this. "It's Gabrielle."

"Gaby? Where are you? I've been calling the house." Her voice was thick.

"That's why I called. I didn't want you to worry. I'm in New York."

"New York? Why?"

Even though Simone couldn't see her, Gaby blushed.

"I guess I ran away from home."

"I've been calling."

Suddenly, an alarm went off. Simone didn't laugh, she didn't scold, she didn't even comment on what Gaby had said. She repeated herself in that odd, thick voice. Simone never repeated herself.

"Tante Simone. What's wrong? Are you sick? Are you all right?"

"I'm fine. Don't worry about me. Tell me about you."

Gaby felt better. Simone sounded more like herself, as if she had just sat up and cleared her head of early morning cobwebs. She is sixty-nine years old, Gaby reminded herself. She is entitled to sleep late.

"I had to get away," she said aloud. "The walls were closing in on me. So I got in my car and here I am."

"Are you staying there?"

Again, Gaby sensed something odd in Simone's voice.

"I don't know. I thought I might try to find a job here. What do you think?"

"I think that's a wonderful idea."

"You do?"

"*Oui*. You need to start again. The old life is dead. Maybe in a new place with new faces, you'll be happy. I only want you to be happy."

Suddenly Gaby felt the tug of love for her aunt. Simone had sacrificed everything for her. Was it fair to leave her now?

"You'll come to New York and live with me," Gaby said, honestly believing that it was a good idea. "We'll get an apartment. I'll get a job and you'll be able to spend your time prowling around the thousands of antique shops here. We'll go to Broadway shows and museums. Steven will visit on his vacations. We'll take him to Radio City. Doesn't it sound like fun?"

Simone laughed. "It sounds exhausting. I'm too old to move again and too tired to be a New Yorker. Besides, you know I've never been a city person. You stay. You find a place for yourself. You find out what makes you happy. That's what's important."

"But I love you, Tante Simone."

"I love you too, *mon chou*, but it's time for you to be on your own."

That was probably what frightened Gaby the most—being on her own. All her life, she had been dependent on someone—her parents, Simone, Brian. Now her aunt was telling her to be something she had never been before—independent.

"Are you saying you don't want me around anymore?" She tried to sound light, but she had too much self-doubt to be casual about being thrown out of the nest.

"No, my darling Gabrielle. What I'm saying is that you have to get used to not having me around anymore. You have to learn to stand on your own, to support yourself, to make it so that you never have to be at anyone's mercy again."

Gaby gave Simone the hotel's number so she could reach her in case of emergency, and then hung up the phone, feeling like a little girl again. She had needed reassurance and encouragement. She had needed a hug and, as she always had, Simone had been there to give Gaby whatever she wanted. Well, Gaby thought, if Simone wanted her to be independent, that's what she was going to be!

Quickly, before she could think twice, she dressed and ran down to the lobby to buy *The New York Times*. She pored over the Help Wanted section and circled the names of those employment agencies with the most appealing ads. For three days, she walked in and out of tall buildings, visiting every personnel agency she could find, from the grimiest to the most glamorous. She entered each one bubbling with enthusiasm. She filled out application after application, sat through interview after interview, but each time, she was rejected. It was no different here from what it had been in Ohio. She was inexperienced and, therefore, unplaceable.

By the fourth day, she had moved out of the Hilton and into a small, inexpensive hotel off Second Avenue. By the eighth day, promise had dissolved into panic. She had seen every sight there was to see. She had visited almost every employment agency listed in the yellow pages and even some that weren't. She didn't know what to do. Her money was almost gone, and she knew that soon she would either have to find something in New York or return to Wadsworth. Yet what was there to return to?

With a leaden step, she trudged up Fifth Avenue, her attention momentarily diverted to the beautiful things displayed in the elegant stores that lined the avenue. Without realizing that a thought was germinating, she wandered through Lord & Taylor and Saks and Bonwit Teller, eventually finding her way to Bergdorf Goodman. She observed the customers as well as the salespeople. She watched. She listened. I could do that, she decided, eavesdropping on a woman who was about her age and trying to interest a wealthy matron in a spangled evening gown. The customer shook her head. Of course she doesn't like it, Gaby thought. She's too heavy for spangles. Show her something simple, something slimming. Sure enough, as if she had picked up on the telepathic message, the saleswoman returned the bejeweled chiffon to the rack and selected a long black velvet sheath with a low, rounded neck cut to display a healthy bosom and long straight sleeves meant to disguise fleshy arms. It was plain, but elegant, with no extraneous details to attract negative attention. The matron's eyes lit up the moment she saw it. The two women disappeared into a dressing room, but Gaby would have bet the last of her savings that the sale would be made.

Spurred on by a revitalized confidence, Gaby located the floor directory and found her way to the personnel department. As she waited for the receptionist to complete a phone call, she assessed her appearance in a nearby mirror. Her hair hung loose about her shoulders, falling into a classic line that framed her face. Over a black sweater and skirt accessorized with nothing but a strand of pearls and a leather belt, her coat served as a basic cover, the charcoal-gray wool providing a complimentary contrast to the creamy cast of her skin. When she checked her makeup, she debated about adding another dash of lipstick, but then decided less is more.

"I'd like to apply for a sales position," she said, as soon as she had gained the attention of the young woman behind the desk.

The woman hesitated, her eyes regarding Gaby through the lenses of her bright red framed glasses, appraising Gaby's appearance as if she were a finalist in the business suit phase of a beauty contest. The first few times Gaby had been forced to undergo this sort of evaluation, she had flinched, uncomfortable beneath the heat of a judgmental stare, but now she was a veteran of the interviewing process. She stared back, perfectly poised.

"The head of personnel is busy at the moment," the young woman said, handing Gaby a small clipboard and smiling. "Would you mind filling this out while you wait?"

"Of course not."

Gaby turned and seated herself on a small couch next to the desk. She didn't know at what precise moment she had decided to lie—before she got to this office, while she was being examined by the receptionist, or after she had studied the application card—but as she set pen to paper, her hand seemed to move without instruction from her brain. She used her middle name, her mother's maiden name. She listed a smart-looking, residential hotel she had passed in her travels as her current address and opted for widowhood as an uncomplicated way of explaining her marital status. As for her job experience, she claimed three years at the Galeries Lafayette in Paris, a store she had been in many times, though always as a shopper, never as a salesgirl. Before that, she said, she had spent two years at the Sonia Rykiel boutique on the rue de Grenelle. (Just last night, she had read an article on Rykiel in one of the fashion magazines.) Before that? She would say that she had been married, traveling, and not part of the permanent work force. The only purely honest statements on her entire application were the fact that she had graduated from Skidmore College in 1968 and was fluent in a foreign language. Yes, she spoke French like a native.

God bless you both, Mother dear, Tante Simone, she thought as she placed the card on the desk.

As she waited for her interview, she considered what she had done. For months, in both Cleveland and New York, she had applied for every available job, from an elevator operator to a short-order cook to an executive assistant. She had been honest every time. Had her honesty been rewarded? Had her forthrightness and eagerness to work gained her employment? No. And why? Because while other women had been engaged in meaningful employment, creating impressive resumes and establishing desirable job skills, she had been wifeing and mothering, two jobs clearly defined by society as completely and utterly meaningless. So, this time, she would lie. Even if Bergdorf's were to check her references, which she doubted they would, what was the worst that could happen? They would find out her resumé was false and ask her to leave? If she told the truth, the likelihood was that they would ask her to do the same thing. The way Gaby saw it, she had no other options.

"Mr. Parker will see you now."

Gaby followed the woman with the red spectacles to a windowless office so white it practically blinded her. The entire boxlike space looked as if it had been bleached. The walls were white, the carpet was white, the desk was white, the chairs were white, even the accessories were white. As she took the seat offered her, she felt conspicuous in her black outfit, as if she had suddenly been transformed into an ink blot on a Rorschach test.

Across from her, Mr. Parker withheld a proper greeting in favor of studying her application. Though his straight posture and assiduous expression defined him as a no-nonsense administrative type, his European suit, boldly striped shirt, satin-silk polka-dot tie, and perfectly pointed pocket hanky indicated that at some weak moment he had succumbed to the soigné atmosphere that dominated Bergdorf's. His appearance prompted Gaby to wonder whether the sterile background was meant to accentuate the person in front of the desk or the man behind it.

Finally, having taken enough time to memorize Gaby's history, Roger Parker looked up. His smile was professional. She returned it nonetheless.

"Ms. Didier. I see you graduated from Skidmore. Were you a business major?"

"No." Gaby was grateful she hadn't lied about something so easy to verify. "I majored in French literature and minored in art history."

"I would imagine that going to school in upstate New York is paradise for a skier. Are you a skier?"

"I used to be. I don't get much opportunity these days." There, she thought, two questions, two honest answers.

"That's too bad. Skiing's a wonderful sport. Occasionally, I indulge myself by spending a weekend on the slopes." As if on cue, he smiled again. "Did you ski while you lived in Europe?"

Gaby had read about personnel managers who deliberately tried to trip up applicants by asking questions unrelated to the job opening. Though her instincts said he wasn't, Parker looked like he might be a skier. She couldn't risk mentioning places she'd never been. What if he was familiar with them?

"My husband was extremely expert," she said, following a hunch, "so we only skied off-*pistes*."

"*Pistes?*"

Gaby's hunch was correct. If this man had ever been on skis, he had never moved far beyond the green circle beginner stage.

"*Pistes* are the Alpine version of groomed trails," she said, cleansing her voice of any pedantry. "They're meant for warm-up or cruising runs. Off-*pistes* runs are rather rugged and sometimes a bit on the dangerous side, but if you can conquer them, the experience is exhilarating."

"According to your application," Parker said, exiting the unsatisfactory detour, doubling back to more familiar ground, "most of your sales experience has been in Europe."

"Yes, it has."

"Have you ever worked in an American store?" He folded his hands, placed his arms on the desk and leaned forward, as if to gain a closer view of his quarry.

Gaby leaned back.

"I did," she said quietly, "but it was years ago, before my . . ." she lowered her eyes and fingered the hem of her skirt, ". . . husband got sick."

Parker retreated to the application card, embarrassed that he had intruded on something so personal.

"I notice you gave the address of a hotel as your place of residence. This is the Christmas season and we do hire extra help for the holidays. Is that what you're looking for? Temporary employment?"

"I would prefer something permanent." Another truth.

Parker nodded and made a notation on her card.

"Would you mind describing what you did at the Galeries?"

"Not at all." As long as you don't ask me specific dates or names, Gaby thought. "Because I spoke English, I was positioned on the second floor, where they carried designer labels that attracted Americans."

Parker nodded. Gaby felt relieved. Obviously, her explanation had sounded feasible. Encouraged, she continued.

"Often, because of my fluency, I filled in wherever they were short of help. Lingerie. Housewares. Shoes. Coats."

Gaby was certain she had detected a glimmer of respect in Parker's eyes.

"Why did you leave Rykiel?"

"Truthfully?" she asked as if she was about to reveal an intimacy. "I got bored. You know how Rykiel is. Though she shuffles her colors around from season to season, her designs rarely change. I wanted more variety."

Gaby's palms began to sweat. Inside her chest, her heart pounded with *mea culpa* insistence. She had just repeated part of a conversation she had overheard the other day in Bloomingdale's. Dear Lord, she prayed, I hope those women knew what they were talking about.

"That's precisely the reason we like to rotate long-term personnel," Parker said, his smile warming. "We don't want anyone to get stale."

"Bergdorf's is such a fabulous store with such a vast selection of merchandise, I would think it would be difficult to get bored working here, but still, it's a smart move."

Parker stood. Had she sounded patronizing? Gaby feared she had gone too far.

"Before we hire anyone, in addition to the normal referral checks, we ask that you meet with a department head and a section manager." He held out his hand. Gaby wasn't surprised to notice that his nails were beautifully manicured. "If you don't mind, I'd like to arrange those interviews for sometime this week."

"That would be fine," Gaby said, swallowing a broad, satisfied grin. "Just fine."

That night, she tried calling Simone. She couldn't wait to share her good news, but each time she called, the phone rang and rang and no one answered. By about eleven, Gaby began to sense that something was terribly wrong. Her head started to throb with twinges of guilt. How long had it been since she had last spoken to Simone? Days? A week? How could she have been so inconsiderate, so self-centered? She remembered how odd Simone had sounded that morning they had spoken. What if she hadn't just awakened? What if she was sick? Why hadn't she followed up? Quickly, she searched her address book for the number of Simone's doctor. She called his office, but his service said he was on call and would get back to her as soon as he could. Not good enough. On impulse, Gaby decided to try the Wadsworth Hospital. As the phone rang, she wondered if she should have called Akron General first. No. Simone always said she hated Akron. It smelled like the inside of a flat tire. No. If she was anywhere, it was either Wadsworth or Cleveland.

"Good evening, Wadsworth Hospital."

"Good evening. I'm calling from out of town and I'm looking for my aunt. Can you please tell me if you have a Simone Boyer listed as a patient?"

Gaby heard the woman punching information into a computer. Her heart pounded. She didn't know whether she wanted a yes or a no. If Simone was there, that meant she was sick. If she wasn't there, where was she and how was she?

"Yes. We admitted Mrs. Boyer on Tuesday."

"Can you tell me what's wrong with her?"

"I'm sorry, madam. For patient information, you'll have to speak to her doctor."

"I tried him. He's not in." Gaby was beginning to panic. "Wait. By any chance, is Dr. Jordan in the hospital?"

"As a matter of fact he is. He came in about an hour ago."

"Maybe you could page him. Please. It's very important. I'll hold."

It seemed as if time had slowed to a crawl before she heard Dr. Jordan's voice on the other end.

"Dr. Jordan, it's Gaby Thayer. What's wrong with my aunt?"

"I tried to call you, Gabrielle," he said. Gaby couldn't tell whether he was defending himself or reprimanding her. "I'm afraid that Simone is very ill."

"What is it? Did she have a heart attack? A stroke?"

"She has cancer."

Gaby felt as if the wind had been knocked out of her. She tried to speak, but at first she had no voice.

"Where?"

"We don't know."

"What do you mean, you don't know!" Gaby hadn't meant to yell, but she couldn't help herself. Fear and frustration were a combustible mix. She was about to apologize for her outburst, but obviously Dr. Jordan was used to hysteria and had ignored it.

"For months," he continued, "Simone has been having trouble eating. As you know, your aunt is a very stubborn woman. Despite the fact that she was losing an alarming amount of weight, she diagnosed her problem as advancing age and left it at that. It was only when she began to have pain that she relented and called me."

"How much pain?"

There was silence on the other end of the phone.

"Enough for her to call me," Dr. Jordan said, finally.

"Can't you operate?" Gaby asked, suddenly recalling that at Thanksgiving Simone's appetite had been much less vigorous than usual and that her color had been decidedly gray. She had asked Simone about it, but Simone had shrugged it off as too much pâté.

"We did. We found a small tumor in the gall bladder."

"And?" Anxiety and hope warred inside her.

"We removed the gall bladder, but a biopsy showed cancerous cells indicating the presence of a larger tumor, which so far we can't locate." Gaby's hopes died as quickly as they had been born. "I'm afraid we're dealing with what's known as an 'occult' tumor, a growth that is so well hidden that none of our sophisticated equipment can find it."

"When you opened her up, didn't you look for it?"

"As best we could, but I'm afraid, Gaby dear, the main growth may be in either the pancreas, the liver, or the stomach, and we're not prepared to explore all three areas in a sixty-nine-year-old woman. Especially when, even if we found it, success-ful treatment is doubtful at best.''

"Are you giving up?'' Concern was becoming disbelief, and disappointment was expressing itself as anger.

"No. We're going to do another series of CAT scans, includ-ing one which does close-ups of the aforementioned areas. In the meantime, we're making her as comfortable as possible.''

Gaby didn't have to ask about Simone's prognosis. That phrase was doctorese for "She's going to die and there's nothing we can do to save her.''

"Does she have to stay in the hospital?'' Gaby said quietly.

"Not now, but in another couple of months she may need more personalized attention.''

"She'll come live with me,'' Gaby said, determined to do whatever was necessary.

"Medical attention, Gaby.''

"A home? Are you talking about a nursing home?''

"Yes. One with a hospital wing that will be able to care for her properly.''

Gaby's stomach lurched. She had visited a nursing home only once, bringing Christmas gifts to the elderly, but she had never forgotten it—the smell, the stuffiness, the overwhelming sense of loneliness and despair. They were places without laugh-ter, without hope, halfway houses for people making the journey between life and death. Simone didn't belong there. Simone was beautiful and intelligent and filled with vitality and élan. Simone ran a business. She took care of a house. She had friends. She . . .

"Gaby. I wouldn't suggest it if I didn't think it was necessary.''

Dr. Jordan spoke gently. He knew what Gaby was thinking. He suspected what she was feeling. He respected her right to question and disagree, but he also knew that when the time came, Gaby would do what was best for Simone.

"I take it you have one in mind.''

"Yes. In Lakewood. It's beautiful, but more important, its hospital facilities are the finest in our area.''

"I'll go see it,'' Gaby said, unable to stop the tears from flooding her eyes.

"Should I tell Simone I spoke to you?''

"No. I'll be there tomorrow.''

Gaby hung up the phone, packed a bag, grabbed a few hours' sleep, and was on the road by four A.M. She called Mr. Parker from a truck stop in Pennsylvania and told him that a family emergency had taken her out of town. She asked if her interviews could wait a few days. If they couldn't, she had decided, it didn't matter. Only Simone mattered. Much to her surprise, Parker agreed. Not only did he promise to set everything up for the end of the week, but he even went so far as to say that she shouldn't worry, the meetings were academic. She could count on starting almost immediately.

The drive from New York to Wadsworth took nine hours. For most of that time, Gaby was taunted by a fiendish whisper that insisted on filling her head with the thought that Simone's illness was punishment for running away; that if she stayed in New York, Simone would die, but if she stayed in Ohio, Simone would live. Over and over again, turning, spinning like the wheels on her car, the voice repeated itself, making her dizzy with the thought that she had done something wrong and that God was going to punish her by taking away someone she loved. By the time she arrived at the hospital, Gaby was certain that when she went to the front desk and asked for Madame Boyer's room, she would be told that Simone had died during the night.

Simone was sleeping. It seemed strange to see her without her rouge or her *poudre* or her netted chignon. Her long gray hair was loose, spread across her pillow like a shawl, and her cheeks were pale, colorless, furrowed with the sunken texture of age and illness. For a moment, Gaby stood at the door, staring at the woman who for twenty-six years had been her mother. It was hard to believe that there had ever been a time when Simone had not been a major force in her life. She had loved her and raised her and been supportive of her, even when she had disagreed with Gaby's decisions. She had cast aside many of her own desires and needs in order to give Gaby what she felt Gaby wanted and needed.

"It's my turn now," Gaby whispered into the silence. "Whatever it takes, *ma chère tante*, you'll have it."

Slowly, she walked to the bed and sat in a small metal chair. She took Simone's hand in hers and held it, wanting to feel the warmth of blood flowing through Simone's veins. According to the doctors, soon that blood would cease to flow, soon Simone's skin would turn rigid and cold and her beautiful, lilting voice would be permanently stilled. Gaby shivered. She could feel death hovering like a dance hall romeo, waiting for its turn to waltz with Simone. As if preparing herself for what was to come, Gaby tried to remember how she had felt when her parents had died. It had been so long ago. She had been so young, and besides, she had had Simone to help her get through her grieving. Who would help her grieve for Simone?

"What are you doing here?"

Gaby didn't remember dozing off, but Simone's voice woke her from an uneasy sleep. When she saw the familiar scowl on her aunt's face, she smiled.

"I had a headache and I thought that a nine-hour drive might be just the thing to clear it up."

Simone patted Gaby's cheek and returned her niece's smile.

"I'm glad to hear that. I thought you might have rushed home because some moron told you that any minute, your old Tante Simone is going to die."

Gaby wondered how Simone could say those words so calmly. Inside, her heart swelled and sank, moving like an ocean swept by a strong, unrelenting tide.

"I did speak to Dr. Jordan," she said delicately, deciding to allow Simone to tell her whatever she wanted.

"Well then, you know I have cancer and you know that they can't seem to find it."

"Yes. He told me."

"Did he also tell you that whether they find it or not, and whether they like it or not, I'm going home next week?" Gaby nodded. "I have things to do. First, I'm going to close Tante Simone. Then, I'm going to inventory all the merchandise and have my friend Claude ship it to Garth's Auctions in Worthington. I've been dealing with them for years and I trust them. With the money, I intend to take care of my own medical bills."

Gaby started to protest, but Simone silenced her.

"You have enough problems. You need to begin a new life, not worry about the ending of an old life."

Gaby could no longer control her tears. "I love you," she said. "I don't want you to die."

"I love you too." Simone took her niece's hand to her lips

and kissed it, knowing that at that moment, Gaby was suffering more than she. "Believe me, I don't want to leave you, especially now when you're so lost, but I may not have a choice. I have to get my life in order. And, my darling, so do you."

Saying that, she pressed the button to raise her bed. When she was comfortable, she folded her hands in front of her, pursed her lips in that special way she had, and turned to Gaby, her face determined and bright, devoid of all depression and gloom.

"Now," she said, as if they were sitting in the back of Tante Simone drinking tea and eating pastries, "Tell me about New York."

3

Once Gaby started working at Bergdorf's, she quickly discovered that one of the major drawbacks to lying was that it took a great deal of concentration to remember what she had said to whom. One of the major benefits was that she never had to tell the truth. Whenever her fellow workers asked questions about her private life—and invariably they did—she could lose herself in the simple, uncomplicated persona she had created in Roger Parker's office—Gabrielle Didier, widow. She gave plausible but insubstantial answers, accompanied by a wobbly smile meant to discourage further probing.

Fortunately, the Christmas rush kept everyone too busy for long, involved conversations. Six days a week, eleven hours a day, with barely a half hour off for lunch. The pace was frenetic, especially for someone so inexperienced, but Gaby learned quickly. In no time, she saw that passivity didn't pay. When one worked on commission, the less one sat, the more one earned. By watching other saleswomen she learned to be aggressive in a gracious way, to distinguish between pushing and encouraging, to differentiate between those who were "just looking" and those who were serious buyers. She learned to swallow her natural shyness and approach women who otherwise would have intimidated her. After a few weeks, she even learned how to initiate a spree.

Once a customer had selected something in the designer department which served as Gaby's base, she quickly mentioned seeing the perfect pair of shoes, or a scarf that would pick up one of the colors in a tweed skirt, or a minaudière that would be the supreme complement to an elegant evening gown. Most women who shopped on the fourth floor didn't need Gaby's help. They knew exactly what they wanted and just where to find it. But every now and then, when she found a customer receptive to the idea of a complete ensemble, Gaby would take her from floor to floor, showing her this and that, enticing her to buy as many pieces as she could. If Gaby was successful, the customer left satisfied, Gaby rang up a substantial sale for Bergdorf's, and she chalked up twenty percent of that sale for herself.

Gaby had never worked so hard in her life. The mornings were fine, but around five in the afternoon, her body mutinied. Her mouth protested having to smile continuously and avenged itself by cricking her jaw and drying her lips until they cracked. Her feet rebelled against the abuse she was heaping upon them. They blistered and swelled until her shoes tightened around her flesh like angry clams, squeezing and pinching with relentless force. Her eyes puffed, her stomach knotted, even her bones hurt. At night, she was so exhausted she barely had enough energy to eat and bathe before falling into a stuporous sleep. But by the start of Christmas week, she realized that in a very short time she had accumulated a very respectable reserve.

Her first thought was to use the money to buy wonderful gifts. It was Christmas, after all, and in the past, Christmas had always been a time of sharing and giving. This year, she had only Steven and Simone to give to, but it wasn't how much one gave, she told herself, or how many people one shared with, it was the fact of the sharing that captured the essence of the holiday. Fearing that if she waited even one more day everything would be gone, she took a full lunch hour and went first to the men's department. Using her employee discount, she bought Steven two sweaters, ties, some shirts, and a leather aviator jacket with a fur collar she knew was the hottest item that season. For Simone, she bought a snuggly velour bathrobe, a hand-crocheted shawl, and pink satin mules rimmed with maribou that she knew would simply delight her aunt.

That night, she took her purchases back to her room and placed them in a pile on the bed. For a long time, she stared at them. Her hand reached out and touched the lavender boxes. Her fingers gently caressed the silver ribbons that glittered atop each package. Suddenly, an indescribable feeling of pride washed over her. She had earned the money to pay for these things. *She*, Gabrielle Cocroft Thayer, former financial dependent, former inexperienced, unemployable housewife, had actually worked for, received, and cashed a paycheck!

Exhilaration charged her with an uncommon burst of euphoria. There was no one to hear her and no one to join her, but still Gaby laughed, filling the air with the glorious sound of self-satisfaction. For the first time in a long time, she felt productive, worthy of respect. Like a familiar scent, the feeling surrounded her, teasing her memory, prompting her to recall that once, long ago—when she had believed herself to be a model wife and mother—she had felt the same way.

Yet now the sensation was different, more internalized, less dependent on the approval of others. Before, her accomplishments had never seemed complete until someone remarked about them. A pie, a dinner, a sweater, a needlepoint cushion—no matter how expertly done, until Brian or Steven or her mother-in-law or a neighbor had validated her efforts with a compliment, the quality of the work remained questionable.

Good Lord, Gaby thought, her laughter stilled with the shock of realization, *did I ever do anything for myself? Was I so utterly tied to Brian that I couldn't function without his say-so?*

In response, she recalled the many afternoons she had spent in The Cleveland Museum of Art studying the masterpieces that hung in the huge galleries. She remembered the many mornings when she had driven to local auctions, examining snuff boxes or paperweights to add to her collections, or searching for unusual pieces Simone might want for the shop. She had gone alone, without Brian, and without Brian's permission. But, a small voice countered, it wasn't the same thing. Those outings were diversions, not an application of talent. They were time fillers, not tests of competency.

Frustrated, she rose from the bed and paced the small room. As if seeking assurance that indeed she was an individual with separate thoughts and singular characteristics, Gaby went to the nightstand and picked up the round, pink-enamelled Fabergé clock that had tracked time for her ever since Simone had presented it to her on her sixteenth birthday. She held the clock in both hands as she sat on the bed, protecting it, cherishing it, not only because of its intrinsic value, but also because, in a way, it provided her with a partial definition of who she was.

Perhaps her love of beautiful objects stood as her signature. Thanks to her mother, Simone, and Bernard, she was knowledgeable about French and English antiques and European art and sculpture. As with a dowry, she had come to her marriage already educated in the appreciation of fine things. It was not something she shared with Brian or had learned at his behest or even pursued with his approval. Hardly, she thought bitterly. He had rarely joined her on her cultural excursions. Instead, he minimized them, just as he had minimized her volunteer assignments at the museum and her occasional hints that she might like to take a part-time job assisting the decorative arts curator.

Gaby's euphoria began to dissipate, slowly fading like a delicious daydream that titillates for a moment and then vanishes forever. Quickly, she got up and walked around, her arms crossed, her hands opening and closing as if she were trying to catch whatever happy thoughts might still be floating about the atmosphere. Damn Brian Thayer! It was when his name had popped into her mind that her mood had begun to spoil. Well, she wasn't going to let him get away with that! She didn't have to kowtow to his whims. She didn't have to accede to his wishes. She wasn't his obedient little wife anymore. She had found a job, she had money in her pocket, and soon she would be with her son.

A few days before, Simone had suggested that instead of Gaby's going home for the holiday, she should invite Steven to come to New York. Though Gaby argued, Simone's rebuttal made sense. Since Christmas fell on a Sunday, Gaby would have only one full day off. A round trip to Ohio was really ridiculous. Gaby would be a wreck, too exhausted to enjoy herself while at home, too exhausted to function back at work. As for Simone's holiday celebration, she assured Gaby that she would not be alone. She and her friend Claude had planned a lovely Christmas dinner with some of their old cronies. Not only would she be fine, but in fact she was looking forward to it.

"Besides," Simone had said, "I think it would be a very good idea for you and Steven to spend some time alone."

Once she thought about it, she realized that, as always, Simone was right. It would be wonderful spending Christmas with Steven in New York. Christmas Eve she would take him to dinner in Rockefeller Center so they could enjoy the confetti-colored resplendence of the huge tree and watch the skaters spin and twirl and cut complicated patterns into the ice. Then, they would go to Radio City Music Hall to see the Rockettes. Surely, Steven would like that. Christmas Day, she would take him to the Plaza, where they would indulge in an unbelievably expensive, totally extravagant, wonderfully delicious meal. After, they would tour Fifty-seventh Street. She would show him Bergdorf's and Bendel's and Tiffany's and Rizzoli's and Steuben and all the other opulent stores with which she had become familiar.

It would be such fun, she told herself, jumping off the bed, bounding for the phone. Her hand touched the receiver, but only for a second. As if she had been jolted by an electric shock, she pulled back, trying to control an unexpected wave of fear. She had thought Thanksgiving was going to be fun. She had believed that that holiday was going to be the mortar that would cement her relationship with her son. Instead, Steven had spent all his time with the Thayers. Though she knew her son had been manipulated, nonetheless, she had felt abandoned, discarded in favor of a plumper fowl and the Cleveland Browns.

This was different, she told herself. Another place, another time—Christmas in New York City. Here, they would have a chance to reroute their relationship. They would be removed from the reminders of what had been, spared the pain of looking at the empty chair at the kitchen table, the unused space in the garage, the closet in the bedroom where naked metal hangers rattled against each other like bare branches in a winter storm. With an intensity that surprised her, Gaby realized how much she wanted to avoid Wadsworth and why. New York certainly wasn't home, but by allowing her to taste even modest success, it had done more for her in one month than Wadsworth had done in thirty-seven years. No wonder Simone had suggested inviting

Steven here. Here, she had something to be proud of. Here, the atmosphere was scented with her achievement as a person. There, it reeked of personal failure.

With a resurgence of optimism, she reached for the phone, but again, something prevented her from picking it up. Though it seemed incredible, she suddenly realized that she hadn't spoken to Steven since that Sunday when she had watched him slide into the front seat of Brian's car. Though she had written to him several times, her notes had been cheerful and brief and had said nothing of all the many things she wanted to say. He didn't know Simone was sick. He didn't even know Gaby was in New York. How could he? No one in Wadsworth other than Simone knew where she was. Had he called? Had he tried to find her? Or had he simply assumed that each time he called she had been out? What if he was angry? What would she say? That at first, she had been too depressed and too angry to talk with him? That later, she had been too busy and too exhausted to expend the energy on the explanations she knew he would expect? It didn't really matter because, now, she had no alternative. In a few days, Steven would be flying home. If they were to have their holiday in New York, she had to call him. She had to do it tonight.

As she waited for him to come to the phone, she sat straight-backed on the bed, smoothing her skirt, combing her hair with her fingers, nervously primping as if readying herself for a blind date. Damn Brian Thayer, anyway! If not for him, she wouldn't be experiencing this horrible apprehension; she wouldn't be worrying about winning her son's approval or his love. She could just see him at that Thanksgiving dinner, as assorted Thayers force-fed him as many criticisms of his mother as they could squeeze in between the turkey and the pumpkin pie, while Brian's mistress gloated and swelled with a sense of false superiority. The thought of it thoroughly enraged Gaby. She felt her hand tighten around the receiver. She had remained silent and passive long enough. She might not have fought to keep Brian—and lately she had wondered why she hadn't—but she was not about to relinquish her rights to her son.

"Mom?"

"Steven. How are you, sweetheart?" Apprehension beat its wings inside her chest.

"I'm fine." He sounded impatient. "Where have you been? I've been calling and calling. You're never home."

Was that concern in his voice? Or disapproval? Resentment because he hadn't been able to reach her? Or relief because he had and she was alive and well?

"Actually," she said, wishing to believe the positives. "I haven't been home for almost a month. I'm in New York."

"What are you doing in New York?" He sounded cold, reproving. It made her edgy.

"Working. You are now speaking to a member of the super-elite, terribly chic, Bergdorf Goodman sales force! Are you impressed?"

Instead of applause, there was silence. Gaby tried to dissect the stillness, cutting through the thick distance that separated them, listening for anger, hoping that what she heard was confusion.

"But why?" Steven said. "Why would you take a job in New York when you're supposed to be home?"

Her lips lifted in a shaky smile. She had been terrified to make this call because she had so desperately wanted this young man's approval. Yet the person on the other end of the line was just a fifteen-year-old boy who simply wanted to call and find his mother at home.

"Why? Because I needed the money. Why New York? Because that's the only place I could find a job."

"Why would you need money? Dad gives you a check every month."

"Things aren't quite the way they seem," she said evenly. "I know we should have discussed this months ago, but you were away and I was having a hard time coping and I just never found the right time. This weekend, we'll talk it all out."

Again, a curtain of silence descended.

"I've planned a fabulous weekend for us," she continued, ignoring the implication behind the pause. "I thought it would be a great idea if you came to New York. Then I could show you the sights and take you around and let everyone in the Big Apple see what a handsome son I have!"

Despite her efforts to the contrary, a large, sad lump lodged in her throat. Quickly, as if Steven could see, she closed her eyes, trying to contain the salty rills that streaked her cheeks and dampened her blouse.

"I couldn't get in touch with you." His voice was low, uncertain. "I tried a hundred times, but you were never there."

"Don't tell me you're not going to see me at Christmas, Steven. Don't! I allowed you to spend your entire Thanksgiving vacation with your father and his family, but I am not a candidate for sainthood. You are my son also, and I think I'm entitled to equal time."

There was no mistaking the rage that heated her words. She had sensed, and accurately so, that Brian had overwhelmed Steven, luring him with expensive, elaborate vacation plans with which Gaby would be hard pressed to compete.

"Dad's arranged for us to go skiing in Aspen," he said softly, apologetically.

"I don't care what your father has arranged. Thanks to his arrangements, I spent Thanksgiving by myself." Her voice trembled and then broke. "I shouldn't have to spend Christmas by myself. After all, I'm not totally without family. I do have a son, you know, a son whom I love very much and who I always thought loved me in return."

"I do love you, Mom. Please don't cry."

She heard the remorse in his voice, the guilt, the youthful frustration about not being able to make things right.

"I know I should be generous and magnanimous and send you off with a hearty 'bon voyage,' " she said, trying to temper her resentment, "but I can't do it. I want to be with you."

"I want to be with you too, Mom. But what should I do? What do I tell Dad?"

Gaby bit her tongue, stifling an urge to provide Steven with what she considered to be an appropriate response to Brian's seedy game of one-upmanship.

"Why don't we try to work out some sort of compromise?" she said, responding to the push-pull she heard in his voice.

"Instead of me coming to New York, could you come home?" He sounded cautious, as if he feared that his suggestion would either stoke her rage or revive her tears. "We're supposed to leave for Denver early on the twenty-sixth. We could spend Christmas Eve and Christmas Day together. Just you and me and Tante Simone. Would that be all right?"

Gaby wanted to insist that Steven come here, that he do it her way, but she couldn't do that. She would be insisting in hopes of ruining things for Brian, yet by doing so she would probably make things worse for herself. Besides, this way, when she told Steven about Simone, it would be easier. He would be able to see her for himself. He would be able to spend some time with her, so that after, he wouldn't have any unnecessary guilt to deal with.

"You leave school on Thursday. I wouldn't be able to get to Wadsworth until Saturday night. The house has been locked up for a month. There's not so much as a slice of bread in the pantry."

"I'll take care of everything," Steven said in a burst of enthusiasm. "You just call me when you get your ticket, tell me your flight number, and I'll pick you up at the airport. How's that?"

"Great!" she said, recognizing that often compromise was the shortest road to victory. "I'll be there with bells on! Maybe I'll add some mistletoe and tinsel. Maybe even a star in my hair. What do you think?"

"I think you're terrific and I can't wait to see you," he said, his voice flecked with laughter and genuine affection.

It was only for a second, but suddenly Gaby saw flashes of Steven as a baby, a toddler, a bandaged, knee-scraped Little Leaguer, a gawky adolescent.

"I *know* you're terrific," she said. "I'll be counting the minutes until Saturday."

Steven felt the pride and the love behind her words, and he too was beset by memories. He saw a woman in sneakers and a baseball hat, cheerleading from the bleachers, screaming and yelling with every ball he pitched, every swing of his bat. He saw a woman showing a den of Cub Scouts how to make papier-maché puppets, gritting her teeth whenever the floury paste fell on the floor or stuck to the walls. He saw a woman tutoring him day after day, sweating out every homework assignment, every test, as if it were her own Day of Judgment. He saw a woman teaching him to dance, setting up foot patterns for him to follow, ignoring his awkwardness, going over steps again and again and again, until he felt a little less foolish and a little more secure. He forgot how betrayed he had felt when he learned that she and Brian were separating, how furious he had been with her for allowing it to happen, how disappointed he had been when she couldn't, or wouldn't, effect a reconciliation. At that moment, all he recalled was the love and the patience and the devotion she had lavished on him over the years. At that moment, all he felt was that he was damned lucky to have a woman like Gaby as his mother.

When Steven James Thayer was conceived, the powers that be must have known that he would be an only child. Not only did he combine the best traits of both parents, but it seemed as if his inheritance had been equally divided. His height and musculature resembled his father's, while his dark coloring and planed facial structure clearly spoke of a genetic donation from his mother. He had Brian's athletic ability, Gaby's artistic eye; Brian's quick mind, Gaby's quick wit. He was ambitious like the Thayers, hardworking like the Cocrofts. In the fall, when Brian preached the rough-and-tumble grit-and-grovel gospel of the football field, Steven proved faithful to his father by displaying his skill as a quarterback. In the spring, when Gaby sermonized about her preference for the play-by-play interplay of the baseball diamond, he converted to blazing fastballs, dipping sliders, and baffling change-ups. There was little Steven did, other than struggle with schoolwork, that was not a tremendous source of pride for his parents. And there was little they did that was not a source of pride for him, which was probably why he still couldn't understand or accept the failure of their marriage.

When Gaby had first told him that she and his father had separated, Steven had listened, but the words had never gone beyond his ears. He blocked. He resisted. He rejected. He denied. He did everything except accuse his mother of madness. But madness he believed it was. How could his father have walked out on his mother? How could he not love her anymore? How could she have let him go? How could she have let it happen? Gaby tried to account for the split, but, she had said with unashamed candor, she didn't really understand all the whys herself. Naturally, it was difficult to explain them to him.

For Steven, the timing had been particularly poor. Though he had started boarding school the year before, it was still strange living away from home, sharing a room, eating in a huge cafeteria-like dining room. It was hard adding special tutorial sessions to an already rigorous schedule of courses. He needed support. He needed encouragement. He needed the security familiarity provides. He needed his parents to supply him with an abundance of love and faith in his ultimate success. Instead, the roles had reversed, and now it seemed as if his parents needed all those things from him.

When he arrived in Wadsworth and told Brian of his plans to spend Christmas with Gaby, it was as if he had sounded a battle cry. Thayers burst from the bushes, descending on him with anguished pleas that he not ruin the family's Christmas by denying them his presence. His grandmother, Ethel, led the attack, with his grandfather, Wally, marching close behind. To listen to them, one would think that the existence of Christmas itself was at stake. If he accepted their invitation, the world would be permitted to celebrate Christmas. If he denied them, the world would have to do without.

At his age, it was difficult for Steven to sound emphatic about serious issues, but the phone call with Gaby had had long-reaching effects. He fought the Thayers valiantly, refusing to surrender to their demands. He would miss them, he said, but this holiday he was spending with his mother and his great-aunt. It vexed him that none of them seemed to understand or accept the rightness of that decision, that none of them seemed to remember that he had spent the last holiday exclusively with them, especially his father, who insisted on taking this as a personal rejection.

As he waited for Gaby's plane to land, Steven cursed the aberration that had infected his existence. He hated the fact that his parents were getting divorced. He hated the fact that his mother was living in New York and his father was living with another woman. But most of all, he hated the fact that all of this was happening to him.

"Merry Christmas, ho ho ho!"

Gaby's arms were around him before he even had a chance to look at her.

"Did you get taller or did I get shorter?" she said, admiring her progeny, her face illuminated by a broad grin. "One thing's for sure. If you get any handsomer, I'll have to hire the National Guard to keep the girls from jumping all over you."

Steven blushed, irked that he would have such an adolescent reaction at a time when he was trying so very hard to behave like an adult.

"You're looking pretty snappy yourself," he said, recovering, noticing that her hair seemed fluffier and that she was wearing more makeup than he ever remembered her wearing.

"Thank you, kind sir."

She curtsied gracefully.

"Can I take those?" he asked, reaching for the two well-packed shopping bags she had carried off the plane.

"You may."

She handed him her bundles and then linked her arm through his and started toward the baggage pickup. As they walked, Steven noted two other changes in his mother. The first disturbed him. She was very thin. Despite the heavy woolen coat she wore, he could see that her skirt hung loosely on her hips, not at her waist the way it was supposed to. She had always been on the slight side, but when he saw how pronounced her cheekbones had become and felt how spindly her arms were, he began to wonder if New York was the Shangri-la she had made it out to be.

The second change was more subtle, but it too disturbed him because it represented a deliberate, conscious break with the past. For as long as he could remember, Gaby had been a Shalimar woman. He had never known her to use any other fragrance. In fact, when he thought about it, he realized that at some point he had begun to believe that the heavy, vanilla-scented essence was part of his mother's very being, not just something she dabbed on behind her ears or splashed on her skin after a bath. Tonight, however, her scent was different. Was it something she had selected for herself? Or had it been a gift from a gentleman?

"How'd you get here?" Gaby asked, keeping her eye on the large hole in the wall that spit luggage onto the snaking rubber treadmill.

"I hired a taxi to pick me up, wait outside while I picked you up, and then take us home."

She turned, looked at him, and patted his cheek affectionately.

"That sounds awfully nice. Thank you." She kissed him, and again he blushed.

"I went shopping, too," he said, with shy pride. "I bought everything I thought we'd need to make a holiday dinner."

"Great! We'll start first thing in the morning!"

She couldn't stop staring at him. He looked so grown-up, and yet there were moments, like now, when the little boy sneaked out and she became conscious of the fragility of the teen-aged personality.

"I probably forgot something major," he said, suddenly panicked that he might have ruined their vacation together before it even began. "What if I did? The stores are all closed by now and for sure, they won't be open tomorrow."

Gaby reached out and grabbed her suitcase, pulling it off the treadmill before it could take another tour of the airport. Steven was too distracted to notice her dragging it toward the exit. He simply tagged along behind, checking items off a mental shopping list.

"Did you buy a turkey?"

Steven nodded.

"Apples?"

He nodded again.

"Bread?"

"Yes. I got sweet potatoes and cranberries and marshmallows too."

Gaby stopped, put down her suitcase, took the shopping bags from him, placed her hands on his shoulders, and with a furrowed brow, spoke in a low, solemn voice.

"You were given a task to do and you have performed it well. In recognition of your princely effort, I dub thee Sir Steven, lord of the supermarket and keeper of the kitchen." She kissed him on both cheeks, handed him the suitcase, grabbed the two shopping bags, and started toward the door. "Now get me to my castle before I have thee beheaded!"

As she and Steven drove up to the French Normandy house they had called home for more than ten years, Gaby realized how grateful she was for the cover of darkness. Without it, she would be forced to confront the large white pine that should have been ablaze with Technicolor lights; and the stone planters flanking the front steps that should have been emptied of lifeless, fall chrysanthemums weeks ago and refilled with sturdy, winterproof yews; and the thick, richly varnished door that should have been outfitted with a red-bowed wreath of fresh evergreens. Gaby found it easier to face the barren landscape at night. Veiled in shadows, it shouted fewer accusations of neglect, produced fewer feelings of guilt.

Why, she wondered, did holidays inspire the creation of so many minuscule habits, so many tiny bits of tradition? Why did people become addicted to the minutiae of holidays, elevating customs like stringing popcorn, or serving creamed onions, or putting candles in the window, to the level of religious ritual?

Ever since Gaby had hung up the phone after her first conversation with Steven, she had set about convincing herself that holidays could be celebrated in many ways, that one did not have to repeat the same things over and over again, year in and year out. Where was it written that Christmas was not Christmas without Ethel Thayer's cranberry relish or Aunt Effie's mince pie? Who had decreed that a tree had to stand six feet tall and be decorated with no less than a hundred and fifty ornaments?

By the time Gaby had boarded the plane for Cleveland, she had actually talked herself into believing that she was emotionally prepared for this homecoming. Yet now, seconds after her arrival, she admitted that she had completely underestimated the insidiousness of her own routines. She missed seeing her delicately curved staircase dressed in its luxurious balsam fir boa. It pained her to see her prized Louis XV console table minus its welcoming bowl of cloved oranges, apples, and chestnuts. Even the ornately carved and gilded mirror that hung above the console looked bare and ordinary without its regal garland of holly sprigs and evergreen boughs.

If those small absences could generate such potent reactions, she asked herself, how was she ever going to deal with the fact that there would be no elaborately decorated spruce holding court in the corner of the living room; no handmade stockings dangling from the white stone mantelpiece; no lavishly wrapped presents cluttering up the flat, pastel-patterned dhurrie rug; no freshly cut logs stacked neatly next to the fireplace.

She held her breath when Steven turned on the lights. Her eyes fixed immediately on the spot where the tree normally stood. It was empty, just as she had expected. Her stomach knotted, but before a single tear could fall, she noticed the skirted table in front of the window. In the center was a short, squat, slightly worse for wear spruce done up as only a fifteen-year-old boy in a hurry could do. Five-and-dime ornaments drooped at the ends of wobbly branches. Blue lights flickered on and off like a garish neon sign. Tinsel hung in uneven silvery bunches, looking like tinfoil ponytails designed for a chorus line of miniskirted Barbie dolls. A clear plastic star with gold-glittered points perched precariously atop the tree and listed to one side like a drunken flagpole sitter.

"It's the most beautiful tree I've ever seen," Gaby whispered, her voice softened with awe at the devotion that had prompted such effort.

"I know it's not the way you would have done it," Steven said, looking down at the carpet. "I mean, it's kind of flashy and cheap looking, but I went all over and, believe me, there wasn't a whole lot left."

Gaby touched one of the red glass balls, causing it to bob back and forth. It bumped the ornament next to it with a light, tinkling sound that broke through the awkwardness that hovered over her and her son. She kissed Steven and smiled.

"It's not flashy at all," she said. "It's rococo and I love it!"

Steven grinned at his mother's approval as if the wish he had made over his birthday candles had just come true.

"Now," Gaby said, taking off her coat, hanging it in the hall closet, and then returning to the living room, suitcase in tow. "You and I don't have much time to be together. If we don't get this weekend rolling, it's going to be over before it ever began!"

She unlocked the huge bag, lifted the top, and rummaged through her clothes, taking out small boxes and bags Steven suddenly recognized as hot chocolate, tea, and a variety of cookies.

"Goodies from the Big Apple," she said proudly. Steven reached for a bag that exuded a definite chocolate-chip aroma, but Gaby pulled it away from him. "Not until you make a fire."

"That's torture." Steven groaned with adolescent pique. Gaby remained unmoved.

"Maybe so," she said, "but we're going to do this right, my boy, or we're not going to do it at all." She collected all the bags and boxes, balanced them as best she could, and started for the kitchen. "I'll handle the hot chocolate. You take care of the fire."

Before long, Steven and Gaby were lounging before a roaring fire, each pajamaed and robed, and sipping the sweet white foam floating atop their cocoa, licking marshmallow goo off their fingertips, and laughing. Without establishing any ground rules, they had restricted themselves to matters relevant only to the two of them, relegating anything that included Brian to the realm of the unspoken. They retrieved pleasant memories and told amusing stories—Steven of pranks he and his friends had pulled at school, Gaby of the trials and tribulations of working at Bergdorf's.

By the time they retired, a cord which had been severed had been retied. Both of them had returned to this house needy and confused, but as the hours passed, they had reached across the strange desolation of their current circumstance and found familiar ground. A marriage had dissolved, and soon Gaby and Brian would no longer be husband and wife. Yet despite the changes that rift had caused, despite the alienation, the just-below-the-surface anger and the doubt, no paper, no decree, no judge, no lawyer, could ever totally divorce a mother from her son.

Christmas Day was better than Gaby had hoped. She roused Steven early, demanding that they restoke the fire and open their gifts. He loved both his new sweaters and refused to select a favorite. He tried to simulate the same level of enthusiasm for the ties and shirts Gaby had brought him, but his performance lacked luster. When he opened the box with the leather bomber jacket, however, his eyes opened so wide, Gaby feared they might fall out. Instantly, he bounded to his feet and slipped the jacket on over his pajamas, pulling the collar up, putting it down, zipping, unzipping, zipping halfway, zipping all the way, running to the mirror in the hall, returning to the living room to ask Gaby's opinion on his latest style variation.

Finally, he settled himself and presented Gaby with her gifts. The first was an illustrated biography of Gaby's favorite eighteenth-century artist, François Boucher. The second was a bottle of Shalimar eau de cologne. He watched as she unwrapped the box. Her eyes darkened, but he was too young to understand how closely associated a scent can become with an emotion or a personality. Brian had given Gaby Shalimar the first Christmas of their courtship. She was seventeen years old and a senior in high school. He had told her that she was his girl and had asked her to go steady. She had agreed, and until that horrible day last September when he told her he didn't love her anymore, she had never worn any other scent.

"I noticed you weren't wearing Shalimar last night," Steven said, watching her face carefully, afraid of saying something that might make her cry. "I can take it back if you don't like it anymore."

"It's not that I don't like it," Gaby said carefully, unwilling to offend him, "I wanted to try something new for a change."

Steven heard the hesitation in her voice. Was the other perfume a gift from an admirer? Had she gone to New York to be with another man? If not, had she met someone there who had convinced her to stay and not return home to Ohio? Though he found it embarrassing to watch his father moon over Pamela, on some semiconscious level he had come to accept their relationship. It was different where Gaby was concerned. She was his mother. She was supposed to remain pure and unsullied by affairs of the flesh. Much as he wanted to cling to that fantasy, he decided that he would listen and wait and, if the opportunity presented itself, come right out and ask if she had a lover.

Gaby's third present was a charming brooch with an enameled oval miniature of two plump, winged cherubs that opened into a locket.

"Steven, this is exquisite." Gaby recognized the piece as late nineteenth century, flawed, but still something that would have cost more money than Steven's allowance permitted.

Steven watched as she examined the piece.

"I sold my watch," he said quickly, not wanting to add that Tante Simone had found the brooch for him and probably had lied about the price.

"The one your grandparents gave you?" She was stunned. She thought he loved that watch.

"It didn't really keep great time, and none of the other kids at school wear things that glitzy. Everyone's into Swatches."

Gaby smiled at the thought of Ethel Thayer's face if and when Steven told her he had pawned a solid gold watch in favor of a plastic-banded timepiece with orange hands, glow-in-the-dark numerals, and a loud tick-tock.

"Besides, I wanted to get you something special."

"This is certainly special," she said, running her fingers over the smooth enamel.

Gaby opened the locket, examining the hinge and the two open spaces meant for pictures.

"It's in excellent condition," she said, looking up at him and smiling.

Steven felt terrific.

"You're supposed to put in pictures of your loved ones," he said, emphasizing the last two words.

Gaby thought he was referring to Brian, that he was trying in a not-so-subtle way to raise the subject of reconciliation. It never dawned on her that he was asking her if she had another man in her life.

"There's space for two pictures." He was getting nervous. She appeared to be considering what she was going to say, measuring her words. Was she trying to find a way to tell him about her lover? Was she planning on getting married again?

"Then I'll put a picture of you on both sides," she said quietly, unwilling to let Brian intrude on this day, unaware that Brian had never been introduced into the conversation. "After all, you're my pride and joy, and, to me, each of those reasons rates a photograph."

"Whew! Thank goodness your rating system doesn't include cooking," Steven said, relief pushing a broad grin onto his face. "Pride and joy I can handle. It's chestnut stuffing that freaks me out."

"Speaking of which," Gaby said, rising and offering a hand to her son, "if we don't hit the kitchen right now, this is going to be a midnight supper."

They worked all afternoon, interrupted only once when Claude brought Simone by on their way to Cleveland. Gaby had told Steven that Simone was ill. She hadn't wanted to tell him how ill, but once Steven had seen his great-aunt, the subject became unavoidable. She sounded the same, sprightly and vivacious. She was as loving and demonstrative as always, hugging Steven, kissing him, holding his hand the entire time she was there. But she had lost so much weight that her skin hung on her bones, altering her appearance, making her look like a wax figure melting in the sun.

"Is Tante Simone dying?" he asked after they had gone.

"Yes."

As much as it pained Steven to hear that, it pained Gaby to say it. She had hoped that the doctors had been wrong, that when she saw Simone this time, she would have improved, that her body would have repulsed the savage illness that was consuming her from within. Instead, where once Simone had been full figured and robust, now she was frail and spindly. Not only did she suddenly look her age, but at certain moments, when her jaw relaxed or her head tilted a particular way, she appeared so many years older that the notion of death no longer seemed premature. Gaby couldn't decide whether God had covered Simone's face with this aged mask as a cruel hoax or an act of kindness. Either way, the facts remained the same: death was inevitable and Tante Simone's death was imminent.

"Should she be living alone?" Steven asked.

"That's how she wants it, and for now it's okay."

"For now?"

"Dr. Jordan has told me that soon Tante Simone is going to be too weak to care for herself."

"Then you'll have to move back from New York and take care of her."

Steven was embarrassed by the hopefulness in his voice, but not by the optimism of his thoughts. He adored Simone and certainly didn't want her to die, but maybe her illness would provide a reason for his mother to return home. If Gaby were home and in the same town as Brian, drawn together by the impending death of Simone, perhaps they would find each other again.

"I've suggested that to both Simone and Dr. Jordan," Gaby said, knowing what was running through her son's mind. "Simone won't hear of it, and her doctors say she's going to need professional medical care. I've already looked into a nursing home in Lakewood."

Steven grimaced and shook his head.

"No! Ugh! You can't put her in there! The thought of Tante Simone becoming one of those dribbling old people who line up in wheelchairs to watch game shows gives me the willies."

"I'm not crazy about the idea either, but I won't allow her to be in pain or uncomfortable for even a moment."

Steven heard the tightness in his mother's voice. He saw the moisture gathering in her eyes. Quickly, he changed tracks, switching from adolescent daydreams to adult reality.

"What about the shop? What about her house? How is she going to pay for all this? Does she have any money put away?"

Gaby laughed. Those questions were pure Thayerisms.

"Not really. You know Tante Simone better than that! She could never hold on to money. Whenever she had a few dollars, she spent it on a *bureau plat* she just couldn't resist, or a piece of jewelry she simply had to have."

"Doesn't she have any investments?"

"She's always felt that antiques were a better investment than stocks or bonds, and that the pleasure she derived from buying and selling them was greater than anything bank dividends could do for her."

"She's not strong enough to work anymore," Steven said, sadly, concerned about his aunt, worried about his mother, thoroughly disgusted with the role of grown-up.

"She's closing the shop at the end of the month. Other than a few special pieces, she's arranged for everything to be auctioned off. She thinks the proceeds will take care of her medical bills."

"Will they?"

Gaby smiled. "Most of them."

Why bother him with the truth? Why tell him that she had already cleaned out her small savings account to pay for the diagnostic tests Dr. Jordan had run? Why tell him the enormous costs of housing a patient in the hospital wing of a nursing home? Why tell him about the limitations of Medicaid and Medicare? Why tell him that Simone's sale would cover only her current bills, but not what was to come? He was young. Simone was not his responsibility. She was Gaby's, and somehow Gaby would take care of her.

"Meantime," she said, rising and heading for the kitchen. "Simone's going to have a gargantuan feast and you and I are going to have peanut butter and jelly sandwiches if we don't get to work. On your feet!"

By six o'clock, dinner was served. They ate heartily, enjoying the food almost as much as they had enjoyed one another's company during the preparation. For Gaby, it was more than she had hoped for. In a way, they had redefined Christmas, taking from the past, adjusting it to the present, maybe even laying groundwork for the future. Yes, there had been uncomfortable moments—when they went to sit in the dining room and Steven avoided taking Brian's seat at the head of the table, and when Steven realized that Simone might never get to use his Christmas gift, a beach robe for her annual *vacances* in Antibes, and when Steven had come in to wake Gaby the next morning and found her sleeping on the chaise instead of in her bed. But they had dealt with their discomfort. All in all, Gaby judged this to be the best Christmas she had ever had.

She told that to Steven as they waited for the taxicab that would take her to the airport and back to New York.

"I loved it too." His eyes grew dark and for an instant, his mouth trembled. "I've missed you, Mom."

Gaby took his face in her hands and gently kissed him.

"I've missed you too, darling. But I'm still going to call you twice a week and I'm still going to come visit. And you're going to visit me in New York. We're going to see a lot of each other, I promise."

His smile was shaky, tentative, as if he wasn't sure how he felt about what she said. Was it good news or bad news?

"I miss having a family," he blurted out, unable to contain his frustration any longer. "I don't want to visit you in New York. I want you to stay here. I want things to be the way they were before, the way they're supposed to be. I want you and Daddy to live together again."

Gaby had been waiting for this. Yet still, she was unprepared for the grief in her son's voice, the desperation in his eyes.

"Things can't be the way they were," she said quietly. "Your father doesn't want to live with me."

"What did you do to make him leave?"

Gaby was stung by his words. She thought they had grown so close. What had happened to make him turn on her?

"I didn't do anything." She felt defensive, compelled to tell the truth, ashamed at what the truth was. "He doesn't love me. He loves someone else."

"Then you must have done something wrong!" Steven's voice rose, crackling with outrage. "It's all your fault!"

Gaby's temper flared. She had been abused by the father. She refused to be attacked by the son.

"My fault?" she said, her voice growing shrill. "You think this divorce is my fault? Well, if you're old enough to make accusations, young man, then I guess you're old enough to hear the facts." She paused, clearly debating about what she would say, what she would keep secret. "I don't know what I did wrong. What I do know is that I wasn't unfaithful. I wasn't sleeping with someone else and then coming home to your father. I wasn't lying and cheating and plotting. I was here, waiting for him like the dutiful little wife that he demanded I be. He said he left me because he finds that twenty-five-year-old infant exciting. Well, so be it. I'm not twenty-five anymore. I'm thirty-seven. For sixteen years I did his bidding, and where did it get me? Struggling to keep my head above water financially, struggling to repair my shattered ego, and struggling to explain something I don't understand to my son." Her eyes welled with tears, but she refused to cry in front of Steven. "I know this hurts you, and for that I'm sorry, but I have to do what I have to do. I need a job, and the only place I could find work was in New York."

Steven felt wretched. He hadn't meant to uncork such a tirade. He hadn't meant to chastise or judge. He had spoken out of disappointment and discontent. He had spoken out of frustration.

"I'm the one who should apologize," he said, stumbling over his words, groping to find the right ones. "I have no right to blame you. It's just . . . well . . . I wanted things to be the way they were."

Gaby took him in her arms and, despite his size, hugged him the way she had when he was a toddler.

"One thing will always remain the same, Steven, and that is that I love you. Nothing can change that." She held him at arm's length, peering deep into his eyes. "We're just going to have to find new ways to enjoy each other, like we did this weekend. I don't know about you, but I had a wonderful time."

"So did I," he said with a shy smile. "Maybe that's what makes me so sad. I'm not sure we'll ever do this again."

"Why do you say that?"

"Because I think you hate this house."

"I admit, it's hard for me to be here. I know there are a lot of good memories inside these rooms, but right now they're overshadowed by the bad memories." She considered elaborating, but decided against it. It was all right for her to hate Brian. It was not right for her to influence Steven to dislike his father. "I have to work things out. I have to sort out my feelings. It's going to take time, but maybe once I get my head together, I'll feel more comfortable. Do you understand?"

Steven nodded. A car pulled up outside the house. The taxi driver honked his horn. Gaby turned. Steven's face fell.

"I'm afraid for you to go," he said. "I'm afraid you'll never come back."

"This is my house," she reminded him gently.

"This is your home!" he insisted.

Gaby longed to give him what he wanted. Instead, she gave him the truth.

"Right now I don't have a home," she said.

4

Transition can be a harrowing voyage marked by numerous false starts and dead ends. For Gaby, life had become a schizophrenic tale of two cities, divided loyalties, split responsibilities, and personal confusion. Habit and predictability had been replaced by chaos and uncertainty. Most of the time, there were no constants, nothing she could count on except the fact that day would turn into night and, if she survived the darkness, daylight would come again.

She returned to New York after her brief Christmas at home, and suddenly, typically, as if someone had thrown a switch, everything was shifted into reverse. What had been positive was now negative. What had been upbeat and exhilarating was now monotonous and depressing. At the store, instead of high-spirited patrons buying wonderful gifts, disgruntled customers returned incorrect sizes and unflattering colors. Displays that had been visual works of art had been disassembled by the grabbing hands of last-minute shoppers, leaving ragtag piles that looked as if they belonged on a Lower East Side pushcart, not a Bergdorf Goodman countertop. Even the mood of the city had shifted. Instead of the accelerated pitch that had charged the atmosphere only a few days before, people on the street appeared to be suffering from postholiday letdown, moving at a slower, more lethargic pace, as if they were exhausted from the entire process of Christmas and were conserving fuel so they could get through New Year's.

Gaby got through, eating takeout Chinese food and watching the crowd at Times Square on TV; but after, she found herself jumping from one mood to another, unable to concentrate on any one thing for very long. She wavered between periods of hope and spells of helplessness, each triggered by how much money she had in her pocket at the time. Though she wanted to change hotels or move into a studio apartment, she couldn't afford to do either. Part of her alimony and earnings maintained the house in Wadsworth, part went into a fund for Simone's care, and the rest supported Gaby's life in New York, which she discovered was frightfully expensive, no matter how frugal she was. Already, she had begun to fall behind.

Once the Christmas rush was over, her work week was cut back to five days instead of six. Plus, January was the slowest selling month of the year. Her co-workers assured her that business would pick up in February, but Gaby couldn't afford to wait until then. Simone was weakening, and within a matter of weeks it would be impossible for her to continue living alone. Gaby was desperate for money, and she knew of only one way to get it.

On her days off, she had amused herself by tracking down the various antiques districts in the city, as well as attending an occasional auction. Though Gaby had always been more of a collector than an investor, Simone had taught her that antiques were friends in need. When she had returned to New York after her weekend with Steven, she had brought much of her paperweight collection with her. Perhaps subconsciously, she had known that sooner or later those precious pieces of glass would become vital to her survival. Though she would have preferred parting with her treasures later, she selected one, wrapped it carefully, hopped on a bus, and went down to Twelfth Street, just off Broadway.

The shop was small and dark, as were most of them in the neighborhood, but she had visited this place several times, cataloguing the inventory. Though the furniture left a lot to be desired—more mediocre reproductions than quality originals—the collection of clocks and glass was superlative. When she walked in, the owner, an unimposing man in a rumpled cardigan and corduroy slacks, was preoccupied with a woman who couldn't seem to make up her mind between two tip-and-turn tables. Gaby busied herself with a clock in the front of the shop, but couldn't help overhearing the discussion in the back.

"This one looks thicker, more substantial," the woman said, pointing to the urn-shaped pedestal of the table on her right.

"You don't buy antiques because they're thick," the man replied patiently, unable to keep a hint of annoyance out of his voice. "You buy them because they're beautiful. This," he said, touching the table on the woman's left, "is just as substantial, but far more handsome."

Gaby had to agree. The one the owner preferred had been here the last time she browsed. She recalled the tag saying it had been crafted in Philadelphia in the late eighteenth century. The top, carved from a single piece of lavishly grained mahogany, had a graceful, piecrust scalloped edge. The pedestal was refined and well turned, with cabriole legs ending in delicate ankles and claw-and-ball feet. Though she couldn't see it clearly from her vantage point, she could tell that the proportions of the table the woman preferred were off. The circular dish top was too thin for the stumpy legs and plump pedestal on which it sat. The color appeared too dark to display sufficient grain, and the feet were not as crisp as they should have been. Still, the woman persisted.

The owner, finally accepting the futility of the debate, opted to make a sale rather than prove a point. He bargained just long enough for the customer to feel she had made a good deal, took her check, wrapped the table in cushioned paper, and helped her to her car. When he returned, he gladly devoted himself to Gaby.

"What can I do for you?" he asked, mopping his brow and then using his handkerchief to dust the clock Gaby had been examining. "Are you interested in this particular piece? It's a Second Empire bronze mantel clock, in excellent condition. It has a silvered dial, as you can see, and an outside count wheel. What I love about it most is the pendulum." He drew her eye to a small gilded cherub on a chain-link swing, pushing it gently, as one would a toddler in the park.

"I'm not here to buy," Gaby said, reluctantly interrupting his sales pitch. The disappointment on his face was immediate. "I'm here to sell you something."

"It must be smaller than a breadbox because you're not carrying anything." He smiled, but only briefly. Obviously, he reserved his charm for buyers, not sellers.

Gaby took the paperweight out of her bag, unfolded the piece of velvet she had wrapped it in, and placed them both on the sideboard next to the clock. Without any change of expression, the man reached into his pocket, took out a small flashlight, and began to study the piece. As he did, Gaby reviewed a few facts in preparation for the negotiation she hoped would ensue. In order to decide on a reasonable opening price, she had considered the valuations he had placed on equivalent paperweights in his stock, as well as the prices of similar items recently sold at auction.

"It's nice," he said, putting it down, making it clear that no attachment had been formed between himself and the object. "What do you want for it?"

Gaby picked up the paperweight and stared at it lovingly. Inside a dome of clear Baccarat glass, a delicate flower blossomed. Six vermillion petals cupped five smaller white petals, the whole growing from a sinuous green stalk bursting with slender leaves.

"Thirty-five hundred dollars," she said, returning the paperweight to the sideboard.

The man shook his head and clucked his tongue.

"You're way off. Weights like this don't fetch as much as they used to. I'll give you a thousand."

If he thought he had another uninformed housewife in front of him, he was mistaken.

"You'll give me a thousand and then you'll turn around and sell it for four. That's a rather hefty profit." She picked up the weight again and wiped it with the velvet cloth. "You had two here a few weeks ago that had surface wear at the base and yet you priced them in the twenty-five-hundred-dollar range. This piece is perfect."

"Okay. Fifteen hundred."

"That was the low estimate on a comparable lot last month at Castleton's." Slowly, she began to wrap the velvet around her crystal treasure. "The least I'll accept is the high estimate. Two thousand dollars. Cash."

"Okay," the man said, relieving her of the paperweight with an eager hand and a toothy grin. "It's a fair price for both of us. Wait here and I'll bring you your money."

Gaby left the store feeling very proud of herself. As she strolled down Twelfth Street, however, she became nervous about having so much money on her. She found a coffee shop, ducked into the ladies' room, and separated the bills into several packets. She stuck one inside her bra, another in her shoe, a third in a zippered compartment in her pocketbook, and the fourth in her wallet. After celebrating her triumph with a quick cup of scalded coffee that she wished had been champagne, she left, continuing down Twelfth. Just before the corner of Sixth Avenue, she passed a stone building with a large banner billowing in the wind—the New School.

Inside the lobby, she noticed a card table with a stack of catalogues on it and a young woman seated behind it, answering questions and directing people to various elevators and doors. Trying to remain as unobtrusive as possible, Gaby walked in, took a catalogue from the table, and found a seat on a wide leather bench near the front window. As she flipped through the pages, it occurred to her that it might be fun to take a course here. It would fill up some of her empty evenings as well as giving her something to think about other than her perpetual financial crisis.

Real estate. Computer technology. Fund-raising. Effective business writing.

I should sign up for all of them, she thought wryly, still turning pages, beginning to lose interest.

Antiques: the Business of Beautiful Things.
(12 sessions) Armand Lafitte and guest lecturers. How does one determine value? How does one go from being a collector to a dealer? What do you have to know about a piece when you're buying? What do you have to know when you're selling?

For months, she had been bogged down by the sameness of working all day, being alone every night, and thinking about nothing other than herself and how she was going to pay for Simone's care. Though she hated to admit it, she knew that without movement and change, even the most beautiful pool of water grew stagnant. Looking through that catalogue, seeing how much it had to offer, she felt stale, unchallenged. This course, however, struck a chord that excited her. Without a second's hesitation, she filled out the application, took the registration fee out of the secret cache in her wallet, and walked over to the young woman at the card table to find out where and how to sign up.

As she left the school and waited for an uptown bus, she debated with herself. Was she throwing out money? Was she behaving foolishly? Perhaps. But at that moment, that class seemed more like a lifeline than an indulgence. She needed to be exposed to fresh possibilities, to walk through newly opened doors. She needed to look at herself in a different mirror, one that reflected more than just a rejected woman struggling to make ends meet. She didn't expect miracles, but she did hope that Monsieur Armand Lafitte would do or say something in his twelve sessions that would change her perspective.

He did more than that. He changed her life.

The class was an interesting mélange of character types. There were several well-to-do suburban women dressed in their coming-into-the-city suits, some borough dwellers with a less casual approach to fashion, a few representatives of the Greenwich Village school of inventive chic, two lower-level Wall Street men with polyester ties and synthetic accents, several decorators-in-training, and a sampling of female junior executives and administrative assistants who were there for the same reason Gaby was—self-improvement.

The first thing Gaby noticed about Armand Lafitte was his eyes. Dark and hooded, they moved like a rifle sight, panning the room slowly, finding a target, then zeroing in and focusing with a steady, unwavering stare. He was a dignified man, about five foot ten, with thick silvered hair and a rounded face that dimpled when he smiled. He dressed with Gallic savoir faire, his double-breasted navy pinstripe suit highlighting broad shoulders and a lean middle. Gaby estimated his age to be early fifties.

"Good evening and welcome to Antiques, the Business of Beautiful Things. I am Armand Lafitte. I am the third generation of Parisian *antiquaires* and currently run the New York branch of my family's business from a shop on Seventy-seventh Street and Madison Avenue. I was born and raised in Paris, educated at the Sorbonne, and apprenticed at the Louvre. I am teaching this course because I have a deep passion for fine furnishings and accessories, especially those which, like me, have a French accent.''

He smiled, but purely as a means of punctuation.

"In my mind, we are all heirs to history. Antiques are our bequests, our connection with those who went before. They tell us how our ancestors functioned, how they dressed, how they governed, how they viewed each other, how the world treated them, and how they treated the world.''

He paused, allowing his words to take effect. Gaby was mesmerized. Listening to him talk about antiques, she felt as if she had met a soulmate. It reminded her of when she was a little girl and she and her parents and Tante Simone had visited her Oncle Bernard's shop on the rue des Saints-Pères. All of them would sit upstairs, crowded around an old stove, talking for hours about Bernard's latest acquisition, his latest sale. They all but ignored Gaby, but she never minded. She was fascinated by the depth of their knowledge, enthralled by the height of their enthusiasm. It reminded her also of the afternoons she had spent in Simone's shop, being tutored over a cup of tea and freshly baked *tuiles*. She hadn't experienced that level of intellectual excitement in years. Not until Armand Lafitte.

"I adhere to the simple philosophy of that great English poet and craftsman William Morris,'' Lafitte was saying. "He once said, 'Have nothing in your house, except what you know to be useful or believe to be beautiful.' In this class, we shall learn how to make our love of beautiful things useful.''

He passed out a mimeographed syllabus detailing how each session would be spent. Several classes were to be held at the New School with Lafitte lecturing on how one becomes a dealer or a more sophisticated collector. Other classes, meant to provide an overview, were scattered throughout the city—the Metropolitan Museum of Art, several antiques shops, a rug and tapestry dealer's showroom, Castleton's, and a store specializing in porcelain.

Once everyone had had time to look over the schedule, he asked that each person give his or her name and the reason for taking this class. As Gaby listened to the others, she began to get nervous. What would she say? That she had signed up because she was lost; because without her consent, her life was changing and if she didn't find direction, she was afraid she'd be doomed to wander aimlessly? Because in some subconscious spurt of sentimentality, listening to a Frenchman talk about antiques made her feel closer to Tante Simone?

Several spoke of wanting to open shops. A few were collectors who wanted to learn more about auctions—which ones to attend, how to bid, what to bid on, what to watch out for. The decorators, Gaby sensed, needed to increase their vocabularies, so that in the course of conversation with their clients, they could drop in a Louis here and a George there. There were two brides in the midst of furnishing their first apartments who wanted to avoid making expensive mistakes. There was one woman who was doing a major renovation in her house and wanted to switch from her previously ultramodern mode to something more eclectic.

Lucky woman, Gaby thought. All she was renovating were three rooms. Gaby was renovating her life.

Two of the men viewed antiques as investment properties and wanted to educate themselves more fully so that they would know when the market was bullish on a particular style or era.

"And you, madame?"

Gaby's face flushed as she realized that Lafitte was addressing her.

"Why are you taking this class?"

His eyes held hers, and for a moment, she felt hypnotized, helpless to do anything except tell the truth.

"I need to find a career and the only thing I know anything about is antiques."

"How much do you know?" he asked with gentle curiosity.

"I'm not sure." She paused, as if doing an appraisal. "A little about a lot, I guess. I minored in art history in college and majored in antiques at home. I had no choice, really. It's all my aunt, who raised me, ever talked about. Her father owned an antiques shop in Paris which her brother still runs. And she herself owned shops both in France and in the United States."

"Apparently," Lafitte said, smiling at her with an odd familiarity, "antiques are in your blood. I know from personal experience that that can be either a curse or a blessing. Sometimes, it's both at the same time."

Though he moved on to the next person, Gaby couldn't shake the feeling that he had connected with her on a subliminal level, that he had been trying to tell her something, but because of the others, had felt compelled to code his message. She tried to speak to him after class, but by the time she reached the front of the room, he was surrounded by a gaggle of impassioned students.

She thought about waiting, but then asked herself, *What for?* What was she going to say, that they were kindred spirits and she understood how he felt? She didn't know this man at all. How could she possibly presume to understand how he felt about anything? He was being polite and she was making a tête-à-tête out of a passing remark.

Suddenly, she felt foolish. She put on her coat and left, yet as she did, she felt certain that his eyes had followed her.

It wasn't until the fourth session that Gaby had a chance to speak to Armand. The class had been held in the French period rooms at the Metropolitan Museum of Art. One of Lafitte's associates, another antiques dealer, had acted as their guide, walking them through the Wrightsman Pavilion, pointing out as many of the glorious details of the eighteenth century as two hours would permit. When the class ended, the bees swarmed around the guest instructor, leaving Armand standing off to the side, alone.

"Monsieur Lafitte, if you have a minute, I'd like to ask your opinion about something."

"Your accent is very good." His comment was so out of context that Gaby had to think before she responded.

"Thank you."

"I've noticed that whenever you pronounce something, you don't sound like an American using high school French. You sound like a native. Did your aunt teach you?"

"Yes. And my mother." She laughed, remembering how, as a child, she and her father had practiced their French together, studying on the side so that when the three of them gathered around the kitchen table, they could surprise Delphine with their accomplishments. "I've spoken French as long as I've spoken English."

"Was your father French?"

"No. He was purebred American, born and raised in Ohio. He met my mother during the war. He was stationed in France. They fell in love and got married, and she moved here."

"But you went back to France regularly?" He sounded like a man who had been stranded on a deserted island and had just come upon a visitor from the outside world.

"For a long time, yes. Unfortunately, I haven't been in years."

Gaby didn't mean to, but she couldn't help growing wistful. It had been five years since the last trip abroad. Brian traveled so much in his job that he wanted to spend his vacations nearer home. She had understood then, but lately she had been besieged by a longing for her parents almost as intense as it had been in the years immediately following their deaths. She knew it was loneliness and the prospect of losing Simone that had resurrected their memory, just as she knew it was a gnawing sense of rootlessness that had rekindled her desire to return to Antibes and Paris.

"You don't have to worry about Paris changing too much," Lafitte said, as if sensing the cause of her melancholy and empathizing with it. "No matter when you go, you'll still be able to find your way around. One of the things that makes the City of Lights so magical is its constancy."

Gaby smiled, aware that he was attempting to be kind, embarrassed that she had put him in that position. Seeking to hide her discomfort behind a flurry of activity, she started to rummage around in her bag, finally extracting a carefully wrapped box.

Lafitte's eyes widened with interest as she folded back the corners of the cloth covering.

"I was considering selling this," she said, trying to sound offhanded and casual. "I wondered if perhaps you knew of a dealer who specialized in this sort of item."

He took the box from her. Turning it over in his hand, he examined the exquisite rectangular case. It was gold and enamel, nineteenth century, he thought, either French or Swiss, obviously designed for snuff. In the center of the lid was an enameled portrait of Napoleon Bonaparte, his likeness contained within a gilded octagon and framed by two sylphlike women in flowing white gowns.

"How much are you hoping to realize from the sale?"

Gaby blushed. She had not done her homework.

"I don't know," she said. "I thought around five, six hundred dollars."

"If I were to hazard a guess, I would say that this magnificent *objet* is worth more like five or six thousand dollars."

Gaby was shocked, but pleased. Three weeks before, Simone had undergone yet another battery of tests. Gaby had assured Simone that with her new job going so well, she could more than afford to pay whatever was necessary. The truth was, she was barely getting by.

"I have a client who collects objects of vertu. If you'd like, I can offer it to him."

"I don't want you to go to any trouble."

Despite her attempts to keep up a façade, her need for money was apparent. Armand studied her closely.

"Would you feel more comfortable if we made it a business deal?"

Gaby nodded.

"You give me this on consignment. If I sell it, I'll take ten percent of the sale price. Fair?" He extended his hand.

"Fair." She shook his hand and gave him the box. It would never have dawned on her to mistrust or suspect him, or to question why his percentage was so low.

"Where can I reach you?"

Gaby hesitated. Her hotel was not exactly the Carlyle. What would he think? Before she could say anything, he reached into his pocket, took out a business card and handed it to her.

"I'll tell you what," he said, again preempting her embarrassment. "I'd like you to see my shop. If you're not busy a week from Saturday, why not come by? I should have spoken to my client by then."

"Sometimes, I have to work on Saturday," she said, grateful that he hadn't pressed her.

"Would an evening be better?" When she had taken his card, he had noticed that she wore no wedding ring.

"Probably."

"If you're not busy, how about that Saturday evening then? Around six-thirty?"

"That would be fine."

"I look forward to it, Madame . . ."

"Didier. Gabrielle Didier."

"*Au revoir*, Gabrielle."

"*Au revoir*, Monsieur Lafitte."

As Gaby descended the grand staircase that fronted the Met, a strange sensation enveloped her. It wasn't unpleasant, nor was it titillating. Rather it was a vague impression, like a thick fog she knew was there, but couldn't touch. Armand Lafitte was going to be a meaningful person in her life, of that she was certain.

That same week, Gaby returned to Ohio to formalize her separation agreement. Considering that this court session was the precursor for her divorce and would establish all financial perameters, she was surprisingly calm as she walked into the small, oak-paneled courtroom and took her place at one of the two tables facing the bench. As she listened to the opening statements, she was a vision of serenity.

It was when her lawyer insisted that Brian maintain the life-style he had established for his wife and child that she felt her composure slip. Brian's lawyer agreed, promising to pay for Steven's expenses. He also agreed to provide enough money for Gaby to run her life—two hundred and fifty dollars a week.

"Your honor, that's outrageous!" Gaby's attorney, Orin Phillips, sprang to his feet immediately, his round face tight with fury. "My client can't possibly maintain her house and her standard of living on two hundred and fifty dollars a week."

"But she has done exactly that," Brian's lawyer said, his face impassive, the slight smirk on his lips almost imperceptible. "If the court pleases, I would like to present into evidence six months of canceled checks, each in the amount of two hundred and fifty dollars. I would also like to present canceled checks in Mrs. Thayer's own hand that clearly demonstrate that on the money given to her by Mr. Thayer, she has managed quite well indeed."

Gaby glared at Brian, all measure of civility gone. "You bastard!" she said in a venomous hiss. Without any change in expression, Brian folded his hands and turned toward the judge, dismissing her.

"They're lying!" Gaby said to Phillips, gripping the edge of the table while trying to control her rage. "What about the cash he gave me? I used that for food and gas and dry cleaning. I told you about that, didn't I?"

"You did, but by that time, my dear, I'm afraid the damage was already done." Orin Phillips shook his head and patted her arm. "We'll do the best we can under the circumstances, but I must be honest, it doesn't look good."

Gaby stared at him, disillusionment and disappointment coloring her eyes.

Brushing a disobedient shock of white hair off his forehead, Orin stood and presented a grim visage to the judge.

"Your honor, I must object. Mr. Thayer and his attorney are not only incorrect about their facts, but they are audacious enough to be perpetrating a hoax right here in this hallowed hall of justice. They know as well as I do that each week, in addition to the aforementioned check, Mr. Thayer gave his wife two hundred and fifty dollars in cash. In her grief over their separation, and her shock at discovering her husband's infidelity, Mrs. Thayer acceded to these arrangements without discussion. At the time, she sought no advice of counsel because she trusted Mr. Thayer. In return for that trust, he is now attempting to defraud her."

The judge listened sympathetically, but as he was bound to do, requested that Orin provide evidence to substantiate Gaby's claim. Naturally, they had no such evidence.

"Your honor." Brian's lawyer rose and slowly walked in front of his table. He faced the bench, clasping his hands behind his back. "I think that at this time I would also like to make the court aware of the fact that Mrs. Thayer is no longer living in Wadsworth. It is our understanding that she has taken up residence in New York City where she is currently employed. Obviously, she has found a way to support herself in a style even grander than the one to which she was accustomed."

Once again, Orin was on his feet, his face a portrait of disgust.

"I object!" He threw up his hands, cast a sideways glance at his opponent, and then spoke directly to the judge. "You know, your honor, Mr. Thayer and his attorney are sorely testing the limits of my patience. They are also reshaping reality to suit their own needs, squeezing it dry of all compassion and charity until it's nothing but ugly innuendo and sarcastic inference. Yes, Mrs. Thayer was compelled to seek employment in New York, but not because she was seeking the glamour and excitement of the big city. She was forced to look for work in a faraway city because of the total absence of opportunity available to her in this area.''

He paused and placed his hand on Gaby's shoulder, reminding the judge that the issue being debated was not where she was working, but why.

"I beg the court to understand the plight of a woman suddenly faced with a need to earn a living, a woman without an impressive resumé, without any experience except that of being a devoted wife and mother. Based on his previous testimony, I would assume that the plaintiff feels that Mrs. Thayer's difficulty in finding a job is her problem and her fault. But is it?''

He turned, glared at Brian, who remained infuriatingly impassive, and then continued.

"Mrs. Thayer has indeed found employment. She is a sales clerk at a department store. She lives in a small residential hotel and for the past several months has been forced to support her life in New York as well as her home in Wadsworth on Mr. Thayer's ungenerous payments of five hundred dollars a week. Now he's requesting that those payments be reduced by half. Your honor, it may not be listed as such in the annals of Ohio law, but I assure you, what this man is doing is a crime.''

Gaby listened to Orin with growing respect. His speech was impassioned. More to the point, it was the truth. As the judge retired to his chambers to consider his decision, she thanked him.

"I wish I could have done better,'' he said sincerely. "Your soon to be ex-husband is a snake. Even though he makes seventy thousand a year, with your son in an expensive special school and Brian's need to establish a new residence, the judge may not be as sympathetic as we'd like him to be. I'm afraid Brian screwed you and there's no way for us to prove it.''

Orin was right. The judge ruled in Brian's favor. Gaby was awarded alimony in the sum of two hundred and fifty dollars a week for one year. After that, since she had already proved herself capable of finding employment, those payments would cease. She would be on her own. If and when their house was sold, she was obliged to give half the profits to Brian. For now, the house was hers.

Gaby left the courthouse in a rage, furious, both at Brian and herself. How could she have been so stupid? How could she have allowed herself to be party to a trick as dirty as the one Brian had pulled? By trusting him, that's how. By foolishly believing he would take care of her, for better or worse.

You deserve what you got, she told herself as she drove from Cleveland to Wadsworth. *The man cheated on you. He lied to you. He violated everything that was good and honest about your marriage, and still you trusted him. What a jerk! You should have trusted yourself instead!*

Hot tears filled her eyes.

Never again, she vowed, feeling a wave of renewed determination washing over her. *Never again will I be such a willing victim.*

Most of the way to Wadsworth, she raged—about Brian, what he had done, what she should have done—but as she neared Simone's house, she realized she had a more immediate problem. Before leaving New York, she had spoken to Dr. Jordan about the results of Simone's tests. The disease was progressing. Simone's resistance to subsidiary illness was decreasing, which meant that the need for professional care was imminent. What was she going to say to Simone? If she told her the truth about her finances, Simone might feel guilty and refuse expensive treatments or another battery of tests. Gaby couldn't allow that to happen. If she had to go into debt, her beloved aunt was going to die with dignity and with as little pain as possible. When she walked into Simone's house and took stock of her weakened condition, it did nothing to lighten her burden, but it did give her an idea.

"I need you to do me a favor," she said delicately. "I think it's become quite obvious that the two of us cannot support three households." Simone nodded, her manner cautious and a bit guarded. "How would you feel about moving into my house?"

"What?" Simone had been afraid that Gaby was going to suggest putting her in Lakewood or moving her to New York, neither of which she wanted to do. "Why?"

"I have to stay in New York because it's the only place I could find a job, and you have to stay in Wadsworth because you need to be near Dr. Jordan. However, on the way out, it dawned on me that maybe you'd be willing to move into my house and take care of it for me."

"What would I do with this house?"

"We'll sell it." Gaby tried to sound light and enthusiastic, but the cloud that shadowed Simone's eyes told her that no matter how she phrased it, having to leave the place you've lived in for a large part of your life was a depressing option. This was the house in which Gaby had grown up under Simone's loving care. "We'd make a tidy profit," she said gently.

Simone nodded again. Maintaining even the slightest semblance of independence was important to her, especially now when, each day, remaining self-sufficient was becoming harder and harder. Already, this carnivorous illness had forced her to close her shop and deplete her savings. She was not about to let it devour her pride. By selling—and she knew this was why Gaby had suggested it—she could pay some of her own bills.

"Dr. Jordan thinks you would be better off at Lakewood, but maybe he would change his mind if we hired a companion," Gaby continued, "a nurse who would come in during the day and see to your needs. What do you think?" Simone could have used a live-in companion, but Gaby knew she'd never agree to that. She also knew that this was only a stopgap. Soon, Lakewood would be the only alternative.

"This house is yours," Simone said sadly. "It belonged to your mother and father. I had hoped you would leave it to Steven someday."

Gaby kissed Simone's cheek and smoothed a stray lock of hair from her face. "It's our house. It's where we've lived and where I've always felt safe and secure."

"That's why you should keep it. So you always have a haven."

"It's not the house, don't you see that? You're my haven. You always have been. It doesn't matter where you are." Simone had grown wistful, as had Gaby. Both of them knew that the page on which they had charted their life together was running out of space. "Let me sell it. Let me take care of you."

"You should be taking care of yourself, not some decaying old woman."

"I don't need taking care of. I'm fine," Gaby lied. "I just don't want to sell my house, because if I do, I have to give Brian half the profits, and right now I wouldn't give that man a prune pit. Please. You'd be doing me a favor."

"But this is where you grew up. This is where you spent your childhood."

Gaby looked around, seeing the faces and hearing the whispers of the many ghosts who inhabited that house—Bill and Delphine, Simone, friends like Amy Ann, neighbors, herself as a little girl, a teenager, a bride-to-be. Some of the sounds were happy, some quite the opposite, but together they created a history as complex and stirring as a symphony.

"I'm not a child anymore," Gaby said, softly. "Thanks to you, I'm all grown up. It's my turn to see to the two of us, which is exactly what I plan to do. Now be a good girl and say you'll go along with me."

"I hate this," Simone said, with the anger of one who has lost control over her life.

"It's not the way I want it either, my darling Tante Simone, but these are the cards we've been dealt, and the same way we handled every other crisis, we're going to play this one out together."

"I love you, *ma chère* Gabrielle."

Gaby looked into Simone's eyes and held her hands tightly.

"Not more than I love you," she said, wishing she could halt the passage of time and make this moment last forever, knowing that no matter what she wished or how hard she prayed, the universal clock that marked life's progress and decline would keep on ticking.

Occupying three floors of a narrow town house just off Madison Avenue, Armand Lafitte's shop overflowed with wonders from the past. Pieces of heroic scale coexisted with less massive but equally splendid items in a carefully chaotic setting. Enormous mirrors balanced the heavy grandeur of Louis XV consoles and commodes. Régence writing desks provided display space for decorative urns and fanciful mantel clocks. Flamboyant ormolu wall lights flanked lavishly framed nineteenth-century tableaus. Bibliothèques showcased porcelains and smaller collectibles. Silk and velvet upholstery covered a mix of chairs and stools known as tabourets, some painted, others gilded, some neoclassical, others very rococo. Vases lush with fresh roses and bowls brimming with potpourri sat atop gueridons and jardinieres, adding softness and scent to the heavily textured setting.

Following Armand through his shop was an educational experience. Each piece had a history, a name, a story that went along with its neatly typed tag. He talked as he walked, stopping to explain a special point of interest, to rearrange a grouping, or just to give an affectionate pat to a particular favorite.

By the time they had reached the third floor, he had given her, among other things, a basic course in the evolution of the chair. He showed her X-shaped stools based on ancient Egyptian designs and early chairs which depended on stretchers and planks for support. He illustrated how costume design influenced furniture design by showing her a seventeenth-century English farthingale—a straight-backed chair with a space between the seat and the back created to accommodate a "farthingale," or hooped skirt. He showed her how, especially in the eighteenth century, architecture and furniture reflected each other by using similar shapes and decorative motifs: the grand, rectilinear style of Louis XIV, with its passion for scrolling; the softening period known as Régence; the curvaceous shapes and undisciplined naturalism of the rococo era of Louis XV; the restrained elegance and classical references that marked the reign of Louis XVI.

One of his finest pieces was a rare English oak panelback armchair, dating from the sixteenth century. Gaby found it ponderous and uncomfortable to sit in, even with the cushioned footrest Armand placed before her.

"It looks like a throne," she said, wriggling around, trying to figure out the best way to position her body. "I always thought it would be fun to be a queen, but if this is what queens have to sit on, I think I'll pass."

"It is like a throne," he said, smiling as he helped her up. "It was where the master of the house greeted his guests."

"A dining room would have to be the size of a barn to fit twelve of these around a table."

Armand laughed and invited her to sit on something more comfortable.

"I hate to disappoint you," he said, smoothing the tassels on the footstool, "but there were no dining rooms in the sixteenth century. Servants simply moved a table into whatever room was most agreeable to the master, usually the bed chamber. It wasn't until around 1772 that dining room tables appeared."

"What about all those bacchanals with knights in shining armor and ladies in velvet *bustiers* and pointed caps? Was that just Hollywood's rendition of a medieval buffet?"

"Yes and no," Armand said, finally seating himself on a gold brocade settee. "They did have dinner parties, but the ones you're thinking of were held in the grand hall, not a dining room. And while the table may have been enormous, it was little more than a huge board on thick trestles. All the guests sat on backless stools, the one chair being reserved for the lord of the manor, who sat at the head of the table. He was the 'chair man of the board.' "

"You're like a walking encyclopedia," she said, truly impressed.

"I love what I do," he replied modestly.

"It shows."

"Do you love what you do?"

Gaby looked at him. She had only been "doing" something for a few months, and she was doing it out of need, not love. The thought that someone might regard her as a professional anything, amused her.

"I sell clothes," she said bluntly. "It's just a job, not a career." She paused, wondering how much she could trust this man. "As you probably guessed, I need the money. Bergdorf Goodman was kind enough to let me work."

"What did you do before you needed the money," he asked gently, wanting to know, but unwilling to pry.

"I was married. Now I'm not married, but I have to support myself, a house I no longer live in, and my aunt who's dying. That's why I signed up for your class. I thought maybe there was something I could do with antiques."

"This may not be exactly what you had in mind, but have you ever done any bookkeeping?"

"Household budgets," Gaby said, again feeling small and inadequate. "Occasionally, I helped keep the books for my aunt's antiques shop."

"That's perfect! I just happen to have an office manager who's due to give birth any day now. I need a replacement. How about working for me?" His face spread into a broad smile. Obviously, he was as surprised at his offer as she was.

"I hope you don't think I gave you that box and came here tonight just to ask you for a job," she said, flushing. "How embarrassing! What I meant was that I had hoped that your class would tell me what the opportunities in this business are and where I might look for them. That's all, really."

Armand felt guilty. He hadn't intended to cause her discomfort.

"I don't know if I'm capable of providing any further opportunity," he said, hoping to counter the impression he had made, "but you're an able student and a lovely woman, and if you'd like, I'd be happy to add you to my staff, show you around, and share whatever knowledge I have."

"Do you mean that?" Gaby asked, her face childlike and trusting.

"I certainly do."

"I would love working here!"

"Well then," he said, pleased with her response, "that's settled. Now for the next item on our agenda."

He reached into his pocket and handed her a piece of paper. It was a check made out to her in the amount of $4,500.

"My client bought the snuff box for five thousand dollars. I took my ten percent. The rest is yours."

Gaby was delighted.

"Well," she said, staring at the check. "It's been a pleasure doing business with you. This is going to make things a lot easier." Her smile faded. "If I have to, could I bring you other things to sell?"

"Anytime. But right now, this calls for a celebration. Do you have plans for tonight?"

"No." She laughed. "I never have plans for anything."

"If you'd like, we can sit and discuss the terms of your employment over dinner. I know a wonderful bistro that serves the best bouillabaisse in town. Interested?"

"With hot, crusty bread and dry, white wine?"

Armand nodded.

Without any further ado, she put her check in her bag, rose from her chair, and started for the door.

"What are we waiting for? *Allons!*"

During the next few months, the friendship between Gaby Thayer and Armand Lafitte deepened. Gaby quit her job at Bergdorf's, joined the staff of Lafitte et Fils U.S.A., and quickly learned the joy of having a steady paycheck that didn't depend on commission. Her income wasn't enormous, but it exceeded her average week's earnings at the store, which was a definite plus. Having a weekly salary not only allowed her to budget more effectively, but also to move out of her hotel room into a small walk-up on East Forty-ninth Street. Though it was near Beekman Place, an area usually associated with wealth and spectacular river views, Gaby's apartment was less than grand. It consisted of a tiny bedroom, a bathroom with aging fixtures, a kitchen too small and antiquated to produce anything more lavish than a bowl of breakfast cereal, and a living room that even the landlord felt compelled to call modest. It was on the third floor overlooking a rear courtyard that permitted little sunlight, but Gaby didn't care. It was cheap, it was furnished, there was a bus stop on the corner, it was in a decent neighborhood. And it was hers.

Neither did she care that most of her working hours were spent sequestered in Armand's office going over debits and credits, filing invoices, checking shipping orders, and typing bills. She loved her job. There was something so comforting about being surrounded by the familiar air of fine antiques. It was a scent that conjured up images and memories—of home, of Tante Simone, of Oncle Bernard, of easier times, of a simpler existence in which she was a child doted on by a loving mother and father, with no cares, no worries, no obligations other than to finish her homework or clean her room. They were illusions perhaps, visions of a distant past, but they helped color a reality that often threatened to fade into impenetrable gray.

The other two people who worked for Armand—Colby Holland, a young man fresh from design school with a bent for Italian tailoring and flamboyant decor, and Solange Vliet, an older Frenchwoman who viewed herself as Armand's personal guardian, protecting him from the classless and the poor—were friendly and helpful. After a short period of initiation, during which they tested her knowledge and inspected her work, they treated Gaby as a peer, assisting and criticizing in equal measure. Eventually, though she had not been hired as a floor person, on the occasions when Armand was out of town and both Solange and Colby were at auction or estimating an item at someone's home or running a personal errand, they let Gaby handle the front. Much to her delight—and their surprise—she managed to sell something each time.

The real joy, however, was her relationship with Armand. She had never met anyone with such an infinite capacity for giving of himself. It was as if he had decided she was his charge and that the quality of her future was inexorably connected to the quantity of his beneficence. She had confided in him about Simone and her constant need for funds, and Armand had held true to his word, selling whatever pieces she gave him so that she could supplement her income. He also kept his promise about educating her in the antiques business. Though Simone had taught Gaby a great deal, Wadsworth, Ohio, was quite different from New York.

He took her to auctions, museums, antiques shows, and even an occasional out-of-town antiques fair. He gave her books to read and pictures to study. At the shop he provided hands-on instruction in how to examine a piece for blemishes, how to use the pads on her fingertips like a detective to search for scratches and imperfections invisible to the eye, how to tell the difference between a reproduction and the real thing.

Immediately, he noticed that Gaby had an instinctive sense of discrimination as well as a photographic memory. She was the type of student every teacher dreams of—inquisitive and attentive. Nothing had to be repeated. Like a computer, she absorbed everything, classifying information, processing it and retrieving it whenever it was called for. After a while, he also noticed that she had a keen sense of humor. Too, he saw that she was pretty, yet self-effacing, sometimes even harsh on herself, and completely unaware of the fact that with the right makeup and a more sophisticated approach to clothing, she could be quite beautiful. It took several months of unconscious study, but in the end, Armand concluded that Gabrielle Didier was like a raw gem, clouded and shapeless, but full of possibility. All she needed to bring out her natural brilliance was a craftsman with the patience to cut and polish. Armand knew he could be that Pygmalion to her Galatea, but the last thing he wanted to do was to insult or hurt her.

The opportunity he had been waiting for presented itself when he asked her to accompany him to Boston to attend a dinner party being given by an old friend of his family's.

"I feel strange," she said. When she hesitated, he could tell she was summoning up the courage to make a confession. "I don't fit in," she said bluntly. "I'm sure your friends are all terribly chic and cosmopolitan. Compared to them, I've got small town written all over me."

Armand laughed. "Is that all?"

"Isn't that enough?"

"This party is a month away, but if you're willing, we can have you looking big city in less than a week."

Her eyes widened and her mouth broadened into a huge grin. "We can?" Armand nodded. "Where do we start?"

The next day, Armand brought her to a friend on Madison Avenue who, using a simple rinse, restored her chestnut coloring and then cut and styled her hair to take advantage of its thick, natural waves. A cosmetician at Henri Bendel's taught Gaby how to apply makeup—subtle for day, a touch of the dramatic for evening. Thanks to a friend's employee discount, Bergdorf's served as her source for a few dresses, some accessories, shoes, and handbags. The best part was listening to Armand reiterate so many of the lessons she had been taught, first by Delphine, then by Simone: quality over quantity, fine over fussy, luxurious fabrics, nothing trendy, and when in doubt, underdo rather than overdo.

True to his word, the night Gabrielle Didier made her debut in Boston, she looked every bit the New York sophisticate. Also true to his word, no one questioned where she was from. They simply assumed she was who she appeared to be. People complimented her on her dress and Armand on his good taste. Beacon Hill Brahmins swarmed around her, seeking her out as if she were one of them, asking her opinion on everything from world issues to the texture of the pâtés being served. For Gaby, the evening was pure fairy tale. She felt like Cinderella, touched by a magic wand that had transformed her into the storybook princess she had always wanted to be. But no matter how intoxicating it all was, deep inside, a small voice reminded her that after a while champagne bubbles go flat and, after midnight, Cinderella's coach turns into a pumpkin.

In July, Dr. Jordan called to tell Gaby that the time had come to move Simone into Lakewood. She had known it was coming. Whenever she visited, at least one weekend each month, two if she could manage, she was forced to confront the changes taking place in her aunt. Simone was losing weight. Her posture was bending. Her skin was losing its tone. And her hair, that once glorious drape of deep, rich brown had not only whitened, but had thinned so much that it was little more than a sheer, silver shroud.

Gaby had expected an emotional weekend, but nothing could have prepared her for the avalanche of feelings that crashed down on her as she readied Simone for the trip to Cleveland. As she packed some of the smaller items the nurse had missed, she was assaulted by so many memories that she could barely hold back her tears. Simone's huge flowered shawls and her ubiquitous gold chains prompted Gaby to recall how eccentric her aunt had once appeared to the Cocrofts' neighbors, how odd and out of place she had seemed when she'd first come to live in Wadsworth. It had taken a while for them to understand and accept the outspoken, rara avis nature of the Frenchwoman, but in time, they had come to love and appreciate Simone. According to the nurse, not a day went by when someone didn't stop in to chat or to visit or to drop off a cake or a pot of hot soup.

Gaby wrapped Simone's portrait gallery in tissue, taking time to study the old photographs of her parents, the even older photographs of Simone's parents, brothers, and sisters. With special care, she wrapped Simone's wedding picture, trying to imagine Simone when she had been so young and so in love with the handsome man at her side. Gaby remembered how, as a teenager, she had fantasized about Simone and Alain, inventing King Arthur and Queen Guenivere–type stories about the heroic and tragic path of their romance. She had wanted to be Simone then. She had wanted to feel the passion and the commitment Simone had felt. She remembered thinking that on her wedding night she would know what Simone had known. When that night finally arrived, she had felt excitement and love and physical satisfaction, but not the torrid, explosive passion she had imagined. Then she had decided that she had been unfair in asking Brian to compete with a fantasy. Now she knew that her whole life with Brian had been fantasy.

Once Gaby finished packing, she set about making dinner for the two of them. It was a simple meal of Simone's favorites— pot au feu and apples à la Delphine. Throughout, Simone laughed and talked, behaving as if this were just an ordinary meal, one that would be repeated many times in the future. She commented on Gaby's appearance, how much she loved seeing her niece looking so beautiful, so sleek and soignée. She talked about

Claude and how hard he had worked to close her store and sell off her inventory. She asked about New York and Armand and even ventured a discussion about Brian. But not once did either of them speak about death or dying or Lakewood.

The ride the next day was an excruciating journey for both of them. As they drove through the gates, the silence that had prevailed continued, except it grew louder and more hysterical as they approached the entrance. A nurse greeted them with a wheelchair. At first, Simone resisted, but after some cajoling on Gaby's part, she acquiesced, allowing Gaby to push her through the lobby and down the hall to her new quarters.

Simone's room was remarkably cheerful. Yet a pastel-striped coverlet and pretty pink sheets covered a hospital bed. Poking out from among the delicate floral bouquets that patterned the wallpaper were the plugs and outlets necessary for medical machinery and life-support systems. There were closets and a pine dresser, a freshly tiled bathroom and a vase of summer flowers. Yet Gaby's eyes were drawn instantly to the guard rails by the toilet and the tub, to the intercom meant to summon help, to the television camera hovering overhead so that the patient could be monitored by an attending nurse. It was nicely decorated, well furnished and well equipped, but it was, first, last and always, a hospital.

While someone helped Simone change and settled her in a chair, Gaby waited in the hallway outside her room, leaning against the scrubable vinyl wallcovering and breathing in the antiseptic smell. It had been many years since Gaby had been moved to prayer, but at that moment she closed her eyes and asked God to be kind to Simone, to reward her for her goodness by keeping her suffering to a minimum.

"You can go in now, Mrs. Thayer."

Gaby took a deep breath and demanded that her mouth form into a pleasant smile. She pushed open the door and walked in, determined to find the brighter side. As usual, Simone was several steps ahead of her. She was seated by the window in a chintz-covered chair, four gold chains hanging from her neck, a brightly colored shawl tossed about her shoulders, her feet propped up on an ottoman, her body wrapped in her favorite afghan.

"I like it here," she stated matter-of-factly. "If that young girl is typical of the personnel at this place, I'm going to be just fine. She's sweet and upbeat and didn't prick and prod at me the way the nurses at Wadsworth did.''

"They say Lakewood is the best.''

"It appears as if *they* are right. Now stop looking so grim. You'll give yourself wrinkles and we can't allow that to happen.'' She shook a finger at Gaby and then pointed to the chair opposite her. When Gaby sat, Simone continued. "I may not be able to cure myself, but I've decided that the best cure for what ails you is a hot romance.''

Gaby blushed and then laughed.

"I didn't know I was ailing,'' she said, feeling as awkward as she had when Simone had first lectured her on sex.

"Well, you are.'' She squinted her eyes and surveyed her niece. "Despite the mascara, the red lips, and the rouge, you look a touch ragged around the edges. I think a lover would do wonders.'' She laughed, and for a brief second a flash of brilliance illuminated her eyes, glowing like a flame that had flickered down until it was almost ash, but had found the strength to fire again. "Lord knows, it always worked for me.''

"Speaking of your gentlemen friends,'' Gaby said, embarrassed and eager to change the subject, "how come you never married again?''

"I don't know,'' Simone said, as if this were the first time she had ever really thought about it. "I guess I'm a stubborn old goat who just likes being independent. Do you know what I mean?''

Again, Gaby felt awkward.

"No,'' she said, "I'm afraid I don't. If you think about it, I've never been independent. I went from my parents to you to Brian.''

"You're on your own now.''

"Not really. Technically, I'm still being supported. I won't be independent until my alimony stops.''

"I'm not talking about money, *mon chou*. I'm talking about an independence of spirit. Standing up for yourself, looking after yourself, caring about yourself. That doesn't mean you don't care about others, but when you like who you are, you can afford to be more generous in your liking of others.''

"That sounds wonderful, but at this point, I don't even know who I am, let alone whether I like who I am.''

"I know who you are, and I love who you are right now. But I'm willing to bet that one year from now, after you've had a good dose of what independence is all about, you're going to be crazy about Gabrielle Didier Cocroft Thayer!"

"I'll take that bet," Gaby said, shaking Simone's outstretched hand. "One year from today, I'll let you know whether I think your precious independence is everything you say it is."

They shook and Simone nodded, but both of them knew that the chances of her being around to collect on her wager were very, very slim.

"She's the bravest woman I know," Gaby said to Armand. "There she is giving me a pep talk about life, while her only hope of relief is a quick and merciful death."

"What do her doctors say?"

"They have no way of knowing, but I can tell you she's not going to lie down easily. Tante Simone is a real fighter."

"I don't mean to be bourgeois, but how are you going to pay for all this? She could be there for months."

Gaby had been thinking about nothing else the entire ride back from Ohio.

"That, my dear friend, is the sixty-four-thousand-dollar question. Frankly, I have no idea."

"Why not sell your house?"

"I can't do that," Gaby said, quickly. "I need it for Steven."

"But he's never home."

"I know, but he still clings to the childish hope that his father and I will get back together again."

"Is there any chance of that?"

Gaby laughed, but it was not a happy sound.

"As much chance as there is of me living in a penthouse on Park Avenue."

"Explain it to him. He loves Simone. I'm sure he'd understand."

Gaby rose from her chair and began to pace, circling Armand's living room.

"I can't explain it to myself," she said honestly. "I guess that house is symbolic to both of us. If I sell it, there's a finality to my life with Brian. Steven is still young. He needs to hold on to his roots. He's having a hard enough time adjusting to our divorce. Selling his home out from under him might be too much for him to take.''

"And you?"

She stopped, thought, and then looked at Armand.

"Maybe it's like an escape clause for me. Maybe, subconsciously, I'm holding on to it so that if things get tough, I have someplace to go."

"Things have gotten tough, Gaby, and yet you've said over and over again you don't want to go back."

"And I mean it," she said, seeing the confusion in her statements. "But it's familiar and it's mine. Besides, too much is happening. I can only deal with so many traumas at once. Simone is dying. In a matter of months, my divorce will be final. And suddenly I'm a stranger to myself. I've accepted the fact that I have nothing there, but I'm not sure what I have here, either. Yes, I have a job that I love and a wonderful new friend, but much as I love you, Armand, I want more than this."

"I understand, but to burden yourself with such debt seems foolish."

"I've already sold the house I grew up in. To sell the house I lived in most of my married life would be like erasing my history, and I'm not ready to do that. My present is too unstable and my future is too unsure. Right now, I can manage. When I can't, then maybe."

She had no way of knowing it then, but Armand, more than anyone, sympathized with her need to cling to the ragged remnants of her past. He understood it was all part of the difficult task of making the transition from being one of two to being just one. He understood because, for years, he had been doing the very same thing.

5

Armand Lafitte had not set out to be a crusader. If anything, his personality had always been more reserved than radical; his history, one of scholarship and study, not political infighting and intrigue; his upbringing, one of elegant salons and gentlemanly agreements, not smoke-filled rooms and shady deals. Yet, suddenly, Armand had found himself in the center of a controversy that would damage his business and his social position, compromise his family name, and put a strain on many of his friendships. And all because he chose truth over repose.

It had begun quite innocently in the autumn of 1985. Armand was lunching with several of his fellow antiques dealers when, by chance, he asked a question that evoked a screeching silence.

"Why isn't the fair vetted?"

At first, no one answered. Finally, Antony Vinter, a specialist in English furniture and decorative arts, stated matter-of-factly, "Because Vincent Prado won't allow it."

"Why not?"

"He feels it's an unnecessary expense and an insult to the dealers who show."

"That's absurd! Everything at the Biennale and Grosvenor

House is vetted and I've never heard any of those exhibitors object." He turned to Dean Conway, a dealer in Oriental art. "Would you feel insulted?"

"Of course not! Vetting is nothing more than a way of guaranteeing authenticity. I don't sell anything I can't back up, so why would I care if they brought in a team of experts to verify what I already know?"

"In a way," added John Davenport, a world-famous dealer in antiquities, "it would be a great help. Not often, but every once in a while, a fake sneaks by me. I'd rather have it taken off the floor than have a customer call me a fraud. That kind of thing can ruin one's reputation."

"Then what's the big deal?"

"Prado doesn't want to offend some of his buddies," Vinter said. "When he has to find a particular piece for one of his less discerning clients, he often goes to dealers who fudge provenances or overlook excessive restoration or pass off repros as the real thing. Vetting would eliminate these guys."

"They should be eliminated."

"Maybe, but not by Prado."

"We're all members of the National Antique and Art Association. Couldn't we band together and confront Prado with our demands?"

"We'd have to have the support of the full membership," Conway said, "and I don't think we'd get it."

Armand looked from one to the other, noting that Davenport and Vinter agreed with Conway's assessment.

"Why not?" Armand had only been in New York for four years. He still felt somewhat new to the ins and outs of the antiques business as conducted in America, and relied heavily on his friends' advice.

Vinter thought before answering. He was a man with little patience for extemporaneous opinion.

"The four of us are unique and very lucky," he said. "Not all dealers have year-round businesses the way we do. They sell a major piece here and there, but for whatever reason, they don't have Rolodexes filled with rich patrons and they've never connected with the high-powered decorators in the city. If not for the fair, most of them would operate in the red and eventually go under. They need the exposure, and I doubt if they would do anything to risk losing it.''

"The bottom line is, you don't mess with Prado," Davenport said. "A few years ago, a friend of mine from San Francisco must have done something to offend Vincent. He'd participated in the show for ages, but the following year his application was denied. When he questioned it, he was told that his merchandise didn't come up to the standards set for the fair.''

"That's ridiculous," Armand said angrily. "There are more than a few third-rate dealers at his precious fair."

"And more than a few first-raters who are refused entry," Vinter said. "All true, *mon ami*. But that's the way it is. Over the years, Prado has managed to turn that show into his own private fiefdom.''

"In Europe, that could never happen. The dealers organize and run the shows themselves. They have committees that vet every single piece exhibited, and no one is exempt. Not only that, but in addition to the dealers offering guarantees, so does the management of the show. That's the way it should be.''

"Maybe so," Vinter said. "But separate yourself from your ancestry for a moment and look at the situation with an open mind. The January Antiques Fair isn't opened by royalty the way Grosvenor House is, and it's not touted as the greatest happening the world has ever seen the way the Biennale is. It was started to raise money for a charity, which is still its stated purpose. Over the years, it's evolved into a rather big business. In Prado's mind, he's acting as a true, red-blooded, capitalistic American and simply guarding the bottom line.''

"But the man isn't a professional businessman. He isn't an academic. He isn't even a dealer. He's a decorator.''

Vinter laughed at the undisguised sneer in Armand's voice.

"Again, *mon ami*, you're denying the differences between the Continent and the Colonies. In Europe, collectors do most of their own buying. Here, decorators do the legwork. Even the wealthiest of my clients suffers from a certain amount of insecurity. If he's going to spend thirty thousand dollars on a Sheraton desk, he wants to be certain it fits the space he has in mind and doesn't clash with the decor.''

"Okay," Armand said, nodding, allowing for transatlantic differences. "I'll admit that the fair requires its own set of operating procedures, but that doesn't alter the basic issue. We are in the business of selling history. Few buyers have the formal education or the expertise to verify the value and provenance of every piece they like. That's our job, and where most of us are too proud to be dishonest, there are those whose pride has been compromised by the lure of the almighty dollar. The public has a right to be assured that what they see is what they get.''

"At the risk of sounding like Rhett Butler,'' Conway said, ''the public doesn't give a damn. If they did, we wouldn't be having this conversation. They would have demanded guarantees and refused to buy without them. If sales dropped, Prado would vet in a minute. But they haven't.''

"They need to be educated. They need to be taught that buying antiques with a guarantee is like buying blue chips versus speculating. It's safer. It's more secure. And in the long run, it's a better investment.''

"We all agree with you, Armand,'' Vinter said. He glanced at his comrades, as if checking to see whether or not he had picked up the right cue, and then leaned toward Armand. ''That's why we've launched a campaign to make you head of the January Antiques Fair.''

Armand looked from one to the other.

"You're joking. This is one of those practical pranks you like to pull on me.''

Davenport shook his head.

"I assure you, we're quite serious.''

"The only way to stop Prado is to replace him.'' Conway looked to see who, if anyone, might be listening. ''We've thought long and hard about it, believe me. You'd be great, Armand.''

Vinter said, ''You're known to be a scholar, so your intelligence is an accepted fact. Your father has run the Biennale several times and always has met with great success, so if the adage 'like father, like son' carries any weight, that part of your resumé sounds good. You're relatively new to New York, which means that you couldn't have too many enemies, yet your name is old and French and inspires instant respect among collectors and dealers alike. You have a reputation for carrying museum-quality merchandise. Your instincts about what's right and wrong with the fair are one hundred percent on target.'' Vinter leaned back in his chair, fisted his hand, squinted, and held up his thumb, moving it from side to side like an artist studying his subject. "Also, you're not bad looking, and the ladies seem inclined to swoon when you kiss their fingertips. What more could anyone want?"

"An alternative plan," Armand said, somewhat overcome.

"There is only one alternative. Plant a crown on Prado's head, declare him king, and forever hold our peace. I don't know about you, but I can't do that." Davenport's tone rang with equal amounts of frustration and determination.

"Neither can I." Vinter, the one closest to Armand, patted his friend's hand. "I know you think we're putting you on the spot, and we are, but only because we really think you can do the job."

Armand's mind hurdled from one thought to another. Why him? Why now? *Why not?* Certainly, he was not immune to the seductive allure of fame. He was not without ego or pride. He had come to the United States with the express purpose of establishing the Lafitte name on this side of the Atlantic, and although his business had been profitable from the first, he had dismissed his success as nothing more than an extension of his father's and brother's success, not as something he had created on his own. But if this plan worked, if he was named head of the January Antiques Fair, it would be *his* accomplishment, *his* achievement.

What if their plan failed? Or what if it succeeded and he failed? What if he couldn't elevate the fair to the exalted level of its European counterparts? Instead of affixing his signature to a triumph, he would be exposing the entire Lafitte family to possible humiliation. Was the risk greater than the reward?

"I don't know if I'm cut out to be Don Quixote," he said, still taking his own emotional pulse. "It's true, I am a bit of an idealist, but even so, I can't say that fulfilling impossible dreams has ever been my forte."

"We're not asking you to fight windmills," Vinter said. "Truly, we're not. There is support for a coup, Armand. There is dissatisfaction in the ranks. Most of the better dealers are fed up with Prado's autocratic manner and want him out. Others aren't quite as hostile, but they too would like some new blood at the helm. What we have to do is find a dramatic way of pulling the undecideds over to our side.''

"What do you suggest?'' Armand's voice was hesitant. He was aware that by involving himself in the conversation he was committing himself to their cause.

"What do *you* suggest?'' Vinter asked, smiling at the unspoken acceptance.

Armand surprised himself with his answer. Obviously, he had given the January Antiques Fair more thought than he had realized.

"One way to focus attention on Prado's iron grip would be to have the first-rate American dealers he's denied entry to in the past apply for booths. Then we'd try to encourage more of the top-quality European *antiquaires* to apply. If he remains true to form, he'd turn them down, but rejecting that many high-caliber dealers would create an awful lot of gossip.''

"I love it!'' Conway's enthusiasm was rewarding. Armand hated to brake it.

"Unfortunately, we don't have the time or the manpower for an onslaught like that. We'll have to save that for next year and find another attention-getting ploy for now.''

"The most sensitive issue is vetting,'' Davenport said. "I say we start there. Let's canvass those members of the association who've already agreed that it's time for a change in leadership. Let's see how many would be willing to have their merchandise juried. Then let's form a committee of experts with unimpeachable reputations to examine the goods.''

"Everyone would have to agree as to their qualifications and be willing to abide by their decisions,'' Armand said.

"Sounds good.'' Vinter nodded his approval. At some point, he had appointed himself recording secretary and was busily writing down everything everyone said in a small notepad.

"I know we can't go so far as to swear anyone to secrecy,'' Davenport said. "But if we could, I would.''

"I don't see that as a problem.'' Vinter continued to write as he spoke. "Most of the dealers said they would do just about anything to replace Prado. They'll understand the need for silence. As for the others, I'd guess that those who go along with us on the vetting will go along with everything. Those who don't have too many ties to the other dealers to snitch. Besides, since no one knows how it's going to turn out, it's not in anyone's best interest to declare sides before the actual battle begins.''

Conway laughed. ''You make it sound as if we're going up against General Patton.''

''Knowing Prado,'' Vinter said, ''he probably decorated the inside of Patton's tank, and when the old man died, he left all his strategy books to his dear friend, Vincent.''

''Can we get back to the subject under discussion?'' Davenport was growing impatient. When he had everyone's attention, he continued. ''What happens after we canvass the membership and complete the vetting? Do we approach Prado before the fair?''

''No,'' Armand said. ''In the first place, we couldn't do that without one hundred percent support, which is something I don't think we'll have. Secondly, a confrontation would constitute a definite attack. We'd be daring him to retaliate. And he would, not only against us, but against innocent people. I suggest we bypass him altogether.''

''And do what?'' Vinter asked.

''Let's print up small signs to put in the booth of every dealer who has submitted his wares to vetting, stating that he has done so. It's simple and noncombative, but public.''

''Meaning that the press will pick it up.''

''Exactly. Once it hits the papers, the best that can happen is that either Prado takes the hint and upgrades the fair or the fence sitters come over to us so that we can unseat him once and for all. The worst that can happen is that I get drawn and quartered. What do you say?''

The three men never hesitated.

''Let's do it!''

Armand's grandmother Yveline was the first Lafitte *antiquaire*. It was not something she had planned, nor was it something she had chosen to do. As the youngest child and only daughter of a renowned French goldsmith whose designs were coveted by both the *ancienne noblesse* and the *petite noblesse*, Yveline grew up pampered and indulged. Her family lived in an elegant *hôtel particulier* on the Île Saint-Louis. Yveline was clothed by the finest *couturiers*, shod by the finest bootmakers, attended by an entourage of servants, and tutored by some of the finest minds in

Paris. Though Yveline was aware of the strict boundaries that existed between classes in the early 1900s, and though she understood that her family's Jewishness was another barrier to social acceptance, she remained indifferent to such impediments. She harbored no secret desires to marry a duke or elevate her position. She carried no private wishes to be anyone other than herself. And why should she? Whomever she spoke to, answered. Whomever she wanted to meet, she met. Wherever she wanted to go, she went. And when, at seventeen, she fell in love, the object of her affection returned her feelings, thricefold.

On May 26, 1909, Yveline Meyer married Michel Lafitte, a handsome young banker who had been, until that day, indisputably the most eligible bachelor of Yveline's set. Nine months and two weeks after their wedding, Etienne Lafitte was born. His birth had been long and arduous, with complications that made it impossible for Yveline to bear any more children without a serious threat to her life. Naturally, to people who came from large families, it was a blow, but Yveline and Michel were not the type to mourn the loss of something they never had. Instead of brooding about what might have been, they concentrated on the fortunate circumstances that were—the love they had for each other and their healthy, handsome son, and their beautiful new house on the Avenue Montaigne. Michel's aptitude for financing successful ventures increased his reputation among the business community, as well as his responsibility at his father's bank. Meanwhile, Yveline was developing her own reputation as one of Paris's more talented hostesses. Once it became obvious that the criterion for being a guest at one of her weekly soirées was excellence in something—business or the arts or physical beauty or personal charm or conversation or wit or even criticism— invitations to the Lafittes' quickly became coveted. Theirs was a pleasant, privileged world in which they were eternally safe, perpetually secure.

But then, Gavrilo Princip turned that world upside down, when, slightly before noon on Sunday, June 28, 1914, in Sarajevo, the capital of the Austrian province of Bosnia, he jumped onto the running board of a touring car and fired three shots. Two hit the Archduke Francis Ferdinand, heir to the throne of Austria-Hungary, and one hit his wife, Sophie. They died almost immediately. World War I began shortly afterward. By October 1914, Michel had joined France's fighting force.

For two years, Yveline camouflaged her constant anxiety by conducting her life as if there were nothing to fear, as if Paris and, in fact, the whole of Europe, had not been infected with a murderous disease, as if she herself were not living with a horrible apprehension that, like a bodily scent, had become part of her being.

In 1916, Yveline's worst fears were realized. Michel became one of the 540,000 casualties of the Battle of Verdun. For three years, she mourned. The house on the Avenue Montaigne, once a mecca of conviviality, seemed to be draped in an invisible black bunting. No one came. No one, other than servants charged with replenishing provisions, went. Gone was the rustle of expensive taffetas and silks. Gone was the tinkle of women's laughter, the rumble of men's concerns. Gone were the arguments and lively exchanges that had always been the music of the manor. So much had been destroyed and mutilated by the war, but for many, one of the most poignant symbols of the devastation was the silencing of Yveline Lafitte.

When finally, in 1920, she opened her doors again, it was like the beginning of a new era. And for her, it was. That first night, in the course of casual conversation, one of her women friends admired a pair of giltwood consoles. It was not a passing compliment. The woman appeared obsessed. Yveline, still subconsciously ill at ease with memories of her life with Michel, still searching for a new focus, offered to sell the consoles to her friend. It was the first of many deals she would make. It started slowly, but because the furnishings of her home were so exceptional, the unusual became the norm. Each time she held a soirée, someone asked about a chair or a painting or a settee or, even, a piece of her father's inventory of jewels. Since Yveline abhorred empty spaces as much as nature abhorred its own vacuums, every piece she sold she replaced with something equally precious. Without being completely aware of what was happening, her home had become her place of business, her elegant evenings her showroom, her eager guests her best customers. By the time Etienne was twenty years old and brought Josette Rosenberg home to meet his mother, Yveline was not only one of Paris's social doyennes, but also one of France's leading dealers in jewelry and antiques.

For Etienne, his life with Josette was a joy. Delicate of visage and petite, she was a bright and well-bred woman whose bearing inspired immediate, and complimentary, comparison with her mother-in-law and mentor, Yveline, with whom she shared an almost insatiable need to be surrounded by all things elegant and fine.

Having so much in common and little extra to spare as the Depression took hold and Etienne saw the Lafitte family bank go under, it had seemed natural for Etienne and Josette to move into the Avenue Montaigne *maison*. Yveline created a small apartment for herself and generously ceded the rest of the house to her son and daughter-in-law, with the proviso that the public rooms remain public so that the Lafitte antiques business—which she had renamed Lafitte et Fils in honor of Etienne—might continue. Etienne and his bride agreed. Etienne began his studies at the university, and Josette assisted Yveline. While Yveline's specialties remained furniture and jewelry, Josette was quite expert in the field of fine art, which was hardly surprising since her father was a dealer in baroque art. Though her favorite painters were the Italians Annibale Carracci and Michelangelo Caravaggio, her knowledge extended to the works of Rubens, Van Dyck, Velázquez, and the Dutch school which followed.

Though it seemed wrong to be content in such doleful times, Etienne was unbelievably content. His studies were going well. Lafitte et Fils had expanded—thanks to his wife's contributions— and his family had expanded. In 1933, Josette gave birth to a son they named Jacques. In 1936, they were blessed with another son, whom they named Armand. For the next three years, the Lafitte household bustled and bubbled with activity. By day, the high-pitched sounds of small children mingled with the low, cultivated tones of those with the desire to own precious objects. By night, it continued to be a meeting place for tastemakers and policymakers, for those who were profiting by, contributing to, helping, hindering, or simply chronicling the progress of the times. But inside Yveline's salon, the talk was not only of the Depression. Mussolini's invasion of Ethiopia, the rapid rise of the Nazi party, the Spanish Civil War—even the most blasé political observers recognized the harbingers of war. It was like watching one tree in a forest catch fire, then another, and another. Soon, there would be no way to stop the conflagration.

In 1939, the blaze began. Once again, the Lafittes were asked to sacrifice their eldest male on the altar of human violence, but this time, those Etienne left behind were not safe within the walls of their home. They were not even safe within the boundaries of their birthplace. Their ancestors had lived in France for generations, but suddenly none of that mattered. They were Jewish, and in Hitler's Europe, that warranted a death sentence. There were no trials, no opening or closing arguments, no presentations of evidence. A single drop of Jewish blood demanded a guilty verdict. Guilty of what? Everything and nothing. But what did it matter? There was no court of appeal. There was only death or escape.

Neither Yveline, nor Josette, nor Etienne trusted Marshal Pétain's repeated assurances. Gossip—evil, horrifying gossip—negated everything he said. At Etienne's insistence, his mother, his wife, and his sons left Paris, while Etienne joined an underground group that would later become known as the Resistance. With their help, his family was set up in a hidden mountain village outside of Aix-en-Provence. They were provided with new identities and assumed names, given jobs that kept them more or less invisible—washing dishes, doing laundry, sweeping—and protected throughout the Occupation by a band of French patriots known as the Maquis.

Etienne's performance during the war surprised many, including himself. He had been reared not as a fighter, but as a scholar, a man whose best defense had always been his mind, not his fists. But Etienne was Michel Lafitte's son, a passionate man with an intense loathing for injustice and a low degree of patience for drawn-out military procedures. He needed to see results. He needed to be involved and to help destroy the very core of the vicious German death machine. Because of Etienne's fluency in French, English, and German, as well as his dedication to research, he was invaluable to the Resistance. His work with them included an alliance with members of British intelligence. There, he met two other men with whom he shared an affinity and with whom he would find himself inexorably involved after the war: Peter Wilson, who would later become the head of Sotheby's, and Garrett Castleton.

After the Liberation, Etienne returned to Paris to find that although she was physically healthy and only in her late fifties, fighting to survive a second war had drained Yveline. Running. Hiding. Lying. Feeling hunted. Always looking over her shoulder. For the rest of her days, Yveline would sleep lightly and walk softly, fearful that one day the darkness that had claimed Michel and so many of her family and friends would bring her face-to-face with an enemy she couldn't fend off.

Sensing her need to withdraw, and having agreed with Josette's decision to normalize their sons' lives by devoting herself to them, Etienne became the sole head of Lafitte et Fils.

From the beginning, the notion of competition was a given to those in the business of selling antiques. After all, there were just so many signed pieces and magnificent works to go around. Yet to a man, if asked, most dealers freely admitted that it was precisely that edging out, that beating-someone-to-the-punch kind of rivalry, that produced a continuously high level of quality, as well as the most pleasure. Occasionally, however, it happened that one particular rivalry became more heated than usual, tempers flared, and competition turned into cutthroat antagonism.

It was in 1959, when Etienne had moved his business out of his home and into a lavish four-story shop on the Quai Voltaire, that he found himself tangled in the middle of a struggle for power. Josette's father, Pierre Rosenberg, had passed away, leaving his only daughter a large inventory of valuable art. Naturally, they kept their favorites, but since they needed funds to renovate the new shop as well as their private apartments, they decided to put most of the collection up for auction. At that time, the unarguable center for old masters was London.

Knowing that, Etienne recognized that he had a problem. After the war, he had retained close ties with both Peter Wilson and Garrett Castleton. Over the years, Etienne had become a regular patron at Castleton's, buying and selling many pieces, most of them furniture and objects of decorative art, through his friend's salesrooms. The previous year, 1958, Wilson, who had worked at Sotheby's before the war, finally had taken over the reins at Castleton's rival and, with the swiftness of a magician's wand, had shifted world attention to himself and the house on Bond Street. Etienne knew that Garrett was hurting. For the first time in its long history, Castleton's had been reduced to second best. Etienne debated long and hard about what to do, but in the end, business dictated his decision. He consigned the Rosenberg collection to Sotheby's. Garrett never forgave him.

"How could you?" he had shouted, his tall, elegant form ramrod straight, his thin, pale face florid with rage. "How could you betray me like that? And for that . . . that . . . ringmaster!"

"I needed to gain the highest prices possible," Etienne explained, hoping that a reasonable, honest response would cap any further explosion. "I needed the money, and Sotheby's is the current art capital of the world. Had I been selling furniture, I would have consigned the sale to Castleton's, just as I've done in the past. You know I would have."

"I don't know anything except that when I needed you, you deserted me," Garrett Castleton practically roared, his wavy blond hair flying about his head. "If I had deserted you when you needed a friend, you'd be dead!"

Etienne had been waiting for that. Not because Garrett had ever used it before, but because it was the truth.

In late September 1944, the Allies, in an attempt to advance closer toward the Rhine, had split the German defenses in that area, but at great cost. By October, restoration of morale and a weakened supply situation had become an overwhelming problem for the European theater. Knowing that his forces needed a comfortable base for their winter campaign, General Eisenhower ordered the Antwerp approaches cleared and installed a special intelligence task force to ferret out information on an expected counteroffensive. Garrett Castleton and Etienne Lafitte were part of that task force, operating clandestinely in occupied Antwerp and employing members of the local underground as part of their team. Nationals had a personal stake in the success of missions carried out on their soil. Normally, that meant their fealty was assured, their silence guaranteed. This time, that policy proved to be a disastrous mistake.

Once Garrett and Etienne had established a safe house near the harbor and tapped into German lines, they and Claus Janssen, the commander of the Antwerp unit, recruited several radio operators and ciphers to intercept, translate, and decode messages. Then, leaving the city, while the First Canadian Army cleared the Scheldt Estuary outside of Antwerp, Garrett and

Etienne conducted their own reconnaisance operation in the forests near the Belgian border, close to Cologne and the Rhine, the mighty river that was still protecting the German front. There, informers told them of Field Marshal Walther Model's code name for the expected assault: Watch on the Rhine. They said it was rumored that Hitler himself was planning the onslaught. They said they had heard that Von Rundstedt, the administrative commander, was setting up an enormous, impenetrable front. They said that Hitler considered this a last-ditch effort and had issued orders that no one was to hold back. What no one said was precisely *when* the operation was to begin.

By late November, when Etienne and Garrett returned to Antwerp, tired Allied troops were fighting to hold their established line, and the first Allied ships had arrived in Antwerp's harbor. Time was running out, but still there was no confirmation of when or where Hitler's counteroffensive would begin.

On the morning of December 12, Garrett and Etienne received a phone call from one of the women in Janssen's unit. She sounded frightened, desperate. Her voice was low, her speech rapid, making it difficult for Etienne, who was conversant in Flemish, but not completely fluent, to understand her. She insisted that they come to Bruges. She had what they wanted, she said, but certain that her cover had been blown, she had fled Antwerp. She was sure she had been followed. They were to meet her inside the Chapel of the Holy Blood on the southeast corner of the square known as the Burg.

Her call was troubling. Was she telling the truth? Did she know the starting date of the offensive? Or was she setting a trap? They couldn't afford to dismiss her, but if it was a trap, neither could they afford to leave their headquarters unguarded. Garrett would go. Etienne would stay.

Garrett entered the basilica from the side. The woman had specified the lower crypt, the chapel dedicated to St. Basil, not the one that housed the rock-crystal phial said to contain a portion of the bloodstained water washed from the body of Christ. Because the jewel-studded reliquary had been hidden to protect it from the Germans, the chapel was empty except for two old women kneeling before a side altar, lighting candles, praying, and weeping. Downstairs, it was dark and dank, the air raw, with a wet, biting cold that hovered inside the barreled arches of the low, vaulted ceiling. Garrett hid in the shadows among the ghosts and waited for an hour. When no one showed, he realized he had been duped. Quickly, he returned to Antwerp.

As he approached the basement apartment, he noticed that the door was slightly ajar. It was a breach of security. Something was terribly wrong. Keeping his back pressed against the wall, he closed the door, pulled his gun, and unlocked the trigger. A backup shiv stood ready in his sock. The hallway reeked of urine and old fish. A rat nibbled at his shoe. Toward the back, a blade of light broke through the blackness.

Garrett slithered down the hall, keeping his movements small and silent. Two voices, gruff and glottal. Suddenly, a laugh—the whoop of a jackal about to feed on its prey. Garrett hunched down and continued toward the door. A slap. A thud. Another thud. He winced. There was no mistaking the sound of human flesh being pummeled. Just outside, he stopped. He had to try to ascertain how many were in the room, who was positioned where, what weapons they carried. But then he heard the click of a switchblade. He burst into the room, his gun aimed at the first face he saw. Within seconds, that face was blown away. Etienne was in a chair, bound and gagged, his face bloodied, his chest concave, probably from broken ribs. Standing over him was a man with a knife, his hand raised, poised over Etienne's heart. Garrett fired. His bullet destroyed the German's hand, but the shot had not been fatal. Clasping a bloody stump to his chest, the man fled. Garrett wanted to give chase, but instead went to Etienne, untied him, and helped his badly shaken friend to his feet. Moving as fast as they could, considering Etienne's battered state, they went down the hall to the secret room where the transmitter was. It was then that Garrett was forced to acknowledge he had been too late. Lying across the desk, a pen still clutched in his hand, a knife sticking out of his back, his shirt dyed with his own blood, was Claus Janssen. His wife, Jeanette, lay dead in the corner, tied to a chair, a bullet hole through her chest, her lifeless eyes still staring in horrified disbelief. The transmitter was gone. The tapes and logs were gone. After all those weeks of work, after sacrificing two valued comrades, their assignment had come down to little more than an educated guess. Unfortunately, the Allies guessed wrong.

On the morning of December 16, along an eighty-mile front,

two of Hitler's panzer units cracked through the battle-weary American Eighth Corps and raced into Belgium. South of that main blow, a third German Army advanced to form a protective wall, sealing off the American Third Army. By nightfall, it looked as if Hitler had scored a tactical success.

On the second day, realizing the magnitude of the German threat, Allied commanders met, reassessed their strategies, and made decisions that turned potential disaster into victory. Blocking one of the main avenues of advance at Bastogne and holding fast at St. Vith, they eliminated a major route of escape. One American force maintained a determined stand at Elsenborn Ridge. Other battle forces were redeployed along a line that stretched from Dinant to Monschau. Hitler's offensive pushed practically to the Meuse River by Dinant and almost destroyed the historically embattled town, but the First Army pushed back. Despite the odds, Hitler refused to withdraw from the Ardennes, fighting it out until finally, on January 21, he retreated. Though the Battle of the Bulge extracted a heavy toll from both sides, claiming almost eighty thousand casualties, the strength the Germans needed for defending the Rhine had been spent in Belgium.

The Allied triumph was little consolation for Garrett Castleton and Etienne Lafitte. The official position on the Janssen deaths and the theft of vital intelligence records was that Garrett and Etienne had acted correctly, since as field officers, they were required to follow up even the most suspicious of leads. Given the same situation, most other agents would have acted in the same manner. For Garrett and Etienne, that was cold comfort. Two valued comrades had died, and though they had been officially cleared of wrong-doing, in the minds of most, including themselves, they had failed. The only positive to come out of that episode in their wartime service was a strong friendship which had remained rock solid until that day in 1959.

"If not for you, I would have been another wartime statistic," Etienne said, those many years later, "just like Claus and Jeanette. You did save my life. And I owe you."

"And this is how you repay me?" Garrett's voice was thunderous.

Etienne struggled, but he found himself hard-pressed to think of any explanation other than the truth.

"I didn't view it as a betrayal, Garrett."

"Well, I do. You have to know that the Rosenberg collection will attract worldwide attention. Many of those paintings are major pieces of history. The three Caravaggios alone are worth a fortune in publicity. And yet, do you give the collection to me at a time when you know I need a boost? No! You turn it over to Wilson so that Sotheby's can shovel yet another pile of dirt onto Castleton's. I'll never forgive you, Lafitte. Never!"

Etienne tried to argue, but Garrett stormed out. Sotheby's handled the Rosenberg auction. It was, as everyone knew it would be, a huge, glittering success. Connoisseurs from all over the world attended. Etienne profited by several million dollars. Sotheby's hold on the art market tightened. And true to his word, Garrett Castleton never spoke to Etienne again.

Though Armand had never been asked to prove himself on the battlefields of war, he quickly discovered that wherever there were disagreements, there were battlefields. Fortunately, he was his father's son. He was a fighter. He was prepared to go the distance.

For the next several months, he immersed himself in his project. When he wasn't having breakfast meetings and luncheon meetings, he was locked in his office making phone calls or conferring with his three comrades. He was also busy every night, but Gaby suspected that was more pleasure than business. Whatever, Gaby rarely saw him. She, Solange, and Colby ran the shop by themselves. Armand had taken them into his confidence, but had specifically asked them not to become involved in the scheme. In case it backfired, he wanted them free of any dangerous fallout.

Though they worried about him and questioned the wisdom of taking Prado on, Armand's enthusiasm was infectious. He talked about victory, about how he was certain that Lafitte et Fils U.S.A. would flourish after the success of the coup, how he wanted them to be prepared for the coming boom. When one or all of them hinted that it was possible for a Benedict Arnold to hide in an *antiquaire*'s clothing, he answered them philosophically, saying that doing something was always better than doing nothing. He believed that if he and his cohorts succeeded in merely exposing the Prado theocracy to the harsh glare of public opinion, it would have been a worthwhile effort.

His unfaltering confidence was admirable, but his absence had placed added pressure on his staff. Suddenly, each one found himself or herself completely in charge of a specific area of the business. Colby ran the shop. Not only was he a natural salesman, but he was the one with the most decorator contacts and the most friends in the young, moneyed set, and by far the one with the best storefront manner. Solange's extensive knowledge of antiques, as well as her ability to gauge market trends, made her extremely effective in doing estimates and courting potential estate bequests. Which meant that, occasionally, Gaby was the only one available to attend auctions.

Despite the fact that Armand and the others reviewed the catalogues and made suggestions, Gaby was terrified that somehow she would let them down. She had attended many auctions in Ohio with Simone and several in New York with Armand, but she had always been an observer, never the one to enter the ring. Like a young filly testing her legs, she wobbled a bit in the beginning, but because she was determined to learn, she quickly gained the poise and aplomb required of those who bid beneath the hammer. She went to previews and examined those pieces she thought would complement items already in stock. She touched surfaces, tested hinges, probed interiors, sat on furniture, and looked in drawers. When she took her seat inside the salesrooms, she learned to bid via a lift of an eyebrow, a tilt of her head, a bend of her finger. By attending so often, she began to spot the regulars, categorizing them by style preferences and bidding techniques. Some were ferocious, unwilling to allow anyone else to get a piece they had decided was theirs. These were usually wealthy collectors in that enviable circumstance of having unlimited funds. Dealers were more circumspect. They bid only to a point and then, when they felt that the sale price added to their overhead would create too prohibitive a price tag, put down their paddles and calmly waited for the next lot. Sometimes, dealers bid up a piece to protect themselves. If they specialized in a particular area and an item in that area had been greeted with an apathetic response, they bid to create interest, to inspire others to bid above them. If they didn't, the pieces they had in their inventory would be immediately devalued and their profit margin would be greatly decreased. Few were willing to allow that to happen.

Naturally, just as Gaby had begun to recognize the habitués of the salesrooms, they had begun to take notice of her. Her frequent appearances, the number of expensive purchases she had made, and her personal beauty had not only attracted attention, but had also spawned an incorrect conclusion on the part of those who stood behind the podium as well as those who sat in front. No one knew she was working for Lafitte et Fils. She had established credit with a bank account Armand had opened in her name, so naturally, everyone assumed she was another socialite indulging a passion for the elegant remnants of the Age of Enlightenment. It was exactly the impression Armand had intended. The worst thing a dealer could do was to declare his wants and needs in front of his adversaries. The world of antiques was a small one and competition for the best merchandise was intense. It was not unusual, therefore, for dealers either to phone in their bids or to send secret emissaries to bid on their behalf rather than entering into public jousting matches over a *bureau plat* or a Gobelin tapestry. If people thought Gaby was a collector, fine. If they thought of her as a *nouvelle* society dilettante, that was fine too. Armand didn't care as long as they didn't associate her with him.

Gaby had no idea that anyone had even taken note of her presence, let alone had begun to ask questions about the identity of the tall, stunning woman with the chestnut hair and the bulging wallet. She was completely unaware of her impact on others because Gabrielle Didier was still new to her, still a persona, still a costume donned for public occasions. When she was Madame Didier, doing business for Lafitte et Fils, she was well dressed and self-assured, perfumed with an essence of competence and effortless style. To the observer, she seemed in control of herself and her surroundings, and in fact she was. But at night, alone in her small apartment, she was still Gaby Thayer, a woman in transit, a woman beset by too many financial burdens and too much emotional baggage. Each day heralded another step forward, but since her vision was blurred by obligation to Simone and guilt about Steven, she moved slowly and with great deliberation.

Armand was the only one privy to the intricacies of her life.

He knew where she lived and how she lived. He knew where she went on weekends and why, how she spent her money and on what. He was her mentor, her counselor, her tutor, her employer, her friend. He continuously gave support and encouragement to help her grow and stretch her wings. He was the one person to whom she could turn for a laugh or a strong shoulder or a word of advice. She depended on him and looked up to him. Which was why she was so devastated when he failed.

For thirty-eight years, on the third Wednesday of January, the attention of collectors and connoisseurs from all over the world traditionally focused on a building nearly as old as the vendibles displayed within. For ten days, the Seventh Regiment Armory, on Park Avenue and Sixty-seventh Street, an aging dowager with a ruddy, timeworn exterior, played host to the January Antiques Fair, the largest, most splendid antiques show in America. The fair, organized for the benefit of the Henry Hudson Community Center, a charity dedicated to helping New York City's unfortunates, not only raised close to four hundred thousand dollars a year for its primary cause, but provided a market which produced twelve to fifteen million dollars in sales.

Naturally, as with any function that caused so much fanfare and generated so much money, there was a certain air of controversy surrounding the fair. Because the armory could house only seventy to seventy-five exhibitors, there were those who carped that the January Antiques Fair was the only show where the waiting list is more prestigious than the list of participants. There were those who complained that the armory was a drafty, dreary relic with little more than its size and prestigious location to warrant its continued use. There were also those who insisted that, compared to the Biennale Internationale des Antiquaires in Paris or the Grosvenor House Antique Fair in London, the New York fair was lacking in grandeur and eminence. But to a small, knowledgeable clique, those were minor flaws. The major shortcoming was something far more insidious and, therefore, far more difficult to correct.

Vincent Prado, they claimed, was a modern-day Romanov, a power-hungry autocrat who granted favors or rescinded privileges based on the what-have-you-done-for-me-lately school of decision making. No one questioned his taste. It was impeccable. No one doubted his scholarship. His expertise on eighteenth-century cabinetmakers, known as *ébénistes*, was unchallenged. No one argued his qualifications as chairman of the event. In his ten-year tenure, the fair had grown in profitability as well as international importance. But still, many resented the talonlike grip he maintained on his position, often repeating the maxim "absolute power corrupts absolutely," to explain their vexation. Over the years, there had been several attempted coups, but all had failed because of lack of support. Though Prado's dictatorial manner was offensive to some, to others, the glamour and excitement he had injected into an otherwise staid presentation of *objets d'arts* was more than worth the price of submission.

For one thing, the moneyed buzzed around him in droves. For some reason—and no one was quite certain whether it had been his great genius as a leader or the greater need among his followers to be led—women sought his approval on everything from their ensembles to their vacation plans. Men studied his style, imitating the way he knotted his ties and stuffed his pocket squares. He was asked to pass judgment on velvets as well as vitrines, to recommend specialists in furniture restoration as well as specialists in rhinoplasty, to create menus as well as environments. He had decorated many of their homes and, at the same time, had insinuated himself into much of their lives. He had become more than a designer. He had become an arbiter of style.

He was also a master of the art of fund-raising. His was the inspiration behind the trio of preview parties that marked the opening of the fair. Five hundred dollars purchased the title of benefactor and invited the ticket holder to attend a tony, uncrowded tea hosted by the likes of Charlotte Ford, Nancy Lady Keith, or Brooke Astor. Two hundred and fifty dollars designated a patron and admitted the bearer to a sumptuous party in a private room adjacent to the great hall, decorated with ruffles and flourishes by Pauline Trigère. And one hundred and fifty dollars dubbed one a friend of the January Antiques Fair and granted entry to a massive cocktail party with an elevated level of elegance undiminished by the enormity of its guest list. Though an indefatigable team of society women worked for months on end, making arrangements and attending to details, whenever they were asked to take credit for their efforts, they deferred to the genius of Vincent Prado and his rarefied standards of excellence. Without Vincent, they maintained, the character of the January Antiques Fair simply wouldn't be the same. Perhaps. But some were more than willing to take that risk.

When Gaby's taxi pulled up outside the armory, it was four forty-five and Park Avenue was jammed with rush-hour traffic and chauffeur-driven limousines jockeying for the best parking spaces. Gaby stepped onto the curb and tucked her head down to avoid being battered by a whipping wind. She pulled her coat close to her body, protecting herself against the ferocious gusts that polluted the air with swirls of soot and loose twigs and flying newspaper. It was only a short walk up the steps into the armory, but still, she felt the biting cold suck the moisture out of her skin, leaving her face pink and parched.

Inside, she relinquished her coat and, taking a deep breath, turned down the hall that led to the entryway, a dark avenue lined with tattered regimental flags and faded paintings depicting faded moments in America's military history.

Turning right, she showed the ushers the gold ticket that admitted her to the Benefactors' Tea and moved swiftly to bypass the receiving line. Though she recognized that not greeting her hosts might be viewed as a terrible breach of etiquette, Gaby was not secure enough to stand and make casual chitchat with women whose position intimidated her.

She skirted the edge of the large crowd, stopping briefly to decline a cup of Earl Grey tea and accepting instead a glass of freshly poured champagne. She elected to begin her tour along the sides, rather than taking the slow march down the center aisle, which was clearly the route preferred by the see-and-be-seen set. Moving down the left allée, sipping her champagne, she found herself growing more excited with each step. Everywhere she looked, she was treated to a buffet of gourmet offerings: smooth, polished woods to delight the touch, brilliant gilding to startle the eye, colorful paintings to tickle the imagination, luxurious floral arrangements to suggest a summer garden, luscious edibles to entertain the palate. Though she was supposed to be watching the clock so she could be in position when the coup began, Gaby soon forgot everything except the joy of being surrounded by such incredible beauty. Little by little, she lost herself in the circus of splendor that was the fair.

There were three main boulevards designed to house about

ten booths a side. At the head and foot of this arrangement was space for a dozen additional enclosures. Each booth was carefully designed to display the dealer's best merchandise to greatest advantage. What astounded Gaby was not the quality of the offerings—she had expected only the finest—but the variety and depth of selection. There were Queen Anne secretaires, Kang Xi porcelains, Louis XV parquetry commodes, Louis XVI giltwood consoles, Bible quilts, Minton's china sets, Chippendale highboys, Hepplewhite breakfronts, Philadelphia sidechairs, English Regency armchairs, marine watercolors, and primitive oils. There were ormolu candlesticks, Bessarabian carpets, tole-top tables, George III sterling, tea caddies, militia drums, turn-of-the-century jewelry, nineteenth-century mirrors. There was even a large display of antique toys.

Just when Gaby thought she had seen the most wonderful article at the fair, she'd turn a corner and see something even more spectacular. It was a glorious evening, she decided, the perfect setting for Armand's triumph. Checking her watch, she moved quickly up the side allée toward the front, spying Colby and Solange across the room. They nodded at each other, lost themselves in the crowd, and waited. It was time.

At precisely six o'clock, twenty-nine dealers placed small white signs at the front of their booths proclaiming that all merchandise within their stalls had been vetted by a committee of experts and was guaranteed to be authentic. Within seconds, pandemonium broke loose, as the whispers of insurgency spread throughout the hall.

Armand, Davenport, Vinter, and Conway remained calm, behaving as if nothing unusual had occurred. They waited on the customers in their booths and ignored the gathering throng. Their patrons, people who had shown both the good taste and the remarkable restraint to disregard the signs and the hullabaloo they had created, also maintained a decorous posture. Yet no matter how hard everyone tried, it was impossible to brush aside the sense that something was about to happen. The air crackled with expectation. Reporters and photographers headed for the indoor park that marked the center of the fair, their pencils poised, their flashbulbs ready. As Gaby positioned herself at the edge of the square, she could have sworn she noticed the leaves on the trees curling under, a sure sign of an approaching storm.

Her palms grew damp and her eyes sought out either Solange or Colby. When, finally, she spotted Solange, she saw that the older woman also had begun to fear the worst. She turned, hoping to make eye contact with Armand, but she was distracted by the noise that accompanied Vincent Prado's appearance.

He marched into the center of the square like a Roman emperor fresh from a victorious campaign and stood facing the Lafitte booth. Behind him were a dozen irate gentlemen Gaby recognized as dealers who had rejected the invitation to join Armand's cadre. Davenport, Conway, Vinter, three of the French *antiquaires* associated with Etienne and Jacques Lafitte, and several of their allies crossed over to where Armand was standing and closed ranks around him. Shutters clicked with the rapidity of a machine gun, and bursts of harsh, white light popped like rocket fire as the two camps faced each other.

"I insist that these signs of disrespect be removed immediately." Prado's voice was low and definite, void of any compromise.

Armand's expression of cool confidence never wavered.

"I see placards offering patrons of this fair written guarantees of quality and genuineness. I see notices stating that each and every item displayed has been examined and assessed by an independent team of experts. I see reputable dealers willing to stand behind everything they sell. But I see no signs of disrespect."

The veins in Prado's neck pulsed as he tried to rein his anger. Lafitte had timed his move perfectly. The armory was packed with the curious and the blasé, an I've-seen-it-all-before upper-crust audience which loved nothing more than an unscheduled event. Hundreds of people jammed into the small square, their numbers leaking into the intersecting pathways. Control was essential. Prado's reputation was riding on what he did now. He couldn't risk losing his temper.

"I'm sure you view this . . . this demonstration as a simple act of nonconformance." His mouth curved upward, but it slumped so quickly it seemed more like a twitch than a smile. "To me, it's a mutinous slap in the face to all the people who labor so diligently and selflessly to put on this fair."

Armand allowed Prado his Shakespearean sense of drama, but refused to respond in kind. When he spoke, his gestures were less broad, his voice less bombastic.

"There is no question that the committees of the January Antiques Fair do a splendid job. Every year, the fair is more spectacular and better attended than the year before. But invitations, decorations, catalogues, and catering are not the issue. The genuineness of every single item sold to the public is." He paused, encouraging those who were nodding in agreement and whispering to their neighbors. "Vetting is a time-honored practice meant to honor the customer, and I for one do not understand the virulent objections to incorporating it into this fair. In other businesses it may be true that 'the customer is always right.' When it comes to antiques, I feel that dealers are duty bound always to do right by the customer. Vetting guarantees that we have."

Prado felt the ancient floorboards of the armory wobble as, around him, the room seemed to separate and divide. Lafitte had appealed to the natural insecurity of consumers about being duped. He had used logic and Madison Avenue turns of phrase. The only way to counter that type of approach was with emotion and guilt.

"You can dress this rebellion in the finest adjectives and attach it to the noblest causes, but you will never convince me that these signs are anything but an act of hostility and cowardice." He stepped to the side and splayed his hand, drawing attention to the men at his back. "Behind me, stands a group of your fellow dealers, Monsieur Lafitte. They did not go along with your plan. They do not agree that vetting is essential to a quality antiques show. Yet your heinous signs create the illusion that perhaps they backed away because their merchandise is substandard or because they are here to intentionally defraud the public. Is that what you really think? If so, do you have the courage to confront them face to face and tell them that?" He waited. When Armand said nothing, Prado sucked in his breath, lifted his chin and blew out his words in a puff of triumph. "I thought not! And now, on behalf of everyone here, I demand a public apology."

Armand never budged.

"I have nothing to apologize for, except perhaps for disrupting everyone's good time. For that, I am sorry. But for trying to elevate the January Antiques Fair to the excellence attained by the Biennale and Grosvenor House, I do not now, nor will I ever, apologize. The public deserves the best.''

"I agree, which is why I am compelled to ask you to leave. You have, as you so readily admitted, disrupted everyone's good time. Our guests have paid a hefty price to marvel at the joy and beauty of the world of antiques, and that is precisely what they are going to do. *Bonsoir*, Monsieur Lafitte.''

Gaby noticed that a tall, cool blonde had appeared alongside Prado. When he had finished his speech, she began to applaud, her eyes daring Armand to try to speak over the din. The clapping was contagious, and soon the sound was deafening. Armand, his head still held high, strode past Prado and out the door. Prado's expression of delight was expected. It was the look on the blonde's face that confused Gaby. Who was she, and why had Armand's exit given her such unabashed pleasure?

Within minutes, aside from the incessant buzz that permeated the atmosphere, it was as if the contretemps between Prado and Armand had been staged entertainment. People began to tour the allées and shop the booths, showing no discrimination toward those who had displayed the signs or those who hadn't. Prado, overjoyed that the attempted coup had been such an immediate and abysmal failure, went to each and every one of the offending dealers. If the sign was not removed, he told them, they would be removed and prohibited from ever showing at the fair again. All of them complied.

For all intents and purposes, it was as if nothing had ever happened. The rebellion had been crushed, the show had gone on, the thousand-eared monster that feeds on succulent gossip had been fed, and life was the same as it had been before. For everyone except Armand. For him, things would never be the same.

The next morning, Armand awoke to find a moving truck in front of his shop and two musclemen unloading the merchandise from his booth onto the street. He also found a stack of newspapers filled with stories about his debacle: "The Unfair Antiques Fair," "Rebels Without a Cause," "The Lafitte Defeat." At nine o'clock, when Gaby arrived with croissants, coffee, and every cheerful thought she could conjure up, she expected to find

Armand exhausted and ashen faced. Instead, he was full of energy and surprisingly pragmatic.

"As my father always says, 'If you put yourself on the front lines, you have to assume you're going to get shot at.' Besides, it wasn't a total failure. Two articles supported the notion of vetting. That's two more than even knew what vetting was before last night."

"I thought you were brilliant," Gaby said, as if a single compliment had the power to reverse the course of events.

"Everyone thought Napoleon was brilliant too. Then he decided to vacation in Waterloo."

"Okay. So it didn't go exactly as planned. It wasn't fatal."

"We don't know that yet," he said ominously. "It's not like Vincent Prado to accept a public challenge graciously. Believe me, he's just waiting for the fair to end before making his next move."

"What could he do?"

"I don't know, but he'll do something, of that I'm certain."

"Who was the woman who started the ovation for Prado?"

"Irina Stoddard."

"Who's she?"

"The ex-wife of Lord Winston Stoddard and the daughter of Garrett Castleton, Sr."

"As in Castleton's of international auction house fame?"

"The very one."

"Well, Lady Stoddard must have caught you raising the wrong paddle or something, because if looks could kill, you'd be lying in a box right now. What is her story?"

Armand sipped his coffee, stalling before answering.

"Don't you remember I told you about the Castletons and the Lafittes being Europe's version of the Hatfields and the McCoys? My father never told me the exact cause of the feud. In fact, he refuses to talk about it, but perhaps that's not true of Garrett Castleton, Sr. Perhaps Irina's dislike of me was inherited, like the family silver."

It sounded reasonable. Almost too reasonable to suit Gaby, but she guessed that Armand wasn't in the mood for complicated responses, so she let it go.

"She's a very elegant, very important woman, but I don't think I'd ever want to take tea with her. Is that right?"

Armand laughed, the sound more knowing than amused.

"Take my word for it. Irina Stoddard is an icicle, and no amount of warmth and sunshine can melt her."

As if emphasizing his point, he rose and walked over to the window, shutting out the morning chill. Before returning to his seat, his eyes lingered on a magnificent pair of ormolu andirons known as *chenets*. They had been part of a display grouping in the Lafitte et Fils booth at the fair. Now they were part of an inventory overage that threatened to destroy his bottom line.

"What are we going to do with all of this?" Gaby said, reading his thoughts.

"Before I was so unceremoniously tossed out, there had been a lot of interest in several major pieces. If I'm lucky, the interested parties will come to the shop to buy."

"What if they don't? Most people are naturally lazy. If it's in front of them, they buy. If they have to walk to it, they think about it."

"True, but real collectors are willing to crawl to get the best pieces, and most of our offerings were the best in their class." Armand smiled, trying to reassure her, but her face continued to register doubt. "Don't despair. After all, we do have a large number of regular customers, and the Lafitte name usually attracts international traffic. We have the option of exchanging merchandise with Paris or London, and if all else fails, we have the auction houses. We simply consign the bigger pieces to one of the big three and recoup our losses. Trust me. There's nothing to worry about."

Gaby did trust Armand, but he was wrong. There was plenty to worry about. Within weeks, there was a noticeable decline in his business. Decorators who used to call him first, weren't calling at all. Clients who had bought from him for years, claimed they were cutting back, but were seen coming out of other shops or frequenting auctions. Friends who at one time would never have thought to have a party without him, didn't think to include him. By the end of March, it was apparent that Armand was in a state of utter disgrace. Solange made a graceful exit, returning to Paris where Armand's brother had generously offered her a position. Colby simply left, unwilling to tarnish his name by hanging onto the railings of a sinking ship. Gaby stayed, but each day it was becoming harder and harder to justify her salary.

To the outside world, Armand supposed, the reasons for his exile appeared obvious, but to him, his complete ostracism was a punishment that did not fit the crime. This was not retaliation for challenging Prado's authority. This was not a reprisal for casting a thin shadow on his fellow dealers. This was a vendetta, and though he knew it would be practically impossible to prove his suspicions and clear his name, he knew exactly who was behind it and why. The questions were, how long would it last and how bad would it get?

Simone died in April. Her will was brief, the first part a standard legal document which instructed her lawyers to sell her property in Antibes and use the proceeds to pay off the remaining balance of an old bank debt—accrued when she had refinanced in order to pay for Gaby's college tuition and wedding—and to take whatever was left and apply it to her medical bills; the second part was a letter to Gaby.

Ma chère Gabrielle,

At last the suffering is over. I no longer have to cope with the unremitting pain or the slow, humiliating deterioration of my body. Though I fought as valiantly as I could, in the final analysis, the cancer was stronger than my ability to survive. The last thing I wanted was to be a burden to you, *ma petite*, and yet, despite my wishes, in death, that is what I have become. Perhaps if I had known, I would have resisted that last *bonheur du jour*, or rejected those giltwood *fauteuils*. I doubt it, but one never knows.

Judging by the number of pin pricks and tests and pills and operations and doctors that I had to endure these last few months, I'm certain that my stay at Lakewood cost as much as a stay at the Ritz. I only wish I could say that one was as enjoyable as the other. However, I'm afraid that I'm leaving you a legacy of indebtedness. What's worse, I'm about to put restrictions on you that will make it even harder to erase those obligations.

Though I brought most of Tante Simone's inventory to

Garth's, I saved the best pieces for you and Steven. For you: a rare pair of early eighteenth-century Chinese Export Phoenix Birds to remind you of the spirit of the Didiers, a fine Louis XV ormolu mantel clock, a museum-quality mid–eighteenth-century marquetry table signed B.V.R.B. (Bernard van Risamburgh, the maître during the reign of Louis XV), and of course, the mahogany gueridon where we sipped our afternoon tea, shared our goûter, and learned to love each other. For Steven, an armoire from the time of Louis XIV. I specifically want my grand-nephew to have something from the Sun King, because although he was a man of excess, he was also a man of vision and achievement.

I know that each of these pieces is worth a small fortune, and certainly I would like to think that I had provided the means to settle my own accounts, but these precious antiques are all I have to leave you. They are the sum and substance of my life. I am vain enough to want to be remembered and nostalgic enough to feel an obligation to your parents to protect and preserve your inheritance. That's why I'm forbidding the sale of any of them for a minimum of ten years. If you sell one during that time, you will have to forfeit the others to The Cleveland Museum of Art. At this moment, I'm sure you think I've gone quite mad. I'm also sure you think I'm quite selfish, demanding that you hold on to such valuable things while you're so hard-pressed to pay my bills. The only explanation I can offer is that, to me, one can always find a way to pay a bill. One can't always find antiques of this extraordinary caliber.

I have kept a small reserve because I have a request I don't want you to deny. I realize this might be a major inconvenience, but I wish to be buried in the same place as my parents, my brother, Stephane, my sister, Denise, and my beloved Alain. I've been happy living in America, but I know that my soul is French and would never rest easy beneath soil that wasn't soaked with *le vin rouge*.

My darling Gabrielle, I know that right now the sky is dark and it seems as if there are no stars to guide you, but keep looking up. You'll find your way. Just believe in who you are. Have faith in what you can do. And once in a while, have the courage to take a risk.

Saying *au revoir* to you is the hardest part of dying. I couldn't love you more if I had nursed you at my breast or cradled you in my arms immediately after birth. Though you are not the child of my womb, you, Gabrielle, are truly the child of my heart. *Je t'aime*.

Gabrielle did as Simone wanted. She and Steven accompanied her body to France. Together with Oncle Bernard, they stood in a small graveyard on the outskirts of Antibes and wept as Simone Vivienne Didier Boyer was laid to her eternal rest.

6

As Armand looked out the window of his parents' apartment, it was easy to understand why lyricists were forever romanticizing April in Paris. Outside, the morning sun dressed the Avenue Montaigne in a pale yellow veil that floated over the street like translucent chiffon. Young leaves fluttered on their branches like ballerinas *en pointe*. Flowerboxes were abloom with vivid reds and pinks. Powerful men in custom-tailored suits traveled the avenue in highly polished, chauffeured Rolls Royces or Mercedes-Benzes, while smartly garbed women strolled in and out of fashionable shops, buying the newest and the latest at Guy Laroche or Christian Dior or Jean-Louis Scherrer or Emanuel Ungaro. They indulged their passion for shoes at Maud Frizon, for jewels at Cartier, Bulgari, or Gerard, and their more basic appetites with lunch at Le Relais in the elegant Plaza Athénée.

April was a time of seasonal renaissance, a time for reaffirming one's faith in the cyclical nature of the universe, in the fact that after life was death and after death was life. That April, however, Armand was blind to the rainbow of hope that normally colored the three months between the vernal equinox and the summer solstice. His eyes saw only a gray curtain of disappointment and failure.

"It will pass, Armand." Etienne had listened with great sympathy to his son's story. His own history had taught him that today's friend was tomorrow's enemy and vice versa. "These things have a way of turning around. Trust me."

"I don't regret taking the stand that I did. And I don't regret forcing Prado's hand. But," he said, turning to face his father and his mother, "I do regret tarnishing the Lafitte name."

Josette was seventy-three now; Etienne was seventy-six. As befit a couple married fifty-six years, their minds had become as one. It was Josette who voiced their shared opinion.

"You could never do anything except embellish our name, Armand. We have always been proud of you. We're proud of you now. And we shall continue to take great pride in whatever you do."

She rose slowly, pushing herself up on the arm of the gilded Régence settee where she and Etienne were seated. Though she walked with the assistance of a cane, Josette Lafitte still carried herself with an air of nobility. She made her way to the window and patted Armand's cheek. He was fifty years old, but he always felt like a sheltered child in this woman's presence.

"Your father and I have survived many attacks on our name. You too shall survive. I promise."

Josette smiled as Armand bent and kissed her cheek. She adored her firstborn, but this son claimed the larger share of her heart. Whereas Jacques was practical, Armand was romantic. Whereas the older one delighted in art as a business, the younger delighted in art for art's sake. Whereas Jacques had learned his trade working alongside his father, Armand had been tutored by his mother. Yet she believed that somewhere, somehow, she had let him down. While he was content with his role in Lafitte et Fils, she sensed that he much preferred his work as an art historian. And while she knew he had had innumerable love affairs, only once had he brought a young woman home, and even then, despite his obvious devotion to her, he had never married. She had no way of knowing how many more days she had remaining to her, but every morning she prayed that before she died, her beloved Armand would taste some of the sweetness married life had fed her.

Armand helped his mother into a nearby chair and went to

retrieve her tea. When she was settled, he joined his father on the settee.

"You sent me to New York to increase our fortunes, not to decrease them," he said with a self-deprecating laugh.

"Ah," Etienne said, patting his son on the knee. "The key word is fortune. Lafitte et Fils is a formidable business. So one of our branches has suffered a setback. London is doing well. So is Paris. Believe me, we can more than afford to support the New York shop until this foul wind has passed and the sky is clear once again."

"It's not just a matter of money, Father. I know we can ride out a slow period. But I've been shoved out of the picture. Nasty rumors are beginning to surface, and frankly, I'm concerned about permanent damage to our reputation."

Etienne grew pensive. His dark eyes dulled, as if he had removed the fire from them to fuel his thinking process. Fingers gnarled with arthritis stroked his chin.

"I've met Vincent Prado. He's not a general. He's a foot soldier. Who's giving him his orders? And why? And is this being directed toward you because you headed this attempted coup? Or because you're Armand Lafitte?"

Armand shook his head, but he could feel tiny beads of sweat at his hairline. Once an intelligence agent, always an intelligence agent.

"I don't know," he said. "His following is huge."

"I'm not interested in hangers-on. Who are the ones closest to him? The ones whose opinions matter to him?"

"Jayne Wrightsman. Brooke Astor. An assortment of Roth-schilds. Irina Stoddard. The Trumps. Mercedes Kellogg. The Kluges."

"Isn't Irina Stoddard Castleton's daughter?"

Armand had known that once he mentioned her name, Etienne wouldn't hear any others. He nodded. His father curled his hands into tight fists.

"I can't believe that after all these years, he's still at it." Etienne's voice was low. Josette's eyes narrowed.

"You don't know that he had anything to do with this," she said with a firm, but cryptic edge, as if within that one sentence was contained an unspoken paragraph.

"Do you really think that Garrett Castleton, Sr. is using

Irina, by getting her to use Prado to hurt me as a way of hurting you?" Armand rolled his eyes back. "It's too convoluted."

Etienne grunted his disagreement. He had seen too much to dismiss an idea just because it seemed too obvious or too difficult to work out or too easy to foil.

"When you find yourself barred from consigning merchandise to Castleton's and barred from holding a paddle at one of their auctions, call me and tell me how twisted my logic is!"

Etienne's words were spiced with anger at an old injustice.

"You may be right," Armand conceded, "but Irina doesn't usually do anything on anyone's behalf."

"She wants control of Castleton's International, doesn't she?"

"That is the story going around," Armand agreed.

"Then she would sweep the streets of London with a whisk broom if her father asked her to."

"Do you really think that Garrett has made his daughter his tool?" Josette addressed herself to her husband. "Do you really think that after all these years, he still hasn't had his fill?"

Etienne looked at his wife. He knew how much she had enjoyed her friendship with Garrett and Charlotte Castleton. He knew how much she had regretted that it was her inheritance that had precipitated this feud. But he also knew that she had participated in his decision, and never once since the day he had consigned the Rosenberg collection to Sotheby's had she questioned it.

"If Garrett isn't behind this, then why would all the animosity and all the venegefulness be centered on Armand and not spread around to all who were involved?"

Josette remained silent. She had no answer. Armand remained silent. Unlike his mother, he could have shed additional light. He could have presented an alternative version. But he didn't.

He had already been responsible for a loss of revenue and possibly a loss of family dignity. The last thing he wanted was to lose his father's respect. Or worse, his love.

"I feel as if I'm losing everyone I love." Steven tried to blink back his tears, but one disobedient droplet escaped and slowly rolled down his cheek. "Soon, it'll be Uncle Bernard." He wiped his face with the back of his hand and stared out the window of the airplane, still seeing his uncle waving good-bye at Charles de Gaulle Airport. "He looked so old and weak."

Gaby squeezed his arm, but because she shared his feelings and his fears, it was difficult to find something comforting to say.

"He's not that old, really. Tante Simone was seventy-one, which means that Oncle Bernard is sixty-five."

"He looked ninety."

"He's grieving, Steven. Other than us, Simone was the last of his family, and he loved her dearly."

"So did I."

It was a quiet comment, softly said, but deeply felt. For Gaby, that admission was an important one. Often, she had wondered whether Steven really appreciated Simone or simply tolerated her for Gaby's sake. Simone was so eccentric, so liberal, so different from the Thayers. To Gaby's way of thinking, that was all the more reason to adore her, but Steven had much of the Thayer conservatism in him. Some he had been born with, but the rest had been force-fed in heaping spoonfuls by Ethel and Wally, their two daughters, and their son, Steven's father. Gaby had always hoped that the Thayer bent for sobersidedness had been balanced by the Didier joie de vivre, but since she no longer saw Steven on a daily basis, and since his adult personality was still being forged, it was hard to tell.

"I wanted her to live forever," Gaby said, recalling how once, very long ago, she had believed that family was a forever thing, holding onto her son as if any moment someone would take him away from her, too. "But I guess 'forever' is a fantasy word. Death is reality."

The last time she had seen Simone had been less than two weeks before, and even to her untrained eye, it had been clear that Simone was in extremis. Her skin had sagged against her skeleton, all flaccid and yellow. Her breathing had been labored and her eyes had taken on the color of aged parchment. Though every external sign pointed to death, the internal spirit continued to fight. Her words had been measured and difficult, yet she had insisted upon conversation. She had wanted to know everything— what was happening with Gaby's job, what she had heard from Steven, how Armand was faring, was there a man in her life. In response, Gaby had done what she had been doing for more than a year, she had lied. She told Simone that Armand's business was better than ever, that the shop was busy and she was busy, much too busy to be out searching for romance.

"Why didn't Tante Simone leave her cottage in Antibes to Oncle Bernard?" Steven asked, snapping Gaby back into the present.

"It was too expensive for Oncle Bernard to keep up alone, I guess. And besides, you know he doesn't like to leave Paris if he doesn't have to."

"We had a lot of great vacations there, didn't we?"

"That we did," Gaby said, allowing herself to reminisce, allowing herself to smile. It had been years since she and Brian and Steven had joined Simone and Bernard for their annual *vacances*, but Steven's recollections were correct. They had been wonderful times, carefree family holidays when everyone had felt connected to one another. "I'm glad you have such fond memories of times spent with your great-aunt and great-uncle. It's important to know where you came from and who you came from."

"Even if we kept the cottage, it wouldn't be the same," Steven said, lost in his own train of thought. "Tante Simone is gone. You and Daddy wouldn't be there together. It would feel wrong. Just like it feels wrong whenever I go home."

She heard the bitterness, but by now she knew better than to try and fight it. She couldn't force him to understand why she had left Wadsworth, why she had abandoned his house, or why, in his mind, she had abandoned him. The law may have adopted a system of no-fault divorce, but few children of divorce accepted it as a no-fault procedure. Steven needed to place blame. He needed to focus on a reason for the horrible disruption of his family and the pull he felt on his loyalties. Unfortunately, his youth, his distance from the situation, and his natural tendency to view the world through happily-ever-after eyes, had confused cause and effect.

"Would it help to know that going home feels wrong to me?" Gaby said quietly. "That I feel as strange and alien in that house as you do?"

He stared at her and though his eyes brimmed with accusations, his lower lip quivered, trembling like a bird caught in the rain. "Then why can't you change it? Why can't you make it like it was?"

"Because I didn't make it like it is."

"Maybe not," he said, coldly appraising the woman seated next to him, "but you don't exactly look like you're suffering."

His sarcasm cut like a sword, slicing into her resolve not to defend herself by denigrating Brian to his son. It took every ounce of restraint she possessed to keep from venting her true feelings. Instead, she forced herself to minimize Steven's affront, to understand it as pain taking the form of an insult. Yes it was a slap, and yes it deserved to be answered, but with well-placed jabs, not a roundhouse punch.

"If that's your way of telling me I look good, thank you for the compliment, left-handed though it was." She tipped her head in a mock bow, but her face exhibited no signs of amusement. "Am I suffering? That depends on what your idea of suffering is, Steven. I'm not living on a park bench and begging for my meals, if that's what you mean, but I wouldn't say I'm living on easy street either. I work very hard for my money and I have to pinch pennies every way I know how. I can't expect you to know these things, since you've consistently avoided visiting me in New York, but I live in a dumpy apartment with rented, second-hand furniture, I make most of the clothes I wear, and," she said, her voice stumbling over the lump in her throat, "if Simone hadn't left the money for these tickets in her will, I would have had to sell the last of my paperweight collection to bury her."

Steven blushed. "I'm sorry. I didn't mean to upset you. I just . . . oh, I don't know. I don't mean to say hurtful things. They just seem to come out," he said honestly. "You do look good. Really good. But . . . well . . . you look different. You don't look like my mom anymore."

Gaby's insides softened, turning to mush the way they always did when Steven's little-boy side revealed itself. She leaned over, took his face in her hands, and kissed him.

"I may have added a touch of color here and there, and I may have updated my wardrobe, but rest assured, I'm still your mom. I still sing in the shower and pig out on chocolate chip cookies. I still cry at old movies and scream my lungs out at baseball games. And I still love you more than anything else in this world. None of that has changed, except that with Simone gone and everything else that's happening in my life, I need to know that you love me.''

"I do love you," he said, embarrassed that she had to ask. "I guess I'm just having trouble adjusting.''

Gaby surprised them both by laughing.

"Me, too," she said. "If I never knew it before, I know it now. Growing up is hell!''

After Gaby accompanied Steven to school, she returned to Ohio, where her first stop was the administrator's office at Lakewood.

"I've come to settle my aunt's bill," she said, her face still gray with grief, her eyes dark from the fatigue of so many hours of travel in such a short time.

"We were terribly sorry to lose Madame Boyer. She was an unusual woman, delightfully charming to the end.''

Mrs. Sloane sat at her desk like a schoolmarm, her hair tightly knotted at the nape of her neck, her gray dress buttoned high despite the excessive heat in her office. Though her smile was friendly, it was brief.

"I'm afraid that her time with us was costly, Mrs. Thayer. In the last two months alone, she required extensive medical treatment. I must assure you that none of this was capricious. We only did what was necessary to maintain a modicum of comfort and dignity.''

"I'm sure you did your best.''

"Naturally, we prefer payment in full, but if necessary, we will be happy to make arrangements for you to pay your obligation over an extended period of time.''

"How much is my obligation?''

Mrs. Sloane paused and riffled through the papers on her desk in what Gaby recognized as a superfluous gesture. She knew to the penny what Gaby owed.

"Eighty-five thousand dollars.''

Though Gaby had been prepared for the worst, this was catastrophic. Whatever limited color clung to her skin drained instantly, leaving her face ashen.

"But I don't . . . I never expected . . . '' she muttered, trying to get control of herself.

"I know it's a shock, dear, and I wish it were otherwise, but you knew the hospital wing was expensive. Medicare takes care of all costs for the first twenty days. After that, from the twenty-first day to the hundredth day, you're only responsible for the deductible. Unfortunately, your aunt stayed with us for six months beyond that hundred-day period. In addition to the three-hundred-dollar per diem charge for board and basic medical attention, there were many additional charges accruing from several surgeries and all the extra treatments and care her condition required."

Gaby nodded, her body numb.

"I know how difficult this is. Your aunt is gone and yet there is such an enormous lingering debt. It's one of the unfortunate circumstances of this business. I regret the imposition of such financial hardship during this time of mourning, but I'm afraid I have no choice."

"I understand."

"Mrs. Thayer, believe me, we will make every effort to accommodate you. Why don't you take some time to assess your situation and then come back and we'll work something out."

Dazed, Gaby left Mrs. Sloane's office and practically staggered to her car. Where was she going to get eighty-five thousand dollars? For a long while, she sat staring over the steering wheel, looking out at the lake, hoping for a divine answer to a very earthly problem. A bank. That's where she would go. She would ask for a loan. She was working. She would pay it back, a little at a time.

Confident that the Cleveland Bank would help her, she drove into the city and asked to meet with Mr. Rodale, the head of the loan department. He was polite and sympathetic, but, as he put it, bound by bank policy to reject her application. She had no credit rating and, therefore, was ineligible for any advancement of funds.

"What do you mean I have no credit rating? I've been doing business with you for years. You hold the mortgage to my house. You held the mortgage on my parents' house. I've had savings accounts and checking accounts here since I was married."

"This is most unpleasant for me, Mrs. Thayer, but in the past, your credit rating was based on your husband's earnings. If he were to apply for the loan, perhaps we would be able to help you.''

"I'm divorced from my husband."

"I'm aware of that. Unfortunately, however, you've never established your own banking history. Your husband was paying the mortgage on your home, and your checking account was joint."

"I have a savings account in my own name."

"Which, according to our records, you closed ten months ago."

Gaby's head was spinning. Ten months ago. What happened ten months ago?

"I had to help pay my aunt's hospital bill," she said quietly, knowing that compassion did not qualify as collateral.

"Be that as it may, at the present time you have no open accounts with us."

"But I'm working. Can't you grant me a loan based on my own income?"

"Your salary isn't high enough and your employment tenure isn't long enough to justify such a sizable loan."

"I can't believe this! I can't believe that I've been dealing with this bank for sixteen years and suddenly, because I'm not someone's wife, I'm persona non grata. That's not fair, Mr. Rodale. That's just not fair!"

"If it will help you at all," he said, disturbing his implacable calm with a brief but sympathetic smile, "before she died, your aunt requested that we sell her property in France. This morning, I received word that that negotiation was satisfactorily completed. Once both sets of lawyers and all the appropriate taxes are paid, you should have about fifteen thousand dollars."

"I need seventy thousand more," Gaby said, an hysterical edge to her voice.

"I wish I could help you, Mrs. Thayer, but truly, my hands are tied."

She visited three other banks and two credit finance offices. Each time, the answer was the same: their hands were tied. If she had had a charge account in the name of Gaby Thayer, instead of Mrs. Brian Thayer, then maybe. If she had taken out a loan and paid it back, it might have been different. If she had been able to produce some sort of acceptable guarantee, like stock or property or insurance policies, they would have had a basis for discussion.

At every turn, the message became clearer—men had collateral, and a woman's only collateral was a man. A slow rage began to build inside Gaby's gut. She hadn't asked to be in this position. All her life she had obeyed the rules: women should be good wives and devoted mothers; they should manage the home and let their husbands manage the finances; they shouldn't "worry their pretty little heads" about money matters. Well, she had lived according to the rules and where had it gotten her? Alone and in debt.

Her last stop—indeed, her last resort—was the executive office building of the Wadsworth Match Company. As she approached the desk where Brian's secretary usually sat, she steeled herself. Instead of finding the pretty young woman she remembered, she found a mature woman with a plumpish body, friendly gray eyes, and a small sign sitting on the shelf behind her that read Happiness Is Being a Grandmother. Inside, Gaby smiled. Obviously Pamela Frost was taking no chances.

"Is Mr. Thayer in?"

"May I ask who wishes to see him?"

"*Mrs*. Thayer," Gaby said as she strode past the startled woman, opened the door, and entered without being announced.

He was on the phone, and judging by the sophomoric look on his face, Gaby guessed that Pamela was on the other end. The minute he saw her, his face flushed with embarrassment, then with anger. She supposed she could have retreated and waited for him to finish, but she was there on urgent business. Pamela could wait. Besides, she was well past the point of caring whether or not her actions upset him. She marched to the front of his desk and stood there, staring impatiently until he hung up.

"What do you want?"

"I presume you heard that Simone died." She had waited for a card, a call, some word of condolence or sympathy from him or any of the Thayers. There had been none. She would never forgive any of them for that.

"Yes, I heard. I'm sorry."

I'm sorry. It's snowing out. We need more milk. With the amount of emotion he had injected into his expression of regret, he could have said any one of those things, and they all would have sounded the same. He spoke with no feeling, no sense of loss, as if Simone had been just another name in the obituary column.

"I need your help," Gaby said without preamble.

"What kind of help?"

"I need money to pay Simone's hospital bills."

"Why come to me?"

Gaby had known this would be difficult. God knows, she would have preferred anything than to ask Brian for help, but she had no other alternative. Expecting a negative response, on the way over she had cautioned herself not to dwell on the antagonism of the recent past, but to remember the better moments: their courtship, their honeymoon, the early years of their marriage, Steven's childhood. Brian had been gentle and kind and loving then. He couldn't have changed that much, she told herself. His basic character must have remained intact. Whether their separation had been her fault, his fault, the result of some midlife crisis, premature male menopause, or a sixteen-year itch, this was different. It wasn't about them. It was about someone who had been very good to Brian.

Surely he hadn't forgotten Simone's generosity during the difficult years after Steven had been born and Brian had been between jobs; the countless times she babysat so Brian and Gaby could have a weekend to themselves; the vacations she had paid for so that all of them could spend the last two weeks in August with Bernard at Antibes. Surely he would understand Gaby's decision to provide Simone with a painless, dignified end.

"I came to you because I don't have anywhere else to turn. The bank turned me down. I've tried to arrange a loan, but no one will give me one. I'm desperate, Brian. The bill was eighty-five thousand dollars!"

"She was your aunt. Your responsibility."

"I don't have that kind of money and you know it!"

Brian leaned back in his big leather chair, plunked his feet on his desk, clasped his hands behind his head, and spread his lips in a slow smile.

Had it been a mean, malicious smile, Gaby might have excused it as part of some male defense mechanism, creating hostility so that he didn't have to feel guilty about leaving her. Had it been that, she might have felt sorry for him. But it was a smug smile, the kind people in authority use when dealing with those they consider subservient. That, she couldn't and wouldn't excuse.

"You have lots of money."

"Really? The last time I looked, I was practically broke. If I have a fortune tucked away underneath a floorboard somewhere, I wish you'd tell me where it is."

"The house. According to the terms of our divorce, you're entitled to half. My guess is it must be worth at least a hundred thou, maybe more. Sell it."

"Sell the house? It's all I've got! I can't do that."

"Why not? You've moved out anyway."

"I haven't moved out. I went to New York to find a job."

"And from what Steven tells me, you found one working at some high-tone French antiques shop. Give me a break," he said. "You're holding on to a house that's worth a bundle and yet you have the nerve to barge in here and ask me for money? You're a real piece of work!"

"Give *you* a break? I'm an office clerk! My alimony, such as it was, has stopped, and this job that you seem to equate with being a corporate CEO, barely covers my expenses, let alone Simone's hospitalization." Gaby's voice had risen, turning shrill. Quickly, she calmed herself. "Simone was dying. I wanted to help her. Now I need you to help me." She waited, but his only response was silence. "For God's sake, Brian, what do you want me to do, beg?"

"No. I want you to sell the house."

He wasn't suggesting, he was insisting, and judging by the eagerness in his voice, this was not a new idea. He had been waiting a long time to exercise this demand. Why was it so important, she wondered. What difference did it make to him? Did he want the house for himself? Did he want to live in it with Pamela? Pamela! How stupid not to see it immediately! Pamela was some kind of executive. She probably drew down a big salary, and Brian was having trouble competing. Of course! That was it! He needed money so he could impress his young lover. How fortuitous that Simone had died and put Gaby in a position where she also needed money. Without wasting the energy it took to expend one more breath, she spun around on her heel and stormed out.

She hadn't wanted to face it before, but on the drive back to New York, the truth insinuated itself into her thoughts and lodged there like a nail in the tread of a tire, burrowing deeper and deeper with each successive mile. She was alone. Simone was dead. Steven was at school. Her divorce was final. Her alimony payments had ceased. Brian was out of her life. Like it or not, ready or not, she was now what Simone had wanted her to become—independent.

Simone had promised it would feel good. All Gaby felt was scared. She had so many problems, so few solutions. Worse, she had no one to turn to, no one to depend on except herself. In her letter, Simone had told Gaby she might have to take a few risks to find her way. Then, Gaby had been too immersed in grief to digest Simone's words. Now she knew that even if she had been thinking clearly, she would have dismissed the idea of consciously courting uncertainty.

The trauma of her parents' deaths had smothered many of the if-it-feels-good-do-it impulses she had indulged as a young girl, transforming her into a look-both-ways-before-you-cross-the-street young woman. Once married and a mother, she had buttoned up even more, taking that sprightly child who used to love the land of make-believe and locking her away in a private closet where well-worn memories hung alongside unrealized hopes and unfulfilled dreams. Since then, she had rarely been adventurous, rarely sought the furthest point on a limb. When given a choice, she had opted for the sure thing rather than taking the chance, the backcourt rather than the net. Life had taught her to protect what she had.

But now it was different. She could afford to take risks. She had nothing left to lose.

"I did what he wanted. I put the house up for sale."

Gaby had returned from her mournful pilgrimage early that morning. After dropping off her luggage at her apartment, she headed over to Armand, who she knew had returned from Paris two nights before. She looked awful. Her skin was pallid and lackluster; her eyes were underscored with gray rings. Though he had anticipated that a journey like hers would exact a physical toll, Armand was unprepared for the amount of weight she had lost. In the short time she had been gone, she had grown perilously thin.

Yet as he listened to her relate the details of the funeral, her meeting at Lakewood and its disastrous aftermath, he noted that she sounded anything but frail. She was anxious and distressed, but she wasn't frantic. She wasn't flailing about or seized with a blinding attack of panic. Somehow, somewhere between Wadsworth, Paris, Antibes, and New York, she had gained a strength of spirit and a resolve that was encouraging, albeit unexpected.

"I wish I had the money to give you," Armand said as he poured a cup of tea for Gaby and urged her to drink it. "I know how much you wanted to keep that house."

"I did, but I just can't. It is now officially on the market," she said with only a slight echo of animosity. "Obviously, Brian had done his homework. According to the real estate agent, we should be able to get a hundred thousand dollars for the house. After taking care of the mortgage and the government, I should net about twenty thousand dollars."

"That's great," Armand said, trying to sound enthusiastic.

"Yeah. Great. That, plus the fifteen from the sale of Simone's Antibes property, and my debt is reduced to a mere fifty thousand dollars."

"But you said Mrs. Sloane was willing to work out an arrangement for you to pay on time."

"True, but I have a feeling her idea of reasonable and mine are two different things." She leaned back and sipped her tea slowly, letting the warmth coax the color back into her cheeks. "I figured out that even if I could afford to pay her one hundred dollars a month, which I can't, it would take me forty-one years to pay it all off. Forty-one years! Is that reasonable?"

She laughed at the impossibility of her situation. Armand laughed too, wishing he could disagree with her arithmetic, wishing he could do something to help.

"Let's forget that for the moment," she said, forcing herself to brighten. "How was your trip to Paris?"

"Inspirational. My parents are extraordinary people."

"Obviously they didn't disown you."

"No, they did not. In fact, my father predicted the latest predicament."

An alarm clanged inside Gaby's brain.

"Did something else happen while I was gone?"

It wasn't often that Armand's façade drooped, but suddenly, like a drape that had lost its swag, the confident cover fell and he looked shaky and vulnerable.

"I thought I'd consign a few pieces to auction. Christie's, Sotheby's, and Castleton's thought otherwise."

The alarm grew louder, screeching until the noise pinched Gaby's temples and she was forced to rub the sides of her head for relief.

"Translate, please."

"In simple English, they said they prefer not to accept any merchandise from Lafitte et Fils U.S.A. When I pressed the issue, a friend at Sotheby's told me on the QT that the word around town is the reason I made such a to-do about vetting was to cover up the fact that, for years, I'd been selling fakes, reproductions that I passed off as the real thing."

Gaby was certain that at some point, when she had been asleep or looking the other way, she had fallen off the face of the earth and was now moving about in an unfamiliar solar system. There could be no other explanation. Eighty-five-thousand-dollar debts! Auction houses rejecting top-quality pieces! People accusing Armand Lafitte of fraud!

"That's absurd!" she said. "They can't believe something like that."

"They can and they do." Armand sighed, absentmindedly wiping a careless drop of tea off the satinwood table next to his chair. "According to my source, the story going around is that I began to flimflam the public because I couldn't produce the bottom line expected of me. Lafitte et Fils U.S.A. was failing and unless I came up with something quickly, I would have been recalled to Paris, the shop would have been closed, and I would have humiliated not only myself, but three generations of Lafittes."

"We can't let Prado get away with this!" Gaby sprinted out of her chair and paced the room, fired by a highly combustible mix of frustration and indignation. She had been a witness to and a victim of so much injustice lately, it was getting more and more difficult to view the scales as evenly balanced. "There must be something we can do."

"I've gone over it a thousand times. There's nothing." Concern pleated his forehead, folding in like louvers, as if to shield him from further unpleasantness. "First of all, this whole scenario has been carefully plotted. For me to prove that all this slander is in fact slander, I'd have to recall every antique I've sold over the last four years. Then I'd have to get signed affidavits both from the owners and from several experts who would verify each article's genuineness. And then—after I had gone to that unbelievable expense and trouble, and exposed myself to those extraordinary depths of humiliation—then I would have to find a forum in which I could proclaim the truth."

"Why not the same newspapers that ran the original stories about the fair?"

"The press is quick to report the appearance of guilt, but, I am sorry to say, they are often slow to print the evidence of innocence."

"But they would, Armand. They'd have to."

"That depends."

"On what?"

"Not on what, but on whom. Prado isn't acting alone. Who and how many have taken up arms against me, I don't know, but it's never the size of the army that assures defeat, it's the power of the arsenal. If key reporters have aligned themselves with Prado, my story will forever remain yesterday's news."

Though everything Armand said made sense, it was what he wasn't saying that intrigued Gaby most. There was something hesitant about his attitude, something guarded, as if he was holding back because, by protecting the enemy, he was protecting himself.

"Is someone pulling Prado's strings? Someone with an old score to even?"

"I've lived more than half a century," he said, busying himself with a disorderly tie, fascinated that she had asked the same questions as his father, the same questions he would continue to leave unanswered. "Certainly, in that time, I've rubbed more than a few the wrong way. Prado's Geppetto could be any of a number of so-called injured parties."

Maybe, Gaby thought, but every instinct she had told her there was one very specific injured party, that Armand knew exactly who was trying to ruin him, and why.

Armand rose from the sofa, walked over to the window and looked out at the street. While earlier it had been crowded with people on their way to work, the pedestrian traffic had dwindled to nannies pushing prams, housewives doing errands, and members of the senior citizenry out for their morning constitutionals. Later, the sidewalks would be cluttered by the corps of voguish women who prowled the elegant boutiques and galleries of upper Madison Avenue.

Habit prompted him to glance down at his watch, even though he knew it would say that soon he should open for business. A part of him wished his watch had stopped, that time would be forever frozen just where it was, that the slim black hands would stay put, insisting that it remain nine-fifty, ten minutes before he had to deal with the reality of his disgrace. He used to love the last few moments before he unlocked the front door. He would dust a bit, move some furniture, refluff a few cushions, rearrange a wilting flower or two, just as if he were readying his home for a party, so that everything would be perfect when his guests arrived. Each day he hoped that some remote miracle had ended his penance and that all his old friends and customers would return, but each day there were fewer and fewer guests, no miracles. No party.

"The genius of this plan," he said, keeping his back to Gaby so she couldn't see the defeat fighting the anger in his eyes, "is that once *I* set it in motion with my bravura performance at the fair, it snowballed until it became an avalanche. Even if we locate the source of the problem, it will take years to dig our way out."

Gaby went to him, slid her arms through his, and gave a comforting hug.

"However long it takes, Armand, I'm with you. You're the best friend I've ever had. I don't know how just yet, but I'm going to help you out of this mess."

He turned and patted her cheek.

"I love you for that, my sweet Gabrielle, but you have your own troubles."

"More than you know."

"What happened?"

"In my mail, I found an eviction notice." Armand gasped. Gaby, like a prisoner who's been beaten senseless, simply laughed. "It seems they want to tear down my little building and put up a bigger building. I have two weeks to get out. So, boss, if you don't mind, I'm going to need extra time. I have to . . .''

Suddenly, Armand's face broke into an enormous grin. He held up his hand, stopping her in midsentence.

"I have an apartment for you. Don't ask any questions, just grab your coat and come with me.''

He left the CLOSED sign on the shop door, hailed a cab, and whisked her inside. Though she pumped him for details, he remained infuriatingly closemouthed. Even after the taxi deposited them before a luxurious building on Fifth Avenue, across from the Metropolitan Museum of Art, he said nothing. When they got out of the elevator on the tenth floor, Gaby waited while Armand opened the door and turned on the lights. When she looked inside, she didn't know whether to laugh or cry. It was the most beautiful apartment she had ever seen.

"Do you like it?'' Armand asked as he escorted her through the exquisitely decorated entry.

As he turned on the lights in the sitting room, Gaby stared. There, before her eyes was a collection of seventeenth- and eighteenth-century paintings, classical furnishings, museum-quality accessories, artfully staged lighting—an ambience brimming with the feel of contained grandeur and Old World glamour.

"Why did you bring me here?'' Gaby asked, standing stiffly in the doorway, too terrified to move.

"Because this is where you belong.''

"In my dreams, maybe.''

"Didn't Tante Simone ever tell you that if you're a good girl, your dreams might come true?'' Armand's entire being was absorbed in self-congratulation. He was so pleased with himself, he neglected to notice how agitated Gaby had become.

She didn't understand any of this, except that she was getting nervous.

"If this is your idea of a joke, I'm not laughing. I can't afford this place and you know it.'' Her tone had sharpened, and her posture had turned defensive.

"You can afford it,'' he said quietly, patiently, not wanting to rattle her further. "While I was in Paris, I ran into an old friend who happens to be the woman who owns this apartment. She's ill and has decided to go out of town for treatment. She plans on being away for an extended period of time, and because of all the valuables, she doesn't want the apartment to remain vacant. When she asked me if I knew someone responsible who might be willing to house-sit for her, I said I would look around. Please say I don't have to look any further.''

Gaby shook her head. Her eyes still looked glassy.

"Don't you see? It's divine providence! You're forced to sell your house. You get evicted from your apartment. You're suddenly in need of a home, and at almost precisely the same time, I run into someone whose home is in need of a person.''

"But I can't afford to live here.''

"You most certainly can,'' Armand said, smugly. "The owner will continue to pay the maintenance. All you have to do is pay utilities. You'd be doing her a favor.''

"God! I'm so confused, I don't know what to do.''

"Well, I do!'' Armand took her hand and led her to the door. "We're going back to that hovel you've been living in; we're packing your bags and moving you uptown!''

For the next few months, life seemed easier. Living in that apartment had worked wonders on Gaby's mood. She woke up happy, and if the rest of the day wasn't perfect, it didn't weigh on her the same way it had when she knew she had to return to that drafty, dusty place. Work was slow, and though it was nice to be running the shop, the long, quiet hours were a bit tedious now that Armand was traveling. With the hope of generating interest in some of the more spectacular pieces in his inventory—those he had hoped to sell at the fair—he went to Texas and California and Chicago and Denver, visiting old customers who might have heard about what had happened at the armory, but who lived too far away to have picked up on all the other tattle that was making the rounds in New York.

For Armand, the time away from the city was a tonic, an escape, a remedial pause. For Gaby, it was a time to take stock, to adjust, to try on her new life, to see where it fit and where it needed alteration. During the day, when she wasn't tending to business or studying books and magazines related to antiques, she watched the women who paraded past the windows at the front of the shop. Subconsciously, she studied the way they walked, the way they put themselves together, the way they held their heads and did their hair. She envied their poise and their attitude of total self-assurance almost as much as she did their ability to buy the best and the finest of everything. Occasionally, when she stopped into a gallery or a competitor's shop on her way home, she'd sidle over to a twosome or a larger group and eavesdrop, listening to the way they spoke and what they spoke about. At night, since she had no friends with whom to socialize, no neighbors to invite in for tea, no family she could drop in on for a potluck supper, she whiled away the lonely hours thinking about those nameless women on the other side of the window. Often, she found herself practicing walking and talking the way they did, fantasizing about what they were doing, where and how they were living.

Without realizing it, Gaby had sought comfort by becoming again that little girl who tested embryonic aspirations by acting out whatever she thought she might want to be when she grew up. When she had been very young, her ambitions had followed parental lines. Then she had yearned to be a brilliant architect like her father or a great chef or a fashion designer or, perhaps, if she were lucky enough to grow up as beautiful as Delphine, a fashion model. Sometimes she had longed to be a great actress, other times a royal princess or—after Bill had brought home a huge aquarium filled with tropical fish—a marine biologist. Once or twice, she had envisioned herself a daring test pilot or a shrewd captain of industry. There was even a period—just after she had started dance lessons—when she had decided she was going to be the next Debbie Reynolds, tap-dancing her way into the hearts and homes of America. But, she realized now, no matter what the occupation or the title, there had been a common thread running through all those idealistic meanderings. She hadn't wanted to be just any woman, she had wanted to be special—someone who contributed, someone worthy of respect, someone of note.

It was the end of June when Gaby stumbled onto an audition for a new role. Like most opportunities, this one didn't knock as much as it slid into place, greased by timing and coincidence. As a way of saving money and sparing themselves sixth-day tedium, she and Armand had decided to close the shop on Saturdays during the summer. That weekend, with Steven away on a teen tour and Armand visiting at the Vinters' house in Southampton, Gaby found herself at loose ends. She thought about staying in and starting a new dress or catching up on some reading, or finishing her ironing, but it was much too beautiful a day to devote to chores.

By eleven o'clock, she was in a cab headed for Castleton's. It was the perfect place to spend a Saturday afternoon. The building was deliciously cool, the entertainment was free, and there was a chance she might pick up more information for a plan she had been toying with.

The viewing gallery was quiet, with only a handful of people examining the exhibit of French and Continental furniture scheduled for auction on the following Saturday. For about an hour, Gaby strolled about, taking her time, lingering over several pieces she found especially intriguing. There was a set of four Italian red-lacquer card boxes, each fitted with an unusual ivory card counter, each gilded and decorated with the symbol of one of the four different suits. There was an odd pair of end tables constructed from a series of triangles which, working on hinges, folded up on top of each other, enclosing a leather writing surface and a drawer. There were several delightful folding screens fashioned from scenic Charles X wallpaper panels. And there was a rare Austrian Biedermeier chest that, when all its drawers and doors and apertures were closed, looked like a big, fat, faceless clock sitting atop a curly-legged table.

As she entered the end gallery, the one closest to the far wall, she noticed a young woman with an engraved name tag and a clipboard trying desperately to converse with an attractive, middle-aged couple who appeared interested in a set of six Louis XV chairs. The young staffer was talking more with her hands than her mouth, gesticulating, pointing first to the upholstery, then to the legs, then to the padded armrests, and then back to the upholstery, enthusing as if she were selling a used car. Quickly, Gaby gathered that the couple spoke little or no English and that the overzealous, underexperienced clerk was equally ignorant of their language. The instant Gaby picked up a French word, she walked over and offered to help.

After answering any questions the couple had and translating any information the Castleton woman had about provenance and estimated sale price, she smiled, excused herself and walked away. Before she could get very far, she was stopped by Giles Deffand, the head of the European furniture department.

"Madame Didier, I saw what you did and I am grateful." He bowed slightly at the waist, which gave Gaby time to recover from the shock of his knowing her name. "I can't thank you enough for being so gracious and so understanding. I'm afraid Millicent was put on the floor too soon. She's fresh out of college and exuberant to say the least, but I'm afraid she forgot that her purpose is to assist and to educate, not to hawk prized merchandise as if it were a pair of marked-down pajamas."

Gaby was certain that along with the apology, she had detected a note of deference in his voice.

"I'm glad I was able to help."

As if performing for an audience of one, Deffand glanced over his shoulder and glowered at Millicent, who was sweating from the heat of his disapproval and her own embarrassment. Satisfied that he had displayed appropriate annoyance, he looked back at Gaby, his pique dissolved in a warm, buttery smile.

"Are you here for today's sale?"

"I thought I might sit in on it."

"Wonderful!" he said. "You had been such a welcome addition to the salesroom that when you stopped coming, you were sorely missed."

"I've been busy," Gaby replied, feeling the need to explain her absence.

Deffand nodded, as if he understood the rigors of an appointment-packed life.

"Do you have your eye on anything in particular?"

He was so respectful, so eager to please. At first, Gaby was flustered, but then, as if awakening from a long nap, it dawned on her that he thought she was someone she was not, that Armand's ruse had worked better than either of them had planned. She smiled quickly, amazed at how adept fate was in setting a scene. For a second, she debated what she was about to do. But only for a second.

"Actually," she said as casually as she could, "I came over today to find out about consigning a piece for auction."

"Something of yours?"

"No. It belongs to a friend." That was true, as far as it went.

"I would be pleased to answer any questions you have."

Deffand's attitude was so encouraging, she reached into her

purse and pulled out a Polaroid of a commode that had recently arrived from Paris. When Armand had gone to visit his family, they had arranged an exchange of merchandise as a way of freshening inventory and, perhaps, reinvigorating sales at Lafitte et Fils U.S.A. Though Gaby had agreed that removing stale pieces from the shop was a good idea, silently she doubted that a new influx of stock would make a difference. If there were no customers coming through the door, it didn't matter what was inside the shop. She had decided that there had to be another way. If the three major auction houses wouldn't accept consignments from him, maybe they would accept them from her. She would act as a sort of broker. Once she received payment from the sale, she would turn the money over to Lafitte et Fils U.S.A. It was simple—if it worked.

"It's magnificent," Deffand exclaimed, holding the square snapshot up to the light for a better view.

"It's signed by Charles Cressent," she said, watching his eyebrows arch as she mentioned the name of one of the major *ébénistes* of the rococo era.

"Who is the owner?"

This was the hard part. Gaby was not a person who wore the gown of deception easily. Telling a small lie was difficult. Weaving a web was tortuous.

"He's a European and, for personal reasons, would prefer to remain anonymous. I have all the information about the history of the piece and previous auction appearances. Must you know his name?" She held her breath.

"No. We're very respectful of our patrons' privacy," he said, as if the honor of Castleton's was at stake. "We need to examine the piece, take the information about provenance from you, and establish a reserve, but other than that, if you're agenting the transaction, we don't require anything else."

Gaby would have to discuss the reserve, or floor price, with Armand. But that would have to be after she had told him of her plan.

"You're most kind," she said, stifling a triumphant giggle.

"Not at all. Recommendation from our more valued customers is the way we prefer to acquire merchandise."

"Then you wouldn't mind if, occasionally, I brought you other pieces?" This was turning out better than she had hoped.

"Certainly not! A woman of your taste could only bring the finest to Castleton's, and that's what we look for." He accompanied his flattery with a smile that appeared practiced, until suddenly his expression changed. His eyes widened and his smile became broader, as if he had a secret which he would reveal only if she said the right thing. "I know that what I'm about to ask sounds bold, and I apologize in advance if by any chance I offend you, but would you ever consider working for Castleton's?"

"Excuse me, please?" She heard the phrasing and the politely quizzical tone and, inside, laughed. All those nights practicing in her apartment had paid off. She sounded exactly like the woman he seemed to think she was.

"Madame Didier, you are a woman who impresses me as being extremely well schooled in the area of French antiques and decorative arts. Your French is superb, you're utterly charming, and quite beautiful, and judging by this morning's spontaneous rescue, I would guess that you're not an idler or a bystander. Recently, my assistant retired. I've been searching for someone to take her place, but everyone who applies for the position is either too inexperienced, too ambitious, or too unpleasant for me to think her suitable. As Goldilocks said, you're just right."

Gaby was stunned. She was also troubled. Ordinarily, she would have jumped at the chance to work with Giles Deffand. His knowledge and his ability were legendary. Having his name on a resumé was an incontrovertible boost to a fledgling career. But, she asked herself, if he knew the truth, would he be as interested in hiring her as she was in working for him? Probably not. Though she was all those things he mentioned, it was not her familiarity with antiques or her fluency with language that had prompted his offer. He thought she was a well-to-do woman with a coterie of wealthy friends eager to recycle their antiques via Castleton's salesrooms. Should she enlighten him? Should she tell him that he had assumed certain things that were not so?

Gaby felt as if a vise were closing in around her. Though she knew Armand would never agree, at the shop she was more of a financial burden than an asset. She needed a new job. Here, she would be working in a field she adored with a man she respected, making a salary that was probably equal to or better than what she was earning. And, she told herself, as if toting up the positives, once she was inside Castleton's, perhaps she could pick up clues as to the who and why behind Armand's exile. After all he had done for her, she said to herself, it was the least she could do for him.

"Would you even consider such an idea?" Deffand sounded nervous, as if he was afraid he had offended her.

"As a matter of fact, I would," she said, trying to sound interested, but not too eager. "Naturally, we'd have to discuss job description and what else would be involved." What she wanted to discuss was money, but to raise that now would be just too, too bourgeois.

"I would be honored if you would allow me to take you to lunch," he said. "Business matters always sound less workaday over a glass of wine. Don't you agree?"

She nodded, smiled in assent, and accompanied him out of the gallery.

Everything sounds better over a glass of wine, she thought, astounded by her good fortune, *especially when you're on as tight a budget as I am and somebody else is paying!*

As she had anticipated, Armand had several reactions to her news. First, he was sad, though somewhat relieved, that she was not going to be working for him any longer. Second, he was thrilled that she had landed such a plum job, one that would put her talents to such good use. And third, he was furious that she would have put herself at risk with her consignment scheme.

"I didn't put anyone at risk," she argued. "I simply opened a door that had been slammed in your face."

"If the people who shut that door find out you fronted for me, you might regret playing good Samaritan."

Again, Gaby sensed that Armand's enemies were not the nameless forces he implied they were.

"The way I see it," she said, leaving that subject for another time, sauntering about, making him concentrate on what she was saying by making him follow her with his eyes. "Until we dig you out of this mess, you need an alternative way to sell antiques. That is what you do, isn't it? This is an antiques shop, isn't it? Or have I been mistaken all these months and this is really a fish store in disguise?"

"Very funny." He tried to sound stern, but he was too

warmed by her efforts to refrigerate his voice. "You used to be such a sweet, naive young thing. Look what a sarcastic wench you've become."

"When I first came to New York, I took a course in Reality 101. Guess what I learned? Sweet, naive, young things get nowhere. Sarcastic wenches command attention, if nothing else."

Armand smiled briefly, but continued to reject her original premise.

"I still say you shouldn't have put yourself on the line. Sooner or later, people will forget the ignominy of Armand Lafitte and remember that this shop carries some of the finest antiques in the world."

"I'm sure that's true, but until then, as Tante Simone always said, you have to do what you have to do." She marched over to the desk where he was standing and faced him squarely. "If we can sell a couple of top-quality pieces in one or two of Castleton's upcoming auctions, what in God's name is wrong with that!"

Armand shook his head.

"Nothing," he said, patting her cheek affectionately. "You're right. It's a very good idea."

Gaby gave forth a satisfied sigh.

"I knew that sooner or later you'd come to your senses."

She reached across the desk to hug him, but he caught her arms and held her off.

"I will go along with this plan on two conditions."

"Name them."

"You accept a percentage of the profits as your brokerage fee and you promise to be careful and not do anything stupid."

"Conditions accepted!" Gaby kissed him and grinned. "Don't worry about me sticking to my part of the bargain. The first thing I need is money and the last thing I need is extra aggravation."

Two weeks later, she started at Castleton's. She loved it immediately, probably because, thanks to Deffand's erroneous perception of who and what she was, she had bypassed every entry-level position and started out on the upper tier of Castleton's staff. Notwithstanding his displays of displeasure when things were mishandled, he had indefatigable energy. Deffand was a joy to work with. He was receptive to change, as long as it was for the better, eager to learn, willing to teach, and the quintessential public relations man at exhibitions and cocktail parties.

It was probably his open-door management style and his almost voracious desire to improve his department that inspired Gaby's creative side. Often, she found herself sitting in front of his desk, bouncing off him some new idea she had thought of to increase auction attendance or Castleton name recognition. The first time he decided to take one of her proposals beyond his office was when she suggested that he schedule a few preseason lectures so that beginning collectors could know more about how and what to buy at auction. When he objected that not everyone was as intrigued with French *ébénistes* as they were, she proposed that they develop a series; each department head would conduct his own lecture. Together, they made up a tentative schedule, having decided that there was still time before the fall season began to run ads in the newspapers and see what kind of interest they generated. Giles presented the plan to Garrett Castleton, Jr., obtained approval to proceed, asked his fellow chairmen for their cooperation, and bought a week's worth of space in *The New York Times*. Within two days after the last ad ran, every lecture had a waiting list.

News of Gaby's success and subsequent successes spread throughout the office like a California brushfire, placing her name on many lips unaccustomed to giving praise. It wasn't until late November, however, at a dinner dance benefiting the American Crafts Museum, that she actually met Garrett Castleton, Jr. He had Giles introduce them so that he could personally thank her for the lecture series. After exchanging a few words of cocktail chatter, he asked her to dance. For the rest of the evening, he rarely left her side.

Though she had never laid eyes on him before that night, after, Gaby suddenly found herself bumping into Garrett Castleton, Jr., with astonishing frequency. Often, he stopped at her office simply to chat. Once or twice, he invited her to lunch, occasionally to join him for a drink after work, but each time, she declined. Then he invited her to be his date for the pre–Antiques Fair gala.

"I felt I had to say I'd go, but now that I have, I'm terrified!"

She and Armand sat across from each other in one of the wooden booths that lined the walls of one of their favorite haunts, a small French bistro in Soho. They had finished dinner and were lingering over a fresh cup of coffee and a plate of warm *tarte* Tatin.

"Why should you be terrified?"

"I know this is going to come as a shock, but we didn't have parties like that back in Wadsworth," she said, her tone laced with the beginning stages of panic. "I don't know how to act. I don't know what to say. And I don't have anything to wear!"

"I'm not worried about you. You'll do just fine. And as for your wardrobe, we'll go shopping this Saturday and get you something memorable."

"Something memorable," she muttered. "Do you know what will be memorable? When he or one of his guests asks me about my ancestors, my trust funds, my wealthy friends, my fabulous apartment, or, in case we have forgotten, my dear, departed husband. *That* will be memorable!"

Armand laughed, but Gaby's expression remained frozen.

"If anyone asks you something you don't want to answer, don't. People are basically superficial, especially at parties. It's like people asking 'How are you?' They don't really want to know about bunions or backaches or sniffles or gas. They're simply asking to have something to do with their mouths in between canapes and cocktails."

Gaby fidgeted with her napkin, uncomfortable, struggling with something.

"What is it?"

"I'm going to this party under false pretenses. I'm at Castleton's under false pretenses." Armand started to protest, but she held up her hands. "They all think I'm someone I'm not. I know that when I went to work there I wasn't so much lying as I was merely neglecting to clarify the truth. But no matter how you slice it, the Girl Scouts would never give me a badge for what I did." She looked down, folded the corners of her napkin again and then unfolded them, flattening the stiff cloth on her lap. "What's worse, I'm not sorry," she said, the fire of the phoenix lighting her eyes. "I've been a tremendous asset to Castleton's, if I do say so myself, and I do. What I am sorry about, is that I put myself in a position where every day, I put on a costume and act out a part. Being Madame Didier is becoming such a habit, I'm not sure I know where the real me ends and the pretend me begins."

"Perhaps they're one and the same."

Gaby considered that thought for a moment, but then shook her head.

"No. Maybe one day they will be, but not yet, not while I'm filled with all this conflict. When I visit Steven, I'm the ex–Mrs. Thayer, a divorced mother trying like hell to stay close to my son. When I'm with you, I'm Gaby, the émigré from Ohio trying to make it in the Big Apple. But from nine to five, I'm Gabrielle Didier, glib, chic, smart woman about town, or so the stories go. Do you realize that people at Castleton's think I have a blue-blooded pedigree, money to burn, and dates five nights a week with every swell on Park Avenue? I've never said anything to substantiate the rumors, but I've never denied them either."

"People assume, Gaby. They see a beautiful, poised, educated woman with a certain savoir faire and they assume they know how you live and what you do."

"Armand, they think I'm filthy rich. Is that a joke! I can barely make ends meet, thanks to my never-ending debt to the Lakewood Home."

"If they think you're something other than who you are, that's their problem and your good fortune."

"Don't you see?" she said, growing more and more exasperated. "I feel as if I'm nothing but a phony involved in some grand game of charades."

"Life has a way of making us all players at one time or another," Armand said, trying to remind her that circumstance had cast her in her current role and was still directing her performance.

"I guess." Thinking about Armand and his personal charade, she was momentarily comforted by the vague notion that she was not the only one stuck in a daily act of impersonation. "So what do you suggest I do?"

"That depends on what you want."

She didn't even have to think before she answered.

"I want a career. I want to be able to support myself. And most of all, damn it, I want what's rightfully mine—my self-respect! I want to be worth something without being Mrs. Somebody!''

"Okay," Armand said gently, "what if, to achieve those goals, for the time being, you have to let people think what they want? Is it worth it?"

She nodded.

"Then just relax and do what everyone else does, Gabrielle. Play the game."

"I want to, but I don't think I can," she said, her doubts and vulnerabilities rising to the surface and challenging her resolve. "I don't know the rules."

Armand's eyes softened for a moment, but then a lifetime of experience darkened the pupils into a deep, hard stare that locked onto her soul and held her with near-hypnotic intensity.

"It's a simple game with only one rule. If you're going to play, you play to win."

PART
TWO

JANUARY 1987

7

Gaby slammed the door behind her and quickly bolted three locks. Out of breath, she leaned against the door, closed her eyes, and breathed deeply, trying to regain her equilibrium. Slowly, she calmed. Soon, it took less effort to inhale, less work to stand without trembling. But the respite was brief. The sharp, sudden zing of a buzzer ran through her like a shot of adrenaline. Her heart raced. Her hands shook. Her palms began to sweat. The buzzer sounded again. Almost fearfully, she flicked the switch that allowed the doorman's voice to filter through the brass-plated speaker of the intercom.

"There's a Mrs. Reynolds here to see you, madame."

"It's late, Roger, and I'm very tired."

"She's rather insistent, Ms. Didier. She claims she will not leave until she sees you."

That woman had followed her home from Garrett's pre-fair party. Gaby wasn't up to this, but it wouldn't do to make a scene. Besides, even if somehow the persistent Mrs. Reynolds were persuaded to leave, she would simply return at some other time. And the plain truth was that no time would ever be convenient.

"Send her up."

A few minutes later, Gaby opened the door and Chelsea Reynolds swept past her, letting loose a long whistle as she dropped her sable on the nearest chair and surveyed Gaby's living quarters. Chocolate suede walls, a seventeenth-century Flemish tapestry, a Régence chandelier, paired Empire chairs with unique swan arms—the entrance hall alone was enough to fill any visitor with awe. Without bothering to ask, the blonde woman wandered in and out of the various rooms, her carefully trained eyes scanning the classical furnishings, the seventeenth- and eighteenth-century paintings, the priceless antiques.

When she returned to the foyer, she blinked her eyes several times in utter amazement.

"Gaby Cocroft, you sly dog!" she said, spreading her arms in a grand, dramatic sweep. "When we were roommates at dear old Skidmore College, who would have thought that you, of all people, would wind up living in a place like this?"

When Gaby offered her no answer other than a tentative smile, Chelsea placed her hands on her hips and screwed her face into a mock scowl.

"Okay," she said, giving her old roommate her moment. "Spit it out! What's with this Gabrielle Didier bullshit!"

Gaby wanted to maintain a modicum of dignity, but she laughed in spite of herself.

"It's a long story."

"And a juicy one, I'll bet."

Again, without concern for propriety, Chelsea stepped out of her shoes, located the bar, fixed two drinks, handed one to Gaby, and seated herself in the living room. Gaby dropped onto a couch and put her feet up, oddly relieved. She hadn't thought about it consciously, but for months she had fretted that someday someone would discover her fakery. Now it had happened. Thank goodness that someone had been Chelsea. Right or wrong, with her, Gaby felt safe.

They had been best friends all through college, and while their friendship had had many strengths, its hallmark was the fact that no matter how angry either of them got, they never betrayed each other's confidences. When they met in 1964, they were complete opposites. Chelsea was light, Gaby was dark. Chelsea played with life, Gaby worked at it. Chelsea trusted no one, Gaby trusted everyone. They might never have gotten along, except that in a few basic areas they were exactly alike—they were young girls growing into womanhood, their early years had been marred by great unhappiness, and each of them desperately needed a friend.

As the semesters passed, they became bound to each other, but inevitably, once graduation separated them, time and circumstance combined to widen the gap. Their lives had always run on separate tracks. They hadn't seen each other in fifteen years.

"I know it was forever ago, but the last time we spoke, you were buried alive somewhere outside of Cleveland," Chelsea said, making Cleveland sound as if it were synonymous with purgatory. "You were married to your high school heartthrob. What was his name? Oh, yes, Brian Thayer. Handsome, very handsome, but mucho macho, if I remember him correctly. You had one son. Steven, right? Your goal in life was to be the next Betty Crocker and you actually tried to convince me that you had found fulfillment in the PTA."

She laughed at the ridiculousness of it all. Then, slowly, her eyes panned the room. Her fingers caressed the velvet upholstery on the Louis XV marquise in which she sat. Her mouth curled in a gesture of approval.

"Obviously, you've left Ohio," she said, "and you've left the PTA. The big question is, have you left Brian?"

Gaby hesitated, but despite the passage of time, instinct warned that Chelsea had not changed. She would accept nothing less than total honesty. Gaby faced her old friend squarely.

"Brian left me," she said.

"Egad! Don't tell me." Chelsea squeezed her eyes shut and pressed her hands against her ears. Her upper lip rose in a disgusted sneer. "Another one-time stud who's afraid he's losing it." She shook her head and clucked her tongue. "How young was she?"

"Mid-twenties," Gaby said, amused by Chelsea's reaction, embarrassed at how quickly her friend had divined the crux of the problem. It unnerved her to think that her situation, which had caused her so much pain, was so typical.

"How did he leave you?"

"He came home . . ."

"I don't mean that," Chelsea said, dismissing the details of Gaby's abandonment with a wave of her hand. "I don't want the bastard's exit line. I want the bottom line. How did he leave you financially?"

Gaby noticed Chelsea's eyes skirting the room, stopping at each expensive object, assessing, estimating, lighting up like the digits on a calculator.

"No." She laughed at the absurdity of what Chelsea was thinking. "This was not part of my settlement."

"Now, why did I know that?"

"Because you seem to be a lot more savvy about things than I could ever hope to be."

"He screwed you, right?"

Gaby wriggled around on the couch. Confession was supposed to be good for the soul. Confessing her gullibility was making her uncomfortable.

"He came to the house three weeks after he had walked out and told me that all he could afford to give me was five hundred dollars a week, two-fifty in cash, two-fifty by check. He apologized profusely, but after all, he said, everything was so costly. He had all of Steven's expenses, *plus* my expenses, *plus* an apartment, *plus* a house . . ."

"*Plus* a mistress," Chelsea interjected.

"Plus a mistress." Gaby still couldn't say that without an acrid taste filling her mouth. "Be that as it may, when he added up all the pluses, I had to find a job. I reminded him that I had no job experience, probably because whenever I had even thought about going to work, he had objected. I was needed at home, was the standard phrase." Gaby laughed, but not merrily. "I guess once he didn't need me at home, there was no reason for me not to work."

Again, Gaby shifted position, as she related to Chelsea the events that had brought her to New York in a virtually penniless state.

"Didn't you go to court?"

"Almost immediately. The man couldn't wait to get me there. Once he did, you would have thought I was demanding the gold fillings from his teeth!" Anger, which had been dormant for some time, resurfaced as Gaby rose from the couch and gave Chelsea her own rendition of Brian's attorney's closing argument.

"This woman, your honor, is a bright, young, intelligent, able-bodied woman with all the qualifications necessary to achieve great things. Why shouldn't a woman like this support herself? Why shouldn't she use her God-given talents to contribute to society? Why shouldn't she join the work force and feel the joy one gets from personal accomplishment?"

Chelsea held her stomach and groaned. Gaby returned to her seat for the final act of her playlet.

"The judge ruled that I was to receive one year's paid readjustment. . . . Don't you just love that term? Paid readjustment. That meant that for twelve months, Brian would continue giving me two hundred and fifty dollars a week. After that, I was on my own. I did get half the house and my car and all the furnishings and half of whatever we had invested."

"I swear, if this wasn't a brand-new dress, I'd throw up!" Chelsea stuck out her tongue and gagged, leaving no doubt as to her opinion of Gaby's settlement. "If only I had known! I would have introduced you to one of my divorce lawyers. They never would have let Brian get away with that shit. They would have taken that creep over the coals and left him with nothing but his jockey shorts, if that!"

"Orin Phillips has an excellent reputation," Gaby protested meekly, defending her attorney.

"For what? Reading wills to widows? The guy sounds like a wimp!"

"He was very kind to me."

Chelsea threw her arms up in dismay and practically jumped out of her chair.

"Divorce lawyers are not supposed to be kind! They're supposed to be sharks, vicious creatures with long sharp teeth and an endless appetite for fresh male blood. Believe me, I know what I'm talking about. I've had two divorces, and both times I hired attorneys who ate ground glass for breakfast." She smiled, showing even white teeth. "Every night, I remember them in my prayers because they made me what I am today—single, independent, and very, very rich!"

"Two divorces?" Gaby was fascinated, more by Chelsea's

insouciant attitude about the dissolution of her marriages than by the number.

"And I was widowed once," Chelsea said, wishing to clarify her marital statistics. "But we'll get to me later. Right now, I would like to fill in a few blanks. Like precisely when did you come to New York?"

"November 1984."

Chelsea was surprised and more than a little concerned. Gaby had been here more than two years. Doing what?

Sensing the unspoken question, Gaby's face grew reflective. In a low voice she said, "I needed money. I couldn't find a job. The whole courtroom thing had upset me. And then my son came home for Thanksgiving. Instead of spending the holiday with Simone and me, he was seduced into spending every waking minute with his father, his father's family, and his father's lover. I don't know what happened, but something snapped. I packed a suitcase, shut the lights, locked the doors, and got into my car." She tried to smile, but her lips wobbled. "I guess I ran away from home."

Chelsea joined Gaby on the couch. As Gaby filled in the details of her odyssey, Chelsea took Gaby's hand, wishing she could ease the pain her friend was trying so hard to bear.

"What about your son? Was he a comfort?"

Gaby shook her head. Large, sad tears welled and her voice quivered as she spoke.

"He was only fifteen when Brian left. Fifteen can be a very difficult age. He blamed me for the split. Mommies are supposed to kiss boo-boos and make the hurt go away. They're supposed to make things better, not mess things up. In his mind, if I had been a better wife, Brian never would have left."

"Ouch!" Chelsea recoiled, feeling the same sting she imagined Gaby had felt.

"Do you have any children?"

"Not of my own," Chelsea said in an even voice which indicated neither regret nor relief. "But I do have a stepdaughter who's almost seventeen, so yes, I know how difficult fifteen can be."

She smiled in the way mothers often do when discussing the antics of their children, but for an instant, Gaby thought she noticed a shadow darkening that smile.

"Does she live with you?"

"No." Suddenly, Chelsea stood and stretched her arms over her head. "I have an announcement to make. It is two o'clock in the morning. In the old days, no one loved all-nighters more than I, but alas, time has taken its toll. Unless my adrenaline is being pumped up by the passionate ministrations of some young buck, I need sleep or at the very least, a cup of coffee. If you don't mind, we shall retire to the kitchen for a much needed dose of caffeine. And then I'd like you to clear something up for me."

Her eyes moved around the room, lighting on a seventeenth-century portrait by Aelbert Cuyp, a pair of rare eighteenth-century Chinese figures, a rare Dutch musical bracket clock, a set of early Georgian girandoles.

"How the hell can you afford a place like this?"

For the next hour, Gaby regaled her old roommate with the story of her relationship with Armand Lafitte—their meeting, their friendship, their business arrangement, the January Antiques Fair disaster, how he found this apartment, how he was helping Gaby find herself.

"That old fox!" Chelsea's laughter pealed like a clanging dinner bell, loud and boisterous, almost indecent considering the fact that it was almost three in the morning. "Who would have thought that the suave and courtly Armand Lafitte was so street smart. I love it!"

"You know him?" Gaby was stunned.

"Of course I know him!" she said, indignant that Gaby wouldn't realize that Chelsea knew *everyone*.

"Then why didn't you ever ask why he had been banished or ask if you could help?"

It annoyed Gaby that Chelsea would have accepted Armand's exile without investigating the cause and coming to her own conclusions; that she would have aided the vicious whispering campaign by not arguing against it; that she would have deserted a friend.

"I did ask, but Armand's state of disgrace was always sloughed off as if it was nothing more than the ever-fluctuating winds of social change. One day you're in. One day you're out. That sort of thing. Then, to be honest, time passed, Armand became old hat, and I moved on to the next scandal." Chelsea paused, as if recalling details and sorting out facts. "I do remember thinking that the whole thing was a terrible shame. Aside from everything else, Armand was one of the better walkers."

"Walkers?"

Chelsea sniffed. Obviously, Armand had left gaping holes in Gaby's education.

"A man who escorts women to social events," she said patiently. "When I was between husbands, Armand walked me to several parties." Chelsea became thoughtful again. She ran her hand through her hair with long, sensuous strokes. Her green eyes softened as they turned upward and watched a reel of memories roll across the ceiling. "Like most walkers, he was a wonderful dancer and a delightful dinner companion. But to know the full extent of his charm, you had to invite him in for a nightcap." A small smile appeared. "Armand Lafitte was one hell of a lover!" An unexpected twinge of jealousy flushed Gaby's cheeks. She had grown very close to Armand, very fond of him, perhaps even a bit possessive. Now she discovered that not only did Chelsea know who he was, but she had known him in a way Gaby hadn't, and probably wouldn't.

"I thought he was gay," she said lamely, as if explaining why she had not taken advantage of Armand's sexual dexterity.

Chelsea issued a lusty laugh that only served to embarrass Gaby further.

"Gay? Hardly, my dear! But don't be upset," she said, noticing Gaby's discomfort. "After all those years you spent buried in the hinterlands, you couldn't possibly be expected to differentiate between the slightly effete elegance of the European man and the limp-wristed affectation of the New York homosexual."

"I thought I was getting better at judging people."

"Don't be so hard on yourself," Chelsea said, responding to the self-criticism in her friend's voice. "It's easy to be fooled. Sometimes it takes an expert to tell the difference between a fag and a fop. Besides, look how many people *you've* fooled. You're not exactly the *duchesse* you appear to be."

Gaby laughed.

"That's true. These days, I spend so much time being a

figment of my own imagination, it's hard for me to remember who I really am.''

"Don't make it sound so tragic. Most of the people I know are figments of someone's imagination.''

Chelsea smiled, but there was little arguing with the fact that the glamorous woman sitting opposite her, so beautifully clothed and coiffed, bore little resemblance to the skinny young girl with the long ponytail, Peter Pan collars, McMullen sweaters, and tasseled Weejun loafers she had lived with for four years. Though Chelsea thought the metamorphosis was extraordinary, and to her sophisticated eye a welcome change, in the penetrating light of early dawn, the fancy wrappings that protected Gabrielle Didier had unraveled, revealing a core of insecurity and self-doubt, and prompting Chelsea to wonder how long it would take for Gaby to feel comfortable in her new skin, if ever.

"How do you do it? I mean, how do you squirrel away money for that Lakewood bill, pay for this place, and still maintain your image?''

"When my back is up against the wall, I sell off some of my paperweight collection or some of the smaller antiques I had in the house in Wadsworth.''

"I know how much you love those things,'' Chelsea said, suddenly remembering all the weekends Gaby had dragged her around Saratoga Springs and Glens Falls and its environs, poking around crowded, dusty antiques shops looking for paperweights or snuff boxes. "You must think this new identity is worth the investment.''

Gaby heard the concern and appreciated it.

"I've never been a person to take risks,'' she said pensively. "I'm beginning to think that's why I married Brian. Because he was safe, a known commodity with no surprises.'' The irony made her laugh. "Come to think of it, that's probably why he left me. Too much safety, not enough surprises.''

"Let's not be so quick to dismiss the idea of safety,'' Chelsea said, feeling oddly protective. "I'm all for flying high, but there's nothing wrong with insisting upon a net, you know. I'd hate to see you hurt yourself, Gaby. What happens if you fall flat on your face?''

Gaby shrugged.

"I'm back where I started, with no job and no money. I came here with a badly bruised ego and very little pride. At this point, there's not much that could humiliate me. If the worst happens, I'll be a few dollars poorer and a few memories richer. Either way, it doesn't matter. I don't have many alternatives."

A gray melancholia clouded Gaby's eyes. Chelsea had seen that doleful look many times when she and Gaby had discussed her parents' deaths, when she spoke of how long it had taken her to realize that they were gone and that no amount of wishing or hoping would bring them back. Again, Gaby was recovering from a loss. This time, it was more than the loss of Simone that was causing her malaise. It was the loss of her own identity.

Chelsea was deeply moved by Gaby's predicament, and that surprised her. She was a woman of many acquaintances and very few friends. Years had elapsed, and yet the sensation of attachment that had once existed between them had suddenly, but definitely, reasserted itself. Sitting and talking in the free, open way they had had when they were roommates, time seemed to evaporate, fading as if its passage had evoked no change, its span had effected no consequence. Yes, they looked different. They were both approaching forty, and though they had retained all the requisite characteristics of beauty—the flattering features, the well-kept figure, the clear, supple skin—the glossy patina of youth had dulled. Yes, they sounded different. Chelsea's voice had acquired a piping stridency that sometimes sounded too shrill, too desperate, even to her ears. Gaby's voice had deepened, reverberating with the painful echoes of hurts that never heal. And yes, they viewed life differently—Chelsea through eyes tinted with cynicism, Gaby through eyes blurred by disillusionment. But something had remained the same, some part of their former selves had continued to exist, because in the space of just a few hours, the space of many years had been erased.

How strange it all was. Chelsea knew nothing about the woman, Gabrielle Didier. Yet she had known everything about the girl, Gaby Cocroft. They had been friends without conditions, without recriminations, and without demands. There had been no secrets between them, no pretenses, no lies. She had known what had made that girl laugh, what had made her cry, what hurt her the most, what bothered her the least. Now she supposed it was that girl to whom she was relating, that young friend who was hidden somewhere inside the shell of this stranger.

"Okay," she said, clapping her hands to dispel the negative spirits that had intruded on their reunion. "You've teased me long enough. It's time to tell Aunt Chelsea why we're playing charades. Who we're playing against. And what we're playing for."

"Actually, it's quite simple," Gaby began, having known from the start that she would trust Chelsea with the details of her plan. "As Gaby Cocroft, I had no chance of ever being interviewed for the job of Giles Deffand's assistant. As Madame Didier, I was offered the position. I couldn't turn it down, so I couldn't tell the truth. Aside from the basic fringe benefits, having entry to Castleton's made it possible for me to consign a series of pieces from Armand's shop for auction. This Saturday, three of them will go on the block and will probably bring huge prices. In the next few months, there'll be more."

"What do you get out of this?"

"I get a fee out of Armand's profits."

"How come no one has traced any of these pieces back to Armand?"

Gaby's eyes grew cold.

"Because first of all, no one knows about my relationship with him, and secondly, to most of them he's a dead issue. They figure they buried him long ago."

"Garrett Castleton is no fool, Gaby."

"I know that, but really, I'm not doing anything wrong. I'm not trying to swindle anyone. I consigned only items of the highest quality."

Chelsea sat back and considered what Gaby had told her. For several minutes she remained quiet, contemplative. Gaby began to worry.

"You know what I love most," Chelsea said at last, her mouth curving into an impish grin. "A fake pulling off a scam like this in a business that prides itself on authenticity. It's fabulous!" She was so excited, she practically giggled. "And to think that all those smug society dragons were killing themselves tonight at the gala, trying to befriend little old Gaby Cocroft from Wadsworth, Ohio. It's just too funny."

For a minute, Gaby couldn't tell whether Chelsea was laughing at her or with her.

"Do you think I'm awful?"

"Are you kidding? I think you're terrific! I'm proud of you, Gabrielle, my dear. You've got guts, and to tell you the truth, I never thought you had it in you. Come to think of it, I never thought Armand would buck the system either." She laughed again. "I guess I'm not as smart as I thought I was."

"You won't say anything, will you?" Gaby was nervous.

"I'll keep quiet on one condition." Chelsea suddenly turned serious. "You let me help you."

"How?"

"I have a lot of money, Gaby. More than I can ever really spend. Let me pay off Simone's debts. That way you can get on with your life. You can begin to have some fun. God knows, you deserve it."

"I love you for offering," Gaby said, sincerely touched, "but I can't let you do that. I'll manage. Lakewood understands. I send them what I can, when I can."

"Instead of paying them off, you could pay me off," Chelsea persisted.

Gaby shook her head.

"Please. I have to do this on my own. For Simone and for me. Can you understand that?"

Gaby's eyes had begun to water and now it was Chelsea's turn to be touched. To Gaby, this was a matter of pride, not money. Though Chelsea said she understood, that was only partly true. To her, most things were a matter of money. Pride was not a commodity to be traded and, therefore, of little worth.

"Okay," she said. "But I know lots of people and lots of ways to get around them. Sooner or later, something is bound to come up where my so-called talents will prove invaluable. You must promise you'll come to me and let me in on whatever's happening. I don't mean to make light of your circumstances, but you know I've always loved playing games, and lately, fun has been sorely lacking from my diet. I just want to be part of the action."

"Why would you want to be part of something that could

smear your name? I don't have any name in this town, and Armand's has already been destroyed. Neither of us has anything to lose. You do.''

"That's where you're wrong." Chelsea's mouth hardened. "That bunch you met tonight? They can't stomach me. I have too much money for them not to pay attention to me, and I've been married to men too important for them to exclude me, but they don't have to accept me, and they don't. Though they'd never say it out loud, deep down, they all think I'm a tramp masquerading as a lady. And do you know what? I am. So in a way, I've been playing charades a lot longer than you. I know the tricks and I know the traps. What do you say?''

"I say you're great!" Gaby rose from her chair and hugged the tall willowy blonde.

"And don't worry about Monsieur Lafitte," Chelsea said with a glint. "He knows I wouldn't screw things up for him. At one time, he and I were very *simpático*. I'd say we still are. Obviously, we both know what it feels like to be on the outside looking in.''

"What about Irina Stoddard?" Gaby suddenly recalled that she had seen the two of them talking together at the party. "Is she a friend of yours?''

Chelsea laughed so hard she almost fell out of her chair.

"Are you kidding? She's part of the reason I want to be involved in all this. There's nothing I'd like better than pulling the old Aubusson over that bitch's eyes.''

"I take it she did something to upset you." Gaby couldn't help being amused. Chelsea's responses were so expressive, so theatrical.

"Actually, I did something to upset *her*. I stole her husband.''

Now it was Gaby's turn to laugh. Not because of what Chelsea said, but the delighted way in which she said it.

"My number two was Lord Winston Stoddard. I met him after my first husband, Roy Patterson, died. I had gone to London so that I could escape Roy's greedy relatives, all of whom wanted to pick over my bones and pick apart old Roy's will. Anyway, I met Winnie at a party. He was handsome, in that tall, lean, aristocratic, British way. He thought I was hot. I thought he was hot. And so we began to have a simply wonderful affair. The only one who didn't think we were hot was Irina. When Winnie divorced her to marry me, she didn't take it well. And that's putting it mildly!"

"Didn't you divorce Lord Stoddard?"

"I had to," she said, closing her eyes, lifting her chin, and resting her wrist against her forehead as if testing for fever. "My health was at stake. If I hadn't divorced him, I would have died of boredom! In the short span of two years, the man had gone from hot to cold, so I took as much of his money as I could get and took off for New York. A few years later, I married Drake Reynolds and Winnie married some German countess who claims to be a distant cousin of the queen's." Chelsea tsked and shook her head. "Unfortunately, poor, pathetic Irina has yet to find someone to warm her bed. Any day now I expect her to start placing ads in the personals."

"That tells me why she might bear a small grudge against you," Gaby said. "But why are you so hostile toward her?"

"For the same reason Armand's nose is out of joint. Nasty gossip. Hurtful rumors. Irina Stoddard whispered ugly stories about me into enough ears to fill a Kansas cornfield. If not for Drake and the prestige attached to the Reynolds name, I would have been pushed so far out, I couldn't have gotten back in with a passport."

"Since I've had more than one fantasy about getting even with those who did their best to humiliate me, I understand how you feel, but for my sake, do you think you can keep your animosity in check?"

Chelsea pouted. "I'll try to view making an ass out of Irina as a bonus. How's that?"

"Fine."

"Now that we've got that settled, let's get back to Madame Didier. The way I hear it, people think you were born with a silver *cuiller* in your mouth. Is it something you said?"

"No. It's something they think." Gaby measured her words. She did know Chelsea's penchant for game playing. She also knew that she was walking a very thin line. She didn't want Chelsea's desire to have a good time push her onto the wrong side of that line. "See this place? You are the first living soul other than Armand to see the inside. I don't talk about my private life, nor do I discuss my finances. The only lie I've ever told is that I'm widowed. Whatever people want to assume from my appearance, they do. I just try to keep a very low profile.''

"You can't expect to keep a low profile in a high-visibility world, my darling." Chelsea's eyes narrowed. "What if someone starts playing who-do-you-know-and-where-did-you-prep?"

"I head for the ladies' room."

"That's fine for an immediate solution, but," Chelsea said, her green eyes darkening, "there are some busybodies who can't start the day without reading the Social Register or the Forbes Four Hundred. They memorize names, dates, and bank balances as if they were defending a doctoral thesis on the relevancy of status symbols in a nuclear age. You meet up with one of them in a dark cloakroom and you're dead meat.''

"I guess I have to take my chances."

"Panic not," Chelsea said, seeing the fear that had paled Gaby's face. "Just listen to the voice of experience. When up against an indefensible truth, attack. Be outraged. Be offended. Be utterly repelled by the thought that someone would be so déclassé as even to discuss such things. There are usually only one or two of these know-it-alls per party. Just play off the fact that most people prefer fantasy to reality.''

"And what happens if all these social savants are in the same place at the same time, oh great guru?"

"Run like hell!"

"I'll have to remember to pack my Reeboks the next time I attend a black tie dinner."

"Speaking of black," Chelsea said, "whatever happened to the late Monsieur Didier?"

Gaby lowered her head respectfully.

"A long and painful illness."

"What a tragedy. I'm sure you were devastated."

"So much so, that I just can't seem to bring myself to discuss it.''

"If someone does ask, I hope you're not going to tell them you've become a nun. No warm-blooded woman remains celibate for all those years unless she's dressed in a penguin suit or she's psycho. Or," Chelsea said, amused at her own joke, "her name is Irina Stoddard.''

"Leave the woman alone," Gaby said. "Judging by her escort tonight, I'd say she's doing just fine."

"I'd bet my latest divorce settlement that Maximilian Richard is walking Irina, not sleeping with her. He's too much of a gentleman to say no, and too much of a man to say yes."

She knew it was ridiculous, but for some reason, Gaby wanted to believe Chelsea's theory. She didn't know if she'd ever see Maximilian Richard again, or what she would do if she did, but still, she preferred the idea that he was unattached.

"Okay, back to you," Chelsea said, noting the sudden glimmer in Gaby's eyes. "What about this apartment? Whose is it?"

"I don't know," Gaby answered honestly. "All Armand told me was that it belongs to a friend."

"Man friend? Woman friend? Man's best friend? What?"

"A woman."

"Did she have a lot of lovers? Did she like to entertain? Is there a chance that anyone has seen this place before?"

"From what Armand said, I don't think so," Gaby said, going on to explain how the apartment had come to be hers. "Evidently, she had been set up in this place years ago by a wealthy admirer, but when they split, her crowd became more downtown than uptown."

"Well, whoever she is, she has exquisite taste."

Chelsea's eyes journeyed around the room, appraising the incredible collection of seventeenth- and eighteenth-century art objects. The paintings, the furniture, the accessories—each was peerless in its own right, but in combination they were utterly glorious. Her gaze stopped at a mirror-backed étagère which held a collection of blue-and-white porcelain obelisks.

Suddenly, Chelsea's face darkened.

"What's the matter?"

"There's something about this that's making me uncomfortable."

"I know it's wrong to lie," Gaby said, "and I've thought long and hard about what I'm doing. But I'm not really hurting anyone and I'm not doing anything illegal."

"That's not what's bothering me." Chelsea's voice was gentle, nonjudgmental. "I'm the first one to say that to get by in this life, you do what you have to do. But I was never a Brownie and you were. I know how hard it must have been for you that first time, when you fudged the facts on your Bergdorf job application. And I know how hard it must be for you now to accept the idea that whether you want to admit it or not, you're passing yourself off as someone you're not. But hey, you needed the money. What's more, I think you needed the excitement this game offers you.''

Gaby's cheeks reddened.

"I hadn't thought about that," she said, "but you may be right. In a way, this is the most fun I've ever had.''

"It's known as living on the edge. Thrilling, but dangerous.''

"Chelsea, spit it out. What's troubling you?''

"Your connection to Armand. I know you think you're helping him, but in the long run you could wind up hurting yourself.''

Gaby was confused. Only a short while ago, Chelsea had been reminiscing about the nights she had spent in Armand's embrace. Now she was making it sound as if Gaby was caught in Armand's grip.

"He was good to me. If I can do something good for him, I fully intend to do it.''

Chelsea eyed her friend and shook her head. Gaby was being defensive, protective. But was she being as cautious as she should be? She had been burned once, and so, most likely, she would avoid sticking her hand into open fires, but Chelsea knew that sometimes the flames of hell burned so white and so hot that they became invisible, and only when their flesh was melting did victims know they were being burned.

"Armand's a darling, but he's human," she said carefully. "He was hurt and humiliated, and my guess is he's out for revenge. Watch yourself, Gaby. I'd hate to see you caught in the middle of someone else's battle.''

"I won't be," Gaby said emphatically, closing her eyes and ears to Chelsea's advice.

Chelsea said she understood Gaby's plight, but how could she? She was rich. She was established. She had cronies and associates and a routine and no one depending on her. Gaby had no money, no friends, and no routine. She had a son whose love she had to recapture, an enormous debt she had to repay, and a time schedule she had to respect. Chelsea meant well, Gaby knew that, but Armand Lafitte had been there when no one else was. He had offered her hope, which no one else had done. Thanks to his tutelage, she was beginning to believe that a career in antiques was possible. More important, thanks to his support, she was beginning to believe in herself.

Was he seeking revenge against those who had tried to ruin him? Probably. Could she suffer any consequences because she was his ally? Probably. But because Armand was the only friend she had—other than Chelsea, whose loyalty had yet to be tested—Gaby didn't care about consequences. Why should she? She had been through so much already, there was nothing that could hurt her. Not even the truth.

8

The disrespectful buzzing of an alarm shattered the fragile walls of Gaby's sleep. The noise was startling, jolting her into that transitional stage of wakefulness where her eyes were open but her mind remained fogged with remnants of the night's visions. Because Chelsea had left so late, she had only slept for a few hours. Exhausted, she should have fallen into a deep sleep, but instead she had been restless, tossing, turning, fighting off faceless demons who insisted upon chasing her, pulling at her, fighting with her. Throughout, she had the sense of trying to hold on to something, but it was vague, shadowy. Still, she closed her hands around the phantasm as if it were a newborn child, clutching it to her protectively, almost desperately. Whatever it was, whether real or imagined, tangible or intangible, she couldn't escape the notion that she had lost it once before and was not about to lose it again.

Gaby rubbed her eyes with the palms of her hands, until the residual fragments of her nightmare were little more than confetti-colored specks. When the brightness faded and the clusters dissolved into blackness, she blinked, slowly opened her eyes again, and stretched, but then steadfastly refused to move another muscle until the aroma of fresh coffee wafted into her room. Instead, she lay snuggled beneath a thick comforter and waited, allowing cold air from a nearby window to tickle her nose and brush her cheeks. When at last she smelled her special mocha-java–Columbian brew, she roused herself, slipped out of bed and into a robe, ran to the kitchen, poured a cup of black coffee, and returned to her warm sheets as quickly as she could.

Just as she had brought a few treasured photographs with her when she had moved into this apartment, she had also brought a parcel of old habits. Habits that were like a cushy easy chair which automatically molded itself to the bodily contours of its most frequent occupant. It hadn't taken her long to discover, however, that certain habits, like certain pieces of furniture, didn't fit into new surroundings. Leaving her front door unlocked wasn't wise in Wadsworth, but it wasn't particularly dangerous either. In New York, it was insane. Having breakfast in the Thayer kitchen had been pleasant because there had been a big table to eat at and, usually, someone to sit across from. In this apartment, there was neither.

While some patterns had been harder to alter than others, Gaby found that having coffee in bed had become a delightful part of her morning routine. It gave her a chance to organize her thoughts as well as to plan her day. It also gave her a chance to enjoy her surroundings. For a woman who, if offered a chance to live in another time and another place, surely would have elected Paris during the Age of Enlightenment, greeting the day in that splendid room did for her soul what multivitamins did for her body—it provided her with ten times her daily minimum requirement of pleasure.

The bedroom proclaimed its love for the eighteenth century. Delicately carved and lightly gilded white boiserie paneled the walls. Blue and white toile draped the windows and the elaborate canopy that hung over the bed. Midnight-navy velvet and gold braiding covered a Louis XIV settee, as well as a plump bergère and ottoman. On either side of the bed, Empire rock crystal lamps sat atop magnificent Louis XV tables, one a graceful fruitwood parquetry with a leather writing surface called a *table à écrire*, the other a small oval-shaped piece with a drawer originally intended for filmy lingerie and consequently called a *table en chiffonnière*.

Each piece of furniture was a work of art, with an impressive provenance or a *maître*'s signature, but if asked, Gaby would not have hesitated to point out that her favorite was the least remarkable of the lot. Across the room, beneath an extravagantly gilded mirror, sat the mahogany gueridon where she and Simone had learned to love each other. Once a week, in honor of Simone, Gaby brought home a bouquet of fresh flowers and fixed them in a crystal vase which she placed on the table. Though the arrangements were varied—sometimes lavish, sometimes spare—and the blossoms were mixed, there were always at least six pink roses included. They had been Simone's favorite, and somehow, having *those* flowers on *that* table made Gaby feel as if Simone were there.

Now, as she sipped the last of her coffee, she performed another daily ritual—she debated with the spirit of the gueridon about whether or not Simone would approve of her new life. She never questioned that her aunt would applaud the changes in the way Gaby looked, where she worked, and the circles in which she traveled; she never doubted that Simone would be thrilled to know that Gaby was assisting a learned Frenchman like Giles Deffand, but there were deeper issues that could be questioned and it was those answers Gaby wasn't certain she wanted to hear.

While her first cup of coffee was accompanied by lazy introspection, her second was devoted to an extensive course in self-improvement. Each day, Gaby devoted at least half an hour in the morning and twice that at night to bettering herself. She read classics in both French and English, devoured books on the history and cultural development of Europe in the seventeenth and eighteenth centuries, studied the works of painters like François Boucher and Antoine Watteau, and immersed herself in magazines that ranged from *Art & Antiques* to *Vogue Beauty Guides*.

By the time she had finished a short article on facial contouring and the last few chapters of Dumas's *La Tulipe Noire*, it was almost seven-fifteen. Reluctantly, she crawled out of bed, straightened the linens, and spent fifteen minutes doing stretching exercises. Then she headed for the bathroom. As she undressed, she went to the control panel near her dressing table, clicked on the stereo, and listened as Handel's *Water Music* began to mingle with the steam from the shower.

"Handel took a bath. Used a lot of soap. La, la, la."

Gaby worked up a rich handful of suds and began to lather her body with lavender-scented foam. She massaged her skin slowly, breathing in the delicate floral perfume, singing silly lyrics along with Zubin Mehta and the New York Philharmonic.

"It's wa-ter mu-sic, ta-tum-ta-ta-tum-tum."

Though her natural alto caught on a few of the high notes, she sang with great exuberance, laughing now and then at her feeble attempts at operatic splendor. Once she was dry and had blown out her hair, she turned down the volume, switched to a Brandenburg concerto, and began to apply her makeup.

Carefully, she lined her eyes and shadowed her lids, blushed her cheeks, and rouged her lips. It seemed odd, even to her, that a woman who was almost forty years old should have to concentrate so hard on something that was supposed to be second nature, but until recently makeup had never played an important role in her life. Previously, she had espoused the natural look, believing that less was best. Now, as she dusted her face with translucent powder and admired her handiwork, she admitted that more could look like less and was infinitely better than nothing.

She brushed her hair back into a low ponytail, tied it with a velvet ribbon, and went to her closet. Rummaging about, she found a white silk blouse, a midcalf black nubbly wool skirt, and a long black wool cardigan. A few gold chains, an antique monocle, gold knot earrings, black leather boots, and her ensemble was complete. As she perused her image in a full-length mirror, she smiled. Who would have ever guessed that the entire outfit had cost less than two hundred dollars?

"Nothing like makeshift chic," she said, winking at the elegant lady in the looking glass.

With that, she grabbed her coat, her gloves, her purse, and an umbrella and left for work. It was almost eight-thirty.

Castleton's was housed in an imposing postmodern structure of polished white stone that occupied the entire corner of Seventy-ninth Street and Madison Avenue. Up, toward Fifth, wedged in between Castleton's and its neighbor, an expensive cooperative, a pocket park provided passersby with a place to sit and rest and contemplate the evocative Henry Moore sculpture that dominated the small city garden. In front, an arched glass canopy jutted out from beneath an enormous half-moon Palladian window, sheltering a bright red carpet that led from the curb to a set of thick stainless steel doors flanked by tall white Doric columns. The entire façade was one of contemporary understatement and traditional grandeur, with only one anachronistic touch—next to the entrance hung a large wooden sign with "Castleton's" carved in Old English letters. Some purists might have thought it out of place, but to those who understood and appreciated the concept of continuity, it was the ultimate provenance. The same sign hung outside each and every Castleton's, worldwide, because it was a sign exactly like the one that had hung outside the first Castleton's on Charing Cross Road in London.

Just five years old, these quarters represented a dramatic departure from Castleton's previous home on Park Avenue. There, the emphasis had been on architectural assimilation and anonymity. Here, a definite architectural statement had been made, one that echoed a change in leadership as well as a shift in philosophical approach. Garrett Jr., the man behind the message, had wanted to make a simple point: while Castleton's heart and soul would always be rooted in the past, its feet were firmly planted in the twentieth century.

When Garrett had first arrived in New York to take over the American operation, he had allowed himself time to observe and to learn. After a year, he had come to the conclusion that Castleton's had to move, both physically and ideologically. Garrett understood and accepted the fact that there was a mystique attached to an auction house, an excitement that came from bidding and winning a sought-after piece of history. But he also understood that he was running a business that generated an extraordinary amount of money. If he was going to be successful in New York—and he had to be if he hoped eventually to wear the Castleton crown—he couldn't afford to limit his reach to the privileged few; he couldn't afford for Castleton's to function as a private club for the mega-moneyed. He had to widen the doors and make the world of fine art and antiques as accessible and as attractive to the average collector as it had always been to the wealthy connoisseur. With that in mind, he increased the public relations budget, injected himself into the social scene, enlarged his audience by doubling the number of Castleton's Annex auctions, and raised the awareness level of the general public about auctions in general—and Castleton's in particular—by traveling to major American cities several times a year, lecturing and making personal appearances. Judging by the noticeable upswing in salesroom attendance and the incredible jump in profits, Garrett had more than made his point.

It took Gaby only fifteen minutes to walk from her apartment to Castleton's. Usually, she enjoyed the journey, using the time to study the buildings, the shops, and the people of her adopted city, but on days like this, when it was bitter cold and snowing, the trip became a trek. She gladly would have exchanged her silk square for the old woolen muffler she used to wear at home, but she knew a long, fringed red-and-navy-striped scarf was a definite no-no for a woman of her stature. She also knew that if anyone saw her trudging up Madison Avenue braving a winter storm with nothing but a small umbrella, she would have been the center of a week's gossip, and rightfully so. Anyone else would have called a taxi or summoned her limousine.

By the time she reached the employee's entrance on Madison Avenue, she felt as if she had just participated in the Alaskan Iditarod, without benefit of huskies or sled. She shook the snow off her coat, closed her umbrella, and took the elevator to the fourth floor. The halls were still quiet. Many offices were still dark and unoccupied. Several secretaries were already at their desks, straightening papers, combing their hair, rubbing the cold out of their hands, changing from dripping boots to clean, dry shoes. Gaby smiled and exchanged bits of small talk as she proceeded to the end of the hall where the European furniture department was headquartered. As usual, she was the first to arrive. She clicked on the lights, hung her coat in the closet, and went to her desk, stopping to look out the window.

The snow persisted. Big, fat flakes that looked like sugar-frosted breakfast cereal fell in such thick clumps that Madison Avenue already looked like the first layer of a wedding cake. Morning weather reports had predicted that the snow would end before noon. Gaby hoped they were right. That evening, the January Antiques Fair was scheduled to have its preview parties, and though a snowstorm wouldn't force a cancellation, it certainly could complicate matters.

Thinking about the fair reminded her that she had planned to leave early so she could go home and change for the Benefactors' Tea. Before that, however, she had a lot to do. With so many collectors descending on New York for the fair, Castleton's, Sotheby's, and Christie's had all scheduled major auctions that week. Castleton's presentation, an impressive collection of important eighteenth-century European furniture and decorative arts, was to be held on Saturday afternoon. Gaby was scheduled to be on hand in the gallery for every one of the exhibition days, as well as to help man the phones at the actual sale. In addition, as she had done so many times before, she had promised to log extra hours helping with new arrivals for upcoming auctions.

Though her title read "department head assistant" and granted her certain privileges, often Gaby volunteered to do a wide range of chores. When merchandise was delivered to Castleton's for auction, the head of the department examined each item thoroughly for excessive restoration or fakery. Assistants—cataloguers and cataloguer trainees—researched the piece, looking to substantiate a provenance, to find a unique reference, or to chart a sales history. Once all the information was gathered and the piece was authenticated, an estimate was made, a blurb written, a photograph taken, and an auction lot number assigned. Then the piece was stored—in a separate warehouse for larger merchandise, in the department's basement storage closet if it was a smaller piece of decorative art. Gaby involved herself in most phases of the process, because to her it was the best hands-on education one could get. At a museum, one saw only the finest. At junk stores or flea markets, one frequently saw the worst the market had to offer. At an auction house, one saw both ends of the spectrum, as well as everything in between, making it possible to learn firsthand the difference between good, better, and best.

Though some outsiders might have questioned her above-and-beyond work ethic, those who worked with her found the answer quite simple: Gabrielle Didier loved antiques. She loved being surrounded by them, touching them, learning about them, caring for them. She loved seeing them admired by others, studied, discussed, coveted, fought over at auction. As far as she was concerned, the only unpleasant part of her job was having to separate herself from special lots once they were sold and shipped.

"I have a present for you."

A young woman with straight, black hair that skimmed her shoulders, light turquoise eyes hidden behind tortoiseshell glasses, and a trim, boyish build handed Gaby an envelope. Bettina Zarlov, nicknamed Beezie, was twenty-five and single, with, as she was fond of saying, "no candidates competing for a serious entanglement at the present time." Like Gaby, she was passionate about antiques. Unlike Gaby, Beezie had had to pass an exhaustive test before being accepted into the department and had moved beyond the trainee level only after she had demonstrated an incredible memory for historical data and a wonderfully flamboyant use of descriptive language.

"Thanks, Beezie." Gaby smiled.

"John said to tell you this is for the clock they sold for you last month."

Gaby tore open an end, took out a check, noted the amount, nodded, and stuffed it into her purse, as casually as if receiving two thousand dollars first thing in the morning was an everyday occurrence.

Beezie walked over to the window and stared out at the snow. After a few seconds, she laughed.

"God is in serious trouble."

"What?"

"I'd bet a year's salary that Vincent Prado didn't order a snowstorm as part of the fanfare accompanying the opening of his precious fair. This must be something God had the audacity to do on His own." Again, Beezie laughed. "The elegant Mr. P. must be having a colossal fit. No one snows on his parade."

"He'll manage."

"Manage? He'll probably fly in some low-pressure system and melt every drop of this white stuff by five o'clock."

Gaby rose from her chair. She didn't like talking about Vincent Prado.

"We have work to do."

"True. Late yesterday afternoon, a shipment arrived tagged for our department. Want to take a preliminary peek?"

Gaby already had her purse on her shoulder and her flashlight and magnifying glass in hand.

"What's in the shipment? Anything interesting?"

"As a matter of fact, there were a few things marked to your attention. A fabulous Empire armchair, a commode, and a lacquered bureau. Are they yours?''

"No. They're part of the collection of a woman I met at a party. She wanted to clean out a few things. I simply recommended that she send them to us.''

"Charmed another old broad out of everything but her socks, eh?'' Beezie picked up a notepad and a pencil and followed Gaby out the door, back down the hall to the elevator.

"That's not exactly how it was.''

"You're right. I'm sorry,'' Beezie said, pressing the button for the lower level. "Knowing you, you got her socks too!''

Much of the storage space for the gallery was housed in the bowels of the building. The receiving area was cool and dim, prompting Beezie to click on the overhead lights the instant they stepped off the elevator. The room was huge and barnlike, with strange shadows created by oddly shaped bundles. Some were wrapped in brown paper and string, others were in wooden crates, still others were in quilted throws. It reminded Gaby of a summer house or a part-time residence where the furnishings sat unused and unloved for months on end until someone arrived to remove their shrouds and give them back a sense of purpose.

Gaby felt her insides fizz with anticipation. She loved coming down here. To her, it was as exciting as it would be for a child allowed to roam about FAO Schwarz. Here, she could go over each item quietly and slowly, examining every inch of those that struck her fancy, taking notes on those that didn't so that she could analyze why they didn't.

Often, she played a silent game with herself. She appraised a particular piece, researched what similar lots had brought at recent auctions or shows, checked key dealers for similar pieces, assigned a price, and then compared it to the one arrived at by Giles Deffand. In the beginning, she performed miserably, with her estimates coming out way on the high side. It took a while before she realized that each time she had made two big mistakes. She had determined prices with her eye instead of with her head, allowing her delight to color her estimates. And she had subconsciously acted like a retailer and attached a profit margin. She had forgotten that, at auction, profit was a percentage of the sale price paid by the buyer, not something paid by the seller and included in that price. Lately, though, thanks to her early morning tutorials, she had been coming closer and closer to Giles's figures. Twice, she had hit the actual selling price on the nose.

While Beezie attacked the rear of the room, Gaby poked around the front. She found an Italian rococo table in excellent condition, a pair of giltwood bergères with exquisite frames but shredded upholstery, a buffet piece she thought too dark and cumbersome for her tastes, a Biedermeier games table in exquisitely burled walnut, and finally, the armchair she had been looking for. It was tub shaped, crafted out of the deepest, richest mahogany, with lion's-paw legs topped by graceful swan supports and a loose seat cushion of yellow and white damask. Nervously, her fingers glided over the smooth wood, on the alert for blemishes or for bruises caused by a disrespectful trucker.

It took a few minutes before she located the lacquered desk and the commode. Quickly, she searched the desk with her magnifying glass and flashlight, looking for nicks or chips that might have marred the chinoiserie veneer. She discovered signs of wear at the juncture of the fall-front panel and the main body and a few chips in the gilding, but in a two-hundred-year-old piece, those were to be expected. She opened the desk and examined the shelves and drawers that were fitted above the leather writing surface, making certain everything slid smoothly and closed tightly. It did.

The third piece was less prestigious than the other two, but equally as beautiful. A neoclassical commode with a marble top, its attraction was the delicate marquetry that festooned the front. Gaby loved marquetry, preferring its pictorial designs and artistic flair to the geometric symmetry of its sister craft, parquetry. Though both involved tremendous intricacy and required exceptional skill, she favored inlaid patterns such as the one before her now—flowering vines, a courtly urn, a decorative oval topped by a ribbon and a floral garland—all worked in tiny, hand-cut pieces of walnut, mahogany, and fruitwood. Again, Gaby checked for shipping damage. The marquetry was intact, which was the most important thing; the brass pulls were all there, but the ormolu *sabots* that booted the legs were missing. She strained to recall what she had noticed the first time she had seen this cabinet. They had been missing then. Everything was as it was supposed to be. No need to worry.

Why was she so nervous? she wondered. Probably because she and Armand had decided that whatever they had already consigned to Castleton's would go on the block, but that Gaby would no longer bring them antiques from Armand's shop. The last thing she needed was for something to go wrong now.

"Beezie, it's late," she said, assuring herself everything was all right. "I have to go. I promised I'd work the exhibition this morning."

"Go ahead, be a drudge. I'm going to stay down here and get a head start on Monsieur Deffand."

"One of these days, you're going to have his job." Gaby pressed the button for the elevator. "And I'm going to be able to say I knew you when."

Beezie grinned, gave a conspiratorial wink that implied intimate knowledge of one of Gaby's secrets, leaned back, and blew a kiss to the ceiling.

"From your lips to Garrett Castleton's ear," she said, teasing Gaby, who scowled at her from inside the elevator. "Next time you see him, you will put in a good word for me, won't you?"

"I'll think about it."

The elevator doors closed, but not before Gaby gave her young friend a sly but forgiving smile. Obviously, the fact that she had been Garrett's date last night at the Castleton gala was common knowledge and item number one on the office grapevine.

Gaby exited on the first floor, home of the real estate sales department. At least once a week, she stopped in and checked out the newest listings. Two oceanfront villas in Palm Beach, a Holmby Hills mansion in Los Angeles, an estate in Grosse Pointe, an industrialist's co-op in Chicago, and a four-story town house on Rittenhouse Square in Philadelphia. As she often did, she noted the names of those she thought might be moving to smaller quarters and, therefore, might be interested in reducing the size of their collections. She gave the list to Armand, hoping to be a few steps ahead of the realtors who gave the same list to other antiques dealers throughout the country.

After she left, she walked up the wide, pale wood staircase that led to the second floor. As she reached the top of the steps and peered out the mullioned window that overlooked Seventy-ninth Street, she noticed that the snow had stopped. She laughed. Beezie was right. Vincent Prado had incredible pull.

With a smile still affixed to her lips, she turned and headed for the main exhibition area, noting as she passed that the crowd around the catalogue desk was already two deep. Neither rain, nor sleet, nor snow, nor traffic snarls could keep an avid collector from examining merchandise before a sale. She nodded to one of the three young women working the counter, grabbed the catalogue for the current exhibition, a pencil, and a clipboard filled with applications for absentee bids, and proceeded down the hall.

The same contemporary mode that had been established on the exterior of the building continued to dominate the interior. Track lighting and recessed spots, their placement and intensity engineered with the technical precision of a Broadway stage set, illuminated exhibition areas and walkways. Smoke-gray carpeting covered the floors while rose-toned, sound-absorbing carpeting softened the walls. Lavish floral displays in marble urns stood atop charcoal-gray pedestals in the main room, while areca palms potted in carved stone planters enlivened dark corners and long hallways.

There were two exhibition galleries, one on either side of the salesroom. Each gallery was divided into three sections, with the center spotlighting the most important items scheduled to go under the hammer. Three-dimensional pieces like *bureau plats*, center tables, and unusual secretaires were augmented by the careful placement of sinuously carved chairs, elaborate torchères, and plump stools called tabourets. Everything was displayed with great style. Large commodes, consoles, mirrors, and candelabra decorated the side walls. Often, magnificent paintings from an upcoming Old Masters auction were hung as a complement to the furniture, creating intimate vignettes of Old World splendor.

As Gaby wandered about, keeping herself available for anyone who needed assistance, she looked and listened, absorbing the aura that was so much a part of Castleton's. It was such a mix of accents and attitudes, preferences and predilections. Fur coats, couture clothes, and hand-tooled boots stood in counterpoint to pile-lined parkas, cardigan sweaters, and rubber-soled Wallabies. Perfume clashed with cologne, sleek coiffures with unruly curls, aristocratic French with suburban New York. So many differences, so many dissimilarities, yet everyone there was bonded by an interest in, a passion for, a curiosity about, relics from civilization's past.

For about an hour, she held court in the center gallery, answering questions and translating for foreigners who found it more comfortable to converse in French. While there were many visitors who were there simply to wander about as they would in a museum, the majority were serious buyers who wanted to know about workmanship, or about the specific details that differentiated this piece from others of its kind, or provenances, or what comparable items had brought at previous auctions.

Gaby was about to leave the end gallery, the one closest to the far wall, when she noticed Garrett getting off the elevator. At the sight of him, her insides fluttered and her palms went damp. Should she go over and say hello? Should she wait and see if he came over to her? Should she have called him to thank him for last night? Should she have let him take her home? Gaby turned away, giving herself a minute to compose herself and think. Why was everything so unsettling? Why did she suddenly have to gauge her responses and deliberate before making even the smallest move? Because, she reminded herself, suddenly everything was new. For so many years, life had been prescribed, patterned, predictable. Then, like balls in a bingo wheel, everything had become jumbled and disordered. There seemed to be no sequence, no logical evolution of experiences. One minute she was married, living in a small town, fully acquainted with the local rules and regulations governing a woman attached to a particular man. The next minute she was unattached, available, and prey to the sophisticated denizens of the New York social scene. Why wasn't there a freshman orientation period for detached, displaced women? Why weren't there classes like Beginning Flirting or Singles 101-102?

Kermit the Frog was right, she thought, smiling in spite of the chaos going on inside of her. *It's not easy being green!*

Knowing that if she continued to stand there she would begin to look extremely foolish, she took a deep breath, fixed a confident smile on her face, and turned around. She started to move toward Garrett, but now his back was to her and he was speaking to a tall blonde Gaby recognized as his sister. For a few seconds, Gaby kept her distance and watched. From the stiffness of their backs, she sensed that the conversation was not pleasant. She had a choice. She could wait until they had finished and then speak to Garrett, or she could leave and hope to run into him later that evening. One look at the grim expression on Irina's face and Gaby's decision was made. She left.

"If you're a good little boy, I'll be sure to tell Mummy and Daddy what a fine job you did last night."

Garrett had been avoiding Irina all morning, but there was no avoiding her now. She had cornered him the moment he had exited the elevator and steered him off to the side for a sister-brother chat.

"Saying something nice about me would certainly be a change," he said, making no attempt to hide his sarcasm.

"How nice that there's finally something nice to say."

"Just don't go overboard. After all, Mother and Daddy are getting on in years. I don't think they could stand the shock of hearing the sound of praise coming from your usually venomous lips."

"No matter what you think, they value my opinion," Irina continued, refusing to do battle.

"Everyone has his flaws," he said finally. "Even Mother and Daddy."

"I wonder what her flaws are." Irina tilted her head in Gaby's direction, nodding toward the other woman's back. "I know that you're too besotted to search, but I'm sure that if one looked hard enough, one could find several cracks in that otherwise perfect exterior. As we learned in the case of your dear Cynthia, few in this world are unsullied."

Garrett's eyes narrowed. Through angry slits, he studied the long face, the high cheekbones, and the hooded blue eyes that mirrored his own. He saw the sandy blond hair that was the same shade as his, the tall, thin frame which bore the same look as his. Even her shoulders-back, chin-up patrician posture was the same as his, and it disturbed him. Why did they look so much alike when what he wanted was to believe that they were completely different?

"Stay away from her," he growled, moving closer to Irina, forgetting where he was, grabbing her by the shoulders.

Irina snapped free of his grasp.

"I'm only trying to help, dear brother."

Garrett shook his head in disbelief.

"Spare me," he said.

"Seriously, darling. What if she's just another opportunist in designer clothes? What if she's using you in hopes of gaining entree into the family vault or climbing some sort of career ladder at Castleton's?"

"Irina. The woman is not a young tuft-hunter fresh out of secretarial school. She's well educated, well off, well connected, and hardly looking to fund her next meal by sticking her hand into my pocket. Deffand had to beg her to come to work for us, and thank goodness he did. She's been invaluable."

"She's terribly clever, I'll grant you that, but that's precisely why I'm so concerned." Irina sighed and patted Garrett's hand. "You don't know very much about her, so how can you be so certain that she's not looking to gain from your relationship?"

"In what way?" Garrett was annoyed, at Irina for making such suggestions, at himself for listening.

"I don't know. Maybe she wants Deffand's job. Maybe she wants a seat on the board. Maybe she wants a department of her own to run. I just think you should be careful." Her eyes widened in mock concern. "You're more vulnerable than you know."

"What does that mean?"

"Simply that you don't handle romantic disillusionment terribly well. After all, this is the first relationship you've had since that embarrassing debacle with Cynthia. I'm sure that, deep down, you're petrified that it might happen again."

Garrett's eyes flamed. "Don't you ever mention Cynthia's name again. If you do . . ."

"You'll do what?" Her lips pressed together in an unbending line. "Scold me? Call me nasty names? Have a tantrum? I couldn't care less!"

She moved forward, walking around him so that he was the one in the corner, not she.

"Actually, I don't know why you blame me for the breakup of your pathetic little romance. I simply presented father with the facts about Cynthia Hawthorne." Irina's face flushed at the memory of her victory. Though her voice remained low, it vibrated with spitefulness. "It's not my fault that father places a premium on purity. It's not my fault that darling Cynthia didn't have the character to admit to her sordid past. And certainly, it's not my fault that you weren't man enough to fight for what you wanted!''

Garrett had heard enough. Without another word, he stormed away and headed for his office, slamming the door behind him, wondering in exasperation why every element of his personal happiness was an issue over which he and his witch of a sister waged war—his position with Castleton's, his involvements with women, his relationship with his father.

The thought of his father drew Garrett's eyes to the double silver frame that sat on a shelf behind his desk.

One side held a photograph of his mother, Charlotte Castleton, a picture of feminine perfection. On the other side, was a photograph of Garrett Castleton, Sr., seventy-two years old, silver-haired, silver-tongued, and remarkably energetic, despite an advancing case of arthritis. With a minimum of assistance, he supervised the European operation, shuttling between Castleton galleries on the Continent and conducting many of the auctions held at the main base in London.

Just that morning, he had called to find out whether or not the gala had been successful. Usually, each year immediately after Christmas, he and Charlotte flew to New York to oversee the Castleton exhibit at the fair and to orchestrate the party at the town house. This year, however, a debilitating flu had kept them both at home. Now, Garrett knew his father would demand a complete account of the evening. Though detail was important to Garrett Jr., to Garrett Sr. it was the marrow of success.

When Garrett had finished his report, he heard his father sigh.

''I wish we could have been there.''

''I wish that also. It didn't seem right that you and mother were not at the head of the receiving line.''

The minute the words left his mouth, Garrett regretted them. He had been hoping to get through the conversation without mention of his sister, her ladyship Irina Stoddard.

''Naturally, I expect that you did as I requested and asked your sister to serve as your hostess.''

''I did as you requested,'' Garrett repeated woodenly.

''I know that you and Irina are not particularly fond of each other, but last night was a business party and, as you well know, this is a business of appearances. I hope you understand.''

Of course Garrett understood. No less than a hundred times, his father had intoned what was becoming his anthem: ''Competition is healthy. Squabbling is demeaning.'' As it always was between father and son, the argument stemmed from a difference in perception. The senior Castleton viewed the schism between brother and sister as natural sibling rivalry, as a repeat of his own youthful conflict with his younger brother, Bentley. To Garrett Jr., it was Armageddon.

Since that time eight years before, when Irina had succeeded in sabotaging Garrett's engagement and almost succeeded in destroying his career, the two siblings had been locked in a fierce struggle. At issue was control of the Castleton empire. As their father's retirement and the naming of his successor loomed closer, the skirmishes between them had become more numerous, the competition more intense. For a while, particularly after he had been given the chairmanship of Castleton's New York, Garrett had felt securely ahead. Then Irina had made the voyage west, bringing with her not only her reputation as an expert in the field of Old Masters, but also, the title of executive vice-president.

Cold wars were never easy and this one had proved no exception. Though at the office they managed to avoid any incident that might result in an overt clash, outside they avoided each other completely. Those close to either one never invited the other to small gatherings. At larger events, they simply nodded and went about their separate business. At company functions, they had a tacit agreement to alternate hosting duties. In Garrett's mind, the gala had been his turn. If his father hadn't implied that her absence would be an embarrassment to the family, Garrett never would have invited Irina. If she hadn't felt that her absence would have been an embarrassment to herself, Irina never would have accepted.

But, Garrett reminded himself, last night had been truly his. The spotlight had shone upon him, just as it did whenever he raised the auctioneer's gavel or announced the acquisition of a major collection to the press. The gala had been his. He had written the script. He had produced the show. And, he thought, a spontaneous smile loosening the tightness around his mouth, he had cast the leading lady—a woman whose quick mind and keen humor had reduced Irina to a supporting role, a woman whose mere presence had added distinction and glamor to the evening, a woman whose delicate beauty and fiery spirit had opened a door to a place he thought he'd never visit again.

His smile faded. Moments ago, Irina had threatened to interfere in his relationship with Gaby. He had threatened to retaliate, but he knew that to his sister, his threats were empty. Though he hated to admit it, she was right about his behavior eight years before. He had allowed Irina to take away what was his without much more than a whimper. Why shouldn't she think that he would allow the same thing to happen now? Because now, he told himself, things were different. He was different. The intervening years had served as a kind of mental retreat, inuring him to her barbs, strengthening his resolve, preparing him for the battle he knew was inevitable. He was stronger now, more certain of his abilities, more definite about his wants. The Dinant tapestry was going to belong to him. Castleton's was going to belong to him. And, if she would have him, Gabrielle Didier would belong to him.

This time, when Irina attacked, no matter how powerful her artillery, no matter how devastating her assault, he would not back off. This time, no matter what he had to do, he would win.

By the time Gaby started home, it was almost three o'clock. The sun was shining and the Sanitation Department had plowed most of the streets. The pristine whiteness of the morning snow had turned to a dun gray slush, forcing her to walk close to the storefronts and away from traffic. As she went, she windowshopped, imagining how it would feel to wear that dress or that gown, picturing herself in those shoes or that coat, though the only indulgence her pocketbook could afford was a chocolate croissant for her afternoon tea.

The minute she returned home, she removed her coat and boots and put some water on to boil. The snow had stopped, but the temperature had remained in the low teens. Her fingers felt numb, to say nothing of the lack of feeling in her toes. When, finally, the kettle whistled, she poured boiling water into an enormous mug, dunked a Ceylon tea bag until the water turned a dark orange, added a drop of milk, put her croissant on a plate, and retired to the bedroom.

Dropping down onto the big bergère, putting her feet up on the ottoman and covering her legs with an afghan, she automatically faced Tante Simone's gueridon. She sipped her tea slowly and allowed her thoughts to drift, to wander without direction or purpose, lighting wherever they wished. She wasn't surprised when she found herself lingering in the past. Though the past was rife with painful recollections, it was familiar and therefore more comfortable than the present. Now was a time of flux and uncertainty, a time of mottled grays and occasional brights. Then had happened. It had been recorded in black and white, written in indelible ink. There were memories too hurtful to deal with, yet Gaby knew they were there, hovering just beneath her consciousness, daring her to bring them to the surface. There were memories of happy times also, times so wonderful she longed to revive and relive them, but they refused to comply, disappearing, fading, eluding her like will-o'-the-wisps flickering in the night.

"I miss you, Tante Simone." Gaby spoke to the empty room, saddened by the silence that greeted her voice. "I'm feeling very alone right now, and I could use someone to talk to."

She ate her croissant slowly, savoring every bite, as if the butter-rich pastry contained a magical elixir instead of a chocolate filling.

If it did contain an elixir, what would I ask for?

She let the idea ruminate for a while, even though her response had surfaced instantly—happiness, a sense of security, someone to love, someone who would love her in return. Was she asking too much? Was any of that possible for Madame Gabrielle Didier? Unfortunately, she had no crystal ball, no way of divining her future, but judging by her past, she knew better than to leave it in the careless hands of fate.

Before she had come to New York and donned the mask of Gabrielle Didier—before, when she had been Gaby Cocroft Thayer, the housewife from Wadsworth, Ohio—she had believed in dreams coming true and happily ever after. She had been trusting and optimistic and unquestioning. She had believed that if you were responsible and honest and steadfast, life would reward you. But then, she thought, life had proved her wrong. Very, very wrong.

As her taxi approached the armory, Gaby reviewed for the tenth time a list of things to do: which hands she was supposed to shake, which names she had to remember, which booths she was expected to visit, and which dealers she should avoid. It was not the chill in the draughty armory that made her shudder as she paused at the cloakroom, but the memory of last year's insurrection and Armand's disgrace.

Summoning up every ounce of courage she possessed, she moved through the receiving line, hoping that no one noticed how her hand shook and how her knees had gone unsteady. She had just finished when Vincent Prado swooped down on her.

"Gabrielle! What a delight it is to see you." How he managed to kiss both her cheeks without dimming his megawatt smile she'd never know, but he did. "Isn't it glorious?"

Gaby tried to respond, but he had grabbed her arm and was turning her in the direction of a slew of photographers who flashed strobes in her face, shouted questions, and asked her to look first this way and then that way, so that each one had a chance to capture her for his particular publication. She smiled at all of them, but refused to speak to any of them. Thankfully, the arrival of Nancy Kissinger diverted their attention long enough for her to break away and move into the main exhibition hall.

As she began her tour, her stomach knotted with bitter admiration for the estimable Mr. Prado. Once again, the fair was, as he had put it, glorious. Each booth overflowed with priceless wonders. It wasn't merely the quantity of quality that astounded her, but the fact that every merchant, even the ones whose stock was normally considered mediocre, had found at least one truly extraordinary piece to display. It was as if each participant had outdone himself trying to prove all over again that the reasoning behind last year's disturbance had been completely fallacious, an aberration, brought about by one man's distorted ego.

As Gaby walked past those dealers she suspected of having been Benedict Arnolds, she swallowed hard, pushing down the bilious taste that had invaded her mouth. She recognized that no one knew about her connection to Armand and that no one cared whether or not she deemed him worthy, but still she staged her own silent protest by refusing even to look at their displays. Instead, she devoted most of her time to visiting the booths of the traditional mainstays of the fair, the major dealers about whom there was never a question of authenticity or support for honesty or guarantees.

As she had expected, each one had unearthed a piece he considered to be not only a masterwork, but also a symbol of his specialty. There was a scarlet lacquer bureau-cabinet from G. Randall, a pair of Kang Xi Fu dogs from Ralph M. Chait, a Regency rosewood library bookcase from Fleming and Meers, an eighteenth-century painted Italian commode from Frederick P. Victoria & Son, a doll-house-shaped wardrobe from Cora Ginsburg, an elaborate Empire center table from Didier Aaron, a simple rooster weathervane from America Hurrah.

Gaby didn't know whether it was the champagne, the dizzying height of the prices, or a touch of aesthetic indigestion from taking in too much in too short a period of time, but as she left A la Vieille Russie and tried to circumvent the crowd gathered around the Victorian garden that marked the center of the hall, she suddenly felt light-headed and off balance. If Max Richard hadn't caught her, she might have stumbled.

He took her arm and guided her to a quiet corner where she could catch her breath and regain her equilibrium. His grip was strong and firm, but his eyes, those magnificent delft-blue eyes, were soft and kind.

"Thank you. You saved me from falling headfirst into the bougainvillea," Gaby said, wondering if the flush rouging her cheeks was because she was still feeling faint or because he was standing so close.

"To the contrary. Thank you." Like a true gallant, he bowed his head respectfully. "It's terrible being a knight in shining armor with no fire-breathing dragons to slay and no fair maidens to rescue. I was beginning to think I'd have to hang around all night before I'd find a damsel in distress."

Gaby smiled. "I'm glad I could be of some help."

He returned her smile, displaying a mouth that was full and lush, teeth that were white and even. His face was square shaped, planed with commanding features that in some other configuration on some other face, might have appeared harsh and sharp. But laugh lines crinkled the corners of his eyes, crescent curves parenthesized his mouth, and a deep dimple in his left cheek hinted at a bit of the imp hiding inside the skin of this utterly sophisticated European gentleman.

"Are you enjoying the fair?" he asked.

"Very much. And you?"

"I always enjoy pageantry. It's the medieval in me."

Gaby wasn't sure whether Max was waiting for a snappy comeback, but she had none, and for a moment a thin veil of silence descended. Before the lapse could become too awkward, the party, which had been relegated to the background, reasserted itself. Suddenly, the small corridor where they were standing, which only seconds before had been quiet and isolated, turned into a major thoroughfare. Ivana Trump and Carroll Petrie stopped en route to Garrick Stephenson's enclave for a brief hello and to find out if Max had thought about their suggestion for a charity walk-a-thon. Mica Ertegun and Chessy Rayner, scouting for their design firm, MACII, paused to ask Max if he might be interested in a Biedermeier mantel clock they had found to add to his collection. Carolyne Roehm and Henry Kravis positioned themselves opposite an enormous painting and proceeded to discuss its virtues with Herve Aaron. Another woman, suited and shawled in black and white checks, waved and blew Max a kiss as she passed by. Though she nodded politely to Gaby, it was impossible to miss the curious upward tilt of her eyebrow.

Inside, Gaby bristled. Whether in suburban Ohio or chic New York, it appeared as if certain things remained constant: inquiring eyes would search until they spotted the unexpected; inquisitive minds would dig for roots even among seeds; and interested ears would listen to whatever inventive mouths had to say. As Gaby watched, the bechecked woman hurriedly gathered two of her cronies around her and began to whisper. Gaby and Max had just become fodder for the gossip mill. Were they a budding romance or an imminent scandal? Was their meeting accidental or clandestine? Was this trio the first to know or the last? Whom should they tell? And what should they tell?

"Have you visited all the booths?"

"Twice." Gaby answered quickly. Watching people talk about her was unnerving. "How about you?"

"Obviously, I work more slowly than you. I've only been around once."

"Have you seen anything you simply couldn't resist?"

"I've seen some wonderful things, but so far, my checkbook hasn't made it out of my pocket."

"I'm surprised nothing caught your fancy."

"I didn't say that."

His eyes held hers with an intensity that seemed to erect walls around them, shutting out everyone except the two of them. There was something undeniably electric about this man, yet Gaby felt compelled to wonder whether her response had more to do with inexperience than with charged excitement. After all, she wasn't the savvy cosmopolite she pretended to be. How could she be? She had been a virgin when she married and she had slept with only one man in her entire life.

"There are some wonderful tapestries in the Chevalier booth," she said, racking her brain for something to say, finally recalling their conversation of the evening before.

"True, but I'm a man with a one-track mind. All the Beauvais and Gobelins in the world can't compete with the splendor of the Dinant tapestries."

He said it with the same concentrated, beatific expression one usually reserves for an obsession, which struck Gaby as odd since he didn't seem to be someone prone to singular preoccupations.

"You make them sound unbelievably special."

"They are."

"I feel like running back to Castleton's just to look at them," she said, making a mental note to ask Giles for permission for a private viewing.

"They would certainly be worth the trip, but they've been around a long time. I'm sure they'll still be there tomorrow."

He smiled in a way that made her feel as if he approved of her growing interest. Whether he did or not, as she had already told him, tapestries were one of her passions. To be ignorant about a set that was obviously so important to a man like him, as well as to Garrett and Vincent Prado, seemed a horrible void in her education, a void she determined to fill as soon as she could.

"Speaking of Castleton's," he said, "last night, other than saying you are invaluable and that, without you, a two-hundred-year-old institution would instantly crumble, I don't think anyone mentioned exactly what your position is at that venerable auction house.''

"I'm Giles Deffand's assistant,'' she said, wondering whether he had assumed she was something more lofty and prestigious, like an international representative, the title bestowed upon socialites who loaned their glittering presence to special functions, allowed the public relations department access to their address books, and encouraged their well-to-do friends to buy or sell their valuables through Castleton's.

"I gather you like your job."

"I don't like being idle and I love antiques. It seemed like the perfect situation."

"Are you good at what you do?"

"I try to be. Are you?"

He paused. "Yes. I am."

His answer, Gaby understood, was not arrogant but a carefully considered reply.

"As long as we're exchanging job descriptions, what is it that you do?"

"I'm a builder."

"That's like saying Michelangelo was a house painter."

Irina Stoddard seemed to appear out of nowhere. "Really, darling. Don't be so modest. You know that without you, your native Belgium would be a collection of thatched-roof huts, to say nothing of the massive construction you've done throughout the rest of Europe."

Without preamble, her arm had snaked through Max's, her lips had bussed his cheek, and her body was clinging to his like clear aspic. Gaby thought Max looked stifled by Irina's possessive aura.

"How are you, Gabrielle?" Irina's thin lips spread in a brief, almost illusory smile.

"Very well. And yourself?"

"Frankly, I'm ecstatic!" Completely ignoring Gaby, Irina lavished her attention on Max, her aristocratic accent becoming more pronounced with every syllable. "I hope you didn't plan an early dinner. I'm having such a marvelous time, I want to stay till the very end."

"Unless you'd like me to select another restaurant, I'm afraid you'll have to tear yourself away when the Patrons' Party ends. Our reservation is for seven-thirty." Without creating a scene, Max gracefully disentangled himself.

"Don't be silly," she said, eyeing Gaby suspiciously, as if it were her fault that Max had dropped her arm. "Seven-thirty will be fine. Actually, I'm quite ravenous."

"Gabrielle and I were just discussing the fair," Max said, looking to change the subject.

"Isn't it simply grand? I think it's the best ever, but then, each year I say the same thing." Irina's face glowed with a rhapsodic pride. "I know I'm prejudiced, being a cochairman and all, but it's such a thrill working with Vincent. He's just too brilliant, wouldn't you say?"

Gaby assumed the question was rhetorical, but when no one spoke and Irina continued to stare at her, it became clear that she was waiting for an answer.

"He's done a fine job."

"Fine job!" Irina's eyes flamed. "Is that all? Really, Gabrielle, I thought you had better taste than that."

Her voice dripped condescension. Gaby had not had much contact with Irina, and she knew that in her position she shouldn't make waves, but the woman's manner demanded rebuttal.

"Your question wasn't about the depth of my taste, but the height of Vincent Prado's brilliance. The way I see it, one has nothing to do with the other."

As she listened to the tone of her own voice, Gaby swallowed a grin. As part of her do-as-they-do self-improvement program, she had taught herself the art of hauteur—how to affect an air of subtle disdain by lifting one's chin, sucking in one's cheeks, and speaking through pursed lips. It was a short-range weapon to be used whenever circumstances called for minor intimidation. In this particular instance, it proved extremely effective. Unable to rebut Gaby's statement without appearing nasty, Irina retracted her claws.

"Well, well, well. A ménage à trois." Chelsea's voice cut the air like a saber. Without waiting to be asked, she centered herself between Gaby and Max. "Is this a private gathering or can anyone join?"

Max welcomed the newcomer with a kiss on both cheeks. Gaby, who, they had decided, was not supposed to know Chelsea well, shook her friend's hand.

"Gabrielle, you know Chelsea Reynolds, don't you?" Max asked without noticing the silent exchange that took place between the two women he had assumed were strangers.

"We met last night," Gaby said.

Chelsea's eyes sparkled as she extended her hand in greeting. Irina, still waiting to be acknowledged, glowered at the tall blonde in the peplumed, winter-white Saint-Laurent suit and canary diamond earrings.

Then, without missing a beat, Chelsea smiled and held out a small plate laden with slices of black bread and roast pork, finally turning to face Irina. "Pig, anyone?"

Gaby was shocked, but it was all she could do to keep from laughing. Obviously, Max was also having trouble keeping a straight face, because despite the lack of movement in his facial muscles, his eyes were twinkling.

"No?" Chelsea motioned to a waiter, handed him the plate, and replaced it with a glass of champagne. "I can't say I blame you. As my first husband used to say, 'a pig is a pig unless it's got an apple stuck in its mouth and a barbecue spit stuck up its rump. Then it's pork.' "

Irina's mouth curled in disgust.

"Your first husband sounds utterly charming. He must have attended the same finishing school you did."

"No, darling. My first husband was filthy rich. My second husband was utterly charming. But then again, you should know. He was your husband first."

"Last night you said you were looking for a mirror. Did you find one you liked?" Max asked, hoping to deflect any further slings and arrows.

"As a matter of fact, I did," Chelsea said, willing to redirect the conversation now that she had had her fun. "A Georgian giltwood that will look positively divine in my drawing room. I also picked up an exquisite equestrian painting by Daniel Clowes, as well as several pieces to add to my collection of Chelsea porcelain."

"You certainly don't waste any time, do you?" Max said.

"Absolutely not. If I see something I like, I grab it."

Irina looked as if she was about to comment, but then apparently thought better of it. Gaby noticed the hesitation and for an instant, actually felt allied with the imperious Lady Stoddard. Chelsea's tongue was lethal, and though Gaby had never been lashed by its sharpness, she could more than understand defending against it.

"Good evening, Max. Chelsea. Irina." Armand had turned the corner and appeared surprised to come upon them.

Some surprise, Gaby thought, watching him shake hands with Max and hug Chelsea. He didn't go near Irina, nor she him.

"I don't believe I've had the pleasure. I'm Armand Lafitte," he said as he bowed and kissed Gaby's hand.

"Gabrielle Didier. *Enchanté.*"

She smiled, but inside, her nerves tightened. Deception was a cumulative act. Sooner or later, Gaby feared she would have to pay a price.

"I can't believe they let you in."

Irina's icy tone froze all conversation. At first, Gaby thought she hadn't been paying attention and therefore, had missed another of Chelsea's barbs, but it was Armand who was the recipient of Irina's wrathful stare and Armand who responded.

"I paid for a ticket like everyone else."

"They shouldn't have taken your money."

"Ah, but they did, Irina, because money is what this fair is all about."

"How would you know what this fair is about? You tried to ruin it!"

"There are those who would disagree. Some say I tried to improve it."

"Well, I'm not one of them."

"You've made that abundantly clear," Armand said tightly.

"I want you to leave." Irina's voice vibrated with malevolent insistence, but Armand refused to be browbeaten.

"At the risk of sounding uncourtly, I don't care what you want. I paid for my ticket and I have every intention of staying. I'm going to drink champagne and eat hors d'oeuvres and view the exhibits and mingle with old friends. And then, your ladyship, when I am good and ready, I will leave."

Having said his piece, he turned to Max, Chelsea, and Gaby.

"Despite the rather low opinion of me held by Madame Stoddard, I am still gentleman enough to know when I've abused my welcome. If our little contretemps has made you uncomfortable, I apologize. Please enjoy the rest of the evening. *Bonsoir.*"

With a commendable display of dignity, Armand walked past the Victorian garden and disappeared into the crowd.

"That man is a maggot!"

"Irina," Max said, "I don't know what the problem is between you and Armand, but I wish you'd keep your hostility to yourself. I happen to like the man. What's more, I have great respect for him. He's a true scholar and a scrupulously honest dealer. I have never known him to be anything but forthright and fair and extremely personable."

Irina had expected Chelsea to champion Armand's cause—they were friends. She might have expected Gabrielle to grimace or express some displeasure at being witness to a mudslinging, but she hadn't expected Max to chastise her in public. His response startled her into an embarrassed silence. As if to make matters worse, the next person to turn the corner was none other than her brother.

After giving everyone an appropriate greeting, Garrett turned to Gaby.

"I've been looking all over for you," he said. "Would you mind if I had a word with you?"

Grateful for an excuse to escape the tension, yet nervous that she had committed some social gaffe, Gaby agreed, allowing Garrett to lead her to the back end of the corridor.

"You left so quickly last night, I was concerned," he said, taking her hand. "Did I do something?"

Gaby had forgotten all about her hasty departure.

"I'm afraid I had too much wine," she said, hoping he wouldn't pursue the issue. "I meant to speak to you this morning and apologize, but I was so busy in the gallery, I never got a chance to call. Forgive me."

"Only if you have dinner with me tonight."

Without meaning to, Gaby looked over Garrett's shoulder at the others. Chelsea had already gone. Max and Irina were beginning to leave. Gaby had nothing to do except go home, nothing to look forward to except another lonely evening in someone else's splendid apartment.

"I'd love to," she said, allowing Garrett to link her arm through his, "but if I ask for anything stronger than Perrier, say no."

*   *   *

Armand tried to appear nonchalant as he wandered in and out of the various booths at the fair, but in truth, like Gaby, he was only there to determine the market value of several pieces he had in his shop and was looking to sell. Having been denied the brisk, steady business that normally kept a dealer aware of the changing importance of certain antiques, he had been forced to use alternative methods of costing his merchandise. Knowing that often prices dropped as shows neared the end and dealers grew anxious to clean out their inventory, Armand had decided that he had no choice but to brave opening night.

"Mon ami!" Antony Vinter shouted his greeting, coming out of his booth to shake Armand's hand. In a softer tone, he said, "What the hell are you doing here? I know it's been a while since I spoke to you last, but I didn't think you'd turned suicidal."

Armand smiled at his friend. Thanks to a diminished income, his weekly lunches with Tony and the others had been all but eliminated. Yet throughout his travail, they had stuck by him, defending him long after the flames from their debacle had decreased to a flicker, meeting whenever he could, sending customers to him whenever they could. Their efforts and their loyalty had earned Armand's undying gratitude.

"I guess I'm just a glutton for punishment," Armand said, noting that Tony deliberately continued to stand in the center of the main aisle, rather than retreating inside his booth. "How's business?"

"It's early yet, but good old Vincent has done it again. He's packed the house with customers."

"Give credit where credit is due, I suppose."

"Our day will come, Armand. You'll see."

"I only hope I'm still around to enjoy it."

Vinter's expression turned serious.

"How are you doing? Are things any better?"

"A little. I retained a few out-of-town regulars. I've gained some new clients, and every now and then I get a call from some Europeans who have decided to furnish pieds à terre in New York. Thanks to my illustrious family in Paris, they know the Lafitte name and somehow have managed to escape Prado's sermon about me being the devil incarnate."

Tony laughed, but only briefly.

"It kills me that you were singled out to be the goat while

the rest of us were let off the hook with no real recriminations. Sometimes I feel guilty that Dean and John and I have continued to prosper while you've suffered such tremendous reverses. I wish there was something I could do."

"So do I, believe me, but you can't. This is just one of those situations I'm going to have to wait out."

Before Vinter could respond, an elegantly coiffed woman suited in Chanel and swathed in sable, came out of his booth and politely interrupted.

"Tony, darling. You can red dot those marvelous mahogany armchairs. I am absolutely mad for them."

"Just as I was always absolutely mad for you," Armand said, having recognized Annabel Montgomery's deep, whiskey voice and clipped English accent immediately. She turned, looked at Armand, reddened for a moment, and then embraced him warmly.

"You sly dog! Where've you been hiding? God knows, I've missed you."

"I didn't know you knew Annabel," Vinter said, noting the intense looks passing from one to the other.

"We're old friends."

"Well then, why don't I let you two get reacquainted while I take care of those chairs."

"Why don't you," Annabel said, refusing to remove her eyes from Armand's face. Once Tony had gone, she took Armand's hand. "I have missed you. Why haven't I heard from you? It's been ages."

"Things have been difficult," he said, surprised at his own spontaneous honesty. "I haven't been to London in a very long time. If I had, I would have called."

"Liar!" She laughed, but continued to hold his hand. "You were probably afraid that if I ever got you back in my bedroom, I wouldn't have let you go. Well, you're right. I wouldn't have. Especially now that Philip's gone." She said the last quietly, watching for the effect her words would have.

"I didn't know."

"He died exactly a year ago. His heart gave out."

"I'm sorry to hear that. How are you?"

"Relieved. I was glad he didn't suffer and I mourned him appropriately, but quite honestly his death freed me." She paused.

"Our union was a loveless one, as you know, and frankly, maintaining the façade of being happily married was becoming a strain."

"You should have gotten in touch with me," he said.

"If I had thought, for even an instant, that you would have come charging up to my door on a big white horse and we would have ridden off into the sunset together, I would have. But the last time we were together, you told me we couldn't continue seeing each other. Then, four years passed without so much as a postcard. What was I to think except that you had forgotten me?"

"I could never forget you, Annabel. I thought you knew that."

"And I thought you'd never stop loving me. We were both wrong." As always, she spoke openly, refusing to hide her sentiments behind socially acceptable patter.

"I never did stop loving you," he said softly. "I just did what I thought was best for both of us."

Annabel barely heard Armand's second sentence. She heard him say he still loved her and her mouth spread in a broad smile. She didn't want to know whether he now loved her as a friend, loved her less than he had, as much as he had, with reservations, or without. She just wanted to hug him, to kiss him, to deny that part of their past that had made her miserable and to revive that part of their past that had made her deliriously, deliciously happy. But, she realized, they were standing in the midst of a party. Clearly, the first order of business was to find more intimate surroundings.

"Now it's my turn to do what's best for both of us," she said, her eyes sparkling with the joy of anticipation. How wonderful, after so many lonely months, to have something to look forward to. "I'm going to drag you out of here and we're going to have dinner and catch up on old times."

"Any preferences?" Armand asked, thoroughly delighted by the unexpected turn of events.

"There's only one great place in New York for a Frenchman dining with an Englishwoman."

"Where's that?"

"My hotel. Where else can we eat takeout Chinese and drink vintage champagne?"

"You always did have strange tastes."

"I fell in love with a Frog, didn't I?" She winked and gave him a quick smile as she went inside Vinter's booth to arrange for the shipment of her chairs.

Once her business was concluded, she and Armand linked arms and walked toward the exit. They moved at an unhurried, seductive pace, drawing out the time until they could be alone. They were old lovers, and with the familiarity that comes from extended intimacy, they knew not to rush, because they knew exactly what the night would bring. They would eat and drink and talk and then, when all their other needs were sated and passion was the only remaining void, then they would make love.

"Annabel, my pet. It's so wonderful to see you." Vincent Prado draped his arm around Annabel's shoulder, shifting her so she faced the cameras, shifting himself so that Armand was completely blocked from view. "You look divine. Are you going to be in town long?"

"That depends," Annabel said, glancing over at Armand.

"What are you doing here, Lafitte?"

"Nice to see you too, Vincent." He extended his hand, knowing Vincent would refuse to shake it. "The fair looks like it's going to be a great success. Congratulations."

Prado looked surprised. He would have thought Armand would have been bitter, bitchy even. After all, they hadn't seen each other more than three times since their imbroglio, and whenever they had, the meeting had been abrasive and unpleasant. Maybe he was putting on a show for Annabel Montgomery. Maybe he was trying to nab her as a client and didn't want to create the wrong impression. Maybe he was trying to worm his way back into Prado's good graces. Whatever, Vincent was leery of carrying on a conversation with a man he viewed as an enemy. He kissed Annabel's hand, mumbled something about calling her for dinner, and moved on to the next guest, the next photograph.

"Do you have the chicken pox or some other communicable disease I should know about?" Annabel said, commenting on Prado's hasty departure.

"Last year, Vincent and I had a little to-do. We've been less than buddies ever since."

Armand took Annabel's arm and tried to lead her out into the hall, but she refused to move.

"Is that all you're going to say?"

"For now it is."

Again, he tried to leave. Again, she refused.

"Armand. Why don't you have a booth here? Why isn't Lafitte et Fils represented at the fair?"

"It's a long story and if you don't mind, I'd rather not spoil our evening by talking about it."

Without pressing him further, Annabel allowed herself to be ushered outside and into a taxi heading for the Pierre. If he didn't want to give her the details right now, she would allow him his privacy. But later, she thought, after they had come together, after they had reestablished their own special means of communication, later, she would prod and poke until he relented and told her why he had left her—and what had caused his soft, brown eyes to turn hard and cold and black.

9

Le Cirque was even more crowded than usual. By the time Garrett and Gaby arrived, the Park Avenue restaurant favored by the ultrachic was overflowing with familiar names and famous faces. The bar, tucked behind a mirrored pillar that reflected a lavish display of *pâtisserie* and *gâteaux*, could barely handle those waiting to take their places in the main arena. Cocktails were served and sipped with extreme caution, everyone on the alert for an errant elbow or excessive gesture that might spell disaster for a printed silk or a cashmere suit.

As Gaby followed the mâitre d' to their table, she tried to imitate Garrett's nonchalance, but it was difficult not to stare. The Lauders were seated across from David and Helen Gurley Brown, who were at a table with Dustin Hoffman and his wife, who were near the Sarnoffs, who were waving to Ann Getty, who was dining with Thomas Hoving, who was saying good night to an exiting David Rockefeller.

As she settled herself on the greige-toned banquette and looked around, she immediately recognized two other couples of note: Irina Stoddard and Max Richard to her right, and to her left, in the corner near the door, Chelsea, with a handsome, silver-haired man who looked like Hollywood's version of the ultimate corporate executive.

While Garrett discussed his champagne preference with the sommelier, Gaby studied her companion. He was an attractive man, tall, elegantly built, and distinctively British, in his bright yellow-and-white striped bespoke shirt, his paisley silk tie, and his charcoal-gray glen plaid suit. His thick blond hair was brushed straight back, its aggressive waves slicked with a substance Gaby guessed was probably a traditional hair tonic rather than a more modern gel or mousse. There was a look of studied perfection about Garrett, as if he believed that one's toilette could compensate for one's deficiencies. Yet Gaby's artistic eye noticed something immaculacy couldn't fix. Because his face was long and oval, his features tended to appear magnified and somewhat flawed by their exaggeration. His eyes were a soft, Wedgwood blue, but matched against pink-tinged skin they came off too pale to speak of strength, too translucent to suggest depth. His cheekbones were high and his chin well-defined, yet due to the lack of flesh surrounding both, they seemed sharp and hard-edged. His lips were thin, albeit not unusually so, yet as he turned to Gaby, she saw that they were easily eclipsed by the breadth of his smile, disappearing behind two rows of well-aligned, perfectly white teeth.

"You're staring."

"I'm sorry. I didn't mean to." She blushed, hoping he wasn't blessed with any telepathic talents that might have betrayed her.

"Is there a spot on my tie? An unruly lock of hair sticking out? A leftover bit of canapé lodged between my teeth?"

"No," she said with a reassuring smile. "You look wonderful."

She thought his comment had been an offhanded jest, but his instant relief made her suspect that despite Garrett Castleton's insouciant manner, he suffered many of the same insecurities she did. Though it was heartening to know that the need for approval was indeed basic, affecting even those blessed with wealth and prominence, his response surprised her. Having watched him in action—controlling a sale from behind his highly polished podium, milking an item until he pulled out a desirable bid, wielding the auctioneer's hammer as though it were a royal scepter—she had assumed he was a man firmly in charge of his own destiny, a man with an innate confidence. Now she wondered if perhaps her opinion had been based more on her awe of his position than on a realistic assessment of his personality.

"The crowd seems especially glittery tonight," Garrett said, looking around, nodding to one or two acquaintances, noticeably ignoring his sister.

"It's the afterglow of the fair. I guess people feel that finding and buying something special is worth celebrating."

"You are absolutely right." He handed her a glass of Cristal and lowered his voice to a conspiratorial whisper. "Do you know what I think we've done? I think that right here in the middle of New York City, we have stumbled upon an ancient tribal ritual. This is no ordinary Wednesday night dinner. No no. This, my dear, is the feast that follows a successful hunt." He lifted his glass and clinked it against hers. "To the hunt."

Gaby laughed and sipped her champagne, enjoying herself immensely. She had seen the glint in Garrett's eye and had understood immediately that his toast had also been a declaration of his intentions. She was flattered. Men like Garrett Castleton had never given Gaby Cocroft a second glance, let alone attempted to court her. But, she reminded herself quickly, it was Gabrielle Didier who interested him, not Gaby Cocroft. Had she made a mistake accepting his invitation? Maybe, but she was having a terrific time. Garrett made her feel beautiful and desirable and witty and captivating and all those things she had always wanted to be and had believed she wasn't. Though she knew she probably should be discouraging him, she decided that tonight she would live the fantasy. Tomorrow, if necessary, she would deal with reality.

Throughout their first course, they chatted easily. Gaby stuck to subjects she knew well, avoided those she didn't, veered away from all things personal, and asked questions rather than putting herself in the position of having to give answers. Fortunately, she was able to center most of their conversation around Castleton business. They reviewed many of the pieces displayed at the fair. They conferred on who would man the floor at Saturday's auction, with Gaby doing as she had been asked and putting in a complimentary plug for Beezie. They discussed a sale of major art works scheduled for March. And they debated the advisability of hosting an auction for the benefit of AIDS research. It was only when the busboy cleared the table and their main course was served that Gaby allowed her attention to wander.

Unconsciously, her eyes gravitated toward Max's, drawn as if by the pull of a magnetic field. His lips curled into a slow smile. Gaby returned the greeting, but then looked away, surprised at the effect this man had on her. She had never thought of herself as a woman vulnerable to infatuation. Yet Maximilian Richard made her feel schoolgirlish, a bit giddy, just as she would have felt if she had been a teenager watching *An Affair to Remember* and Cary Grant had left Deborah Kerr, stepped off the screen, and asked her to join him for an ice cream soda.

By the time she allowed herself to look in his direction again, Max had left the table, and she found herself chilled by the wintry visage of Irina Stoddard. Gaby tightened. Garrett, sensing the change in mood, accurately guessed the cause, looked to his right, and met his sister's stare with an unflinching eye. He continued to hold her in his sight until she turned away and began to fumble with her purse. To Gaby it was a relief. To Garrett, it was a triumph of wills.

"Do you know what I find fascinating?" he said, trying to divert Gaby's attention. "Even the most innocuous of customs can claim the privilege of ancestry."

"Excuse me?" Gaby tried to focus on what Garrett was saying, but Irina had upset her. Though they rarely ran into each other at the auction house, whenever they had, their meetings had been polite and cordial, not particularly friendly, but not particularly hostile either. Then, last night, at Garrett's party, the woman had cold-shouldered her. She had been cool at the fair and was glowering now. Why?

"I know you think that these velvet-covered status benches we're sitting on are modern-day contrivances," Garrett said, forcing himself to sound light and chatty. "My dear woman, you couldn't be more wrong. These banquettes are the direct descendants of the most common seating arrangements used in the early sixteen hundreds." Gaby's look of amused interest encouraged him to continue. "Back then, the host sat by himself under a canopy while his guests sat at huge oblong tables that faced each other across the great chamber. According to protocol, principal diners were seated at the center, lesser guests on the ends." He splayed his arm in front of her. "Look around. Is it any different today? The favored customers are still placed in the middle, the not-so-favored on the ends, the least favored toward the back or near the kitchen. Except for the fact that one no longer has to carry one's own cutlery and the risk of ptomaine poisoning has been greatly reduced, little has changed in over three hundred years. Isn't that a comfort?''

Gaby laughed. ''Only to those sitting in the center of the banquettes. If enough of those in the back and on the ends get word of this, we could have a revolution on our hands.''

''Do you know what I say to that?'' he asked, relieved to see her smiling again.

''No, what do you say to that?''

''Let them eat home!''

Three words—*excellence, exclusivity,* and *status*—defined Irina Stoddard's life: an elitist credo that influenced everything she did. She refused antiques, jewelry, and works of art that fell short, just as she rejected people in whom she found one or more of her requirements lacking. To her, there was no such thing as a fine reproduction. There was the original, the only, the first, the best. Second was second-rate and, in Irina's mind, the same as being last.

To be fair, this dedication to superiority wasn't something she had decided upon arbitrarily, but rather something she had been taught. Her parents, her father in particular, had always been very firm in their insistence upon the finest of everything. Owning a portrait by Gainsborough, a Cartier jewel designed by Jeanne Toussaint, a commode by Charles Cressent, or a gown by Balenciaga was not indulgence. It was simply a preference for the nonpareil. ''After all,'' Irina had been told over and over again, ''Castleton is a name that's been associated with excellence for over two hundred years.''

Because of what they viewed as their responsibility toward their ancestors, Garrett Sr. and Charlotte's expectations were beyond high. They demanded quality work and stellar performances, from themselves, from their business associates, and especially from their children. Sometimes, that constant demand for the exceptional worked for Irina, oftentimes against. As a child, pleasing her parents had been a nearly impossible task. While other parents who urged their children to perform for company applauded no matter what ditty or shuffle step was presented, Irina was critically reviewed. While other little girls were encouraged to play in sandboxes or frolic on swings or push their dolls around the park in miniature prams, Irina was discouraged from engaging in such mindless entertainment and was taken instead to museums and concerts and appropriate theater. Before she was ten, all sense of fun and spontaneity had been siphoned from her core. Though they hadn't meant to, in their efforts to teach Irina how to distinguish between activities that educated one for accomplishment and hobbies that simply filled unproductive time, Garrett Sr. and Charlotte had created an excessively serious, introverted child with a severe case of overdrive.

School had been torturous. She had had no social life, no friends, no free time to think or to dream or to explore or to grow beyond the confines of her curriculum. Every waking moment had been devoted to maintaining her grade average. She had succeeded, graduating at the head of her class, honored with several prestigious scholastic awards, but even she knew she had sacrificed much in the effort.

By the time she had reached marriageable age, Irina had begun to view men the same way she viewed objects: one had to search through the chaff in order to find the best. Though she hadn't dated very much at boarding school, just after her debut she found herself besieged with suitors, out several nights a week, wined and dined and courted and wooed. Suddenly, she felt desirable and sought after. Certainly, her family's position and wealth was a draw, but she didn't see anything wrong with that. As far as she was concerned, one's place in society was as much a part of one's resumé as was the color of one's hair and the size of one's teeth. Unfortunately, there were those who didn't care for the color of her hair or the draw of the Castleton name. As the glow of Irina's coming out faded, so did her popularity. The field narrowed and her choices became limited. By the time she reached her early twenties, her love life had been reduced to an occasional liaison with a less-than-perfect romeo.

How natural that her father, who had played overseer to every other aspect of her life, should have been the one to introduce her to her future husband! The two gentlemen had met at Castleton's when Lord Stoddard had come to discuss the sale of several pieces from his great-aunt's country estate. They struck up a friendship, Garrett Sr. invited the young lord to dinner, and the rest, as they say, was history.

Winston had not been her ideal man, nor was he the great love of her life, but at the time, none of that mattered compared to the fact that he met Garrett Sr.'s qualifications as a son-in-law. Winston was titled, wealthy, gentrified, educated, cultured, and possessed of enough physical appeal to allow positive speculation about the successful issue of a marriage between him and Irina. What was more important, Winston actually claimed he loved her. When, once, during a moment of weakness and insecurity, she confided to a couple of girlfriends that she had misgivings, they said she could do worse. Irina wasn't certain she could do better. And so, in 1963, she became Lady Winston Stoddard.

As she watched Garrett and Gaby clink glasses and quaff champagne, she realized that the only time her parents' standards had worked for her was in her battle with Garrett for control of Castleton's. Despite the fact that Irina was the elder and had, on more than one occasion, protested his incredible chauvinism, Garrett Sr. had remained a firm believer in male primogeniture, a point that rankled Irina no end. Growing up, she had had to live up to the same ideals as her brother; she had been expected to perform as well as her brother; she was even expected to marry better than her brother. Yet she was, because of her sex, considered less qualified than her brother to run the family business.

She might have argued longer and louder, except that another of her father's traits was consistency. After Charlotte and Garrett had married, the young Mrs. Castleton had asked to be included in the business. Charlotte was a bright, able woman with an eye for fine ceramics and porcelain. While others who claimed expertise needed time to study the subtleties that distinguished one from another, she could tell at first sight the difference between creamy-white soft-paste porcelain and the more glasslike hard-paste porcelain, between authentic seventeenth- and eighteenth-century Japanese Imari and the cheaper imitation Imari exported by the Chinese during the same period. She knew the alphabetical dating system (A = 1753, B = 1754, C = 1755, and so on) and therefore could interpret the ciphers on the bottom of pieces from the famous Vincennes factory. She knew which painters influenced the design of Sèvres porcelain, which craftsmen made the factory at Meissen famous. She knew Saint-Cloud soft-paste by its thick potting, Mennecy soft-paste by the way the enamels fused with the glaze rather than sitting on top as with hard-paste. What she didn't know was why the breadth of her knowledge impressed everyone except her husband. She had wanted to contribute to her marriage, to serve in a more meaningful way than simply functioning as Garrett's hostess. Her request was denied. In fact, it was deemed unthinkable. Then, only women who had to work did. Charlotte would have been breaking ground Garrett preferred she leave undisturbed. She might have insisted, but she was a woman of standing, a woman of breeding, a woman who—for better or worse—understood and accepted the rules of her day.

To the young Irina, Charlotte was the living symbol of perfection. She seemed to have everything—beauty, charm, intelligence, and a remarkably winsome way. She had exquisite taste. She gave wonderful parties. She was a witty conversationalist and an excellent dancer. She had wealth and position and all the power and influence that came with that particular package. She was what every girl aspired to be.

As she got older and ambition began to assert itself, Irina's opinion changed dramatically. Her father became a symbol of power and success, a man worthy of respect. Her mother, on the other hand, suddenly seemed to epitomize Victorian subservience. The way Irina saw it, Charlotte acquiesced instead of arguing. She retreated instead of defending. She gave in instead of getting even. The day she had acceded to Garrett's demands and left Castleton's, content to be his wife and mother to his children, was the day she had declared herself powerless. Whether or not she felt she had made the right decision and that her life had been a good one, to her daughter she appeared weak. And Irina had decided that the only way she was going to win her father's approval was to be strong.

At the university, Irina had studied art. Because she didn't marry immediately after graduation and because she loathed idle time, she begged Garrett to let her work at the gallery. Viewing it as a harmless interlude between schooling and mothering, and because Charlotte had intervened on her behalf, he agreed, allowing her to apprentice with the head of the Old Masters department. To everyone's surprise—except Irina's—she was found to be smart, well-tutored in her field, and a quick learner. Within a very short time, she was given the responsibility of cataloguing several major auctions. A year later, she was being considered for another promotion when her marriage intervened. Winston Stoddard was a graduate of the same school as Garrett Castleton—he wanted his wife at home.

For a while, Irina shelved her ambition and concentrated instead on different pursuits, such as presenting her parents with grandchildren—Charles Castleton Stoddard and Sarah Remington Stoddard, now twenty-three and twenty, respectively. She decorated her two homes and conducted her life along approved Castleton guidelines. She joined committees, did good works, made a name for herself in all the important social circles, and watched as her younger brother struggled to make a name for himself in the business.

It didn't take long for boredom and sibling rivalry to take hold. Though Garrett Jr. worked fiendishly, with little time to himself and little energy for anything other than trying harder to do better, he was doing something of note. In contrast, Irina's obligations were few—Sunday dinner with her parents, holiday functions, hostessing at major Castleton events, and calling her mother three times a week. She became restless and irritable, sniping at everyone around her. For a time, she shopped compulsively, buying anything she saw, leaving the packages unopened in the hall. She took piano lessons and a sculpture class. She read. She did needlepoint. Nothing soothed her. Finally, she concluded that the only cure for what ailed her was to return to Castleton's. Though both her father and her husband objected, Irina insisted upon taking her place in the family business.

When the head of the Old Masters department retired shortly after Irina's return and she took his place, she interpreted it as a sign that she was right. At some point in time—she couldn't remember when it had come to her or why—she had decided that she, not Garrett, was her father's natural successor. Brother and sister had never been close, but once she had determined that he was the only thing standing in her way, in her mind they became enemies.

At work, she allowed her ambition to burn unchecked. She insinuated herself into as many facets of the business as she could. She solicited estates, arranged auctions, wrote catalogues, hostessed parties. The only thing she refused to do was take the hammer. Though she didn't like the notion of giving Garrett an unchallenged advantage, auctioneering, no matter how elegantly done, was still haggling, still a task better left to men. She contented herself with manipulating her position on the inside. She ran her department with an iron hand and a cost efficiency that became a model for other departments. While Garrett remained loyal to longtime employees and often allowed people to stay on past their most productive years, Irina viewed everything from the perspective of the bottom line. When Irina petitioned her father for a seat on the board and was put off, she decided to advance her cause by taking a circuitous route. Instead of pestering her father, she mastered the intricacies of boardroom politics, wooing board members until not only was she voted onto the board with a clear majority—her brother was the only dissenter; her father voted only in case of a tie—but she became an immediate power broker. When Garrett Sr. congratulated her on her victory and welcomed her to the upper echelon of Castleton's International, it was one of the finest moments of her life.

When her marriage failed, she was stunned. She believed she was a woman attuned to details, aware of even the smallest changes of rhythm in her family. She believed her home life was secure, that she more than fulfilled her obligations toward Winston and her children. What she neglected to see was that while she had been pursuing her own success, she had neglected her husband. Winston Stoddard didn't want a driving, striving career woman by his side. He wanted a soft, sensuous, attentive bed partner, an ego-flattering, fun-to-be-with, cater-to-his-every-need woman. A woman like his mother. A woman like Irina's mother.

Though she tried to reason with him—think of the children, your reputation, my reputation, all we've meant to each other—Winston was beyond reasoning. He was involved with someone else. He humiliated Irina by leaving her for a brassy blond American slattern, lusting after her in public in a way he had never displayed toward Irina even in private. Irina never forgave him, or her.

At about the same time as Irina's marriage was unraveling,

Garrett had become involved with Cynthia Hawthorne. Although Garrett Sr. had understood and accepted his son's unspoken decision to postpone his personal life until his status in the business community had been established, he had begun to worry about the perpetuation of the Castleton name. When Garrett announced his intention to marry, his father was ecstatic. He viewed the young woman as the perfect mate for his son and heir. Cynthia was beautiful in a delicate way, with a creamy, cameolike complexion, soft gray eyes, and light brown hair that she always wore pulled up in a loose topknot with gentle wisps trickling down her neck. She was a graduate of England's finest schools, a recognized scholar in the field of Renaissance art, and an award-winning equestrienne. Adding to her cachet, the Hawthornes were a family of merit, her father head of an enormous business conglomerate and an honored patriot, her mother a well-known patron of the arts, her sister a baroness and a familiar name on the charity circuit, and her brother a lieutenant in the Royal Air Force. Garrett's betrothal gave the senior Castletons just the opportunity they needed to bury their disappointment with Irina's collapsed marriage and move on. His standing increased. Irina's decreased. Instead of asking her to hostess teas or cocktail parties at special auctions as they had always done, suddenly Cynthia Hawthorne was being drafted. At Sunday dinners, instead of Garrett Sr. and Charlotte doting on Irina's children, they doted on Cynthia.

Winston's defection had done more than simply wound her pride. It had labeled her a failure. She could not tolerate being whispered about or looked away from or pitied. Having witnessed other falls from grace and attempts at reinstatement, Irina knew that the only way she could right the wrong that had been done to her was to accomplish something extraordinary. That was when ambition became obsession. To gain control of Castleton's overrode everything else. To do that, however, she had to discredit and destroy her brother.

Actually, taking the first step had been easy. Her naturally suspicious nature had told her that no woman of twenty-eight years living outside of a convent had a history of purity and piety. It took her private investigator less than a month to strip away the veneer and uncover the truth of Cynthia's past. Not only was she not a virgin, but in her youth during the sixties, she had been part of a cult which thrived on chemical dependence and sexual independence. Knowing her father's position on the importance of purity and authenticity, Irina could hardly wait to present him with her findings. But wait she did, holding out until exactly the right circumstance presented itself.

It happened when she least expected it. One afternoon, she and her father were having tea together, a rarity in itself. He seemed preoccupied with his current grandchildren and his future grandchildren. He expressed pride in both Charles and Sarah, another rarity, pleasure in their academic achievements and their general good nature. Suddenly, he began to wonder aloud about the kind of children Cynthia and Garrett might have. Irina looked away, busying herself with a troublesome spoonful of clotted cream. Garrett Sr. had spent too many years training his daughter to look at someone directly when they were speaking not to notice her inattention. The more she fumbled with her scone, the more curious he became.

"Do you know something I should know, Irina?"

She looked at him, being careful to hide her mounting excitement.

"I dislike repeating myself. Is there something you wish to tell me?"

Again, Irina feigned discomfort, hesitating just long enough to establish her reticence.

"You probably won't approve," she said innocently, "but recently I heard some stories about Cynthia that prompted me to delve into her past. What I found disturbs me."

"Tell me."

"After university, Cynthia spent a great deal of time in Paris with a group of people who were not a nice sort. They all lived together in a ramshackle building where they experimented with hallucinogens like LSD and exercised a rather free-spirited approach to sex. From what I understand, it was all quite raunchy."

Garrett Sr. said nothing. His narrowed eyes and tight lips said everything.

"She only stayed there for two years, but during that time she had a child. Now, I don't know if it was the drugs or something else that caused the problem, and the man I had looking into the matter couldn't find anything that gave a definitive answer, but the baby was born with Down's syndrome. He was placed in an institution in Switzerland, and shortly after, Cynthia returned home to England."

Garrett Sr. never spoke, never raised an eyebrow, never took an extra breath. He simply rose from his chair and left the room. Within two days, Garrett Jr.'s engagement was broken. That was eight years ago. Sister and brother had hardly spoken since.

Now she sat and watched Sirio, the owner of Le Cirque, stop and pay court to Garrett and his new lady friend. Irina rarely paid any mind to the women he dated. His experience with Cynthia had left him gun-shy, and as far as Irina knew, he had not been seriously involved with anyone since the unfortunate Miss Hawthorne. He did, however, seem extremely interested in Gabrielle Didier, and that was of major interest to Irina. If he followed his usual pattern, he would date her several times, perhaps take her to bed once or twice, and then drop her before either of them could think of a future together. If, however, he deviated from this pattern, Irina would be forced to take steps. The battle between them had to be confined to their abilities alone. She couldn't allow the possibility of another Castleton heir to influence her father's decision.

From what she had observed so far, the relationship was more business than pleasure. Garrett was smitten, but she suspected he was as intrigued with the mystery that seemed to surround the woman as he was with the woman herself. Mystery, indeed! The only time Irina believed in mysteries was when they were between the covers of a book. In real life, mysteries were nothing but cover-ups for tales one didn't want to be told.

As Max returned to the table and stole a glance at the woman across the way, Irina wondered, as she had wondered aloud to Garrett the night before, what might an investigation of Madame Didier's past reveal?

Chelsea had barely touched her food. For more than an hour she had been trying to convince her ex-husband, Drake Reynolds, to allow his daughter, Belle, to move in with her.

"For the last time, no!" His gray eyes hardened into steel. "She's not your child. You have no rights where she's concerned."

"But Drake. She's desperately unhappy. Maybe if she stayed with me for a few months, she'd be able to sort out whatever's troubling her."

"Living with you would be the worst thing for her. You're no role model for a young girl. You have the morals of an alley cat. Everyone knows you'll fuck anything that walks, as long as it has a full wallet."

Chelsea was numb to his insults. She had heard them all before. At least here, in a public restaurant, he couldn't emphasize his point with his fists.

"She came to see me today. She was very upset. She couldn't stop crying, yet when I asked what was bothering her, she wouldn't tell me. Do you know what it is?"

Drake sighed and looked at Chelsea as if she were a simpleton.

"I can't believe you'd let yourself be manipulated by a spoiled seventeen-year-old. Her grades were atrocious. I grounded her and she came running to you for sympathy. If you had ever had a child of your own, you could have figured that out for yourself."

"How bad was it?" she said, ignoring the snide tilt of his mouth.

"She's failing three out of four subjects. Is that bad enough?"

"Doesn't that tell you something? Belle is a bright girl. She's always been a conscientious student. If she's failing, it's because something is terribly, terribly wrong."

Drake laughed, but it was hardly mirthful.

"I'll tell you what's wrong," he said, grabbing Chelsea's wrist under the table and squeezing it until it hurt. "Her mother is a drunk and her stepmother is a slut."

"And her father is a bully." Chelsea pulled her hand away and rubbed her fingers, momentarily regretting her decision not to meet him at his apartment. Right now, she would have welcomed the privacy. She was having difficulty reining her temper.

"But I am her father, and so what I say goes."

Chelsea backed off, knowing that if she didn't, he would make a scene. She remained silent while the waiter poured coffee and produced a selection of desserts. Chelsea declined. The conversation had taken away her appetite. All she could think about was Belle.

The first time they had met was five years before. Actually, it had been right here at Le Cirque. Belle had been twelve then. Chelsea had just had her second divorce finalized and had begun to date the handsome, extremely eligible Drake Reynolds. He had spoken of his daughter so often, and always in such a protective way, that when he asked if Chelsea would mind Belle joining them for lunch, she agreed.

Despite Drake's explanation that his first wife, Belle's mother, was a hopeless alcoholic living in an institution on a posh estate in Connecticut that catered to wealthy inebriates, Chelsea had expected to meet a very spoiled, very arrogant debutante-to-be. Instead, she encountered a shy, withdrawn child of incredible beauty. In that one afternoon Belle had managed to touch a part of Chelsea that no one had ever touched before.

Belle looked nothing like her father. Before he had grayed, Drake had been dark, with dark eyes and a ruddy complexion that always retained a Palm Beach tan. Belle was the image of her mother—pale, well boned, with thick, lustrous flaxen hair, eyes the color of new grass, and a tall, lithesome body that had obviously developed long before Belle was ready to deal with the impact it had on others. She had a small, straight nose and a long, swanlike neck that combined to make her profile a photographer's delight, and lush lips so naturally pink that lip rouge would have been redundant.

She was extremely polite and displayed manners which would have made her headmistress at Dalton very proud, but Chelsea couldn't help noticing how deferential she was to Drake. She didn't order without his approval. She didn't eat until he had eaten. She didn't speak unless he spoke to her. Whenever Chelsea asked her a question, she looked at Drake as if seeking permission to answer. Admittedly, Chelsea's experience with children was limited to avoiding them in stores, ignoring them on airplanes, and watching them perform on television, but nonetheless, Belle's behavior struck her as odd. Afterward, when she mentioned it to Drake, he reminded her about Louise, his ex-wife. Belle had been traumatized by her mother's illness, he said, and, he pointed out, it had been less than a year since Louise had been committed. Chelsea had believed him then. It was only later that she began to suspect that something else, something much worse, was wrong with Belle.

"Drake. Please. I'm only asking for a few months. Just until I can find out what it is. Then, maybe together, we can help her."

Drake motioned to the captain to bring a check, treating her appeal with the same indifference as he might a request to go to the ladies' room.

"You relinquished your rights to do anything together the day you sued for divorce."

"I didn't divorce Belle."

He turned to her, moving his face so close to hers she could smell the coffee on his breath.

"We're a package deal. You leave one, you leave both."

"You sound like an idiot. Our marriage wasn't any damn good and you know it. You said so often enough."

"And who's fault was that?"

"Mine, okay? Does that make you happy?" She looked at him with disgust, trying to figure out what she had ever seen in him in the first place. Then she looked at herself with disgust. She knew the answer and it didn't make her happy. "We are not the issue," she said, steering the conversation back on track. "Belle is the issue. She needs help and I think I can help her."

"No."

"I love her and she loves me!" When she had first heard about the impending divorce, Belle had thrown herself at her stepmother's feet crying, pleading with Chelsea to stay, begging her not to leave. "That's why I went to court to petition for joint custody."

Drake stood. Chelsea began to slide off the banquette, but Drake blocked her way.

"I guess with you, love only goes so far," he said. "In case your memory needs jogging, let me remind you that your so-called devotion lasted until I offered you a co-op and five million dollars to drop your custody petition. You took the money and ran, as fast and as far as you could. And you left me to explain your sudden change of heart to my daughter."

Without another word, he left the table, retrieved his coat, and walked out of the restaurant. Chelsea moved away from the table slowly, not caring who was looking or whispering. She was used to being the object of gossip. What she wasn't used to, nor would she ever get used to, was being slapped in the face with the truth, especially this truth. Belle had trusted her. She had loved her without conditions or reservations. She had come to her with her hopes and fears. And Chelsea had paid her back with a Judas kiss. She had promised to fight for her and protect her, and then had sold her out for five million pieces of silver.

As she walked out onto Sixty-fifth Street, a strong swirl of frigid air made her stop where she was. She pulled up the collar of her coat and turned her back to the wind. Across Park Avenue, she could see Drake heading up the block to his apartment where Belle was waiting. Chelsea watched him walk inside his building and shivered. Though she pulled her coat tighter against her body and hugged herself to keep from trembling, she knew it could have been a hundred degrees outside and still she would have felt cold.

Gaby had been so absorbed in the drama being played out at Chelsea's table that she had not noticed Irina and Max until they were standing directly in front of her.

"The chocolate mousse cake is the kind of wonder wars are fought over."

"I was leaning toward the plum tart, but inasmuch as Belgians are known for their flair for desserts, I think I'll take your advice, Richard." Garrett smiled. He liked Max, despite the fact that the man was in the company of his sister. Everyone makes mistakes, he reasoned. He hoped Richard would come to his senses sooner rather than later.

"And you, Gabrielle?"

Gaby smiled also.

"I think I'm just going to have coffee."

"You're too thin to be a slave to the scale, and that cake is too mouth-watering for any human to resist it without a very good reason. Are you philosophically opposed to after-dinner excesses, or are you simply allergic to chocolate?"

"Neither, but my stomach and I have an understanding. When it's hungry, I feed it or it growls. When it's full, I stop feeding it or it becomes surly."

Max shook his head, offering Garrett playful sympathy.

"You have a problem. Not only are you dealing with a woman who knows her own mind, but one who knows her own stomach as well."

"We have to go." Irina made no attempt at small talk. She made no attempt at any conversation whatsoever. She tugged on Max's arm and repeated her request to leave until, reluctantly,

Gaby thought, Max said his good nights, turned, and followed her out.

"I would apologize for my sister's rudeness, but then you might assume that I care what you think of her and I don't. I only care what you think of me in light of her insolence."

Exposing his animosity toward Irina had been difficult for Garrett. Not only was he personally embarrassed by her behavior, but clearly, his ego was not strong enough to buffer guilt by association. The insecurities Gaby had suspected before were more evident now.

"I think you're a very nice man in any light."

He nodded, as if to say, thank you, that's just the answer I wanted to hear.

"If you don't mind my asking, has it always been this way between you?"

Garrett sipped his coffee, thinking, wanting to give her as honest an answer as he could.

"Perhaps not as blatant as this, but yes, I would say our relationship has always been a bit off."

"That's sad."

"Do you think so?"

"Yes, but that's probably because I'm an only child and when I was growing up I longed for a brother or a sister."

"I'll tell you what's sad," he said, his voice underscored with a sudden anger. "*Having* a sister and growing up feeling like an only child."

Gaby had no response that would explain or soothe, so she remained silent, allowing Garrett to struggle with memories of his childhood. While he did, Gaby found herself returning to hers. What she had said was true. Over the years, she had witnessed the closeness among Simone and Bernard and her mother, Delphine, even between Brian and his sisters, and had felt the lack. More than anything, Gaby had wanted siblings for her son, a house full of children for herself and Brian. She had longed for the laughter and tumult she saw in other women's homes, the full feeling of connection that came from having a big family. But for reasons she could never fathom, life had decided once again to deny her her dreams.

"I've spoiled your evening. Forgive me."

Gaby had drifted so far away from Le Cirque and New York, that Garrett's voice sounded muffled and distant.

"I didn't mean to burden you with family arguments."

"You didn't. I guess my mind wandered."

"You never had any children, did you, Gabrielle?"

The question took Gaby by surprise. She started to answer, but then remembered whom he thought she was. She had to think. To say no was to add another lie to a list she felt was already far too long, but to say yes was to open a door to a room crowded with complications. It had taken almost a year of scrimping and saving and doing without for her to be able to send Lakewood a check for a mere eight thousand dollars. She needed her job. Much as she wanted to opt for honesty, she couldn't afford for Garrett or anyone to question her position at Castleton's. And, she realized, that meant she couldn't afford to offer Garrett explanations about Steven.

"No."

"That's a shame. I'm sure you would have been a wonderful mother."

Gaby looked away as if the subject was too painful to confront.

"You must have loved your husband very much."

Instead of answering, Gaby asked a question of her own.

"Were you ever married?"

"Almost. I was engaged once, but there was no wedding."

Gaby had feigned pain. Garrett's was real. He remembered how hurt and disillusioned he had been when he had learned of Cynthia's transgressions. It wasn't that he cared about the drugs or the retarded child, although he had been horrified when first he had heard, it was that she had lied to him, that she had left him vulnerable to Irina's attack. If she had only told him, he might have been able to arm himself better, but no, Cynthia had deliberately withheld information. She had willingly walked onto the gallows, placed the rope around her neck, and given Irina permission to kick the stool out from under her.

"What happened," Gaby asked gently, hesitant about trespassing on private property.

He looked at Gaby and offered her an unconvincing smile.

"Let's just say my fiancée and I disagreed on the subject of forthrightness. There were things I would have preferred to know and she preferred to keep to herself. As it turned out, she wasn't very good at keeping secrets.''

Guilt affected Gaby like an injection of curare. Her muscles froze and her chest tightened, making it almost impossible for her to breathe. The waiter brought the check. As Garrett filled out the credit card receipt and they prepared to leave, Gaby struggled to regain her mental balance, but she felt as if suddenly the world was moving in slow motion, decreasing its pace so her brain had time to formulate a thousand niggling questions.

What had the other woman been hiding? What were her secrets? Who had uncovered them and why? Had this woman allowed herself to be careless because on some level she had wanted to be discovered? Or was it that what had been discovered was only terrible in the eyes of the beholder, not in the mind of the accused? Perhaps it had all been a matter of interpretation and manipulation. If so, who had done the interpreting and the manipulating and why? Was it Garrett himself? Another woman in love with Garrett and motivated by jealousy? Someone whom Garrett had scorned and who wanted revenge?

It could happen to me, she thought as she allowed Garrett to help her with her coat and escort her outside.

Gaby hiked her collar, defending herself against the cold. But how, she asked herself, would she defend against the coldness of those who would certainly feel betrayed if it was discovered that she was pretending to be something she was not. Would she fare better than Garrett's fiancée? Probably not, she realized with a flash of sympathy for that unknown Englishwoman.

For herself, she knew that despite her personal discomfort, despite her concern for others, and despite the possibility of unfavorable consequences, until every cent of her debt was paid, she would continue to be Gabrielle Didier, letting others think what they wanted to think, telling the truth whenever she could, bending the truth whenever she had to.

As the taxi neared her building, Gaby experienced yet another sensation—dread. What if Garrett expected the proverbial nightcap? What if he wanted to escort her upstairs? See her apartment? Ask about the different antiques? Make love to her? She wasn't ready for any of it.

For once, the gods were with her. As they entered the lobby, she pleaded fatigue. Garrett was gentlemanly enough not to press. Later, lying alone in her bed, staring up at the ceiling, she couldn't shake the feeling that, like the parables of old, the story of Garrett's broken engagement contained a lesson.

For hours, she dissected the tale. It was almost four in the morning when Gaby decided she had solved the parable. In this case, there were two lessons. The first was obvious. Deceit, like nuclear energy, could be contained, and yes, some of its uses were good not evil, but with something that continued to gain strength and momentum even in its confinement, there was always the risk of a leak, always the danger of a ruinous explosion.

The second lesson involved the revelation of deceit. If a secret was vital to someone's security, really vital, nothing short of a momentary episode of madness would precipitate a casual confidence or a deliberate act of carelessness. That left the task of revelation to outsiders. But why, Gaby asked herself, would someone take the time to go out of his way to dig and dig and dig until he had unearthed a hurtful truth about someone else? There were only two motivations powerful enough to inspire that kind of malevolent dedication—love and hate.

To survive, Gaby had to guard against both.

10

Her breasts had lost the firmness of youth, her waist its waspish silhouette. Her stomach had slackened, the flesh on her arms had loosened. Her skin tone had grown soft, her hair had grayed. But despite the imperfections of age, in Armand's eyes, Annabel remained Venus incarnate. He stood before her in worshipful awe, not because her form was as exquisite as it once had been, but because her being still exuded a sensuousness that made any response other than passion an act of disrespect.

As he watched her walk toward him, her lips arched in a knowing smile, he recalled the first time he had seen her unclothed. Then, as now, she had rejected the coyness of disappearing into the bathroom and reappearing in a filmy negligee. Instead, she had paraded across the floor of his tiny flat dressed in nothing but a susurrant veil of confidence. Now, as then, he waited like an anxious groom, flooded with a mix of feelings that ranged from shy questioning of his own ability to please to an unalterable belief that only he was capable of providing her with the ultimate joy she expected and deserved.

The room was dim, illuminated by a small bedside lamp and a single wedge of light that had bullied its way through the door that opened onto the sitting room. The celadon damask drapes had been drawn. The pale green silk bedspread had been folded down by an attentive maid, exposing crisp white linens dotted with a delicate floral design of peach blossoms and fresh spring leaves. Across from the bed, a fragrance candle burned on top of a white-manteled fireplace, its cypress scent perfuming the air, its flame reflected in the golden pier glass that hung behind it on the moiré silk wall. A half-empty bottle of champagne and two glasses rested next to a vase of roses on the dressing table, waiting for Armand's attention. But his attention was elsewhere. His eyes were riveted on the woman who had been his first love, his only love.

With other women, Armand always adopted the role of the aggressor, the conductor who orchestrated the way they made love, the pace, the intricacy, the mood, when it began, when it ended. It was as if he didn't trust his partners to appreciate the lyricism of the sexual act or to reach the proper crescendo without his explicit direction. With Annabel, he allowed himself to be a player and not just a leader, to succumb to temptation, to be seduced as well as to practice seduction. The difference, he supposed, was that with other women, even at the height of his ardor, he was conscious of being judged, compared, held up against an image of what they thought he was or wanted him to be. With Annabel, he was free to be himself.

Without ever taking her eyes from his, Annabel began to unbutton his shirt, her fingers moving leisurely, deliberately. Armand bent forward and traced the line of her mouth with his tongue as her hands removed his shirt. His mouth drifted behind her ear and feasted on the warm flesh of her neck. Her arms dropped to her sides and she tossed back her head, lifting her chest, broadening the canvas on which Armand's lips painted abstract bolts of lightning, stripes of heat that seared her skin and left her trembling with desire.

Just then, Armand stepped back. Annabel smiled. Only he made love this way, teasing, tantalizing, offering and then recanting, approaching and then retreating. Instinctively, she went to the bed and sat in the center, waiting. Armand filled the champagne glasses, brought her one, and turned on the suite's stereo system. In the background, the overture to Mozart's opera *The Marriage of Figaro* began to waft through the air. Within seconds, the lilting music, the aromatic scent of the candle, and the earthy tang of arousal had blended together to produce an environment heavy with atmospheric aphrodisia.

Armand slipped out of his trousers, removed the long-stemmed red roses from the tall crystal vase on the dressing table, placed them on the nightstand, and joined her on the bed. Neither of them spoke. Each drank champagne while drinking in the sight of the other's nakedness, sating their thirst while their hunger grew. When the bottle was empty, Annabel put down her glass and brought Armand's face to hers. Her lips pressed against his with an urgency he recognized as matching his own, yet still he pulled back.

Annabel reclined against the pillows, her patience strained. Armand retrieved the roses and sat astride Annabel's legs. Gently, he deplumed the deep red flowers and went about creating a bower fit for a queen. One by one, he tossed the velvety petals onto the sheets, onto the pillowcases, against Annabel's white skin, into her long black hair. A fragrant aura began to diffuse around them as silky blossoms gathered on Annabel's body, touching her, exciting her until all thought evaporated and she became nothing except a vessel of sensation. She thought she would go mad with frustration, but then, finally, Armand's hands met her skin.

As he rubbed rose petals against the pale pink aureoles that tipped her breasts, she shivered with the sheer rapture of it all, sliding further beneath him, wanting to get closer to the most vital part of this man whom she loved so fiercely. She felt him harden against her as he leaned down and charted the length of her with his tongue. When at last his mouth covered hers, his hands slipped underneath his own body to find the deepest part of hers. Her hands moved also, but there was no method, no design to her caresses. She was controlled only by the desire to touch him. She stroked his neck, his sides, his back. She felt his face, his ears. When her fingers caught in the wiry hair on his chest, and his fingers tangled in the web of her femininity, her back arched and she moaned. He removed his hands and started to pull away, but she groaned and grabbed at him, hot and wet with wanting.

This time, he didn't withdraw, but entered her slowly, as if hoping to prolong that special moment of joining for as long as he could, but Annabel had waited too many years for this reunion. With uncharacteristic eagerness, she pulled him down onto her and held him tightly, as together they stripped away time and recaptured their youth. Annabel clung to him, needing to feel him inside her, needing to know that he belonged to her and her alone, that there was no one else, that there had never been anyone else, that it was just them, just now, just this exquisite pleasure of their bodies linked in a symphony of movement, rising higher and higher, culminating in this incredible instant of fiery climax and violent release, this wonderful, inexplicable, undeniable feeling of delicious contentment.

After, even when they slept, Annabel continued to cling to Armand, because she loved him as much as she had when she was twenty and she was just as afraid of losing him now as she had been then.

Annabel Griscom spent 1952 as an art student living in Paris on a modest allowance sent to her by parents who didn't want her stay in the City of Lights to be all that pleasurable. Though the Earl and Countess of Swindon were normally generous to the point of overindulgence, this deliberate penury was designed to bring Annabel to her senses. After she had completed her studies at Cambridge, they had hoped that their only child would embrace her role as a daughter of the peerage, settle into the life of an eligible debutante, and chart her future around the task of providing a suitable heir for the earldom. Instead, Annabel bartered for a year's tuition at the Sorbonne, promising that if, after twelve months, she had not attracted favorable notice from anyone prominent in the art field, she would return to Willowsgate, the family estate, and confine her painting to family portraits or local landscapes.

She had been in Paris just over a month when she first met Armand. It was July, and inside the Louvre it was beastly hot. What little air there was seemed to hang like a heavy canopy, cloaking the atmosphere with an almost woolen thickness. Though several other students had elected to stay in the larger halls where an occasional electric fan manipulated the stagnant mass, Annabel had closeted herself in one of the chambers housing paintings from the neoclassical period. She had positioned herself and her easel near the window, intently copying *The Oath of the Horatii,* by Jacques-Louis David. Her thick black hair was piled on top of her head, but several tresses had resisted imprisonment by a barrette and defiantly stuck to the skin on her neck. She wore the sheerest cotton blouse dignity would permit and a full skirt which she had hiked onto her knees so that if a merciful breeze wafted by, it wouldn't neglect her.

All morning, guided tours had filed in and out of the small space, poaching Annabel's oxygen and replacing it with the stale smell of dried sweat and damp clothing. Annabel willed herself to concentrate. Though the bodies of her four main figures were almost completed, she was having difficulty duplicating the skin tone and musculature in the legs of the leather-thonged Romans. The last thing she needed was some septuagenarian tourist clucking his tongue in her ear and shaking his head with disapproval.

After what seemed like an interminable time, the latest guide managed to ferry the last of the stragglers into the next room, leaving Annabel free to struggle on in relative peace. For the next hour, she worked at a furious pace, taking advantage of the strong yellow light that filled the sky and poured into the room. She mixed and remixed her colors, stroking the canvas, looking, comparing, remixing, and repainting until, finally, she had completed one limb to her satisfaction. She wanted to smile, but sitting in front of that window during the height of a summer's day had intensified the heat until it had become almost unbearable. Her skin felt scorched, her throat dry and parched. Every part of her felt wet. Every part of her ached. Using the back of her hand, she mopped her forehead and upper lip, wiping the moisture on her paint-stained skirt. Then, she held open the front of her blouse and blew downward, trying to dry the valley between her breasts. She thought about continuing, but the light was changing and her stomach was pleading for attention. She stood, but as she went to stretch she stumbled backward, turning over her small chair and tripping over her paintbox. When her head cleared and her eyes opened, she was on the floor, cradled in the arms of the handsomest man she had ever seen.

"Bonjour. Comment ça va? Avez-vous des vertiges? Allez-vous mieux?"

Annabel couldn't speak. She was entranced by the deep brown eyes that were staring at her with genuine concern.

"Comprenez? Parlez-vous français? L'anglais?"

"I'm fine," she said at last. "I was just a little light-headed."

"British, yes?" He smiled, his lips broadening into a delicious curve.

"Quite. And yes, I do speak French, but I suspect that your English is probably a far sight better."

Suddenly, she realized that she was still lying in this man's lap. Had they been formally introduced, she might have remained there, but since they hadn't been, she thought it only proper to sit up and exchange names. She loosened herself from his grip, but when he made no move to stand, she simply slithered backward a bit and faced him, both of them sitting crosslegged on the wooden floor.

"I'm Annabel Griscom," she said, extending her hand.

"Armand Lafitte." He took her hand and pressed it to his lips, which felt cool against her hot skin.

"I'm not usually this clumsy."

"Then I'm glad you chose today to be unusual. I'm very pleased to meet you."

His eyes drifted over her, taking in the porcelain whiteness of her skin, the rosy tinge on her cheeks, the dark, undisciplined tendrils that danced about her face. Her eyes also danced, but they changed colors the way a ballerina changes costumes, going from a soft, sparrow brown to a light, meadow green. As his gaze wandered, he couldn't help comparing her to the odalisques that had fascinated the painter François Boucher. The same filmy, gauzelike fabric that veiled her body, veiled Boucher's fabled love slaves. The same provocative blend of innocence and sensuousness that Boucher's women expressed by their poses, was expressed in hers. The same naked frankness that stared out from those eighteenth-century canvases, stared at Armand now. She was barefooted, with long, graceful toes splattered with paint. One side of her blouse had drooped, baring a shoulder and falling low enough to hint at a full, lush bosom. Her skirt was long and loose, draped between her legs like the folds of a curtain, behind which were hidden a thousand mysteries.

Annabel remained silent throughout his inspection, conducting her own survey. He was seated, but she could tell that his height was average, his build broad shouldered. His hair was dark and wiry, curly without looking boyish, thick without appearing matted. Though his eyes had an eddying, hypnotic quality about them, it was his lips that attracted her most—fleshy, ripe, the lower one protruding slightly more than the upper, pursed slightly, looking as if they were poised for a kiss she wouldn't have minded returning. She couldn't decide whether it was because his linen jacket and white shirt were unrumpled or because he had been unruffled at finding a strange woman in his lap, but she concluded that he was a man of sophistication, a man who had already tasted more of the world than she had dreamed.

"If I don't clean this mess up before the guard comes," she said, springing to her feet and squeezing them into well-worn sandals, "he's going to ban me from the Louvre."

Armand rose also, helping her retrieve stray tubes of paint and brushes. As she returned her tools to her wooden box, he noticed that once again, the color had drained from her face.

"You're not still feeling faint, are you?"

"No. I'm fine. Really. I just forgot to eat and I think that little swoon was my body's way of punishing me for being so neglectful."

"Since your body and mine have gotten so close recently, I feel a certain obligation to make sure that it's well fed. If you don't mind, I'd like to treat you to lunch."

Annabel remembered the bread and cheese at the bottom of her knapsack. She also remembered that she had to go to the bank and cash a check to pay her rent. Oh, well. The bread and cheese would keep until the next day. So would her landlord. Armand Lafitte might not.

They spent the rest of the afternoon at a small café on the rue du Bac and the rest of the summer falling in love.

Never had Annabel felt such completeness, such total rapport. Armand made her think; she made him laugh. He gave her books to read. She gave him records to play. He taught her to cook. She taught him to ride. He introduced her to French antiques. She introduced him to English toffee. As the days passed into weeks, and the weeks passed into months, Annabel felt herself growing closer and closer to Armand. She felt as if they were becoming part of each other, as if their very blood was somehow mingling, linking them together for the rest of eternity.

To Armand, Annabel Griscom, madcap heiress, sometime art

student, and full-time love, had untangled the threads of his youthful confusion and sewed the seams of his life together with tight, even stitches. No wonder when, at the end of Annabel's year in Paris, they went to Willowsgate to announce their engagement, they were shocked to find that in the eyes of the Earl and Countess of Swindon, they were not only totally unsuited, but that marriage was completely out of the question.

"He's Jewish."

Annabel's mother practically whispered it. In front of Armand, she and her husband had managed to sidestep the central issue, making polite references to background and expectations and responsibilities, but now, in the privacy of Annabel's bedroom, Claire Griscom felt her daughter deserved to hear the unvarnished truth.

"What bloody difference does that make?"

"It makes a great deal of difference, especially when you consider all the other negatives."

"What other negatives?"

"Armand is a charming young man, but he's a commoner and he's French and his family are merchants."

"And he's Jewish."

"Yes. That too." At least Claire had the decency to look embarrassed, Annabel thought. "Your father and I are of the opinion that marrying out of your religion creates an additional strain. We feel you'd be happier with your own kind."

"If I were any happier, I'd burst!" Annabel felt the color rising in her cheeks. "I am madly in love with Armand and he's madly in love with me. Can't you see that?"

"I do see, darling. But really, it's probably just a summer fling that has lasted a bit longer than most. You'll get over him. Once you've gotten back in the swing of the young set in London, Monsieur Lafitte will become little more than a pleasant memory."

"I can't believe you're doing this to me."

"What I'm doing, darling, is attempting to spare you the heartbreak I know you would eventually suffer."

Annabel glared at her mother.

"No. What you're doing is trying to protect your precious title. It would be simply horrid if the next Earl of Swindon was half Jewish, wouldn't it! Why, you and father would never be able to show your faces at the club. Uncle Albert and Aunt Jane would have a field day chatting you up behind your back. That's all you really care about. You don't give a rat's damn about me being happy."

"That's untrue." Claire was on her feet, her hands on her hips, her face twisted with indignation. "All we've ever wanted was your happiness."

"All you ever wanted was for me to be a brood mare. You're just upset because I've brought home the wrong stud!"

"Don't be crude."

Annabel laughed.

"You and father sat in the drawing room and boldfacedly told the man I love he isn't good enough for me, and you're calling me crude? What a joke!" She paced back and forth in front of her mother, trying to work out the rage that was filling her body. "I just want you to know how humiliated I was by your behavior. You think you're so much better than everyone else, don't you? Well, I've spent a great deal of time with Armand's family. They might've objected to my *not* being Jewish, but if they did, I don't know about it. They were always warm and welcoming. They're delighted that Armand and I want to marry."

Claire's back stiffened at the challenge.

"They're not members of the peerage. We are."

"And I'm supposed to sacrifice everything that's important to me on the altar of the precious House of Lords?"

Claire Griscom loved Annabel fiercely, but right now she was angry. There were certain givens in her life, and being a countess was one of them. It was more than a title granting status, it was an historical connection, a relevance, a position within the Commonwealth, an ancestral promise of perpetual security. Maternal devotion aside, there was no way she was going to give all that up for what she considered to be an illicit, insignificant dalliance.

"Aren't you asking your father and me to sacrifice everything that's important to us on the altar of your misguided lust?" She practically spit out the last word, as if she couldn't wait to cleanse her mouth of such filth.

"Mother, please. He's such a fine man. Why can't you see that?" Annabel altered her approach, retreating a bit, hoping to appeal to her mother on another level. "His family is highly respected, not only in France, but all over Europe, here in England, even in the United States. The Lafittes are hardly the simple merchants you and father are portraying them as. And besides, Armand is a scholar." She knelt down in front of Claire, her posture begging for attention. "He's so fascinating, mother. I just wish you'd give him a chance."

Claire's expression refused to soften. "I gave you a chance and look what happened! I allowed you to go to Paris so that you might indulge this artistic whim of yours. I had hoped that you would use the year either to study and prove yourself or to work this compulsion out of your system. You did neither. Instead, you threw yourself into this man's bed like a common trollop!" Her lower lip curled downward in disgust and she averted her eyes, avoiding Annabel as if the sins of the flesh had permanently disfigured her daughter. "And now, simply because he's managed to satisfy your prurient urgings, you think he should be accepted as a member of this family. I'm offended."

"If Lord So-and-So had been the man to satisfy my prurient urgings," Annabel said quietly, "would you be less offended?"

Claire looked deep into Annabel eyes. She saw the child her daughter had been, the woman she still hoped she'd become. She also saw trust and the belief that no matter how difficult it was, Claire would answer with the truth.

"Yes," she said, clearly and distinctly, leaving no room for misinterpretation or argument. "Had your lover been a lord and an Anglican, I would be less offended."

Having said her piece, she turned and walked out of the room, like a magistrate who had just pronounced sentence and refused to hear any further appeal. Annabel remained crumpled on the floor beside the bed, confused and shaken. All her life, she had believed that her parents were reasonable people. She could never remember any subject being barred from discussion or any request being denied a fair hearing. Yet now, for something as important as her future happiness, her petition had been dismissed.

Now her mother had left Annabel's bedroom, having given Annabel what she claimed she had wanted—the truth. The problem was, now that Annabel knew the truth, what was she going to do about it?

Later that night, after she was certain her parents had retired, she sneaked into the guest wing and into Armand's room. She flew into his arms as if their separation had been years instead of hours. She pressed her body against his and felt her soul being infused with a new strength. As long as they were together, she thought, everything would be all right. She kissed him and caressed him, wanting him to make love to her, wanting him to excite her to the point where all guilt and doubt would be burned to ashes in the heat of their passion.

Instead, Armand gently pushed her away and led her to a settee, far away from the bed.

"Did you speak to your mother?" he asked, keeping her hand in his.

She nodded.

"What did she say?"

Annabel struggled, trying to condense all the distasteful things her mother had said into something palatable.

"Genes."

Armand smiled and squeezed her hand.

"Are they afraid that a frog and a bulldog won't make for pretty grandchildren?" Annabel didn't answer. "I can't say that I blame them. After all, who wants to cadoodle a tadpole that barks?" He was trying to be light, but having had his own private talk with Annabel's father, he knew the reasons.

Annabel smiled, but only briefly.

"It's all too ridiculous, Armand. Their objections are so Old World and unfair. They've got their priorities all tied up in property and peerages and appearances and obligations. I love you. You love me. Isn't that what's important?"

"To us it is."

She began to weep and he held her to him, trying to comfort her, knowing he was powerless to do so.

Annabel drew back and sniffled. Her eyes had turned a pale green that reminded Armand of fresh, spring grass. Strands of her hair had matted on her cheeks. He brushed them back, took her face in his hands and gently kissed her lips. The salt from her tears stung the open wound that was his heart. As if to salve his pain, he held her closer and pressed his lips harder against hers, waiting for the response he knew would come. He had promised himself he wouldn't make love to her in her parents' home. He had vowed not to violate the wishes of his host and hostess. But his love for Annabel and the knowledge of what he intended to do erased all resolve, leaving nothing but a raw, aching need that only this woman's love could heal.

Annabel returned to her own room just before dawn and fell into a deep, contented sleep. When, finally, she roused herself, it was early afternoon. She dressed quickly, expecting to find Armand in the garden or in the solarium or at the stable. He wasn't in any of those places. She searched the house, the grounds, everywhere she could think of, refusing to admit what she had already begun to suspect. She went back to his room. His closet was empty. Conveniently, her parents were nowhere to be found, and as she might have expected, the servants remained stubbornly mute. Shaking, she planted herself next to the telephone, staring at the black instrument, willing it to ring. When, despite her efforts, it remained silent, she began to call Paris, every hour on the hour. By ten o'clock, she was frantic. In case something had happened to Armand, she refrained from calling the senior Lafittes, but dialed Jacques's flat instead. He had no idea where his brother was. Yes, he would call if he heard anything. No, he wouldn't alarm his parents unnecessarily. Yes, he thought Armand was all right. No, it wasn't like him just to take off.

By the time her parents returned home from London, shortly after midnight, Annabel felt as if all emotion had been pummeled out of her.

"What happened to Armand?" It wasn't a question. It was an accusation.

Claire looked uncomfortable, squeamish in fact. She stole a glance at her husband, imploring him to take charge. Walter sat next to his daughter on the sofa and faced her squarely.

"Armand is gone, my dear. He left early this morning."

Annabel sat up, her head reeling from too little food and too many angry thoughts.

"Why did he leave?"

"Because he's a gentleman and it was the right thing to do."

"Right thing to do? What are you talking about?"

Walter patted her hand.

"He and I discussed the situation at some length. He's quite a sensitive and sensible young man. Together, we came to the conclusion that perhaps a separation would clear the air enough for both you and he to do some thinking.''

"Separation? Clear the air?" Suddenly, she felt dizzy. Her head began to spin. "What are we supposed to be thinking about?"

"How you really feel about each other."

Annabel felt Armand's arms around her. She felt his lips on hers, his body inside hers, his heart beating against her chest.

"I don't have to think about a thing," she said, feeling fresh tears gathering in her eyes, refusing to shed them lest they be mistaken for a show of childishness. "I love him. He loves me. I can't live without him."

"We think you can. That's what this separation is all about."

Months passed and still Annabel heard nothing from Armand. From Jacques, she learned that he had left his studies and joined an archeological dig somewhere in the Middle East. Jacques knew nothing else. He said Armand had refused to discuss Annabel with him. Though there was a part of her that was furious with Armand for abandoning her, a small voice pleaded with her to understand the pressure that had been placed on him. For a long time, she nurtured the hope that he would call or return unexpectedly or, at the very least, write to her from wherever he was, asking if perhaps the ban had been lifted. But if he did, what would she answer? Her parents would never change their minds. She knew that and she guessed he knew it too.

Eventually, her parents and the continued silence from Armand, wore Annabel down. A year and a half to the day after Armand disappeared, Lady Annabel Griscom married Philip Montgomery—a future duke, an Anglican, a wealthy financier, a man fifteen years older than she. A man she didn't love.

For four years she tried to bury her hurt by being a proper wife to Philip and an obedient daughter to her parents. She reasoned that if she had given up the one man she would ever love because of family obligations, then she might as well do her best to fulfill them. She and Philip tried and tried, but Annabel could not conceive. She went from one doctor to another, submitting to all sorts of poking and prodding. She visited psychiatrists as well as gynecologists, trying to see if external pressure was responsible for internal resistance, but still she couldn't get pregnant. Finally, Philip agreed to be tested, and once again she was tested. The results proved to be more painful than any actual birth could ever have been. Annabel was barren. She would never be able to provide an heir for the House of Swindon. She would never contribute to the continuation of her family line or Philip's. The irony of it all hit her like a leaden mallet. She could have married anyone. It wouldn't have made any difference. Because being infertile, *she* didn't make any difference.

Naturally, she was devastated by the news. She couldn't bear to witness Philip's disappointment and the disappointment of her parents. She told Philip she had to go away for a while. Where? She didn't know. How long? She didn't know that either.

In truth, she had been completely honest with him. Flying to Paris and calling Armand had been a subconscious reaction to a trauma, not a subversive plan for a tryst. More than anything else, she had needed comfort and the assurance that even without the ability to breed, she was indeed a woman. Only one person could give her the affirmation she sought.

Armand was so shocked to hear her voice and so disturbed by the melancholy he heard in it, that he rushed to her side. When she saw him, she cried for the first time since the doctor had told her his findings.

"What a waste," she said after telling her story. "What a disgusting waste."

She stood at the window, staring out at the Place Vendôme, her posture as upright as the Egyptian obelisk that marked the center of the seventeenth-century square. To Armand, despite the gray lines under her eyes and the sallow color of her skin, she looked more beautiful than he had remembered. True, she had exchanged her paint-stained skirts for white gloves and a prim suit, but somehow he sensed that beneath her ladylike veneer, the spontaneous, life-loving woman who had bewitched him almost six years before still existed.

"I don't know what to say, Annabel."

She turned. She saw the pain in his eyes and the confusion. For a second, she too wondered what she wanted him to say.

"That you loved me. That you really, really loved me. That you left only because you felt you had no other choice."

Tears rolled down her cheeks, releasing evidence of heartbreak arduously supressed. Armand rose from his chair and went to her, hesitating for only a moment before he took her in his arms and allowed her tears to wash away all the years they had spent apart.

She stayed in Paris for two weeks, her days occupied with mindless errands that freed her to anticipate being with Armand and to contemplate her future. Though she would have preferred spending every waking moment with Armand, his time was no longer his own. He wasn't a student the way he had been when they had first met. He was on staff at the Louvre now, oversee-ing delicate restorations and advising on new acquisitions. He had begun to make a name for himself and was often asked to travel to other museums to offer opinions on the authenticity of certain works. Although she was proud of his accomplishments, in a strange way, when he left her bed in the morning to go to the Louvre, she was jealous of his enthusiasm and his involve-ment, envious of his sense of purpose and commitment.

She had no purpose other than rebuilding her damaged psy-che, no involvement except in finding herself. She'd stroll along the Faubourg St.-Honoré and imagine herself living in Paris as Armand's wife. She'd wander around her old haunts on the Left Bank and wonder if she could, or should, pick up her brushes and oils and return to painting. Though she wanted to convince herself that the time was right for both dreams finally to be realized, a nagging feeling inside her told her that the years she had spent away from Paris, Armand, and her art had widened the gap between what was and what might have been.

"I'm going home." She said it quickly and quietly and then waited for a response.

She and Armand were in bed, their bodies still moist from lovemaking. Armand untangled his legs from hers and sat up. Annabel moved only her eyes. He didn't appear angry or even surprised.

"I know," he said.

Annabel pulled the sheet around her and sat facing him. She reached for his hand, and for a few minutes they just looked at each other.

"I love you, Armand. More than life itself," she said at last. "In my heart, I'm certain that I'll never love anyone else, but something is pulling me away from you." She looked down, fingering the sheet with her free hand, measuring her words.

When she looked up, her face was damp. "I guess I feel I owe them. I owe Philip and I owe my parents. I let them down. I didn't give them the one thing they wanted. If I were to divorce Philip and marry you, which, God knows, is what I want to do, I'd be adding disgrace to disappointment." She bit her lip, trying to keep it from quivering. "I can't do it."

Armand pulled his hand away from hers. The lines on his forehead deepened and he began to rub his temples, as if he could massage away what she had said, what he had been thinking. When he looked at her, his eyes had darkened with the hurt she had inflicted. Yet his voice, which she had expected to explode with anger, was more unnerving, because it was flat with resignation.

"You're the only woman I'll ever love, Annabel. These past years have proved that to me. There hasn't been a day that I haven't thought about you or dreamed about you or ached for you. But somehow, we've offended the gods and we seem fated to be apart." He paused, leaned forward, and caressed her cheek. "You're too passionate a woman to be imprisoned in a loveless marriage. It's like taking a flower and daring it to blossom inside a darkened closet. I'd like nothing more than to take you away and find a private island where the only important thing was the love two people feel for each other, a place where family and obligation and loyalty didn't matter. But there is no such island." He paused again, this time pulling her toward him and kissing her softly. "I'll always love you, Annabel. And if ever you need to feel loved, I'll always be here for you."

For almost thirty years, the same forces that had insisted upon keeping them apart conspired to throw them together. They'd meet by chance and it would start again. Sometimes it would last for days, sometimes for years. They'd separate, and then, just when they both thought the gods had triumphed, once more fate would intervene and their love affair would continue. The only difference between this chance meeting at the fair and all their other meetings, was that now there were no more obstacles. Annabel's parents and her husband were gone.

"Philip knew about us," she said over breakfast. "He never said anything, but I know he knew. Whenever we were involved, he distanced himself from me, as if giving me permission to be with you.''

"If I were your husband, I wouldn't have been that noble,'' Armand said, allowing some of his resentment over all the lost years to surface.

"It wasn't nobility, my pet, it was guilt. He was not without his *affaires d'amour*.'' She nibbled on a croissant, her face reflective. "I used to hope he would fall madly in love with someone else and leave me. But he didn't. Or he wouldn't.'' She picked up her napkin and wiped the corners of her mouth. "Did you ever fall in love with anyone else?''

Armand smiled. She looked like an insecure teenager just then, with her fingers crossed under the table, hoping that his answer was the one she wanted to hear.

"No. There have been many women in my bed, Annabel, but no other woman has ever occupied my heart.''

Her mouth spread in a wide, satisfied grin.

"Good,'' she said. "Since you love me, I suppose you will also be honest with me?''

He nodded, curious.

"First, what happened between you and Prado?''

He sipped his coffee, taking the time to compose his answer.

"The clash of the Titans,'' he said with a wry smile. "When two enormous egos do battle, it's always bloody.''

"Explain, please.''

Armand retold the saga of the Antiques Fair without attempting to shield himself from criticism by extensive editing. He told it as it had happened, including those instances when he felt he had been blinded by his own ambition and those times when he had allowed himself to feed on the flattering encouragement of others.

Annabel listened quietly. She tried to restrain herself from giving a response, but periodically her face registered varying degrees of anger and pain. When Armand had finished, she took a few seconds to organize her thoughts.

"I take it that the reason there was no Lafitte booth at the fair is because you've been excommunicated by his holiness Pope Prado.''

"That's about it.''

In front of anyone else, Armand might have felt some embarrassment, some need to defend himself or to color the truth so as to maintain his image. Annabel had known him too long and too well for fiction.

"It's a matter of pride," he said simply. "I didn't mind failing. I had gone into this knowing that defeat was a distinct possibility. But this exile has besmirched my family name, and that is a difficult pill to swallow."

"No one knows better than I," she said with a trace of bitter irony, "the sacrifices you've made protecting your family, and mine. But this goes beyond a simple tit for tat. I always knew Vincent was vengeful, but this expulsion from the garden is too complete, the intricacy of the plan too diabolical for the workings of his mind alone. Who are his confreres?"

"The dealers who benefited from the ban on vetting, I suppose." He answered quickly, hoping to shift her onto a different track.

His voice had remained calm, but as she listened, Annabel had studied his eyes and they had betrayed him. His explanation was too simple. The dealers he spoke of were small time. They didn't have the power or the influence to squash a Lafitte. The architect of this ostracism was someone who not only had a penchant for details, but also had the power to demand that others bend to his will.

Annabel's first instinct was to probe deeper, but she restrained herself. Armand had his reasons for hiding the truth from her, and for now she would respect his privacy, but only because she had another question to ask.

"What happened four years ago to make you decide that suddenly, after thirty years, you had to make an honest woman of me?"

Her shift caught him off guard.

"Philip came to see me," he said, as surprised as she that he had allowed the truth to come out so easily.

"And appealed to your sense of morality, I suppose."

He saw the anger in her eyes and wondered whether it was directed toward him, her late husband, or both.

"No. Actually, he appealed to my code of honor. You were quite right. He did know about us. Not all of it, but enough to confront me with the tawdrier aspects of our relationship. He told me how humiliating it was for him whenever he knew we were involved. How hurtful it was and how demeaned he felt every time you returned to his bed." Annabel's face flushed with a growing rage, but still Armand continued. "He said he felt that it was my fault that your marriage had been so unfulfilling, that if I had taken myself out of the picture, you would have allowed yourself to be happy with him. He pointed out that you had married him freely and willingly, at a time when I was long gone from your life and that perhaps if I had had the character to turn you away when you first sought my solace, things would have been different between you."

"And you believed him?" Annabel was on her feet. Her body shook with fury. "How could you?"

Armand faced her squarely.

"Because having to look your husband in the eye as he told me how he felt being cuckolded made me feel guilty. That's why. Because he made me think that perhaps there was a grain of truth to what he said. That maybe if I had been stronger, your life with him would have been happier, and that, my dearest Annabel, was all I ever wanted for you."

"My life was happy, thank you very much, but only when I was with you." She was pacing, her fists clenching and unclenching as if keeping time with the rhythm of her rage. "He came to you because I told him I was leaving him." She paused, grabbed hold of the chair facing Armand and gripped it as if she would fly away if she let go for even an instant. She might have continued to rant, but when she looked at Armand, she saw how painful his confession had been, and so she forced herself to calm down. "It was just after my father died. Mother had died a few years before, as you know. There seemed to be no reason to stay with Philip any longer. We had no marriage and I didn't care about what his family would have thought. They certainly never cared about me. From the moment they discovered I couldn't give them a little Montgomery, they treated me like an unnecessary accessory to Philip's life. I told him I wanted a divorce, that I wanted to be free to marry you. He told me he'd never allow it, that before he'd let me go he would feed me to the Fleet Street sharks. He swore he would give the papers every smarmy little detail about our affair and make us the laughing-stock of the Continent." She offered Armand a weak smile. "Obviously, he never understood how much I loved you. He never realized that I would never have allowed him to hurt you. So, not trusting me, he went to you, knowing, I suppose, that you would do as he asked. You would do the right thing.''

Armand raised his hands to his face and rubbed his eyes, as if he had been lost in a bad dream and could erase it with a few twists of his fists. When he looked at Annabel, there was no anger, no frustration, no disbelief, no apologies, just regret.

''That's when I agreed to come to New York,'' he said simply. ''I figured that if I increased the distance between us, I would decrease the possibility of going back on my word.''

''I feel as if I've ruined your life.''

Armand laughed, but somehow it sounded strangled.

''Annabel Griscom Montgomery, you magnificent fool! You're the only thing that's made my life worth living. Without you, the past four years have seemed like an eternal winter, an endless season filled with nothing but an empty, lonely cold. There's been little warmth and no heat, at least not the kind I feel whenever we're together.''

Annabel went to him and lowered herself onto his lap, burrowing her head into his neck, sliding her arms around his waist.

''I love you, my sweet frog,'' she whispered, feeling his flesh against her lips as she spoke. ''And despite them all—my parents, Philip, his family, the world at large—we've survived. It's our time now.''

Instead of an embrace or a kiss or an enthusiastic expression of agreement that, yes, at last they could do as they had wanted to do thirty years before, there was silence.

''In case you missed it, that was a proposal of marriage, Monsieur Lafitte.''

''I know. But it's not that easy.'' Annabel pulled back so she could see him as he spoke. ''I don't want to drag you into this mess. Just give me time to straighten it all out.''

''If we give each other any more time, my darling, by the time we say 'I do' and finally crawl into our nuptial bed, we'll be too old to do it!''

This time, Armand's laugh was genuine.

''Somehow, I don't think that will ever be one of our problems.''

''Then what are our problems?''

"The problems are not ours, they're mine; and as much as I want to marry you, my first obligation is to resolve them." His voice reverberated with intent. It was as if he had taken a holy vow. "What I did was on the side of right. It may have been ill-advised, but it was not wrong. This punishment, this banishment, is unwarranted, and I'm not going to accept it for one moment more than I absolutely have to. Until I redeem myself and my family, I'm not free. Can you understand that?"

She thought about offering to help by going to Prado and pleading Armand's case, but she rejected the idea before she had a chance to give it voice. His pride had been battered enough. He had to fight this battle in his own way and in his own time. The only choice she had was to wait. She had been waiting for so long, another few months couldn't possibly matter.

"Of course I understand. It's who you are and why I love you so fiercely." She took his face in her hands and kissed him. "If you want me to do anything, I will. If you want me to do nothing, I'll abide by your wishes and do nothing."

She spoke with conviction, but in her heart she too took a solemn oath: whoever was behind this blackballing, whoever had dared tarnish her beloved's name, whoever was preventing her and Armand from being together, was going to pay dearly for what he'd done—if not by Armand's hand then by hers.

11

"What, will no one offer any more?"

With those words, spoken on October 15, 1958, Peter Cecil Wilson, better known as PCW, altered the personality of the auction forever. From the late 1700s, when Castleton's, Sotheby's and Christie's sprang into existence selling coins, stamps, etchings, books, and "fictile manufactures" like china and porcelain, until that stunning moment on New Bond Street when the hammer came down on the sale of Cézanne's *Garçon au Gilet Rouge*, the final lot of Jakob Goldschmidt's prized collection, it seemed as if auction houses had existed for the sole purpose of providing a neutral site for aristocratic gentlemen to trade personal property without having to resort to the indecorous practice of face-to-face haggling.

The Goldschmidt auction changed all that. Not because the painting sold for $660,000, a record at the time, and not because all the other offerings far exceeded the printed estimates, but because it was the first auction by one of the venerable three to be held at night and the first to be choreographed as total spectacle, complete with a glittering assemblage of more than fifteen hundred invited guests, television cameras, and full media coverage. It was also the first auction PCW commanded as head of Sotheby's.

Wilson was an ambitious man, but more than that, he believed that without the addition of splash and showmanship, the art of the auction would stagnate and eventually die. For centuries, auctioneers had viewed the people who came to their salesrooms as nothing more than potential buyers. Wilson saw them as an audience, a group to whom he could play, a group easily manipulated as long as he targeted his appeal to the two major instincts of every buyer: collecting and competing. He understood the souls of those who gripped bidding paddles in their hands waiting for their moment of glory, because he, like them, was a gambler. He relished the sport of auction, the theater of auction, the thrill of battling and winning, the utter joy of owning something the value of which had been established then and there at the very instant of triumph.

On that magical night in 1958, playing to the glittering crowd, he cajoled, he enticed, he beseeched. Then, when the bidding on the Cézanne slowed at $616,000, Wilson had the audacity to lean over the side of his rostrum, plant an incredulous look on his face and scold, "What, will no one offer any more?" Not only was he given what he asked, but the entire audience stood and cheered.

Peter Cecil Wilson had succeeded where many before him had failed. In one night, he had shifted the limelight away from the dealers and made it into a spotlight for the new rich. From then on, instead of buying fine art and antiques in private, anonymous viewing rooms, the wealthy, especially wealthy Americans, sought to parade their desires, and their ability to indulge those desires, in public. PCW wooed them with the ardor of an insistent suitor, flattering them, tempting them, seducing them into visiting Sotheby's more often than Harrod's. The golden era of the auction had begun.

Garrett Castleton, Jr., like his counterparts John L. Marion of Sotheby's and Christopher Burge of Christie's, felt he owed an enormous debt to Peter Wilson. Without him, Castleton's might not have enjoyed the profits it had in recent years. But Garrett secretly envied Wilson. He envied him the Goldschmidt auction, the stupendous success, the influence, the international celebrity, that had flowed from that one night. Though he had presided over many important auctions in his years behind the Castleton podium and had brought the hammer down on many record-breaking sales, Garrett still longed for his night of nights, his spectacle, his coronation.

Perhaps it was that subconscious desire to recreate Wilson's coup that accounted for Garrett's preoccupation with the Dinant tapestries. If he could find *The Marriage of Brussels*, he would have three of the most famous, most sought after tapestries in the world. The fact that he didn't own the other four was irrelevant. Long ago, he had decided he didn't need them. His plan was simply to unite the three he had under a provocative, marketable title: *The Love Trilogy*. He would retell the romance of the Flemish lord and his Walloon bride via the press. He would flesh out their story until they seemed real and every detail of their difficult courtship and eventual marriage had become part of the public consciousness. He would, in essence, weave them into the fabled fabric which held other classic starcrossed lovers, like Romeo and Juliet, Lancelot and Guenivere, Napoleon and Josephine, the Duke and Duchess of Windsor. He would make his auction as much of a must-attend as Wilson's Goldschmidt offering or Sotheby's Jewels of the Duchess of Windsor or Christie's selling of the Van Gogh *Sunflowers*. If people were willing to pay for objects that gave them elegance by association, and clearly they were, he would give them love by association.

What disturbed him was that so many others were tracking the missing Dinant. Max Richard was open about his desire to own the piece. Vincent Prado had announced his intent the other night. And because his own search for it was well-known, it was likely that his sister, Irina, had also called out the hounds. Who else, he wondered, was clogging the trail? As with most things that suddenly come into vogue, he had to assume that his natural competition, Sotheby's and Christie's, were also intrigued with the possibility of finding such a treasure. If one of them located it, they wouldn't have the trilogy, but what if they had unearthed the name, or names, of those in possession of the other Dinants? What if they had already cut a deal? They, too, could create a package. It might not have the mass appeal of a love trilogy, but when one was selling a true bit of history, there was more than enough romance attached to it to prompt a museum or a dedicated collector or even a government to pay a king's ransom.

As Garrett studied himself in his office mirror and slicked back a wandering shock of hair, he determined to broaden his search. In addition to prodding his contacts in Europe to intensify their sleuthing efforts and upgrading his own investigation in the United States, he decided that perhaps he should extend his reach to South America. The problem there was that—although no one would admit it outright—several of the major collections were known to contain pieces believed to have been smuggled out of Europe by Nazis during the war. It was even rumored that one or two of the better-known collectors were former Nazis themselves. That made most dealers and agents loathe to press for information on provenances. What they didn't know, they reasoned, couldn't hurt them. Garrett couldn't blame them, but it was worth a try.

Another splash of cologne, another tug on his tie, and he was ready. In just a few minutes, he would mount the polished mahogany rostrum and open Castleton's winter sale of important French furniture and decorative arts. Judging by the crowds at the fair, the auction should be a success. The most important *antiquaires* from Paris were in town. Thanks to a strong deutsche mark, a large contingent of well-to-do Germans had come ready to buy. The other night at the fair, he had recognized half the population of Dallas and Houston milling about the armory, as well as members of the tony set from San Francisco and L.A. His New York friends, none of whom could resist anything labeled important, would certainly be there. And, he reminded himself as he made his way to his private elevator, Gaby would be sitting beside him handling telephone bids. Other than finding *The Marriage of Brussels* on his doorstep, what more could he ask?

"Showing here!"

The electric stage turned. A team of spotlights hit three lapis-blue vases of Chinese porcelain, two smaller, one larger, all mounted on glistening ormolu. They were rare pieces, a garniture from the time of Louis XV, estimated between seventy and ninety thousand dollars. Garrett glanced down at his catalogue, the one that listed the reserves on each lot in a code known only to him and his immediate staff, and opened the bidding at forty thousand dollars.

"Will someone start me off with forty? Thank you to the gentleman in the center. Do I hear fifty? . . . I have fifty thousand from the woman on the left . . . sixty from the back. Thank you . . . seventy from the phone on my right . . . eighty in the corner."

Gaby strained to hear the voice on the other end of her telephone.

"Ninety from the woman on my left."

Gaby's bidder went silent for the moment, giving her a chance to study his competition. Grouped in front, whispering to each other while plants throughout the room did their bidding for them, sat the clique of old-guard Parisian *antiquaires*, minus one of course—Etienne Lafitte. Doris Leslie Blau, a New York rug and tapestry dealer, was seated on the aisle toward the rear, her wild red hair fluffed around her face like a devilish halo. Leon Dalva, a dealer in grand eighteenth-century antiques, sat across from her, calmly taking in the action through scholarly, round metal glasses. In the center, near Sister Parrish, the doyenne of New York decorators, Gaby noticed Max Richard, his head lowered as he checked his catalogue for upcoming lots. The woman on the left to whom Garrett kept referring was none other than Chelsea Reynolds. Gaby watched in utter fascination as her finger twitched in answer to a gentleman who had nodded a bid of one hundred thousand dollars.

"One ten. Now we're getting someplace," Garrett said, flashing an appreciative smile to his audience. They responded with a collective laugh and a bid for one hundred and twenty.

The man on the phone instructed her to bid again, which she did, but when Chelsea upped his offer to one hundred and forty-five thousand dollars, he told Gaby to cease bidding.

"I have one hundred and forty-five thousand dollars. Do I hear more?" Garrett paused. He raised his gavel. "Fair warning!" The gavel was about to come down. "Going once. Going twice. Sold! To Mrs. Reynolds."

In a space next to the lot number, he noted the selling price, the number of the winning paddle, and in this case, because she was known to him, the name of the buyer. The stage rotated once again, his eye noted the reserve, and without delay he opened the bidding.

Gaby was seated between Giles Deffand and Beezie, at a

long desk that flanked the auctioneer's podium. Three others manned telephones across from them, while three more from their department stood at the front of the salesroom, their eyes trained on the audience, alert for every motion from a raised paddle to a raised eyebrow. Gray-smocked spotters were strategically placed along the sides and the back, holding long wooden pointers in their hands, ready to direct attention to tapestries pinned onto fabric-covered walls, or to chandeliers suspended from sturdy metal chains, or to bidders whose subtle moves might otherwise be lost in the crowd. Above, an electronic toteboard recorded the bids in six currencies: dollars, pounds, French francs, Swiss francs, German marks, and Japanese yen. Also above the selling floor, contained behind large glass windows and looking like booths at a baseball stadium, were several computer rooms operated by staff trained to record every centime bid on the level below.

It wasn't like this for all auctions. For most, the toteboard stayed dark, the booths remained empty, half the telephones were unmanned, and the mammoth, movable walls weren't wedged out the way they were now, but rather held to straighter lines, making the gallery smaller so that the number of bidders appeared larger. Today's auction, as most labeled important did, went beyond a mere sale. Today was a show, and therefore the stage had to be properly set. Though the full wattage of the enormous spotlights fixed on whatever appeared on the revolving platform, the real spotlight was on the players.

As Gaby watched in genuine awe, Garrett worked the room with a maestro's touch, building to crescendo after crescendo, until the feeling of wealth and power that permeated the atmosphere was so strong it was almost palpable. In a voice that constantly hinted at restrained emotion, Garrett encouraged his flock to respond to his call. He moved them, inspired them, preached to them as if he were a modern-day Elmer Gantry at a revival meeting. Lot after lot was sold far beyond the estimates listed in the catalogue. A pair of Louis XVI consoles, both with marble tops resting on magnificently carved ormolu ram's heads, went for more than half a million dollars, as did an eighteenth-century desk attributed to the workshop of *ébéniste* Jacques Dubois. Two sets of three-light ormolu chimneypieces bearing the "crowned C mark"—a tax mark used from March 1745 to

February 1749 on any alloy using copper—went for more than three hundred thousand dollars per set. The amounts were staggering, and though Garrett appeared to take them in stride, each time the hammer came down on a spectacular round of bidding, Gaby's heart pumped a little faster—especially when a pair of Chinese Export phoenix birds similar to the ones left to her by Tante Simone brought thirty thousand dollars and a clock, not as old or as fine as the one she had inherited, brought twenty-five. The price of the desk had almost knocked her out of her seat. Her *bureau plat* had been crafted by the ultimate *maître*. If a Dubois warranted half a million, what might a Bernard van Risamburgh bring? She couldn't help but fantasize about how much easier it would be if only she could offer even one of those pieces for sale. She could wipe out her debt to Lakewood and begin to live her life free of encumbrance, free of the horrible, cramping feeling that at any moment the walls of her hastily built fortress might come crashing down on her. But Simone had forbidden her to sell. In her heart, Gaby understood. She knew that, in essence, what Simone had done was right, that to own these treasures and to enjoy them for a lifetime was far better than to sell them for a quick profit. But still.

While Gaby had been lost in her own reverie, Garrett had started the bidding on another example of Jacques Dubois's artistry. This time, it was a fine pair of *bois satiné bibliothèques*, grille-work bookcases crafted from polished woods and mounted on the ubiquitous gilded ormolu feet that seemed to be the very symbol of the eighteenth century. They were magnificent pieces, almost modern in the simplicity of their design. The bidding was fierce, moving quickly past the hundred thousand mark, on up into the quarter-of-a-million-dollar range. Though Gaby had an anxious customer barking instructions on her telephone, her eyes were drawn to Max Richard, who appeared committed to owning this set. What interested her was that unlike most other bidders, Max was not subtle or shy about proclaiming his offers. He raised his paddle almost defiantly, letting his competition know that they were, indeed, involved in a battle.

"Two hundred and seventy-five . . . I have two hundred and seventy-five thousand dollars. Do I hear three hundred? . . . I'm listening. Do I hear . . . yes, I do! Three hundred thousand dollars from the man in the center. Thank you." Garrett smiled at Max. Gaby's caller dropped out, as did Beezie's and Deffand's. "Are we finished? Or do I hear three and a quarter? . . ."

Up and up, the bidding continued, but now it appeared to be a duel between Max and an agent Gaby recognized as someone who frequently represented Japanese industrialists.

"Four hundred and fifty thousand, says the gentleman in the center. Does the gentleman on my left have another bid?"

Gaby watched as six hundred thousand dollars hit the toteboard. She listened as Garrett asked if Max would go higher. She looked at Max's eyes, which had an amused glint. He shook his head and held up his hands in a gesture of surrender.

"Fair warning," Garrett said, still staring at Max, hoping to squeeze out yet another fifty thousand dollars. He raised his gavel slowly, allowing Max time to reconsider his silence, but when the wooden mallet came down, it hit hard. A sale was a sale. The new owner of the Dubois *bibliothèques* was the slight, balding gentleman busily punching numbers into a pocket calculator, computing the final sale price plus the buyer's premium and converting it all into yen.

"You seemed so intense," Gaby said to Max later at the *après*-auction cocktail party Garrett was hosting in the private gallery behind the salesroom. "For a moment, I thought you were going to offer your grandmother in exchange for those bookcases."

Max laughed.

"I came close, but I only put Granny on the block for very special pieces."

"Besides," Gaby said, wondering what he would have bid for a very special piece if he was willing to bid five hundred thousand dollars for something he obviously considered less impressive, "I thought you collected mostly Biedermeier."

"I do, but I house that collection in New York. In Europe, I have mostly French and Continental furnishings."

Gaby was embarrassed. How provincial! She should have guessed that he had more than one address.

"And where is your castle?" she asked, trying to recover from her gaffe.

"Sorry, no castle, no moat, no drawbridge. Just a simple apartment in Brussels and a place in Geneva."

Somehow Gaby sensed that his definition of simple and hers came from two different dictionaries. It did intrigue her, however, that he called his home in Geneva a "place." What did that mean? A villa? An A-frame? A manor? A cottage? Despite the fact that her dealings with him had been brief, he seemed to be a very direct person, not one to muddle meanings or cloud issues with euphemisms or metaphors. She debated pursuing the matter, but before she could come to any decision, Garrett interrupted.

"I tried, old man, but I think Frucht's ceiling was well beyond the ozone layer." He clapped Max's shoulder, a sympathetic pat from one who understood the displeasure of occasional loss. "From my side of the podium, the strength of the yen has been a tremendous boon, but from the seats, I suppose it's been a royal pain in the butt."

"It does tend to cramp one's style," Max said dryly. "But enough about my loss and a comment on your gains. Congratulations, Garrett. You did a superb job today. As usual."

"Thank you." Someone called his name and, excusing himself, Garrett moved on to socialize with another cluster of satisfied customers, leaving Max and Gaby alone.

"I don't know about you," Max said, handing his champagne glass to a nearby waiter, "but spending money, or trying to, gives me a ferocious appetite. I need to feed the savage beast, but I hate to dine alone. Would you care to join me for dinner?"

Why was this happening to her? Had she walked under a ladder? Broken a mirror? Spilled salt? Put shoes on her bed? Other than her two evenings with Garrett, she hadn't had a date in two years. Plus, if asked, Gaby would have admitted that in her fantasies, Maximilian Richard was far and away the number one candidate for the ultimate Prince Charming, yet she was about to reject his invitation. Armand was coming over for dinner. They had planned it ages ago as a way of celebrating— they hoped—the profits made from those pieces Gaby had consigned to Castleton's.

"I would care to very much," she said, "but I can't. I'm sorry. I already have plans."

"Another time?"

"I'd like that."

He took her hand, squeezed it lightly, and made his way to the exit. Gaby watched him go, unaware that someone was watching her.

At the press of a button, a mechanical lift hoisted a long metal bar fitted with sawtoothed grips. Gradually, one of the fabled Dinant tapestries, *The Garden of Love*, was unfurled. The pace was slow and dignified, a stately tempo suited to the revelation of one of history's more glorious survivors, though an accompaniment of heraldic trumpets might have sounded more appropriate than the metallic squeaking that marked the lift's progress.

Once the antique weaving was fully exposed, Gaby simply stared, her eyes drinking in the refulgence of color, the complexity of design. For a few moments, she forgot that she was standing in the bare, brightly lit inspection area, where new arrivals were examined and assessed. She forgot that she was wearing plain woolen slacks and a turtleneck sweater. Rather, in a flash of fantasy, she indulged her imagination and pictured herself the chatelaine of a medieval castle, garbed in sumptuous velvets and brocades, her hair coiled beneath a loosely arranged, ornately jeweled veil, her bodice girdled within a full-sleeved, tight-fitting gown.

She had been removed from the present, transported back in time to the late Middle Ages. Instead of standing in a windowless corporate cave, she saw herself in the great hall of a seigneurial household.

As Gaby moved closer and the splendor of *The Garden of Love* drew her deeper into its spell, her mind's eye insisted upon envisioning the tapestry in its original surroundings—proudly warming the stone wall on which it hung. By day, it must have been exquisite, with the sun's golden rays washing its rich rainbow with a xanthic glow. By night, illuminated only by the limited reach of flickering candelabra and occasional lambent banners of moonlight that floated in through small, high-set windows, it must have appeared haunting, mysterious, almost spectral. How much more fitting than its present reality—dangling from a pole like a piece of half-dried laundry, its intricately worked surface blanched by the harsh, abusive glare of modern-day electricity.

"Extraordinary, *n'est-ce pas?*"

Giles Deffand waited for an answer. When none was forth-coming, he stepped back and studied his protégée with amuse-ment. For at least ten minutes, Gaby had not spoken or moved more than a few paces. Deffand was not certain she had even breathed with any regularity since she had first laid eyes on the Dinant. Though he would readily admit an acute admiration for the tapestry's technical brilliance and would also confess an almost awesome respect for its remarkable richness of detail, Gaby's response exceeded admiration and respect. She appeared mesmerized, practically bewitched. It was as if the sight of this fifteenth-century garden had unleashed a rush of subconscious recognition and connection. Her back straightened. Her chin lifted. Her hands affected a stiff, peculiar pose. Her face approx-imated the same cautious yet flirtatious look that marked the visage of the lady from Dinant. It was as if a gene full of ancestral memory had suddenly exploded and the woman in the garden accepting a young gentleman's offer of a goblet of wine was not simply the interpretive work of a Flemish weaver but, in fact, one of Gaby's antecedents, one of the women linked to her in an unbroken chain of genealogic succession.

Deffand watched as Gaby's fingertips touched the silken threads that had woven the delicate face of the comely gentle-woman. They were tender, almost loving, even when they moved on to the thicker woolen strands that had fashior d the woman's gold brocade gown and purple veil. He noticed that when she came to the unicorn playing in a grassy field outside the lady's castle, Gaby stopped, hesitated, and then, with almost religious deference, traced the milky-white threads that had sketched the fabulous one-horned creature that so dominated medieval lore.

"It's really quite exceptional," she said at last. "Years ago, when I first saw pictures of the Dinants, I remember thinking that they looked as if they were especially beautiful. But now, seeing this in person, I must admit, this is just so far beyond the mere definition of beauty, I'm at a loss."

Deffand laughed.

"Now you know why some people are killing themselves to find tapestries like these, and others are willing to kill or bank-rupt themselves to own them."

"Where does this particular one come in the series?" Gaby

asked, again moving within inches of the tapestry so she could examine the detail.

"Third. First is *The Meeting*. Then, *The Courtship*. And then, *The Garden of Love*."

Gaby nodded, his recitation prodding her own memory to recall the proper sequence.

"They look so in love and so happy here," she said, noting the shy smile on the maiden's face, as well as the bashful, albeit hopeful, expression in her suitor's eyes. "Yet the fourth tapestry is called *The Battle of the Lion and the Unicorn*, isn't it?"

"It is. But remember, the very heart of the Dinant legend is based on the concept of love conquering all, of good being victorious in the age-old battle with evil. Although their association with the lion and the unicorn elevate them to symbols of sides in a conflict, these two young lovers were real people who triumphed not only over the objections of their families, but also over the bloody political wars being waged at the time."

Deffand took Gaby's arm and walked her backward so they could take in the huge piece.

"In the late fourteen hundreds, the Flemish who controlled the northern duchies of present-day Belgium considered the Walloons of the south to be enemies." He raised his arm and pointed at the tapestry. "Do you see the two castles?"

Gaby's eyes were drawn to the top part of the piece. On either side were two distinctly styled castles, each bearing its own flag. The one behind the lady was blue with three yellow fleurs-de-lis. The one behind the man was red with a golden lion standing on one hind leg with the front paws raised, a symbol known in heraldry as a "rampant." Deffand explained both symbols, as well as the history behind the looming of the Dinants.

The tale of the tapestries began when Edouard de Rosier, one of the lords of Flanders, came upon the young Walloon woman in a forest during a hunting expedition. She was en route to Namur on the border of the Ardennes, to become affianced to the son of another gentried Walloon. One of the horses in her caravan had stumbled, toppled her carriage, and overturned a supply wagon. Ever the gentleman, Edouard stopped and offered to help. The lady's escort, entrusted by her father with her safety and viewing the northerner as an enemy, resisted at first, but finally, having no alternative, accepted his assistance. That night, they all shared a meal and by the time the last tankard was raised, the two young people had fallen hopelessly in love.

The next day, the leader of the caravan decided they had to return to Dinant. Because the lady had not arrived in Namur on schedule and, therefore, had caused her future betrothed considerable embarrassment, and because Edouard de Rosier had secretly waylaid the messenger sent to Namur to report the cause of their unavoidable delay, the engagement was canceled.

Edouard became obsessed with the fair maiden and courted her despite the fierce objections and threats of her father. She, too, appeared to ignore whatever parental restrictions had been placed on her. Frequently, she slipped out to meet her beloved in a nearby clearing.

Deffand nodded toward the tapestry on the wall. "I give you *The Garden of Love.*"

Gaby smiled. It was just so pleasingly sentimental, so universally appealing. For several seconds, she indulged the romantic in her while the inquisitive side of her personality idled, holding back the hundred or so questions that had come to mind during Deffand's narration.

"I thought that historical parallels were a major part of the significance of the Dinant tapestries," she said, gulping down the last, lingering lump of mawkish romanticism so that her intellect could surface and continue the investigation of these weavings. "So far, I don't see too many."

"They're there, but they're subtle. Let's say that the first three provide a prologue to the remaining four," Deffand said. "The first two introduce us to the landscape and the characters. In *The Garden of Love*, the designer of the series wanted us to see the clear division of the country as symbolized by the two castles and the river running in between, commonly assumed to be the Meuse. It was probably his way of trying to prepare us for the eventual conflict, but surely he knew, as we now know, that nothing could prepare a person for the horror portrayed in *The Battle of the Lion and the Unicorn.*"

Like a little girl absorbed in a wonderful fairy tale, Gaby's eyes widened as she gratefully accepted a chair and sat opposite Deffand. With his gaze returning often to the tapestry, he continued the story of the sacking of Dinant.

In 1466, the Duke of Burgundy, known for most of his reign

as Philip the Good, responded swiftly and sternly to political unrest in the south. Considering the martial mentality of the times, the razing of the town was hardly unusual. It probably wouldn't have rated so much as a footnote, if not for the extreme cruelty exercised by some of his soldiers. A cadre of overzealous Burgundians decided to teach the people of Dinant a lesson. They took eight hundred citizens, tied them back to back, and drowned them in the Meuse.

"Eight hundred people! That must have been most of the town," Gaby said.

"It was. If not for the courage of Edouard and others like him, the entire town would have perished. Despite the fact that he was pledged to support Philip, he hid the lady of Dinant and her entire family until the sacking was complete and Philip's army had gone. Miraculously, because their castle stood on a distant bluff and not directly in the line of fire, it was spared total destruction."

"Does the tapestry depict the drowning?" Gaby asked, wondering whether or not designers or weavers of the time would have been bold enough to make such political statements.

"I know what you're thinking, and believe it or not, yes it does. I saw *The Battle of the Lion and the Unicorn* before it was auctioned off, and I must confess I was shocked. Not only does it show several townspeople standing in a river tied back to back, but if you look closely, done in very small scale, as if standing off in the distance watching, is one yellow ram, clearly meant to represent Philip's Order of the Golden Fleece."

"Good for Edouard. Obviously, he had the guts to tell it like it was!"

"Our Monsieur de Rosier was quite a fellow," Deffand said, smiling at her intense involvement. "That's probably why he won the hand of his lady."

"What was her name?" Gaby asked.

"Marguerite." Again, Deffand pointed. "Notice the bunch of daisies in her left hand? In all the tapestries, she's either wearing a crown of daisies, holding a bouquet, or standing near a flurry of white-topped flowers."

"Because," Gaby said, displeased with herself for overlooking the obvious, "in French a *marguerite* is a field daisy."

"Exactly," Deffand said. "In medieval times, it was also called the 'maudlin daisy' in honor of Mary Magdalen."

"What was Marguerite's family name?"

"No one knows for sure." He directed her attention once again to the unicorn. "See the collar around his neck? It bears a unique monogram. Though I've never seen *The Meeting* or *The Marriage of Brussels*, it's said that the same monogram appears in those two pieces also."

Gaby rose, walked over to the tapestry and leaned over to examine the two initials. They were large, royal-blue Roman M's, abutted and tied together by a thick, spiraled gold cord.

"Frankly," Giles continued, "it's one of the unsolved mysteries of the Dinants. Despite voluminous research, no one has ever been able to come up with a verifiable name."

"What about the de Rosiers? Didn't they have any old family documents?"

"Possibly, but it appears as if the last of the de Rosiers were wiped out in the First World War when the Germans decided to imitate dear, old Philip the Good and make Dinant into a parking lot. As far as anyone knows, no one survived. The assumption is that whatever papers they might have had either disappeared or are hidden away somewhere in the keeping of people who have no idea what they have or how valuable it is."

"So Marguerite's maiden name is simply lost to history," Gaby remarked, momentarily awash with bittersweet feelings of regret for the forfeiture of Madame de Rosier's identity.

"They didn't have hyphens back then," Giles said as he stood and made his way to the control panel where he pressed a button that initiated the tapestry's descent.

"Has anyone ever placed an inquiry ad in a newspaper?" Gaby said above the squeaking. "Maybe it would turn up a de Rosier or someone who knew a de Rosier."

"As a matter of fact, Garrett did exactly that. Several years ago, he ran three ads. One in Antwerp. One in Brussels. And one in Dinant."

"Any responses?"

The lift stopped. Giles hunkered over the tapestry, smoothing the gentle folds and then bundling it into a tidy, fat square.

"Only one and that was from a Baron Pieter von Gelder who wanted to know if Garrett had had any other responses."

"Could he be a de Rosier?"

Deffand shook his head.

"We thought of that, but von Gelder's line is well documented. He's practically pure Flamard with a touch of German thrown in every couple of generations. There's not a drop of Walloon or French blood in that man's body. More's the pity, I say."

Gaby turned contemplative, her index finger absently tracing the line of her chin.

"Doesn't it seem strange," she said, half to herself, "that there weren't *any* other responses, even from quacks? And that the only respondent was someone who claimed to have no information but instead was looking for information?"

Giles had asked similar questions of Garrett at the time, and the two men had discussed the matter ad nauseum, exhausting just about every possibility.

"Baron von Gelder is a collector of some repute," he said, giving Gaby the answer he and Garrett had settled on, "so if you assume that he knows about the Dinant tapestries and perhaps is interested in owning them, and you assume he knows that de Rosier is the name of the man who commissioned them, then I suppose it's not strange at all."

"Could he have been one of the anonymous buyers of the three sold at auction?"

"It's possible," he said, reconsidering that point while he lifted the tapestry and prepared to go. "Unfortunately, we have no way of knowing."

"Is he a player?" Gaby asked as they entered the private elevator that led to the executive floor and the vault where the two Dinants were kept.

"If you mean can he afford high-ticket items, the answer is decidedly yes."

"Then for all anyone knows, he could own one or two or all three of the Dinants."

"Or he could own none of them," Giles reminded her. "He's not a de Rosier, but he is Belgian. Perhaps his call was what he said it was—just idle curiosity about an errant national treasure."

The elevator opened. Gaby and Deffand walked down a short hall, turned right and entered another large room, this one wired and outfitted to house on-premise valuables like jewelry, certain artwork, an occasional piece of furniture, and, of course, the Dinants. As Deffand returned *The Garden of Love* to its place, Gaby watched with distracted eyes.

"I don't buy that," she said, feeling a bit like one of her girlhood heroines, Nancy Drew. "The most obvious explanation is an acquisitive interest in the Dinants. But if that's the case, why didn't he express his interest openly? If he's a collector, surely he recognized the Castleton name. Why didn't he just tell Garrett that if and when the missing Dinant appears, he wants to be contacted?"

"Perhaps he felt a declaration like that, before the tapestry was even found, would have been not only premature, but bad business. After all, to lay his cards on the table so early gives Garrett the upper hand. Having someone like von Gelder already announced allows Garrett to use him as bait. With enough big fish in the pond, the floor price would probably become inflated way beyond any measure of reality. Maybe von Gelder was simply protecting the bottom line."

"Or maybe he was reconnoitering," Gaby said in a tone that made it clear she had been off on her own track and only half listening to Deffand. "Maybe that call was his way of finding out the sort of company he was in."

"What do you mean?" Giles led her out of the security office, back into the hall, closed the door behind them and locked it.

"My guess," Gaby said, her face pinked with Dinant fever, "is that he was trying to find out how many other players are in the game and how close any or all of them are to the jackpot. My guess is that the name of Baron Pieter von Gelder should definitely be added to the list of people hunting *The Marriage of Brussels*."

"It's already a long list," Deffand said, noting the accelerated pitch in Gaby's voice and smiling to himself. "And it seems to get longer every day."

Irina Stoddard was not having a good day. She had broken two nails. The hairdresser had shown up an hour late for her appointment. Max was in Europe and had phoned to say he wouldn't be returning for at least another week. A source she had counted on for information about the missing Dinant tapestry had come up empty. Chelsea Reynolds and her trashy entourage had been seated at the next table at lunch. The Sweetheart Ball was less than two weeks away and her Lacroix hadn't arrived. And now there was a message to call her father. Could an earthquake be far behind?

As she waited for Garrett Sr. to come to the phone, she wondered what might have prompted this rare call.

Recalling that her brother had left for London the day after the auction and had been there for more than a week, Irina speculated that perhaps something he had said had provoked the call. It would be just like him, she thought, to take father aside and with that well-meaning, goody-two-shoes manner of his, fill the old man's ear with tales. Irina comforted herself that there wasn't much to tell—at least not much that Garrett knew.

Had Charles or Sarah caused another fuss? A scandal this time, perhaps? Though it was true her parents were more relaxed with their grandchildren than they had ever been with her, their expectations remained dizzyingly high. The last time Irina had spoken to her mother, Charlotte had fretted that Sarah was running with a crowd that bordered on unsuitability. Translation: there wasn't a royal in the lot. She disliked the flat Sarah lived in, the two young women she lived with, the hirsute sculptor she was afraid her granddaughter was—God forbid—sleeping with, the hours she kept, and the trendy clothes she wore. Other than that, Charlotte supposed, the child was a delight.

As for Charles, other than declaring himself a homosexual or shaving his head and becoming a Hare Krishna, nothing could possibly be as traumatic as his recent announcement that he wished to leave his job at Castleton's and become a furniture maker. Winston, delighted that Charles was extricating himself from the clutches of the Castletons, immediately responded with an offer to bankroll his son's new venture. Irina, unwilling to be cast in the all-too-familiar role of villain, mouthed acceptance and encouragement, but secretly harbored a sense of ineffable embarrassment. For, whenever Garrett Sr. complained, "How could he do this to me?" as he frequently did, Irina knew he was really asking of her, "How could you fail me?"

"Irina, darling. How are you?"

His booming basso startled her.

"I'm fine, Father," Irina said, collecting herself, adjusting her posture, readying paper and pen in case note taking was required. "And yourself?"

"Couldn't be better. Your mother and I are about to take off for Morocco and give these old bones a bit of sun, but before we left, I wanted to tell you how pleased I was to hear about the success of the auction and about how well things are going in New York."

He sounded jubilant, almost as pleased as when she had told him of Winston's proposal and her acceptance.

"Whatever do you mean, Father?" she said, doodling Max's name on her notepad.

"Garrett's been regaling us with all the snappy innovations behind the booming success of our youngest branch."

Her mood descended as quickly as it had elevated.

"There have been so many changes," she said flatly, erasing Max from her thoughts if not from her notes. "Which ones has he been telling you about?"

Even before he spoke, Irina felt certain that her own contributions—cutting back on unnecessary staff, reorganizing credit check procedures, arranging for extra storage facilities, and overseeing the care and feeding of Castleton's elite corps of international representatives—had not met the lofty criteria required for inclusion on her brother's list of "snappy innovations."

"Things like the charity auctions. The dinner dances. The lecture series. The clothbound catalogues for special auctions. The celebrity ski race."

Irina's face blanched and then flushed red with anger.

"Ski race? What ski race?"

"I think they've dubbed it Castleton's Celebrity Classic."

"How precious," Irina said, unable to quell the derisive undertone in her voice. "Funny that I don't recall hearing about it."

"That is a bit odd. Especially since Garrett was so enthusiastic and so full of details. Perhaps it slipped his mind."

"That must be it," she said, again restraining herself, but allowing a dab of sarcasm to perfume her words.

"It's scheduled for sometime in late March," her father continued, "out in some godforsaken place called Steamboat Springs, Colorado. I don't know exactly how they've organized it, but since it's for AIDS research and since it's another brainstorm from that new woman . . . what's her name? Gabrielle . . .''

"Didier," Irina said impatiently.

"Didier. That's right. Gabrielle Didier. Well, with her in charge, I'm sure it'll be a spectacular event. She certainly does seem to have a talent for public relations."

"That she does." Irina's pen floated like the pointer on a ouija board, scrawling Gaby's name here and there on her doodle pad, then Garrett's name, then thin lines connecting Gaby to Max to Garrett.

"How well do you know her?"

Her father's voice had a faintly familiar ring to it, a curious, excited, perhaps-wedding-bells-will-be-ringing-soon-and-I-can-finally-have-a-grandson-named-Castleton tone Irina had only heard once before—in the halcyon days preceding Cynthia Hawthorne's disgrace. Had Garrett announced his intention to marry that Didier woman already? Irina had thought they were only in the preliminary stages of a relationship. Since when had it become a courtship? Was it possible that the pace of their involvement had quickened so rapidly? Or was it more probable to assume that Garrett was again being presumptive, behaving like a lovesick pup blurting out premature hopes. Either way, Irina was uncomfortable with her father's interest in Gabrielle Didier.

"I don't know her terribly well," she answered honestly. "She's attractive and obviously quite clever, but I am puzzled as to why someone of her standing would deign to accept an assistantship." When in doubt, raise doubt in the minds of others. "Surely, if she had wanted to have her name on the letterhead, she could have done what other women of our station do. She could have volunteered to be an international rep instead of tagging after one of our staffers."

Garrett Sr. swallowed a laugh.

"I would hardly call Giles Deffand a staffer, Irina. And the way I understood it, Madame Didier was working *with* him, not tagging after him."

They were certainly seeing eye to eye a few minutes ago when they had passed by her office. They were so deep in conversation that they hadn't even looked up when Irina's secretary had brushed by them carrying a stack of folders.

"It was an observation, Father, not a condemnation."

"I'm glad to hear that, because looking at our year-end figures, I tend to agree with Garrett. We're damn lucky to have her."

"Mmm," Irina mumbled, "damn lucky."

With broad, black, deliberate strokes, she scratched out Gaby's name, inking over it again and again until the paper ripped. As her hand moved, her mind raced, considering the fact that her brother was scheduled to spend another week in London and then several days first in Amsterdam and then in Monaco.

On the other end of the phone, the skin on Garrett Sr.'s forehead rutted as he listened to the silence and wondered what was going through Irina's mind. He knew there was no love lost between his children, and on some level he was even willing to claim a certain responsibility for their intense rivalry, but long ago he had decided to ignore much of what went on. That didn't mean he was oblivious to their bouts of gamesmanship or that he approved of them, but unless or until their tug-of-war interfered with the conduct of Castleton business or caused his darling wife to suffer any undue distress, his attitude was to let it be.

"Well, my dear," he said, suddenly eager to be finished with the call, "I'm sure Garrett will be delighted to know that you have everything under control."

"Not yet," Irina thought as she put down the phone, crushed the overworked piece of notepaper in her hand, and slammed it into a nearby wastebasket. "But I will."

Within the hour, Gaby found herself seated in a chair facing the imperious Lady Stoddard, wondering why she had been summoned. As she entered, Gaby had the strangest sensation that, perhaps, instead of walking into an office, she had walked into a carefully painted portrait. The damasked walls, the brass torchères, the throne-back chair, the golden desk appointments, the scepter-straight posture, the tightly combed twist of hair, the multistrand choker of pearls, the ruffled lace collar that rose high on the back of her neck with a starched, self-confident arrogance —it was Elizabeth I redux, the court of the Virgin Queen, reduced in size perhaps, but not in importance. Recognizing the allusion for the conceit that it was, nonetheless Gaby felt intimidated. As she waited for her royal highness to speak, she folded her hands in her lap in an unconscious gesture of obeisance. For what seemed like an interminable stretch of time, there was no conversation, no small talk, no sound other than the cadenced silence of two soldiers at attention. Then Irina's lips spread apart in what Gaby supposed was intended to be a smile, but in truth appeared to be little more than a baring of teeth.

She began. Her voice was soft and cultured, her words clipped and precise. At first, there was a curious monotony to her speech, a metronomic quality that lulled Gaby a bit. But then, as she listened more closely, as Irina's patter became more substantive, she felt herself growing cold, as if an arctic wind had suddenly changed course, wrapping itself around her.

" . . . and in going over the year-end analysis, something terribly disturbing has come to light. There's a chink in the structure of the organization."

Irina paused, hoping for a visible response on Gaby's part, but there was none. Gaby remained infuriatingly calm and composed.

"At first, I couldn't believe it. I guess I didn't want to believe it, but facts are facts. Castleton's New York is teetering beneath the weight of a staff bloated with redundant personnel. We've always prided ourselves on our operational efficiency. Can you imagine how horrified we were to discover that we have a number of people doing exactly the same job?"

She shook her head and lowered her eyes, hoping that when she lifted them, she would be rewarded with fidgeting fingers, or a gnawed lip, or fluttering eyelashes, or one single strand of hair out of place. There was nothing.

"Needless to say, we've decided we must act swiftly in order to forestall a possible crisis. Since we are not without compassion, our general policy in these matters is to cut back where it's the least painful. Naturally, we try to protect those who need protection, those with families to support, those who would be devastated if relegated to the unemployment rolls."

Her lips moved again in that odd curl designed to convey amity and goodwill.

Though Gaby was determined to deny Irina the satisfaction of a reaction, inside, her emotions rollercoastered. Interspersed between spells of utter panic, Gaby experienced small pockets of amusement at the farcical nature of Irina's performance. Her gestures were so broad, her verbiage so pretentious, her use of the royal "we" so overworked, that if not for the catastrophic consequences of what she was doing, and Gaby's suspicion that she was thoroughly enjoying herself doing it, she might have applauded.

"It goes without saying that the notion of losing your particular brand of, how shall I put it . . . enthusiasm? esprit? Yes, 'esprit' sounds right. Well, it's simply tragic, but as can be said about so many tragedies, this one is completely unavoidable."

Her voice dropped an octave, underlining the word "unavoidable," making it clear that there was to be no discussion, no argument, no changing of her mind.

"You see," Irina continued, resting her elbows on the green leather writing surface of her desk and delicately tenting her fingers, "though I would like to think there is another way to ease our current financial pinch, I know from past experience that trimming staff is the quickest way to bolster the bottom line. I hope you understand, Gabrielle, but despite your 'snappy innovations,' I regret I must ask for your resignation." She sighed. It was a deep inhalation of breath, a thorough filling of her lungs, a dramatic expression of rue.

Gaby had to concentrate in order to fight back the fear and anger raging inside of her. It had taken her so long to get where she was. It had been so difficult, so demeaning. The thought of starting over again paralyzed her. But only for a moment. Somewhere deep in her soul, a flame stirred within the ashes of defeat.

Gaby unfolded her hands. She leaned back in her chair. She smiled, crossed her legs, and ran her fingers through her hair—the image of a woman in charge of herself.

"I'm as shocked as you are," she said, deciding that before Irina buried her completely, she would grab hold of the shovel and do a little digging of her own. "It was my understanding that profits were up at Castleton's New York. It was also my understanding that *I* was largely responsible for that upswing."

It was Irina's turn to feel off balance. She had expected some sort of confrontation. After all, wasn't that the underlying purpose of this meeting? To face off against a potential enemy? To challenge, to test one's strength, and then, ultimately, to triumph? But while she had been prematurely relishing her victory, interpreting her opponent's stony silence as a disgruntled yet quiet acceptance of her fate, it appeared as if Madame Didier had been taking aim so that she, too, could fire off a few shots.

"Really, Gabrielle! No one person is ever singly responsible for a large company's success," Irina said, lifting an eyebrow and raising her voice to a deliberately high and patronizing pitch. "That's a rather egotistical delusion, don't you think?"

"You weren't listening, Irina. I never said I was singly responsible for the company's success. I merely reminded you of the fiscal results directly attributable to my contributions and questioned your assessment of those results."

Irina stood. Her hands gripped the front of her desk. Her eyes narrowed. The veins in her neck tightened. This was no longer fun.

"I know how much you enjoyed your tenure here and I'm terribly sorry about all this unpleasantness, but I have no other choice. I'm sure you understand."

Gaby stood also, praying that Irina would not see that her knees were shaking.

"By the way, does Garrett know about this personnel crisis?" she asked.

"I don't make these decisions by myself," she said. "This is a family business, you know."

Gaby tried to hide her disappointment, and while most others would have missed the quick twitch of her lips, Irina caught it. Like a snake's, her eyes were always open, always alert.

"I wish there was another way," she said, adopting the pose of a gracious winner, reaching across her desk and offering to shake Gaby's hand. "But . . . well . . . do you think you could clear out your desk as soon as possible? It's bad for office morale to have someone who's leaving linger."

"I'll be gone by this afternoon," Gaby said coolly, ignoring Irina's gesture, exiting before her real feelings surfaced.

As she reached the door, she turned. Again, Irina smiled. This time, it was genuine.

"Can you believe it? She fired me!"

For the better part of an hour, Gaby had been pacing, letting off steam, ridding herself of pent-up anger and frustration. Armand and Chelsea, called in a moment of weakness, witnessed her soliloquy. They didn't rebut anything she said. They didn't add to what she said. They simply let her rant.

"What garbage that was, all that stuff about the value of my enthusiasm and my innumerable contributions and my fabulous sense of esprit! Bull! She wanted me out of there! O-U-T! Out! But why? I still don't understand. I thought I was doing such a good job. People told me I was. Garrett said I was. Garrett! What hurts is that she claims he knew all about this. That he agreed with her. I thought he cared about me. Am I such a horrible judge of character?" she asked, stopping, looking at Armand for a second, and then returning to her march without waiting for an answer.

"And what about Giles? Why didn't he defend me? Why didn't he tell them what a help I was, what a great job he thought I was doing? I spent the whole morning with him. He was so friendly, so nice. He didn't say a word. I wonder if he knew. I wonder if he cares. I wonder . . ."

"Stop!" Armand moved directly into Gaby's path. As she went to step by him, he took her by the arm and escorted her to a chair, where he stood until she sat. "It's ridiculous to waste all this energy beating yourself and trying to analyze the Mephistophelian mind of Irina Stoddard. Obviously, you've threatened her in some way and she's decided to strike back."

"I barely know the woman."

"To know her is to loathe her," Chelsea said with a disdainful chuckle.

"Okay, so she's not Miss Congeniality," Gaby said. "I still don't know what I did to make her so mad."

"For one thing, you look better in those department store slacks than she does in her finest couture ensemble. And for another, you'd have to be deaf, dumb, and blind not to see that Garrett is ga-ga over you. Since she hates him and he's not exactly president of her fan club, my guess is that you've been caught in the middle in a nasty little game of sibling rivalry."

"If Garrett is so ga-ga, how come he allowed her to do this?"

"You don't know that he did. You only have Irina's word for that, and you can take it from me, her word isn't worth the price of a subway token."

"I couldn't agree more," Armand said, handing Gaby a

brandy and returning to his seat on the couch, "but knowing the clannishness of the Castletons, I hate to say that it would not be out of character for Garrett to put business concerns first and his personal feelings second."

"You think he knew and approved?" Gaby said, wondering whether it was pride or the beginning of passion that was behind her need to know the depth of Garrett's involvement.

"Let's say there's some truth behind what Irina said. Let's assume there was some in-house study of the New York office and it showed a potential problem. This branch is Garrett's baby, and frankly, I can imagine him doing whatever he thought was necessary in order to bring it into line, including approving personnel cuts. That doesn't mean he okayed each and every name, but to take this a little further, what if he did see your name on the list? You have to remember, he thinks you're independently wealthy. In his mind, for you to lose this job would mean that, yes, you'd be disappointed and perhaps a bit put off, but truly, the worst problem you'd have is too much free time."

Gaby nodded. "You're right. I painted my way into this corner and somehow, I have to paint a way out." She punctuated her sentence with a heavy sigh. "It doesn't matter why or how this happened. It did. And I have to find a way to pay my bills. Despite my grand surroundings and my limited, but very well-to-do circle of friends, I'm flat broke."

"I could . . ."

Gaby held up her hand and stopped Chelsea before she could continue.

"No loans. It's tough enough repaying strangers. I don't want to have to worry about repaying friends. Thanks anyway."

"How about coming back to the shop?"

Gaby shook her head. "I hate to remind you of unpleasant truths, but you don't have enough traffic in the shop to require a staff."

"Well then, what if I call some friends and see if they need any help. You are experienced now, you know."

"That's a lateral move," Chelsea said, nixing the idea. "I don't like lateral moves unless I'm in a horizontal position."

"I suppose I could go back to Bergdorf's."

"Back being the operative word." Chelsea grimaced. "Up is where you should be headed, darling. Up!"

"Where? How? And to what?"

"I don't know yet. Let me think."

"What about Europe? Your French is perfect. Your knowledge of antiques is superb. And there's nothing like a sojourn in Paris to lift the spirits," Armand said. "Perhaps Jacques needs some assistance. Or one of the other *antiquaires*. Come to think of it, what about the Hotel Drouot? I know someone there, and certainly Castleton's is the perfect reference."

"I'd love that," Gaby said honestly, "but I can't move further away from Steven. Not now, anyway."

"I've got it!" Chelsea bolted off the couch. "A broker! Gaby could be an antiques broker!"

"That's not a bad idea," Armand said, letting the concept take shape in his mind. "Not bad at all. What do you think, Gaby? You've seen how brokers work at auction and you've seen them in my shop, scouting for pieces clients have requested. It's really no more difficult than being a personal shopper. The difference, of course, is that what you're seeking isn't always easy to find, but if you do find it, the rewards can be enormous."

"I think the standard fee is twenty percent," Chelsea said, her face still contemplative, still working the notion through. "That's not bad when you consider that most people who take advantage of the service are looking for major pieces with big price tags."

"It does sound good," Gaby said, feeling a bubble of excitement but keeping a rein on her emotions. "It sounds like something I would love doing. There's one small problem, however. Being a successful broker takes high-powered contacts and time to build a reputation. I don't have either of those things."

"Ah, but I do." Chelsea giggled. "I've had three rich husbands, and thanks to them I have more high-powered contacts in more places than the CIA. As for reputation, have you forgotten who you are? The elegant, swellegant Madame Didier of upper Fifth? I keep telling you, this is show biz without the footlights, darling. You look the part. You sound the part. And what's most important, people think you *are* the part."

"Okay," Gaby said, pacing again, "so I've created an impression. Why should anyone pay me to find precious antiques or *objets d'art?* Why don't they look for themselves or hire already established brokers?''

''Because most major collectors are obsessive. If they devoted every waking minute to antiquing, they still wouldn't have time to search for everything on their lists. And as for hiring you, the collectors I know would hire Howdy Doody to shop for them if they thought he could find that one elusive piece. Besides, most of them owe me favors. Trust me, you'll get more commissions than you can handle.''

''You make it sound so simple.''

''It is simple.''

Gaby turned to Armand. ''What do you think? Can I do it?''

He smiled. ''Of course you can. You know how to check for authenticity. You know how to check prices and provenances. Your knowledge of antiques is broad enough to handle a diverse clientele. And if you're not sure where to find something outside of New York, you have me, my family, and your Oncle Bernard. You're a bright, talented woman, Gaby. You can do anything you set your mind to.''

Just then, Gaby's mind was spinning. Positives and negatives bumped into each other like snowflakes in a storm until they blurred into one blinding sheet of white. She walked to the window, pulled aside the thick brocade drapes, and stared across Fifth Avenue to Central Park. It seemed like forever ago that she had stood at a window and peered out at New York City. Then she had been a naïf, a country girl running away from the pain of a bungled marriage and a vacant home. She was still somewhat naive—she recognized that—but this time it felt different, she felt different. At some point, she wasn't sure exactly when, she had stopped running away and started running forward. Moreover, she realized as she turned and looked at her two friends, she was no longer running alone.

''I have two favors to ask,'' she said, addressing herself to Chelsea.

''Name them.''

''Would you be willing to throw a party so I could meet these bigwig collectors?''

Chelsea grinned. ''Would I be willing to throw a party? Will Bloomingdale's take back absolutely anything? Of course!''

"How quickly can you arrange it?"

"Would the end of next week be too soon?"

Gaby laughed. "No. That would be great."

"What's the other favor?" Chelsea asked.

"Can I borrow a dress?"

12

Chelsea Harper Patterson Stoddard Reynolds believed in laughter and caprice and spontaneous festivity. She believed that without wide, exuberant brushstrokes, the world paled to a numbing shade of gray. She saw nothing noble about penury and nothing praiseworthy about restraint. Money was a commodity. It was meant to be traded, exchanged for packages of pleasure, and whether those packages were material, emotional, spiritual, or sexual, her attitude was the same: you got what you paid for.

She was also completely honest with herself. She knew that certain people disapproved of her, but Chelsea didn't care. She not only relished controversy, she welcomed it. In a small pond stocked with only big fish, you had to fight for attention. And if you were splashy enough and arrogant enough and confident enough and unusual enough, even when the tongues wagged, eyebrows also lifted in a respectful salute.

Certainly, there were those who thought having small shopping bags and satin ribbon imprinted with one's initials was terribly gauche. There were those who felt that only invitations engraved on the finest vellum were truly comme il faut. And there were those who thought it a horrible solecism to allow less than six weeks between the invitation and the event. Yet not a single person who received one of Chelsea's high-gloss, lipstick-red bags didn't sift through the tuft of crimson tissue paper like an excited child, searching for whatever treasure Chelsea had stuffed inside. Beneath the tissue, wrapped in Chelsea's trademark English garden chintz, were small Battersea boxes from Tiffany's emblazoned with a spray of snowy white roses. Within was a sprinkling of dried rose petals and a short, handwritten note requesting that the recipient join Chelsea "at her apartment on Thursday next, at seven-thirty in the evening for a black tie dinner." Who the honoree was and why he or she rated a salutatory dinner was left to the imagination.

Not a single person declined. On the following Thursday, fifty people—from Texas, New York, and London—arrived at Chelsea's Park Avenue apartment practically panting with anticipation.

Though most of the guests had been to her home before, those who hadn't found themselves in a gracious, cultivated surrounding reminiscent of an English country house. In the entrance hall, where a chamber music trio played Bach, a softly swagged ceiling, a Regency table, a Venetian looking glass, and a collection of wooden canes in a porcelain umbrella stand set the tone that continued throughout the spacious, ten-room apartment.

The drawing room, a riot of cherry-red walls and various printed fabrics, created a portrait of an eighteenth-century manor. Despite the vividness of color, there was a reticence to the design, a conscious effort to reproduce an era without belaboring a point. Two nineteenth-century Aubusson rugs, each replete with lush roses muted by time, established seating areas. At one end, a fire blazed in a wooden-manteled hearth garnished with small vases of fresh roses, a George I giltwood mirror, a mantel clock, porcelain candlesticks, and two pen-and-inks. Flower-strewn chintz, parchment-pale damask, and ribbon-striped silks upholstered loveseats and cushy chairs, filling the room with a profusion of pigments and patterns. Chinese Chippendale side tables, Oriental porcelain lamps, petit-point throw pillows, and part of an impressive assemblage of Chelsea botanical plates added to the period setting.

It was into that room that such names as Lady Philip Montgomery, Vincent Prado, Mario Buatta, Maximilian Richard, Mark and Duane Hampton, Armand Lafitte, Saul and Gayfryd Steinberg, Lord and Lady Pembroke, Oscar de la Renta, Annette Reed, John and Susan Gutfreund, Laura Hunt, Vincent Forcade, Bill Blass, and Lynn Wyatt came to mingle with other stars of the social set.

Gaby had to struggle to maintain a façade of calm assurance. Inside, she trembled with near phobic terror at committing some terrible gaffe. The party was barely five minutes old when it appeared as if her premonition would be realized. Chelsea introduced her to a cluster of new arrivals, one of whom, Bill Blass, offered compliments about the elegance of her appearance. Gaby smiled. She nodded politely. She offered what she believed was an appropriate thank you and was about to move on when a sharp, pointed jab from Chelsea's elbow prodded her memory. The short, sequined, leopard-print skirt and side-tied black cashmere sweater she was wearing had been designed by none other than Bill Blass.

The incident left her weak with insecurity. Needing a lift, she sought a friendly face.

Armand had come alone. They had decided it was best for them to continue the charade of mere acquaintance. When she spied him standing in a far corner, she was disappointed to find him deep in conversation with a woman unfamiliar to her. She started to turn away, but he had spotted her and smiled invitingly.

"Madame Didier. What a pleasure to see you again." He bussed her hand, holding onto it for an extra moment, squeezing it to let her know all was well. "May I introduce Lady Philip Montgomery."

"Annabel, please." The woman's smile was warm, her grip firm.

Gaby returned the smile and the handshake, noticing how creamy her complexion was, how clear, how moist, how stereotypically, enviably English. She noticed, too, the delicacy of the older woman's maquillage: a faint blush of pink rouging her cheeks, a splash of peony painting her lips, a soft smudge of celadon haloing her eyes, their normally hazel shade greening in favor of the peridot tone of her dress. Then, subtleties registered and appreciated, Gaby's gaze fell to the shoulder of Annabel's dress. There, pinned to a simple drape of chiffon, was an emerald and diamond brooch that positively dazzled. The emerald, a sugarloaf cabochon, was the size of a quail's egg, its color so dark, so rich, so full of fire, it seemed to smolder within its glittering nest.

"Armand tells me that you're the reason we're all gathered here this evening. He said that you used to be associated with Castleton's but you've left in order to launch a new career. How marvelous!"

Gaby forced herself to refocus, to concentrate on Annabel, to take her eyes off that fabulous jewel. As she did, she secretly acknowledged that no matter how long she stayed in New York, or how many of these parties she attended, or how many lords and ladies she met, she'd never lose her bourgeois fascination with the everyday opulence of the upper class. This was Thursday night. Thursday night in Wadsworth might have brought out a bingo board or a deck of cards or a board meeting–city council–PTA type of dress. But never tuxedos and never jewelry the likes of this.

"It is marvelous," Gaby said, noting that when Annabel smiled, Armand smiled. "I love antiques, and the idea that I might be able to help find that one rare, important piece to complete or enhance a collection is truly thrilling."

"How fortunate for both of us that you feel that way."

Gaby tilted her head quizzically.

"You see, I've developed a sudden, inexplicable passion for things fussy and French." She paused. Her face remained inscrutable, but Gaby had caught Armand's self-conscious weight shift, an added lilt in Annabel's eyes. "André-Charles Boulle, in particular," she continued. "You see, my dear, there's a wall in the drawing room at my family estate in Swindon that seems to be positively screaming for one of his masterpieces. Unfortunately, my energy level doesn't quite meet the level of my passion, and while I used to love visiting the salesrooms and antiques shops myself, I'm afraid it's become far more exhausting than exhilarating. If you're willing to take on the task, I would love to commission you to find it for me."

Gaby's heart double pumped, one beat with excitement, the next with gratitude. Someone had actually entrusted her with a commission! And something as grand as a piece by Boulle! Though she knew that Armand had initiated the suggestion—she wished she could hug him right then and there—she plumped up her confidence by reminding herself that Lady Montgomery didn't have a gun pointed at her back. She didn't have to go along with him. After all, something like a cabinet by Boulle involved a great deal of money. She didn't have to agree.

"I'd be delighted." Did she sound too eager? Too desperate? She had to be more businesslike, more professional. "Do you have a preference for first part- or second-part boulle work?"

André-Charles Boulle, one of the most famous *ébénistes* in the court of Louis XIV, veneered his cabinets with a combination of tortoiseshell and brass, sometimes mixed with pewter, lapis lazuli, or wonderfully exotic woods. Intricately patterned, delicately cut, the veneer was an artful blend of dark and light, a chiaroscuro contrast completely unique at the time. First-part boulle work used the darker tortoiseshell as the background, the lighter brass pattern laid into it. Second-part boulle work was the opposite, the brass forming the ground, the dark becoming the overlay.

"To be honest," Annabel said, having given Gaby's question a few moment's thought, "I'm not interested in parts. I'm interested in the whole." She smiled again. Armand smiled again. "I want the best, most outrageously glorious piece you can find. How does that sound?"

Almost impossible, Gaby thought. "Challenging," she said.

Under Armand's pleased, avuncular eye, Gaby and Annabel discussed the details of their arrangement. As Chelsea and Armand had suspected, when the group standing next to Annabel heard snippets of the conversation, one woman, a Houstonite resplendent in an off-the-shoulder gold satin sheath and diamond choker, decided to be the next to claim Gaby's attention. After some conversation, she too offered a commission, hers for late-nineteenth-century Berlin painted porcelain plaques. Another Texan, a dark-haired beauty in head-to-toe black with the unlikely but, as it turned out, befitting name of Lush, couldn't be in town when Sotheby's auctioned off an enormous Beauvais tapestry she had her eye on, so the job went to Gaby. The gentleman standing with her, a huge person with a linebacker's body and a sepulchral, bass voice, confessed an incongruous love of paperweights. Minutes later, Gaby had concluded her first sale. He was looking for St. Louis fruit weights. She owned six. He wanted three.

"If you don't mind," Chelsea interrupted, bringing yet another commission to a conclusion. "I'm going to steal my guest of honor and introduce her to those on the other side of the room." With a light tug, she took hold of Gaby's arm and steered her out of the corner. "How're things going?"

"Great, I guess."

"Why the question mark?"

"It's fabulous, but it's happening so fast and coming so easy."

"What did you expect? These people are not dumb. They know why they're here and, yes, their requests are favors, just as I told you they would be. You just do your thing, get them what they want, and believe me, they'll be happy to hire you again."

"I know. I just hope I'm not in over my head."

"Why would you think that?"

"Because it's going to take a miracle to find some of the things they're looking for!"

"You don't need a miracle, darling. You've got Uncle Bernard in Paris and Armand and me here."

"That's true." Gaby reached out, forgetting that she and Chelsea were supposed to be recent acquaintances. "I can't tell you how grateful . . ."

"Please." Chelsea held up her hands, fending off Gaby's intended embrace. "One never gushes when wearing cashmere. It's simply not done." She grimaced, stepped back, and surveyed her friend. "By the way. How come that outfit looks better on you than it does on me?"

"Does it really look good?" Gaby asked, needing confirmation.

"It must be the dark hair."

"Seriously. Does it fit? Did I tie the sweater right?"

"We're the same size, almost the same height. You're thinner, damn you. You've always been thinner. That must be it."

"I only had these plain gold earrings. Everyone here is bedecked and bejeweled. Am I underdressed?"

Chelsea sighed.

"Gabrielle. Trust me. You are to die from. You have quickened the pulse of every man in this room, including most of the waiters, who, I can assure you, have never ever felt a single flutter for a female in their entire lives. And for your edification, a seven-thousand-dollar outfit can never be considered *under* anything. Now follow me. I want you to met Belle.''

''Seven thousand dollars? My God! Does this come with snow tires or a warranty?'' Suddenly, Gaby was afraid to breathe, let alone sweat. ''What if I spill something on it? Or someone else spills something on it?''

She had barely recovered from one shock when she was gifted with another. Belle Reynolds, Chelsea's stepdaughter, was one of the most beautiful young women Gaby had ever seen. Tall, blond, with a heart-shaped face and pale sea-green eyes, she looked amazingly like Chelsea, except that Belle's mouth was rounder, distinguished by a slight overbite which pushed out her upper lip, exaggerating its fullness, accentuating its ripeness. Her hair was flaxen, naturally streaked, and shiny, like the silken strands inside a husk of corn. It was long, brushed back off her broad, high forehead, hanging down her back in gentle waves. Her dress, a short, sleeveless tube of black velvet, was high necked and somewhat prim, but underneath, the sinuous curves of her body asserted themselves, the voluptuousness of her form contrasting with the innocence of her face. The only jarring note was the uncharacteristic excess of Belle's perfume. One would have thought that someone of her age would have preferred something lighter, something woodsier, something more elegant than the heavily floral scent she wore. She positively reeked.

''I've told Belle all about you,'' Chelsea said, placing an affectionate, protective arm around her stepdaughter's shoulder, lowering her voice to a conspiratorial whisper. ''She knows we're old buddies and she knows that no one else knows.''

They hugged and giggled, like two little girls sharing a delicious secret. For a moment, Gaby allowed Steven to intrude on her thoughts. She wondered what he was doing, who he was with, if he missed her as much as she missed him.

''I've given Belle permission to ask you anything she wants about my sordid past. However,'' Chelsea said, furrowing her brow and shaking a finger at Gaby with mock menace, ''I haven't given you permission to tell her the truth.''

''Your reputation, such as it is, is safe with me.'' Gaby crossed her heart, put her pinky to her lips, and reverently held it up to heaven.

"Okay, my pets. I'm off to hostess. Be good." With a dramatic flourish, Chelsea turned and, like a guided missile, sighted another group to entertain, projected herself into the center, and then allowed the force of her personality to explode.

Belle and Gaby watched with undisguised admiration. It was difficult to believe that someone so electric, so volcanic, could look so delicate. But she did. With her light, near-white blond hair, her honey-gold lace dress, and the brilliance of the canary diamonds sparkling at her ears, neck, and wrists, Chelsea looked like a fragile concoction of spun sugar, the friable crown on a *gateau St. Honoré*. Her dress, a spare sheath which hung loose from her shoulders with no discernible shape, appeared modest and reserved, like a lace curtain sheltering one's private quarters. Even the hemline, which curved up at her outer thigh and rose high on long shapely legs shimmering beneath golden hose, failed to destroy the angelic illusion. If not for the startling slashes of vivid red on her lips and fingertips, she would have been the ultimate vision of auric splendor.

"Was she always this elegant and special?" Belle asked, her gaze still trained on Chelsea.

Gaby had to grin. In college, diamonds and lace were hardly bon ton. The vogue then was dungaree skirts, ponytails, Bass Weejun loafers, white socks, sweatshirts, and, for Sunday dinner, McMullen sweaters and cotton blouses with cutesy-pie floral prints and Peter Pan collars.

"Elegant? No," Gaby said truthfully. "Special? Yes."

Belle turned. The yellow in her eyes cooled as they moved from Chelsea to Gaby, as they became less adoring, more analytical. She was studying Gaby, evaluating her, probably deciding whether or not to trust her.

"How come you and Chelsea stopped seeing each other?" If not for the openness on her face and the unpretentiousness of her manner, Gaby might have found her question too blunt, almost rude. Instead, she took it as Belle's crude way of determining Gaby's level of loyalty.

"Circumstances, I guess. Life pulled me in one direction, Chelsea in another." Belle nodded, as if life was tugging at her also. "Believe me, I would've liked nothing more than to have kept in touch. More than once, I needed a friend like Chelsea. I've missed her."

"Me, too." Belle turned away, as if she had said something wrong. When she looked at Gaby again, she looked embarrassed. "What I mean is, well . . . she and my father are divorced."

"I know." Once again, Steven was there, hovering over the conversation. "And you're not happy about it because you wanted them to stay together."

Belle nodded, a little surprised at the sadness in Gaby's voice.

"I'll bet every now and then, though you don't say it out loud, you feel real selfish because you think that hoping for a reconciliation means you're only thinking of yourself. Right?"

Again, Belle nodded, her eyes widening, warming.

"My son feels the same way." It came out before she could stop herself.

"Chelsea told me," Belle said softly. "I won't say anything."

"Thanks." Suddenly uncomfortable, Gaby tossed her head, throwing her hair off her shoulder, as if that simple gesture could brush away the past, erase all the pain the divorce had brought both her and Steven. "You know, Belle, we seem to have an awful lot in common. Something tells me that's why Chelsea brought us together. What do you think?"

"I think you're right." She smiled, even if only briefly. "Chelsea told me I had to come tonight so I could meet you."

"Well, I'm glad you did. I like you. I'd like to be your friend."

"I'd like that, too." Her eyes brightened, but then the sunlight left. "I'm not very good at making friends."

So shy, so needy. Did the divorce do this to her? Had her divorce done that to Steven?

"Don't be so hard on yourself," she said. "Not everyone is a social butterfly, especially when they're young. Some people need more solitude than others. They need space to grow, quiet time to think. I know I did. My son does."

Like a piece of colored glass refracting a ray of light, Belle's face displayed several emotions at once, from grateful to thoughtful to hopeful.

"Maybe someday I'll get to meet him."

"Why not?" Gaby said, wishing she could arrange something immediately, wondering why she felt an undercurrent of urgency about helping Belle.

"Why not what?"

He seemed to come from nowhere. How long had Max been standing there? What had he heard?

"Why not sample the champagne?" she said lightly.

"Great idea!"

Max found a waiter and, within seconds, the three of them were clinking glasses and chattering like old friends. Most of the time, Max's attention was directed to Belle. He seemed to know just which questions would elicit a spontaneous, positive response, just which conversational path would make Belle feel relaxed and safe. He asked about school. Not generally, but specifically about her art classes. He asked if she was involved in a particular project. When she said yes, that she was working on a large-scale oil painting, he asked if she had stopped doing watercolors.

"I didn't realize you and Belle knew each other," Gaby said, a bit confused.

Max smiled.

"We didn't before tonight. But I'm honored to make her acquaintance." He bowed and Belle blushed. "Your stepmother allowed me to view your work. You're a very talented, very sensitive artist, Belle, and I'm impressed. Watercolor is a difficult medium, but you've managed to convey remarkably strong emotion even with a pale palette." All at once, he laughed. "Do I sound like an art critic or a fan?"

"A little bit of both," she said, with a look of infatuation dusting her face. "But it's okay, since everything you've said is so nice."

"How did I miss them?" Gaby asked, feeling remiss and a bit left out. "Where are they? I don't remember seeing a group of watercolors."

"You're the guest of honor," Max said. "You're supposed to be nervous, not observant. Besides, Belle's paintings are in Chelsea's bedroom." He paused, letting both women play Victorian and feign shock. Then, in a stage whisper, he said, "I told her I had to make a very private call." He snapped his fingers. "Instant access to the bedchamber of Madame Reynolds." He turned to Belle and winked. "Women love mystery. It works every time." Max's eyes continued to tease as he turned to Gaby. "Remember that," he said. "So the next time I tell you I have to make a private call . . ."

"I'll know what you're really after," Gaby said, suddenly feeling giddy and more adolescent than Belle.

"Speaking of what I'm after," he continued, "let me congratulate you on your new venture."

"Thank you."

"If you would allow me, I'd like to add my requests to your shopping list."

"That's very kind."

"It's also very self-serving. Collectors never have enough eyes, ears, hands, or time to find everything they want. That's why people like you are so necessary." He smiled, and suddenly Gaby felt necessary. "You already know I collect Biedermeier. I'd like you to keep your eyes open for anything and everything you can find."

"That's rather broad."

"True, but since Biedermeier only had a twenty-year surge of popularity, it's a rather limited category to begin with. The key is to look for the exceptional. Decorative arts in particular. If you find something, call me. I'll give you numbers so you can reach me anytime, anywhere. And if it would make it easier, it would be my pleasure to invite you to my apartment and show you what I have."

"It would be helpful," she said, thinking that under different circumstances, from a different man, in a different setting, that line could easily have come off sounding like a typical come-on. But there was nothing typical about Max Richard.

"We'll arrange something soon," he said.

Right this minute. After dinner. Tomorrow morning. Anytime, day or night.

"Whatever's convenient," she said.

"I've come to rescue you," Vincent Prado said, whispering in Annabel's ear. "Excuse us, Lafitte."

Without waiting to hear whether or not she wanted to be rescued, Prado spirited Annabel away from Armand and into the entry.

"How could you waste your time with him?" Prado tsked.

"Such a bore. I hope you haven't bought anything from him. Oh, Lord, you haven't, have you?"

Though Annabel thought him thoroughly distasteful, she fought the urge to walk away. Perhaps Prado could help fill in a few of the blanks in Armand's story.

"And why wouldn't I? The Lafittes are world-renowned antique dealers."

"The main branch, perhaps. But not this transplanted sapling. He has been bilking his customers ever since he settled in New York by selling overly restored pieces as well as"—he shook his head, as if what he was about to say was too astounding for words—"passing off reproductions as the real thing. It's just so, well, tawdry."

"I find that difficult to believe."

"I did, too, but Irina Stoddard . . . do you know Irina?" Annabel nodded, more than a little intrigued. "Well, she told me that Castleton's had had to turn away several lots consigned for auction when, after being examined by their experts, they were found to be bogus. Each time, the provenance had been Lafitte et Fils U.S.A."

"How dreadful! Who were those unfortunate souls? Were they friends of yours? Were they friends of mine?"

"I asked Irina, but you know how discreet she is. Her lips were sealed. She refused to say anything, even to me, and we're very, very close."

Annabel couldn't help but wonder about why Irina had been so closemouthed. Was it because she was protecting other people's reputations or was she simply destroying Armand's? Were there names? Had anyone in fact been defrauded? And if not, why had she made up such a destructive tale?

"You know, Vincent, I remember hearing about a long-standing feud between the Lafittes and the Castletons. Perhaps this is an offshoot of that bitterness."

"I didn't know about any feud," he said, piqued that Irina had kept him so uninformed. "But now that I think about it, when Armand staged that foolish mutiny at last year's fair, Irina did say something about loyalty, something to the effect that he was no better than his father. I didn't understand it then. I'm so glad you explained it."

I still don't understand it, Annabel thought. *And really, it doesn't explain a thing.*

Why would Irina be fanning the embers of such an old fire? What would she have to gain? Her father's approval? But for what? Disgracing Armand? That would only make sense if making Armand look bad made Castleton's look good. No. This had to be something personal, something between Irina and Armand.

Prado was still rambling on, but Annabel was no longer listening. She was thinking about Irina Stoddard and what personal ax she had to grind. She was also thinking that Irina had best watch her step. Because if she had conspired in any way to hurt Armand, Annabel would take it personally.

". . . and after the smoked salmon with caviar, Madame Didier will change seats. When she does, clear her place, remove her chair so there is no empty space, and set her up at table number three. After the sorbet, she'll move into the library to table four, and for dessert, number six."

As she spoke, Chelsea's gaze wandered about her vast kitchen, where men and women in white coats and *toques blanches* bustled about, each tending to his or her specialty. The master chef tasted and critiqued. The sous chefs stirred and blended. Cuisinarts whirred. Whisks slapped against the sides of huge copper mixing bowls. Steam perfumed with the scent of herbed stock floated to the ceiling from stainless steel pots. Knives thunked against wooden chopping boards as vegetables were sliced and cut and sculpted for garnish. In a far corner, corks popped as white wine bottles were opened and readied for pouring, red wine decanted and allowed to rest.

Next door, in the breakfast room, dishes were piled on two long tables, each stack arranged as to their order of service. Handsome young men in crisp white shirts, black moiré bowties, tight pants, and short black jackets raced in and out, carrying soup plates to be filled with the *crème de moules au saffron* Chelsea had chosen as her first course.

Leo, her majordomo for the evening, listened patiently, copying her instructions onto a small pad, not because he needed to write them down to remember them, but because he knew it was expected of him. Over the past six months, he had managed several parties for the demanding Mrs. Reynolds. While she could be difficult, often fastidious to the point of fetish, in all fairness she had put him and his crew on the social map.

When he first met her, he had been one of several maitre d's for a chichi caterer. Then Chelsea Reynolds had called and requested his services. He thought she had made a mistake and had offered to transfer her to his employer. He had made the mistake. She didn't want that caterer, but she did want Leo and his staff. When he explained his situation—that he was an employee and couldn't do private jobs—she offered a rather simple solution. Quit. Everyone he worked with was a freelancer who hired out for any caterer who needed him. Why not start his own business, she suggested. Why not become a freelancer himself? With her encouragement, and her backing, he had taken her advice, created Bonhomie, and used her party as his premiere. Within weeks, his calendar had been booked. In return for her patronage, Leo made himself available whenever she wanted.

"Leo! Are you listening to me?"

"I am, madame."

"You look as though your mind is elsewhere."

"It is, madame."

His dark eyes rolled slowly over her body, moving like hands, stopping, lingering, touching each erogenous zone with an intense expectancy. He felt his own body respond. He saw her look at him. He saw her watching the bulge in his pants grow. He thought he saw the side of her mouth curl into a lustful smile. But then her eyes lifted. There was no passion, no carnal desire, no red-hot anticipation. Only cold green anger.

"Get your mind out of my bed and your ass back to work!"

As she spun on her heels and left, Leo laughed. With mock gallantry, he bowed his head toward the door she had just passed through and salaamed with one hand, while pointedly rubbing his groin with the other.

"Certainly, madame," he said, ever the perfect toady. "Your every wish is my command."

Espionage was a tedious business. It wasn't anything like the James Bond movies. There was no wonderfully efficient, blindly devoted Miss Moneypenny to rely on for unearthing trivial but lifesaving bits of research or ironing out the otherwise endless details of planes and trains and time zones. There was no Q to dream up mind-boggling inventions like lethal toothpaste or a car that converted to a submarine, and very few luscious female agents afflicted with chronic nymphomania. More often than not, the real James Bonds floated in and out of the ordinary world, unnoticed.

Max couldn't remember a day when he wasn't a spy. There was never a time when he wasn't hiding from one camp, ferreting out information about another. First it was the Germans. Then it was the postwar "them." Then, it was the Bahutu and Watusi tribes in Africa. Then the Russians. And now, as a special agent for Interpol, it was anyone who had committed a crime against Belgium or the other nations of Western Europe.

Because of the demands placed on him by his huge real estate development business—a business which also provided his cover—and because he bore too many psychological scars from previous missions for superpower political espionage, Max had limited himself to occasional cases, predominantly white-collar crimes, but only those with a dirty, grimy ring around the collar. Usually, his cases involved financial wrongdoings that had their genesis in Belgium, but had then crossed national borders and in some way threatened to undermine the government or weaken the prevailing peace.

Currently, he was involved in a case that had been assigned nearly three years before: to expose an international network of diamond smugglers who were stealing diamonds off ships docking in Antwerp and then smuggling those same diamonds into the United States. To date, though Max had strung together a passel of possible names, lead after lead had dead-ended and he had failed to uncover anything conclusive, anything concrete enough to warrant arrest.

There were several attributes essential to spying: an eye for details, an ear for conversational slips, a mind capable of patching together seemingly mismatched facts into a cohesive pattern, an ability to stay calm and in control no matter how great the provocation, and above all, unwavering patience. Right now, Max's patience was strained. For two courses, he had been forced to listen to the gospel according to Vincent Prado, a lengthy sermon on the need for elegance in an increasingly tacky world. Though his listeners were already believers, Prado droned on.

It was at times like these that Max longed for the early days, when, instead of having to spend hours sifting through meaningless palaver hoping for one tiny grain of insight, a few shiny coins in the right pockets guaranteed a string of loosened lips. During his first tour for Belgian intelligence, in Burundi, the exchange rate had been simpler: a bushel of vegetables bought a quantity of information. Quick. Easy. Painless.

It was different now. In this world everything moved at a slower pace. Social-register spying functioned according to its own rules. In order to infiltrate, one's camouflage had to be perfect. An intruder couldn't be intrusive or obvious; one had to be visible, but not so exceptional as to attract unwanted attention; one had to be private, yet make enough appearances at enough of the right functions so that one's presence was accepted and above suspicion. You had to be one of them. Max was. But still, at that moment, he would have given half his holdings for a reliable mole.

Now, as the dinner progressed and Gaby joined his table and settled herself next to Max, her scent drifted past his nose. It was light. A definite contrast to the heavy-handed Joy favored by most of the other female guests. Feminine. Delicate. His guess was Moulinard de Moulinard. Not the parfum. The eau de toilette.

"And how was table number one?" he asked, delighted at having been provided with such a lovely distraction.

"Terrific!" Her eyes glowed like a little girl's at her very first birthday party. "The conversation was lively, and thanks to the generosity of several of my dinner companions, my shopping list has grown appreciably."

"It appears as if your decision to leave Castleton's was a wise one."

"Yes, I suppose it was."

She tried to smile, but a taste of bitter irony puckered her lips. The decision may have been wise, but it hadn't been hers. She hadn't yet forgiven Irina for firing her. She wasn't certain she ever would. She was practically broke, deeply in debt, without any income she could count on, and though she appeared flushed with the prospects of a flourishing new business, she knew better than to count her commissions before they were earned. All she had were requests. Not one dime had exchanged hands, nor would it until she had located and delivered the merchandise. Worse, in order to find the items on her list, she would have to dip into her meager reserves to finance a European hunting expedition.

A sudden burst of laughter spread through the room like a summer shower. Max turned. Belle Reynolds and Annabel Montgomery appeared to be sharing a private joke.

"Belle and Annabel have become fast friends," Gaby said, as if explaining their behavior. "She used to paint. Annabel, that is. So, naturally, she and Belle have become engrossed in a discussion of schools and mediums and colors and hues and whatever else is of interest to artists. Annabel's also a great storyteller. She's probably . . ."

"Gabrielle, my dear." Vincent Prado's voice rose. He knew it was a bit too loud, but he wanted to attract her attention and he hated to repeat himself. It made him feel foolish. "I haven't had a chance to offer my felicitations on your new career."

"Thank you, Vincent." She still had trouble speaking to him without gritting her teeth.

"As you well know, I'm not a man of empty blessings." He paused and smiled, like an orator about to deliver an important punchline. "My business has expanded so rapidly that where I used to do all my own legwork, lately I've found it impossible to keep up. I utilize the services of many brokers, both here and abroad." Another pause. Another meaningful smile. "I would like to add you to my organization."

People oohed and aahed, and though Gaby hated the adulation he inspired, they were right to be impressed. His was a large organization. He was a famous man with an impressive client list. His favor was worth a great deal of money to her. Gratitude was in order, even if she choked on it.

"I'm honored, Vincent." She offered him her most beguiling smile as well as a slight tip of her head, but then, in a conflicting gesture, she lifted her chin as if to remind him that she was not some common bootlicker, but rather a woman of culture and breeding, a woman whose name added as much prestige to his staff roster as his name added to her resumé.

The move may have been subtle, but Prado caught it. He

spent the next few minutes trying to ingratiate himself with a mix of flattery and bluster. Each time he complimented Gaby, he invited praise for himself by bringing up the January fair or mentioning one of his more stellar clients or discussing his investments. If not for Gaby sitting beside him and a light that had snapped on in a corner of his brain, Max would have made an unnecessary trip to the men's room. Instead, he stayed put.

". . . and so, though I'll be leaving for Europe next week, it's for vacation, not business." Prado turned to the woman on his left. "The fair just exhausts me so." He turned back to Gaby, without missing a beat. "Naturally, I'd like us to sit down sometime before I go. I have so much to talk to you about, so many things to spell out. My clients expect the best, you know." Again, he turned to the woman on his left. This time, he pinched her cheek. "Because *they're* the best." And again, back to Gaby, "But of course, you of all people understand, don't you, dear."

What she understood was that the question was rhetorical and required no verbal response. It didn't matter. She had nothing more she wanted to say to him now, anyway. Tomorrow morning she would call and set up a proper appointment. Once they were secluded in the privacy of his office, she would pin him down as to exactly what he wanted, as well as price ranges and delivery dates. Even before they started, she could tell it was not going to be a pleasure doing business with him.

Having finished with Gaby and feeling assured that he had control of the table, Prado opened another discussion.

"I've decided to buy a villa on the Riviera," he announced, giving it the momentous importance of a decision to donate his organs to science.

"Does this mean you're giving up your flat in London?" Lady Pembroke asked with obvious disappointment.

"No, no. I have too many friends in London, too much work there to ever give up that glorious apartment." He reached across the table and patted her hand. "But I do so love the sun. I almost bought a darling cottage in Antibes last April. I put a bid in, but, well, *c'est la vie*."

He shrugged. Gaby choked. Could he have been talking about Simone's cottage? The thought made her break out in a cold sweat.

"Are you all right?" Max asked, patting her on the back.

She nodded, took a quick gulp of water, and wiped a few tears from her eyes.

"I swallowed wrong," she said, wondering how she would have swallowed seeing Vincent Prado in Tante Simone's home.

"But you know how they say that all things work out for the best," Vincent continued, as if Gaby's coughing had been nothing more than background music. "Recently, I heard about a smashing villa in Cap Ferrat. I won't mention any names because I don't like to speak of those who've hit on hard times, but it used to belong to one of Wall Street's more lustrous stars."

"How much are they asking?" Lush, the dark haired Houstonite with an affinity for Beauvais tapestries and Swedish vodka, repeated her question when she realized she had slurred her words, but she needn't have worried about her enunciation. Prado had intended to talk price from the moment he raised the subject.

"It's hard to believe that a mere three-quarters of a million could buy such a palace." He sighed, as if this magnificent villa were a key setting in a Proust novel. "But imagine the fun I'll have furnishing it! It'll be a pure busman's holiday!"

"It sounds to me as if the deal's already been made," Max said.

Prado tried to look sheepish, but it wasn't part of his repertoire.

"Actually, yes. I bought it to celebrate the enormous success of this year's fair." He bowed his head. Max wondered if he was waiting to be knighted or blessed. "I'm closing on it next week."

"Congratulations, Vincent. Homes in three countries. That's impressive. You've become a bona fide member of the jet set."

Max lifted his wineglass. Everyone else followed suit. Prado beamed. Had he not been blinded by the incandescent glow from his own ego, he might have noticed that while he looked from one tablemate to the other, gauging the level and sincerity of their admiration, there was an odd tilt to the toastmaker's lips.

Gaby noticed. At first, she had accepted Max's toast at face value. Now she wondered. Had the toast been genuine? Had it been meant as mockery? Or was it something else, something beyond her understanding? Did Prado have a weakness she and

Armand had overlooked? And what about Max? Did he know what that weakness was? How did he find out? And why did he care?

The noisette of veal had been served and enjoyed. The glasses of Chateau Laroque had been drained. The plates had been cleared, the stemware replaced. As coffee and dessert—individual, cold Grand Marnier soufflés topped with raspberry *coulis*—was being brought out from the kitchen, and champagne was being poured, two magicians dressed in the classical costume of the French clown Pierrot roamed from table to table, one entertaining in the dining room, the other in the library, both astonishing the guests with examples of sleight of hand. Only two people felt it necessary to leave—Chelsea, to check with Leo on when he planned to serve the petit fours and cordials, and Gaby, who suddenly felt claustrophobic.

It had come on her all at once, that inexplicable anxiety, that horrible feeling that someone had shut off the air and that soon the walls would close in around her. She felt odd. Her skin tingled. Inside, her head felt like a thousand plastic bubbles were popping. People who sat next to her seemed far away, illusory almost, their voices indistinct and unclear. Laughter, which had sounded so bright and gay at the beginning of the evening, had begun to seem tinny and forced. Conversations which had seemed interesting had turned repetitive and shallow. Faces and names had begun to blur.

Excusing herself, Gaby left the library. Bypassing the powder room in the entry, she made her way down the hall to Chelsea's bedroom, hurrying, hoping no one had followed, praying no one would stop her. Her body was trembling, sweating, as if her blood sugar had taken a drastic plunge. Her hand shook as she turned the brass knob, but the instant she opened the door and looked inside, she felt relieved.

It was a large room, lavishly furnished, but as Gaby closed the door behind her, her first sense was of the intense femininity of its mistress. The colors—a warm butterscotch for the walls, a caramel and vanilla for the geometric-patterned rug, the pink and peach and rose tones, the vibrant greens, the massive doses of white—said a blonde lived there as clearly as if a sign had been posted. Chelsea's obvious fascination with chintz continued, upholstering a chaise and an ottoman, skirting a table, draping the windows, encasing the throw pillows. The queen-size bed, dressed in white sheets and shams appliquéd with a single sprig of pink roses, was nestled inside a modern-looking steel frame which had been transformed into an eighteenth-century bower thanks to yard after yard of ruffled, diaphanous organdy hanging in lush gathers behind the headboard and at each of the four corners. On the dressing table, ably guarded by a dark Regency armchair cushioned in yet another floral, sat an assemblage of antique silver hair accessories and crystal perfume flacons, the grouping flanked by two small lamps, everything centered around a gold Empire vanity mirror.

It was all beautiful, but at that moment it was Chelsea's chaise that drew Gaby. Folding a hand-crocheted afghan and putting it to the side, she slipped out of her shoes, lifted her legs, lay back, and closed her eyes. Whether it was the profusion of fresh roses or the lingering scent of a recently burned fragrance candle, the aromatic ambience acted like a sedative, calming her, soothing her. Within seconds, she felt safe and at ease, as if she were in an efflorescent spring garden, a place where flowers bloomed and birds sang and the air was clean and pure. The mirage was so edenic, so enchanting, that she couldn't resist drifting. She dozed, but lightly.

The sharp ring of the telephone jolted her awake. Instinctively, her hand reached out to answer it. She picked up the receiver and put it to her ear. At first, there was no sound except a faint clattering that Gaby soon recognized as coming from the kitchen. She was about to ask who was calling and for whom, when she heard Chelsea.

"What do you want?"

"I want her home." The man's voice was cold and deep.

"She's spending the night. That was our arrangement."

"I've decided I don't like that arrangement, so I'm changing it."

"But why? She's having a lovely time."

"I don't have to give you any explanation. She's my daughter and she'll do what I think is best."

"You're being pigheaded and childish and deliberately cruel." Chelsea spoke so softly that if not for the loathing underlining her words, it would have sounded like a whisper. Instead, it seemed like a hiss. "She hasn't finished dessert. Let her stay."

"I'm coming to get her."

"I have a house full of guests, Drake. I don't want you here. I'll have her home first thing tomorrow morning."

"You'll have her home tonight."

He said no more, but Gaby heard the "or else . . ." as clearly as if he had shouted it.

"Whatever you say."

The phone clicked. Chelsea had hung up. On the other end, Drake Reynolds held for a minute longer, listening to the silence. Then he, too, hung up the phone. As Gaby turned and replaced the receiver in its cradle, she found herself facing the wall behind the chaise.

There she saw a collection of six watercolors, Belle's watercolors, all matted in white and framed in thin, stem-green painted wood. The grouping was a study on solitude, or so it appeared. In each painting, there was one thing separate and apart from the whole: a single shell lying in the sand, a piece of driftwood on a beach, a lone leaf fluttering on a naked tree, a sagebrush lost in the vastness of the desert, a fir tree nearly buried beneath a mountain of snow. She recalled what Max had said about Belle's work and agreed. Her palette was tender and subdued, as only watercolors could be, yet the subject matter was highly charged. What moved Gaby most was the way the landscapes flowed, one hue blending into another with no defined beginning or end, as if each belonged to the other. Not so with the focal point of each painting. That was more intense, its color sharper, its borders more finely edged, a broad halo of white space exaggerating the extent of its separation from its natural surround.

Unexpected tears trickled onto Gaby's cheeks. Belle's paintings spoke of such ineffable loneliness, such complete lack of connection, such permanent isolation, it would have been inhuman not to have been touched by them. But Gaby's response went deeper. She felt as if an enormous cloud of sadness had canopied the room, making the world appear dark and hopeless and depressing. Though at first she wanted to believe she was crying only for Belle, Gaby finally acknowledged that her stream of tears flowed for far more personal reasons.

Within those stark, desolate scenes, Gaby recognized herself.

She, too, was adrift, lost, estranged from the world she had known, unfamiliar with the ways of the world in which she now lived. She, too, felt tossed aside, discarded by those who should have loved her no matter what, by those who had promised to be with her no matter when. While once she had been part of a family, a community, a group of friends, now she was a woman alone, an outcast, a fifth wheel.

She dabbed at her eyes and, catching sight of herself in the small mirror, stared, unblinking, unbelieving, as if she didn't know who the woman in the glass was. The woman looked stunning, despite her tears, but the picture was wrong. She was wrong. She was in a borrowed dress with a borrowed name with a borrowed resumé with a borrowed future. No wonder she had felt so cornered earlier, so strangled, and so panicked. Everyone had been treating her as if she were one of them. She wasn't. And if they didn't know that, she did.

All her life, Gaby had been an honest, forthright, plainspoken woman with simple, basic values. She had never thought much about the future because, as a wife and mother, her future had seemed set. Now nothing was set, nothing was sure. She wasn't even certain what was basic anymore. All she knew was that while she had been hibernating in the warm, dry, safe cave of marriage, the world had changed. When she had been pushed out of her cave, she had discovered that the rules had changed as well. And now, whether she liked it or not, she had changed.

What the hell am I doing? she asked the frightened woman in the mirror.

She sat, folded her arms on the dressing table, and for a few minutes did nothing except stare at her image, feeling guilty and defensive. Then, as if she had just figured out the answer to her own question, she snapped open her purse and began repairing her makeup.

"You're starting over again," she said, making a declaration rather than offering an explanation. "That's what you're doing." She wiped off her lipstick and then relined and rerouged. "You're trying to make a life for yourself. Not for a husband. Not even for Steven. But for you, Gabrielle Didier Cocroft Thayer." A fresh swipe of brown pencil. Additional blush. "Okay. So you're alone. So it's scary. So it's a bitch trying to make ends meet. Guess what? Crying isn't going to help. Neither is feeling sorry for yourself." A spray of cologne. A touch of powder. A quick flick of her hairbrush. "You're not the first woman to find herself in this predicament, and God knows you won't be the last. Others have made it and so can you."

With renewed courage, she stood, smoothed out her skirt, and prepared to face the party again.

The party lasted another hour. By midnight, most of the guests had bid their hostess good night. Though Chelsea had overheard Max offer to take Gaby home, and though she knew how disappointed Gaby would be, she prevailed upon him to escort Belle home. Drake wouldn't harass Max. Also, he wouldn't subject him to a barrage of stupid questions. Had Gaby gone along, Drake might have said or done something that would have embarrassed Chelsea. She and Gaby had just renewed their friendship. She didn't want to risk creating a distance by exposing Gaby to one of her bigger mistakes. Had she brought Belle home herself, there would have been a scene, and that was the last thing she wanted or Belle needed.

By twelve-thirty, the last guest had gone. The help was still clearing and cleaning up. Chelsea poured a brandy and took it to her room. Closing the door behind her, she put the snifter on a table near her bed, stripped, returned her jewels to the safe, her shoes and clothing to the closet. She relit her fragrance candle, shut the lights, and slid naked beneath her sheets.

Veiled by shadows and serenaded by street noises, she sipped her brandy, letting the alcohol slowly anesthetize the pain of her guilt about Belle. Something was terribly wrong. Chelsea knew it. She could see it in the girl's eyes when she had told Belle that Drake had called and her eyes had widened into huge green orbs of fear. She could hear it in her voice when she had pleaded for Chelsea to call him back and force him to let her stay the night. But knowing, seeing, hearing—it didn't matter. She was unable . . . no . . . not unable . . . unwilling to do anything about it. Why? She loved Belle, probably more than she had ever loved any other single person, including her husbands. She wanted Belle to be happy. She wanted to do the right thing. Yet each time her instincts advised her to take steps, Chelsea pulled back. She shut her eyes. She walked away.

She had to. Each time she came close to committing herself

to someone, really committing herself, the dybbuk that had haunted her since childhood appeared, warning her about what would happen if she allowed herself to become attached. She'd suffocate. She'd wither and grow old before her time. Slowly, she'd weaken, sapped of her strength and her spirit by whatever life-sucking whelp she had unwisely taken to her breast. And if she argued? If she tried to explain how much she needed, how badly someone like Belle needed her. If she demanded proof of the demon's claims? With devilish glee, he'd flash before her incontrovertible evidence of the ravages of dependency, evidence she had witnessed firsthand and therefore couldn't deny.

He'd paint a portrait of her mother.

"Chelsea?"

Without her hearing the door open or close, Leo had walked in and stood by her side. He could see that her eyes were blurred from the brandy, but he also noticed that she looked uncommonly vulnerable sitting there in her bed, her pale hair glistening in the dimness, her breasts dappled with dusky, mobile patterns. Quietly, not wanting to break the mood, he removed his clothes, curtained the bed by pulling the organdy falls together, and climbed inside. He had already downed two brandies. The sight of her silky body and the thought of what pleasure that body was capable of giving aroused him almost immediately. He wanted to grab her, but this was Chelsea's bed and she controlled what happened here. Leo waited. Usually, she slithered next to him. Tonight, she didn't. Not knowing whether something was really upsetting her or if this was just a new game she was playing, he shifted toward her, gently wrapping his arm around her shoulders.

"You look so sad." He kissed her cheek. Still, no response. "If something's bothering you, Chelsea, we'll talk. Whatever it is, you can tell me."

She turned, looked at him, and then leaned across him to place her empty brandy glass on the table. Slowly, she opened a small gold box. She took something from it, closed the box, and sat back against the pillows.

"I don't pay you to talk, Leo," she said as she handed him a condom. "I pay you to fuck."

*   *   *

"If you'll leave your name, telephone number, and a brief message, I'll be happy to get back to you. Thank you for calling."

He had to listen to ten self-conscious messages before he got to the one he wanted.

"I found what you've been looking for: an Empire marble-top gueridon that's an utter joy to behold. I tried to buy it for you, but yesterday, Heathrow Antiques, some bloke in Montclair, New Jersey, outbid me. I suppose it's just as well. The plinth was loose. Better luck next time."

Stop. Rewind. Play.

He replayed the message, copying it, and then erasing the tape. Though his instructions were in code, one didn't have to be a trained cipher to understand them. Tomorrow, he would drive out to his contact in Montclair and pick up a gueridon shipped from Heathrow Airport in London. When he got it home, he would jimmy open the base, remove the diamonds, put them in his safe, and wait. In a few days, he'd contact one of several fences. They'd meet. They'd negotiate a deal. And a few days after that, he'd deposit a cashier's check into his Swiss bank account.

As he looked at his memo pad, he felt beads of sweat forming under his shirt collar. He reached inside his pocket, extracted an expensive linen handkerchief, and swabbed his neck. He wondered if he'd ever get used to the idea that he was, in effect, a smuggler. Probably not, but when he had agreed to take part in this operation, he had accepted the idea, just as he had accepted the terms of his employment. It was very risky, very dangerous, but in its way, very exciting.

Though he had asked himself a thousand times why he was doing this, why he was putting his name and, yes, perhaps even his life on the line, each time he received one of those checks, he had his answer. He was doing it for the money, and in his mind the end justified the means. Did he fear being caught? Of course. But more than that, he feared being poor.

Belle sat scrunched in the corner of her bed, knees propped, blankets tucked around her waist, pillows plumped behind her back. Throckmorton, her white Persian cat, slept contentedly by her side. Because she was reading by flashlight, she held the paperback closer than she ordinarily would, distracted somewhat by the reflected image of her eye on the lens of her thin, wire-frame glasses. She was reading a novel, the one all the girls at school had been talking about, the one with all the explicit sex scenes in it. To a person, they had claimed that reading the sex in that book was better than actually having sex. They said it got them hot. Belle was halfway through with it, and not once had she had the promised reaction.

Carefully, so as not to disturb Throckmorton, she turned the page, telling herself to concentrate on the story and forget trying to force herself to feel something she didn't or be something she wasn't. And one thing she wasn't was one of the girls. Though she belonged to the same socioeconomic group—one didn't go to Miss Fulton's without a large bankroll and a long, distinguished lineage—and shared an equivalent family history, including at least one divorce, Belle was quite different from her classmates. For one thing, she was serious. She read, she painted, she liked to listen to the opera or visit museums on Sunday afternoons. Rarely did she party with people her own age. She didn't disco, didn't do drugs, didn't drink enough to get more than a buzz, and for all intents and purposes, didn't date. Not that she wasn't asked. No one as beautiful as Belle could arrive at her senior year in high school without having had a spate of eager suitors. But she wasn't comfortable with young people.

She preferred being with people much older than herself. Like tonight. She hadn't felt out of place being the only young woman at Chelsea's party. She had felt safe. True, everyone had fussed over her, but because they existed on such disparate levels, a distance had been maintained. They didn't ask her questions she didn't want to answer. They didn't badger her to tell them every last detail of her private life. They didn't pry beyond the basics of politeness. They didn't judge her on anything more than her appearance and her table manners. To them, she was a youngster. As long as she looked pretty and behaved herself, her presence was welcome. To the kids at school, she was a peer, and according to them, that gave them the right to push and prod and intrude into places Belle considered none of anybody's business.

Chelsea was Belle's best friend. In a way, she was her only friend. She could talk to Chelsea about almost everything. They laughed and giggled and gossiped. They shopped and lunched and, frequently, toured the art galleries together. Belle loved it when people mistook them for mother and daughter. She cherished the resemblance, as if looking like Chelsea's child meant that somehow, in some mystical way, she had been re-created in Chelsea's image—strong and independent—not weak and helpless and ineffectual the way she really was, the way Louise, her mother, was.

"Belle. Are you still awake?"

Quickly, she clicked off the flashlight and threw it under her bed. The book she tucked in between the bed and the wall. Throckmorton got pulled closer, the blankets higher. She tossed her glasses onto her nightstand and turned toward the wall, keeping her eyes tightly clamped.

The door opened, and for a moment a slash of light fell across her body. Then the door closed and the light disappeared. She heard him coming closer. As he did, she began to shut off, to lock away her emotions, to close off her sensibilities, to hide her pride and to empty her mind of as much conscious thought as she was able. He sat on the bed. She felt his weight push down the mattress, slanting it in his direction. Even though she knew it was useless, she held the blankets closer, hanging on as if they were a life raft.

His hand stroked her hair. When he leaned over and kissed her cheek, she could smell the liquor on his breath. He wasn't drunk, though. Sometimes she wished he were. Then perhaps she could excuse him by saying he didn't know what he was doing, or that after he did, he didn't remember it. But he knew and he remembered. How could he forget? He did it again and again and again.

"I know you're awake, Belle. Turn over and let me see how pretty you look. Come on, baby. Let Daddy see you."

Slowly, she turned her face toward him, keeping the blankets securely wrapped. She opened her eyes, but she couldn't bear to look at the lust on his face, so she focused on his hand. She watched it come nearer to her, watched it pull back the covers, watched it unbutton the top of her pajamas, watched it fondle her breast.

"Please, Daddy. Don't," she whispered, looking into his eyes, pleading with him to stop.

"Daddy loves you, Belle. Show Daddy how you love him."

She shook her head from side to side, protesting, all the while knowing it meant nothing, made no impact, would change nothing, would stop none of the ugliness that was about to happen. He pushed back the thin cotton top, baring her chest and sighing, as if in awe of what lay before him. His hands hovered over her breasts, poised worshipfully. Then he covered them. He rubbed, kneaded, and plied them, pinching her nipples until she wanted to cry out in pain. His breath quickened, coming in that awful way, those short bursts, those explosive puffs of hot, stale breath blowing in her face. She tried to turn away, but his lips found her mouth. They pressed down, pushing her lips against her teeth. His tongue jammed its way inside her mouth, darting about like a lizard looking for a rock to hide under.

The first few times he had done this, she had fought back, she had punched him, wrestling with him, jerked and twisted beneath him. Instead of inhibiting him, it excited him. Since then, Belle had trained herself simply to lie there, limp, passive, unwillingly willing, like a tissue he could take, use, soil, crumple up, and leave behind. She had learned to transcend the reality keeping her mind active, centered on something else, something wonderful, something so far removed from that room that no matter what he did, she was insensate. Like now, he had ripped off the blankets and was straddling her, his penis red and swollen, hanging over her like a pendulous prod. She knew he wanted her to touch it, but she was thousands of miles away, at Willowsgate, summering with Annabel Montgomery, painting on the lawn, laughing and joking, having tea and scones amidst the verbena.

"Say you like it," he said in that strange garbled voice. "Go on. Say it. Tell me you want it."

"I like it," she repeated obediently.

"Say you want it."

"I want it."

She felt his hands slide her pants off and for a moment, as the night air licked her skin, she stiffened. *Think about something else. Anything else.* He hunkered lower, resting that pulsating shaft on her leg, tangling his fingers in the soft, blond triangle that deltaed her womanhood. *Concentrate,* she screamed to herself as he took her hand and placed it where he wanted it, moving it up and down in his own private, triballike rhythm. His eyes rolled back as he too entered another place.

She tried to return to Willowsgate, but the image was gone. Lunch with Gaby. She tried to conjure up lunch with Gaby, but the picture was faint, disjointed, full of static. It was so very difficult to escape from the disgusting feeling of his fingers invading her body, his tongue lapping at her flesh, his hands grabbing as if she were his to do with as he wished.

The worst was when he lowered himself, dropping his weight onto her as he dug his way into her. He lunged and thrusted until her inside ached with the physical and emotional agony of it. But that didn't hurt nearly as much as when his lips touched her ear and he whispered, "I love you, Louise."

After, he never said anything. He simply put on his robe, bent down, and lightly kissed her forehead as if he had just told her a bedtime story and listened to her prayers. Then he left.

Belle didn't move. She lay there, her legs still spread, her body still wet with his semen. Throckmorton, who had napped in a corner during his mistress's ordeal, jumped onto the bed and licked Belle's face. She wanted to cry, but she had no tears. She wanted to scream, but other than her cat, she knew there was no one to listen. Besides, what would she say? How could she tell anyone something like this? What would they think of her? They would be sickened. They would turn away from her. They would shun her. And rightfully so. She had to be a bad person to do such bad things, to make him want to do such bad things to her. Fathers were supposed to protect their daughters. They were supposed to love them and cherish them and call them "princess," and walk them down the aisle at their weddings. Fathers weren't supposed to do this. But her father did and had since she was eleven.

She reached over to her nightstand and grabbed the perfume bottle that sat next to her lamp. Her finger pressed up and down on the atomizer as she sprayed her entire body with the cloying scent. Throckmorton started to pull away.

"They can smell it," she told him. "Even after I shower and scrub and scrub. They can smell him on me. I have to cover it up. I have to hide it."

As she pulled the blankets up over her nakedness and her shame, and drew Throckmorton even closer, she looked at the

entire five thousand dollars. Morris, impressed with her apartment as well as with the quality of the rest of her paperweight collection, asked her to call him if ever she found any other examples of St. Louis weights. Too, he told her that his wife, Jocelyn, who had not made the trip east, adored snuff boxes. Their twenty-fifth anniversary was coming up in July and he would love to be able to present her with something exceptional. He was willing to spend up to fifty thousand dollars if Gaby could find just the right thing. She promised to try.

The auction at Sotheby's for Lush's Beauvais tapestry had been held the previous Saturday. Before Lush had left town, Gaby had established a ceiling price. Fortunately, the woman was as free with her money as she was with her liquor. Because the tapestry was truly a magnificent piece, the bidding had been fierce, but when the gavel went down, Gaby had bought the Beauvais for forty-two thousand dollars. Since she had decided that when she bought at auction she would take her percentage off the sale price, without the ten percent buyer's premium added on, her take from those few minutes of absolute, unadulterated joy was eighty-four hundred dollars!

Knowing that often instant success was more tease than trend, Gaby quickly banked most of her money. Since she had no salary coming in, it seemed only prudent to create a fund that covered her everyday expenses as well as an additional fund to support the traveling essential to her new business. She did, however, splurge on a new dress for Steven's eighteenth birthday party, a round-trip plane ticket to Cleveland—supersaver nonrefundable of course—and for her son, a watch to replace the one he had sold so he could buy her Christmas locket.

As she reviewed her list of unfulfilled commissions, her eye lingered on the name Max Richard. As he had said he would, he had called and invited her to brunch the Sunday after the party so that she could view his collection of Biedermeier. As he had said, it was an impressive collection, incorporating not only numerous examples of the warm-wooded, cleanly elegant product of early-nineteenth-century Europe, but several pieces from its antecedent, French neoclassicism, as well.

As Max conducted his tour, taking Gaby through his apartment —a terraced penthouse atop the Bruxelles, the most luxurious of Max's string of New York co-ops—Gaby's attention was divided. She was fascinated by what he said about the history of the period, but equally so by what his recitation was saying about him. His love of simple yet cultivated forms and his insistence upon meticulous workmanship was evident as he showed her the living room, a huge space dominated by a wall of bookcases on one end, an expanse of undressed windows on another. Columns abounded, some built in and ceiling high, others shorter, standing free-form and topped with Egyptian-style bronzes or Grecian urns. A fruitwood daybed with gently curved sides and soft, earthy brown suede upholstery looked almost feminine facing a brawny, hobnail-tufted leather couch. Small cherry tables, a pair of fruitwood tub chairs cushioned in brown, an imposing secretary in Russian birch, a black and white Portuguese needlepoint rug, recessed lighting, bunches of fluffy white chrysanthemums, and an assemblage of both modern and ancient statuary created a portrait of a man appreciative of the past, but not so overawed as to dismiss the accomplishments of the present.

The other rooms were similar, all caramel and chocolate, all unruffled and intensely masculine, all a carefully conceived contrast of austere design and rich materials, formality and intimacy. Seeing Max here, in these specific surroundings, Gaby couldn't help thinking it was as if these remnants of the Age of Reason, that time in man's history when, finally, he was viewed as a creature fully in command of his own destiny, had been gathered together as a decorative resume, a visual explanation of who and what Maximilian Richard was.

"The difference between the early neoclassicists and the later proponents of the style," he had said when pointing out the Italian lyre-back chairs encircling his dining room table, "was discipline and refinement. Napoleon would have gilded almost every inch of these chairs. The designers who followed were far more sober in their tastes. In fact," he had continued, affectionately stroking the front of a magnificently burled armoire, "if you really look at most Biedermeier pieces, they're Empire without all the fuss."

That too, Gaby decided, aptly defined Max. The brunch he served—croissants and sweet rolls, assorted confitures, fruit, and coffee—the conversation that accompanied the meal, the manner in which he discussed what he wanted in the way of antiques, was straightforward and honest, with no superfluous extras meant to overwhelm or bedazzle.

But he had overwhelmed her. From the moment she had seen him at the Castleton gala he had refused to leave her thoughts and her dreams. Although he was undeniably one of the best-looking men she had ever met, extraordinarily successful, and, judging by the various discussions they had had, an intellect well schooled in many subjects, it was Max's essence that acted like a magnet, his gentleness and compassion that conspired to draw her to him. The way he had defended Armand at the fair, the way in which he had dealt with Belle at Chelsea's party, his spontaneous chivalry, his seemingly limitless generosity—the man seemed practically perfect.

At one time, Brian had seemed perfect, too. She had known he had faults, just as she knew Max had to have flaws hidden beneath that handsome exterior, but with Brian she had been young and naive and unwilling to tempt fate by looking too closely at reality. She was no longer young, no longer naive. As smitten as she was with Max, and she was, she couldn't afford to be distracted by the mere possibility of romance. Though Max had been charming and flattering and extremely attentive whenever they had been together, in truth he had yet to demonstrate any inclination toward moving beyond a basic flirtation. Gaby had no time to chase will-o'-the-wisps.

The plane continued its ascent, climbing up through the thick white fog of a cloudy New York morning, finally leveling off within the infinite blue that existed above the weather. As Gaby gazed out her window, she wished she could reach out and grab a handful of that blue tranquility. Just then, she felt anything but placid.

The flight from La Guardia to Cleveland's Hopkins Airport was short, just under two hours. While part of her wanted to accelerate time, to land, to get this unpleasant reunion with her ex-husband and his family over with, another part of her wanted to stretch time, to elongate the flight, to remain airborne and forever avoid the confrontation she knew awaited her. Had it been any occasion other than Steven's eighteenth birthday, Gaby would have declined Ethel Thayer's invitation. But it was her son's day, and besides, she wouldn't give any of them the satisfaction of staying away.

Gaby clicked open the antique locket that hung around her neck and studied the face of the handsome young man in the small picture. He had displayed enormous courage while he had been in the Wadsworth schools. It was never easy to defend a deficiency. There was never an explanation adequate enough to still the taunts that followed a failing grade or a humiliating performance. Yet Steven had persevered, refusing to concede defeat. It had not been his choice to go away to school, but he had gone, packing a host of reservations in one suitcase, a heart full of hope in another. He was a senior now, making application to top-grade colleges. His record was excellent by any standards, stunning if one considered the obstacles he had had to overcome. Pride swelled Gaby's chest, forcing a smile as well as a tear.

Despite the fact that she had spent much of the flight thinking about him, when she deplaned and saw Steven standing inside the terminal, she was shocked. Not that he was there—he had told her he would pick her up—but that he had changed so much since his Christmas break. Was it possible that he had gotten taller? Was it possible that his face had lost even more of its boyishness? Was her ·baby truly becoming a man? As they hugged and she felt the strength of his arms around her, a fleeting sense of regret surfaced. Sending him away had been in his best interest. She knew that. It had been necessary and, judging by the results, correct. But in doing what she had to do for Steven, she had denied herself the pleasure of his company. Would it have been different if she had remained in Wadsworth and not moved to New York? Having given that question endless consideration, the answer came quickly—not appreciably. She spoke to him twice a week, wrote at least three times a month. She had visited him at school several times and seen him on his vacations. Had she lived in Ohio, he still would have divided his time between her and Brian. He still would have wanted to take his summers away. So if it didn't make that much of a differ-ence, why did she feel so guilty?

"Have I got a surprise for you!"

He took her suitcase and practically pushed her through the exit toward the parking lot.

"I'm too young to be a grandmother, Steven," Gaby said, actually fearing that waiting outside was a young girl with a big smile on her face, a tiny diamond on her finger, and a suspicious bulge in her abdomen.

"Cute, Mom. Real cute." He shook his head as if what she had said was completely absurd, but his blush told her it wasn't as impossible as he wanted her to believe.

"Is that the most awesome thing you've ever seen?"

He had stopped in front of a brand-new, bright red convertible. Surrounded by cars tainted and dulled with winter's grime, glistening in the sun, it stood out like a jewel among coal, red and rich.

Gaby walked around it, touching the canvas roof, the chrome trim, the shiny hood ornament, the black vinyl upholstery. She opened the door and sat inside, gripping the wheel, testing the comfort of the seats, checking the glove compartment and the radio. She remembered how it was when she was eighteen and Brian had owned a convertible. Every afternoon from April until October, they'd cruise around town with the top down, her ponytail whipping into her face, Brian's eyes shaded by dark glasses, his arm draped over the side of the door à la James Dean. The wheels were hot and that made them cool.

"It is definitely awesome." She grinned, knowing how excited Steven was, knowing without asking that Brian must have bought it, feeling for a moment a twinge of competitiveness and jealousy about Brian's ability to give with such largesse.

"Do you think so?" He helped her out and walked her around to the passenger side, all the while reciting passages from the owner's manual. "Last night, when Dad gave me the keys, I freaked. I mean, like this is mine! Can you believe it?"

Once Gaby was settled and her suitcase was in the trunk, he jumped in, slipped on a pair of sunglasses, and started the car. Gaby watched as he listened to the engine hum. His profile was striking. Like a young Apollo, his jaw jutted forward, its squared shape forming a strong base for the rest of his features: a high, wide forehead; deep blue eyes thickly fringed and heavily browed; a straight nose, narrow at the bridge, broader at the tip; and a generous mouth that, more often than not, was curled upward in a smile. With his short-cropped hair, his bleached-out jeans, plaid button-down shirt, scruffy sneakers, and aviator jacket, his image was startlingly like that of a young Brian. As he put the car into drive and accelerated, Gaby felt as if she had shifted into reverse. The boy next to her was not her son, but instead her son's father, the sexy football hero she had fallen in love with, the fun-loving, handsome, free-spirited man Brian had been then.

Most of the way down Interstate 71, Steven extolled the virtues of his new driving machine, demonstrating its ability to handle curves and highway speeds, jockeying in and out of traffic. While he rambled, Gaby's slow regression continued. She read road signs for places like Berea, Strongsville, Sharon Center, Chippewa-on-the-Lake, and suddenly, as if she had been injected with a heavy dose of nostalgia, her body relaxed as her mind drifted backward. This was real. This was clear. These were names she knew, places she had been. This was a world she could relate to. This was a world she understood. She had been part of this landscape for most of her life. She belonged here. New York seemed foreign and unfamiliar. Her life there lost its immediacy. Its reality diminished as everything she had done in the past two years faded behind a filmy screen of soothing, deliberate forgetfulness.

As Steven drove into Wadsworth, he must have anticipated her request because the first place he stopped was in front of the old Tante Simone. It was still an antiques shop, but now it was called Kensington Square and featured English collectibles rather than French.

"Do you want to get out?" Steven asked.

Gaby barely heard him. She couldn't take her eyes off the sign above the door. It was glossy, black enamel with fat gold letters, slick and, to Gaby's mind, pretentious. Tante Simone's sign had been hand carved out of bleached wood, its name painted a friendly Mediterranean blue. It had been more personal, more country, more conducive to the notion of browsing and chatting about the peculiarities of one piece or another. It had been more like Simone. But the sign was gone, just as Simone was gone.

It had been almost a year since she had buried her beloved aunt, but just then, sitting outside her shop, that place which had been their special clubhouse, Gaby had never missed her more. She fought an overwhelming urge to go inside. She knew it would break her heart if she did. She wanted to find Simone there, to sit at the gueridon and have tea and a chocolate *goûter*, and listen as Simone rhapsodized about her latest acquisition. Her eyes welled, filling with tears that spoke of loss and an ever-present loneliness that Gaby knew might fade in time, but would never ever go away. The tears fell, and as they did, another fantasy was washed away. Seeing this shop with that new name and those unfamiliar things in the window, knowing that inside were different people and different *objets*, Gaby had to face the fact that as hard as she worked and as long as it took, when that day came that she paid the last of her debt to Lakewood, she would not have bought back Simone's life. She would have simply paid for her death.

"No," she said, wiping her eyes and shaking her head. "I don't want to go in."

"I know how you feel, Mom. I hate it, too."

He pulled away, but slowly, almost respectfully.

"Would you mind going by the house?" she asked.

Instinctively, Steven knew she didn't mean the house he had grown up in. She wanted to see the house she had grown up in. As they drove onto the street, he could feel his mother tense. He knew how much this small, dormered Cape with the oversized kitchen meant to her. At the time she had sold it, he hadn't understood her reasons. She had said it was because their house was bigger and more comfortable for Simone and a companion, but the more he had thought about it, the less sense that made. Especially since Simone's stay there had been so brief and it was only a few months later that she had been moved into Lakewood.

When she had sold *his* house, he hadn't understood that either, but then, because he had been so angry, so bubbling with rage, he had sought an outlet. He had allowed himself to confide to his roommate. Once he began, it was like a dam opening up. He told Frank everything, about how he blamed his mother for the breakup of his parents' marriage and how awful he thought she was for moving away and for selling the only home he had ever known. He remembered how embarrassed he had been when Frank, whose parents had been divorced for several years, sided with Gaby.

"My parents belonged to a country club. They traveled to Europe twice a year. My old man drove a Mercedes, my mother a BMW. We had a housekeeper and a gardener and a huge house in Scarsdale. We lived like royalty. And then, suddenly, guess what? My dad declares personal bankruptcy. And why? Because suddenly he forgot how to make money? Because suddenly his law practice folded? No way José. He did it so that he could screw my mom to the wall and not give her a dime, that's why! Hey,'' Frank said, poking Steven in the chest for emphasis. "I bet your mom wasn't lying at all. I bet that whatever she did, man, she did because she needed the bread."

"My father gives me everything," Steven had said, knowing that if what Frank said was true, as a defense that sounded feeble.

"Sure he does, but don't buy into that. He gives you because you're his son and heir, and because he's into this game of which parent are you going to love best. He's fucking your mom, Steven, just as sure as he's fucking the young chippy he lives with."

Frank's words had been painful, but they had had a certain ring of truth to them, and in that truth was also an element of relief. Though he had never consciously admitted that he believed Gaby had deserted him, this allowed him to dismiss the idea altogether. Though he had never wanted to believe that she had stayed in New York because she preferred it to Wadsworth, this allowed him to understand that she had had to stay there because that's where her job was.

The one remaining confusion was why, whenever Gaby talked about money, there was an edge to her voice. Okay, so maybe Brian wasn't Mr. Generosity. Why did he sense an air of desperation surrounding her, an urgency to earn as much money as she could as quickly as she could? She said she lived plainly and he believed her. She said that her apartment was a loan and her contribution to its upkeep was minimal. She said she had a good job at Castleton's. What was the problem?

"You know, Steven, sometimes you are truly dense. Did it ever dawn on you that your mom's footing the bills for your great-aunt's stay in that vegetable patch called a nursing home? Did you ever think that she might be working to pay them off?"

Frank was right. Steven felt dense. He had never thought about bills and debts and who was paying for what, but he had thought about it a great deal since, and now, sitting with his mother outside where Simone had lived, where her parents had lived, he knew it had to be true. Gaby was transfixed. She had not been able to tear her eyes away. It was as if an ancestral magnet had demanded her attention, pulling her back to her roots, gripping her soul, refusing to let her go. No. She would never have sold this house unless it was absolutely necessary.

"I hated moving her out of here," she said quietly. "She loved this place."

"It wasn't something you wanted to do," Steven said, hoping she had caught his veiled apology for his pique over other things she had said she hadn't wanted to do.

She heard the unspoken, turned, smiled, and patted his cheek.

"What I want to do now is stop being maudlin and start being happy. This is my son's eighteenth birthday, you know."

Steven reached over and hugged her. She clung to him for a moment, reminding them both that as long as they continued to love each other, neither distance nor age nor even differences of opinion could loosen the basic bond that existed between them.

"Do you want to go anywhere else?" Steven asked.

"No," Gaby said, knowing he wanted her to go by their house, knowing that was the last place she wanted to visit. "I've had just about enough of memory lane for one afternoon. Besides, I have to conserve my energy for tonight. Let's go to the inn."

As Steven drove away and the white-shingled Cape began to shrink, Gaby looked back, wondering if it was ever possible to go back, to revive old relationships, to recapture lost feelings.

"She's not coming tonight," Steven said flatly.

"Who?"

"Pamela."

Gaby's head bobbed slightly as she considered this bit of news. It couldn't be because Ethel hadn't extended an invitation. Ethel had never and would never champion Gaby's cause. Had Steven requested that she not be invited?

"Is she away on a business trip?" she asked, trying to sound casual, somewhat startled to discover that she didn't feel casual.

Steven's mouth spread in a slow, satisfied smile. Though his eyes looked straight ahead, Gaby could see by the crinkles at the side that they were twinkling.

"She and Dad aren't seeing each other as much as they used to."

"Oh?" She hadn't meant to show any interest. She didn't

want to get Steven's hopes up. *What about your hopes,* a small voice asked.

"He told Grandma he didn't want Pamela there tonight. He was afraid you might be uncomfortable."

"How considerate." How she did it she didn't know, but she had actually managed to eliminate all trace of sarcasm.

"He even asked if I thought he should pick you up and escort you to the party."

"And what did you say?"

Actually, it had been Steven's idea that maybe his father would bring his mother. He had planned to spring it on Gaby, see if he got a positive response, and then go to Brian. He wasn't sure whether the agitation in Gaby's voice was positive or negative, but he decided the best course of action just then, was no action.

As he pulled up to the Wadsworth Inn, parked, and shut off the ignition, he said, "I told him, no way! Mom's *my* date."

Why was it that every five minutes since she had landed in Ohio she had felt like crying? Fighting off yet another welling of tears, she reached into her tote and pulled out a long box wrapped in red paper and tied with a red cloth ribbon imprinted with the Cartier name.

"I don't like my dates to be late," she said, handing him the gift.

He tore off the wrapping, impatient to get to the gift within. When he opened the box and saw the watch, his eyes doubled in size.

"This is . . . wow! . . . like it's just too great," he said, holding it against his wrist, studying the square face with the black Roman numerals, the lizard band. Then he turned it over. Engraved on the back was the inscription: *To Steven. On your 18th and for all time, my love. Mom.*

He smiled, but this time it was shy. The man had become the boy again, the little child whose heart would always be moved by his mother.

"I love you," he said as he kissed her.

"You're a wonderful son, Steven," Gaby said, gulping back yet another impulse to cry. "And because you are, I am going to buy you lunch. We're going to catch up on what's happening in each other's lives and then I'm going to take a nap so that I can look particularly special for my date this evening.''

"You alway look special to me, Mom.''

"Thanks,'' she said, silently thanking God for having blessed her with this young man. "But right now, you look hungry to me. Let's eat!''

Brian downed the last of his scotch. It was only seven-thirty and already he had had two full, stiff drinks. Though he would never have admitted it to anyone—he was having a hard enough time admitting it to himself—he was nervous. Even here in his mother's house, that bastion of security, that font of perpetual ego fulfillment, he felt odd, strangely awkward. He couldn't seem to find a place to settle. No room felt right. No chair felt comfortable. He couldn't find anyone interesting to talk to or think of anything interesting to talk about.

The front door opened. As he had done each time the bell had chimed, his head turned and he held his breath waiting to see who walked in. Two more neighbors. A friend of Steven's.

Steven had left to pick up Gaby over an hour ago. It took ten minutes to get from here to the inn, fifteen if there was traffic. Where the hell were they? They were supposed to have been here before the guests arrived. What had detained them? Had Gaby changed her mind about coming?

Actually, Brian thought, he wouldn't blame her if she had. He had been awful when she had come to see him about helping out with Simone's bills. He had squeezed her until she had had no choice but to sell the one thing she had wanted to keep. He couldn't imagine that she was too eager to be in his company or, as long as he was confessing, the company of his family. But, he reminded himself, it was Steven's birthday. She might not want to see him or his parents or his sisters or anyone else, but if Steven wanted her here, she'd be here. She had always been that kind of mother.

Brian went into the dining room where the bar was set up and fixed himself another drink, lighter this time, so that when she did arrive he wouldn't fall down drunk at her feet. All day he had been trying to put a finger on his feelings, to figure out why he was so anxious about seeing Gaby again. Was it curiosity?

Was he simply interested in seeing if New York had changed her and, if it had, in what way?

Or was it curiosity about the degree of change in him? Was he counting on her to act as a plumbline, to measure the depth of his maturity, the height of his achievement? She had always known him better than anyone else. Who better to gauge whether or not he had grown in stature, whether his success at Wadsworth Match had translated into a perceptible aura of importance? She would be able to detect nuances. But only if she was willing to speak to him, which was questionable.

Like a schoolboy at his first social, he turned and studied himself in the mirror over the sideboard. It wasn't immodest, he decided, to think that he was still ruggedly good-looking, still sinewy, still boyishly appealing. A mirror reflected the facts. What the mirror couldn't do, unfortunately, was to tell him why Pamela's interest in him had waned. More to the point, why his interest in her had decreased until it was practically nil?

When they had first met, his response to her had been carnal, chemical, purely animal. She was young, but he had dallied with lots of young women before her. She was exciting, with exotic tastes and effective techniques; but she was aggressive, and every once in a while that disturbed him. He had always thought of himself as a major stud. He wasn't used to a woman taking charge in bed, initiating sex, directing him as to what she liked and what she didn't. She was one of those women of the eighties the media were always talking about: take-charge women who wouldn't take a backseat either on the job or in the home; superwomen who wanted it all—career, marriage, family; independent women who didn't need a husband to have sex, money, or security.

He had never been with anyone like Pamela before. Gaby had been a woman of the sixties, a woman who still saw the man as king of his castle, the breadwinner, the dominant figure. His on-the-road one-night stands had always been secretaries or waitresses or stewardesses or convention groupies. Pamela was an executive. Was that the turn-on? Was it the power that had attracted him to her? Her job? Her title? Certainly, that had been a big part of it. He had liked accompanying her to office parties, meeting the upper echelon of her advertising agency as well as the top brass of the companies she represented. He had liked discussing business with her, politics, the changing economy, the dynamics of a changing world. He had liked watching men cater to her, envying him.

What he didn't like was the feeling that he had to keep up, that each time she landed a new account, he had to do the same, that each time she got a raise, his salary level had to rise another notch. What he liked even less was the suspicion that when she traveled, she cheated on him. Clearly, whether he liked it or not, he was a sixties man.

The front door opened again. This time, the woman framed in the portal was the person he had been waiting for—his wife. Ex-wife. He corrected himself, noting the regret that had accompanied the thought, noticing the stares and audible gasps that accompanied her entrance. The Gaby he and everyone else in that room had known had always been nice looking. The prettiest girl in Wadsworth. This woman was strikingly beautiful. Her dark, chestnut hair was shiny and lush, combed away from her face, a few strands softly wisping about her forehead, the rest tumbling below her shoulders in subtle waves. Her body—how could he have ever thought of her as thin—was enveloped in a printed silk sheath which hugged her tiny waist, girdled her hips with small, sensuous pleats, and stopped inches above her knees, making her legs look longer and shapelier than Brian ever remembered. A fantasy of apple green, pink, and white, she appeared a ravishing harbinger of spring thrown into a boring sea of basic black dresses and traditional navy-blue suits.

Brian's eyes indulged in the sight of her, traveling the distance of her slowly, drinking her in, savoring the sensations that flooded his body. When his gaze reached her face, he felt as if someone had pushed a pause button. All emotion was suspended, all feeling put on hold. Her face was totally different. She was wearing more makeup than she had ever worn, but that wasn't it. It wasn't the mascara or the soft, celery-green shadow or the faintly rose blush or the fuchsia lipstick that held him entranced. He was responding to a look, an air, an attitude he had never seen before. Arrogance? No. There wasn't an arrogant bone in Gaby's body. Boldness? Pluck? Confidence, perhaps?

He wanted to approach her, to examine her, to take her aside and talk, but his path was obstructed by a crush of old friends who also wanted to investigate the new Gaby Thayer, so instead, he held back and watched.

"Do you think those earrings are real?"

Brian spun around and glowered at his sister. Enid's question had been posed in a stage whisper loud enough to catch her brother's attention as well as that of several others standing nearby.

"I thought you had a manicure this afternoon," he hissed.

"I did." She held up her hands, displaying ten freshly enamelled, Fire & Ice fingertips.

"Too bad they forgot to trim your claws."

Enid sniffed, admired her nails once again, touched the pearl clusters that graced her lobes for assurance that she too was properly jeweled, and then looked at Gaby.

"They couldn't be real." Though she had no way of knowing for certain, she had correctly assessed the cabochon of pink tourmaline and its crown of diamonds as costume. "And even if they are, they're so gauche they scream New York."

"Go check your makeup, Enid. Your face is turning green."

"Well, excuse me! And since when are you Gaby's knight in shining armor? The last I heard, you were sleeping in any bed that had clean sheets on it just so you could get away from her."

Brian spun on his heels, walked out of the dining room, and headed toward Gaby, eager to escape the mocking tone of his younger sister. As he wended his way around the tables and chairs and people crowded in the living room, he tried to control the anger he felt. Gaby had been right all along. Enid was an audacious twit who had always looked at Gaby through jaundiced eyes. But, his conscience asked, was he angry with Enid for what she had said or angry with himself because what she had said was true?

"Welcome home!" He took Gaby's hands, drew her to him, and kissed her cheek before she could pull away. Though she had stiffened at the sound of his voice, her skin felt soft against his and she smelled as delicate and feminine as she looked. That, too, he realized with a sense of deflated pride, was different. She wasn't wearing Shalimar. "I'm glad you're here."

"It's Steven's birthday," she said, freeing herself from his grasp, but looking directly at him so that he didn't miss the point.

"Isn't she the most gorgeous thing you've ever seen?" Steven had been gushing ever since she had come down the stairs at the inn.

"That she is."

Brian felt himself ogling, but he couldn't help it. If he thought he had felt awkward before she arrived, it was nothing compared to how he felt now. Suddenly every social grace he had ever possessed deserted him. If not for Ethel impatiently ushering Gaby and Steven inside, he might have stood in the entry for the rest of the evening shuffling his feet and searching for the right thing to say. Instead, he followed the procession into the living room.

Ethel also appeared to have been sprinkled with stardust. She was Gaby's new best friend, clucking over her and introducing her around as if she were a visiting celebrity, which was amusing because other than Frank, Steven's boarding school roommate, Gaby had known most of these people all her life. Brian stood off to the side as she worked the room, reluctantly accepting the role of spectator. Despite the fact that outwardly she seemed like a stranger, certain movements, certain idiosyncratic bits of behavior were familiar enough to remind him that the woman inside that exquisite package had been his wife for sixteen years.

When Holt Thompson put down his cigar so he could kiss her and she quickly averted her head, Brian laughed. Gaby had always said Holt smelled like a dirty ashtray. When Loretta Phillips effused about how marvelous Gaby looked and how excited she was to have her back, Brian saw the right side of Gaby's lip tilt upward. That was her I-can't-stand-you-but-we're-in-public-so-I-won't-make-a-scene smile. When Steven introduced her to Frank, Brian saw the caring, child-loving side of Gaby. She greeted the young man warmly, bussed his cheek as if he were a member of her family, and talked to him, laughing occasionally, linking her arm through his and Steven's, letting them both know that since they were important to each other, their relationship was important to her.

When he noticed Enid approaching, Brian's antennae went up. Gaby's spine straightened, her eyes narrowed, and her face blanked. Brian expected to see her retreat rather than expose herself to a lashing from his sister's venomous tongue. To his surprise, Gaby didn't back off. She stood her ground and waited for Enid to get closer. Just as they were nose to nose and Enid was about to speak, Gaby deliberately and with great hauteur turned her back. Brian almost applauded.

"Boy, if looks could kill." Steven chuckled as he whispered into his father's ear. "I don't think Aunt Enid is a happy camper right now."

"I think Aunt Enid had it coming."

"Yeah, but who would've thought *Mom* would've given it to her?"

"Your mom seems to be full of surprises."

"That she is!" Steven said, his face illuminated with genuine admiration and affection.

That afternoon, after Gaby had given Steven his new watch, she had presented him with an even greater gift. She had taken him into her confidence. Over lunch, she had told him about being fired and having to start over again and what she was trying to do and how her old college roommate had come to her rescue. She had spoken of her friendship with Armand Lafitte and of Chelsea's stepdaughter, Belle. She explained what being a broker meant and how nervous she was about succeeding. He asked about Simone's care and if Gaby had been left with any debt. Though she wouldn't reveal the extent of that debt, she did admit that, yes, she had an obligation she had to clear up. And when he asked if there was a man in her life, she told him that, no, there was no one and that, in fact, she was quite lonely and wished she had someone to love and to love her in return. Naturally, Steven had one particular someone in mind, but being the grown-up that he was, he had opted for discretion rather than disclosure.

"How's she doing in New York?" Brian asked, hoping he sounded solicitous but not overly interested.

"She's had some rough times, but she's come through them like a champ. A month ago, with the help of some friends, she started her own business."

"Doing what?" Brian no longer cared how interested he sounded.

"Mom's an antiques broker now. The way she explained it, she's like a personal shopper for really knowledgeable collectors."

Brian nodded as if he knew what an antiques broker was, which he didn't. It didn't sound like much to him, but Steven seemed impressed, and the last thing Brian wanted to do just then was to appear to be denigrating Gaby.

"And who are these friends? Boyfriends? Girlfriends?"

"One of each," Steven said, delighted with his father's reaction. "A Frenchman, Armand Lafitte, and Chelsea Harper, Mom's old roommate. Do you remember her?"

Brian nodded again and tried to smile, but he and Chelsea had never gotten along very well, so his attempt ended in a sneer.

"Who is this Lafitte character?"

"According to Mom, he's a friend. That's all."

He had heard that one before. Pamela always insisted that the men she worked with were friends and that if she went out with them for lunch or dinner or away on business trips, it didn't mean anything. While Brian didn't think of himself as parochial, neither was he progressive. He was forty years old and somewhat set in his ways. To him, men and women were sexual creatures. They could be lovers, ex-lovers, or would-be lovers. But they couldn't be "just friends." It went against nature. So while Gaby might have wanted her son to believe that her relationship with this man was platonic, Brian believed otherwise.

"Does she have many male friends?"

Steven wanted to tell Brian about Gaby being lonely and wanting a man in her life, but again he decided less was more.

"I don't know. Why don't you ask her?"

Brian looked at the numbers of people still hovering around the woman he had walked out on. He envisioned the numbers of men who now hovered around her in New York.

"I will," he said somewhat ruefully. "But I guess I have to wait my turn."

Plus ça change, plus c'est la même chose. The more things change, the more they stay the same.

Over the years, Simone had repeated that phrase so often, Gaby had come to think of it as Simone's personal anthem. Tonight, sitting on Ethel's couch, listening to her old friends offer explanations as to why they hadn't been more supportive when Gaby was going through her divorce, while at the same time offering advice about why she should take advantage of the breakup of Brian's affair to try and win him back, Simone's anthem pounded inside her brain.

She had been away from this town and these people for more than two years. They hadn't gone out of their way to see her in the months after Brian had left. They hadn't gone out of their way to keep in touch in the months since she had left. Yet now that she was back among them, they felt they had the right to tell her what she should or should not do. To them, despite the time that had elapsed or the changes that passage of time might have wrought, she was the same. Perhaps because they were the same. They had the same interests, talked about the same things, had the same problems, and spread the same gossip, only the names were different.

Though Gaby found that disturbing, she refused to find fault. These women had been her friends. She had been one of them and would be one of them still if circumstance had not plucked her from their midst. She understood them, even if they no longer understood her. She knew what pleased them and what frightened them. She knew that the status quo represented security. Change posed a threat. Routine was comforting. Newness demanded adjustment. They lived in their own structured, clichéd world, where a bird in the hand was worth two in the bush, one good deed deserved another, there was no sense crying over spilt milk, and there was strength in numbers.

Even now, they repeated the same pat, self-protective phrases she had heard before.

"I don't like to place blame."

"I didn't think it was right to take sides."

"I refused to have dinner with him and Pamela, but then you moved away. What could I do?"

"I would have invited you, but Bill works with Brian. I had no choice. You understand, don't you?"

Gaby understood all too well.

Now that Brian and Pamela had split, Gaby was being wooed back to her home town with promises of inclusion. For the mere price of going back with her husband, she could have her Thursday tennis game, her Wednesday bridge group, dinners with every couple in the room, a seat on several boards, invitations to parties galore, and a welcome-home from everyone in downtown Wadsworth. Gaby was beginning to think that, had she asked, she could have had a parade down Main Street.

Oddly enough, the picture they painted was appealing. They were familiar. The life they were describing was familiar. Certainly, coming home would be easier than fighting for survival in New York. Certainly, being with someone she had once loved a great deal would be better than having no one to love. Wouldn't it?

Adding to her confusion was Brian's attentiveness. Ever since he had wangled a place next to her on the buffet line, he had remained by her side. He had been solicitous, complimentary, amusing, courtly—all the things she remembered him being when they were kids. As she described her life in New York to him—leaving out the downside, concentrating on the upside—he appeared genuinely interested. He asked questions and seemed to listen to her answers. When she asked about his job, he seemed pleased and described it in greater detail than she would have guessed he would. All in all, it was the most civilized exchange they had had in years. When he asked to drive her back to the inn, she said yes.

As he led her into the cocktail lounge at the rear of the lobby, Chelsea's words ran through her head: "Beware of Greeks and ex-husbands bearing gifts."

Chelsea had taken Gaby to lunch that past week to prepare her for, as she had put it, Gaby's return to the scene of the crime. In between bites of her green salad and broiled fish and sips of her Montrachet, she had lectured Gaby on the pitfalls of postmarital reunions.

"Don't be suckered by sweet talk. He doesn't want you back. He wants to get you into bed and play Humpty-Dumpty. He's going to be hot for you, but not because he's discovered how much he loves you or how stupid he was to let you go. He can't stand the idea that he doesn't control you anymore. He wants to be Tarzan and he wants you to be Jane. Don't let him do it. Don't let him take away all that you've gained. You're in control of yourself now, Gaby. Keep it that way."

Now, Brian steered her toward a quiet, dimly lit corner, inviting Gaby to sit beside him on a Wedgwood-blue loveseat centered within a curtained bay. He ordered two brandies. While they waited, he appraised Gaby, a slow, deliberate process that vacillated between the cool, unfeeling assessment of a business-man calculating his prospects for a sale and the ardent, sensual adulation of a man desirous of consummating a relationship.

Gaby fought it, but the primal, female urge, stifled for too long, began to assert itself. A hectic flush warmed her cheeks. Her palms went moist, and for a second, she thought she felt a slight tremor. Inside, her blood churned, oscillating like the evening tide, agitated by the force of Brian's stare. Quickly, she lowered her eyes and fussed with a speck of dirt on her shoe, pleading with her body to be still.

The brandies came. Brian leaned forward to clink his glass against hers.

"I've never seen you look more beautiful," he said.

Gaby smiled and then retreated behind the snifter, taking another sip, letting the warm amber liquid restore her calm.

"Judging by everyone else's reaction tonight, I wasn't the only one who thought so. They hung around you like flies." He laughed. "It was like when you were crowned Miss Wadsworth. Remember? I couldn't get near you then, either."

Gaby nodded. She did remember. He had stood off to the side throughout the pageant, refusing a seat, claiming that he wanted an unobstructed view of his girl. After the coronation, he had tried to run up onto the stage, but by the time he got there it had filled with photographers and reporters and relatives and well-wishers.

"Your friends have missed you," he said, the smile fading in favor of an expression of sincerity.

"I've missed them."

"You'd make a lot of people awfully happy if you moved back." He leaned forward again and rested his hand on her knee. "Your friends. Steven. Me."

Gaby shifted position. Brian pulled his hand back.

"Besides, think how great it would be when Steven comes home for visits. We could do things together, the way we used to. We could give Steven a sense of family again."

He was tugging on all the right strings. He spoke and Gaby's fears and insecurities made her song of independence and self-reliance sound strident, atonal, unpleasant. He spoke about friends and family and togetherness, and suddenly his was the voice of harmony, his was the carol of concord. He spoke and she could hear Steven in the background, crooning, prodding, encouraging her to make things the way they were.

"There've been so many disruptions in his life. Our divorce. His going away to school. Simone's death." Brian shook his head, his brow furrowed. "What a tragic loss. I know I didn't seem very sympathetic when you came to my office that day, but, well, you took me by surprise. I bungled it and I'm sorry. I cared about that woman. I really did."

He looked mournful. He might have felt mournful. But Gaby's memory was long, and when it came to Simone, her patience was short. The spell was broken. The music stopped.

"You have an odd way of showing concern, Brian. Simone was ill for months. You could have called or gone to visit her. You could have sent a card. A flower. Something."

"Hey! I know." He held up his hands, fending off further criticism. "Let me try and make up for my rudeness. Let me help you out. How much do you need to take care of Simone's bills?"

Again, Gaby was feeling flushed, but this time the heat came from a different fire. This time, it was anger mixed with indignation. His tone sounded patronizing, much too don't-you-worry-your-pretty-little-head-about-it to suit her. Though it was true that it could take years to pay off that debt—especially if her new business floundered—pride demanded that she reject his offer. And so she did.

"It's my obligation and I'm handling it. Thank you, anyway."

At first, Brian was relieved. His generosity, he realized, had been hasty, a spur-of-the-moment ploy to impress. Once said, he regretted the gesture and prayed that she wouldn't take him up on it. When she didn't and the wave of relief had passed, he was surprised to find that what he felt was a backwash of dejection. By refusing his offer, she had rebuffed him. Whether he had meant it or not, whether he would have honored it or not, he believed his overture had sounded earnest and bountiful. Obviously, he was wrong. What he had said was wrong. Maybe being here was wrong.

Suddenly, Brian felt uncharacteristically confused. He felt clumsy and inept. He didn't know what to say or how to act. Before, when they had sat down, he had sensed a renewed closeness, an easy familiarity, even a hint of rekindled emotion.

Now he felt a distance, a draft, a coolness that came from a door being opened, being prepared for an exit.

"I don't mean to keep stepping on your toes, babe. Really I don't. I guess it's just I don't know who you are these days. It's like we're strangers." He rested his arms on his knees and clasped his hands. His face grew thoughtful, his eyes wistful. When he spoke, his head was bowed, his voice soft. "It's not right. It's just not right." He shook his head. "I think we made a mistake, Gaby."

Gaby was too stunned to reply. *We made a mistake*. The words banged against the sides of her brain like a bell in a campanile.

"No, Brian," she said, unwilling to let that pass without comment. "*You* made the mistake. You were the one who cheated. You were the one who walked out on me. Remember?"

"I do remember. And I confess. Mea culpa." He pounded his chest as if to emphasize his contrition.

Gaby knew he was trying to keep it light to prevent an argument, but despite his intentions, she resented his cavalier attitude.

"I hurt you," he continued, hoping to stem the rage he sensed rising in her. "And I'm sorry. There's no way to excuse my actions. Call it a sixteen-year itch, a midlife crisis. Call it whatever you want. The truth is that I was looking for excitement and Pamela provided it. I was blinded by her youth and the fact that she held such an important job and knew such important people."

"When *I* wanted to go to work, you forbade it. You found it insulting and demeaning and a turnoff and a thousand other things that made no sense. How ironic that Pamela's job should be such a turn-on." She leaned back, narrowed her eyes, raised her hand to her chin, and tapped her index finger against her lips. "Tell me. Was it the job itself? Or was it the woman? If I had wanted to be an advertising executive would you have allowed that? Would I have been exciting then? Or didn't it matter?"

Her sarcasm sliced into his heart like a shiv, drawing blood. The sharp sting of her assault forced him to look at her as he never had before, to see her as his victim, the bearer of his abuse.

"It was *me*," he said, washed in a wave of guilt. "I never should have let myself get so carried away. We never should have gotten divorced."

"But you did get carried away and we did get divorced."

Her voice shook. Hot tears pooled in her eyes. When, she wondered, would she shed the coat of humiliation? When would she remove her defensive armor? When would she feel like a woman again?

"Yes, we did, but in a way, maybe it was for the best. Maybe it gave us each a chance to grow. I mean, look at you." His eyes traced a line from her ankle to her lips. It was a sinuous line that snaked about the landscape of her body. "You're gorgeous," he said in a husky voice, "and right now, I'd like nothing more than to rip your clothes off and make love to you."

His face moved closer to hers. His hand slid beneath her chin, drawing her toward him. His mouth brushed hers.

"Move back," he whispered. "Come home. You could get a great apartment in one of those new buildings we passed. We could spend time together. We could get to know each other all over again."

His hand descended. As it came to rest and began to trace the curve of her hip, Gaby halted his progress.

"And what about my job?" she asked quietly. "How am I supposed to live while we're getting reacquainted?"

"The way you explained it, you're a free-lancer. You could be a broker anywhere. Why not here?"

"Because there aren't enough potential clients or sources here."

"So do something else. Take a job in one of the antiques shops. Or work for the museum."

Gaby pulled away from him. He didn't understand. She wasn't certain that he was capable of understanding or that he even wanted to, but just then, what he wanted was irrelevant. All she could think of was how much money she had wasted on this dress, on trying to impress him and his family and everyone else who had turned their backs on her. All she could think of were the months of scrimping and saving and doing without, of the many months ahead filled with uncertainty and continued denial. She stood and faced him.

"When you walked out on me, Brian Thayer, you left me

with nothing. No money. No way to support myself. And last, but far from least, you left me with little self-respect and no sense of pride. It hasn't been easy. I've struggled and I've suffered. I'm still struggling and still suffering, but slowly I'm winning the battle. I've begun to carve out a life for myself. It may not be much, but it's mine, and right now it's in New York."

Gaby picked up her purse, looped it onto her shoulder, and looked at him, her expression mirroring her incredulousness.

"No matter how appealing you or your proposal are, if you honesty believe I'd come back here and take some dinky job just because you've decided it might be fun to play house again, forget it! Never again will I allow myself to be in a position where you or any other man can decide my fate without my vote."

Brian stood, bringing himself to his full height, looking down on her. His jaw was granite, his eyes embers smoldering with resentment.

"You'll regret this," he said, knowing that no matter what she said, this wasn't the last of it, that their relationship wouldn't end until he ended it.

"Maybe," Gaby said nonchalantly, "but I doubt it."

With that, she turned and slowly walked away, knowing all too well how much he hated her for rejecting him, knowing how close she had come to buckling under and accepting him, thinking, *Plus ça change, plus c'est la même chose.*

14

"**I** don't know whether to be ecstatic or devastated to finally hear your voice. Five more attempts and I would have made the *Guinness Book of World Records* for the most times any single phone number has been called in uninterrupted succession. I believe the total is somewhere around seven thousand four hundred and twenty-three, give or take a dial or two."

Gaby laughed. Garrett did sound thoroughly exasperated.

"I was out of town for the weekend," she said, surprised and pleased at his persistence, but hoping he didn't ask a lot of questions as to where she had gone and why.

"You've been out of town and I've been out of my mind. I just want you to know that, time zones be damned, I tried to call you from every major city in Europe. Unfortunately, each time I called the office, you were out. Each time I called your home, that blasted machine was on, and Neanderthal that I am, I refuse to carry on conversations with mechanical objects. When I returned to New York last week, however, I discovered why you were never at your desk. Irina told me you've quit Castleton's! Is that true?"

Irina. Quit. She should have known. The question was, how should she answer Garrett's question. With the truth?

"What did Irina say?"

"To make a long, distressing explanation short, she said that you wanted to branch out, to do your own thing."

Actually, what Irina had told him was that Gaby had said she found Castleton's too limiting, her position there less than satisfactory. When he had asked for Irina's interpretation of Gaby's sudden and untimely resignation—and he was immediately sorry he had—Irina painted it as a sign of Gabrielle Didier's unbounded ambition, that her leaving was a thinly veiled suggestion that they dismiss Giles Deffand and put her in his place, that she had done this during the height of the winter auction season to make replacing her more difficult, that this was a test of the extent of Garrett's affection. And if none of those theories seemed cogent or palatable, then, Irina had said, clearly, she was what Irina had suspected from the start—an insubstantial dabbler.

"I've become an antiques broker." Gaby decided to leapfrog the issue entirely. Whatever had motivated Irina to fire her had also motivated her to lie to her brother. Was it as simple as Chelsea would have her believe? That Irina was caught up in the competitive swirl of sibling rivalry, that, for whatever reason, she viewed Garrett's attentions toward Gaby as threatening and, therefore, would go to any lengths to tarnish her image? Or was it more complicated?

Gaby quickly concluded that the cause didn't matter. The effect was that she was out of Castleton's. Looking on the bright side, it appeared clear that Garrett had not been consulted about or informed of her circumstance before last week. A thought teased. Could she play on his displeasure and attempt to get her job back? Should she take advantage of his obvious caring? To what end? Garrett would question Irina. Irina would become infuriated and Gaby would be firmly entrenched in the middle of a battle, which was exactly where she did not want to be. She had started her own business. Why start trouble?

"Though I can't stand the thought of not seeing you every day, I suppose my loss is the collectors' gain," Garrett said. "You'll be a marvelous broker."

"Thank you. That's sweet."

"What can I do to help?"

Gaby's brain crackled with a flash of déjà vu. Just last night, Brian had offered to help. His offer had sounded tinny, hollow, and self-serving, like the rest of his after-dinner speech. Had she accepted, she knew she would have been obligated to him in unimaginable, untenable ways. Garrett's suggestion also measured the man. It sounded solid and sincere. Without saying so, she knew he had established limits. He would promise no more than he was able to give and take in return, no more than was honorable to ask.

"Actually, there is something you can do," she said.

"Name it."

"Might I count on you for advance notice on special items?"

"I'll call you personally."

"Which will make doing business with you a distinct pleasure."

"How about skiing with me? Would that be a pleasure?"

"You've lost me. Skiing?"

"How quickly they forget," he tsked. "The Castleton Classic? The charity ski race in Steamboat Springs? Your brainchild? Your winter western extravaganza?"

Gaby had forgotten. It seemed like ages ago that she had planned that outing, but now it was only two weeks away.

"It was a momentary lapse. Of course I remember."

"Good. Now, since one hand washes the other, I have two favors to ask of you."

"Which are?"

"First, would you do me the honor of being my lady for the festivities?"

Though she knew there had to be personal complications included in this package, Gaby's immediate concern—her constant concern, it seemed—was money. She had skis and boots—old, but serviceable—but what about everything else: clothing, goggles, hats, gloves, socks, underwear? And how about her room? Food? Lift tickets?

"I've booked a penthouse suite overlooking the mountain for you at the hotel where we're housing our celebrity guests," Garrett said, concluding that her hesitation was prompted by concern over the nature of her accommodations rather than the cost. "Naturally, everything's carte blanche, including equipment rental. In addition, I do solemnly swear to allow you plenty of time to ski without me."

"Why would I want to do that?"

"I am an intermediate skier with an advanced fear of death. From what I've gathered, you're quite expert. If you decide to jump off cliffs without me, I promise not to be insulted. Fair?"

"Fair," she said, knowing that it would be awful if she refused him, knowing that she hadn't skied in several years and was simply dying to go. "Under those circumstances, Mr. Castleton, you have yourself a date!"

"Excellent!" He was so overjoyed, he was certain Gaby could hear him smiling. "And now for favor number two."

"Ready."

"Even though you set up almost everything before you left, there are a host of last-minute details that need attending to. If I paid for your time, would you consider taking charge of this project and seeing it through to its grand and glorious conclusion?"

"You're a very persuasive chap," Gaby said, admitting that, for her, "paid" was the operative word. "Not only do you have a date, but a tournament director as well."

The land had once belonged to the Utes, and it was said that once one knew the Yampa Valley one was forever bound to that parcel of earth, to the sound of aspen leaves quaking and trembling in the stiff breezes that whipped down through the mountains, to the rich land just west of the Great Divide.

The Utes had controlled the valley around the Yampa River, then called the Bear, for more than a century before the first white settlers arrived, coming every summer, when the ground grew verdant and lush, to hunt the game that roamed the lowlands fed by the river's drainage, and to farm the vegetation that greened the vale until the land glowed in the sunlight like a vein of emeralds. They also came for the springs, the hot, healing mineral waters which bubbled up from far below the ground, smelling of the deepest, dankest part of the earth.

Though the Utes called the area "the Stinking Springs," another legend credits three Frenchmen with providing the name the town bears today. Sometime around 1855, three men trekked along the Yampa River. Trappers, they had been in the mountains for months and they were tired, anxious to sell their bounty. While two trudged along behind, guarding their provisions and their packs, one man took the lead. As he walked ahead, checking the trail, scouting for Indians, he thought he heard a *chug-*

continuously, hurrying the porters along as if they were African bearers. She didn't check in so much as she announced her presence. And she didn't offer to help those at the Castleton Classic welcoming table so much as she added them to her entourage.

"There are several rather large cartons outside which need to be brought in and unpacked immediately. Be a love and see to it, won't you?"

Having instructed Beezie Zarlov—whom Gaby had named head of the Host Committee—on her next task, Irina turned to several other staffers, commanding each to perform a different chore. In addition to a welcoming packet containing instructions for the race, lift tickets, and a schedule of activities, each guest was to receive a royal-blue duffel imprinted in red with CASTLETON CLASSIC/STEAMBOAT SPRINGS and stuffed with woolen headbands similarly imprinted, splits of champagne, and tins of caviar. Irina had decided that no matter what was in that bag, without her input it was lacking. To fill the void, she had brought boxes of chocolate skiers especially molded for her by Kron, samplers of sunscreen and after-sun moisturizer, and new, hot-toned, disposable cameras she thought would be fun. Also, she had printed up a letter of greeting under her signature, and her signature alone. The fact that each duffle had been packed and tagged and stacked in alphabetical order was not, as she told them, her problem. It was theirs.

Once she had dispensed with the distribution of her favors, she turned her attention to the schedule of activities. Grabbing a sheet from the table, she bit her lip in a display of innocence, raised an eyebrow in a show of disbelief, and sighed, an expression of exasperation dabbed with pity.

"Garrett, dear," she said, addressing her brother, ignoring Gaby. "Is this written in stone? I mean, is there any flexibility in these plans?"

"Why do you ask?" Garrett's voice lacked interest, but Irina wasn't listening to what he was saying, let alone to how he was saying it.

"To me, the torchlight parade, whatever that is, should be the finale of the event, not the opener. Also, I loathe buffet brunches. They're so, well, *American* and, therefore, completely wrong for an occasion waving the Castleton banner. Besides, buffets are gauche. Who wants to stand in line holding some silly tray as if he's in the army or begging in some soup kitchen? I, for one, would rather go hungry! We should serve more European fare. Don't you think?''

Garrett refused to dignify his sister's pettifogging with an answer, but his silence did little to deter Irina. She continued to ramble on about how ill advised this was or poorly timed that was, while Gaby stood off to the side and fumed. Though she was angry with Irina, she was furious with herself. She had allowed this Attila to invade her territory. She had allowed her crew to be bossed. She had allowed her carefully laid out plans to be picked apart.

Why was she so easily cowed by this woman who had dismissed her? Feeling the fire of the phoenix rising inside of her, Gaby determined that if she had buckled under when Irina had fired her, or been intimidated by her in previous encounters, that was in the past. It wasn't going to happen again. Step by step, inch by inch, slowly but surely, Gaby was coming up from the ashes, gaining strength. She felt it first when she decided to go out on her own. She felt it again when she rejected the idea of going home. She felt it now when she decided that Irina deserved a proper response.

"In answer to your question," Gaby said, lifting her voice just enough to attract attention and interrupt Irina's diatribe, "there is no flexibility to this schedule. Everything has been planned down to the last snowflake. If you had any suggestions, Irina, we would have been happy to entertain them when the classic was in its initial planning stages, months ago. Your ideas may be well intentioned, but they're late." Gaby's smile was plastic, but it refused to melt under the heat of Irina's stare. "Since you did go to the trouble of buying and shipping all those lovely little goodies, however, we'll do our best to include them. As for the letter, that's up to Garrett. He's already written one on behalf of Castleton's International, but if he thinks your singular hello is called for, we'll stuff that also. Now, if you'll excuse me, I have a date with a ski slope."

Without waiting for a reply, Gaby headed for the elevators and her room. Grumbling to herself all the while, she changed into white stretch pants and a hot-pink parka, skied down to the gondola, snapped off her skis, hoisted them onto her shoulder, and took her place on line inside the loading station. Every few seconds, six more people climbed into a gondola, dropping their skis into outside slots before they did. Gaby was so involved in her own feelings of rage, she was oblivious to whatever was going on around her. Just as the door to her car was about to close, the sixth passenger lumbered in.

"Well," Max said, "fancy meeting you here."

She had known he was coming, of course, but that didn't lessen the shock of seeing him there, seated across from her, in a matte black jumpsuit, his goggles strapped to his arm, a black headband covering his ears, mirrored sunglasses hanging around his neck.

"Is this your first run?" she asked, conscious of the fact that the other passengers were listening and watching.

"No. I've been out for a while. The snow is wonderful." He looked at her face. It was pale, not yet pinked by the cold. Her hair, drawn up into a thick, high ponytail that bounced above her headband and goggles, had no snow peppering it, no ice beading its ends. He glanced down at her boots. The buckles were tightly snapped, instead of loosened or hanging open so that her feet could breathe and relax between runs. "You look too warm for this to be anything but your virgin voyage. Yes?"

Gaby smiled and nodded, noting, as she had several times before, Max's habit of deduction. On the few occasions she and Max had been together, he had impressed her as a consummate observer. It wasn't that something as simple as figuring out whether or not she had skied once or ten times that day struck her as astounding—she too was addicted to the study of minutiae—but the fact that the process was a persistent pattern of behavior did intrigue her.

"Actually, this will be my first run in several years," she said, thinking back to that last trip, that week in the Laurentians the Christmas before Steven had gone away to school, the year before her entire life had changed. "I haven't skied in a long time. I hope I haven't forgotten how."

"If you'd like, I'll hang in alongside, just in case."

"I don't want to hold you up."

Her skis were long, fast, quick-cutting slaloms; her boots front buckle, stiff, high performance.

"Somehow, I don't think you will," he said.

He started her out on easy blues, intermediate trails that let her get the feel of her skis and a sense of the mountain. Within no time, he noticed that she was moving into the turns with greater confidence, shifting her weight, planting poles, rolling her ankles. They moved on to the more difficult, black diamond runs, tackling chutes and trails with names like Vertigo, Concentration, and Oops. She was a graceful skier, swift and smooth, with little noticeable movement, yet enormous, obvious power. When she cruised, her skis were perfectly parallel, carving textbook cuts into the freshly packed snow. On the steep, she challenged the fall line, skiing straight down, edging for control, letting her skis run. On moguls, she crunched down, forcing her legs to absorb the impact of the punishing mounds, using her poles to propel her forward, riding the tops, then slicing around the sides, hitting, bumping, bouncing, sliding from one snowball to another.

Ability aside, what affected Max most was her unselfconscious, unadulterated delight in the sport. As they skied, he could hear her humming or laughing or singing to herself. Once, when she caught an edge and fell, instead of clambering to her feet, she stretched out on her back, winged her arms, and fashioned an angel in the snow, giggling like a four-year-old.

"How about heading up to Storm Peak?" Max asked, pointing to their left.

"Whatever you say." She grinned and pushed off in the direction of the chair lift.

To Max, it seemed as if her mouth was caught in a perpetual smile. He was getting caught in the spell of that smile. Her effervescence was difficult to resist. It was as if she existed within an electromagnetic field, a highly charged atmosphere that drew others to her, galvanized them, energized them, mesmerized them. Yet as he raced to catch her, Max cautioned himself. He couldn't afford to be distracted by Gabrielle Didier. She was not a woman designed for a mere dalliance. And just then, he was not a man capable of commitment.

The Storm Peak chair was a triple. As Gaby and Max moved to the front of the line, they were joined by a single, Belle Reynolds.

She was dressed all in black, and Gaby thought she looked exceptionally beautiful. Her pale blond hair hung free and loose.

She wore no hat, no headband, only earmuffs and sunglasses. Her parka, a long, full, quilted parachute silk tied just below her hips, drew attention to the young, lithesome body in the shiny black stretch pants.

She was excited to see them. On the way up, she was animated and smiling and chatted easily about the weather, the snow, and the skiing. Then Gaby asked about Chelsea.

"She's taking a private lesson."

Private lesson in what? Gaby thought with a silent chuckle. Chelsea had never cared one single whit about the mechanics of skiing. Though she was a fair skier, she had always been far more interested in the ambience of the sport. To her it was a means to an end, a way of meeting men, wealthy men in particular. Gaby recalled that when they were at Skidmore, every Friday afternoon Chelsea took off for one ski area or another; and every Sunday night she returned to the dorm with the name of another absolutely devastatingly handsome, wildly rich young man.

Chelsea had met Terry Kirkpatrick on one of those jaunts. Gaby had always thought Chelsea would wind up marrying Terry. He was a terrific guy—bright, quick-witted, good-looking— and they had seemed so much in love. But Terry lacked Chelsea's requirements for the role of prince consort. His parents owned a bar in Boston. He was at Dartmouth on scholarship. He planned to work after graduation while attending law school at night. And he wanted at least three children. Though Gaby had spent endless hours preaching to her friend about the importance of love and making a long-term investment in character and potential, Chelsea had remained adamant. No money. No marriage. No children.

"And where's your father?" Max asked.

Belle turned away. She looked out to the side, her face hidden, her voice oddly pitched.

"Over on Sunshine Peak with Lady Stoddard."

Gaby's eyebrows arched. Irina and Drake Reynolds. She could hardly wait to hear what Chelsea had to say about that combination.

"Who are you skiing with?" she asked.

The wind shifted. In place of the clean, crisp air of seconds before, a thick, cloying floral scent polluted the atmosphere. Again, Belle had showered herself with perfume.

"No one."

"Would you like to ski with us?"

"Thanks, but no. I like skiing alone, and besides, I don't want to intrude."

"You're not intruding, Belle. We'd love to have you." When Max smiled like that, Gaby couldn't imagine anyone resisting his charm, but Belle managed. They left the lift, and without so much as a good-bye, Belle skied off as quickly as she could. Too quickly, in fact. As Gaby watched her descend the trail directly below the chair, she thought Belle was being a bit reckless, skiing very fast and very close to the tree line. One mistake, one errant tuft of snow, one misplaced edge, and she could slam into a tree trunk and incur serious bodily harm.

"I don't like what I see," Gaby said, her eyes glued to the young girl's back.

"Neither do I. She's too fine a skier to be taking risks like that."

"There's something very sad about her. She rarely smiles. I wish I knew why."

Max watched Gaby's eyes narrow, her jawline tighten with concern, as Belle faded from sight. A distinctly maternal air had settled around her. What a shame, he thought, that so many who don't deserve the privilege were granted parenthood, while others with the gift of giving were so cruelly denied. But better than most, Max knew that life wasn't always fair and that divine judgment wasn't always just.

Belle's melancholia had upset them. Without the need to communicate, they took a blue trail and fell in beside each other, skiing slowly, allowing themselves time to think, time to shed the residual grayness Belle had left behind. As they rode upward again, their conversation lightened, as did their moods. Gaby felt that in some inexplicable way, some infinitesimal way, she and Max had grown closer.

"Have you ever skied the glades?" Max asked as they disembarked.

"No. Is it tough?"

"Not tough, tricky. But great fun. Are you game?"

"Sure. Why not?"

"That's the spirit!"

He grinned, exchanged his goggles for his sunglasses, adjusted his headband, and loosened his boots' grip around his ankles. Gaby did the same. When Max stood, he looked squarely at her and leaned forward. His eyes never moved from hers as he fixed her gaiter, untangling it from the cord of her sunglasses, straightening it, pulling it up under her chin. The nearness of him affected her with a hot, flushed sensation. Though it disappeared as quickly as it came, inside, where no one else could see, Gaby felt a weakness, a vulnerability, a softness she thought she'd never feel again.

"Just stick close," he said, backing away. "Follow me and don't get into an argument with a tree. They have a habit of winning."

Before they traversed into the forest, the snow-covered evergreens at the top of Storm Peak had been just another prop on a magnificent stage. Thickly frosted from the recent blizzard, the tall, stately pines seemed unreal, like sugary adornments on a birthday cake. Juxtaposed with the cloudless blue sky, the brilliant sun, the valley below, the hot-air balloons suspended in the distance—it had all looked too perfect, too planned, almost fake, as if a carnival photographer had pulled down a huge sheet of scenic paper as backdrop for a shoot.

Inside the glade, it was different. There was dimension and depth and the reality of being confronted with nature. The trees were no longer wintry wonders to be observed from afar, they were formidable objects to be respected and carefully circumvented. Though widely spaced, they created shadows, broad shafts of flat, gray light that alternated with blinding white spots where the glint of the sun disguised the roll of the terrain.

As they skied, Max made gentle turns, drawing parentheses in the powder, slaloming his way deeper into the woods. At first, Gaby found it easy to follow him. She used the same techniques she used on the open trail, poling, shifting her weight, making her turns. But then the complexion of the landscape changed. The evergreens had disappeared. Now, clumps of tall, spindly aspens crowded the glade, their light, greenish-white bark taking on an eerie, spectral cast. The snow was deeper here, requiring smaller, tighter, almost nonexistent turns. Fighting to keep up and maintain her balance, Gaby cleared her mind, set her sights on Max, and simply tuned in to his rhythm.

"How're you doing?" he shouted over his shoulder.

"I'm not sure. Are we having fun yet?"

She heard him laugh, but she also noticed that he slowed his pace, trying to accommodate her inexperience and her nerves. Suddenly, he veered to the right, leading her out of the aspens into another group of pines. Because they lived at a lower altitude, these trees stood closer together. Their boughs wore less snow than those on top of the mountain, but their trunks were cupped with huge drifts, creating dangerous troughs and mounds. In addition, every so often, a green-needled branch or a bouquet of naked twigs reached out from the snow, announcing to the world that a shrub or a bush or a sapling slept beneath winter's blanket.

It was growing late. The light had gone almost completely flat. The ground had lost its consistency. Here it was crusty. There it was soft. One minute the powder was just to the top of Gaby's boot, the next minute it hit midcalf. What looked level was not. What looked like a solid mound was not. Gaby was finding it more and more difficult to negotiate. Up ahead, even Max was struggling.

"I can see the trail," he yelled. "We'll be out of here in a minute."

"Don't take it personally," she shouted back, "but I can hardly wait!"

He turned sharply left. She tried to do the same, but her ski caught the tip of a peekaboo bush. She tried to edge, but as she did she slid into a drift, lost a pole, tumbled past a tree, and finally came to rest in a high bank. Her left leg was twisted uphill at a bizarre angle, pushing the tip of her ski deep into the snow and straining her calf. Her right leg was pretzeled the other way. She tried lifting one and then the other. She tried yanking them out, using her remaining pole as a lever. Finally, giving in to frustration and nerves, she used her pole to snap open her bindings and release her skis.

"No. Don't do that!" Max shouted. He was no more than fifty feet from her, but he couldn't get to her in time to stop her. "It's harder getting out without your skis. The powder's too thick."

"Sorry, Max. I couldn't move. I couldn't get my ski out."

"It's okay. Really. Don't get upset. Try to get up." As he spoke, he trudged toward her, using his skis like snowshoes, stomping through the snow, poking his poles into the ground to reconnoiter his route.

Gaby pushed her hands down alongside her, hoping to gain enough leverage to lift her upper body. Her arms sank up to her shoulders.

"Throw yourself backward, toward the tree behind you. Then grab onto it and try again."

She did as he said. She arched her back and hurled herself up into the air and then down into the snow. Again and again she flung her body upward, backward, onto the higher ground. She was exhausted and frightened and all she had gained was a few feet. But instead of being closer to the tree, she had shifted to the left of it, too far to grab on to the trunk. Luckily, however, when she reached down, her hands found a table to push off. Slowly, she hoisted herself up. The next step was to stand.

She bent her right leg, pushed on her right hand, and made it up into a lopsided crouch. As she hunkered awkwardly over the snow and started to bend her left leg, she thought she heard Max shouting at her, but she was too involved in what she was doing to listen. She stepped down. She searched, but there was nothing there. No snow. No bush. No tree. No ground. The space below her was empty. Her boot was dangling in a dark, black, bottomless void.

"Max!" she shrieked. Frantically, she snatched at anything she could. Her fingers found a small, scrawny young branch reaching out to her from the base of the tree. She clutched at it as if it were a lifeline. When it slipped out of her grasp, cold tears of fright welled in her eyes. She could feel her body tilting toward the crevasse. "Max! There's nothing underneath me!"

He was only a few feet away. He looked at her, the ground, the treeline, the slope. He considered the situation, possible courses of action, possible alternatives.

"Don't move," he said. "I think you're over a ravine. Just hang on."

He retrieved her skis, found her errant pole, and picked his way around so that he was at her back. Dropping her skis to her right, close to the tree, he balanced himself, reached down, wrapped his arms around her waist, and tried to hoist her to her feet. Using all the strength she had, she pushed herself out of the snow, but several times the drift pulled her back. When, finally, Max had her upright, she had trouble getting her footing.

"Stand on my skis," he said, his mouth next to her ear, his voice calm, his hold steady and secure.

Gaby stumbled. The packed ice on the bottom of her boots made them slippery. She faltered. He tightened his grip, drawing her up against him.

"Lift your boot so I can scrape the snow off."

Again, she obeyed. She held her foot so that he could clean the bottom.

"Don't put it down." Still holding onto her, he took one of her skis, snapped open the binding, slid it in between his legs and guided her foot into place.

"Jump on it."

"I'm afraid."

"I've got you. Jump on it!"

She did. When she heard the binding click and felt it lock around her boot, she practically cried with relief. They repeated the process, and within seconds Gaby was up on both skis. He handed her her poles, but told her to wait. Gently, he backed away and retraced his steps, coming around in front of her.

"Hold out your poles," he said, grabbing them with one hand, holding onto the nearest tree with the other. "Now keep your feet spread apart and your weight evenly balanced. I know you're scared, but I'm going to have you out of here in a minute."

"The last time you said that, I wound up buried in ten feet of snow."

He laughed. "I guess I deserve that."

"At least," she said, offering him a wobbly smile.

Gingerly, he pulled her toward him. At first, her skis moved in fits and starts. Once she relaxed, they settled into a track and began to glide. Having nowhere else to go, she slid into him. Again, his arm swept around her waist. For a moment, they allowed their bodies to rest against each other. With his free hand, Max dusted snow off her face and out of her hair. They were so close, nothing but a breath could come between them.

Suddenly, Gaby kissed him. It was a light kiss, a mere

glancing of lips, but for some reason—the setting, their nearness, a danger shared and now past—it tasted more intimate than a simple gesture of gratitude.

"That's the second time you've rescued me," she said, a bit startled at her boldness, but smiling nonetheless.

"I'm either a hero or a jinx."

"Whichever you are, I seem to be a perpetual damsel in distress. It's embarrassing."

They both smiled, but neither moved away from the other. They seemed suspended in time, held by the magic of the moment. They were alone in a frosted paradise, a snowy Elysium that felt totally removed from the civilized world. The sun was beginning to set, but every now and then, the wind parted the trees and invited a golden ray inside its private glen. The air was chilled. Gaby, whose body was coated with snow, shivered. The mood was broken.

"I think I'm freezing," she said, and then, feeling a twinge, "I also think I hurt my back."

"In that case, it's time for a hot toddy." Reluctantly, he released her. "Come. Let's head back."

"Great idea! Only this time," she said, peering through the trees, spotting a nearby trail, and pointing her skis in that direction, "I lead, you follow. Okay?"

Max saluted. *"Oui, mon général!* Whatever you say."

To the casual observer, it was an innocent tableau: two men drinking coffee in a back booth in a busy coffee shop on the corner of Forty-seventh Street and Sixth Avenue, the heart of New York City's diamond district. It was twelve-thirty in the afternoon. The restaurant was busy. Almost every table was filled with neighborhood people on a lunch break. Salesmen. Secretaries. Merchants. Jewelry designers. Cutters. Polishers. Women in luxurious furs grabbing a quick bite between visits to jewelers. Orthodox Jews in black hats and long black coats, conducting business over hot bowls of soup and glasses of tea. Yet despite its appearance, the tableau was anything but innocent.

They were an odd couple, the two in the back booth—one, an elegant chap in a European suit, the other, a small Indian in a loose-fitting shirt and green cloth turban. The European tapped his fingers nervously. The Indian smoked a foul-smelling cigarette and loudly slurped his coffee. Neither spoke. Every now and then, the Indian put down his cup, opened an attaché case sitting next to him on the red vinyl bench, and examined the contents of five velvet boxes.

Ten minutes passed.

The man in the suit was growing impatient.

"Look," he said with an edge to his voice, "if you want them, pay up. Otherwise, give them back. I can't sit here all day."

The Indian refused to be rushed. "I have two more to go," he said calmly. "Order a doughnut or something."

"I don't want a doughnut!" the more elegant man said. "I had these cut exactly the way you wanted. Either you give me the money we agreed on, or I pack up my goodies and take them elsewhere."

The darker man downed the last of his coffee and stubbed out his cigarette. Quickly and quietly, he locked the attaché case, reached inside his shirt, and handed the other gentleman an envelope under the table. Without another word, he slid out of the booth and out of the coffee shop, his head down, his face away from the curious. The other man stuck the thick envelope into a deep pocket inside his coat, grabbed the check, and made his way to the cashier. Paying, he turned and headed for the men's room.

Once locked safely inside a stall, he removed the envelope and began to count. Fresh thousand-dollar bills. Three hundred and sixty of them. Exactly the price they had agreed upon. The Indian was slimy, but honorable in his own way. So were the Pakistani he was meeting later that afternoon and the old man he was meeting tomorrow.

Then again, he reminded himself as he greedily calculated his take from all three transactions, as long as an arrangement remained profitable for everyone involved, there would always be honor among thieves.

Gaby spent most of the evening alone in her room. By the time she and Max had skied back to the hotel and finished regaling those gathered in the bar with their man-against-the-mountain adventure, her back had stiffened. She had hoped a hot bath and a couple of analgesics would remedy the situation, but when Garrett came to get her, she was still hurting. While it pained her to think that she wouldn't be able to see many of her efforts realized, she knew it would pain her more to sit in a straight-back chair for a long period of time. Garrett offered to stay with her, but they both knew that he had to serve as host at the welcoming banquet, and so she shooed him away in favor of a heating pad and room service.

She did get to see the torchlight parade and the fireworks. From her window, she could see the line of skiers snaking down the mountain, one after the other in perfect rhythm, their torches held high, their lights forming a string of flaming pearls. The fireworks display was equally dazzling. Skyrockets and flares hissed into the night, exploding into spectacular balls of confetti-colored sparks. Fiery pinwheels spun high above the mountain-top, swirling about the sky like a blazing lasso. And at the end, a hundred lances attached to a wooden frame burst into a sizzling silver billboard that proclaimed this the Castleton Classic.

After, while everyone else was being wined and dined and entertained by Billy Crystal, Gaby nibbled at her soup and sandwich and watched a medley of sitcoms. She was beginning to feel sorry for herself when someone knocked on her door. Maybe it was Max! She slipped on her robe, pulled her hair into a neat, low ponytail, pinched her cheeks, and hobbled to the door.

"If I were a Jewish mother, I'd have brought you chicken soup, but being a proper Englishman, I've brought tea and sympathy."

It was fleeting and she hoped it didn't show, but she was disappointed. She hadn't been able to keep Max out of her thoughts for a single second all evening. Yet seeing Garrett so concerned, so handsome in his black leather slacks and yellow cashmere sweater, standing before her with a silver tray in his hands, she couldn't help but feel a pang of guilt about thinking of him as second best. Especially since Max hadn't even called.

"Tell me all about it!" Like someone who had been ship-wrecked for years, she hurried Garrett into the sitting room, impatient to hear everything. "Did they love the torches and the fireworks? Was dinner all right? How was the wine? I know Billy Crystal had to be great. He's always great. Was he good?"

Garrett couldn't stop laughing.

"Calm yourself. You were a smashing success! Everything was glorious! As a matter of fact," he said, handing her a cup of tea, "your name has been permanently inscribed in the annals of the party planners hall of fame."

Gaby was overjoyed. She tucked a small pillow behind her back, sipped her tea, and then pestered Garrett with a thousand questions. Once he had answered the basics, she prodded him to give her the gossip—who sat with whom, who showed, who didn't, who left early and with whom, who stayed late and with whom. With all that she managed to drag out of him, there were only two surprises: Max was a no-show and though Gaby had feared he might have been closeted with Irina, according to Garrett *her* latest fascination was Drake Reynolds. As for Chelsea, according to the rumor mill she was still taking a "private" with her young instructor.

"Was Belle there?"

Garrett had to think. "No. Maybe she hooked up with some other teenagers."

"Maybe," Gaby said, but somehow she doubted that. Belle wasn't aggressively social with anyone, but she seemed particularly shy with people her own age.

"I've called the weather bureau," Garrett said. "You'll be happy to know that it's snowing now and will continue until the morning, at which time Mother Nature will follow your instructions and give us a perfect racing day: brilliant sunshine and temperatures in the twenties."

"Remind me to give her a call and say thanks, won't you?"

"I hope you're scratching yourself from the race."

"We'll see. Right now, I'm feeling okay. By morning, I expect to be better than okay. Now tell me what else has been happening. When I was up at the office, Giles said things at Castleton's are terrific."

At first, Giles had been extremely standoffish. In Gaby's mind, she was the one entitled to a fit of pique. After all, he had been her superior. He should have defended her or at least warned her about her impending departure. When Gaby interrogated Beezie, however, she discovered that Giles had also been told that she quit, but the story fed to him had included the gibe that Gaby's leaving was because she found him lacking. Gaby went to Giles immediately. She took him out for a very long lunch, during which she assuaged his ego, reassured him of her respect, her trust, and her friendship, and then recommended that he replace her with Beezie, which he did.

"Yes, Castleton's New York is doing very well. I know modesty prevents you from agreeing, but much of that success is due to your contributions." She started to protest. "All right, we won't discuss how wonderful you are. We'll talk about something else that's wonderful. One of my sources in South America has come through with some information on the missing Dinant!"

Gaby's eyes widened. Garrett was so excited he was rubbing his hands together with unabashed glee.

"According to my man in Argentina, several years ago an ex-Nazi bragged to his cronies that he had coerced someone into giving him *The Marriage of Brussels*. Clearly, he was aware of its value, both historically and financially. My source asked around a little more and found out that this guy, whoever he was, had been highly ranked and stationed in either Belgium or the south of France. Unfortunately, he died two years ago, and since he had no family and had used a number of aliases, we haven't been able to get a fix on his real name or his post during the war."

"Did he sell the tapestry?"

"No, it doesn't sound that way. But he could have. This was a clever man. Most Nazis who stole or extorted works of art as payment for security or services, took them for their intrinsic value, not because they wanted to shop them. During the war they had no market, and after the war they were stolen goods and, therefore, incriminating. This bloke, obviously anticipating an unfavorable end to Hitler's reign, demanded a note from the Dinant's owner stating that he was giving this to the German as a gift, free and clear. He also demanded that the man sign it and stamp it with his seal."

"Where is the note?"

"No one knows."

"Does anyone know the name of the signator or anything about him?"

Garrett shook his head. "Another vagueness. All my source could find out was that the original owner was a collaborator. We don't know his nationality, nor do we know the extent of his involvement, but my guess is that it was rather deep. The tapestry was in payment for silence about his activities. Since we all know how much that tapestry was worth, he must have had plenty he wanted to cover up.''

Gaby grew contemplative as she tried to fit pieces together.

"If he's still alive, I'll bet he'd love to reclaim that Dinant,'' she said quietly, thinking aloud. "If you could find out about this Nazi's death, so could he.'' She looked at Garrett, knowing that he had already come to the same conclusion she had. "Forget about Max or Prado or anyone else. This man, whoever he is, is your most serious competitor. If he was what they say he was, he'll do whatever he has to do to get what he wants.''

"I agree.'' Garrett too had grown quiet. "Collaborators tend to be an extremely nasty lot.''

Gaby looked at him. She knew how much he wanted to find the Dinant. She had even guessed some of the reasons why it was so important to him. But she cared for Garrett, and the last thing she wanted was for this quest to put him at risk.

"Maybe you should abandon the search. With this man in it, it's dangerous. It's not a grown-up game of hide-and-seek anymore.''

Garrett leaned forward, took her hand, and kissed it gently. Then he looked into her eyes. In his gaze, she saw something she had never noticed before: absolute, unwavering commitment.

"I can't give up,'' he said, his tone a mix of resignation and resolve. "Because, you see, finding the Dinant has never been a game to me. It's been the key to my future.''

"We got a tip. The diamonds are being smuggled into the United States via antiques.''

Even though the operative on the other end of the phone couldn't see him, Max nodded. Antiques. It was so logical it made him angry. He should have thought of that. Although antiques have to be checked through customs, rarely were they subjected to an exhaustive examination.

"Did you get a name?'' he asked.

"No, but we're working on it.''

"What about that other matter?''

"The surveillance?''

"Yes.''

"Your man's been real active lately. He's been back and forth between Antwerp and Brussels a dozen times."

"Business?"

"Seems that way."

Max could hear the questions in the other man's voice. *Why am I following this upright citizen? Why am I recording his telephone calls? Why am I watching his family? What did he do?*

Max heard the questions, but offered no answers. He also knew that none would be demanded of him. In exchange for his participation in tracking the diamond smuggler, he had bartered with Interpol for assistance on a private matter. He had assured his superiors that the case fell within Interpol's boundaries, but had insisted that the conduct of the case be left to his sole discretion.

"Stay on him," Max said.

"He's got a twenty-four-hour tail. I just wish you'd tell me what I'm supposed to be looking for."

"A slip," Max said, knowing the man didn't understand. "A tiny, almost invisible slip. That's all I need."

Gaby couldn't sleep. Her back was tight. And she couldn't stop thinking about Garrett and the Dinant tapestries and dead Nazis and live collaborators. She needed to clear her head. Maybe a walk would do it. She threw on a sweatsuit and sneakers and headed for the elevators and a midnight stroll through the lobby.

The main floor was quiet and dim, except for the reception desk, which remained brightly lit. In a leisurely way, she wandered about, stopping and looking inside shop windows, lingering in front of a craft store that featured a wonderful display of glazed ceramics, checking out the T-shirts and mugs in a sundries shop, stopping also to admire a luscious red suede dress and a white ski jumpsuit decorated with rhinestone snowflakes and a fox-trimmed hood that looked like something out of a Sonia Henie movie.

Along the enormous glass wall that faced out onto the mountain, there were small seating areas with butter-soft black leather chairs and granite-topped tables, each suite flanked by large faux-Chinese pots planted with tall, leafy ficus trees. The cleaning staff must have just been by. The furniture was freshly dusted. The cushions on the chairs were neatly fluffed and perfectly positioned. Even the sand in the ashtrays was raked.

It was probably that studied perfection that drew Gaby's attention toward the grouping at the end of the hall. It was filthy. There were magazines strewn about the table. There was a large beverage container, its plastic cap speared by a half-chewed straw, a crumpled brown paper bag and a crinkled ball of waxed paper. On the floor, alongside one of the chairs, was a pair of fuzzy, black *après*-ski boots and a big, red canvas pouch.

Gaby approached quietly, uncertain as to what she might find. What she saw tugged at her heart. Curled up inside a makeshift crib was Belle Reynolds, hugging her parka the way Gaby used to hold her blankies. Gaby sat on the edge of the table facing the annexed chairs, gently trying to rouse the sleeping girl. Belle sat up with a start. Her body went rigid. Her eyes widened, and her hands flew up in front of her face.

"It's all right. Don't be frightened, Belle. It's just me, Gaby."

Belle exhaled, letting go of pent-up air, releasing her muscles from their state of alert. Then, like a baby, she fisted her hands and rubbed her eyes.

"What are you doing here?" Gaby asked softly, knowing that whatever had prompted Belle to sleep here would also prevent her from telling the truth.

Her eyes darted about, searching the area as if she were afraid she was under surveillance.

"I was reading magazines," she said. "I guess I dozed off."

"But you're still in your ski clothes. Didn't you go to the dinner?"

She blushed. "No. I never made it. I'm sorry."

Gaby looked more closely at the waxed paper. It looked as if it had once held a sugary donut.

"Did you eat? Other than this, I mean?"

Belle nodded. Clearly, she was embarrassed. Gaby didn't want to press. After all, Belle's reasons for camping out were none of Gaby's business. But she looked frightened and alone and confused.

"Actually, I did. You see, Chelsea must have been looking for me. She must have said something to Max because he tracked me down at the Inferno. You know, that hangout in the square? Well, he was going to bring me back, but I told him I didn't want to have dinner at the hotel.''

"Why not?"

She paused. Again, Gaby felt the sadness that surrounded this child.

"I'm the only kid here, Gaby. I feel strange. Max said he didn't really want a big dinner either, so he invited me to go with him to Dos Amigos, that little Mexican place across the street.''

Gaby smiled. Maximilian Richard: one-man rescue squad.

"That sounds great," she said, wishing she could draw Belle out, knowing there was something else, something she kept hidden, something that needed to be said. "But why didn't you go to your room after dinner? Is there something wrong with it?''

I have to share it with him, Belle wanted to say.

"No. I just didn't want to be there.''

A chill ran through Gaby, a cold almost-thought that refused to gel.

"I'll tell you what. I have this huge suite which is going to waste. How about keeping me company?''

"I . . .''

"You're not intruding. You're not putting me out. You're not any trouble. You're not in the way. You're not anything but a pleasure, and I don't want you to be anything except my guest.''

Suddenly, impulsively, desperately, Belle threw her arms around Gaby's neck and hugged her tightly. Gaby stroked her hair and patted her back, hating whatever it was that had provoked the hot tears on her neck.

Irina lay next to Drake Reynolds, her body still warm from the heat of their sex. He was not the best lover she had ever had—only one man could claim that crown—but neither was he the worst. Truthfully, he hadn't even been her first choice, but despite her efforts to the contrary, Max Richard seemed positively determined to avoid consummating their relationship. That left Drake, who was, she reminded herself, hardly a leftover scrap. He was incredibly handsome, well positioned, a marvelous skier, a sensuous dance partner, and rich rich rich. Odd, she thought. Sexually, he had been merely adequate, quite a surprise, considering that he had been a former bedmate of that money-hungry, title-grabbing nymphomaniac. No matter. She had been spectacular. Now, watching the rise and fall of his back, the gentle undulations of a contented man at rest, she recalled the ecstasy on his face and the uncontrollable passion in his responses when she had treated him to the full extent of her expertise. He had been shocked at what she knew, what she was willing to do, and how well she did it. But then again, he, like most other men, viewed her as the consummate Victorian, a woman with sexual tunnel vision, a woman whose forays into the realm of physical exploration followed a very narrow path, thin and restricted, just like the veins which carried her cool, blue, aristocratic blood.

Once, they would have been correct. Once, she had been a sexual naïf. She had been a white-glove lover who allowed herself to be touched but never reciprocated with any enthusiasm. Then she met a man who unfolded the petals of her sexuality, a man who taught her the fulfillment of giving pleasure. Their time together had been pathetically brief. If she were to be honest, and about this she was, even if only to herself, Irina would admit that she had mourned his absence every minute of every day since that horrible moment when he had told her good-bye. She had been hysterical. She had demanded an explanation, a reason, a way to win him back. He had claimed she was smothering him with her possessiveness, with her constant demands on his time and his being. She had disagreed. She had argued, pleaded, begged him to stay, but to no avail. After he left, her obsession grew. She fantasized about him constantly. So much so that, in a way, he became a spectral companion, a ghostly lover who followed her and haunted her, especially at night, especially when she was in bed with another man. Like tonight. It wasn't Drake Reynolds she had made love to. It was *him*. It was *his* face she had seen across the pillow, *his* body she was ministering to, *his* mouth which had sucked her flesh, *his* orgasm that had filled her void.

But what about me? she thought, feeling a familiar ache in her groin. Why was it that no other man could complete her arousal, that no other man could scale the height of her passion? Had he ruined her forever? Had he made it so she would never experience another moment of complete physical satisfaction again?

She hated him for that. She hated him because, without him, she couldn't feel longing or desire or warmth or pleasure or joy. She hated him because, without him, she felt nothing but pain.

The crowd was loving it, cheering as each pair of racers came onto the course and the announcer called their race as if it were the Kentucky Derby.

"They're off . . . and they're coming through the first gate . . . Don Johnson on the red course is out ahead by a length . . . the youngster on the blue, Belle Reynolds, is catching up, coming up from behind, dropping to a tuck, taking the lead . . . Johnson adds more steam, but Mr. Miami will need to give it all he's got . . . into the stretch, way ahead, is Belle Reynolds who is . . . yes! The schoolgirl from New York City has just skied herself into first place. What a race!"

Having taken Garrett's advice and eliminated herself from the competition, Gaby stood at the bottom, checking details and observing. Watching Belle was both disturbing and exhilarating. She was a beautiful skier, but this was a celebrity race, not the Olympics. She had pushed herself coming down the course, sideswiping flagpoles, refusing to edge, allowing her skis to pick up speed to the point of recklessness.

"Her time is unbelievable. I don't think anyone's going to catch her."

Gaby had been so absorbed in her own thoughts, she hadn't heard Max come up behind her.

"Hi. No, I guess not."

"What's wrong?"

Gaby grimaced, as if searching for the right words. "She worries me."

"Me, too. Any ideas as to what it is?"

"No, but I think it's something serious. I found her sleeping in the lobby last night. I know you took her to dinner, and that was great," she said, smiling appreciatively. "But afterward, for some odd reason, she refused to go to her room." Now it was Max's turn to frown. "Did she happen to say anything while she was with you that might explain her behavior?"

"Nothing specific, but I did tiptoe around a few different possibilities."

"And?" She could tell he didn't like what he had discovered.

"For some reason, she appears to be terrified of her father."

"Do you think he beats her?" The thought hollowed Gaby's stomach. "Was she in the lobby because she was afraid he might punish her for having dinner with you?"

"I certainly hope not. Unfortunately, I don't know Drake Reynolds well enough even to hazard a guess," he said, silently promising to find out as much as he could.

"Neither do I," Gaby said, silently promising the same thing.

"Meanwhile, how are you? I see you're not racing, which I assume means your back is still hurting."

"Twinging. Not hurting."

"I feel responsible."

Why was it that when he looked at her with those deep blue eyes, the rest of the world went out of focus?

"Don't be silly," she said. "You're my knight in shining armor."

He smiled and then, with great ceremony, bowed low at the waist. When he spoke, it was with exaggerated pomp.

"Well then, fair lady. I hereby dedicate my race to you and pledge to give you my best effort. But please, if I lose, don't take it personally."

Gaby laughed. He kissed both her cheeks, said good-bye, and started for the lift.

"Don't deny it. The man turns you on."

"What's true is true," she said, keeping her eyes on Max while answering Chelsea.

"Have you slept with him yet?"

Gaby shook her head.

"Are you sleeping with Garrett?"

Again, she shook her head.

"Have you taken a vow of celibacy?"

Gaby faced her friend and laughed.

"Not by choice."

Chelsea paused and considered the matter.

"You've never slept with anyone but Brian, have you?"

While Gaby might have expected Chelsea's tone to be accusing or condescending or even critical—in view of her own obvious insistence upon the need for an active sex life—instead, it was gentle and understanding.

"No. And yes, I'm scared to death about jumping into bed with someone new, in case that was going to be your next question."

Chelsea nodded, as if confirming her own conclusions.

"Listen," she said quietly so that no one could overhear, "you're not a virgin. You don't have to play 'I'll show you mine if you show me yours.' You've seen it before, and believe me, darling, no matter how much they'd like you to believe otherwise, everyone has the same equipment. Men are men and women are women. Some are smaller in places than others. Some are bigger. But basically, it's all the same. Screw one and you can screw them all! Trust me," she said, patting Gaby's arm and grinning. "All you have to do is lie back and enjoy it."

Gaby tried to heed Chelsea's advice, but all evening she was as nervous as a bride on her wedding night. She knew Garrett was going to come to her room. He couldn't stay away from her. He was attentive and affectionate. His eyes rarely left her and his manner grew more intimate as the hours lengthened. When the awards banquet ended, he linked his arm through hers and never removed it until they were standing at her door. Then he turned her to him, slid his arm around her back, and drew her close. His lips nuzzled her ear.

"Don't send me away," he whispered. "Let me stay with you tonight."

So many conflicting feelings buzzed inside of her.

I want to. I don't want to. I can. I can't. I'm embarrassed. I'm frightened. I'm inexperienced. I'm inadequate.

His mouth found hers. His kiss was gentle, filled with caring.

I need to feel loved. I need to be touched.

Shyly, she handed him her key. As he opened the door and stood aside to let her in, she shuddered. She felt so awkward and horribly unsophisticated. What was she supposed to do now?

"I hope you don't mind," he said, closing the door behind them, locking it, leading her into the sitting room where a crackling fire warmed the room with a faintly orange glow. "I took the liberty of having a bottle of champagne sent up."

The curtains were drawn. On top of the fireplace, in gilded three-point candelabra, long, white tapers flickered in the dimness, their yellow flames licking the air with an elegant sensuality. Music played softly in the background, a full, lush orchestral sound that Gaby recognized as a Brahms serenade. She couldn't help but be impressed. Obviously, Garrett was not going to simply bed her. He intended to romance her.

She sat on the sofa, positioning herself safely in a corner, watching as he popped the cork on the champagne and poured the bubbling ecru wine into two crystal flutes. She felt as if perhaps she had given him the key to the wrong room, that instead of being in a hotel on a mountain in Colorado, she was in a high stone tower in a medieval castle in a magical, faraway land. She was a princess, he was a prince. She had been asleep for a very long time and he had come to awaken her.

But her fairy tale rang with the harsh undertone of reality. Part of her had been asleep for a very long time. Her femininity, her sexuality, the core of her womanhood, had lain dormant for more than two years. Sipping the champagne, watching the fire, feeling the heat and desire emanating from the man seated next to her, slowly she felt a stirring begin. Garrett moved toward her. He took her glass, put it on the table, and took her in his arms. His kiss was deeper, more ardent now. As his tongue flicked inside her mouth and his fingers combed through her hair, she was certain she could feel the thump of his heart against her chest. He needed her. He wanted her. Every movement, every sigh, everything he did, told her so. She had no reason to feel afraid, no reason to feel self-conscious or hesitant. Yet she did. She felt all those things and more.

"Why don't you change?" he said, his whisper hoarse with longing. "I'll meet you inside."

Afraid her own voice might betray her, she rose without saying a word, taking her champagne with her to the bathroom. Once inside, she downed whatever remained, wishing she could empty the bottle of its liquid and fill her body with courage, any kind of courage. Slowly, with shaking hands, she removed her clothes, averting her face from the mirror, not wanting to watch herself disrobe. Once she had, she couldn't resist. She turned and looked, perusing herself slowly, critically, trying to see herself as he would see her.

She didn't notice how taut and firm her body was. All she noticed was that years of daily exercise hadn't thwarted the advancement of age. The simple fact was that she wasn't a young girl anymore, and suddenly that seemed less an irrefutable fact of life as it did a reason for rejection and scorn. She saw the extra flesh on her arms, the slight sag in her breasts, the waxy-looking lines that stretched across her hips, reminding her that once she had been pregnant and had borne a child.

She touched her skin. Thanks to the cold, it was dry, more like linen than satin. Quickly, she reached for body lotion and slathered it all over herself, rubbing it in, trying to restore a youthful, baby-soft feel. She powdered herself and perfumed herself. She brushed her teeth and gargled with mouthwash. She fluffed her hair, tipped her lashes with a flick of the mascara wand, and retinted her lips. Finally, when she had run out of ablutions and could find no further acts of purification or beautification to perform, she reached for her nightgown and slipped it on.

It was old—she had bought it during that last year of her marriage, when she had been silly enough to believe that an expensive negligee might actually make a difference. It was a rich yellow, like the deepest part of an iris; long and silky with two thin straps and a heartshaped bodice, it caressed her body, clinging to her the way she had wanted Brian to cling to her. But the man waiting in the bed was not Brian. He was a stranger. How was she ever going to face him wearing something this revealing? How was she ever going to let him take it off her?

Please, let it be dark.

She opened the door. He had been merciful. The room was black except for the low light near the bed. She could see that he had brought her another glass, as well as the rest of the champagne. She could also see that he was naked under the covers. As she walked toward him, his blue eyes traced the lines of her body with a scorching heat, as if they had been fired with acetylene. Quickly, she slipped beneath the blanket, maintaining a slight distance.

"You're beautiful." He said it simply and ingenuously. It was not a line in a script written for seduction. It was how he felt.

He handed her champagne. Quietly, they drank. Gaby could feel the air thickening. She was nervous, but she was needy. She wanted a man's hands on her, a man's mouth pushing against hers, a man's strength pushing into her and letting her know again the joy of being a woman. Sensing that Garrett was waiting for a sign from her, she placed her glass on the table alongside the bed. He did the same. Then he shut the light.

As Garrett came nearer, Gaby's breath lumped in her throat. *Please let me be all right, let me please him,* she prayed.

His face hovered above hers. Slowly, he found her mouth. He kissed her, tasted her, luxuriated in the feel of her lips against his. He was eager, but hesitant, not wanting to rush her, wanting to demonstrate his respect for her. His hands stroked her arms and then moved down the sides of her body, the silky gown slithering against her skin. He seemed to like feeling the contours of her body beneath the cool, sleek fabric. She liked it too. Inside, way inside in that dark place that housed the most primitive of responses, she felt a tingling, a kindling. As his hands touched her breasts, mingling flesh and silk, she gasped. He too was short of breath. He moved closer, pressing against her, kissing her, rubbing her breasts until he could feel that her excitement matched his. Then he raised himself up and lifted her gown like a groom lifting his bride's veil. She raised her arms and felt his legs straddle her as he removed the yellow negligee. For a brief second, the cool air kissed her skin, but then the heat returned as his mouth savored her breast. He lowered himself onto her loins and undulated against her, his other hand groping about, seeking entrance to the well of her passion.

Gaby returned his embraces. She touched him, kissed him, fondled him. And though she sensed a certain reserve to her responses, she found that her body had a mind of its own, that it trembled and stiffened, hardened and softened, sizzled and pulsed according to how and where she was touched. Yet all the while, that small, observant, thoughtful part of her brain that always remained aloof and active marveled at how much she was enjoying the sex. She wasn't in love with Garrett—more than once, she had seen Max's face flash before her eyes, and yes, even Brian's image had insinuated itself—but the sex, the physical rutting about, the joining of bodies, the hot, steamy, lustful sating of the libido was truly delicious.

She reveled in the way Garrett lavished her with displays of affection, stroking, caressing, worshipping her body as if he were a supplicant. He wanted her. If she didn't want him with the same intensity, she needed him nonetheless. She led him to her, feeling him enter her, feeling her own body close around his. They ground against each other, sliding, pumping, pressing into each other until, finally, Garrett seemed to explode. For Gaby, it was a quieter quake.

He kissed her softly, rolled off her, and brushed a tendril of hair from her face.

"You're a remarkably beautiful woman, Gabrielle Didier." He kissed her again, planting little pecks on her cheeks and lips. "I think I'm falling in love with you."

She tried to smile, but the most she could muster was a wobble. If only she knew what was expected of her.

"You don't have to say anything," he said. "Just know that I care and know that I'm a patient man."

Soon after, he fell asleep. As he lay beside her, spent and sated and grateful, Gaby grew anxious. Instead of feeling warm and satisfied, the way she should, she felt cold inside, empty and lacking. Something was terribly wrong with her. It had to be. When she had experienced this rumbling, low-voltage climax with Brian, she had thought it was the natural course of a marriage, that after years of making love to the same man, passion simply dissipated, changing from the volcanic eruptions of the early years to a less vigorous thundering. But Garrett was not her husband of many years. He was a suitor, an admirer, a man who clearly wanted to move their relationship forward. Making love to him should have been overwhelming, if for no other reason than it was new. Instead, it had felt medicinal. She had reacted by rote, as if a doctor had prescribed sex as a remedy for built-up tension. He had touched her, but only on the outside. He hadn't reached the heart of her sensuality. Gaby was beginning to doubt anyone ever would.

Hoping not to disturb Garrett, she slipped out of bed and made her way to the bathroom. She switched on the light and immediately caught sight of her reflection. Her hair was mussed. Her lipstick had been kissed off. Her skin was pale. And her eyes were flat, save the two lone tears that fell onto her cheeks. A man had just told her she was beautiful and remarkable and sexy and desirable and that he was falling in love with her. Yet Gaby had never felt lonelier. She felt isolated and unworthy and unfulfilled and like a total failure as a woman. Not because he had been left wanting, but because she had been left wanting.

She turned on the water and washed her face. She sponged herself and then repowdered her skin until she smelled sweet and soft and untouched. She started to brush her hair and then stopped.

"You don't love Garrett," she said to the disheartened woman in the mirror. "And I'm beginning to think you didn't love Brian as much as you thought you did." She stood back, studying herself, allowing the thought that had taken seed to develop. "That's what's wrong! It's not a physical deformity or a missing part. You're not some kind of freak. You just need to fall in love with the right man."

Feeling as if she had lifted an incredible burden off her shoulders, her mood buoyed. She brushed her hair and her teeth, sprayed a bit of perfume on, and slipped into her robe. As she did, she concluded that how much or how little she had felt in bed with Garrett was important only to the moment. Beyond that, it was irrelevant. If she was ever going to get on with her life, she had to grab hold of other feelings and think of other things.

Like how many new clients this outing had added to her roster. Like how she had felt earlier this evening, when she had opened the congratulatory telegram from Garrett Castleton, Sr., and had read his words of praise and gratitude. How she had felt when she read that he wanted her to be his honored guest at his pre–Grosvenor House reception at Shefferd House, the Castleton family seat. Like how she had felt when the entire audience had stood and applauded her efforts on behalf of the Castleton Classic. And yes, she had to remember how she had felt when Irina Stoddard had taken her aside, abandoned all subtlety, and warned her against trying to muscle her way back into Castleton's.

In each instance, she had felt strong and confident and able. She had felt triumphant and maybe even powerful. With Irina, she had simply drawn herself up into an indignant huff, planted a sardonic half smile on her lips and tossed off a casual, "I'm too busy minding my own business to care about minding your business."

But more than anything, she had to remember how she had felt after Irina had laughed and called her an opportunist in sheep's clothing.

"You want everyone to think of you as a nice guy. Just remember what they say about nice guys. They finish last!"

"Only if they allow it," Gaby had retorted. "And I won't!" she had added silently, and she had meant it.

So what if there was no passion in her life, no special man, no special joy? So what if her body and her heart ached with an emptiness as vast and as deep as a canyon? She was growing, changing, developing into that independent person Simone had envisioned. She was determined to make that vision a reality, to make a success of herself, to make certain that she would never again have to rely on anyone other than herself for her well-being. It wasn't going to be easy and it wasn't going to happen tomorrow. But it *was* going to happen.

Maybe later, there would be time for love.

PART THREE

PART
THREE

15

It annoyed Garrett Castleton, Sr., that he wasn't a lord or, at the very least, a knight. Certainly with his vast fortune, he could have taken over the titles of any number of down-at-the-heels nobles who had been forced to open their estates to tourists in order to pay expenses. Shefferd House, built in the latter part of the sixteenth century, had been the Castleton family seat for two hundred years. Though it had burned and been rebuilt twice during its history, and had been redecorated and refurbished dozens of times, its maintenance had never depended on the profit from a turnstile. A Castleton had always paid the bills.

If service to the crown or stellar achievement in business or the arts was supposed to earn investiture, then how, he wondered, could the Castleton clan have been overlooked for so long? Surely, someone must have noticed that since 1743 the Castleton name had been equated with superior quality, influence, and continued success. Surely, someone must have been paying attention when Castleton's made news with record-breaking sales and historic auctions. Had the crown been sleeping when Castleton's held the first significant auction resulting from the Settled Lands Act of 1882 and started a trend in which landed aristocrats—practically impoverished by the agricultural crisis of the 1870s—sold off many of their artistic treasures for the first time and gave a much-needed boost to the London art market? Had everyone been out of town when Pierpont Morgan, then the acknowledged expert in the field, bought three of the finest tapestries in his collection from a single Castleton auction or when, in 1917, William Randolph Hearst began his famous assemblage of armor by buying his first two lots from Castleton's?

And what about military service? At least one Castleton had served Britain in every major battle since the Seven Years War and, with only a few exceptions, had served with distinction. There was Nigel Castleton, who deserted during the Napoleonic Wars after his lover, and commanding officer, had been killed. There was Albert Castleton, who had been part of the unit Disraeli had sent to Egypt to guard the Suez Canal in 1875. He had been there less than six months when he began to complain of headaches and visions and then one day simply disappeared. There was George Castleton, who, during the First World War, was dishonorably discharged after he decided he knew a quicker route than the one he was supposed to take and led his troops directly into an ambush. And while Garrett Sr. firmly believed that he should have been knighted for his efforts during the Second World War, he knew there were those who held that his exemplary record in British intelligence had been nullified by the operation he and Etienne Lafitte supposedly had bungled during the Battle of the Bulge.

They hadn't bungled anything, he thought angrily, quickly rising to the defense of himself and his old comrade. They had been betrayed. Why didn't those in a position to confer titles concentrate on what he and Etienne had accomplished? Why didn't they list their successful missions? The lives they saved? The military maneuvers they assisted? No! One incident— admittedly horrible—had erased all the good he and Etienne had done. And they had been good. They had worked so well together. Maybe because they had so much in common—antiques, running a family business, being newly married—they had liked each other right off, quickly becoming *simpático*, establishing a sense of being completely in tune with each other. Each knew without words what the other one needed or wanted. They protected each other. They cared about each other.

"Is something wrong, dear?"

Garrett was so far away that, at first, Charlotte's voice merely tickled his consciousness. Without turning around, he lifted his arm and invited his wife to join him at the window of their sitting room to enjoy the dusky end of an early summer's day.

The sky was soft, washed with pale patterns of pinks and blues and violets and white. Below, the grounds of Shefferd House sparkled. It had rained off and on that afternoon. Thick, gray, moisture-laden clouds had alternated with periodic bursts of brilliant, yellow sun. The massive lawn that surrounded the Georgian estate glowed with a rich viridescence. Flower-filled gardens, both formal and wild, splashed the pastoral landscape with broad strokes of vivid color. Boxed squares of peonies, phlox, delphinium, and evening primroses balanced stately rows of sculpted yews and neatly contained beds of vivacious, pink dahlias. Stone walls were dressed in ivy. Grassy paths were framed by leafy trees. Archways studded with roses marked the way to the house, where each entry was flanked with huge Versailles planters abloom with summer's bounty.

"Are you thinking about this evening's party?" Charlotte asked, trying to divine the cause of her husband's frown.

"No," he said, his eyes blinking as if he had just come out of a trance. "I was thinking about things that happened a long time ago." His gaze drifted back outside, to the boundaries of his property and the horizon beyond. "It seems as if the older I get and the less future I have available, the more I find myself dwelling in the past."

Charlotte knew by the pained look in his eyes that he had been thinking of Etienne Lafitte. Not wishing to disturb the memory, she didn't speak, but instead simply remained by his side, just as she had throughout their forty-eight years.

"So many mistakes," he muttered, more to himself than to her. "So many terrible mistakes."

"Mistakes can be remedied, you know."

"Some, not all."

"A great deal of time has elapsed, Garrett. Surely you realize that however grievous your past wrongdoings, eventually anger loses its heat. Can't you abandon your hostility toward Etienne?"

"I have." He took his wife's face in his hands and gently kissed her. He was so fortunate to have married her, so fortunate that she still saw fit to love him. "I miss Etienne and there's nothing I'd like more than to have him back in my life."

"But?"

"Pride, I suppose. Fear of rejection, perhaps. So often, I've thought about calling or writing, but somehow the words stick in my throat.";

"Knowing Etienne, he wouldn't demand a lengthy apology. 'I'm sorry' is all it would take. Two words, Garrett. Two simple words."

"As always, my darling, you're right." He patted her cheek and smiled. "Soon I shall make things right between Etienne and myself."

"Just don't put off for tomorrow what should be done today," she said pointedly. "I hate to sound grim, but at this stage in our lives we don't know how many tomorrows we have left."

Garrett's eyes darkened as he looked away and wondered, "Were there ever enough tomorrows to make up for the sins of yesterday?"

"Can you believe the way they're carrying on? You'd think that woman was God's gift!" Irina looked toward the end of the receiving line, where Gabrielle Didier stood flanked by the two reigning Castletons, the Garretts Sr. and Jr.

Bentley Castleton's wife, Phoebe, who was standing next to her niece, discharged her duties with even less enthusiasm than Irina. Unhappy with the secondary role given her husband, Phoebe resented feeling like a ceremonial horse, being trotted out on state occasions, asked to perform in a particular way, and then trotted back into her stall until the next time her presence was required. Her greetings were so brief they were almost terse, her handshakes so short it made the recipient feel as if he should run to the nearest clinic and check for signs of plague.

"What do you know about her?" Phoebe asked, eager to hear whatever gossip Irina wanted to dispense. "Where did she come from?"

"I have no idea. One day, she simply appeared and *voilà*! Vincent, how delightful to see you." Irina changed gears with the agility of a Grand Prix driver, kissing Vincent Prado on both cheeks and promising to speak with him later. She shook hands with Dame Something-or-Other and then continued her conversation. "For all I know, the woman was birthed in a seashell. What difference? Garrett is positively besotted. I wouldn't be at all surprised if he chose tonight to announce their betrothal."

"I did overhear him ask your father if they might have a few moments together sometime during the evening."

"Oh, splendid." Irina grimaced, especially after she spotted her ex-husband with his latest wife. "As if my life were not complete."

Sensing that it was wiser to avoid even a minor confrontation with his former wife, Winston steered the current Lady Stoddard away from the receiving line and into the ballroom. Irina was too involved in what Gaby was doing to care.

An ancient rage mounted in her gut. Why was she positioned at the lower end of this receiving line when, by rights, she should be near the head? Why was she made to feel like a guest in this house when, one of these days, she should be its mistress? And why was she viewed as the challenger in the battle for control of Castleton's when she should be the natural successor?

Again, she fixed her gaze on her brother and his current lady. Garrett was truly besotted. Worse, it appeared as if her father was equally entranced. Both men seemed glued to the American's side. Admittedly, Gabrielle Didier looked beautiful. Her tall, lean body was encased in a golden wand of Fortuny pleats that fell from her shoulders to her toes like an Athenian toga. Elegantly spare, except for two twisted, tasseled cords of silk that crisscrossed her midriff and waist, plus minimal accents of gold on her ears and wrists, she appeared uniquely unadorned in a forest of jeweled bibs and long, watery chiffons. Even Irina felt overdone in her floor-length hyacinth silk and voluminous Queen Mary pearls.

Without bothering to bid anyone adieu, Irina abandoned the receiving line. As she made her way down the long hall toward the ballroom, moving with the slow, deliberate step that was her style, only peripherally aware of the ancestral portraits that lined the damask walls, she thought about what was and what was to come.

Irina believed she had been charged with the task of restructuring destiny. Though she believed that her cunning and perseverance would effect a victory, she was not a woman to trust fate. She had to discredit her brother in such a way as to completely destroy his chances of being named head of Castleton's International. To do that, she had to take a lesson from the Cynthia Hawthorne episode: everyone has at least one dirty piece of laundry hanging on his line. Gabrielle Didier had to have something she didn't want anyone to know. All Irina had to do was find out what that was.

As she approached the portrait of her grandfather, she stopped and stared at his cold, arrogant visage. Just as he had in life, he ignored her, his blue eyes focused on a spot above her head. When they were children, the old man had favored Garrett. Just as she had when she was a child, and then again as a young woman, she wanted to scream, to demand his attention, his affection, his respect. But back then, out of fear of chastisement from her father, she had remembered her place and kept her thoughts to herself.

Suddenly, she clenched her fists and laughed, emitting a mirthless, vengeful sound.

"I'm going to make you notice me," she said to the man in the gilded frame. "You may have been able to convince my father to talk my mother out of Castleton's, but it won't work with me. I'm going to take what you refused to give. I'm going to be all that you wouldn't let me be. And if I have to destroy your precious grandson to do it, *c'est la guerre!*"

The grand ballroom was at the eastern end of Shefferd House, an enormous domed space that stretched the full width of the mansion. At either end were deep, bayed windows that helped create the illusion that the room was oval rather than rectangular. Redecorated by Charlotte five years before, the color scheme was restful, receding into the background like a gracious hostess wishing to spotlight her guests. On the walls hung a rich yellow and vanilla striped paper that flattered complexions, but politely demurred to the more fanciful fabrications of ladies' evening wear. Intricately carved doorways and moldings painted a soft eggshell glowed in the reflected light of three ornate crystal chandeliers. A muted celadon-blue silk draped the windows, its delicate shading echoed in both the upholstery and the Savonnerie carpet that covered the floor when the room was not used for dancing.

Exuberant George III gilt-framed mirrors faced each other across the broad expanse, looking down over elaborate chimney-pieces carved from stark white alabaster. Populating the room were a number of elegant gueridons, consoles, and end tables. Reflecting Charlotte's passion for colored stones, each boasted a surface of porphyry, agate, jasper, blue john, or lapis lazuli. The other furnishings, pushed back against the walls for this evening's festivities, were a mix of influences. The English chauvinism of both Charlotte and Garrett was evidenced by a predominance of Robert Adam's slender, disciplined neoclassicism. But here and there were pieces in the more flamboyant rococo style of the French from the same period, reminders of the close friendship the Castletons had once enjoyed with an *antiquaire* on the Quai Voltaire.

In a corner by a window that afforded glimpses of Charlotte's prized rose garden, a five-piece orchestra played "Dancing in the Dark." As Garrett Jr. stood on the sidelines and watched his father expertly lead Gaby around the floor, he couldn't help but notice that Garrett Sr. was still, at seventy-three, extremely swank, tall, and slender with silver hair and a ruddy complexion. His body moved with the easy, unselfconscious grace of a man who knew he didn't have to impress anyone with feats of terpsichore.

"Why is it that he can dance and converse at the same time? When I dance, I have to count."

"You have other talents, Uncle Bentley," Garrett said kindly, trying to gauge how much his uncle had imbibed.

"Name two."

"You're a gifted pianist and a patient teacher. If not for you, I might never have learned to ride a bicycle or to swim."

"Both extremely important disciplines," he said with a self-deprecating laugh. "If you never learned either one, it wouldn't have mattered one whit."

"It would have mattered to me, because you matter to me."

Bentley looked confused and then surprised and then deeply touched. His eyes moistened, and when he smiled, his upper lip quivered.

"I know it's undignified and probably not in keeping with

the occasion, but . . ." He threw his arms around Garrett's neck and hugged him. "I'm proud to be your uncle and I'll be even prouder when you're named head of Castleton's."

"*If* I'm named head of Castleton's."

"Do you really have any doubt?"

"As a matter of fact, yes, I do." Garrett proffered an insecure smile and shook his head in frustration. "I had a rather long heart-to-heart with Father not more than an hour ago. Like an apprentice applying for his first job, I listed my qualifications for the post. I was modest about my achievements, honest about my shortcomings. I laid out my hopes for the future, my plans for the present, and my philosophy on the direction I felt Castleton's should take over the next several decades. I wanted his approval. I wanted him to show appreciation for my efforts. For God's sake, I wanted him to give me the job then and there. But all he said was, 'We'll see.' Hardly a vote of confidence, wouldn't you say?"

"He's toying with you. Who else is he going to select? Her?"

He nodded in the direction of Irina, who was standing near the door talking to her ex-husband and the current Lady Stoddard, a statuesque redhead draped in clingy white jersey and dripping rubies. Irina's face was tight. Her back was so straight she looked as if she had been stapled to the wall.

"Big brother rarely consults me on anything," Bentley said with uncharacteristic pique, "but if it even looks as if he's entertaining the notion of elevating that piranha, I shall feel compelled to voice my objections. I may not be a major force in this family, but I am a Castleton, I do care, and for once I shall make damn sure I count."

Garrett squeezed Bentley's arm affectionately and then turned to watch Irina. She must have sensed him studying her because, just as he was about to turn away, she caught his eye. He saw the hostility. He felt the challenge. But it was when she looked at Gaby, returned to him, and gave him a slow, sinister smile, that he felt the depth of her intent.

"I may need you, Uncle," he said, keeping his eye on Irina, refusing to retreat.

"I'll be there, Nephew," Bentley said, pledging his allegiance to the one and only Castleton who had ever claimed to need him. "But let's go slowly. I have a feeling that calling up the troops would be a mite premature. I know he's not free with praise, but your father's quite proud of you. You've made Castleton's New York a smashing success."

"Thanks in large part to her," Garrett said, smiling at Gaby, who was still dancing with her host.

"She is as graceful as she is charming," Bentley agreed. "I suggest you nab her as quickly as you can."

"If she would agree, my dear uncle, I would marry her in an instant."

"Have you asked?"

"Not yet, but I will. Soon."

"Judging by the silly expression on your father's face, I think he'd be delighted to have her as a daughter-in-law and, if you don't mind my sounding crude, if marrying her would help ensure the chairmanship, run, don't walk, to the nearest altar!"

Garrett chuckled and then grew serious.

"Your suggestion is both valid and personally pleasing, but I was thinking more along the lines of a spectacular coup, one that would shake up the antiques world and attract international attention."

Bentley's eyes widened. "Like what?"

"Like finding the missing Dinant tapestry, grouping it with two I already own, and auctioning off the trio as a package."

"Can it be done?"

"I'm working on it. Let's hope it comes through in time."

"Would you like an alternative?"

"Of course."

"Find a way to reunite your father and Etienne Lafitte."

Now Garrett's eyes widened.

"I thought they loathed each other."

"Ancient history. And besides, it was your father who did all the loathing, not Etienne. That's why he's searching for just the right opportunity to apologize. Bended knee is not his best position."

Garrett could hardly believe what he was hearing. After the Antiques Fair debacle, Irina had told him Garrett Sr. had issued a directive that Armand Lafitte was to be barred from Castleton's, both as a buyer and as a consignor. According to her, their father had been outraged at Armand's conduct, but yet, not at all surprised. Irina related how Garrett Sr. had gone on at great length about the lack of loyalty on the part of the Lafittes, their selfish tendency to do whatever was good for them without care or consideration for anyone else. At the time, Garrett hadn't questioned her because the feud between his father and Armand's father was part of the family legend. He couldn't recall Garrett Sr. giving any indication of a thaw, and so he had accepted Irina at her word and had carried out the so-called directive. Now he wondered.

"Are you quite certain about this, Uncle Bentley?"

"Quite. As a matter of fact, your mother and I were talking about it earlier. She was hoping that Etienne and Josette were in town for Grosvenor House. If they were, she was going to try to arrange an accidental meeting."

"But?"

"We decided that was not the way. A reunion such as theirs requires a dramatic denouement on a grand stage. But where and when and how?"

It was as if the answer had been there all along, but hidden, submerged beneath a bog of incidental, inconsequential diversions. A slow smile began to grab hold of Garrett's lips. As the thought grew and took shape, his smile expanded.

"The where is Castleton's New York," he said quietly, but with an air of anticipatory triumph. "The when is the night I auction off the Dinants. I shall send a personal invitation to the entire Lafitte family: Josette, Etienne, Jacques, and Armand. And I promise you, Uncle Bentley, before the hammer comes down on the first sale, the hatchet will have been buried."

"Do you have a background in public relations?" Garrett Sr. asked, guiding Gaby down the hall to his library.

"I don't have a background in anything," Gaby said truthfully. "Castleton's was my first foray into the working world."

"If that's so, you had a rather impressive debut. You have a creative spark and a wealth of enthusiasm, both very rare commodities. You gave us a much-needed boot in the pants, and for that I'm grateful."

"I enjoyed it," she said simply.

He opened a door and led her into one of the most beautiful rooms she had ever seen. She loved books, and this room was filled with them. Shelf after shelf of leather-bound volumes lined the walls, their timeworn hides and gilded spines forming a rich but muted facade. A deep crimson Aubusson carpeted the floor. Crocus-yellow silk swagged cornices that topped large but gracious French doors. Gilded chairs upholstered in dark red leather sat before a Sheraton mahogany desk. Plum-toned porphyry pilasters segmented the shelves, standing like sentries at evenly spaced intervals. Burled walnut and mahogany occasional tables provided display space for magnificent *objets d'art*, ranging from blue john candelabra and ormolu clocks to tortoiseshell tea caddies and obelisks.

It was all splendid, but clearly the special treasures had been reserved for a place of honor on top of an extravagantly carved George I gilt-gesso side table. Reflected in a heavily scrolled pier glass were two tall, eight-light eighteenth-century candelabra aglow with candles and two Meissen figures mounted on Louis XV ormolu bases. Gaby felt drawn to them, reaching out with a hesitant finger to touch the cool ceramic. Something about them was vaguely familiar. One was a woman clad in a white cloak and a puce and white dress. She held a scepter and an orb and sat before a dappled horse. Scattered around her were books, a palette, a hammer, a cuirass, a shield, and a globe. Her companion, who was seated on the back of a crocodile with sharp fangs and a pink tongue, wore a feathered headdress, skirt, and cape, and held a parrot in one hand, a flower-filled cornucopia in the other.

Unable to recall where she had seen those two pieces before, Gaby took a seat on one of two cream velvet sofas and watched as Garrett Sr. walked toward a wall, pressed a button, and stood aside as a trompe l'oeil door swung open and revealed a hidden bar.

"Brandy?" he asked, amused by the somewhat startled look on her face.

"Please," she said, suddenly busy with a loose tendril, quickly retreating behind her mask of nonchalance. She knew she was supposed to be used to luxury. She knew he was supposed to think she was to the manner born. But while Gabrielle Didier might be blasé about secret panels and English mansions, Gaby Cocroft wanted to giggle.

Serenaded by the faint sounds of music coming from the

ballroom, they sipped their brandies and talked about Castleton's. He seemed fascinated with her opinions on the business of antiques.

"It's like any other business," she said. "You have a product to sell. You have competition. In order for you to garner the lion's share of the market, you have to advertise. You have to promote yourself. You have to create an image."

"Ah, but Gaby my dear, ours is a world of authenticity and provenances and history, not one of image and illusion."

"I disagree. Today, antiques are vendables. Once they enter the storerooms at Castleton's or Sotheby's or Christie's, they're salable merchandise, just like cars or dresses. There are trends and top-of-the-line items just as there are staples and come-ons. Castleton's is like a department store. A buyer comes in, looks over what you have to sell, and then either buys or passes. The only difference between you and Harrod's is that at Harrod's the price on the tag is fixed."

He laughed, a booming sound that seemed more appropriate to someone larger.

"I never thought of it that way, but you're right." He laughed again and then shook his head. "Things are so different nowadays. When I first came to work for my father, auctions were hushed, gentlemanly affairs. They were tea parties without the biscuits. There was never a raised voice. Even the auctioneer maintained a definite decorum. Now, I watch Garrett in amazement. The way he works the crowd, talking to them, cajoling them, deliberately trying to incite frenzy."

He smiled and though Gaby thought he was responding to a vision of his son at work, his eyes had grown hazy and distant.

"Did you ever hear of Peter Wilson?" She nodded, not speaking for fear of intruding on whatever moment he was reliving. "He was the genius who singlehandedly brought auction houses into the twentieth century. Some of us came kicking and screaming, loath to give up our narrow attitudes and limited perceptions of who we were and who our customers were, but his success placed the rest of us in an awkward position. We couldn't fight him, so we had to join him."

He didn't seem to require a response, so Gaby continued to remain silent, listening and being as companionable as she could.

"You would have liked him," Garrett said. "He was quite

charming." Again, the past seemed to take over. His eyes clouded as the room before him faded and another time asserted itself. "He and I served together during the war. We were intelligence agents." He paused. His eyes narrowed and his mouth tightened. He looked confused, as if struggling to decide whether or not to continue his journey backward. "There were three of us. We called ourselves the Furies because just like those three mythological spirits, we thirsted for revenge against those who wanted to destroy our world. Sometimes we succeeded. And sometimes we failed."

Gaby saw his pain and, in her own way, understood. He must have been witness to enormous carnage. Though she was a pacifist at heart, probably because she was mother to a son, she could never look away from or abandon those who had been asked to fight and had agreed. She was safe, thanks to them. Her son was safe, thanks to them. But if asked, her heart spoke instead of her head. War was ugly and evil and had already caused the deaths of too many mothers' sons.

"Did the three of you remain friends?" she asked.

Garrett stood and walked to the bar, refilling his brandy glass and taking a healthy swig of the amber liquor before answering.

"Unfortunately, no. Peter and I grew apart toward the end of the war, and after, once we became competitors, the chasm widened. Often, I thought about making peace, but I waited too long. He died from leukemia in June 1984."

"And the third Fury?"

"I'm embarrassed to say that I managed to alienate him also."

"Is he still alive?"

He nodded.

"Is the rift irreparable?"

"I hope not." He forced a smile.

Gaby knew it was none of her business, but she couldn't contain her curiosity. "Do I know him?"

"Etienne Lafitte."

Gaby was thunderstruck. Armand's father! And Garrett's father! Friends. Now enemies. Had any of this influenced Armand's current situation? Did Armand even know about this? Was this another one of his secrets? Was this the reason he was barred from Castleton's? She had a thousand questions. She knew she couldn't ask Garrett Sr., but the next time she saw Armand, she intended to subject him to an intense interrogation.

"I've never met Etienne Lafitte," she said as offhandedly as she could. "I only know him by his fine reputation."

"Which is well deserved." He walked toward his desk, opened a drawer, and extracted a small box, which he handed to her. "And speaking of well deserved, Garrett told me you collect paperweights. Please accept this as a thank-you for all that you did for Castleton's."

Stunned by both the rapidity with which he had changed the subject and the shock of receiving a present, she unwrapped the box slowly. Inside, was a magnificent Baccarat paperweight, one she recognized immediately as being a prize, probably worth somewhere around four thousand dollars! It was a starry, blue and white ground with beautiful millefiori canes mixed with silhouettes of a deer, a dog, a rooster, and a butterfly. On one cane, she made out the date, 1848.

"It's gorgeous," she said breathlessly, "and I thank you, but it's completely unnecessary."

"Perhaps. But that's when gift giving is the most fun. When it's unnecessary." He bowed and smiled, the true gallant.

"I agree." She returned his smile, stood, and kissed his cheek.

"Good. Now that we've given and received, I wonder if we could have another dance?"

"I'd be honored," she said.

As they strolled back into the ballroom and rejoined the party, she felt deliciously buoyant. But later, strange sensations began to distract her. She was having a terrific time, but despite the thrill of being feted and gifted and complimented and pursued, something continued to gnaw at her. Was it Garrett Jr.'s frequent and public displays of affection? Was it Garrett Sr.'s unexpected display of admiration? Was it Irina's continued display of hostility?

Or was it that each time she managed a step forward, she felt her foot slip a little deeper into the soft, wet quicksand of duplicity and deceit?

16

If Gaby had gone to sleep feeling like Cinderella, fairy tale princess, she woke up feeling like Kitty Foyle, working girl. Last night had been a starry dream filled with champagne and caviar, a splendid evening of being applauded in the spotlight and courted in the moonlight. Today, the Grosvenor House Antiques Fair opened. To collectors all over the world, it was a greatly anticipated event. For Gaby, it loomed as a watershed in her budding career. If she was to establish her credibility, it was crucial that she satisfy the requests of at least three of her most influential patrons. Therefore, at eleven o'clock this morning, Filofax in hand, she would attend the private, by-invitation-only viewing. If she was lucky, perhaps she would have completed several major transactions by the time the general public was admitted at five.

As she pored over her list of commissions and tried to create a schedule of priorities, she thought about the last few months and how much she had learned about her chosen field. Antiques brokering, she had discovered, was an odd business. In most other businesses, the product came first. Once enough goods had been stockpiled, orders became the prized commodity. People courted them, begged, bribed, or bartered for them, because without them they couldn't move stock or reduce inventory. Gaby's job was the reverse. Thanks to Chelsea's party, contacts made at the Castleton Classic, and referrals, she had plenty of orders. Her problem was finding merchandise.

Fine antiques were as far from assembly-line items as Detroit was from Paris, and those who coveted them were not merchants looking to buy, tack on a profit percentage, and resell as quickly as possible. Her clients wanted very specific things, special things, items that required papers and pedigrees and stamps and guarantees. Her clients wanted things so limited that every other collector of that particular category was looking for precisely the same things. That meant that Gaby not only had to locate exactly the right merchandise for each customer, but she had to find it and buy it before anyone else.

Since her baptism at Chelsea's, Gaby had attended innumerable auctions and estate sales. She had haunted the stores that lined Madison Avenue, Fifty-seventh Street, and Greenwich Village, quickly becoming a recognizable fixture. She had been persistent and it had paid off. Dealers called her if they thought they had something she needed. Decorators called her to ask if she knew where to find something they needed. Too, her photographic memory had proved, once again, to be a valued asset. While she scouted particulars, she catalogued extraneous items for later use, sorting them into lots and filing them on a mental Rolodex. Several times, a referral called and commissioned her to purchase something, and almost immediately she was able to recollect whether or not she had seen the item, where she had seen it, and when. In each instance, she had been able to execute a quick and profitable turnaround.

The more she shopped, however, the more evident it became that many of her big-ticket items could be found only in Europe. For Gaby, that predicament was classic. In order to make money, she was going to have to spend money—and a lot of it—on a buying expedition, money that should have gone to dear, old, patient, reasonable Mrs. Sloane at Lakewood. Gaby debated, but in the end she knew she had no choice. She was going to have to dip into savings to fund her trip.

At first, she had wanted to take Steven with her. She wasn't sure how she would have explained his presence, but she missed him and she had thought that as a graduation gift she would take him to London and then to Paris, where they would be able to visit Oncle Bernard. He refused her invitation.

She asked him the night of his graduation. She and Brian and the senior Thayers had attended the outdoor ceremony, all of them putting aside their personal hostilities to watch a very special young man receive his diploma. Afterward, they had gone to dinner at a local restaurant. Frank and his family had been there and, for the most part, despite the strain of bringing together those who had chosen to separate, it had been a lively, fun-filled evening. When Steven drove her to the motel where she was to stay, she handed him a ticket and told him of her plan.

"I can't go," he said, his voice registering honest regret. "In two weeks, I start a summer job Dad got for me at Wadsworth Match."

"It would only be for a week. Couldn't you start after that?" She was disappointed and didn't mind showing it.

"I need the money, Mom. College is expensive, especially Brown. I can't ask Dad to foot the entire bill."

"But I wanted to give you something. I thought you'd like this. I thought we'd have a wonderful time."

"We would, but I just can't. Frankly, if you don't mind, I'd rather cash in the ticket and use it for books."

Gaby had nodded numbly. Giving him money for books was like giving a woman a vacuum cleaner for her birthday. It was utilitarian and boring and she hated it.

Yet painful as it was, Steven's rejection of her gift had not been the worst part of the evening. That came when he had asked her why she had refused Brian's suggestion that she move back to Wadsworth.

"He was asking for a reconciliation. You shot him down, Mom. Why?"

In the back of her mind, she had always known that that little scene in the rendezvous room at the Wadsworth Inn would come back to haunt her. She had always known that Brian would have edited the story to favor himself. She wanted desperately to tell Steven that Brian had not in fact asked for a reconciliation, but instead had simply wanted to play house and test the waters and add her to his harem. However, just as she always did when she was tempted to berate Brian to his son, she forcibly restrained herself.

"I have no job in Wadsworth, Steven. I can't earn a living there."

"I don't see why not," he persisted, going on to repeat the same speech Brian had delivered.

Gaby tried to remain patient, but it wasn't easy. She had thought Steven's anger over her divorce had dissipated. Obviously, it had just gone underground. For a while, they argued without arguing, discussing in near-inimical tones the reality of her life versus the fantasy about her life that Steven had constructed.

"It's another man, isn't it?"

"No, Steven. I've told you, there is no one." She deliberately avoided saying *no one else,* just as she avoided commenting on his use of the word, *another,* which made it sound as if she and Brian were, in fact, a still-married, still-devoted couple and this mythical man was the third arm of some steamy love triangle.

"Dad says that's not true. He says that Armand, that French guy, is your boyfriend."

"Let me give you a piece of advice," she said hotly, wondering why she was shocked at Brian's audacity in concocting a fictional affair for her rather than owning up to all his own nonfictional romances. "Unless you're in the next bed and can see what's happening, you have no way of knowing what's going on. And if you don't know something, it's best to keep your mouth shut!"

She felt as exasperated now as she had then. When was it ever going to be better between her and Steven? Each time she thought they were resolving their differences, something reopened the wound. Time. Circumstance. Rumor. Fact. It was always something out of her reach, out of her control, making her feel as if there was some mysterious, cosmic plot to punish her by keeping Steven distanced from her.

It seemed so unfair, so unnatural. Weren't children supposed to be permanently bonded to their mothers, bound by an invisible cord that stretched out over distances, allowing space while at the same time retaining that unique connection forged at birth? Wasn't there supposed to be an unspoken language between mothers and their children, a telepathic method of communication that transcended the nonsensical babble of everyday? Perhaps, but with her and her son, she feared the cord was losing its elasticity. The further apart they grew, the fainter their chances at reconciliation.

Maybe when she was firmly on her feet things would change. After all, if this trip was successful, if she could find several of the more expensive items on her list, she would be able to reduce her debt at Lakewood and feel more comfortable about the future of her business. If she were more relaxed, perhaps he would be more relaxed, more receptive to what she had to say, more forgiving of what she had done, more tolerant of what she had to do. She might even be able to convince him to visit her on one of his school breaks. Then she would introduce him to her new life, her new home, and the hundreds of pleasures a big city like New York could provide. And if he was open minded and flexible and allowed himself the luxury of enjoying what was offered without feeling compelled to defend Wadsworth or make unnecessary comparisons, he might be surprised. He might find that he actually liked it.

It was nine o'clock. Gaby finished the last of her coffee and jumped into a shower. She dressed carefully, in a light, candy-pink wool suit, a pert hat, pink kid gloves, pale hose, and low-heeled shoes. London was a city with a strict fashion code that had less to do with hemlines than with tradition. Wimbledon meant all white. Royal Ascot meant morning dress for men and elegant, well-bred ensembles for women, spiced with a dash of millinary bravura. At church services, weddings, formal teas, and any event graced by a royal, gloves were a must, hats de rigueur, and pearls the bauble of preference. It didn't matter whether Italian couturiers were preaching minimalism or Parisien ateliers were advocating a newer, freer, less cumbersome chic, the English would always be English, and if that meant capping a Givenchy with a bonnet or an Armani with a cloche, they did. By ten-thirty, confident that she was appropriately clad, Gaby raced for a taxi, arriving at Grosvenor House just after the doors had opened.

If Gaby had ever had any reason to question the innately British love of pomp and grandeur, Grosvenor House dispelled all doubt. It was spectacular! Nearly ninety exhibitors showed their wares at stands that filled not only an enormous Great Room, but a balcony level as well. As she wandered inside and caught her first glimpse of the magnificent space, her mind flashed to the armory where the New York fair was held. There, shoe-leather brown was the predominant color, dark sobriety the dominant mood. Here, daylight prevailed in an airy, pale gray surround that spoke of polished sterling and cooing doves and feathery cirrus clouds. All about, there were elaborate floral displays, as lush and sumptuous as those in New York, but here, the flowers blossomed beneath eight enormous crystal chandeliers that sparkled and glittered like the crown jewels. Here, the booths were backdropped with especially coordinated decorative fabrics that enhanced the overall look of the Great Room as well as the merchandise displayed within. Here, lush carpets absorbed the clatter of thousands of high heels and wingtips, creating an appropriate atmosphere of quiet reserve. Here, though several major dealers occupied honored stations, every single booth was a paean to quality.

Grosvenor House was a vetted show. The organizers, in concert with the British Antique Dealers' Association, took seriously their responsibility to maintain the fair's international reputation for integrity. To them, guaranteeing authenticity and thereby safeguarding the public against fraud and fakery was more than a job, it was a national trust. Each year, some one hundred and twenty-five experts—academics, auctioneers, and dealers—formed eighteen specialized vetting committees. Those committees examined not only every single piece offered for exhibition, but the merchandise appearing in nonexhibitors' ads as well. There were stringent guidelines about what was and what was not antique. For exhibition in the 1987 fair, an article had to have been made before or during 1887. Pictures, bronzes, sculpture, book bindings, and manuscripts were admitted if made prior to or during 1914. Anything from a later period was admitted at the discretion of the proper committee, and then only if it was deemed important or exceptional.

There were rules about regilding, repainting, and replacing damaged or missing parts. There were rules about refurbishing the inner workings of clocks as well as the surfaces of desks and the upholstery of chairs. There were standards relating to condition and quality, descriptions and dating. There were also definite critera for exclusion, all of which dealt with the abhorrent notion of altering the original character of an antique: extensive restoration, marrying sections of different pieces, enrichments, additions, subtractions—all were verboten.

Gaby could feel excitement percolating as she walked about the balcony, touching, looking, experiencing. The aura of excellence was nearly overwhelming, like a pricey perfume, arousing an almost lustful desire to own or possess the items on display. She lingered over the Bilston enamels at Susan Benjamin's Halcyon Days, oohed at the mahogany breakfront bookcase at John Keil and aahed at the vibrant floral paintings at Rafael Valls. At Earle D. Vandekar of Knightsbridge, the Qianlong *famille rose* baluster vases decorated with phoenix birds caught her eye. At Richard Courtney, she saw a George I walnut bureau that would more than satisfy a commission granted her by one of Lush's friends in Houston, but before she bought, she wanted to complete her tour, just in case she found something better or something comparable for less.

Taking one of the curving staircases down onto the main floor, she smiled when she saw the loan display from the Royal School of Needlework: the train worn by Her Majesty the Queen at her coronation in 1953. A massive field of plush, royal-purple velvet, lavishly embroidered with gold, edged and caped in ermine, with a crown and E II R embroidered at the end—for Gaby, it revived a long-forgotten childhood memory.

She was only five when Elizabeth ascended the throne, but she remembered sitting in front of the television set with her parents watching the coronation. She remembered hearing her father say that the crown of St. Edward weighed close to twenty-five pounds and that the world was waiting to see if the young monarch was going to bow—both literally and figuratively—beneath the weight of her new office.

She remembered she had held her breath when Elizabeth took her place in the Chair of Estate and was presented by the Archbishop of Canterbury to the people in Westminster Abbey as the true ruler of the realm. She had straightened her shoulders when Elizabeth had moved to the Coronation Chair, was anointed, cloaked in gold, and presented with the orb, the Coronation Ring, the scepter with the Star of Africa diamond, and the rod with the dove symbolizing the Holy Ghost. But when the Archbishop of Canterbury had lifted St. Edward's Crown and held it over Elizabeth's head, Gaby had stiffened, forcing her neck to go taut and rigid. For some reason, Gaby had identified herself with Elizabeth, perhaps because at five years old if your daddy called you Princess, anyone else called Princess was a sister of sorts. She had closed her eyes, clenched her fists and concentrated harder than she ever had before, willing Elizabeth's head to remain high and firm. When it did, Gaby had cried, as if she had shared in the new queen's accomplishment.

Moments later, she was laughing. Her father, not certain about the cause of Gaby's tears, had gone into the kitchen and returned with a plastic colander, a wooden spoon, and a bulb baster. With farcical broadness, he replayed the coronation, seating Gaby in the center of the room. Speaking in his version of the King's English, he presented her with her makeshift scepters and then, with Delphine pressing her lips together to imitate the sound of heraldic trumpets, placed the bright yellow colander on Gaby's head. Once he had crowned her, Bill lifted Gaby onto his shoulders and bounced her around the room as Delphine curtsied in honor of Gabrielle, queen of the United Kingdom of Cocrofts.

"A tuppence for your thoughts."

It took Gaby a minute to return to the present. When she did, she turned and greeted Armand with a wistful smile.

"I was lost in the land of once-upon-a-time."

Armand shook his head. "I'm sorry, but this is the opening of one of Europe's grandest antiques shows. There can be no melancholia today. In fact, anything less than total euphoria is unacceptable."

Ordinarily, Gaby might have responded with a playful grin, but not now. She had a question that needed answering.

"Speaking of once-upon-a-time, didn't you tell me that your father and Garrett Castleton are sworn enemies?"

"I did, because they are. Why do you ask?"

"For months, I've been agonizing about what happened to you after the fair, about who might have spearheaded your blackballing and your exile. When you first told me about that feud, the pieces seemed to fit. Garrett Castleton, Sr., had motive and opportunity. Therefore, I believed he was the one responsible. But last night, that same man spoke quite fondly of your father.''

"So?" Armand's face remained void of expression.

"So I got the impression he was looking for a way out, a way of making up with your father. If that's true, the last thing he would do is sabotage his old friend's son.''

"I never said that Castleton was the ringleader.''

"No, but you alluded to it. Now I'm thinking you might have exaggerated the rift to get me to lay off. That you wanted me to believe in Castleton's guilt so I wouldn't look elsewhere. That you know who's behind all this and for some reason are loath to point a finger. Is that true, *mon ami*?''

"I may be many things, Gaby dear, but I'm not a masochist. If I could erase the blight on my name, I would.'' He took her arm and steered her into a corner beneath the stairs. "I appreciate your concern, but time will take care of everything. Don't focus on the feud. It goes back too many years for it to matter.''

Armand was making sense, but Gaby remained unconvinced. Her instincts told her that something was off.

"If it wasn't Garrett Castleton, Sr., who was responsible for your current persona non grata status, who was?''

"If I knew, I would tell you," he said, taking her hand and kissing it gallantly. "Any other questions I can't answer?''

Gaby knitted her brow and narrowed her eyes.

"Who are you staying with here in London and why are you keeping whoever it is a secret?''

Armand laughed.

"You've become a regular Sherlock Holmes, haven't you?''

"Don't change the subject.''

"I'm staying with Annabel Montgomery. It's another long, long story which I'll tell you at another time. All I can tell you now is the reason we're keeping our relationship quiet is that until my name is cleared, I'd rather it not be linked with hers.''

"Fair enough.''

She should have known, she thought. That night at Chelsea's. Armand's unavailability since they arrived in London. Annabel's nonappearance at the Castleton's party. Maybe subconsciously she had known and didn't want to pry. Whatever, she was happy for Armand because, quite obviously, when he was with Annabel he was happy.

"Speaking of fair, have you taken the full tour?"

"Just the balcony. I haven't started down here."

"Then go to it and enjoy yourself. I'll be at the Lafitte stand if you want me."

"Is your father here?" she asked, eager to meet Armand's family, even more so after Garrett Sr.'s revelation.

"He is. I'd like you to meet him and my brother, Jacques."

"That would be terrific. I'll be over as soon as I finish my rounds."

It took Gaby close to two hours to visit the booths in the Great Room. Starting at Hotspur, she made her way around the outer allée toward Apter-Fredricks, further around toward Garrard & Co., down the other side past Alistair Sampson, Paul Mason, and Armitage, up again to Stair & Co., Jonathan Harris, and Christopher Clarke, and finally, down another allée past Didier Aaron, Grosvenor Antiques, Jacob Stodel, and Bourdon-Smith. Everywhere she stopped, she subjected much of what she saw to intense examination, jotting down names and prices, dimensions and descriptions.

By the time she had completed her first go-round, she had pinpointed several items she definitely intended to buy, including the walnut bureau she had found on the balcony, an exquisite German gold and mother-of-pearl snuff box for Jocelyn Morris, a Dutch musical bracket clock, dated 1765, for a Los Angeles collector she had met in Colorado, and a fabulous, late-seventeenth-century William and Mary mirror bordered by *verre églomisé* panels—glass panels decorated on the back with a layer of engraved gold—that Chelsea, in Texas for a board meeting of Patterson Oil, specifically had asked her to broker. Though Gaby thought the fifty-thousand-dollar tag was high—she was certain that if it wasn't sold that very day, in two days the price would drop—the dealer was an old friend of Chelsea's and she had seemed quite anxious to own the green-tinged looking glass. So Gaby bought it.

She also found two pieces she knew Max would love: a Biedermeier games table with graceful swan supports and an Austrian neoclassical mantel clock, beautifully arched and columned, that perfectly complemented his collection. But before she could conclude any deal for Max, she called the number he had given her.

As she waited for someone to answer, she found that suddenly, she felt awkward. She hadn't spoken to Max since the Castleton Classic. She had heard that he had left for Europe shortly after and, as far as she knew, hadn't returned. Was it business or a woman keeping him here, she wondered.

"It doesn't matter," she reminded herself, blushing at her burst of unjustified jealousy. "Our relationship is business. Nothing else." Yet as she listened to the ringing on the other end of the phone, she could see Max coming to help her out of the snow. She could feel his arms wrapped around her body, his lips pressed against her mouth.

"Richard Limited. Good afternoon."

"Is Mr. Richard in? This is Gabrielle Didier."

"I'm sorry, Madame Didier. Mr. Richard is out of town, but he left word that if you called, I was to ask for a number where he might reach you. If it's all right, he'll return your call sometime this evening."

He left word. He was expecting her to call. He hadn't forgotten about her. She smiled and gladly gave the young woman her phone number.

It was almost three o'clock by the time Gaby was able to visit at the Lafitte London stand. She was nearing the miniature park that acted as the fair's center when Vincent Prado stopped her.

"What do you think?" he asked, clearly expecting a pat on his back.

"It's positively outstanding!" The sentiment was honest, but her enthusiasm was deliberately exaggerated.

"It's the place," he said as if the disparity between the two shows was obvious and surface. "Personally, I prefer a more antique setting, if you will allow the pun. To me, the armory has a unique charm, but I realize that not everyone is as enamored of its brooding interior as I am. There are those, like yourself, who seem to prefer a more modern environment, one that's brighter, more sanitized, perhaps."

His upper lip curled as if someone had just breathed garlic into his face.

"It's not the place or the look, Vincent, although that helps. It's the consistently high level of the exhibitors that sets this apart from New York. There are no second-rate dealers here."

Prado visibly bristled. Gaby couldn't have cared less. He was a phony and a bully, and she had decided months ago—when she had visited him after Chelsea's party and he had suddenly realized that he had leaped before he had looked and had no commissions for her—that while she might not seek actively to antagonize him, neither did she have to kowtow to him. No one knew of her connection to Armand. She wasn't a dealer who needed Prado in her corner so that she might gain admittance to his precious fair. And since she viewed her acceptance in the upper social strata as tenuous, she didn't have to worry about being in or out of his favor.

"And you think I admit second-rate dealers?"

"I think it must be very difficult to chair this type of event year after year and stay on top of every detail, especially when you have your own business to run," she said, shifting to a less strident, more diplomatic tone. "Grosvenor House is not a one-man show. It's run by professional organizers who work hand in glove with the BADA. They delegate responsibility, and that, I think, is one of the keys to its success. Vetting, of course, is another."

It was as if she had snapped her fingers and returned him to an hypnotic state. His face blanked. His eyes moved like blips on a radar screen, scanning, probing, stopping when they spied Armand, who was busy with a customer.

"Why do you feel that vetting is so important?" His eyes never left Armand.

"Because it would be impossible for me to walk through any exhibition of this magnitude and be certain that every single item is exactly what it's purported to be. I'm a professional, Vincent. If I feel more comfortable with guarantees, imagine how the beginning collector or first-time antiques buyer feels."

"The reputations of the individual dealers should be enough."

"In a perfect world, maybe. But if I were spending thousands upon thousands of dollars for a seventeenth-century whatnot, I'd want more than just a handshake and one man's say-so. I'd want something in writing, something that says if it's not a seventeenth-century whatnot, I get my money back!"

Gaby's voice had risen. Prado's face flushed. With an anxious finger, he traced the curve of his collar, pulling it off his neck as if the silky Sea Island cotton had suddenly become a hangman's noose.

"Of course," Gaby said, "that's just my opinion."

She smiled benignly, but she knew she had annoyed him. A consummate showman, however, Prado quickly recovered, restoring a look of bored indulgence to his face, a touch of condescension to his voice.

"Well, *chacun à son goût*, as I always say. Each to his own."

"Precisely," Gaby said, deciding that she had played long enough. "And now, Vincent, if you'll excuse me, I have places to go and things to buy."

Armand had signaled her not to come to his stand after leaving Prado, so she turned and headed directly right, into the huge Stair & Co. exhibit. Prado, standing alone, alongside a topiary rooster, looked momentarily lost. Then Irina Stoddard appeared.

"What were you two buzzing about?" she asked, in a way that made it obvious her question was prompted by more than simple curiosity.

"This fair. Our fair. What difference does it make?" he snapped.

Irina pursed her lips and clucked her tongue, mocking his exasperation.

"Did she say something to upset you, Vincent dear?"

"I always find the subject of vetting upsetting!"

Tiny beads of sweat dotted Prado's temples. Irina looked away, glancing over his shoulder, trying to avoid staring at his perspiration, which she viewed as a sign of weakness.

"Maybe you should simply accede to the desires of the masses, abdicate, and let Armand Lafitte run the fair," she said, her eyes fixing on the Frenchman just beyond the garden where she stood.

"And maybe you should remember that you have cast your lot with me, Lady Stoddard, and if I go down, you shan't be far behind."

Irina stepped closer, bringing them nose to nose.

"Don't threaten me, Vincent, because if push ever comes to shove, I promise you, you'll lose. Now," she said, stepping back and behaving as if they had been discussing nothing more than the weather, "what news do you have for me about the missing Dinant?"

For the second time in less than an hour, Prado felt as if he were choking. His finger worked feverishly to loosen his collar.

"Did you hear me?"

"Yes. Yes. After extensive research, my source tells me he believes it never left the country, that it's still somewhere in Belgium."

Irina nodded. "That makes sense. Where in Belgium?"

"He doesn't know, but I'm flying to Antwerp in a few days to meet a dealer who was born in Dinant. Maybe he'll be able to help."

"I certainly hope so. The clock is ticking, Vincent."

"I'm running as fast as I can, Your Ladyship."

Irina rolled her eyes and let loose a sigh of impatience.

"Don't be boorish. Just call me the instant you know something," she said, dismissing him with a flick of her hand, turning, and walking away.

Again, Vincent was left with the tall, proud, green-leafed rooster. He chuckled, petted the carefully clipped barnyard creature, and muttered under his breath, "I'll let you know what I want you to know, when I want you to know it! And if you don't like it, cock-a-doodle-do!"

"It's been too long. How've you been?"

Though it should have been no surprise to hear Max's deep baritone on the other end of the phone, Gaby was flustered nonetheless.

"Fine. Just fine." She closed her robe and fluffed her hair as if he could see her. "And yourself?"

"Unbelievably busy."

"That's good, isn't it?"

"Well, perhaps, but you know what they say about all work and no play."

"Sorry Max, but you could never be dull."

He laughed. "If I gave you some phone numbers, would you call my detractors and repeat that?"

"Gladly." She was smiling like a fool and she knew it. "Although I can't believe you have any detractors."

"You're too kind."

"I'm buttering you up."

"Should I take that to mean you've found something so extraordinary that I simply can't live without it?"

"Two things."

She described the games table and the clock in great detail, trying to be as professional as she knew how, ticking off provenances, personal impressions about the condition of both items, future salability, information about the offering dealer, and finally the prices.

Without a moment's hesitation, Max declared the items "Sold!"

"Tomorrow, just call Prudence with the amounts and the dealers' names and she'll arrange for certified checks to be hand delivered to you at your hotel or wherever you wish. As for your fee, I'd like to take care of that in person. Do you plan on staying in London?"

"I'm heading to Paris day after tomorrow."

"Perfect! I'll be in Paris then also. What hotel are you stopping at?"

"The Ritz."

"If you don't mind, I'd like to call and take you to dinner."

"No," Gaby said, feeling as if Santa Claus had just filled every request on her Christmas list, "I don't mind at all."

Annabel Montgomery's London flat was a melody sung in only one note. Every room in the spacious duplex was painted a cool, luminous ivory. Every fabric—whether silk or wool or damask or chintz—wore the same creamy wash. Every flower, every candle, every ashtray, every carpet, was bridal white, soft and virginal. Occasionally, mahogany tables and chairs interrupted the monophonic atmosphere, their dark, resonant tones adding harmony and a sense of structure. Though the starkness of the decor might have seemed odd, out of keeping with the ruffle and flourish style usually associated with the English, within seconds upon entering, the rationale behind the apartment's sterility became evident: to showcase an exceptional collection of art.

When Philip Montgomery had inherited his title, he also inherited a great deal of money and very little to do. His family's holdings were primarily stocks and real estate, requiring some management, but hardly a yeoman's work week. Many men faced with the same blessed predicament created new businesses to challenge themselves; others increased the breadth of the businesses they already owned; still others did whatever was necessary to maintain the bottom line while indulging personal passions. Philip's passion was art. He loved owning fine paintings and sculpture. He loved looking at art, living with art, talking about it, studying it, buying it, selling it, trading it. To him, especially since he had been denied children, the accumulation of art was more than a hobby, more than a preoccupation, more than the subject of cocktail party patter. It was his immortality.

When he had first met Annabel, aside from all the other reasons he had for being attracted to her, it was her artistic bent that intrigued him most. He respected her talent, but more than that he admired her ability to spot talent in others. From the start, all their leisure time was spent in the pursuit of art. They visited galleries and art fairs, museums and estate sales. They read books and attended lectures. They bought at auction and through dealers, and sometimes—if a painting struck their fancy and Annabel felt the artist had promise—they bought on the street.

Philip preferred the darker palette of the seventeenth-century Italians and the Dutch School. Annabel favored lighter canvases with frolicsome color and romantic subject matter, like the Impressionists or the eighteenth-century French painters Boucher, Fragonard, and Watteau. Philip responded to the fervor and intensity inspired by religious and mythological themes. Annabel was fascinated by portraits and pastoral landscapes. By investing wisely and following their instincts, sating each one's individual appetite, they had amassed a collection of such quality and depth that it had attracted the attention of museums all over the world.

Armand was impressed. It was an awesome assemblage. Constable, Carracci, Rubens, Degas, Barocci, Pisarro, Millet, Reynolds, Vermeer, Velázquez, Van Dyck, Bonnard, Monet, Léger, Caravaggio. As Annabel took him around and recited the names of the artists represented in the flat, as well as the larger number housed in Blandings Castle, the Montgomery estate in Gloucestershire, he thought he understood for the first time why Annabel had remained with Philip long after their relationship had disintegrated to an arrangement in name only. Having been denied many of the usual benefits of marriage—love, companionship, passion, children—Annabel had opted to create something that would bear her mark, something that would prove she had existed, something that would authenticate her worth. From what he could see, she had done a miraculous job.

"It's incredible. I'm very proud of you, Annabel," he said as they returned to the living room.

"I didn't do it alone," she said, pouring red wine into two big-bellied goblets. "I must give credit where credit is due. Some of the more spectacular pieces, like that Caravaggio, were Philip's doing."

She nodded toward the wall opposite them. There, centered within a gilded frame, was a gypsy holding the hand of a young man, stroking his palm as she read it, staring somewhat shyly into his eyes as she spoke.

"*The Fortune Teller*," Armand said quietly. He approached the painting with a reverent step. He squinted and examined the canvas. "Caravaggio painted three versions. One hangs in the Louvre, another in the Musei Capitolini in Rome. And this one, which is from the famous Rosenberg Collection."

Annabel smiled. "I thought you might enjoy seeing it."

Armand nodded. Now he understood her uncharacteristic insistence that they dine here. Throughout their many years together, they had rendezvoused either in a hotel or in his apartment. Without ever putting it in words, they had mutually agreed that they would never insinuate their love on her home with Philip. Since he had come to London a week ago, they had stayed out at Willowsgate, but he had made it clear that London and Gloucestershire were out of the question. In Armand's mind, Willowsgate was Annabel's. It was hers to do with as she pleased, with whom she pleased. This flat and Blandings Castle, however, were Philip's, and even with him gone, Armand refused to intrude.

"Come sit with me," Annabel said, patting the space on the sofa next to her. She had snuggled into the corner and curled her legs up beneath her, looking like a cat about to purr. Her dark hair was held with a thin grosgrain ribbon that matched the pale pink of her long silk shirt and wide-legged pants.

Armand joined her, taking the wineglass she offered.

"To you," he said, clinking crystal.

They drank, and then Armand leaned over and kissed her gently on the lips.

"Thank you for understanding why I didn't want to come here. And thank you for understanding how happy I am that you made me come."

"Save your thanks, my darling. I have a surprise for you and I don't want you to have exhausted your supply of gratitude."

With that, she put down her wine, rose from the couch, and disappeared into another room. When she reappeared, she was carrying a cake aflame with candles. She set it down on the coffee table, reached behind a chair, and handed him a box wrapped in green paper and tied with a huge green bow.

"Happy anniversary," she said with a broad, self-satisfied smile.

He looked at her quizzically.

"I decided that married or not, it's right that we celebrate that glorious moment in the Louvre when, thirty-five years ago, we first fell in love. I know we met in July, but this is a rather special occasion that demands a special gift, and since you won't be here next month, I decided to give this to you now."

Armand laughed. Surprises like an unscheduled anniversary, an unexpected gift, her unending desire to give to him—no wonder he had loved her for so long. Taking a deep breath, he blew out the candles on the cake.

"Well done," she said excitedly. "Now go on and open the box!"

Realizing that she wouldn't tolerate a slow but neat unwrapping, he ripped off the bow and the paper, opened the box, and took out what looked like a leather photo album. On the cover was an engraved card that read THE MONTGOMERY COLLECTION. Inside, were two sections, the first showing one hundred photographs of paintings, most of them Old Masters, all of them masterpieces. The second contained pictures of splendid furniture and decorative pieces.

"I don't understand," he said, having gone through the entire album twice.

"I love you," she said quietly, gently caressing his cheek. "And I want to spend the rest of my life with you, but I want our life together to be just that—our life. I want us to be free of the past, to start out as fresh as we can, without excess encumbrances. To that end, I intend to sell this flat along with many of the paintings Philip and I acquired during our marriage. For me, that was another time. It's past. You and I are what's now. It's our present and our future I want us to concentrate on: what is and what will be, not what was.''

She had tears in her eyes, but her mouth maintained its smile.

''That first year, when we loved each other, we talked about where we wanted to live and how we wanted to live, about building a collection, about focusing our excess energies on art. We had so many dreams, Armand. It's time to make them come true.''

Armand was too touched to speak. Annabel understood, and so she continued.

''I want you to sell these things for me.''

Armand started to object, but Annabel held up her hand, silencing him.

''I want you to publicize the fact that I've entrusted Lafitte et Fils U.S.A. with both the art collection and the furnishings. I want you to host a huge cocktail party for the hoi polloi to view the paintings. I want enormous press coverage—TV, newspapers, magazines, whatever! I want firecrackers and hoopla and every bit of excitement we can generate. This collection is too important to be ignored, which is why I'm giving it to you. You're too important to be ignored, and I want the world to remember that.''

Armand shook his head in amazement.

''This really is my problem,'' he said. ''You don't have to do this.''

''I know I don't have to. I want to and I will.''

''Once a bulldog, always a bulldog,'' he said.

''I simply feel that the situation needs a good swift kick in the ass. The Montgomery Collection is that kick. You'll see. People will be killing themselves to get to you. As well they should.''

''You're sure about this? About selling all these paintings? All those antiques?''

''I'm determined to marry you, and since you refuse to march down the aisle until your reputation has been restored, damn right, I'm sure! One way or another, Monsieur Lafitte, by this time next year, I'm going to be Madame Lafitte!''

''That would be nice.'' He kissed her. ''You're nice.'' He

kissed her again. "This is nice." She moved nearer to him and slowly undid the buttons of her shirt. "What did I ever do to deserve a woman as spectacular as you?"

"It's not what you do, Froggie, but the way you do it that keeps me loving you." She took off her shirt, unhooked her bra and let her breasts fall into his hands. "Now, I don't believe you've thanked me properly for my gift."

"Where are my manners," he said, burrowing his face in her flesh, running his hands down the sides of her body, reaching beneath the silken waist of her pants.

"I don't know," Annabel said, undoing his shirt as quickly as she could, "but wherever they are, you can be sure I'm about to find them."

It was almost two in the morning when Max left Interpol Headquarters in Saint-Cloud and started back to Paris. Though he should have been exhausted, his body and mind were running on overdrive, pumped with the belief that finally he was closing in on his smuggler. Operatives in both Amsterdam and Antwerp, the two largest diamond-dealing cities in the world, had reported that within the month a large shipment of gems from a major South African mine was due to arrive in Amsterdam. If the smuggler followed his usual pattern, he would have paid off either a dockworker or someone on board the ship so that, somehow, a container of diamonds that had appeared on the cargo manifest at the start of the voyage disappeared before it could be checked off at the end of the voyage. Then he would have the stones cut to his specifications, hiding them until he could arrange delivery to the United States. It had taken a long time to infiltrate the tight web surrounding the diamond industry, but finally Max had informers planted at various junctions along the smuggler's route. Now, all he could do was hope that his men were in the right places at the right time.

As he maneuvered his Citroën in and out of the fast-moving lanes heading away from the suburbs toward the Périphérique that encircled the city, he allowed his thoughts to drift to the other case occupying his mind. The man he was tracking was a criminal of the worst sort—the kind whose crimes affected not only his immediate victims, but made society his victim as well. This man's entire life had been one of villainous behavior, yet he had managed to cover his sins with a thick cloak of respectability. His evil was masked by wealth, his treacherous soul disguised behind a costume of loving family man, pillar of the community. He was neither of those things, but so far Max had not produced any tangible evidence that would convict him of his sins.

"One of these days I'll get what I need to punish you for what you've done," Max muttered to himself, renewing his vow to continue his search.

But how would he feel when that case ended? he wondered. Would he finally be able to put the past behind him and begin to create a future? It was so difficult to know. This particular matter had been haunting him for so long, it had overwhelmed his life, determining what he did and how he behaved. Other than the conduct of his construction business, anything that threatened to interfere—emotional involvements, long-term sexual liaisons, friendships—was disallowed. Anyone who tried to force a relationship or in any way distract him from his mission was dismissed.

Rarely did he regret his self-imposed monasticism. The end, he reasoned, more than justified the means. But every now and then, he felt the oppressive weight of a heart too full of hate to love. As he had tonight, when he had spoken to Gaby and heard her voice and visualized her face with those big, cornflower-blue eyes that had the ability to hold him captive beyond his will. He was glad she had called. He wanted to see her. He wanted to take her to dinner. But he was afraid.

To Max, commitment was anathema. Experience had hollowed out his soul, eviscerating him, leaving a void where once an abundance of trust and faith had lived. Over the years, he had grown suspicious of people and of feelings, and most of all, suspicious of love. Love in almost every form had hurt him. It had betrayed him. It had sliced into his being, leaving scars too deep, too profound ever to fully heal. Unwittingly, almost unconsciously, he had become a man of many tests, a man who placed deliberate obstacles in the path of anyone who dared to approach him.

He tried not to be rigid in his grading. He tried to remain fair. Sometimes, he succeeded. Like that last morning in Steamboat Springs when he had seen Garrett leaving Gaby's room still in his clothes from the night before. Max had felt a switch shutting down his emotional furnace. He had felt a familiar chill invade his bones as someone who had interested him had seemed to disappoint him. He had left the hotel and left the country feeling blighted and let down. Yet Gaby's face had continued to insinuate itself on his thoughts. He recalled how open she had been with her affection in the glade, how open she had been from the first time he had met her at the Castleton gala. He was the one—he was always the one—he realized, who had been secretive and closed and inscrutable. He had made no advances. He had issued no invitations. Garrett had. What did he expect? That she would reject Garrett and throw herself at him? That she would assume he was being tentative because circumstance warranted distance? That for some bizarre reason she would join him on the sidelines of life and wait until he was ready to ask her to jump into the game?

He blinked. He had been so lost in thoughts of Gabrielle Didier that he had missed the Porte Maillot exit. Now it would take at least twenty minutes longer to wind his way around to the Place Vendôme and the Ritz, where he maintained a private suite of rooms. Only New York and Paris have traffic jams in the middle of the night, he groused as he tried to weave his way in and out of the ribbons of cars. He blinked again, clearing his head of everything except getting home safely. He couldn't afford an accident any more than he could afford a serious romance. Not now. Not when he was so close.

The taxi moved away from Claridge's and lazed through the snarl on Brook Street, inching its way toward Park Lane and the Grosvenor House Hotel, where the exhibition was housed. Neither London traffic, nor a stubborn gray sky, nor a steady, cold rain could dampen Gaby's spirits. She felt positively buoyant. Last night after Max's call, certainly a contributing factor to her good mood, she had telephoned Preston Morris about the snuff box, the collector in Los Angeles about the Dutch clock, and the couple in Houston for whom she intended to buy the bureau. She had also reviewed her commissions to be certain that she hadn't overlooked anything. She hadn't. Most of the other requests were for French period furniture, and that she would have to look for in Paris.

On the way to her first stop, Richard Courtney's booth, Gaby passed a small stand which she had somehow missed the day before. It was off in a corner of the balcony with only one piece on display: a magnificent late-fifteenth/early-sixteenth-century tapestry. Carefully lit so as not to fade the colors, it seemed to shimmer in the shadows, like a garden caught in a shaft of moonlight filtered by a cloud.

"It's very special, don't you think?" A young woman with shiny black hair, a round, unmade face, and sparrow-brown eyes smiled as Gaby approached.

"That it is."

"You look as if you've seen it before. Have you?"

"No. I don't think so."

"It's Flemish, woven in Brussels around 1498. It's entitled *The Troth* and it was commissioned as part of a trilogy commemorating a marriage."

Gaby smiled and nodded. Even then, before diamond rings and elaborate weddings, there were trends and status symbols.

"I've been doing a bit of research on the Dinant tapestries. I guess because this one is of the same era, it caught my eye."

"You have a good eye," the woman said appreciatively. "I saw the Dinant counterpart to this piece, *The Betrothal*, when it exhibited in Amsterdam. The themes are identical and much of the imagery is the same, but truly, the Dinant was superior."

"In what way?" Gaby asked, with an appetite for information that bordered on hunger.

The young woman, who introduced herself as Emma Clarkson, the daughter of the owner of Clarkson Galleries on King Street, launched into a dissertation on the similarities and differences between the two tapestries. She spoke of the overall design, about the intricacy of the Dinants, the use of the unicorn as a symbol, the intertwining of Flemish and Walloon icons.

"In the Dinant," she said, pointing to the maiden standing in a castle doorway, "the lady is prettier, more delicate. She has a crown of daisies on her head and in her hand, she holds the pink carnation that was the fifteenth-century symbol of betrothal and marriage."

The woman in Emma's tapestry not only held a carnation, but had several of them bunched in a basket crooked over her arm and one poking out from the bodice of her gown.

"It was customary for a bride to hide a carnation on her

person," Emma explained. "The understanding was that the groom was free to search for the flower, and upon the word of the bishop could even open her clothing to ease his search."

"Before or after they said their vows?" Gaby asked, as amused as she was curious.

"I don't really know," Emma said with a smile. She took a book she had on a desk and flipped through the pages. "This is more typical," she said, pointing to an engraving of a Flemish allegory. "It's the classic act of betrothal. The man presents the woman with a bouquet of roses and pinks. In return, she holds out a single carnation as a gesture of acceptance. That's the way it's portrayed in *The Betrothal*."

"Were you at the auction when that Dinant was sold?"

"I was there with my father. It was a major sale, but unfortunately, the buyer chose to remain anonymous."

"Did you bid on it?"

"Every dealer on the Continent bid on it, but the ultimate victor had more money than all of us, I suppose." Emma tilted her head and looked at Gaby with a new curiosity. "Are you a dealer? Is that why you're so interested in the Dinants?"

"No. I'm an admirer, and for some reason, of late, there's been a great deal of talk about the missing Dinant. Do you know about it?"

Emma laughed. "I think my father dreams about it. It's every tapestry dealer's fondest wish to get hold of that piece. It's worth a fortune! I mean, think about it. If *The Betrothal* sold for half a million dollars, which was a record for tapestries at the time, can you imagine what *The Marriage of Brussels* would bring?"

"It's beyond my pocketbook," Gaby said.

"Mine too, but there are those who would pay just about anything for it."

"Have you had any inquiries?"

"I haven't personally, but I know my father has received several calls from people who would like to be notified if he does hear anything."

"Offhand, do you remember any names?"

"No."

A tall man wearing tinted eyeglasses entered the booth and stood in front of the tapestry. He was an older man, seventyish,

Gaby guessed, but with that suave, European elegance that consistently attracted attention. As she glanced over at him, Gaby decided that in his youth he must have been extremely handsome, probably quite athletic. She watched as he walked to the tapestry and touched the thickly woven piece, stroking the stitches, checking for signs of restoration. He tipped up his glasses so that he could study the condition of the piece more closely. As he did, Gaby noticed that his eyes were a striking blue, deep, but cold, like a bottomless pool of freezing water.

Emma and Gaby were exchanging addresses when they were interrupted by the sound of a foot tapping. He was frowning; his arms were folded across his chest in a show of impatience.

"It's been delightful talking with you," Gaby said, hastening to leave.

Emma glanced at the man and then back at Gaby.

"I've enjoyed it as well, but . . . ." She shrugged as if to say, business first. "Before you go, take this book. It's one of the best on medieval tapestries and is simply chock full of information about the Dinants."

The man's head turned sharply. The small muscles in his forehead tightened as he watched the two women. Gaby sensed him staring. She didn't like the way it made her feel. She had no idea who this man was or why she felt the way she did, but he made her uncomfortable. Quickly, she thanked Emma for the book, promised to stop by later, and left, turning back onto the main section of the balcony, headed for booth number thirty-three.

The fair was crowded, but today, there were many more average collectors roaming the stalls, more suburban dealers, more spectators who were truly just looking. There were also even more Americans than the day before. What fascinated Gaby was that the Americans were buying on their own. In New York, that would have been the exception. At the January Antiques Fair, it was rare to see a major purchase being transacted without a third party in tow, usually a decorator. Was it greater confidence on the part of the buyer thanks to the vetting? Probably. But too, as Armand had explained, in the States, American dealers built a twenty-five percent secret commission into their prices as a bonus for the decorators. In Europe, that overage was reduced to ten, which probably accounted for the poor attendance on the part of the interior design population at the larger

European shows like Grosvenor House and the Biennale in Paris. Gaby didn't really care. To her, the fewer decorators wandering about, the less competition she had.

She reached Richard Courtney Ltd. and stood open mouthed in front of his booth. The bureau was gone. In its place was a desk, an exquisite piece of furniture to be sure, but not the piece she had come to buy.

"Excuse me," she said to the gentleman in charge. "I'm Gabrielle Didier, Mr. Farnsworth. Do you remember we spoke yesterday about the George I walnut bureau? I told you I wanted to purchase it."

Clive Farnsworth smiled and his upper lip disappeared.

"Ah, yes, Madame Didier. I do recall our conversation. You were going to discuss the price of the bureau with your client and get back to me."

"Yes. And here I am, check in hand. Where is the bureau?"

"I'm afraid that shortly after you left, someone else took a fancy to the same piece. The gentleman in question was prepared to purchase the bureau immediately. I'm sure you understand that I was obligated to sell to him, rather than compel him to wait for your client's decision."

Gaby nodded numbly, her head bobbing like a plastic doll with a spring for a neck. She had spent fifteen minutes describing this piece to the Ardels, convincing them that it was exactly what they had asked her to find. Now she had to call and tell them they couldn't have it.

"Would you mind telling me who bought it?" she asked. "Just in case he decides it looks dreadful in his library and wants to sell?"

Company policy forbade giving out that kind of information, but Clive Farnsworth saw how disappointed Gaby was. Yesterday, they had had a lovely time together. They had chatted about the bureau and about the fair. She had told him she was new to the brokering game. He had confessed that he too was working his way up in the antiques business. He knew how he would feel if he had been charged with buying something for Courtney Ltd. and had had it fall through.

"I shouldn't," he said, with a conspiratorial wink, "but I will."

Her next stop was downstairs toward the back. There, too,

she found herself stymied. The neoclassical clock she had intended to buy for Max had already been sold, crated, and shipped. At the booth next door, the Biedermeier games table was gone also. What was going on? Was there a curse on her? Was there a reason that out of the thousands of items on display at this fair, the three she needed to buy had been sold?

Suddenly she felt woozy and off balance, as if the world was listing left and she was tilting right. Wobbling, she found her way to Lafitte et Fils, London.

"I've been trying to reach you all morning," Armand said, his excitement stilled a bit by her pallor.

"If it's bad news, save it for another rainy day," she said, accepting the chair he offered her.

"Actually, I am the bearer of exceptional tidings," he said with indisputable glee. "Within the next six months, your money troubles will be *tout fini*!"

Gaby looked at him with wide, blank eyes. "Gee," she said sarcastically, "if I don't have to worry about money every single waking moment of every single day, what will I do for fun?"

Armand laughed. "I see you've had a bad morning."

"Only mildly disastrous. Not serious enough to warrant calling out the National Guard, but upsetting nonetheless."

"Would you like to tell me what happened?"

"Actually, I was hoping someone could tell me what happened. Yesterday, I put a hold on three items. Last night, I contacted my clients and received the okay to buy. This morning, there was nothing to buy. All three pieces had been sold out from under me." Frustration pooled in her eyes. She tried to raise a smile, but like a sail on a sea that had suddenly calmed, her lower lip collapsed. "I just lost about eleven thousand dollars in commissions, Armand. To a woman who has no salary and debts that amount to fifty-some-odd thousand dollars, that's a hefty loss! Not to mention loss of faith. I mean, what do I tell these people? What do I tell the Ardels and Max Richard?"

"You tell them the truth. They can't fault you if someone else has good taste."

"I suppose."

She looked like a little girl in need of a hug. He obliged, for once deciding that he didn't care who was watching.

"Now," he said, lifting her chin so he could look directly

into her eyes. "Are you going to let me give you my good news?"

"Yes. I'm sorry. Absolutely."

"Annabel has given me the Montgomery Collection."

Before she could ask any questions, he handed her the album and watched as she flipped the plastic sleeves holding the photographs of all the paintings, antiques, and decorative arts.

"This is unbelievable!"

"I know!" Armand said with a broad grin. "Which is why I said that within the next six months your money troubles could be over. Because I adore you and because you've been such a good friend, I want you to have the chance to prebroker as much of this as you want to your clients. Between the art and the antiques, you just might wind up a very wealthy woman."

Quickly, he explained what Annabel was doing and why. As he spoke, he noticed that although Gaby remained nominally attentive, she appeared to be distracted, as if she were working something out.

"What's the matter?" he asked gently. "I thought you'd be ecstatic about all this, and instead you look as if someone died."

Gaby rose and paced the small booth, taking her time before returning to face her friend.

"What if you retained the antiques but consigned the art collection to Castleton's?"

"Even if I could—which I can't—why would I want to do that?"

"You can't, but I could, and there are several reasons you would want to do that. The first is money. Annabel's gift is extremely generous, but you and I both know that the only way for her to maximize this collection is to bring it to auction."

Armand agreed. In the past few years, art had become the ultimate chic. Auctions had started to resemble feeding frenzies. Prices had escalated beyond reason. And why? Because thanks to a boom economy, the rolls of the ultrarich had become too crowded. There were too many with too much for cars or boats or private planes or precious jewels to be sufficient marks of distinction. And so the rich had turned to art. Instead of putting their wealth into garages or hangars or vaults, now they hung their money on their walls.

"The second reason is good old-fashioned revenge. Castleton's took an unreasonable stand against you. They embarrassed you in front of your peers. I think they deserve to be squeezed."

"And how do you intend to squeeze them?" Armand asked, noting that not only had the color returned to her cheeks, but she was beginning to flush with exuberance.

"If it's all right with you and Annabel, I'd like to offer them the Montgomery Collection. Naturally, they'll make it into an event with all the media attention that goes along with major art auctions these days. I want them to get all excited about it, all committed to it, and then, just before the catalogues are ready for the printers, I'm going to tell them that I'm not the actual consignor, you are. In effect, I'm going to tell them the truth, that because they barred you, the only way to get this collection in house was to use an intermediary. If they refuse to reverse their policy—which they won't—we'll be forced to pull the collection."

"This could hurt Garrett," Armand said.

"It could, but it won't because he won't let it happen," Gaby answered confidently. "I don't believe Garrett was behind the decision to banish you from Castleton's. He'll simply squeeze whoever was responsible for your exile until the policy is revoked. He'll have his auction and you'll have your redemption."

Armand folded his arms across his chest and smiled. Gaby had come a long way from the frightened, insecure woman he had first met in that classroom in the New School. She hadn't had it easy since then, but she was toughing it out. She was maturing, changing, becoming savvy and sophisticated. But most important, she was becoming confident enough to take chances.

"Reason number three for doing this," she continued, "is that it just might be a way to reunite your father with Garrett Castleton, Sr. Last night I spoke to Garrett Jr. and casually asked about the start of this feud. He told me it had something to do with your father's giving the Rosenberg Collection to Sotheby's instead of to Castleton's. If you gave them the Montgomery Collection, perhaps everyone involved would feel that all scores had been settled—theirs as well as yours."

Armand's face turned contemplative as he evaluated options and alternatives. Gaby could almost see him thinking.

"I'm impressed. This is a very ingenious plan. Do you know that?"

"It's ingenious if it works."

"If it doesn't, there might be serious consequences. You might be leaving yourself open to harsh criticism, not to mention exposure."

"Is that a yes or a no?"

"Do you understand the personal risks involved in something like this?"

Gaby straightened her shoulders, tossed her hair back, curled her lips in a strong, resolute smile, and saluted.

"I understand them and I accept them."

"You're being flippant."

Gaby's expression softened, yet Armand was certain that, amidst the determination and calm, he spotted a ripple of fear.

"No, I'm not," she said. "It's just that, finally, I see the light at the end of the tunnel for both of us. Tante Simone once told me that sometimes one has to take risks in order to survive. This is one of those times, Armand."

"I admire your courage, *ma petite*."

"Well," she said with a fatalistic shrug of her shoulders, "as they say on the slopes, 'No guts, no glory!' "

It didn't seem possible for Shefferd House to look more beautiful than it had the night of the pre-Grosvenor gala, but in the light of day, bathed in the golden tones of natural sunlight rather than the harsh blue-white of electric spots, the Georgian mansion asserted its symmetric elegance. The enormous brick structure dominated the landscape, proudly centered within its own park, like a jewel in a velvet box. Ivy scaled the walls of the side wings, rising high, up to the roofline, wrapping the house in a fleecy green cloak that fluffed and fluttered in the summer breeze.

Inside, with the carpets and furniture organized in their everyday pattern and the space devoid of people, the front rooms adopted an extremely formal air, museumlike, Gaby thought, as if there should be a rope cordoning them off from the public. Yet what was more evident now, more impressive, was the care that had gone into the furnishing of this home, the loyalty to history, the dedication to detail, the desire to create and continue a legacy.

As Gaby accompanied Garrett into his parents' private sitting room, she noticed an immediate change in ambience. The scale was more manageable, less intimidating. The chairs and sofas were plumper, plusher, more suited to long, comfortable, unbuttoned interludes with a book or a piece of embroidery. The *objets* were still precious, but less pompous, mixed in with family photographs and more whimsical indulgences than were exhibited in the rest of the house. Even the flowers—blossoming within baskets or pottery instead of Meissen or silver—presented a less arranged, more natural aspect.

As tea was served and Gaby, Garrett, and his parents waited for Irina to arrive, Charlotte entertained Gaby with charming anecdotes about the history of several of the heirlooms in the room. Most of them were from her side, and as she told about how her great-great-grandfather hoodwinked an adversary out of a pair of girandoles or how her great-uncle had won a marquetry table in a card game, Gaby's eye took its own visual tour. Again, as she had felt in Garrett Sr.'s library, she noticed several pieces which looked vaguely familiar and oddly out of place. An urn that should have had a mate. Two glass paintings that seemed to be telling a story without an end. A carved jade Fu-dog with eyes of black stone and an outstretched paw that seemed to reach for someone or something that wasn't there.

Suddenly, the door opened and Irina wafted into the room. Like everyone else, she had responded to the break in the gloomy weather that had dominated the spring and had dressed for the sunshine. Wearing a frothy cerulean-blue silk dress and a wide, flower-trimmed hat, she appeared delicate, feminine, like one of the women on a Fragonard picnic. All she lacked was a parasol and a petticoat.

One look at Gaby, however, and the image was destroyed. The painting faded and in its place stood a piece of sculpted marble, its features cast in an expression of implacable distaste.

"What a . . . surprise," she said, pausing so that no one missed the deliberate omission of the expected adjective, "pleasant."

Gaby allowed the slight to pass, knowing that more than rain clouds had shifted. So had the advantage. In a few minutes, Irina was going to find out exactly how big a surprise Gaby's visit was.

After the butler had poured tea and everyone had taken a

plate of scones and biscuits, and after the usual small talk had petered out to an expectant silence, Gaby put down her cup, folded her hands on her lap, and waited. When she had everyone's attention, she began.

"The reason I wanted to speak to all of you is that I've been given the honor of consigning a monumental art collection to Castleton's." She paused, allowing them to project and anticipate. "It's Lord Philip Montgomery's collection, given to me by his widow, Annabel. Naturally, there are a few conditions."

"Name them." Garrett Sr. could barely contain his elation. Montgomery's collection was legendary. Without doubt, an auction with his name attached would be an international event.

"First, is that the Montgomery Collection be auctioned by Garrett in New York." She smiled at Garrett, whose face had flushed with controlled jubilation. "With all due respect, sir," she said, turning to the Castleton *père*, "I think Garrett's handling of the gavel is masterful, and an occasion such as this requires his unique brand of virtuosity."

Father looked at son with unmistakable pride.

"I couldn't agree more," he said.

"The other conditions are these: that the Montgomery Collection be accorded all the publicity and media attention it deserves and that I be allowed to oversee all arrangements regarding this auction."

"With pleasure," Garrett Sr. said, allowing no space for questions, no room for doubt about his confidence in Gaby's ability. "Knowing your adeptness in matters such as these, I feel perfectly content to have you running this particular show. What do you have in mind?"

"For one thing, I'd like to develop an elaborate viewing. If we traveled several of the more extraordinary pieces, setting up mini exhibitions in major cities on the Continent as well as in the States, we could build international enthusiasm. I recognize that something like this is expensive, what with security precautions and all, but in the end I feel Castleton's will be more than compensated for its expenditures."

"One way to defray some of the cost, is to host these exhibitions in our own galleries wherever we can," Garrett said, trying to home in on particulars even though his attention was splintered—reviewing staff, selecting a team, scheduling, calculating, planning. "This tour should be launched here in London, however. This is, after all, the Montgomerys' home as well as Castleton's base of operations."

"Marvelous idea!"

"Perfect!"

They all chimed in with suggestions and encouragement. All except Irina. When she spoke, her voice rang with derision and demand.

"These arrangements are fine if you're looking to host a sideshow," she said, smiling quickly and perfunctorily at her parents, glaring with contempt at Gaby. "If, however, you wish to offer the public a thoughtful, well-planned exhibition of important art, the collection must be properly curated. As the acknowledged in-house expert on Old Masters, I must insist upon a personal review of the collection and the authority to oversee the writing of the catalogue."

She spoke directly to her brother, pushing him squarely in between her and Gaby. Before he could respond, Gaby spoke.

"Not only is that unnecessary, it's totally unacceptable," she said. "The Montgomery Collection is world renowned. To question its quality, even in the subtlest way, would be an insult to the Montgomerys. I won't allow it."

Irina's eyes burned with anger.

"*You* won't allow it?" she said in a tone that left little doubt as to her opinion of Gaby's credentials. "It's standard procedure for someone from Castleton's to examine each individual piece in a collection so that we may be certain that there are no forgeries and no low-quality paintings that could bring down the level of the auction."

"I have Annabel Montgomery's written assurance that the collection has been authenticated and evaluated by several independent scholars," Gaby said, refusing to back down. "That will have to suffice."

"That's absurd!" Irina turned toward her brother. "Are you going to go along with that?"

"Yes," Garrett said without hesitation. "Since I want to schedule this auction for early December, a lengthy review would be a waste of time."

"A waste of time," Irina repeated, making it clear that she considered the phrase a criticism of her ability as well as a comment on expediency. "You think it would be a waste of time."

"Yes, I do," Garrett said firmly, ending that discussion and then initiating another with his father on the logistics of a December sale.

Irina glared at Gaby. For an instant, their eyes met. A palpable heat passed between them like a current. Then, issuing a sigh that signaled boredom, Gaby twisted her mouth into a triumphant arch and turned toward the others, dismissing Irina as Irina had once dismissed her.

For reasons she still couldn't comprehend, Irina had declared them enemies. She had slammed a door in Gaby's face. She had lied to her and about her. She had tried to undermine her at every turn. For a while, Gaby had tried to fathom why Irina bore her such hostility, but the seed of that anger continued to remain deeply buried. Eventually, without being conscious of it, Gaby had ceased caring about Irina and her constant state of petulance. But today, sitting there, feeling again the sharp edge of Irina's disapproval, her pride had demanded that she deliver a message: she would not suffer any further indignity at the hands of Irina Stoddard. Not now. Not ever again.

Irina seethed. The woman was a nothing, an interloper, a stranger, and yet she was being showered with compliments and praise, treated in a way normally denied the daughter of that family. Irina's rage began to puff up, expanding, enlarging, growing in size until it threatened to overwhelm the space. Long ago, she had learned to sublimate her wrath about being overlooked by her parents. Long ago, she had learned that to place blame elsewhere was far less painful than to deal with the fact of their negligence. Now she blamed Gaby.

How dare she dismiss her? How dare she think she could cow Irina with a stare and a sigh? How dare she interfere in family business? How dare she think she held the power to decide who would take over the reins of Castleton International?

Silently, Irina composed a response to Gaby's message—one that would not be lost on anyone.

17

If London was a civilized, bespoke, and brollied gentleman, and Rome was a grande dame whose age was just beginning to show, Paris was a woman, a sensuous, seductive, forever youthful woman with the capacity to bewitch all who visited her. Her parks, her bridges, the grandeur of her architecture, even the drama of her history, created a banquet of such incredible richness, it was difficult to know what to taste, what to leave until another time.

Gaby and Bernard Didier spent the morning strolling through the Musée d'Orsay, the lavish new setting for nineteenth-century French art. The spectacle of space, the elegance of design, the dramatic use of sculpture as both display and decoration, the artful interplay of shadow and light, glass and stone, gild and granite—the whole, as well as each of its parts, became such an overwhelming experience that Gaby found herself stopping to pause every now and then to refresh her body and replenish her emotional stores.

While the soaring height and massive sculpture of the ground floor took her breath away, it was the smaller alcoves housing the paintings from the Jeu de Paume collection that held her captive. Ever since she had first visited Paris as a tiny girl hanging on to Delphine's hand, she had loved the art of the Impressionists and Postimpressionists. She couldn't count the number of times she had viewed the Monets and Degas and Pisarros and Sisleys, the Cézannes and Van Goghs, the Renoirs and Gauguins, but then again, neither could she weigh the amount of joy they had given her at each viewing. It was as if those painters had spoken to her in a special language. She hadn't needed anyone to interpret meanings or explain techniques. They had communicated a sense of happiness through their exhilarated brushstrokes and vibrant colorations, their pretty women, their playful outings, their dreamy landscapes.

As they moved through the museum, up the stairs, in and out of the various recesses, she and Oncle Bernard discussed the lesser-known artists of the time, like Blanche, Boldini, and Helleu, debated the relative importance of Bonnard, Vuillard, and Roussel, agreed upon the long-term impact of Ingres, Delacroix, Millet, and Corot. Although Gaby found them interesting, Oncle Bernard turned up his nose at the Art Nouveau exhibits, declaring the curvilinear style with its preoccupation with squiggly representations of plant life too fussy for his taste. Gaby tried to elicit a favorable comment about the era by reminding him of the work of Louis Comfort Tiffany, Beardsley, Toulouse-Lautrec, and some of the other more famous proponents of the style, but as she had known he would, Bernard remained firm in his dislike.

After three and a half hours, they had had enough. Once outside, a curtain of sunshine blinded them. Their pupils had dilated to accommodate the veiled light inside the museum, and now even sunglasses felt inadequate. Standing in the shadows next to the building, they chatted while watching the glass-canopied *bateaux-mouches* motor up the Seine on their way toward the Eiffel Tower. Then, when their vision had adjusted, they walked arm in arm along the embankment, down the Quai Voltaire toward *le quartier des antiquaires* and Bernard's shop on the rue des Saints-Pères. They proceeded slowly, accommodating Bernard's lameness, which was now aided by a cane. Each time Gaby sensed a wave of fatigue and suggested they stop, he growled, tapped his cane impatiently, and forged ahead. His spirit had not aged at the same pace as his body.

They lunched at a small café on the corner of the quai and the rue du Bac, just across from the Pont Royal. Bernard was a regular, and the madame greeted him like a celebrity, kissing him, escorting him to his usual table near the front window, fussing over him and Gaby. Bernard made a show of introducing his beautiful niece from New York, beaming, even as they teased that she was much too fluent to be a Yankee, much too good-looking to be blood related. He ordered a bottle of chilled Pouilly-Fuissé and a bottle of Evian. After, he and madame tried to entreat Gaby to sample his favorite *déjeuner: rouget* with boiled potatoes and *haricots verts*. Though she was certain the two took it personally, Gaby declined the small red fish in favor of a simpler, lighter *salade niçoise*.

During lunch, Gaby filled Bernard in on what had happened since they had last seen each other. Though she called and wrote to him often, she had never been able to describe fully how she had gone from struggling unemployed divorced housewife to struggling high-powered antiques broker. Verbalizing it now, she tensed. Bernard was the first person, other than Chelsea, who had heard this tale of deliberately mistaken identity, and Bernard was family, which made his approval all the more important. He listened quietly as she told him about her involvement with Armand, her job with him, her employment at Castleton's, her apartment, her dismissal by Irina, her decision to go out on her own. When she explained the use of her mother's maiden name, people's assumptions about her wealth, her background, and her status, she cringed, waiting for his response.

"You do what you have to do," he said, sounding exactly like Simone, echoing her attitude that life often demanded compromise and inventiveness. "If others choose to deceive themselves, so be it."

Though he had accepted the reason for her masquerade, several times his eyes squinted quizzically, as if he knew something was missing from this story, some essential plot element that would clarify the central character's motivation, yet he let her go on uninterrupted, assuming that sooner or later whatever was being suppressed would surface.

Since he had offered to contribute to Simone's care when he had first learned of his sister's cancer, and had repeated his offer several times during her illness and again after her death, and since, each time, Gaby had assured him everything would be taken care of, he assumed that what she was withholding was something personal, something related to Brian and their divorce. Having been in the United States only once—when Delphine and Bill had died—he had no concept of rising medical costs or nursing home bills or the effect of catastrophic illness on the survivors. He had no way of comprehending the extent of Gaby's burden. And she had no intention of telling him.

What she did tell him was that she was feeling pressed, that she had come to Europe in hopes of establishing herself and had been roadblocked in London. She told him who her clients were, what she needed to buy, what she had not been able to buy at Grosvenor House. Immediately, as if trumpets had just sounded a call to battle, he declared their afternoon agenda canceled. They could visit the Picasso museum some other time. He knew dealers all over the city. By the end of the day, or by the end of the next day at the very latest, he assured her, she would have found everything she needed.

Their first stop was to be Bernard's. On the way, Bernard critiqued each shop they passed, including Lafitte et Fils. He considered Etienne the only serious rival of Didier Aaron and Bernard Steinetz. He was a man of stellar taste, Bernard said, with a knack for finding pieces that were *insolite*, which, loosely translated, meant not just unusual, but provocative as well, and *fastueux*, both noble and showy. He knew Armand and respected him, confiding that he felt the Lafittes were wasting his talent by having him manage a shop so long on antiques and so short on art. Jacques, he claimed, was good, but lacked his father's fineness of eye and his brother's scholarly mind.

He praised the Chevalier twins, claiming their *galerie* had the best tapestries and antique rugs in all of Paris—which to him meant in all the world—and raved about Jacques Perrin, an aggressive dealer who was one of the first foreigners to exhibit at Burlington House—the London show that alternated years with the Biennale and admitted more foreign dealers than Grosvenor House. Alain Demachy of Galerie Camoin didn't fare quite as well. Bernard was a purist and naturally suspicious of antiques dealers who specialized in everything, calling that a contradiction in terms. He especially questioned those whose real occupation was decorating.

"Most good *antiquaires* have a sense of design. But not all decorators have a knowledge of antiques."

Bernard's shop was just off the corner of the rue des Saints-Pères and the rue de Lille. It was as Gaby remembered it, with bottle-green enameled wood framing two huge windows, each of which displayed only one grand piece, and a thick, hammered-bronze door that set the tone for the elegant *galerie*. Bernard specialized in the Directoire, Empire, and neoclassic styles of the late eighteenth and early nineteenth centuries. He was addicted to columns and gilded swans and ormolu friezes and tapered, fluted legs. He felt passionate about classical lines, Greek motifs, and marquetry. And when it came to the works of J. H. Reisener, the most famous *ébéniste* of the latter half of the century, and Georges Jacob, the most accomplished *menuisier*, or chair maker, of that same period, he was more than an adoring fan. He was, to use the vernacular, a groupie.

But most of all, Bernard was commited to tastefulness. He tolerated contemporary fads and fashions as long as they presented some sort of style. He didn't foist his preferences on the rest of the world, but rather looked to influence by example. Despite his infirmity and his age, Bernard remained a handsome man. His tall form had stooped with the weight of his years, but his sartorial sense had retained the snap of youth. Ascots had always been and still were his trademark, and rarely, if ever, did he exchange one for the foolish invention he called the fancy man's noose. His hair was silver now and his skin lacked the firmness of long ago, but his dark eyes still crackled with curiosity and intelligence, and his full mouth still widened with easy humor, especially when he wondered whether it was the gauntness of his face that had made his nose appear more beakish, or if, perhaps, "I've told so many stories that I've incurred the awful curse of Pinocchio."

"And now . . ." he exclaimed, having dispensed with the business of introducing Gaby to his assistant. He led her inside and turned her so she might face the interior wall. "For Monsieur Richard," he said with a dramatic sweep of his arm. "This should more than compensate for the loss of that games table."

The snobbery in his voice was unmistakable. As with most *antiquaires*, especially those of the French variety, he considered his own pieces—and those of a very select few others—prime.

Others were grade A perhaps, but lesser. In this instance, he was right. If Max would have liked the games table—and Gaby believed he would have—he would adore this secretaire.

Closed, it was a striking but simple, unpretentious piece with a flat, unembellished façade crafted from the honey-toned woods favored by Biedermeier artisans. It stood quietly among the more ornate pieces, like a rose in a bouquet of orchids. Once the front panel opened, however, simplicity bowed to intricate woodworking and whimsical design. To Gaby, it looked like a doll house, with miniature doors and windows and columns and pediments, with stairs, a stoop, a brick foundation—everything cut from different woods, pieced together to create an amusing illusion behind which were hidden small drawers and cubbies for desk necessities.

"It's fabulous!" As she toyed with the drawers and stroked the smooth, blond burled wood, delight dancing in her eyes, Bernard leaned against the wall and watched, his arms crossed across his chest, his mouth spread in a satisfied smile.

After several minutes, she turned, affected an exaggerated pose and a businesslike visage, and said, "And so, Monsieur Didier, let us discuss price."

"Fine, Madame Didier," he said, addressing her by her alias, happily playing the game. "What did you have in mind?"

"Five thousand less than you did, that's for sure!"

Once they had acted out a negotiation, Bernard made several phone calls, provided Gaby with names and addresses, and sent her on her way. It took hours, but in the end "le search," as antiquing was known in Paris, yielded a bureau for the Ardels, a Savonnerie rug for Lush, and a Régence console for another client. But no clock for Max.

When she checked with the concierge at the Ritz, she found there was no message from Max, either.

"That's okay," she told Bernard—and herself—later, after dinner in his apartment, "I had wanted to spend tonight with you."

Though her face wore a bright mask, disappointment hung in the air like a wave of August humidity, refusing to be dispersed by a weak wave of the hand.

"Besides," she added, quickly, "let's not make something

out of nothing. Max is a nice man, but I have no time for schoolgirl crushes.''

"From what I've heard about Maximilian Richard, he's not the type to be interested in schoolgirl crushes, either. I'd say grown-up affairs are more his style. Tell me, would you make time for that?'' Bernard asked slyly, downing the last of his Beaujolais.

Gaby blushed. She had never discussed anything this personal with her uncle before, and though she knew he meant well, his frankness was almost as discomfiting as the directness of his gaze. Instead of answering, she took refuge in the wine, making a show of refilling his glass and then hers, drinking, and then savoring the light, fruity flavor of the Gamay grape.

They had moved from the dining room overlooking the small garden that fronted the rue de Ville into the living room, a large, oddly shaped space with lofty ceilings that curved and bowed according to the mandate of a mansard roof. Amidst the requisite antiques and collectibles, Bernard had, over the years, introduced cozier pieces into his predominantly formal decor, fitting oversized armchairs alongside his stone Burgundian fireplace, allowing throw pillows to grace his Directoire sofa, filling a corner with a plump chaise that transformed reading into a sensuous activity.

"How do you feel about dead-end projects?'' Gaby said, after a few minutes, making it clear she did not want to discuss her sex life.

"That depends on how dead the end,'' Bernard said, making it plain that he understood.

"Lately, there's been a lot of talk about the Dinant tapestries, especially the one that's missing, *The Marriage of Brussels*. Do you know anything?''

Bernard sipped his wine slowly, thoughtfully.

"Personally, no, but now that you mention it, I have heard rumors about a search. What's your interest?''

"I'm not sure," she said with an honest shrug. "Curiosity, I suppose. Gambling on a long shot. The thrill of the chase.'' She sat back in her chair, folded her legs and hugged her knees, her eyes lost in a dream of chance. "I mean, what if we were to find it? Can you imagine? What a coup!''

Bernard laughed. "It wouldn't be a coup, my darling niece. It would be a miracle!"

If he thought he was going to defuse her, he was mistaken. Instead, her eyes became incandescent, glinting with near-electric light, reminding Bernard of the little girl who used to love exploring the countryside around Antibes, who loved building sand castles and making up stories about the wee folk who lived inside them.

"Maybe so, but if you had told me a month ago I would be brokering the Montgomery Collection, I would have said that was a miracle."

Bernard shook his head. "Don't compare the two. For Annabel Montgomery, selling this collection is an act of love. Armand's giving it to you is an act of friendship. Your giving it to Castleton's is an act of revenge. Finding the missing Dinant is none of these things. It's a quest. It's like looking for pirate's treasure, which means it has the potential for danger."

"It's a risk I'm willing to take," Gaby declared, not knowing when she had decided that or why. "What about you?"

As impressed as he was with her spunk, as intrigued as he was by her daring, Bernard hesitated. He knew she was inexperienced, naive about the ruthless element that populated the underbelly of the art world. He wondered about the extent of her bravery, the limits of her determination. How far was she willing to go? How far was he willing to take her? Yet no matter how many questions he asked, there was only one answer—she was blood, and if she wanted to have a go at life's windmills, he would gladly play Sancho Panza to her Quixote.

"I must admit," he said, his mouth promising a smile, "it sounds like fun."

She jumped out of her chair and hugged him.

"I knew you'd help."

She sat on the floor and stared up at him, like an apostle at the feet of her master.

"Where do we start?" he asked, somehow knowing she had a plan already mapped out.

"Right here in France and then in Switzerland."

"Why there? Why here?"

"I'm certain it's not in Belgium. Max Richard's been looking for it for years, and if his resources and contacts in his native land haven't turned up anything, I'm convinced there's nothing to turn up. One of my sources claims the original owner sold it to a Nazi. Much of the art hidden away by the Nazis in Germany has already been found, but many of those in the know say the bulk of the loot was hidden in France during the Occupation and in Switzerland, where neutrality protected even stolen national treasures.''

"You've done your homework."

"I've tried, but now I need to tap into your network of sources. I need you to call anyone you think has a pipeline to information about the whereabouts of contraband art. In the meanwhile, I'll keep listening and reading. Maybe an old history book or a new acquaintance will provide a clue. Who knows?''

She lifted herself up off the floor, fetched the bottle of Beaujolais, and once again refilled their glasses, never noticing how quiet Bernard had become.

"Here's to us," she toasted. "Here's to the Didiers! May we both get a chance to celebrate *The Marriage of Brussels*." She raised her glass, took a hearty sip, and returned to the comfort of her armchair, still unaware of the cloud that had drifted into the room.

"Simone loved Beaujolais," Bernard said suddenly.

His quick change of subject caught Gaby completely off guard. It was as if she had been on an up escalator and then, without warning, it had started moving in reverse. The instant she heard the name, her mind emptied. And her heart paused. A door inside her soul flew open and exposed the cold empty room where once her aunt had lived.

Simone. All day, all night, Gaby and her uncle had deliberately avoided talking about her. Looking at him now, she knew why. It was obvious that he, too, still suffered the hollow, nagging pain of loss. He, too, had experienced emotional hallucinations, moments when Simone had seemed so alive and so near that when the reality of her permanent distance reasserted itself, the chasm containing his grief had widened. He, like Gaby, still had not fully accepted the fact of her absence. But while they shared much, some burdens each of them bore alone.

Gaby watched as Bernard examined his hands, turning them over, touching the knuckles gnarled with arthritis, the skin dotted with brown spots. She watched as he rose from his chair and limped over to a table laden with family photographs. He lifted one in a Victorian filigree frame. It was a young Simone on the beach at Antibes. Her hair was covered by a flower-printed scarf. Her long, bare legs were spread out in front of her, her toes digging into the white, pebbly sand. Stacks of her trademark bangle bracelets dangled from her wrists. Piles of gold rings circled her fingers. Her dark eyes were shaded by large glasses, but her lips were pursed as if someone off to the side were counting and, at the exact moment the shutter clicked, she was to kiss the air with the full passion of her being. He put the picture down. One by one, he looked at the other photographs, the other reminders of those he had lost. Lastly, he picked up one of Delphine. He looked at his baby sister's face and then at Gaby.

"You look just like her." He tried to say it softly, but his voice came out like a sob etched in pain.

He looked so alone, so adrift standing by that table of celluloid tombstones. Gaby wanted to go to him and hold him, but instinct said she could offer little to counter the ponderous threat of one's own mortality.

"I miss them, too," she said, in a way that invited him to speak, yet allowed him to be silent.

"I don't mean to minimize your devastation," he said after a while, "but you have Steven. You have suitors. I have no one. I have no family. And yes, while I have my work and a few friends, nothing seems powerful enough to illuminate the darkness."

"You have me," she said meekly, wishing it were enough, knowing it wasn't.

"But you're so far away." Too far away to fill in the blanks left by death. Too far away to lend a sense of family. Too far away to call in case of trouble or sickness.

She heard what he said as well as what he didn't say, and because she understood, because she felt the same way, she crossed the room, sat next to him, and lay her head against his chest.

"I don't have anyone either, Oncle Bernard. Garrett Castleton is my only suitor, and no matter what he feels for me, I don't love him. Worse than that, though I hate to admit it, I don't have Steven either. He doesn't love me the way he once did."

Bernard looked shocked. "Don't say that! Of course he loves you. He's your son."

Gaby shook her head.

"Unfortunately, blood doesn't guarantee eternal affection," she said, lifting her head, seeing her own sadness reflected in her uncle's eyes. "He's angry. He blames me for the divorce, for the breakup of his family, for just about everything that's gone wrong in his life. Yes, I know that maybe someday his anger will pass, but right now there's a bigger ocean between him and me than there is between you and me."

"Perhaps you should build a bridge," Bernard said quickly, the distress he felt evident in his voice.

"I've tried, but it's a difficult task."

"Then for the time being, let it go," he said in an abrupt, pragmatic about-face. "Let him work out whatever he has to work out. Meantime, you concentrate on constructing a happy life for yourself. Build your business. Give yourself some security. Find someone to love. Then, when Steven is ready to be part of your life again, you'll have a life for him to be part of."

Gaby was truly moved. She looked at him and caressed his cheek, brushing a silver strand of hair back into line.

"Thank you, Oncle Bernard," she said, kissing his forehead.

"For what?"

"For lending me your shoulder and your support. For reminding me how wonderful it is to have a family. For loving me."

"It is I who thank you, my sweet Gabrielle," he said, taking her hand and squeezing it, letting both of them feel the connection of ancestry. "Because without you, I would have no one to love."

The next morning, the concierge handed Gaby two messages. One was from Chelsea. She was arriving that afternoon and would speak to her the minute she got in. The other was from Max. If it was all right, he would call for her at eight and they would dine right there at the hotel in L'Espadon.

Gaby was busy the rest of the day, visiting dealers, filling commissions, introducing herself to the antiques community of Paris, but if anyone had asked her exactly what she had done or where she had gone, she couldn't have provided a coherent response. All she could think about was seeing Max. By eight o'clock, she had changed her dress three times, had tried no less than five different hairdos, and had vacillated between red-red, red-orange, and fucshia lips. The end result was a short, black strapless dress topped with a bolero jacket aswirl with red passementerie, a soft, straight ribbon-tied ponytail, smoky eyes, red-red lips, onyx earrings, sheer black hose, and high-heeled patent pumps. A few squirts of Les Quelques Fleurs parfum and she was ready. Fortunately for her nerves, Max was prompt. The bellman called up and announced Max's arrival at precisely eight o'clock.

When the elevator door opened and she saw him waiting for her, the impact was like an earthquake that rumbled deep inside her core, upsetting the surface calm, rocking it, releasing such strong, unexpected waves of emotion that even after they settled, she sensed that all her attitudes and preconceived notions as to how she was going to act were off the original mark. She had forgotten how stunning he was, how strong and tall and virile. She had forgotten the power of those delft-blue eyes, how hypnotic they were when they fixed their gaze as they did now.

When he approached, gently took her in his arms, and greeted her by kissing both her cheeks, she had to fight to remember that he would have greeted anyone that way. It wasn't special. It didn't mean a thing. Linking her arm through his, they walked through the mirrored *salon de thé*, down the eighty-yard corridor of lavishly stocked *vitrines*, or showcases, that connected the Vendôme side of the hotel with the rue Cambon side. Small talk dominated, but for Gaby it was a blessing, alleviating much of her self-consciousness, so that by the time they were seated, she felt composed and in control.

Max ordered a Chablis Grand Cru. After it was poured and they had had a few moments to enjoy it, he raised the question Gaby had been expecting, but dreading.

"What happened? You never called Prudence. Did you run a credit check and discover I'm a bad business risk?"

"Hardly."

She told him what had happened, succinctly and honestly, and then described the secretaire she had seen at Bernard's.

"I'll look at it tomorrow. How's that? And don't feel badly.

It's not unusual for things to be sold out from under your feet, especially opening day of a fair like Grosvenor House.''

Something Max said clicked, and a thought that had nibbled at her consciousness for days suddenly took voice.

"Maybe not, but there was something unusual about these sales.''

"What do you mean?''

"I asked for the names of the purchasers of all three items. In each case, they were American dealers whose names sounded incongruous with the items being shipped to them.''

"How so?''

"The clock was going to a shop called Village Green Antiques, in Larchmont, New York. The George I bureau was being shipped to Plaza Suite, in Montclair, New Jersey. And the games table was headed for The Manor, in Bedford, New York. First of all, in my humble opinion, all three of those shops carry inferior merchandise. These items were superior and not in keeping with the rest of their stock. Village Green specializes in folk art, not fine neoclassical pieces. Plaza Suite doesn't usually carry English furniture and The Manor deals in Americana. Where would they come to a Biedermeier games table?''

They wouldn't unless they were receiving diamonds, Max thought. "How would you account for it?'' he asked, interested to see if she had a theory.

"The only connection I could find is the obvious one. All three show at the January Antiques Fair and all three have been criticized for their lack of quality. Vincent Prado has gone on record defending each of them, but my guess is he told them to shape up.''

My guess is he's bartering participation in the fair for a safe shipping address. Max made a mental note to pull the tails off some of his other suspects and assign a surveillance team to cover the three shops Gaby mentioned and alert customs. Prado already had a tail.

"Well, well. I guess it's true what they say. This is where the elite meet to eat.'' Chelsea swept across the room like a diva taking a curtain call. She bussed both Max and Gaby and then stood gaily chattering away while, behind her, a very handsome, very young man waited. Gaby also waited, but it soon became clear that there was to be no introduction. At one point, in the middle of Chelsea's monologue about what it was like dealing with her late husband's family, she turned, pointed to a nearby table, and practically commanded the uncomfortable gentleman to sit. Gaby was almost as embarrassed as he was.

Eventually, Chelsea joined her companion, but throughout the evening, snippets of their conversation drifted over to Gaby and Max's table. It wasn't pleasant. Chelsea's behavior could only have been described as rude. She asked him to order a bottle of wine and then changed the order, scoffing at his choice as if he were an idiot. The captain listed the evening's specials, but before her young gentleman could express a preference, she ordered for both of them. Though occasionally she smiled and petted him, lowering her voice to a more seductive tone, giving him the full thrust of her attention, the mood was fleeting and short-lived.

Listening upset Gaby. There was a shrill, shrewish edge to Chelsea, an attitude of extreme impatience, as if she were merely tolerating this person—whom Gaby had guessed was a paid escort—merely marking time until they would leave and go to her room and he would do what he was hired to do and she would make certain she got her money's worth. When had she become so debauched, so myopically self-indulgent that she couldn't muster even a smidgeon of common decency? Had three failed marriages done this to her? Or was it something else?

"Have I lost you?"

Max reached across the table and took her hand. His voice was soft. So was his touch.

"Not at all," she said, trying not to get lost in his eyes.

"You're a very compassionate woman, aren't you? I see how pained you are, how sympathetic. That's very sweet."

He kissed the tips of her fingers, lightly, casually, as if they had already been intimate and this was one of those private pleasures lovers allowed themselves in public.

"You're also very beautiful."

His eyes were like magnets, so forceful, so strong that at first, she tried to look away, to avoid becoming entangled in his web, but she couldn't.

"Either I'm flushed from the heat of your compliments or it's gotten very warm in here," she said.

He sipped his wine and smiled appreciatively as she slipped

out of her jacket and dropped it on the back of her chair. Her skin looked almost pearlescent, as if the moonlight had crept past the French windows that overlooked the garden so that it might dance on her shoulders. Her face was flushed, dusted with a delicate pink that made her eyes seem deeper, her lips riper. As she leaned forward and rested her arms against the table, her breasts strained against the confines of her dress, creating a valley that begged to be explored.

"Do you have any family? Brothers? Sisters?" Gaby asked, keenly aware that he had been reconnoitering her body.

"Unfortunately, no. How about you?"

"I was an only child."

"Are your parents still living?"

"No. They were killed in a car accident when I was twelve. I was raised by an aunt, but now she's gone too."

"It appears as if we have more in common than simply an interest in tapestries and antiques." He smiled, but this time it lacked his customary brightness. "I thought I recognized a kindred spirit."

Gaby's expression requested an explanation.

"Being orphaned, being forced to face the world alone when one is young and somewhat defenseless, creates a special breed of independence. One that relies on toughness. Resilience. Determination."

"And you think I have those qualities?"

"Don't you?"

A few years ago, Gaby's immediate response would have been no. She never would have recognized those things in herself, and if she had, she never would have admitted it, fearful that to do so would upset her carefully ordered existence. Yet, slowly, she was coming to understand that her dependency on Brian had been little more than a defense against the reality of a poor marriage, a denial of her unhappiness, a denunciation of an obvious mistake. It was different now.

"You bet I do," she said with conviction.

Max laughed and raised his glass in a toast just as Chelsea's escort brushed by them and out the door. Gaby looked over at Chelsea, who was paying no attention to his exit. She tried to see if the young man was leaving the hotel or going to the men's room, but the maître d' was talking to someone, blocking her view. Without giving it any more thought, she turned back to Max and watched as he tasted the Saint-Julien '70 he had selected to accompany their main course and declared it superb.

"Would you like me to seat you in the grill?" the maître d' asked politely, turning toward the room next door.

"I don't think so," Irina said, her eyes darkening as they moved from Gaby and Max to Chelsea and then back to Gaby and Max. "I think I prefer to dine in my room this evening. Send up my usual broiled fish and a bottle of white wine."

"Very well, madame."

Twenty minutes had passed. Gaby and Max had just about finished their *noisette de veau* when the waiter serving Chelsea's table tried for the second time to serve her dinner. It was becoming obvious to everyone who cared to notice, including Chelsea, that her companion was not coming back.

"There doesn't seem to be any reason to wait," she said coolly. "Apparently, my friend decided he wasn't hungry."

With that, the silver cover was lifted, and her plate was placed in front of her. With admirable aplomb, as if being stood up was an everyday occurrence, Chelsea finished her dinner, instructed the captain to add the check to her bill, and bid Gaby and Max good night.

"You seem upset," Max said.

"I feel sorry for her. I don't think she meant to do what she did."

"Do you know Chelsea well?"

Gaby almost told the truth. Then she remembered she couldn't. She wished she could.

"We met at the Castleton gala. You introduced us, I believe."

"That's right, I did." He nodded, but Gaby sensed he had known that all along. "I guess because she gave you that dinner, I thought you two were fast friends."

"We are now," Gaby said, wondering why her relationship with Chelsea was of such interest to him. Was it because he suspected she was a fraud?

He raised his glass. "Here's to Chelsea. May she never have to spend another evening alone." Gaby raised her glass. They clinked. They drank. "And here's to us," Max said, his eyes locking on hers. "May we spend many more evenings together."

*   *   *

It was dark, save for the light shining through the window from the garden below. Vivaldi wafted through the air, the lilting sounds of a baroque concerto spilling out into the elegant suite from speakers hidden in the ceiling. In the bedroom, an empty wine bottle rolled against the door as a blanket fell from the bed.

Irina Stoddard moaned, her silk nightgown pushed up above her waist, her naked body writhing against the sheets. Her jaw was tight. Her eyes searched the dimness as a hand kneaded her breast. Nimble fingers massaged her groin, stroking, caressing, tugging at the small, sensitive knob that controlled her passions. She was sweating. Her skin felt clammy and her hair was beginning to mat. Her head throbbed from too much wine, but she didn't care. It felt so good to be touched, to be fondled, to feel her nerve endings sting and prickle with excitation.

She loved it, especially now that she felt the hardness against her, pressing, pumping, making her pulse with wanting. If only she didn't have to do this to herself. If only she didn't have to rely on devices and alcohol. If only he would come back.

As she worked the plastic shaft, moving it against her, then inside her, she forced her mind to go blank, to allow her body the freedom to find that paradisic oasis of absolute physical pleasure. Her eyes clamped shut. She puffed and panted. Her heels dug into the bed. And at its peak, as always when she had scaled that wondrous mountain and felt the frenzied approach of climax, she saw his face and heard his name burst from her lips in a sob.

"Armand!"

On the other side of the hotel, Max escorted Gaby to her room. She handed him her key and watched as he unlocked and opened her door. She walked inside the tiny entry and turned around, expecting him to return her key and say good night.

"I'll go only if you want me to," he said quietly, his eyes asking the question another way.

Without needing to think, she stepped aside and allowed him in. Gently, immediately, his arms wrapped around her waist and pulled her toward him, bringing her face near enough for his lips to cover hers. He kissed her softly at first, then deeply, all the while holding her against him, giving their bodies a chance to meet, to become familiar. He loosened the ribbon that held her hair. As it fell onto her back and his hands combed through the thick, luxurious mane, something happened to Gaby, something magical, something new.

All night, she had been feeling strange, tingly, almost edgy. Every time he touched her or looked at her or spoke to her in that near whisper he sometimes used, she had felt her insides hollow, as if all her vital organs had been removed, leaving nothing but an odd blend of space and sensation. Now she understood. It was wanting. It was lust. It was a craving to be physical with this particular man. She wanted him, just as much as he wanted her. She wanted him to touch her, to make love to her. But more than that, she wanted to touch him, to make love to him, to possess his body while he possessed hers.

As he held her, she laced her arms around his neck and kissed him, letting him know his desire was shared and that his ardor would be returned. When they parted, his eyes burned into hers as, slowly, he removed her jacket. Softly, his hands caressed her skin, smoothing over it as if she were as fragile as a cameo. She leaned back into his arms, lifting her chest as he lowered his head, offering him the softness mounded above her dress. She had never felt like this before, not with Brian, not with Garrett. They hadn't moved beyond the hallway and yet she felt such a powerful longing, it was almost beyond her control.

Without taking his hand off her waist, Max led her into the bedroom. He removed his jacket. She undid his tie, unbuttoned his shirt. All the while, they continued to kiss—mouth, cheek, neck, chest, nose, eyes—it didn't matter as long as their lips touched flesh. Gaby felt Max reach behind her and unzip her dress. She felt his tongue dart about her mouth as his hands pushed the silk off her skin and onto the floor. Quickly, she removed her hose and lay down on top of the bed, waiting.

She had made love to Garrett several times since Colorado. Each time, he had felt the need to set a scene, to ply her with champagne or candlelight or romantic music. Each time, she had felt satisfied, but not fulfilled. With Brian, there had been too much role playing—he the aggressive male, she the passive female—and too little honest passion. She had always believed that she was the one lacking, that whatever incompleteness she felt was her own fault, but the second that Max lay beside her and hungrily buried his face in her body, she knew she had been wrong.

It was as if this were the first time, the only time she had ever been with a man. He made her quiver and tremble. He made her ache. He made her feel hot. He made her feel as if every cell, every corpuscle, every pore was a center of delight, a sleeping sensation that required only his touch to be awakened and aroused to extraordinary heights. He made her want to crawl inside his skin, to be so close, so intimate that one heartbeat would be indistinguishable from the other. When finally they joined, Gaby wished that for once, time would stop at exactly that moment. That moment just before, that moment when passion had accelerated to its maximum, cresting to a point where there could be no more feeling, there could be nothing except a delicious numbness. That moment just before the whirlwind ended.

For Gaby, the whirlwind lasted most of the night. She and Max made love over and over again, feasting on each other until their bodies were exhausted and begged for sleep. When finally she did sleep, her dreams were simple. They were of Max.

It was when she awoke and turned toward the other pillow that she wondered whether or not the entire night had been a dream. Max was gone.

"How could I be so stupid?"

"How were you stupid?"

"We made love all night long."

"Did you enjoy it?"

"It was unbelievable."

"Did he enjoy it?"

"He certainly seemed to."

"So what's the problem?"

"For me, it was more than just sex. I mean, God help me, I think I'm falling in love with that man."

"That's a mistake. You don't have to love everyone you sleep with."

"Oh! It's better to hire some stud so that you can abuse him in public and he can abuse you in private? That's better?"

"Are you suffering? Are you hurting right now?"

"Yes, but . . ."

"I'm not. Case closed."

Gaby and Chelsea were touring the rue du Faubourg St.-Honoré. Actually, Gaby's attention was divided between sight-seeing and self-doubt. Chelsea's attention was clearly focused. She was buying. They'd move ten feet down the narrow side-walk and Chelsea would disappear inside a store. Angelo Tarlazzi. Lanvin. Walter Steiger. Chloë. Louis Féraud. Laroche. Lagerfeld. Gaby was dizzy. She was also depressed and needed to talk. With Chelsea, she had only half an ear, but she supposed that was better than none.

"Why did he leave without saying anything? Without leaving a note?"

"He had things to do. Don't be a baby. Is that fabulous or what?" Chelsea had fixed on an outfit in the window of Sonia Rykiel. It was all white—pants, undersweater, cardigan, sailor's beret, and oversized purse. "I must get it for Belle. She would look terrific in it, don't you think?"

Before Gaby could answer, they were inside the store. Within minutes they were outside again. As she had done everywhere else, Chelsea had directed the packages to the hotel.

"Otherwise, you begin to look like a bag lady," she had said.

"Speaking of Belle," Gaby said, trying to pick up at least one conversational thread, "why is she always so sad?"

"Because Drake Reynolds is a bastard, that's why! I'll give you an example. I wanted to bring Belle with me. I begged him. I pleaded. I tried to reason with him. But no. He said she'd rather stay with him. Get serious! What young girl would turn down a vacation in Paris?"

Gaby knew of a young man who preferred being in Ohio.

"Is he abusive?"

"Why do you ask?" Chelsea stopped walking and turned to Gaby. "Why would you think that?"

"Because I get the impression she's frightened of him."

Chelsea flashed on the beatings she had suffered at his hands. The verbal lashings.

"He is quick with his fists. I've had more than my share of black-and-blue marks thanks to him."

"Does he beat her?"

The color drained from Chelsea's face. Her green eyes went dead.

"Probably," she admitted.

"Then why don't you do something about it?" Gaby's outrage was immediate.

Chelsea's response was just as immediate.

"And what would you like me to do? Fight him for custody of his child? I'm not her natural mother. Her mother is alive and living in Connecticut."

"Why haven't you spoken to her about this?"

"Because she's a drunk who's in and out of sanatoriums. She dries out, gets out, stays out for a few months, maybe even a year, and then, boom, she's back in."

"Do you care about Belle?"

Chelsea looked away, embarrassed, chagrined, as if Gaby had caught her doing something wrong. "I love her," she said simply.

"Then help her."

"I can't."

"You must."

Chelsea's hands began to shake. "I don't know if I can," she confessed. "I'm selfish. I'm spoiled and I'm not very good at making commitments or living up to those kinds of responsibilities."

Gaby stared at her friend. It was rare to see Chelsea exposed like this, stripped of her hard, protective shell.

"If you love her," Gaby said gently, but with a certain insistence, "at least you have to try."

Chelsea nodded. "You're right. I know you're right. Will you help me?"

Gaby smiled, her face lit with gratitude and relief.

"My pleasure. Now, you help me figure out what went wrong with Max."

It was almost five when Chelsea and Gaby returned to the Ritz. Before going to their rooms, they checked for messages. Three men had called Chelsea, old flames who were always open to the idea of restoking the fire. Bernard had called Gaby. Max had stopped by early that morning to look at the secretaire. He loved it.

"Why didn't he call me?"

"There could be a thousand explanations. Maybe he plans to call you later. Maybe he had to go out of town. Maybe he's just a love-'em-and-leave-'em kind of guy."

"That's comforting."

They were so engrossed in their own conversation, they never noticed Irina watching them from inside the magazine shop. As they waited for the elevator, Irina noticed how easily they talked and laughed, how chummy they seemed. Discounting her near-phobic dislike of Chelsea and her growing dislike of Gaby, their closeness piqued her interest. They seemed so opposite. Yet they had become friendly so quickly.

As she watched the elevator door close behind them, she couldn't help but wonder whether there was more to their relationship than met the eye. She had too many other things on her mind just then to take the time to follow up on her hunch, but one day she would. Because something told her that once she started to dig, she would turn up dirt on both of them.

There must have been two hundred roses in Gaby's room. As she opened the door, the first thing that struck her was the powerful fragrance perfuming the air. It was thick, but delicious, making her think of English gardens and scented bath water, Valentine's Day and lacy sachets. Everywhere she looked—on the nightstands, the fireplace, the desk, the windowsill—there was a vase filled with dozens of long-stemmed roses. White. Peach. Gold. Pink. Yellow. Red. Each bouquet was an explosion of color, a spectacular burst of nature. She stood dumbstruck, her eye traveling from one to the other, back and forth, finally catching on a white card tied to the vase nearest the door. Once she had noticed that one, she looked around again and realized that several vases bore notes. Picking up the first one, she saw, too, that they were numbered. Smiling, hoping, unable to quell the tumultuous fluttering inside of her, she did as she was supposed to and read them in sequence.

My dearest Gaby . . .

I took the liberty of making plans . . .

Please be packed and ready by seven P.M. . . .

My car will pick you up and take you to the plane . . .

Tonight, we're having dinner in Geneva . . .

Tomorrow, you'll meet my children . . .

Love . . .

Max.

18

Accompanying Max on his mysterious odyssey was somewhat akin to falling through the looking glass. He wouldn't permit any questions about where they were going or what they were going to do when they got there. After a great deal of prodding, he did explain that though the children weren't really his, he looked after them. Gaby asked how many there were, whose they were, and how they had gotten to Max, but he had given her all he intended to give. The crew served champagne and caviar. He talked about the secretaire, her day, Chelsea, his day, the weather in Geneva, the weather in New York, the weather in Paris, everything but their eventual destination. He held her hand, lavished her with attention and affection, and, through it all, smiled like a Cheshire cat with a yummy secret.

They checked into a suite at Le Richemond and ordered a late dinner at Le Gentilhomme, the hotel's restaurant, but barely touched their food. They drank, but the wine must have contained more aphrodisiac than alcohol, because they danced until two in the morning, clinging to each other, unwilling to separate even when the band took its break. When they went to bed, they made love as they had the night before, devouring each other time and again, as if an inner voice warned them to seize the moment before it disappeared.

There was an undeniable chemistry between Max and Gaby, a potent mix of combustible fuels that needed little more than a spark to precipitate an explosion. From the moment they were reunited, Gaby's insides fizzed and bubbled, as if someone had injected her with champagne. She felt reborn. She felt alive. She felt as if someone had decreed that the world be a place of perpetual sunshine and blue sky, that the universe be transformed into a vast philharmonia where violins and harps played romantic serenades, that the air be forever redolent with the scent of hyacinths and lilacs. She had forgotten how exquisite it was to fall in love, how exciting a look could be, an accidental brush of the hand, an unplanned moment alone. It wasn't just the physical, although for her, being loved by Max was almost more than she could stand, it was the way they laughed, the way they talked, what they laughed about, what they talked about, the way they slipped in and out of French, their common interests, their different interests. Though she had sensed it coming and had fortressed herself against an attack of emotion, she had been powerless against the tender tug of Maximilian Richard.

If, however, she had managed to reserve a smidgeon of restraint, that too crumbled when, early the next morning, they drove outside Geneva, up into the hills past Coppet, just outside of Céligny to Max's La Maison des Enfants du Monde. It was a huge complex of alpine chalets that formed a community of caring for children orphaned by war. Everywhere she looked there were children—little ones, teenagers, toddlers, young adults— from Lebanon, Afghanistan, Africa, South America, Central America, Iran, Iraq, Israel, Asia, Ireland, India, Europe. There was a four-story main house which served as both school and recreation center. There were smaller three- and two-story chalets in which the children lived. There were garages, barns, silos, and acre upon acre of grazing land for the cattle and crops that were raised there.

"We're entirely self-supporting," Max explained as he drove Gaby around in an old army jeep. "During the summer, everyone works with the livestock or tending the crops, even the youngest members of the family. In the winter, after the dairy cows are brought down to the valley and the planting's done, school is the number one priority.''

"How many children live here?"

"Right now, almost two hundred and fifty live on the property. We have twenty-five in university, forty partners working here or in my construction business, and at least seventy-five graduates working throughout Europe and Africa."

"What do you mean by 'partners'?"

"After the children finish high school, they're allowed to decide their future. If they wish to learn a trade, that's fine. If they choose college, also fine. But for all of them, once they graduate or are qualified in their trades, if they want, they can come to work here. Instead of making them employees, they become part owners. They receive a salary as well as a percentage of profits. If they choose to work for Richard Construction, they receive a salary and a graduation gift of stock which can only be sold to me or another graduate. Many of the teachers and chefs and mechanics and carpenters and accountants that you see here today grew up here. Many of the engineers and architects and plumbers and interior designers who've worked on Richard projects grew up here. It's my way of giving them a start in life. Or making up for the way their lives started. I'm not sure which.''

He smiled, but there was no question about how serious he was about his children and the quality of their lives.

"You must be very proud of them." Gaby spoke softly, feeling an awesome reverence for this remarkable man.

"I am." He parked the jeep, took her hand, and led her to where they could look out upon the small mountain village that was La Maison.

It was a heavenly landscape painted with God's sure touch. They stood high above the world, looking out at the brooding mass of snow-capped peaks that were the Alps, down over verdant, undulating mountains spiked with dark green firs and pines, kissed with fields of bluebells and narcissus and edelweiss. The air was crisp and cool. The sky felt close enough to touch. The sun, full and bright and glorious, seemed to concentrate on La Maison, spotlighting this cluster of honey-toned wooden chalets with peaked roofs, French doors, gingerbread-trimmed balconies, lush gardens, and windowboxes exploding with color.

"How do they come to you?" Gaby asked, truly overcome.

"The Red Cross. Various relief organizations within their countries who can't find adoptive parents for them and can't care for them anymore."

"What happens to the ones who don't come to you."

Max's eyes deepened until they were so blue they were almost black.

"Lots of things, few of them good. They starve. They die of terrible diseases. They become beggars or thieves. They get bounced from one relative to another or they stay in refugee camps waiting to be deported to another strange and unfriendly place." He shook his head woefully, as if trying to fathom how anyone could let that happen to innocent children. "I wish I could do more."

"Look around you, Max," Gaby said, splaying her arms, encouraging him to view his surroundings through her eyes, to drink in the magnificent panorama, the heartwarming sight of healthy children laughing, chatting, going about their chores. "Look at how happy these kids are. They feel safe and secure and wanted. Yes, it would be wonderful if every war orphan could have this same opportunity, but you can only do so much. And from what I can see, you do more than most."

With an impatient nod that she was coming to recognize as Max's typically self-conscious response to a compliment, he started up the hill toward the main house. As they walked, his arm draped her shoulders, her arm encircled his waist. Like perfectly meshed gears, they seemed to fit together, easily, comfortably. Since that first dinner—was it only two nights ago?—when she had invited him into her room, into her bed, and into her life, there had been few awkward moments, no strained silences. Even here, visiting a place she'd never been before, Gaby felt oddly at home. She wasn't a guest. She was with Max, and therefore she belonged.

During the rest of the afternoon, Max introduced Gaby to most of the staff and many of the children. They wandered about the grounds observing the extent of La Maison's operation. They toured the dormitories, which functioned like private homes, with kitchens and dining rooms and family rooms replete with a television, a stereo, and shelves of books. Gaby couldn't resist lingering in the house where the youngest ones lived. She insisted upon staying during their dinner hour, sitting in one of their tiny chairs, singing French ditties, encouraging them to tell her everything they had done during the day. By the time Max pulled her away, she had a child on each knee and three more glued to her side.

They dined in the main house at a table of staff and partners. The room was huge, designed to function as both dining hall and social hall, but with that warm, cozy feeling that came from wood siding walls, lofty, stuccoed, and beamed ceilings, balconies, and round tables all covered with crisp white cloths, all decorated with freshly picked flowers in hand-crafted bowls. Though Max tried to keep the conversation impersonal and topical—La Maison, politics, the latest additions to their family—every so often one of his charges insisted on reciting a personal history as a way of making sure Gaby understood the extent of Max's generosity.

At steady intervals throughout dinner, young people found an excuse to walk by the table and stop. They welcomed Max home, shared a tidbit or a laugh, and waited politely to be introduced to Gaby. She was an object of intense curiosity and speculation. Judging from the whispers and stares and various other reactions, Gaby guessed that Max rarely, if ever, brought anyone here. For most of them, Max was father-lover-brother-confessor-friend. He was their fantasy come to life, but more important, he was their anchor. Their entire sense of security revolved around him and his interest in them. Gaby or any other outsider was a threat, a way to divert or dilute his dedication. Having been orphaned, Gaby understood how they felt. She had felt the same way about Simone. They had to be protective of him. It was their only way of protecting themselves.

During coffee, Max was called to the phone. Suddenly, Gaby was besieged by youngsters crowding around her, bombarding her with questions about who she was, where she lived, how well she knew Max, and how long she planned on staying at La Maison. Before she could answer, one of Max's aides asked if she could join Max in his office.

"I have to fly to Antwerp." Gaby's disappointment was swift and visible. So was his. "I'll leave you a number. If you need me, call." He tried to smile, but his mouth refused. "I'm not sure when I'll be back. Probably, sometime late tomorrow."

He put out his hands and invited her into his arms. They kissed, and immediately the passion that simmered just beneath their skin surfaced.

"I miss you already," Max said, nuzzling the soft flesh of her neck, sliding his hands down around her hips, pressing her to him. "I don't know how I'm going to stand being away from you."

Gaby couldn't speak. Her voice was lost, caught in the tornado of emotion that swirled inside her whenever they touched. Instead, she found his lips and spoke to him without words. She tasted him slowly, clinging to him, wanting to remember every sensation, wanting to hold onto him until the last possible moment. He, too, seemed loath to part. His arms had locked around her, imprisoning her in his embrace. When their lips separated and he spoke, they were so close she could feel his breath mingling with hers.

"Will you be all right here?" he asked.

She smiled and nodded.

"I'll be back as soon as I can."

She smiled and nodded again.

He opened his mouth as if to say something else, but instead he kissed her, softly, quickly. Then he left. As he did, she whispered to the air what she hoped he had wanted to say to her, what she knew she wanted to say to him: "I love you."

The sound of the organ filled the massive cathedral, its enormous brass pipes trembling with the power of a Bach toccata and fugue. The pews alongside the main altar were filled with more than three hundred and fifty guests. Baskets of white flowers dotted the long aisle, softening the somber angularity of the Gothic interior. Outside in the Groenplaats, curious onlookers gathered to watch one of Antwerp's most prominent families arrive at the Onze Lieve Vrouwekathedraal in an elegant caravan of eighteenth-century horse-drawn carriages. Aided by liveried footmen costumed in blue and gold silk, the members of the wedding party stepped down onto the cobblestone street, taking their places for the processional. Twelve groomsmen in morning coats. Twelve bridesmaids in long gowns of blue silk. Four flower girls adorned with petticoats and ribbons. A young ring bearer in navy blue breeches and white knee socks. The best man. A maid and matron of honor. One by one, the carriages deposited their passengers and moved to the side, clearing the way for the bride, who arrived in a gilded brougham.

The organ signaled the start of the ceremony. Heads turned as the front doors of the cathedral opened and the groomsmen began the long march to the altar. Max stood toward the back, in the last row of guests. Though he was as impressed by the grandeur of the proceedings as any of the others, he had not been invited. He wasn't a friend or close relative or business acquaintance of either family. He was an intruder, analyzing details, watching with an intensity incongruous to an occasion such as a wedding.

He had arrived early that morning, positioning himself off to the side, remaining in the shadows so that he could study the wedding party without being seen or recognized. As people entered and took their seats, Max took notes. Belgium's finest families were represented. There were numerous dignitaries from France and West Germany. There was a contingent from England as well as a row of visitors from the United States. Though he wasn't surprised by the stature of the assembly, he was surprised at the anger he felt.

How could they pay honor to a man like this? he asked himself. *Because they don't know what kind of man he is*, he answered, knowing that the stripping away of this man's artful camouflage and the revelation of his true character was the reason Max had stayed on this case for these many years.

When the music began, he maneuvered himself into a spot at the far end of the pew. As the wedding party walked by, he studied every face, recognizing some, straining to connect others to a list of names compiled by Paul van der Hamme, senior Interpol agent in the Brussels office. Nothing clicked.

The music stopped. Two young men in the same livery as the footmen lifted a large roll of white satin and, beginning at the altar, unfurled the shiny fabric all along the aisle, continuing out the front door of the cathedral and down the steps, stopping when they had reached the glittery brougham. When they returned, the organist began the wedding march. The bridesmaids filed in, each of them carrying a bouquet of blue and yellow blossoms. The maid of honor followed, then the matron and then the four small flower girls who, their faces marked with the seriousness of their task, sprinkled the white satin with delicate petals of bluebells and daisies. When all the attendants had taken their places alongside the altar, the organist announced the arrival of the bride and her father.

Max stood transfixed. She was quite lovely, gowned in layers of handmade Belgian lace, her strawberry-blond hair tucked behind a lace mantilla, held in place by a glittering diamond tiara. Her skin was fair, her eyes as blue as the Schelde. She was of medium height, around twenty-five, the only child of her father's third wife, the youngest of three. Her two older half-brothers were groomsmen, but Max had been unable to pick them out. Her name was Annette and as she progressed toward Ian, her groom, her face glowed with the joy of a woman about to wed the man of her heart. Ian was an Edelhof, scion of a family which controlled most of the coal production in the Kempen basin. According to Max's research, he was a wealthy young man with a bright business mind and a serious intellectual bent, a man with little capacity for fun, but one who was clearly in love with the delicate woman walking toward him.

Max watched the way the bride gripped the arm of her father, as if she had grown up knowing that no harm could ever come to her as long as he was by her side. He noticed the way her father rested his hand over hers in a gesture of unselfconscious paternal affection. He noted how old the man looked, much older than most men who accompanied twenty-five-year-old brides to the altar. His current wife, standing at the pew nearest the altar, appeared to be around fifty. She was turned toward her daughter and her husband, smiling proudly as they took their slow walk down the aisle.

How could you be proud of him? Max asked, silently speaking to the lovely woman in the filmy chiffon in the front pew. *You're a decent woman from a decent family. Were you in love with him? Or did you marry him for his money? Even so, how could you not know?*

His eyes fixed on the father of the bride, his gaze too heated to be ignored. Unexpectedly, the man turned. He sought the source of the heat. Their eyes met, and for a moment Max thought he saw a flicker of recognition. But that was impossible.

They had never met. Though Max knew all about him, he knew nothing about Max.

But you will, Max thought, continuing to stare, wishing he could telegraph his thoughts. *One of these days I'll find the proof I need. And when I do, you'll pay for what you've done.*

As the groom came to meet the bride, her father bent down and kissed her cheek. It should have been a precious moment in his life, but he had been distracted. As his daughter linked arms with her future husband, he turned and searched the crowd. The man he was looking for had gone.

It was late by the time Gaby said good night and retired to Max's apartment. She had spent a lovely evening listening to stories about Max, about how much La Maison had changed in the ten years of its existence and how much they loved and admired their benefactor. Despite the hour, she felt energized and knew that sleep would be slow in coming. Instead of forcing it, she changed into nightclothes, slipped on a robe, and began to explore the lair of Maximilian Richard.

His apartment, built beneath the eaves of the main house, consisted of two large rooms and a bath. The decor was rustic and simple, with hand-hewn furniture Gaby knew must have been made by La Maison carpenters. There was a bedroom with a wide-planked wooden floor spread with two strongly patterned Persian rugs, an enormous four-poster bed dressed in an English quilt, a white stone inglenook and fireplace, big comfy chairs upholstered in bold plaid fabric, and beautifully mullioned windows that looked out across the mountaintops at a moonlit infinity.

The other room was a library with a thick-legged, big-drawered desk, two small leather sofas plumped with throw pillows, another huge hearth, and shelf after shelf of books and mementos. It was here that Gaby chose to begin her education, because it was here that she found photographs that provided clues as to who he had been, insights as to who he had become.

On the mantel were several snapshots of a young Max and a tall, comely redhead. Gaby recalled Chelsea saying that Max had been married briefly, that his wife and a child had been killed. This woman must have been his wife. She was fragile, delicately structured, yet knowing Max, Gaby guessed that, in fact, she was strong and resourceful. There was a small silver frame with a photograph of a baby no more than six months old. It was black and white, yet Gaby could see that the boy had deep blue eyes like his father. She saw the child again as a toddler being held by Max and his mother. All three had smiled into the camera, and in that captured instant, the love they shared appeared powerful and binding. There was one more picture of the boy. He was approximately four years old, grinning at the photographer, standing alongside his mother, who was seated and quite pregnant. This must have been just before they were killed. Gaby shivered at the thought.

On a nearby shelf, she found other pictures, older ones, ones that showed Max as a little boy. In two or three of them, he was with a woman with dark hair and dark eyes, an extremely attractive woman with full, bowed lips and a heart-shaped face. The smile, the shape of the eyes, the dimples, the lips—this woman had to be Max's mother. But how could she be? Max had said he had been orphaned by the war. Maybe she was an aunt or just a woman who looked as though she could have been Max's mother. Gaby was confused.

She moved on, looking at the *objets* that decorated the tabletops and bookshelves. Instead of priceless porcelain and valuable antiques, there were framed crayon sketches, animals crudely whittled from wood, lopsided vases, papier-mâché masks, and hand-carved bookends. They were delightful, but the one item that caught her eye was an embroidered emblem that sat in an old frame in the center of his desk. It was fussy, scrolled and embellished with gilded acanthus leaves and petaled flowers, leading Gaby to think it had been part of an ornate family crest. At first, she had difficulty making out the letters, but when she picked it up and examined the piece more closely, she saw it was two intertwined M's. They were fashioned differently from the simple monogram on *The Garden of Love* tapestry, but the coincidence of finding an emblem bearing the same two initials on the desk of a man so determined to find the Dinants struck Gaby as too bizarre to ignore.

Later, as she crawled into Max's bed and tried to sleep, her mind insisted that she review the photographs, the people in them, who they were, how they fit into Max's life. Too, she pondered that emblem, that monogram, the flowers on the crest, those books on tapestries that filled Max's shelves. Were there discrepancies between what Max had told her and what she thought she had discovered in that room? Or was it her imagination working overtime? He didn't seem to be hiding anything, she told herself, but then again, to the outside world, neither did she.

Her head reeled. Curiosity and guilt tumbled over each other like acrobats in a circus. There were so many things she wanted to know. But how could she ask him anything until she was honest, until she told him her real name, her history, the fact that she had a son and an ex-husband, that the man whose shop he had visited was her uncle and not just a dealer coincidentally endowed with the same last name, that she had been raised by that man's sister, that she had no money, no social standing, and no fancy background, and could lay claim to no title other than that of Miss Wadsworth?

As much as she wanted this affair, this romance, this whatever it was they were having, to continue, and as intense as things were between her and Max, the truth was, their intimacy had existed for only a few days. Thanks to Brian, Gaby was gun-shy about investing her trust in anyone, let alone someone she barely knew. Also, though she didn't think so, a tiny part of her brain demanded that she consider the possibility that she was simply a midwestern girl being swept off her feet by a smooth, suave European who was an extremely accomplished lover. There was no denying that she had come to his bed physically needy and had left it physically satisfied. Maybe once her libido was sated and the flush of awakened passion had calmed, she would find there was no deep, abiding feeling there. She didn't believe that, but just in case, she decided not to jeopardize her delicately crafted façade for the sake of an explanation of a few nagging inconsistencies.

If Max had secrets, and she believed he did, he was entitled to them. After all, she had secrets too.

Max found Gaby sitting on the hillside telling stories to a gaggle of small children. She was dressed as they were, in the standard La Maison khaki shorts and white T-shirt. Her hair was braided. Her feet were bare. Though her eyes were shaded with sunglasses, it wasn't hard to see how animated she was. She was gesturing, changing voices, looking almost as young and delighted as her audience.

Instead of joining them, Max hung back, indulging himself in the sight of her. He had missed her. It felt as if he had been gone for weeks, instead of hours. On the flight back from Antwerp, he had thought about nothing but seeing her again, being with her, touching her, holding her. Being the analytical animal that he was, he tried to step back, to categorize his feelings for her. It had been a long time, but the sensations were too familiar and too potent to deny. He was falling in love with her, and in truth, he wasn't sure he wanted to deny those feelings anymore.

For years, he had lived an emotionally celibate existence. He had chained his heart inside a cold, impersonal prison which permitted no visitors, no escape. He dated. He partied. He satisfied his physical urges. But he consistently, deliberately avoided entanglements. In an odd way, it had been easy. First, he had suffered the aftereffects of his family's murders for a very long time. Too, no one had ever come into his life who affected him as Gaby had. No one had ever burrowed her way inside his soul the way she had. From that night at the Castleton gala when he had witnessed her subtle but definitive put-down of Vincent Prado, he had known that she was an unusual woman. Nothing she had said or done since had dissuaded him from that point of view.

If anything, she had continued to impress him, in both large and little ways. Gaby seemed softer than most other women he met. She wasn't as cynical or as blasé. She didn't affect boredom or offer unnecessary criticism. She seemed more open, more genuine, and more honest than most, which to Max was more important than anything. She was a terrific skier, a compassionate friend. She could look drop-dead glamorous or down-to-earth fresh. She knew the difference between fine and faux, between a fair price and a bargain. She was a caring, giving lover, and from what he could see—Gaby picked up a cranky, sleepy four-year-old, comforted him, and resettled him on her lap—she would make an equally caring, giving mother.

Max stopped himself. He knew where he was headed, but he also knew it wasn't time. Not yet. Maybe when this business was all over. Maybe then. For now, he cautioned himself, just enjoy her.

He tiptoed up behind her, holding a finger to his lips. Quickly, before anyone could give him away, he removed her sunglasses and placed his hands over her eyes. He put his face next to hers and said in a deep, gruff basso voice, "Guess who."

Gaby's insides lurched at his touch. Her mouth spread in a broad smile as she answered, "Mickey Mouse?"

The children shrieked with laughter, shouting "No, silly. It's Max!"

"Max?" Gaby feigned shock as she turned to him. They grinned at each other as half a dozen excited, giggling children climbed all over them.

For twenty minutes, Max divided his time between Gaby and the youngsters, weaving an elaborate tale about where he had been and what he had done. Though his story was an adorable one about a magic plane and a mermaid in distress, something in his manner told Gaby that had she asked the reason for his trip, she too would have been told a fable. She might have ruminated on that except that when, finally, the children left for their afternoon naps and Max took her in his arms and kissed her, she couldn't have cared less where he had been, as long as now he was there with her.

"I missed you," she said when he released her.

"Sure, you say that now," he quipped with mock indignation, "but when I showed up, you were too busy to say so much as hello."

She laughed. "I'm sorry. I couldn't help myself. The kids are terrific. I loved spending time with them."

"I know. I saw."

They stretched out on the grass, facing each other and holding hands. For a while, they talked about Gaby's day at La Maison. Max asked for her impressions. Basically, she offered nothing but praise, but she did suggest that he bring in an educational diagnostician to test for learning disabilities. She was sure some of the older children suffered from them, that because of the diversity in languages, it was assumed that their problems were in translation. She suspected there were other causes.

"You seem to know a great deal about this. Were you ever a schoolteacher?"

Gaby laughed, but inside, her nerves tightened.

"Hardly," she said, as coolly as she could. "I'm just interested. I knew a boy once who had a learning disability. Both his teachers and his parents thought he was stupid or slow or, worse, not trying. He was ignored by the system and made fun of by his classmates. What he really needed was specialized tutoring. When he finally got the training he needed, he flourished. He's now a freshman at Brown University."

"Good for him," Max said, wondering who this boy was to have had such a lasting effect on her.

"Good for any kid who overcomes a problem. I mean, you'd think that knowing that someone like Albert Einstein suffered from dyslexia, educators would be sensitive to children who seem to be struggling. Unfortunately, that's not always the case."

Max placed a gentle, appreciative kiss on Gaby's cheek.

"I only wish I had known someone like you when I was a little boy."

"Speaking of little boys," she said, grateful he hadn't pursued the matter further, fearful she had gone too far, "last night I noticed pictures of two handsome little boys in your study. One was you. Was the other your son?"

"Yes."

It had been many years, but the pain in his voice neither shocked nor surprised her. She acknowledged the hollow ache she still felt whenever she thought of her parents. But horrible as that was, she recognized the utter devastation she would suffer if she ever lost Steven.

"Would it be out of order for me to ask you to tell me about him, about what happened to him and your wife?"

Max hesitated. A shadow passed over his eyes. She noticed a tightness in his jaw, as if he was making a decision. She fretted that perhaps she had overstepped her bounds, begging entrance to a place too private for strangers. But slowly the cloud lifted, and in a voice weighed down by painful memories, Max began to tell her the story of his life.

On May 10, 1940, German forces invaded Belgium. Hoping to avoid the wholesale bloodletting and destruction of the First World War, the Belgian army surrendered eighteen days later. Seven months later, on December 10, 1940, Maximilian Richard was born in a barn on a dairy farm outside Oostkamp, a small town on the Brussels–Oostende road, to a woman who had already lost her husband to the Germans.

The farm was owned by his mother's friends, Jacob and Berthe Glucksmann, Jacob's two younger brothers, and their families. During the Occupation, however, the small farm lay fallow as the Glucksmanns hid from the German SS. For five years, the farm appeared deserted, but in fact, it was very much alive, functioning underground as a way station on the human railroad used to ferry Jews from Belgium and the Netherlands to safety. Whether Max wanted to or not, he was born into a world that required spontaneous saviors, and whether he liked it or not, surreptitious charity was to be his destiny.

From the first, Max was taught to understand the importance of silence, the necessity of keeping his movements minimal and basic. Even before he fully comprehended the meaning of what was going on around him, he learned that to some, human rights were arbitrary bonuses granted by a whim or as a favor. But living with the Glucksmanns, he also learned about courage and daring and demanding what was rightfully due a member of God's society on earth.

He used to watch Jacob and Jan and Joseph blacken their faces and tie provisions to bicycles for the perilous trip to Nieuwpoort, a tiny fishing village near the French border. He'd watch as Berthe and Tess and Sarah and his mother dressed the children in burlap and hid them under piles of hay in small wagons strapped to the backs of the bicycles. His job—once he was a walking, talking toddler—was to check the sky. Being the smallest, he was able to crawl out of the vent that let air into the elaborate storm shelter the Glucksmanns had built beneath the barn. He pushed aside the grating camouflaged with sod and slid out on his belly. Lying face up, he studied the heavens, waiting to see if nature was going to provide the starless, moonless night needed to smuggle human cargo out of the country. Once he was certain that the cloud cover was not a temporary umbrella, he scurried back down the vent and alerted the travelers.

It took most of the night to pedal the back roads to Nieuwpoort. Just before reaching the harbor, they hid the bicycles in the garage of a friend and completed their journey on foot. Still using the cover of darkness, the frightened refugees were spirited on board one of four fishing boats owned by sympathizers. Down in the bowels of the boat, beneath thick, slimy nets that smelled of fish, they hid, waiting for first light, when they could push off with the rest of the fleet. While others scouted the North Sea for mackerel and cod, the Samaritan vessel detoured and rendezvoused with another small boat. Exchanging people for provisions, the Belgian trawler quickly retreated, throwing out its nets, hoping no one had noticed its brief disappearance.

For the Glucksmanns waiting back at the farm, those nights were torturous. The men had to hide in safe houses in and around Nieuwpoort and wait for another dark night to travel home. Max and the others never knew until they actually arrived whether or not they'd ever see Jacob, Jan, and Joseph again. For five years they lived with the ax swinging over their heads. They never knew if a neighbor spotted near the house or the barn was simply curious or a collaborator. They never knew when or if waterfront rats had snitched and set up an ambush on the road between Oostkamp and Nieuwpoort. They never knew whether or not the families who came to them had been followed. But it didn't matter. The Glucksmanns were Jews, and in the late thirties, when Hitler's virulent anti-Semitism was exposed, they knew they had a choice to make. They decided to stay in Belgium. For that dubious privilege, they risked their lives every day, but by the time the war ended, they had saved more than five hundred people.

After, the family returned to the business of farming. Max was sent to school with the Glucksmann children. Every day they arose at four, ate their breakfast, packed a hearty lunch, and rode their bicycles the five miles into town. When they returned home in the afternoon, they did chores, helping with the milking or the plowing or the harvesting or whatever else was needed of them.

As Max got older and the Glucksmann children began to marry and bring their new families to live on the farm, Max began to look for alternate sources of income. All around, towns and cities were rebuilding and expanding. Construction crews welcomed young, strapping teenagers like Max, even part-time. When he graduated from primary school, knowing he couldn't afford university, he signed on full-time with a construction company building in the environs of Brussels. For two years, he learned, literally from the ground up, the trade that would eventually become the foundation of his empire.

In 1960, however, Max needed money. Though he had managed to squirrel away some cash, between sending home half his paycheck and having to pay for room and board near the job, it was becoming clear that the only way he was ever going to accumulate enough for tuition to the university was to join the army. He was nineteen years old. His assignment: Urundi.

Urundi was one of the smallest and most crowded countries in Africa. South of the equator, east of Zaire, west of Tanzania, bordering on the northern part of Lake Tanganyika, when Max arrived Urundi was still the southern part of Ruanda-Urundi, a mandated territory under Belgian administration. They were unsettled times, with each half of the territory arguing for independence. Though he had been sent as part of the regular army, it didn't take long for his superiors to transfer Max into intelligence.

For a year, Max traveled throughout Ruanda and Urundi doing reconnaisance, getting to know the two ethnic groups that dominated the population. The Bahutu were the farmers and the original settlers of the region. The Watusi, the cattle owners, were the tall, agile warriors who, about four hundred years before, had invaded Ruanda from the north, swiftly defeating the meeker Bahutu. As a means of settlement, it was decided that in return for protection and a cow, each Bahutu would serve a Watusi "lord." This rather primitive, master-slave form of domination continued until 1959. It was then that the Bahutu of Ruanda rebelled, massacring thousands of Watusi, forcing the Watusi *mwami*, or king, and more than one hundred thousand of his followers south to Urundi. Naturally, there was concern that with the influx of Watusi, the same sort of bloody uprising would befall Urundi. It was the job of the Belgian forces to try to prevent such a disaster.

With Max's background, it was easy for him to infiltrate both groups. He knew about farming and he knew about livestock. He also knew about respect and diplomacy and was immediately accepted by the leaders of most enclaves. In army parlance, he established contacts. In Max's mind, he made friends. He listened to stories, tracked down rumors, put to rest harmful gossip that, given the inflammatory environment, could have turned combative. Through his efforts and the efforts of men like him, tribal disputes and pocket battles were contained. By 1961 when Urundi voted to become an independent monarchy, renamed Burundi, and Ruanda voted to become a republic, renamed Rwanda, Max had moved up in rank and established himself as a friend of the Burundian government. By 1962, when he was discharged from the army and returned to Brussels to attend the university, he had become a permanent fixture in the intelligence community. Max spent the next four years studying political science, economics, and business. Summers, he returned to construction work, helping to build office buildings in downtown Brussels. What bothered him was to see how little attention was being paid to adequate housing for middle-income families. From speaking to his army pals, he learned how difficult it was to find a decent place to live within commuting distance of the cities. Slowly, he began to formulate a plan for suburban cluster communities that would be both comfortable and affordable.

During his last year of university, Max fell in love for the first time in his life. Her name was Catherine Bonné. She was a Walloon from Namur, finishing a degree in history. Max was taking advantage of a particularly beautiful spring day. He took the tram out to Laeken so that he could indulge himself in the splendor of King Leopold's botanical gardens. He was in the Azalea House, letting the refulgent waves of blazing color splash at his senses, when he noticed her. She was bending over, touching a delicate spray of blossoms. Her skirt was sheer and as it hung down and the sun peeked through, lithesome legs and a slim, sinuous body revealed themselves. She stood and, as if she sensed him watching, turned, presenting a pale face framed by long, rusty-red hair. Her eyes were blue, but light, like larkspur, and her gaze was steady. With a quick, graceful flick of her hand, she pushed her hair onto her back, dismissed Max as little more than a presence, and returned to studying the intensely coral flowers on the bush nearest her.

"You have to leave," he said, walking up behind her. "It's a matter of national security."

"I beg your pardon." She spoke in French, refusing, as many Walloons did, to answer him in Flemish.

He switched to French.

"These are Belgian azaleas, grown, fed, and paid for by Belgian taxpayers. If you don't leave, thousands of innocent flowers are going to wilt and die from the shame of being second best.'' He shook his head in an expression of great dismay. "They just can't compete with beauty like yours. Please. Come with me. If you don't, it's going to be terrible. A national calamity.''

"Really!'' A hint of smile kissed her lips.

"Absolutely. Look,'' he said, encouraged, grabbing a sprig of blossoms and inviting her to examine them. "They're beginning to fade already. Can't you see it? We'd better hurry. Any second now, they're going to call in the guard.''

"Then I guess you're right. We have to leave. But where are we going?''

Max grinned. "To the Great Geranium Gallery.''

"I thought I was a threat to the flowers?'' Catherine said, wondering why she had agreed to go anywhere with this strange man, knowing that he wasn't strange at all.

Max took her hand and began to lead her out of the glass and wrought-iron structure.

"Only to azaleas,'' he said, matter-of-factly. "They're sensitive. Geraniums are arrogant. Nothing bothers them.''

Max and Catherine toured the rest of the gardens, talking and walking until the sun set and their tour led to dinner, which led to plans for breakfast, which led to three more dates, bed, and then, four days after his graduation, to the altar.

For two years, they boarded on the Glucksmann farm, living in a single room in the attic. Catherine got a job teaching in Bruges. Max took out a loan, hired a crew, and tested his dreams. Over the next two years, the first cluster community—apartments and stores around a central green—was built by Richard Construction on the commuting road between Oostkamp and Bruges. By the time it was completed, Max was up to his neck in debt. Within three months, he had paid off all his loans and had broken ground on two more clusters, one in Asse on the old road from Brussels to Ghent, the other outside Ypres. Also, he and Catherine had become the proud parents of an eight-pound baby boy, Theo.

Theo was six months old when the Richards moved into their new apartment in Brussels. They felt secure and successful and thoroughly blessed, as if life had nothing but good to offer them. Six weeks later, Max was asked to return to Burundi. Serious problems existed between the Bahutu and the Watusi. Since independence, there had been continual unrest. The Bahutu objected to Watusi rule. In 1965, assassins had killed the prime minister. Later that year, his successor had been shot. In 1966, the *mwami* was overthrown and Micombero, the new military leader, had declared himself president. Now, in 1968, the Belgian government, in conjunction with the United Nations, decided that perhaps with some experienced intelligence intervention, further bloodshed and upheaval could be prevented. Max was drafted.

It was early 1969 when Max, Catherine, and Theo arrived in Bujumbura, the capital. Max had decided that the less Catherine knew about the real reason for their transfer, the safer she and Theo were. He had also decided that he could maintain a cover and do some good for the people of Burundi if he helped bring the country into the modern age. With financial aid from the Belgian government, as well as from several private investors, he began to construct office buildings and apartments and, outside the city, the same kind of cluster housing he had put up in Belgium. Catherine taught French in the elementary school and occasionally accompanied the missionaries when they went out into the countryside to dispense medicine and food. Most of the time, Theo was by Catherine's side, but when he couldn't be, he was cared for by a kind Bahutu woman whose husband worked on one of Max's crews. For the Richard family, life settled into a strange, watchful, yet not entirely unpleasant routine.

Catherine and Theo remained shielded from Max's intelligence activities. For them, his meetings with tribal leaders or government personnel were part of his job, something he had to do. Their excursions to remote villages like Rutana or Nyanza-Lac were looked upon as vacations or diversions, a way for Catherine and Theo to practice their Kirundi, to sightsee, and to shop the outdoor markets. Even when they remained in a village for weeks at a time—sometimes with Max, sometimes without—it didn't concern them. They had grown very fond of the gentle Bahutu. They liked visiting the coffee plantations where arabica coffee was grown, or climbing to the higher elevations where robusta coffee, the kind used for instant coffee, was grown, or watching the fishermen haul in their catch from Lake Tanganyika. They could never get used to the Watusi habit of drinking animal blood, but the high jumps and acrobatic dancing of the tall, limber Africans never ceased to thrill them.

In 1972, when the Bahutus revolted against the Watusi, and one friend took up arms against the other, Catherine was appalled. Max was concerned. He wanted to ship her and Theo home. She was eight months pregnant. Theo had just turned four. Max had to stay, but his family didn't. Catherine chose that time to turn stubborn and recalcitrant. The most she would agree to was to leave Bujumbura, where much of the fighting was taking place. Thanks to her Bahutu amah, she and Theo were spirited safely out of the city to a small village near Gitega in the heart of Burundi.

Officially, Max was a European businessman with no governmental position or influence. Unofficially, he was a mediator trying to bring both sides to the bargaining table. Each time he thought he had arranged a meeting, something happened, the meeting was canceled and hundreds more men were slaughtered. It wasn't long before it dawned on Max that there was an instigator at work, an outside party with a vested interest in the continuation of the civil war. He began to hear about arms being shipped across the lake from Zaire and smuggled across the borders on the other side from Tanzania. Whether the arms were coming from the Russians or other Africans interested in staking out further territory for themselves, he didn't know. Nor did he have time to find out. When he heard that the fighting had radiated well beyond the environs of the capital and threatened to overtake the entire country, all concerns faded compared to his fear for the safety of Catherine and his son.

Grabbing a jeep, he headed for central Burundi, over plateaus, up steep slopes, down into the swamps that lay at the foot of the escarpments. He could smell war in the air. The pit of his stomach was tight, as if soft muscle had been replaced by rock. Just ahead of him, he heard the pop of rifles, the boom of grenades, the screams of people in the throes of death. His hands sweated as he gripped the wheel and pressed down on the accelerator. He drove as fast as he could, but he was too late. Fire was everywhere. Grass huts had been torched. Women and babies had been shot where they stood or sat, their lifeless bodies slumped onto the ground, slowly being cooked by ravenous flames. The bodies of the men and boys were scattered in and among the huts, their hands still gripping guns, spears, rocks, even pitchforks. Max found several Watusi among the dead. He removed a bazooka from one, a rifle from another.

Max threw the guns in the back of his jeep and drove on. Mass murderers were never content with destroying just one village. They built up a heinous momentum, a thirst for more and more blood, a need to justify the first kill by killing again and again. As he neared Gitega, he could smell the burning sulfur and charcoal of exploded gunpowder. He could see puffs of smoke rising in the distance, smoke that signaled fighting. He grabbed his gun, checked to be sure his ammunition belt was secure, and bolted from his jeep, running in the direction of Catherine's hut. He saw her. She was running away from him holding Theo in her arms. Her gait was lumbering, her body cumbersome and awkward. He called to her, shouting her name, wanting her to know he was there to protect her, to protect Theo. He was oblivious to the gunfire around him, the grenade that hit just to the left of him. He spotted two Watusi with rifles aimed at Catherine. He fired immediately. One. Two. He killed them, but in doing so he had taken his eye off Catherine. Just as he turned back to her, she turned and saw him. He tried to reach her. Theo was crying. He jumped out of Catherine's arms and started running toward his father. The grenade hit right in front of him, blowing off half his head, splattering his body all over the ground. Catherine had been shot, but she continued to stumble toward her son, screaming, holding her abdomen, which was bleeding. Max was almost there. He could almost feel her touching him, but then, he felt nothing except a shooting pain in his chest.

When he woke, he was in a hospital in Bujumbura. The bullet had missed his heart by inches. Another bullet had found Catherine's heart, and she had died next to her son, four feet from her husband. Max had been brought to the hospital by the few Bahutu who survived the attack. They had also had the decency to bring his family so that he could decide where to bury them. Though the doctors warned he wasn't well enough to travel, Max left Burundi immediately, taking with him his son, his wife, and his unborn daughter.

It took a while for Max to recover from his losses, at least on the surface. He left the army and threw himself into his business.

Within five years, he was a multimillionaire with a string of office buildings and apartment houses and cluster communities all over Europe. It was then, in 1977, that he decided to open La Maison as a tribute to the memory of Catherine and Theo.

Gaby's face was streaked with tears. His recitation had been so controlled, so restrained, but there was a wretched resonance in his voice that spoke volumes about the pain he felt and the bitterness he continued to harbor. For a long time, they didn't speak, they didn't move, they simply let the past drift over them like a cloud dark with rain.

Gaby was so caught up in the emotion of the moment, it wasn't until later that night that she realized he had never explained what had happened to his mother or the Glucksmanns.

So many questions. So few answers.

19

During the fifteenth century, at the zenith of its glory, Bruges was an important trading hub. It boasted access to the North Sea via the Zwin inlet, as well as two deep canals that linked it with Oostende and with Sluis in Holland. As a shipping center it attracted wealth, and wealth begot a surrounding of magnificently gabled guildhalls and merchant houses, charming squares, narrow cobblestone streets, and elegant church spires that soared high above the city. Bruges was a seat of power, a base for the exchange of goods and ideas. It was a favored resort of the dukes of Burgundy, a magnet for agents of princely banking houses and commercial traders. Art flourished there, as did Flemish literature, the making of lace, and the production of wool. But when the Zwin began silting up with the sands of the Schelde, Bruges, the victim of a series of circumstances beyond its control, earned the somber sobriquet, Bruges-la-Morte. The inlet clogged. Trade shifted north to the larger, more accessible harbor at Antwerp. Its power dwindled, its fountain of influence dried up, and much of its wealth sought other venues.

Though it eventually found its way into the twentieth century and is now an industrial city, the look and feel of Bruges remain medieval. It is a city caught in a time delay. Cars are banned from many of its streets. Bicycles are a major mode of transportation. Strict laws protect the ancient façades from capricious change or from high-rises blotting the skyline. More than fifty bridges—Bruges means "bridges"—criss-cross the numerous canals that snake through the city. At religious festivals and pageants, the locals don medieval costumes. And every day, tourists flood the streets, eager to submerge themselves in the distant past, happy to regress to a simpler time.

For Gaby, it was love at first sight. She was overwhelmed by the unique beauty of the town. Its canals sparkled in the summer sun. The waters rippled from the regal progress of snow-white long-necked swans. Green, lush willows and lime trees reached over stone walls to shade the boats that wended their way along the intricate waterways. Flowers were everywhere: in windowboxes, climbing up trellises, filling pots that flanked doorways and alleyways, in patches of garden fronting stores and squares. On windowsills, wooden shoes decorating shutters or filled with blossoms reasserted the historical connection between the Flemish and the Dutch. And every fourth store, or so it seemed, was a bakery displaying yet another of Belgium's culinary talents—mouth-watering pastries and huge platters of marzipan shaped and colored to look like pieces of freshly picked fruit. More than once, Gaby asked Max to stop so she could watch the making of bobbin lace. Just as women must have done in the fifteenth century, the lace maker, usually an older woman, sat with a huge pillow on her lap. Pinned to the pillow was a parchment pattern. As she worked, she stuck pegs into the pattern and flipped the bobbins over and around the pegs, pulling the threads so that they formed a design. As the lace was made, she moved the pegs and continued patterning her cloth. Her hands worked almost too rapidly to follow, taking two bobbins with one hand, twisting them, bringing over two held by her other hand, always working with multiples of four, sometimes having more than forty bobbins on a pillow.

They visited the Hospital of St. John where the work of Hans Memling, Bruges's best known painter, was housed along with the world's oldest pharmacy. They saw the Grote Markt, the cathedral of St. Sauveur with its Gobelin tapestries and choir stalls emblazoned with the sign of the Golden Fleece. They also stopped at the Chapel of the Holy Blood, where, because it was Friday, they were able to see the golden reliquary studded with jewels, one a black diamond said to have belonged to Mary, Queen of Scots. But for Gaby, the most interesting place on their tour was the Princely Béguinage.

As they crossed the Bridge of the Vine, which spanned the Lake of Love, Gaby's gaze was drawn just beyond the gateway into a mystical compound of ordered tranquility. Arm in arm, they strolled around the grassy quadrangle, looking at the austere white cottages with their stepped roofs, keeping their voices low so as not to disturb the pervasive serenity. Here and there Benedictine nuns distinguished by their traditional fifteenth-century black habits and white *béguins*—medieval peasant headdresses tied under the chin—walked silently from one building to another, their heads bowed, their hands clasped and hidden beneath their robes. Though most Belgian towns had *béguinages*, or *begijnhofs*, few of them functioned as actual convents. Some were museums. Others were known for their manicured gardens. Some, like this one, had been turned over to the Benedictines on the condition that they wear the dress of their predecessors and that they maintain the *begijnhof* as an historical monument.

As they walked, Max explained the differences between a traditional convent and a *béguinage*.

"Originally, these were places designed to care for widows of Crusader knights, peasant women with no way to maintain themselves without the protection of a husband. Later on, widows from the upper classes began seeking the safety and companionship provided by the *béguinage*. Back then, women married very young, and because men wanted brides of childbearing age, it was possible for young widows to remarry. Once they had passed their productive years, however, they became burdens. Many of them were religious, but wealthy. They wanted to feel useful and part of a community, but they didn't want to take vows, especially the vow of poverty, which they would have to have done if they entered a convent. The *béguinage* was the answer. They moved into the houses that you see rimming the quad, bringing their female servants and their possessions with them, and spent the rest of their lives doing charity work."

"What happened to the servants when the widow died or became too old to work?"

"See those larger houses?" he asked, pointing to a group of dwellings in the center of the cloister that looked like small, two-story apartment houses. "The servants moved in there. Usually, the widows remembered them with bequests for their lifetime care."

"It's so peaceful," Gaby said in a near whisper, listening as the song of a bird interrupted the silence.

"That's its main purpose. To provide peace for the soul and a restful haven for the spirit."

"What kind of woman enters a *béguinage* today?"

Max grew thoughtful.

"A woman alone, in need of companionship, in need of privacy. A woman looking to escape the pressures of a modern-day world, perhaps."

"It is a great place to hide."

Max's head jerked involuntarily. He stared at Gaby, whose expression seemed wistful, as though she felt envious of those living in this sequestered nunnery.

"You've been watching too many late-night movies," he said, studying her carefully.

"I don't mean hide from the police or anything like that," she said. "Haven't you ever wanted to run away? To leave the world and all its problems behind you and start again?"

"I suppose after Catherine and Theo died I did, but instead I threw myself into my work."

"You were lucky. Not everyone has a career to help absorb his pain."

It was as if a window shade had snapped up, allowing Max a look inside the place where the private Gaby lived. He had never realized just how closemouthed she had been about herself and her past until that moment. Now he was curious.

"Is that how you felt when your husband died? Like running away?"

When your husband died . . . Gaby cringed. She hated lying, especially to Max, but just then she had no idea what to say, how to explain what she had done and why. Besides, this wasn't the time or the place.

"Yes," she said, deciding that half a truth was better than no truth at all. "When my marriage ended, I had nothing but time on my hands, and when you're grieving over what you've lost, time is your enemy, not your friend. I wanted to work, but no one wanted me. Willingness is not considered adequate qualification for a job.''

''It would be to me.''

Impulsively, Gaby kissed him. ''That's because you're unbelievably special, Max. There are not too many in this universe like you.''

He returned her kiss, but out of respect for their surroundings, kept it light and brief.

''I hope you're not planning on making a comparative survey,'' he said, half teasing.

''I wasn't,'' she said, warmed by the undertone of jealousy in his voice, ''but now that you mention it, it might be a lot of fun.''

''I guess I'm just going to have to eliminate my competition by plying you with food and wine and romance.''

He slid his arm around her waist and pulled her to him. She looked into his eyes and allowed a slow smile to curl her lips.

''Ply away,'' she said.

They walked back over the Bridge of the Vine, ambling toward their hotel. They were quiet, comfortable enough to have no fear of awkward silences. Along the way, they passed a compound, one of a series built throughout Flanders by guilds or wealthy families to house the poor and the old, called ''God's houses.''

''The only requirements for residency are 'honesty, good character, and a peaceable nature,' '' Max said as they stopped to admire the village within a village. ''What's nice is the way these people express their gratitude. They maintain their homes beautifully, they take care of each other in a loving, familial way, and they begin and end each day with prayers for the generations who lived and died before them.''

''That's lovely,'' Gaby said admiringly. ''You Belgians are certainly a charitable lot.''

There were twenty-four houses, each with its own garden, several of which were being tended by their owners. One woman was bending over, loosening the dirt around her flowers with a small hand rake while trying to hold a cascade of necklaces against her chest. She wore a floral-printed scarf on her head, and for a moment her silhouette was so like Simone's that Gaby felt overcome. The woman turned and smiled. Gaby looked at her face and the image disappeared, but not the emotion it had aroused.

"This is so much nicer than a nursing home or an old-age home. It's more loving and more respectful of a human being's instinctive need to maintain dignity and pride and a touch of independence."

Again, Max sensed that Gaby was speaking from experience. Her voice had resonated with such feeling that he was certain tears lurked just below the surface. He didn't know who was the cause of those tears, but although she had asked him about his past, he would wait until she chose her moment to tell him about hers.

He took her hand and led her across another bridge. As they neared Huidevettersplein, the small square where their hotel, the Duc de Bourgogne, was, they passed a shop with a huge window. Max stopped and turned Gaby toward the window.

"Now that is a handsome couple, don't you think?" he asked, grinning foolishly at their reflection, hoping to chase the cloud that had darkened Gaby's mood.

She looked into the glass. "Very handsome," she said.

"Except that woman looks like she's in desperate need of a hug."

"She is," she said, taking refuge in Max's arms, grateful for his sensitivity and comfort, even more grateful for his patience and lack of interrogation.

When they separated, she glanced at the glass again. Behind them, two youngsters passed, their arms intertwined, their bodies extremely close together. She stared at them and then at the reflection of Max and herself, also with their arms intertwined, also with their bodies touching. She saw her face and, in it, the depth of her feeling. Though she hadn't spoken the words aloud, she loved this man. She loved him with the same intensity and vigor as that young girl loved that boy. Because it was as fresh and new for her as it was for them. Because the fire of passion didn't require innocence as fuel. Because love had no age limit, no lessening of effect due to the passage of time, no rules for denial due to past experiences. Knowing that, knowing that love was by its very nature refreshing and rejuvenative, a potent elixir of youth available to anyone willing to drink from its fountain, she smiled.

"I guess the hug did it," Max said, continuing toward the square, noting her change in mood and acknowledging it with a squeeze of the hand.

Gaby desperately wanted to stop, to ask Max how he felt, if he shared her feelings, if he felt the same delirious excitation whenever they touched, if he felt the same growing sense of intimacy she felt, if he loved her. But she couldn't, so instead she simply said, "I guess it did."

The next morning, over croissants and tea, Max announced he had a business appointment in Diksmuide. He said it would probably run into the early afternoon.

"Will you be all right on your own?" he asked.

"I won't have as much fun without you as I'd have with you, of course," she said dreamily, reminding both of them of the night before, another night when only exhaustion ended their lovemaking. "But I'll muddle through."

"Would you like me to hire a guide for you?"

"No, thanks. Actually, I think I'm going to spend the morning in the library. From what I hear, they have several fabulous volumes on the history of the Dinant tapestries."

Max leaned back in his chair and looked at her, a bemused expression on his face. "Since when are you so interested in the Dinants?"

"Since I met you."

"And what is it you hope to learn in the library?"

"How they were made. What the original owners were like. The history, the significance, of them, maybe even a newspaper article that would give a clue as to who bought the three sold at auction and where *The Marriage of Brussels* might be."

Max laughed. Generally, he judged enthusiasm an appealing quality, but the way Gaby wore it, it was positively provocative.

"I probably shouldn't do this, but staring at you in that skimpy negligee has probably caused me to go slightly daft."

"Good. I'd hate to think that in the cold light of day, my negligee and I had lost our appeal."

"Hardly," he said with a blatantly lustful leer.

Gaby was torn between curiosity and the desire to respond to the invitation in his eyes.

"What shouldn't you do?" she asked, deciding that perhaps she could satisfy both urges.

"Save you a little time by telling you I own the three Dinants sold at auction," he said, enjoying the spontaneous surprise and delight of her response, hoping nonetheless that he hadn't made a mistake.

"You do?"

"I do. I bought *The Meeting* at Christie's in London, *The Battle of the Lion and the Unicorn* at Castleton's in Amsterdam, and *The Bethrothal* at Sotheby's in Geneva."

"Why did you keep it so secret? Why don't you want anyone to know?"

"Because I don't want to negotiate where the Dinants are displayed. I intend to find and buy *The Marriage of Brussels*. When I do, I'll make Garrett an extremely appealing offer on the two he owns and present the series to the Belgian government."

"What about *The Triumph of Chastity*?"

"Even without it, having six of the Dinants together and available in one place is better than having them hidden away in vaults all over the globe."

"I couldn't agree more," she said, endlessly impressed with the intensity of both his desire to give and his determination to get. He was a complex man, but to her, each new facet of his personality was simply another cut on a perfect diamond. "At the risk of repeating myself, there aren't many like you, Max, a fact which makes me feel like a very lucky woman."

Max rose from his chair, walked over to where Gaby was sitting, leaned over, and took her in his arms.

"I'm the one who's lucky." His mouth covered hers, and as though an electric current were racing through her body, she felt every cell come alive.

"You have a meeting," she said, instantly breathless. He opened her peignoir and ran his hand across her breasts, casually, as if both of them needed no more than a gentle reminder of how good they were together to elicit a response. Then he picked her up and carried her back to bed.

"I know," he said, sliding her silken garments down her legs, throwing them aside, indulging himself in the luxurious feel of her flesh. "But something tells me I'm going to be late."

* * *

Gaby would never know what had prompted her to follow him, but she had, and again she found herself confronting more questions than answers. She had fully intended to go to the library, but as she left the square outside the hotel and approached the bridge that led to the center of town, she noticed Max getting into a taxi. If he had been going to Diksmuide as he had said, he should have headed south. Instead, he was headed north. On impulse, she too flagged a cab, asking the driver to follow the taxi in front of them.

Damme was only four miles away. On the edge of the tiny townlet, Max's cab stopped at a *begijnhof*. Though it looked like the Princely Béguinage with its black and white houses and verdant central lawn, unlike the one in Bruges, a high gate surrounded the property, a gate that remained securely locked until a presentation of credentials was made to the sentry on duty. Gaby waited until Max had entered. She watched him walk toward the back. He knocked on the door of a corner house and after a few moments was let in. The door closed behind him. Gaby paid the cab driver, asked him to come back for her in an hour, and got out. She donned sunglasses, tied a scarf around her head, and approached the guard, deliberately distraught and babbling.

"Excuse me. That man who just walked in. Max. I was supposed to come with him today, but I slept late and by the time I got up and got dressed, he had already gone. I feel so embarrassed. I mean I'm not usually late. In fact, I hate being late, don't you? It's not polite, but well, sometimes, you just can't help it. You've slept late now and then, haven't you? Of course you have. Everyone has. Well, but that's not the point. The point is I'm here and he's here and we're here to visit and the only thing standing between me and him is you. So what do you say? Will you open the gate?"

"What is the number of the house you are going to?"

Shielded by her dark glasses, she squinted to try to make out the number on the first few doors.

"There are no numbers here," she said, realizing he had been trying to trick her. "I'm going to the one in the corner. That one down at the end." She stretched her arm out in front of him, waving her finger in front of his nose. "See it? The one in the shadow of that big old tree. Is that an oak? We have oaks all over at home. Anyway, it's that house and I have to get there. They're probably wondering where I am. Worried. They're probably worried. I hope they're not angry. They could be. I mean look how late I am. It's . . .''

The gate opened. The sentry's eyes looked glazed. Gaby prayed she had made him so dizzy he wouldn't think of following her. She walked past his kiosk and down the lane a bit and then took a quick left, losing herself behind the center apartment buildings, doubling back and heading for the chapel. There she could remain out of sight, yet still have a clear view of the house Max had entered.

The chapel was cool, almost cold. Made completely of stone, sheltered by an awning of tall, voluptuously leafed trees, it was a decided relief from the summer's day outside. Gaby untied her scarf and loosened her hair, shaking it, lifting it off her neck, waiting for her body temperature to lower and the heated flush to leave her cheeks. All the while, her eyes remained fixed on that single white door with no number and heavily curtained windows. Who lived there? Whom had Max come to see? Why? Why had he lied to her? What was he hiding?

After about fifteen minutes, Gaby's vision began to blur from staring so hard. She decided that a fast tour of the chapel would be all right. Trying not to stray too far from the chapel's entry, she wandered further inside. As soon as she did, she stopped. Hanging to the left of the small altar, fronted by a table filled with half-burned candles, was a huge tapestry. Within seconds, she knew it was *The Triumph of Chastity*, the seventh Dinant.

In the center of the tapestry was a chariot being drawn by a team of smiling unicorns. Standing atop the chariot, was a beautiful maiden, the virtue Chastity, holding aloft a book Gaby assumed was a Bible. Her gown was a flowing creation woven in madonna blue with golden threads decorating the wrists and hem. Her head was crowned with a simple band of marguerite daisies. Inside the chariot, its arms bound behind its back, was a winged pagan, a vice, an angel of earthly temptation.

Gaby moved closer, touching the piece, caressing the woolen background, the silken faces. Even in the dimly lit chapel, Gaby knew this was a Dinant—the symmetry of the composition, the flowery foreground, the richness of color, the types of flowers in the garden surrounding the chariot, the style of clothing worn by the maidens attending the lady Chastity, the blue banner at the back of the chariot marked with three golden fleurs-de-lis. She might not have been a Dinant scholar, knowledgeable enough to affirm its provenance with absolute certainty, but she was expert enough to hazard an extremely educated guess.

This tapestry was presumed lost or destroyed. Just that morning, she had asked Max about it. What had he said? *Even without it* . . . She had assumed he too believed the piece no longer existed, but obviously he knew it did. Did he own this one also? Was he allowing the *béguinage* to borrow it until he found *The Marriage of Brussels*? Was he hiding it here because it gave him some bargaining advantage? It didn't make sense. He had told her about the other three. Why not this one? Gaby was confused. More than that, she felt shaken. His trust was conditional. Why? Was he suspicious of her? Or simply not completely honest? Was he not who she thought him to be? Was she seeing in him only what she wanted to see? Was she deliberately blind to something obvious because she wanted so badly to love and be loved?

Her eye caught movement across the courtyard. She ran to the entry just in time to see Max exit and the door close. Who lived there? Gaby was dying to knock on that door, but she knew she didn't dare. She also knew she had to get back to Bruges. She waited until Max's taxi drove away before leaving the chapel. Her cab was at the gate. Now all she had to do was get past the guard.

"I can't believe he was that mad," she muttered as she approached his kiosk. "I mean, really, making me take my own cab back. What ever happened to chivalry! I apologized. What more does he want?"

The gate opened instantly.

That night, as she lay in Max's arms, she felt unusually vulnerable. Before that afternoon, she had felt safe with Max, secure in the belief that he was a man of honor, a man of probity and principle. Certainly, discovering that he had deceived her didn't falsify everything else she knew about him, but it did raise doubt. Doubt about whether his passion was sexual or emotional, about whether their moments together were meaningful to him or an insignificant, albeit pleasant, passing of time. Doubt about whether there could ever be any real future with Max.

How could there be? Love had its foundation in truth. Commitment required honesty. Though they lay naked beside each other, their identities remained heavily cloaked. Gaby had her reasons for secrecy, and if she accepted the fact that, to her, they were sound, solid reasons, necessary for her very survival, she had to accept that Max had reasons too. Yet the fact remained that neither of them had been completely honest with the other. Neither was brave enough or strong enough or enough in love to tell the truth.

It was almost eight o'clock when Belle let herself in. The house was empty. She called out to Drake and the housekeeper, but neither one answered. A note was taped to the mirror in the entry: *Went to a dinner party. Be home later. See you then. Love you, Daddy.*

Belle ripped the note off the mirror, crushed it in her hand, and dropped it into her purse. In the kitchen, Mrs. Moore had left a dinner plate for her. If she wanted, all she had to do was pop it into the microwave and zap it for two minutes. Belle left the plate where it was. She hadn't eaten all day, but even the thought of food made her sick.

With Throckmorton by her side, she walked down the hall to her bedroom. As she passed her father's room, she looked in. It was so different now from the way it used to look when Chelsea lived there and all the fabrics and wall coverings had been celery green and peach. Different, too, from the way it had looked when her mother had lived there and the ambience had been yellow and sunny. But everything was different, especially now. For Belle, life had turned as dark and muddy as the browns that pervaded her father's room.

She closed the door, unwilling to recall the few happy times she had spent in that room, unable to forget the horrible fights she had witnessed there. She could still hear the screaming, the name calling, the sounds of punches landing on soft flesh. She could still see her father roughing up her mother, pushing Chelsea, shoving one or the other of them around because in some way they had disobeyed him or denied him.

Drake had never beaten her. He had never even spanked her when, as a little girl, she had done something naughty. She had never thought about that before, but now it struck her as odd.

Maybe it would have been better if he had beaten her. Maybe he would have left bruises or cracked a few teeth. Someone might have noticed and called Chelsea or her mother and one of them would have called the police and demanded that she be taken away from him. But her bruises were internal. No one noticed and no one called anyone for help.

Once in her own room, Belle tried to sit, to think things out, but she couldn't. She felt agitated, edgy, unable to stop moving. She desperately needed to talk to someone, but Chelsea was in Europe and her mother was back in that sanatorium. All afternoon, she had avoided confronting the truth. She had purged her mind of all thought, walking around the city until she was so fatigued, she was practically senseless.

"I can't," she said to the fluffy animal in her arms. "I can't do it anymore. No. I can't."

Throckmorton jumped onto the bed, bored with his mistress's problems. Belle paced, her mind moving faster than her feet, but with the same unfocused lack of direction. She rambled, voicing disconnected thoughts and ideas to a disinterested cat, a disinterested silence.

"I'll move. I'll leave town. I'll go far away. That's it. Where he won't find me. Where he can't hurt me. Money. Oh, God, what'll I do for money? Work. That's what. I'll get a job. I can't. Who would want me? I'm no good. I'm no good at anything."

By ten o'clock, Belle's pacing had become frenetic. Her breathing had grown rapid and shallow. She saw visions before her eyes, visions of the future. She hallucinated about Drake using her body, taking her by force, demanding that she comply with his wishes over and over and over again. Her eyes teared. Her throat grew tight.

So tired. So confused. So frightened. So alone.

By eleven o'clock, Belle's mind had splintered into a thousand fragments—bits and pieces of terrifying thoughts with no coherent pattern, like the shards from a shattered kaleidoscope. Yet in the midst of her mental chaos, one thought continued to reassert itself. It seemed right. It seemed easy. It seemed to be her only way out.

She sat at her desk and quickly, before she lost her nerve, penned a letter. Only a few lines. Even now, she didn't have much to say because she was too ashamed to tell the whole truth. She licked the envelope, stamped it, and ran to the hall where there was a mail chute. For a minute, she held it halfway in, halfway out. She stared at it, knowing that once she let it go, she couldn't take it back. Her heart thumped inside her ears, filling her head with loud demands. Obediently, she dropped the letter into the slot and watched it through the glass as it whizzed down to the lobby. She was proud of herself, probably for the first time. Proud because she had made a decision. The most important decision of her life.

"It's just too ugly," she mumbled over and over again as she returned to her room and locked the door behind her. "He'll do it to me and then to her. I can't. I won't let that happen."

She went to her bathroom and filled a glass with water. All the while, she continued to shake her head and mutter.

"Ugly. I'm ugly. He's ugly."

Slowly, she opened the drawer by her bed. She took out a small orange plastic bottle. The name on the prescription: Chelsea Reynolds. The contents: Seconal. The directions: one before bedtime, as needed. Belle opened the container and spilled thirty tablets into her hand. Without any hesitation, she opened her mouth, threw the pills back into her throat and quickly drained the glass. She sighed with relief. It was done. Soon it would be over.

She changed into pajamas and climbed into bed, letting Throckmorton nestle in the crook of her arm, wanting to feel him near her at that final moment when she would pass into that world where one never felt anything again. The pills took effect, but the total, instant lack of consciousness she had wanted was not be be. Instead, she was attacked by nightmares. Drake. Animals. Masks. Being tied to a table. Metal stirrups. Straps. Things being stuck into her and pulled out of her. Chelsea watching. Her mother watching. Drake laughing. Everyone laughing . . . laughing . . . laughing.

The sound filled her ears, waking her, prodding her out of bed and onto her feet. She pressed her hands against her ears, trying to shut out the laughter, the humiliation, the scorn.

Hot. I'm so hot. And scared. So scared. Soon. He'll be home. He'll find out. Angry. He'll be angry. Can't let him find me. Got to get out. Got to . . .

She stumbled toward the window, opening it, letting the air hit her face. She closed her eyes, feeling the sweet good-night kiss of a summer breeze on her cheeks. She leaned on the sill, stretching out over the street. She extended her arms, reaching toward the welcome serenity of open space. Further and further she reached. Her eyelids blinked, but everything was black. Her head was woozy, her balance skittish. She felt the void and longed to be part of it, to be surrounded by it, by its nothingness, its painlessness, its peacefulness. Finally, mercifully, she slipped into it, falling, drifting, flying, feeling free, truly free, truly safe.

In the last instant before her body crashed onto the pavement twenty floors below, she smiled, knowing that she had stopped him. Her father could never touch her again.

"Belle's dead." Gaby heard herself repeat what Chelsea had told her over the phone, but still she couldn't believe it. "She jumped out her window."

She shivered. Max took her in his arms and held her tight against him.

"I have to go home. I have to be with Chelsea. I have to say good-bye to Belle."

"I know," Max said; he, too, was rattled by the news. "I've already called my pilot. You'll take my plane."

"Are you coming with me?"

She looked frightened, the same way most people did when faced with the reality of human frailty.

"I have to finish up some business in Brussels first. I'll follow you to New York. Don't worry. I'll be there."

Gaby nodded. She was too upset to question what he was doing or where or why. All that mattered was Belle. Why had she done such a horrible thing?

"We all knew something was wrong, but no one did anything about it. Do you remember how she was in Steamboat Springs? How reckless? How frightened?"

Max shared Gaby's sense of frustration and guilt, but more than that, he felt a certain complicity in Belle's death. He had recognized a dangerous isolation in the young woman. He had seen it in her art. He had heard it in her conversation and observed it in her manner. Yet he, the supposed protector of victimized children, had done nothing. He had let it pass as if it would simply go away. He knew better. He knew that hurts like hers never healed without enormous doses of care.

"She was troubled. Now she's at peace," he said, hating the vacuousness of those words, recognizing that at a time like this words were all that remained to hold on to. "Come. Let's get ready."

Within the hour, they were packed and in a cab on their way to Brussels. For most of the ride, they sat pressed against each other, holding hands, needing the closeness, needing the reassuring touch of warm flesh against warm flesh. Gaby wept. Max's face was dour, his eyes veiled. The only time they spoke was when they passed Oostkamp. Max had promised to take Gaby there to meet the Glucksmanns. Now that visit would have to wait.

At the airport, Max settled Gaby on board the plane, kissed her good-bye, and promised to call the minute he arrived in New York. He waited on the tarmac until the 727 was airborne before returning to his taxi.

"Brussels, sir?" the driver asked.

"No. If you don't mind, I'd like to go back up north to the *begijnhof* in Damme. Do you know where it is?"

The driver laughed.

"Not only do I know where it is, but I took the lady there just yesterday."

"Which lady?"

"That one. The one you just put on that plane."

"She went to Damme?"

"Yes, sir. We followed you. She said she wanted to surprise you. She waited until you were inside, and then she went in. I picked her up an hour after I dropped her off. So, was it?"

"Was it what?" Max's voice was flat and lifeless, like the straight, unwavering line on a failed EKG.

"A surprise."

"Yes," Max said, feeling a bubble inside his heart deflate. "Her visit was a big surprise."

How could she? No. The real issue was how could he have been so naive, so careless? He should have known. He never should have opened himself up to her, told her about himself, his family, his past. Why did he think it would be different with her? For as long as he could remember, love had either betrayed him, abandoned him, or made a fool of him. What made him think the gods had decided to rewrite the story of his life? Again, love had hurt him, reaffirming what he had always believed, that love demanded commitment and along with commitment, confession, a reckless act: a bared soul provided a target. Love was too volatile an emotion to be trusted. Not like hate. Hate was a constant, a steady, steely sensation that demanded a watchful awareness.

Yet, somehow, Gaby had managed to scale those barriers and bypass his misgivings. Was it her ingenuousness, her warmth, her ability to give of herself without condition or compromise? Whatever it was, Max now had to view her with suspicion. After all, he was too involved in the world of espionage to take chances, to discount the possibility that she too was involved in the business of subterfuge. He wouldn't be the first operative to be seduced by the enemy, the first man to be victimized by his own weakness. But now that he had been warned, he would become armed.

Until he knew why she had followed him, until he knew who she was and what she really wanted from him, there would be no further entanglement with Gabrielle Didier, no further emotional complications. He would close his heart and his mind to her. He would protect himself and those he was sworn to protect. But he would miss her.

Because no matter who she was, he loved her.

20

Chelsea Reynolds's father was a drunk. He never slept in the streets or fed off soup lines at men's shelters. He didn't spend his days on a park bench swigging booze from a brown paper bag, or his nights staggering from one strange bar to another, but he was a drunk just the same. He denied it. His wife denied it. His two sons denied it. And for most of her childhood, Chelsea had denied it too.

She was in her early teens when she was forced to confront the beast that was Jack Harper's alcoholism—the beast that had grown larger and larger until there was no ignoring its existence. It loomed like a hideous, black-biled monster that raged out of control one minute and lolled about in a mellow stupor the next. When it possessed her father he smacked her for no reason, embarrassed her in front of her friends, screamed obscenities at her mother until she was reduced to tears, humiliated her younger brothers, and then had the audacity to demand the respect that was due him as head of the household.

A social drinker, that's how he viewed himself. No better or worse than anyone else. Sometimes he had one too many, but who didn't? He wasn't an alcoholic.

Jack Harper never admitted that he *needed* his drinks, but he thought about drinking all the time. He thought about when he could have a drink, what he should drink, where he would drink, with whom he would drink. And when he wasn't drinking, he hurt. He physically ached from the lack of alcohol in his blood. He felt weak and dependent, unloved, undeserving of love. Most of all, he hated himself. What he never realized, what he never wanted to see, was that his family hated him too.

As Chelsea stared out the window of the limousine taking her to Louise Reynolds's sanatorium, and watched the scenery glide by her window in a greenish blur, she saw her father's face as it had been just before he died. He had been a handsome man once, but by then he was bloated, his features distorted. His skin was pasty, spongy like uncooked dough, and his eyes, jade like Chelsea's, were too watery and yellow to look anything other than rheumy. He was only fifty-three years old, but to a stranger he appeared at least fifteen years older than that.

Chelsea was twenty-nine then. She had been married to Roy Patterson, a man one year younger than her father, for six years. She remembered when her mother had called to say that her father had collapsed and had been rushed to the hospital. She remembered hating the fact that her mother had sounded so guilty and so panicked, so certain that his condition was somehow her fault, and not the fault of the bottle. Her mother thought of herself as a martyr—after all, what could a woman with three children and no other means of support do but stay?—but to Chelsea, her mother had been not a victim but a volunteer. The reality was that Maude Harper lacked the courage required to take the steps needed to extricate herself. She lacked the strength to tough it out. And because she did, she was stuck with the responsibility of her children, and all of them were stuck in a situation that would improve only if Jack sought help or died.

Chelsea was determined not to repeat her mother's mistakes. Control was key. Control, planning, and discipline. By knowing precisely what she wanted and what she didn't, and by leaving nothing to chance, she would avoid the traps her mother had fallen into—the burden of children and a marriage made for love at the expense of money.

If she had wanted to do that, she thought with no small amount of regret, she could have married Terry Kirkpatrick.

Certainly, she had loved him and he had loved her. But Terry came from the working class. Even with his lofty ambitions, it would have been years before he would have made the kind of money Chelsea wanted, if ever. Besides, he was a man she would have loved intensely enough to have forgiven his faults and mistakes, and she couldn't have that. She had seen what forgiveness allowed. What she wanted was the freedom money allowed.

At twenty-one years old, however, there were only two ways to obtain big money: inheritance or marriage. Enter Roy Patterson, father of a Skidmore classmate who made the fatal error of inviting Chelsea to her wedding in Houston. It was an extravaganza billed as the party of the decade. Chelsea took one look at the Patterson mansion, the bedazzling jewels Roy's wife and daughter wore, and decided that was where and how she wanted to live. For three days, she flirted with Roy. Something about him had tickled her antennae. This was a man who wanted to have an affair. She smelled it. She sensed it. And she took advantage of it. The night of the wedding, while his daughter was being deflowered by her groom in the bridal suite of Houston's fanciest hotel, Roy Patterson was in a guest room down the hall from his wife, being initiated into the world of uninhibited, unlimited sex as practiced by the children of the sixties.

Chelsea left Texas the next day and, for a month, avoided taking calls from Roy. In desperation, he flew to New York. She was having an attack of conscience, she said. He was the father of a friend. He was old enough to be her father. He was married. What kind of girl did he think she was? Luckily for her, he didn't think beyond his pants. For six months, she teased his libido until he was crazed at the thought of losing her. She slept with him one time, refused him the next. He bought her lavish presents, all of which she rejected. She offered him gifts of the flesh, none of which he could resist. When she told him she was in love with him and he said he returned her feelings, she gave him a choice: his wife of twenty-five years or her. He chose her.

Oddly enough, Roy Patterson was the best thing that could have happened to Chelsea. Aside from the obvious, he was a caring man, one who quickly intuited her need for security. He settled a Texas-sized sum of money on her immediately and then went about trying to repair the wounds of her childhood. Though his manner was often outwardly gruff and oilman crude, with Chelsea he was paternally patient. If she expressed an interest in something, he encouraged her to pursue it. When she wanted to learn about the stockmarket, he arranged for his broker to tutor her, and when she finished he gave her fifty thousand dollars to invest. When she thought she might like to try her hand at interior design, he gave her carte blanche to redo all thirty-five rooms in the Patterson mansion. When she felt snubbed by Houston society, he threw a party in her honor and made sure it was well attended. When she worried that her brothers, Rob and Christopher, were in trouble—drinking, being surly and disrespectful to Maude, doing poorly in school—Roy arranged to have them transferred to Rice University, where he and Chelsea could keep an eye on them. And when Jack Harper died, Roy not only brought Maude to Texas to live with them, but established a generous trust fund in her name.

Chelsea hadn't loved Roy when she married him, and throughout their eight years together, more often than not her passion had been contrived, but she had grown very fond of him, and his kindness had spawned a genuine devotion. When a sudden heart attack felled him two years after her father died, she truly mourned his passing.

What would he think of her now? she wondered, as the limousine drove through the gates of Cheshire Greens and up the gravel path to the entrance? He had warned that someday she would regret the distance she placed between herself and her emotions, that eventually she would suffer if she remained locked up inside the icy palace where she kept her heart. She had disagreed then and for years afterward. After all, she hadn't regretted her ability to detach during her marriages to Winston Stoddard and Drake. If anything, it had helped her escape two bad situations without any noticeable scars. She didn't regret her decision not to have children. She didn't feel she had come out a loser by exchanging motherhood for mobility. She didn't regret being aloof when it came to dealing with the slings and arrows of a high-profile social life. If you didn't care what people thought about you, you didn't get hurt when they talked about you. But what about Belle? What effect had her concrete wall had on Belle?

As she followed the nurse into the garden and waited for

Louise, she shivered, recalling her visit with the police officer assigned to Belle's case. He had come to her apartment late the night before, just after she had arrived home from Europe. He had shown her grisly pictures of a mangled, bloodied body that bore absolutely no resemblance to her beautiful Belle. Mercifully, a sheet of long blond hair shrouded her face, shielding Chelsea from having to see the agony and shame that had permanently branded the young woman's features. It was when she had asked, ''Why?'' that the policeman told her he had come to her for the answer to that same question.

''I know you've been away, Mrs. Reynolds, but if you wouldn't mind, we'd appreciate it if you'd look through your mail. Perhaps she wrote a note to you. I understand you were very close.''

Very close. How close could they have been if Chelsea had had no inkling that Belle was even considering something as gruesome as suicide? Feeling as if she were moving in slow motion, she took the stack of mail the doorman had saved and began rifling through it. Midway through the pile she found it—light lilac stationery with a flower on the bottom left-hand corner. With trembling hands, she slid her silver letter opener into the envelope and slit open the top. She hesitated, paralyzed by fear. If the officer hadn't coughed and shifted his weight impatiently, she might have remained entranced indefinitely. Slowly, she opened the folded note.

> Dear Chelsea,
>
> I don't know how to tell you this. I'm so ashamed. I'm pregnant. Almost four months. Too late for an abortion, the doctor said. I've thought about it and there's no other way. I can't let it be born. What if it's a girl? He'd do it to her too. I know he would. You know too. Daddy doesn't like it if you say no to him. You said no and he beat you. I couldn't say no and now look. His baby's having his baby. It's just too ugly.
>
> I love you like a mom, Chelsea. I only wish I could have been a better stepdaughter. Then maybe you would have loved me enough to help me get away from him. Now I have no choice. I have to help myself.
>
> Belle.

Sitting on a bench facing the gray stone hospital where Belle's real mother lived, she read the note yet again, wishing again that the words would order themselves on the page so they said different things, less hurtful things, less telling things. But they didn't. Belle's death was a cold, hard fact. So was the knowledge that the sleeping pills Belle had swallowed were hers, that the suicide note had been sent to her, that she had been the last person to whom Belle had reached out—and Chelsea had not been there.

It seemed impossible to shake the notion that she could have prevented this, that she *should* have prevented this, but hadn't. Not because she was away in Europe, but because she had been absent when Belle had really needed her, during those awful early years when Belle had been trying to adjust to her mother's alcoholism, during those terrible nights when Drake was sexually and psychologically abusing her. What better ally could Belle have had than another child of an alcoholic? None, except that to have helped Belle would have meant helping herself, and Chelsea had begun to make a career out of denial. And what about Drake? For a long time, she had suspected he was mistreating his daughter, though she had never suspected sexual abuse. Why hadn't she pursued it? Because she had denied that, too.

As Chelsea watched Louise Reynolds and her nurse approach, she noticed that Louise was frail, thinned by too much alcohol and too little attention to her health, but in her own way still quite lovely. She had her blond hair knotted at the nape of her neck, and it was easy to see where Belle had gotten her fine bone structure. Her color was surprisingly good, peachy almost, leading Chelsea to believe Louise was well into the recovery cycle of her stay here. Her gait, though slowed by medication, retained a certain patrician rhythm, gliding rather than walking, and she had a way of perching lightly on a seat rather than sitting squarely on the bench. Chelsea had lived among the upper crust more than half her life. She was wealthy and sophisticated and worldly. Louise Reynolds was a humble patient in a rehabilitation clinic, and yet, even through her plain cotton hospital-issue dress, her aristocratic ancestry proclaimed itself with such authority that Chelsea felt like an arriviste.

"You've come about Belle," Louise said simply.

Chelsea was grateful. She hadn't known whether or not

anyone had notified Louise of her daughter's death, or whether that terrible chore had been left for her.

"Yes. If it's all right with your doctors, I'd like to bring you home with me so you can attend the funeral tomorrow morning."

Louise's eyes darted about, looking for her nurse, who had stepped back to afford the two women privacy. Seeing Louise's distress, the nurse moved closer, whispered something in her patient's ear, and patted her shoulder in comfort.

"I'm not sure I'll be present at my daughter's burial," Louise said. Her voice broke slightly, but her posture remained straight and firm. "I don't know if I'm up to handling the press and the crowds and all the questions that come with a sordid situation like this."

"Louise, you have to go. You have to do it for Belle."

"And what did you ever do for Belle?" Her tone had changed. It was snippy, accusing. It took a minute before Chelsea remembered her own father's mood swings and put her defense mechanisms on hold.

"I didn't know what was going on." *Yes, you did*, a small voice said. *You knew. In your heart, you knew*.

"And if you had?"

"I would have taken steps." *Would you? When Belle begged you to fight for her in court you backed down the minute a dollar bill was waved in your face.*

"Like what?"

"It doesn't matter now, Louise."

"It matters to me." She was insistent, strident.

"Maybe I would have called a lawyer. Maybe I would have had it out with Drake. I don't honestly know."

"You would have done nothing." The words fell off her tongue hurriedly, heatedly, as if they had been singed by fire. "In all the years you knew Belle, you didn't lift a finger to help her. You only do what helps you."

Chelsea heard the voice of utter disapproval and felt her carefully fashioned veneer begin to crumble. Few penetrated Chelsea's fortress, but Louise had blasted her way in with the truth. A familiar sense of self-loathing crawled on Chelsea's skin like an army of ants, making her squirm in her seat. Her hand touched Belle's letter, which lay next to her, and discomfort turned to pain as she realized that Belle's last words confirmed her mother's bitter sentiment.

"Did you know that Drake was using Belle sexually?" Chelsea wasn't sure whether she was trying to wriggle out of a difficult spot by deflecting the guilt or trying to obtain important information, but the sentence popped out of her mouth before any sort of censure could be applied.

Louise's face clouded. Her eyes rolled backward, and for a moment, she looked as if she was going to faint. Again, she sought the support of her nurse, who urged her to breathe deeply. When she looked at Chelsea again, she studied her, as if making a decision.

"I'm an alcoholic," she said in the pitifully desperate tone of someone fighting a battle against a chronic disease. "I'm not offering you that as an excuse, merely as an explanation. Also, if you're assuming I blame my drinking on Drake, don't. I'm a child of an alcoholic who lost control."

Child of an alcoholic. The words triggered so many powerful images and memories. Louise didn't have to explain or excuse herself. Chelsea knew all about her. She knew that Louise had accepted unacceptable behavior in Drake because she never felt she deserved anything more. She knew Louise had probably spent her childhood covering up and cleaning up from a drunken mother or father. She knew that to Louise, Drake's inability to perform well sexually probably didn't seem out of line either. Chelsea recalled hearing her mother complain about her father's ineffectiveness often enough to understand that not every bed was a bower of passion. But Louise's biggest problem was thinking that Drake's problems were her fault.

"Did you ever suspect he was molesting Belle?" Chelsea asked gently.

Louise nodded. "I confronted him about it. He denied it, but from then on, at least once in every argument he told he that if he was drawn to other women it was because I was so unappealing, so undesirable, so totally unworthy. I believed him."

She paused, sighing, breathing deeply again as if needing additional oxygen to continue. Her eyes glistened with gathering moisture. Her voice remained whisper soft, but without any noticeable tremor.

"I drank because it was the only way I knew to anesthetize the pain. I ignored my friends' advice to leave Drake. I ignored the sounds I heard in the middle of the night, the pathetic weeping I heard behind the closed door of my daughter's room. I ignored it because I was just too weak to deal with it.''

Her face was streaked with the wet agony of honesty. Her hands were clasped into a tight ball, her knuckles white with shame as she struggled to hold onto that slippery crutch, control.

Chelsea was struggling too. She felt as if someone had dragged her in front of a mirror, ripped the flesh from her body, and demanded that she look at the vacuum that existed where her heart and soul should have been. Listening to Louise was like listening to the whispers that haunted her in the night, the whispers that recited her credo of self-preservation over and over again like a mantra: *Accept the unacceptable. Look away. Detach. Blame. Control. Judge without mercy. Reject intimacy. Deny the hangover. Deny the pain. Deny the loneliness. Deny. Deny. Deny.*

"There but for the grace of God," she thought as she took Louise in her arms and encouraged the woman to vent her grief.

As she felt Louise's body rock with the ineffable sadness that only a mother who had lost a child could know, Chelsea felt her own spirit tumble lower and lower, careening downward until, at last, she hit bottom. Listening to the other woman keen, Chelsea heard nothing but a frightening silence from herself. For once, there was no reflexive defense springing to her lips, no quick explanation or apology to get her off the hook. There was nothing to say because, sitting in that garden in that sanatorium, Chelsea knew with sudden, stunning clarity that her life was just as sterile, just as empty, and just as tenuous as Louise Reynolds's. Louise might have a long road ahead of her, but at least she had taken the first step. She had admitted she had a problem. True, she had taken that step many times before and failed, but she continued to take it. She continued to reach out for help. Chelsea never had.

How many times had she discounted alcoholic support groups? How many times had she told herself she didn't need help because she wasn't a drunk? That she was different, that she could have a drink here and there because she had always been able to maintain control? But, she wondered now, what had been the point? Was she any healthier than Louise Reynolds? Was she any happier?

Her head throbbed. Her vision blurred. When it cleared, she

saw her father's face just before he died, just after he had told her he loved her and asked for her forgiveness. She saw the expression of self-hatred that had insinuated itself on his face when she had refused to grant him absolution. He had died seconds afterward, his face forever frozen into a mask of loathing. She had thought it appropriate then. Now she wished she had behaved differently, that she had allowed him the compassion she was giving Louise, that she had accepted his alcoholism as an illness instead of a curse. Then the curse might not have followed her. She might not have been so irresponsible about the conduct of her life. She might not have felt so responsible for the end of Belle's life.

"How could we have let this happen to her?" Louise said, pulling away slightly but continuing to hold Chelsea's hand.

"I let it happen," Chelsea said, feeling her own grief well up within her and fill her throat with a painful lump. "I was too selfish to risk losing what was mine. Instead, I lost Belle. I have no right to ask, but please forgive me, Louise. I never meant to hurt her. I loved her."

For a long while, the two women clung to each other and mourned the loss of their delicate, beautiful Belle, their only child, their shared child. Then, wiping her eyes and purposefully straightening her back, Louise spoke.

"I thank you for your offer," she said, as if their tears had cemented a bond between them, "but I think I need to be here tonight. Tomorrow, I will go to the funeral. Nurse Garth will take me. But I can't speak to the press and I won't speak to Drake."

"That's fine," Chelsea said, rising from the bench, tucking Belle's letter into her purse, and snapping it shut. "You don't have to say a thing. I'll speak to Drake for the both of us."

I owe that much to Belle.

It seemed inappropriate for the sun to shine on the day that Belle Reynolds was to be committed to perpetual darkness, but nature showed little respect for the dead. It was hot, but not humid, cloudless, bright, typically June, a perfect day. Outside the Frank E. Campbell Funeral Chapel on Madison Avenue, reporters and TV cameramen jostled for position, elbowing their way in and around the glittering crowd which had come to bid farewell to one of its own. As taxicabs and limousines discharged their passengers, cameras rolled, flashbulbs popped, and microphones were thrust under noses along with eager requests for comments on the tragedy. Everyone had questions. No one had answers.

"Why would someone who had it all—money, looks, social position, brains, talent—want to end her life?"

"Was it drugs?"

"Rumor had it she was pregnant. Any word as to who the father was?"

"Her friends say she was a loner. Wasn't she close to anyone?"

"Her mother's an alcoholic. Was she?"

Gaby stood by the door and listened with a growing anger. Though she understood they were only doing their jobs, it sounded vulgar hearing them shout at bowed heads and veiled faces. Then again, everything about this day was vulgar—the reason they were here, the reason Belle was here.

Gaby had come with Chelsea an hour before so that Chelsea could be here when Louise arrived. Their visit had upset Chelsea tremendously. She had called Gaby when she got home and asked her to stay over. All night, she had rambled on about how she had let Belle down, how unresponsive she had been, how deliberately uninvolved. She reviewed her life as a series of mistakes, listing her offenses coldly and clinically, as if she were reading them off a police department rap sheet. For the first time, she spoke openly about her father's alcoholism, how much she hated it and him and how his constant insobriety had affected her. Years before, when they had been in college, she had talked about her father as a drinker, but then she had painted him as more of a weekend inebriate than a chronic drunk. Never had she connected herself to him emotionally, never had she related her problems to his. Also, for the first time, she spoke of signing up for a support group like Alanon or Adult Children of Alcoholics. Though she was resistant to talking about her father and herself in front of strangers, she was frightened that if she didn't, someday she might wind up like Louise.

When Gaby met Louise, she understood her friend's fears. The woman was swathed in black and thickly veiled, but her fragility showed in the unsteadiness of her walk, the hesitancy in her speech, the tight grip she maintained on her nurse's arm. Mrs. Garth told Chelsea that after she had left, Louise had spent three hours with her doctor and then had required sedation. She was medicated now, at her request, so that she could honor her daughter in death with a dignity she rarely managed while Belle was alive.

Chelsea had arranged for Louise to have a private receiving room, one that would remain closed to all except her family and closest friends. When it was time for the service to begin, Chelsea would escort her into the chapel and then later to the cemetery. Drake was forbidden to go near her. So far, however, Drake hadn't arrived. Neither had Max, which was why Gaby had posted herself outside. She hadn't heard from him, and although it was only two days, she missed him so terribly, she was afraid that when she did see him, she would throw herself at him.

Just then, a long black limousine pulled up. The door opened and out stepped Drake Reynolds. Exiting behind him and quickly taking his arm was Irina Stoddard. Both of them were hidden behind dark glasses. Drake was pale, his skin almost as gray as his hair. His posture was stooped, and despite Gaby's expectation that he would be surrounded by a malevolent aura that would display his evil to the world, she had to admit that all she saw was honest grief. Did he know about Belle's pregnancy? Did he realize that he was responsible for his daughter's death? Or was he so deranged that he was able to block out his culpability for his child's desperate plunge?

Irina, never one to miss a photo opportunity, had outfitted herself in a smart, photogenic black suit and black straw cloche decorated with a pale pink fabric rose. While her hair was neatly chignoned and she had kept her accessories and makeup discreetly minimal, her sorrow had been daubed in such thick strokes that it appeared almost garish. As she and Drake swept past the throng of onlookers who had gathered on the corner, she lifted her hand as if to shield her face from the cameras, but for some reason it never moved higher than her shoulder.

Inside, the chapel filled. Outside, mourners continued to arrive. Gaby waited, but still no sign of Max.

"Read this."

Chelsea shoved a copy of Belle's letter into Drake's hand and stared as his dark eyes drank in his daughter's last words. She had insisted that he follow her into a small anteroom off the chapel. She had originally planned this confrontation for after the burial, but watching him play the guiltless, bereaved father, seeing Irina hanging on his arm like his lover-in-waiting, watching him as he was showered by the comforting condolences of friends and relatives while, in another room, Belle's mother sat alone, bravely struggling to deal with her role in the making of Belle's tragedy, so angered her that she was moved to act immediately.

"It's not true." He returned the letter without so much as a blink. "Except, of course, the part concerning your negligence."

Chelsea had steeled herself to expect retaliatory gibes.

"You're a sick man, Drake. Sick and disgusting."

"Isn't that a little like the pot calling the kettle black?"

He stood before her, infuriatingly cool. She studied him, seeking a sign, a twitch, a mistake of the tongue, something, anything that would show deep regret for his actions instead of surface remorse over Belle's.

"Did you love her, Drake?" She stood directly in front of him, daring him to look away, daring him to lie.

"Very much."

There it was. Pain. She heard it. She saw it. And a part of her was glad. Even the monster felt pain.

"Didn't you realize what you were doing to her?"

"I didn't do anything." The mask was back. It had slipped for a second, but now it was firmly affixed to his face. "She was disturbed. She must have imagined it."

"Did she imagine the fetus inside her womb?" Chelsea's entire body shook with rage. "You put that baby there!"

He pushed her, trying to shove her aside so that he could move toward the door, but she blocked him.

"How did you feel when you slept with her? Like Rambo? Like some big, virile stud all potent and strong?" Her throat was so tight she was certain that she was shouting, but actually, her voice was low, frighteningly quiet. "Well, take it from a grown-up woman who did sleep with you, Drake, you're not. But you know that, don't you, you bastard! That's why you preyed on that poor innocent child. So you could feel masterful. God! It's so perverted. You're her father. How could you? I could kill you for what you did to her!"

Her fists pounded at his chest until the back of his hand crashed across her jaw. She fell against the door. Her face throbbed, but she refused to give him the satisfaction of touching her wound.

"She jumped out of a window to get away from you. She died rather than live with you one more second. And you know why? Because you're slime! Because you're a child molester! A pedophile. A man who can't get it up for women so he fucks children!"

"Shut up," he said, raising his fist.

"Does the truth hurt?"

"Shut up, I said."

"I'll shut up. But only after I bring this letter to the police and they shut you up in prison, which is exactly where you belong."

His eyes narrowed into slits. His teeth clenched, his breath came in short, hot puffs, and his entire being took on the posture of a predator about to move to the kill.

"You wouldn't."

"Oh, yes, I would."

Suddenly, his whole demeanor changed. In an instant, he became calm and cool again, his frenzy locked up inside a persona. It was the first time Chelsea had ever recognized his madness.

"Do it," he said with the confidence of one who knew he couldn't be trapped. "Show the police the letter. Belle's dead. She can't be questioned. It's my word against that of an obviously troubled girl."

"Louise will testify that you molested Belle."

"Louise is a drunk. No one would take her word for anything."

"I'll testify to the fact that Belle was afraid of you. She came to me a number of times. She was desperate to get away from you!"

"And what did you do about it? You gave her a bottle of sleeping pills, a pat on the head, and sent her on her way. You didn't fight to get her away from me. You did nothing! Which proves you didn't believe her. And guess what! Even if you did, no one's going to believe you. You have no credibility. You're nothing but a whore in an expensive silk dress, and everybody knows it. Now get out of my way."

He pushed her aside, opened the door, and walked out, leaving Chelsea alone and shaking. His words bounced off the walls of the small room, smacking into her from all sides. The truth did hurt, and everything he had said was the truth. No one would believe Louise. Or the suicide note of a pregnant teenager. Or the words of a woman who had listened to the sounds of coins jangling in her pocket rather than the sound of a troubled child crying in the night.

It was difficult for Irina to maintain a façade of intense mourning. Too much was going on. The press was hounding her for information about her relationship with Drake—"No comment" —Drake's reaction to his daughter's suicide—"No comment" —her reaction—"No comment." To her friends, however, knowing that their network was more important than the media, she hinted that, yes, she and Drake were involved and, yes, she intended to remain by his side throughout his ordeal.

As she took her place in the front pew and waited for Drake, she looked around the room, searching for Vincent Prado. She had spoken to him several days before. Their phone conversation had been unsettling.

"My source is certain the tapestry is nowhere in Belgium," he had said when she asked what he had learned in Antwerp. "He did say that new rumors have surfaced about *The Triumph of Chastity*."

"The one everyone thought had been destroyed in World War One?"

"The very same. It seems as if a few of the old people of Dinant remember hiding a woman and a small girl whose names were de Rosier. They recall that the woman seemed as protective of the tapestry as she was of the child, and since they knew the value of the tapestry, they understood her concern."

Irina was barely able to contain her excitement.

"So where is it? And where is that child? Who is she? Who was she? Where is she?"

"That's all I could find out," he had said.

"You're useless, Vincent."

"No, Irina, I'm not!"

"You're keeping something from me. I can tell." His assertiveness had surprised her.

"I've given you all I have to give. And all I'm ever going to give."

"What is that supposed to mean?"

"It means that if you wish to find missing tapestries, you'll do it on your own. If you wish to know something about someone, you'll find it out on your own. If you wish to play dirty pool, you'll do it on your own. I am no longer at your service. Now, if you'll excuse me, Your Ladyship, I'm going out to dinner."

"Where will you be if I need you?" she had asked, ignoring his declaration of independence.

"Here. There. Everywhere. But don't call me, darling. I'll call you."

Irina could still feel the anger she had felt when she heard him hang up the phone. How dare he be so insubordinate? So ungrateful? So uncooperative? Vincent Prado had made a terrible mistake. She didn't take kindly to being dismissed. She would have to find a way to punish him. Not now. Now, she had to concentrate on Drake Reynolds. But soon.

"I can't tell you how sorry I am about what happened to your stepdaughter."

Round face. Blue eyes. Light brown hair, now flecked with gray. Dimples. Stocky frame. Bostonian accent. "Terry Kirkpatrick!" Chelsea said, her voice ringing with relief. "I knew you'd come."

She had called him, as she had done frequently in the past when she had been in trouble and had needed a friend. And as he had done each of those times, he came as a friend. He put out his arms. She fell into them eagerly, allowing him to comfort her, knowing that even after all those years, his embrace still connoted comfort and safety.

"I can't begin to tell you what your being here means to me," she said. He took her hand, and as if he had pressed a button releasing her emotions, her eyes flooded with tears.

Gently, he steered her off to the side and into the room where she and Drake had squared off. Closing the door, he brought her to a chair, encouraged her to sit, and waited until she had calmed.

"I didn't mean to upset you," he said, kneeling in front of her.

"You didn't." She touched his face as if to assure herself he was real. "I guess it's just I know it's okay for me to let go when I'm with you."

He smiled and dabbed at her eyes with his handkerchief, carefully avoiding the purple welt on her cheek, wondering who had put it there and why.

She looked at him and, again, wondered what life would have been like if she had said yes instead of no. "Will you stay with me?"

She sounded so frail, so afraid of being alone, so unlike her image.

"Of course."

"Is it painful for you being here? I mean, because you lost your wife and all?"

"No. It's been five years. I've adjusted."

Chelsea nodded. Suddenly she felt shy, as if they were strangers and she had asked something very personal. She didn't like to think of Terry and herself as strangers.

"Did you bring your children?"

"No. I didn't think it was appropriate."

She nodded, her eyes watering all over again.

"Are you all right?"

She shook her head. Her lips quivered.

"You have two girls and a boy. I only had Belle. And she wasn't really mine."

Fresh tears dotted her cheeks. She took his handkerchief and wiped her face, wincing as her hand grazed her jaw.

"Chelsea, there are some ugly rumors flying around town. Are they true? Was she pregnant? Is that why she killed herself?"

"Four months."

"Who's the boy?"

Chelsea stared at him. His immediate assumption was that the father of Belle's baby was a classmate. If he had concluded that automatically, so would everyone else. Drake's name would never even come to mind. He would be free. While Belle lay dead.

"What's the matter?" He could see her mind working, sorting facts, examining them, evaluating options, selecting, choosing. "Is the kid someone you know?"

It was an impulse, one of Chelsea's few uncalculated moves,

one she would regret as soon as she made it. She reached into her purse and withdrew Belle's letter, handing it to him. As he read it, his face grew dark. When he looked up, she saw that familiar storm raging in his eyes, that storm that always accompanied the onslaught of an attack of Irish temper.

"Is this true?"

"Drake denies it, but yes, I believe it is."

"And you want to nail him, is that it?"

She knew he would react this way. He had always been a marcher, a civil libertarian, a man with a cause. He had gone into the law because he believed in rights and hated wrongs.

"I'm not sure."

"What aren't you sure about? That he did it?"

"I'm not sure I want to get involved."

Terry stared, unable to disguise his astonishment or his disappointment.

"You are involved. She wrote you this letter because she wants you to do something. She's begging you to do something," he said, his voice strained.

Chelsea looked away, avoiding, denying, relying on all her usual defenses to justify her actions. "I don't want to see my name splashed all over the tabloids."

"Why? What are you afraid of?"

"You read the letter," she said with panic in her voice. "I didn't get her out of there. It's my fault she killed herself. They were my sleeping pills she took. At a trial it would all come out. Think of how it'll look."

"How it will look? Chelsea, please! That man abused his child. He made her pregnant. She killed herself because of him, not you. He should be locked up!"

"Why do you care so much about what happens to him?" she asked, knowing that he was thinking, *Why do you care so much about yourself?*

"Why do I care? Because I have two daughters. And because something like this shouldn't happen to any child! That's why!"

"I can't do it." Fresh tears dampened her cheeks. Her hands trembled.

"Now's not the time to discuss this." He put an arm around her and held her until she stopped shaking. Later, he decided, feeling her body rock against his. Later, they would talk. The wound was too fresh. She needed time to think things through. To think about Belle's letter. To think about the right course to take.

Terry Kirkpatrick wasn't a patient man, but he saw her turmoil and he felt her pain. He would give Chelsea time. But he wouldn't give up on the idea of bringing Drake Reynolds to justice.

Gaby couldn't believe her eyes. When Chelsea walked into the chapel with Louise on one arm and Terry Kirkpatrick on the other, she was certain she was hallucinating. Terry escorted both women to their seats and then moved into the pew behind them. He was several people removed, making it difficult for Gaby to catch his attention, but that was all right. She was still searching for Max.

There was standing room only in the chapel, but as yet Max was not among the mourners. Armand had suggested that perhaps he was detained in Europe on business or had had difficulty getting here in time, but Gaby rejected all of that. She now knew Max well enough to know that he did what he wanted, when he wanted. If he wasn't here, it was by choice.

Drake walked in. Before he took his place beside Irina on the other side of the aisle, he stopped in front of Louise. Suddenly, it was eerily quiet. The crowd held its collective breath, waiting to see what would happen. He bent down to say something to his ex-wife, but she turned her head. Her sob echoed throughout the room. He went to take her hand, but Chelsea hissed at him. Quickly, he backed off. Instead of taking his seat, he approached the flower-strewn mahogany coffin in the front of the room. Reaching behind and retrieving a ribbon-tied blossom, he solemnly placed a single red rose on top of the blanket of white roses that draped the casket. Leaning down, he lifted the white velvet pall and kissed the polished wood. Then, with every eye trained on him, he took his seat, bowed his head and covered his face with his hand. Louise wept. Chelsea was certain she was going to be sick.

As the minister intoned the benediction, Gaby turned just in time to see Max walk in. She had to fight to keep from smiling. He looked directly at her. Then he looked away. Had he seen her? Of course he had. She had felt it. Then why had he turned away?

"Whatever you're thinking about, stop. You're out of sync with the rest of the crowd. Sit down." Armand's voice snapped her back to attention.

Guiltily, she sat, trying to shelve her troubles so she could concentrate on the minister's eulogy. Unfortunately, the man's words were uninspired. He hadn't known Belle, and so his oration consisted of platitudes. Gaby's mind wandered.

Involuntarily, she turned, again seeking Max out. Her eyes fixed on his face, practically demanding that he look at her, but he remained stony, staring straight ahead. Gaby could hardly believe it. How could someone who only forty-eight hours before had made love to her with such volcanic passion be so cold, so distant, so hard. Surely the world had lurched off kilter. That was the only way to explain the fact that a young woman her son's age had decided life had nothing to offer but pain; that the man who, only an hour before, she had been certain was going to be the focal point of her future was pretending she didn't exist.

What happened? Was it something she said? Something she did? Going back over the week they had spent together, she could recall nothing that wasn't idyllic, not a single moment when she wasn't certain that he was as deeply involved in their relationship as she was. The only thing that had spoiled their stay in paradise was Chelsea's call about Belle. Was it that? Had Belle's death revived bad memories concerning the loss of his son? Not that she had noticed. He hadn't retreated from her or withdrawn. If anything, he had been the one in control, not she. He had been solicitous, caring, loving, offering her his plane, promising to join her as soon as he could. On the ride to the airport he had held her hand, comforting, consoling. While he had stood next to the taxi waiting for the plane to take off, his face had been . . . Taxi! The taxi driver! She couldn't believe that she had let a detail like that escape her. He was the same driver who had taken her to Damme. She hadn't given it any thought then, other than a passing acknowledgment of coincidence, but now that detail loomed as something more serious. What if he had let it slip that he had taken her to Damme? That she had followed Max? Her head was swimming with what-ifs, with truths and their consequences. That must have been what happened. He knew, and now he had decided he couldn't trust her, he couldn't believe her or her feelings. She had to get to him. She had to explain.

But, she thought frantically, feeling the strings of her self-knitted web tightening around her, *what do I say? Yes, I followed you, but it was simple curiosity. Otherwise, I'm an upstanding, Girl Scout kind of gal? Or do I confess all my other sins of omission?*

The service had concluded. Gaby felt Armand's hand on her arm, guiding her out of the pew and into the aisle behind Chelsea and Louise, behind Drake and Irina, behind Belle. Gaby craned to find Max. He had gone. Slowly, heavily, she inched along, leaning on Armand. As they walked out into the street, the sun stung her eyes, yet she felt enveloped in darkness. She was oblivious to the television cameras zooming in on her, to reporters invoking her name. She was oblivious to the venomous stare being directed at her from Irina Stoddard, who was mesmerized by the sight of Gabrielle Didier arm in arm with Armand Lafitte. She was oblivious to everything except the gnawing, naggingly familiar sensation of being lost and alone, of not knowing who she was or what she was going to do with her life.

That night, however, when her picture was replayed on the nightly news in city after city, and her name—*Madame Gabrielle Didier, close friend of the young woman's stepmother*—was mentioned as one of the mourners, millions of people were introduced to the glamorous, well-to-do, sophisticated woman New York thought she was.

One of those people was her son.

21

"How are you?" Armand asked.

It had been less than a week since Belle's funeral. Though they had spoken every day, this was the first chance Armand had had to visit Gaby in person. He didn't like what he saw. She looked thin and drawn.

"I'm still a little rattled," she said.

Armand nodded. He too had been unnerved by the news of Belle's death, even more so by Gaby's explanation of what had pushed the girl over the edge.

"It's going to take a while for us to get over this tragedy."

"If we ever get over it," Gaby said, thinking of Chelsea.

"Is there something else disturbing you?" Armand asked, noticing the thick veil of sadness shadowing her eyes.

Max was disturbing Gaby, but much as she wanted to talk about what happened—what she had done, what, if anything, she should do now—she couldn't bring herself to confide in Armand. For one thing, she felt foolish repeating the story of the taxi driver and her capricious expedition to Damme. For another, in her heart she suspected that Max's reasons for making a secretive trip to the *béguinage* must have been intensely personal. To expose that visit would be a betrayal of the worst kind.

"It's nothing," she said, forcing herself to brighten. "Probably just nerves. After all, I've put all my eggs in one basket. If the Montgomery auction doesn't live up to our expectations, I'm in trouble."

Armand visibly squirmed in his seat.

"What's the matter?" Gaby asked, suddenly alarmed.

"I'm afraid my visit isn't going to help your nerves. When I was in Paris, I found out that my friend, the woman who owns this apartment, has died. A few days later, I received a letter from a solicitor writing on behalf of the woman's lover. He wants to sell the apartment."

"When?"

"I convinced the solicitor to let you stay through the summer definitely, possibly to the end of the year, depending on how quickly the estate is settled. He did say that if you wanted to buy the apartment—as is, except for certain antiques—you were welcome to do so."

"Did you laugh? I mean, what a joke! I can barely pay the utilities, let alone the million or so I'm sure the owner wants."

"Don't worry about it," Armand said, forcing a smile. "We'll find something else. Something better. We have plenty of time."

Gaby shook her head. "I don't think so, Armand. I have a sinking feeling that, for me, time is running out."

"I don't know if you remember me, Mrs. Reynolds. I'm Steven Thayer."

"It's been too many years for me to remember the face, but the name is definitely familiar. Come in."

Chelsea ushered Steven into her living room, trying to study the young man as they walked. Like his father, he was tall and well built, handsome, yet distinguished by a less brutish bone structure than she remembered Brian having. Just then, however, as he took the seat Chelsea offered him, his features were hardened into a tight mask.

"I don't mean to bother you," he said politely, "especially at a time like this, but I'm looking for my mother. Mom had given me your address and telephone number in case of an emergency."

"Is this an emergency?" Chelsea asked, suspecting a slight exaggeration.

Steven looked embarrassed.

"I don't know where she lives. I called from the airport, but her machine was on."

Once, Gaby had remarked that Steven had consistently refused to visit her in New York. She had assumed it was his way of avoiding the reality of the finality of her divorce from Brian.

"No problem," Chelsea said, rising. At her desk, she scribbled the address on a piece of notepaper. When she handed it to him, she watched an uncontrollable sneer curl his lip.

"Do I ask for Mrs. Thayer or Madame Didier?"

"Your mom's not Mrs. Thayer anymore, Steven," she said gently, suddenly understanding the reason for his unannounced visit—and his anger. He must have seen a news clip about Belle's funeral in which Gaby's New York name was used.

"Okay, but that's no reason to change her name. And if she wanted to change her name, why not go back to being Gaby Cocroft? What's with this Madame Didier stuff?" He was trying to maintain a respectful attitude, but the confusion and outrage mixing inside him was setting off sparks.

"Let's say it's a *nom de guerre*."

"It's a lie. Why not tell it like it is."

Chelsea didn't like his tone of voice.

"You want me to tell it like it is, okay, I will," she said, deciding not to coddle him, knowing that even if she wanted to, she didn't know how. "Your mother came to New York needing a job. No one in Ohio would hire her. No one here wanted her, either. She had no money and no one to help her out. One day she walked into a store, filled out an application, and lied. She invented an employment history and used Didier because if she used Thayer or Cocroft, a reference trace would reveal the truth: that she had never been anything other than a housewife and a mother, which, in the real world, my dear young man, doesn't count for much."

He was squirming, shifting his weight from side to side, uncomfortable in her presence, uncomfortable with what she was telling him, but most of all, uncomfortable with the conflict churning inside of him.

"I think being a wife and mother counts for a lot," he said loyally, defensively.

"Sure it does. In the house. To the husband and the child. In the marketplace, to an employer, it's a big fat zero. Your mom found that out the hard way."

"And so she lies about who she is?"

"So what! Your mother isn't stealing. She isn't practicing medicine or law or designing airplanes. She's working with something she knows, antiques, and working damn hard to make a success of herself. What's wrong with that?"

"Nothing, I guess."

He looked properly chagrined. Chelsea softened.

"Steven, your mother is a wonderful woman who did what she had to do. Now she's finding herself, fulfilling herself. These past few years have been tough on you, I know, but believe me, they've been a lot tougher on her."

"I haven't helped very much," he said in the soft voice of one confessing a sin.

"You were busy growing up and adjusting. She understands that, but she misses you."

"I miss her, too," he said, clearly anxious to leave, "so if you'll excuse me, I think I'll go see her now. Thanks for the address and, well, for what you said."

He blushed. Following an unaccustomed impulse, Chelsea raised herself up on her tiptoes and kissed his cheek.

"You're more than welcome, Steven. Enjoy your visit."

It didn't take long for the taxi to travel from Park Avenue to Fifth, but within that short span of time, Steven and his conscience engaged in a lengthy debate. There was something to what Chelsea said, he decided. In truth, despite her many efforts to tell him about it, he had never really considered the new circumstances of his mother's life and how they had affected her. He knew she had debts, but now he realized he had simply assumed that everything would be all right. After all, mothers took care of things, that's the way it was. But Chelsea was telling him that wasn't the way it was, that his mother had been in a hole with no one to pull her out. Was it such a big deal to change a name to get a job? And even if it was, was he in any position to judge?

Stop thinking like a child, he told himself. *View this like an adult. Accept the fact that you don't live here, you don't know what prompted her to do what she did or what she was doing.*

Still, something didn't feel right. Was it that he had expected Gaby to be living in a tenement and, instead, the taxi had stopped in front of a very swell looking building facing the Metropolitan Museum of Art? She had told him she had an arrangement where she took care of an apartment for someone out of town, but he had pictured something older, something more modest and less intimidating.

As he waited for the doorman to buzz up to Madame Didier's apartment, he looked around the lobby. It was a far cry from Wadsworth, Ohio, that was for sure. Maybe that's what was bothering him, that he felt out of place in her new world, that he might not fit in with her new life. He didn't think of himself as a hick, but this building, Chelsea's apartment, that crowd outside the funeral home—it was all so different from the way he lived, the people he had grown up with, the people Gaby had grown up with.

On the ride up in the elevator—carpeted, mahogany paneled, piloted by an impressive gentleman in a smart burgundy uniform—he wondered who had answered the buzzer and who would come to the door. Was his mother home? Would she be happy to see him? And if she wasn't there, who was?

When the door opened, an older woman in a white-aproned, pink maid's dress smiled and invited him inside. She was his first shock. The apartment was his second. As Tante Simone's grand-nephew and Gaby Thayer's son, he was not ignorant about the value of antiques. Standing in the entry, looking at the Flemish tapestry and the French chandelier, peeking into the living room at the paintings and classical furniture, he grew jittery. Women struggling to make ends meet didn't have maids and didn't live amidst such grandeur.

"Hello, Steven. I'm Armand Lafitte."

Unless, of course, Steven said to himself, too stunned to reject the man's handshake, *they have wealthy lovers.*

"Your mother had an errand to run, but she should be back shortly. In the meantime, come inside. We can get acquainted over a cold drink."

Armand couldn't help noticing the instant rigidity in the young man's posture or the absolute hostility etched on his face.

At first, he didn't understand, but then he remembered Gaby saying that Brian had told Steven she and Armand were more than just friends. Gaby had denied it, but in Steven's eyes Armand's presence had just confirmed his father's suspicions.

"I can't tell you what a pleasant surprise this is," Armand said, determined to keep his end of the conversation upbeat. "I've wanted to meet you for a long time. Your mother only speaks of you in glowing terms."

He smiled. Steven's face remained set.

"Do you live here?"

"No," Armand said, shaking his head emphatically, happy to supply an answer to that particular question. Maybe now, the boy would relax. "I have an apartment above my shop."

Steven nodded, still unconvinced.

"I don't mean to be rude, but what's your relationship with my mother?"

"We're friends. Good friends, I'd say, but that's all."

Steven nodded again.

"Since you've never been here before, how would you like to look around while I ask Mrs. Booth to fix us some iced tea?"

Steven agreed, Armand exited, both of them relieved to be away from each other. Steven moved around the living room carefully, hesitantly, keeping his hands at his sides, afraid to touch anything, as if each item carried contagion. He progressed to the hall and then to the bedroom. When he entered, he permitted a brief smile to graze his lips. His mother must love it in this room, he thought. It was so her. The white woodwork. The canopy bed. The froufrou French furnishings. And Tante Simone's gueridon.

Drawn to it, he walked over to the small mahogany table festooned with a bouquet of summer blossoms and touched the edge. The feel of the wood elicited memories and tears. His eyes brimmed as his mind retraced the happier moments of his childhood, times spent with his eccentric great-aunt, his Oncle Bernard, his parents. He considered himself a man, yet standing there, needing his mother, missing Simone, he knew he was still very much a boy.

But the boy was curious, and so he began to look more closely around the room in which his mother slept. He walked to a closet and opened it. Then to another. At the third, he stopped.

He felt as if his heart had stopped also. There were several hangers of men's clothes. A drawer of shirts. Armand had lied to him. His mother had lied to him. They lived here together. They were lovers. Brian had been right.

He stormed out of the room into the hall. At the entry, he ran smack into Armand.

"The iced tea will be right out."

"I'm not staying." His jaw was fixed, his eyes icy.

"Is something wrong, Steven?" Armand couldn't imagine what had happened, but clearly, something had.

"I have to go home."

"I'll have your mother call you."

"Don't bother," he said as he banged on the button for the elevator. "We have nothing to talk about."

The elevator doors opened. Steven marched in and refused even to turn around until the doors closed. What had set him off?

He drew a blank until Mrs. Booth approached with a tray of tea and cookies.

"Where is Madame Didier's son?" she asked putting the tray down on the coffee table.

"He left."

"Maybe it's just as well," she said, spotting an offensive smudge on an end table and using her apron to polish it away. "If we don't finish packing Mrs. Duvall's things, I'm never going to have time to tidy up at your place. We still have to clean out the bedroom, you know."

"The bedroom! Steven saw the men's clothes." *He thought they were mine.* "How could I have been so stupid?"

"I beg your pardon? Stupid about what?"

Armand shook his head.

"About perceptions, Mrs. Booth. About the way things seem, which is sometimes different from the way things are. Very different."

For a week, Gaby felt as if she were chained to her telephone. If she wasn't waiting for Max to call, she was trying to call Steven. Armand's description of Steven's mood and their conversation had been upsetting, but the fact that Steven refused to respond to the messages she continued to leave for him at his job and his grandmother's house was beginning to make her angry. Why, she wondered, was he so unwilling to let her present her version of whatever story he thought he had uncovered? Had she been such a terrible mother that he would immediately believe the worst of her? Didn't she deserve at least the benefit of the doubt? Max, too, she thought, should not be so quick to judge. After all, the only reason she had followed him was because she had caught him in a lie. Why was his lie okay, her lie a crime?

By six o'clock, she had worked herself up to such a pitch that she knew she could not stay in that apartment a moment longer. Earlier, Chelsea had invited her to have dinner at La Côte Basque with Terry Kirkpatrick. She had said she wasn't sure. Now she was. It would serve both Steven and Max right to call and find her out.

Knowing Chelsea's tendency for tardiness and knowing how much she disliked waiting at a bar, Gaby timed her entrance so that when she walked in, Chelsea and Terry were already seated. As in most of New York's chichi restaurants, La Côte Basque had a very definite pecking order to its tables. The front banquettes were prime. The bar area was choice. The back of the original restaurant was acceptable. The rear of the addition was Siberia. Joseph, maître d' and ringleader of the circus, escorted Gaby to a corner table and invited her to slide in next to Terry.

"I'm so glad you came," he said, kissing her cheek.

"Me, too," she said, honestly happy to see him, happier still that he had reentered Chelsea's life at such a critical time.

"Would you like something to drink?"

Terry had scotch in front of him. Chelsea's glass was filled with a clear, carbonated liquid with a slice of lime. Perrier, probably.

"White wine would be fine," Gaby said, noticing that Chelsea was not only not drinking, but was very subdued. "Are you all right?"

"Not really." Her mouth twitched, as if she were trying to smile but lacked the muscle tone to do so. "Each day is worse than the one before. I can't seem to shake this awful depression, this terrible feeling that I'm responsible for what happened to Belle."

"You're not," Terry said tightly. "He is."

The two women turned in the direction of the door. Standing there waiting for Joseph were Drake and Irina.

"If I thought it slightly inappropriate for us to be having dinner out, imagine how I feel about *him* being out in public. Especially with her!"

Chelsea's eyes had turned so dark and foreboding, so filled with shadow and menace, they reminded Gaby of the interior of a forest at dusk.

When Joseph led the twosome into the bar, away from Chelsea's group, Irina looked positively furious. Drake must have said something to mollify her, however, because they took their places calmly and without incident.

"If I didn't hate her so much, I'd feel sorry for her." Chelsea said it without sarcasm or the usual antagonism that accompanied a discussion of Irina. "She thinks he's a great catch."

"I wouldn't worry about Irina Stoddard," Gaby said. "From what I know of her ladyship, she's not into being a victim."

"Belle wasn't either, but look what he did to her." Chelsea's fragile façade shattered. Her eyes welled immediately, as if a dam had cracked.

"Isn't there some way to make him pay for what he did?"

Gaby had turned to Terry, knowing he was an attorney, not knowing that he was trying to convince Chelsea to let him explore the possibility of an indictment.

"I think Belle's letter would be enough to spur an investigation," he said pointedly.

"Then why not do it?" Gaby asked, innocently aligning herself against her friend.

"Because . . ." Terry started.

"Because there's no way to prove the baby was his," Chelsea interrupted, repeating to Gaby the same arguments she gave Terry in private. "Drake denies he assaulted her sexually. No one else saw him do it. Belle never actually told anyone what he was doing to her. And simply offering unfounded suspicions is inadequate."

"It's unfair," Gaby said. "One way or another, he should be held accountable for what he's done."

"That's what I say." Terry smiled at Gaby and then at Chelsea, who softened long enough to smile back.

"I do have some good news," she said, returning her attention to Gaby. "Max came to see me a few days ago." She said it quietly, sensitive to the fact that Gaby hadn't heard from Max since his return from Europe. Still, the mention of his name caused Gaby to wince. "We got into a discussion about emotionally needy children and how to help them and about the fine results La Maison was achieving. He suggested that we try to establish a center for abused children here in New York similar to La Maison. He also offered to help fund it."

Gaby juggled her annoyance at Max with admiration for his generosity.

"Do you really plan on running this center?"

Chelsea nodded.

Gaby reached over and squeezed her hand.

"It's a wonderful idea. I'm proud of you."

Chelsea responded with a shy smile.

"Not yet, but you will be. I promise."

"I don't believe you," Terry said with the gruffness of a teddy bear. "You promised me dinner, and so far I haven't even laid eyes on a menu."

"Forgive me." With uncharacteristic coyness, Chelsea bowed her head and smiled.

Gaby noticed that under the table, Terry had taken Chelsea's hand and was holding it. It was when she looked up and across the table that she noticed a new couple standing at Joseph's station—Max Richard and a striking Englishwoman Gaby remembered meeting at the Castleton gala at Shefferd House.

Max turned and their eyes met. He turned away and said something to Joseph. Seconds afterward, he and his date were escorted to a table in the bar, facing Drake and Irina. Gaby began to shake. How blatant could he be? Chelsea and Terry continued to discuss dinner, oblivious to the flush heating Gaby's skin. Suddenly, she put down her menu, picked up her purse, and slid out from the booth.

"If you'll excuse me, I have to go home."

"What's the matter?" Both of them spoke in unison.

"I'm not feeling well."

Terry started to follow. "We'll go with you."

"No. Please. Stay. I'll be fine. Good night."

She practically ran to the door, brushing past Joseph and the small crowd gathered at his desk.

"What happened?" Terry asked, truly concerned. "Two minutes ago she was fine. Suddenly, she's ill. Was it something we said? The wine? Does she have a headache? A bad stomach?"

Chelsea rubbernecked in the direction Gaby had glanced just before pushing through the revolving door. She spotted Max deep in conversation with an adoring blonde.

"Worse," she said. "She has a broken heart."

Irina felt as if she was sitting in front of a large television screen, clicking her remote control and tuning in to one fabulous show after another. There was the general Thursday night scene that was *Dining Out in New York*. That show was one of her perennial favorites. She loved the tiny waves the women gave each other, the knowing nods exchanged by the men. Checking out the clothes and jewels of those who merited the front tables was always fun. Counting face-lifts was worth at least ten minutes of entertainment, as was ticking off the number of young, voluptuous second—and third—wives who flaunted jumbo diamond rings and spoon-fed their happy hubbies puppy-dog devotion.

Then there was the Drake and Chelsea show. Irina was a player in that one, so of course she rated it highly. Every once in a while, Chelsea's eyes zeroed in on Drake with an odd look Irina couldn't interpret. Drake seemed intent on pretending Chelsea didn't exist, which was fine with Irina. He hated Chelsea. Irina was certain of it. All the more reason for her to cozy up to this poor pathetic man who was grieving over the loss of his only daughter.

Ever since Colorado, when she had sensed that her being with Drake had been a definite annoyance to Chelsea, Irina had decided to set her cap for him. After all, she reasoned, she could use a husband. From what she could tell, he wasn't opposed to another wife. She liked living in New York, and if, for some catastrophic reason, things didn't work out and she wasn't made head of Castleton International, she certainly wasn't going to subject herself to further humiliation by moving back to London. She didn't love Drake, but since when was love a requirement for marriage? Drake was handsome, well positioned, rich, and able to order a bottle of wine without sounding like a peasant. What more could a woman want?

Speaking of wanting, another of the shows she was enjoying was the one starring Max Richard and Gabrielle Didier. It had been short-lived but dramatic. He walked in. She ran out. Glancing at Max, she could see that he was upset, but recalling the look of near tears on Gaby's face, not nearly as upset as she was. While there was no doubt Irina loved witnessing Gaby's acute discomfort, there was something troublesome about it. Only a onetime lover could be so thrown off balance at the unexpected appearance of the other.

Irina had seen Gaby and Max dining together at the Ritz. A day or so later, she had tried to call him, but the concierge had said Monsieur Richard had checked out. Curiosity had prompted her to ask about Gaby. She too had gone. Had they gone off together? It certainly seemed that way. But tsk tsk. It appeared as if the fire had died rather quickly. Paris was less than a month ago. They weren't speaking at Belle's funeral, which was almost two weeks ago. Their little romance hadn't gone on long enough to qualify as an affair, she decided. It was more like a fling, and judging by the way Max's date was hanging on his arm, the fling had been flung.

Irina allowed herself a moment's regret that she had never managed to snag Max Richard. He was without question one of the world's more appealing creatures. But in the long run, it worked out better for her that he and Gaby had been involved, even for a short time. The thought of telling Garrett was so delicious, she almost burst into song.

And then there was the matter of her father. The man was positively besotted. He talked about Gaby incessantly, about how fortunate the Castletons were to have her in their circle, how wonderful it was that she had brought the Montgomery Collection to them, how generous it was of her to offer her services in the preparation of the auction. If it was going to be a high bursting Garrett's bubble, it was going to be ecstasy finally to reveal a gap in her father's judgment. Except—although Gaby's two-timing Garrett was naughty, knowing how excited her father was about the Montgomery auction, he would probably excuse her infidelity. Irina needed something far more serious to invalidate the woman in the eyes of Garrett Castleton, Sr.

Her eyes traveled from Max to Chelsea and stopped. Chelsea and Gaby. Their closeness confused Irina. From what Irina had gathered, they'd met at the Castleton gala and become instant best friends. Thinking about it, it was too tight too fast. Irina couldn't know whether or not such intimacy was typical of Gaby's behavior, but it certainly wasn't typical of Chelsea Reynolds. No one—including her staunchest supporters—had ever defined her as the warmest of women. Maybe there was more to that relationship than met the eye. Maybe it was worth looking into.

If I'm lucky, Irina thought as she absentmindedly stroked Drake's inner thigh so he didn't feel neglected while she plotted, *I can get two birds with the same stone.*

Gaby let herself into her apartment just in time to hear the telephone. Stumbling about in the dark, she ran to pick it up, hoping it was Max or Steven.

"Mrs. Thayer, it's Mrs. Sloane from Lakewood. I hate to call you at this hour, but I didn't want to chance missing you during the day."

"I understand," Gaby said, pretending that Mrs. Sloane called frequently enough so that this particular call didn't signal trouble. "How may I help you?"

The responding hesitation was not friendly.

"Mrs. Thayer, you owe us a considerable sum of money."

"I'm aware of that, Mrs. Sloane." Gaby began to sweat.

"We've allowed your debt to linger for what we would consider an extraordinarily generous amount of time. However, we are entitled to be paid for services rendered."

"You're absolutely right and I do intend to pay in full."

"When?"

"Soon."

"How soon?" Her tone was insistent.

"Mrs. Sloane, I'd love to take care of this immediately, but due to circumstances beyond my control, I can't. I'm not a rich woman. I'm working, and in my business the summer is very slow. I can send you some money tomorrow, but . . ."

"How much?"

Gaby had made slightly over twenty thousand dollars in commission for the items she had purchased in Europe, but her reserves had dipped below the danger level. She had to retain half that for living expenses.

"Ten thousand dollars."

"That still leaves a balance of thirty thousand dollars!"

"I know, but I'll be able to pay that off by the end of the year." The Montgomery auction was scheduled for the second week in December, five months away. If she could hang on until then. If all went well. If . . .

"I'd like to believe you, Mrs. Thayer, but your credit rating at Lakewood is rather poor."

"Please, Mrs. Sloane. I know I have no right to ask, but could you be patient a little longer?"

Again, there was a silence.

"Okay, Mrs. Thayer. You have until the end of December. If by then, we haven't been paid the monies owed us, we will be forced to take legal action."

The phone clicked. A switch inside of Gaby clicked. She had to come up with thirty thousand dollars! She had to find a new place to live! Her business, such as it was, had slowed to a virtual standstill. Max had dropped her. Steven was avoiding her. Frustration, hurt, disillusionment, and anger boiled inside her like the ingredients of a stew. She slammed down the phone and threw a cushion across the room.

"Why is this happening to me?" she screamed, feeling hot tears roll down her cheeks. "What did I do to deserve this?"

With clenched teeth, she stormed around the apartment, ranting and railing, venting months, perhaps years, of pent-up rage.

At first, she didn't hear the buzzer, but then it became insistent. Gaby stopped and stared at the wall, fixed on the spot making the sound. Instinctively, she wiped her eyes as if the person at the other end of the intercom could see her distress. Someone was downstairs. Ever the optimist, her mood turned hopeful. Maybe it was Max. He had seen how upset she was at the restaurant. He was coming to talk things out, to make things right between them. It had to be him. It couldn't be anyone else. Without waiting to hear a name, she instructed the doorman to "send him up."

When she opened the door and found Brian standing in the hall, she decided she had gone mad.

Without waiting for her to invite him in, Brian strode past

her and indulged himself in a tour of the apartment. Gaby closed the door and waited.

"Steven wasn't kidding," he said, whistling like an over-awed tourist visiting St. Peter's for the first time. "This place is outrageous!"

"Would you like to come in?" she asked, showing him into the living room, suddenly feeling uneasy, almost embarrassed for him to see the grandeur of her surroundings, while on the other hand, finding the look of shock and, yes, even admiration glossing his face immensely satisfying.

When he took a seat on the sofa, she saw immediately that he was uncomfortable. He crossed and uncrossed his legs. He shifted position two or three times. He draped his arm over the back, looked around, and then dropped his arm into his lap. Finally, he retreated into the corner, bolstering himself on two sides as if he was afraid that if he didn't he would topple over.

Inside, Gaby smiled. Usually, Brian overwhelmed furniture. He was a big man, and his size frequently diminished chairs and couches. But Gaby knew it wasn't the dimensions of the sofa that intimidated him, it was the aura of the room, the ambience, the overpowering sense of extreme wealth that had him cowed. What struck her also was the glaring incongruity of seeing Brian in this type of setting. Somehow, he didn't fit. It wasn't right. He wasn't right. He seemed out of place, out of sync. Was it that she wasn't used to seeing him here? Or was he the first true mirror she had looked in since coming to New York? Had she been deluding herself all this time? Brian was from Ohio, just as she was. He was sophisticated—not on a par with Armand or Max or Garrett—but far beyond being a bumpkin. He traveled. He was educated. If he appeared inappropriate and disharmonious with finery such as this, what made her so certain she was not?

"I have to hand it to you, Gaby. You've done all right for yourself." He splayed his hands as if showing her proof of her success and laughed self-consciously. "No wonder you didn't want to move back to Wadsworth."

"It wasn't a matter of wanting to, Brian," she said, wondering why she always felt the need to defend herself to him. "I couldn't move back. I have no job there. I have a job here."

"And quite a job it is, from what I can see."

"I get by."

Again, he laughed, this time with a cynical edge.

"Thanks to that monsieur you live with."

"No," Gaby said, truly annoyed with Brian *and* Steven for making such wanton assumptions. "Thanks to me and a sublease that allows me to house-sit this wonderful place for the cost of my utilities."

"The Frenchman doesn't live here? That's not the impression Steven got."

"Steven jumped to conclusions. Armand Lafitte is a friend, not a lover, and he lives on Madison Avenue, not here. If Steven had taken the time to ask, he would have been told the truth."

Brian looked dubious, but rather than aggravate her further, he changed the subject as well as his approach.

"He's young, impressionable. And it was probably too much for him. You know, seeing you on television surrounded by all those socialites. Hearing you called Madame Didier. Then coming up here, seeing this, seeing *him*. I guess he didn't know what to think."

"I guess not," she said, regretting that her son had had to discover his mother's duplicity on national television, regretting also that their relationship had eroded to such a degree that simple communication between them had become impossible. "But believe me, it's not the way it seems."

"Frankly," Brian said, his eyebrows raised, his mouth widening into a broad grin, "to me, it seems very exciting. I wish I were part of it. I wish I were sharing it with you."

"Are you in New York on business?" she asked quickly.

"No. I wanted to see you." He leaned forward, resting his arms on his knees so that his body was close to hers. "I wanted to talk to you."

"About what?"

He leaned back, his face thoughtful, concerned about the way what he wanted to say next would be received.

"When you came back to Wadsworth and we had that drink at the inn," he said, "I tried to tell you how I felt, but I bungled it. I mean, I really blew it, asking you to give up your job and come home just because I thought it might be fun to give us another try. You got angry, and let me tell you, you had good reason. I was a jerk!"

He gave her his most endearing little-boy smile.

"Since then, I've done a lot of thinking. Maybe we both needed a change. You're happy here in New York. Maybe we could both be happy here. I could get a job, move in here, meet your friends, become part of your life. It would be great, don't you think?"

"No. I don't think it would be great at all."

"Why not? We used to be good together," he said with a distinct leer.

"We used to be married. We're not anymore."

"A technicality. Besides, this is the eighties. Judging from the looks of this place, the looks of you, and the fact that you're using some fictitious name, I'd say you've loosened up quite a bit. What would be so horrible about us living together? People do it all the time."

"I don't do it at all. And even if I did, I don't want to do it with you."

His eyes narrowed.

"Suddenly I'm not good enough for you? Is that it?" He lifted his lip and sucked on his teeth, an action Gaby recognized as a signal that his ego had been attacked. "I remember a time when you followed me around like a lovesick puppy. I remember a time when you thought I was the best."

"And I remember a time when you thought I was second best," she said, countering his offense, "that I wasn't good enough or young enough or exciting enough. That's when you walked out on me. Or don't you remember that?"

The rapidity with which her anger surfaced and the intensity of its flame surprised both of them. Gaby had thought she had put her life with Brian into perspective, that she had relegated the demise of their relationship to a small corner of her emotional house. Yet her response had been instantaneous and subconsciously driven, like the answers to a psychologist's word-association test. It left her on guard, Brian on the defensive.

"Sometimes a man can't fight his urges," he said, offering whatever excuse came to mind first, no matter how lame it sounded. "I chased another skirt, that's true. But you have to admit our sex life had grown stale."

She didn't answer. She didn't have to. He was right. Max had proven that.

"And yes, I guess Pamela seemed very tantalizing, what with her title and the kind of work she did, and, well, she was young and . . ."

"Brian, we don't have to go through all this. It doesn't matter why our marriage soured. It did. We're divorced. We share a son, and for his sake I want us to be friends. But that's all I want us to be."

He digested that slowly and with great difficulty. Rejection was never his favorite dish.

"By the way," he said, his face suddenly illuminated with a confidence Gaby found slightly unnerving, "I got a call from Mrs. Sloane the other day. I guess she thought we were still married. She threatened to put a lien on *our* property because we've been delinquent on our payments. When I told her we were divorced, she apologized for bothering me." He let that sink in before continuing. "How much do you owe?"

"Thirty thousand dollars," Gaby said without hesitating. He asked. Why shouldn't he appreciate the enormity of the debt?

"Whew!" He was genuinely astounded, making it obvious that Mrs. Sloane had not divulged any details. Also obvious was his refusal to offer help. "You're telling the truth, aren't you? You really don't have a sugar daddy taking care of you."

"No, I don't." His expression changed. Gaby read what she wanted to read—respect for and appreciation of her independence— which was why his snide laughter pushed her off balance.

"I wonder what your fancy friends would think if they knew that the elegant Madame Didier was a down-at-the-heels housewife from Ohio who couldn't pay her debts."

Gaby's skin prickled. She felt as if she had just spotted a snake crawling on her floor.

"What exactly are you trying to say, Brian?"

"Oh, I don't know," he said, rubbing his chin and grinning malevolently. "I was just wondering if anyone might be interested in meeting the husband of the widowed Gabrielle Didier. You know, TV reporters, the folks at *People* magazine. I know everyone back in Wadsworth would get a big kick out of reading about your fairy tale life here in the Big Apple."

Gaby sprang to her feet.

"I want you out, Brian. Now!"

He rose also, following at an infuriatingly slow pace. Gaby

wanted to throw something at him, to hit him, to hurt him, to wipe the supercilious look off his face. Instead, she opened the door and stood there, the picture of self-assurance.

"The people who matter to me, really matter, already know the truth. There's nothing you can do *for* me or *to* me, Brian. So once and for all, get out of my life."

He hiked himself up to his full height and glowered down at her.

"This is your last chance, Gaby. Are you sure that's all you have to say to me?"

She looked at him, trying to remember the young man she had revered, the young man she had willingly devoted her life to, but all she could see was the man who had tossed her aside like a lifeless tennis ball, the man who now had the nerve to threaten her with exposure and ridicule.

"I do have something else I'd like to say."

"I thought so." He smiled smugly.

Her mouth remained set. Her eyes fixed on his face as she said, "Brian, go fuck yourself!"

The door slammed, immediately setting off another explosion of anger. Her body trembled. Her eyes teared. Racing, she exited the hallway, refusing to look in the living room, refusing to revisit the place where Brian had stood and tried to humiliate her.

Once inside the bedroom, the traumas of the evening—the sight of Max with another woman, the phone call from Mrs. Sloane, the confrontation with Brian—swooped down on her. Tears of frustration and anger streaming down her face, she ripped off the bolero jacket she had worn to dinner, the same one she had worn on the night she and Max had dined in Paris, and threw it on the floor. She kicked off her shoes, propelling them across the bedroom, knocking into a dresser and rattling a pair of Meissen figures that held court in front of a huge mirror. In that mirror, she caught sight of herself. Her face was streaked with mascara. Her hair was puffed and wild. Her eyes were wide and unfocused. She was a woman unhinged. The sight of it, the weakness and surrender implied by it, brought her up short.

"I'm not weak," she said, gripping the edge of the dresser, defending herself to her reflection. "I didn't surrender. For once in my life, I gave as good as I got!"

Instantly, as if the tap had been shut off, her tears dried. Her breathing remained labored, but she inhaled deeply, closing her eyes, letting the fresh oxygen cleanse the destructive vapors from her system. In a few moments, the tremors quieted.

Removing her dress so that she was clad only in a slip, she sank into the chair beside Tante Simone's gueridon and put her feet up. For a long time, she felt as if her mind was blank, as if her tantrum had exhausted her to the point where even thinking was too strenuous. But she must have been thinking, because when her trance lifted, she realized she had made several decisions.

First, whatever she had to do in order to survive until the Montgomery auction, she would do. If she had to pinch pennies, clip coupons, scrimp and save even more than she already had, she would. If she had to go back to work at Bergdorf's or get a job as a waitress or take in alterations, she would. The Montgomery auction represented her financial salvation, and much as she hated placing so much importance on one single day, that's the way it was.

Second, she was going to take Oncle Bernard's advice about Steven. Much as she loved her son, he was convicting her without a hearing. Just then, she had neither the resources nor the strength to batter against such resistance. If he was going to insist upon licking his wounds and feeling betrayed, so be it. Whether he knew it or not, he had betrayed her. Whether he cared or not, she too had wounds.

Third, she decided she was going to confront Max Richard. If she allowed Max simply to end their relationship without so much as a whimper, she deserved to be alone. Though she didn't believe they had been nothing more than bed partners, he owed her an explanation. He could say she was an extended one-night stand, that she meant no more to him than any other vacation companion, that they had been nothing more than a brief affair. He could say all that and more, but he was going to say it to her face!

Tonight had proved something to her. In her past life, she had been passive, allowing herself to float like a raft along with the tide. But when the raft had capsized, she had run away from that life. She had made changes, and those changes had changed her. In her new life, she had been forced to face up to the necessity for control, for measured aggressiveness, self-confidence, and the courage to stand up and say, "You can't take that. It's rightfully mine!" It hadn't been easy thus far, nor would the road ahead of her be without bumps, but Gaby remained a determined optimist.

She loved Max and she hoped that the distance between them was a misunderstanding. She hoped that when she next saw him, he would be the man she had known at La Maison and in Paris and in Bruges. But if he wasn't, if that man had been a mirage, if there was no future with him, she would adjust, as she had done when she discovered she no longer had a future with Brian. She would create a future for herself, by herself. Where? Doing what? She wasn't sure. Would she stay in New York and perpetuate the role of Madame Didier, antiques broker and woman of the world? Or would she take her profits from the Montgomery auction and set up elsewhere?

Long into the night, she wrestled with those questions, trying on answers like so many pairs of shoes, hoping to find the one that felt most comfortable. Just before she fell asleep in the chair by the gueridon, she made her decision: she was going to move to Paris. Oncle Bernard was there and so was the opportunity to start over, with no lies, no unhappy memories. Maybe in The City of Lights, maybe there in the country of her mother and Tante Simone, she could find the happiness and contentment that had eluded her up to now.

It was eight o'clock in the morning. Gaby had been up and dressed since six. The doorman to Max's building had assured her Mr. Richard was definitely alone. The elevator had let her off in the small foyer outside the penthouse. The gold button that buzzed inside the apartment taunted her. Her heartbeat quickened. Her breathing became shallow and erratic. She raised her hand, tentatively pointed her finger, brought it close to the buzzer, and then retreated, pulling away as if some heat-seeking device might detect her presence and set off an alarm before she was ready.

Gaby could not believe she was doing this. Confronting Max had seemed like such a good idea last night, but now she wasn't so sure. What right did she have to demand anything of him? He hadn't made any promises. He hadn't spoken of commitment or proposed any sort of arrangement between them. He had never even whispered any terms of endearment. But he had made love to her with a passion abounding with promises. He had touched her in a way far more tender and loving than any verbal endearment could ever possibly be. And he had introduced her to his children. She pressed the buzzer and waited.

When the door opened, an expression of complete surprise engulfed Max's face. Though he wore a bathrobe, Gaby could tell he had been awake for some time. He was shaven. His hair was brushed. And he smelled of sandalwood. He was barefoot and, if she had to hazard a guess, had very little on underneath his robe.

"Gaby! Good morning. Come in."

He stepped aside, his eyes glued to her back as she strode purposefully into the living room and seated herself on one of the leather couches. On the table in front of her, a half-filled cup of coffee, *The New York Times,* a plate speckled with toast crumbs, and a wrinkled napkin formed an unframed still life.

"How about if I make us a fresh pot of coffee?"

"That would be nice. Thank you." The last thing she wanted was coffee. She already felt overdosed on caffeine, but her nerves had buckled at the sight of him and she needed time to regroup.

Max cleared the table and headed toward the kitchen. As he left, Gaby couldn't help noticing the way the soft paisley fabric of his robe clung to him like silk against steel, outlining the strong musculature of his body. It shocked her to think that she was lusting after him, but she was. If this were a fantasy, she would have followed him. She would have stripped off that robe, ravished him with a hungry mouth, stroked him with eager hands, tempted him with her flesh, and aroused him to the point where whatever barrier had been constructed between them collapsed beneath the weight of their mutual wanting.

But this was not a fantasy. Fidgeting, she rose from the couch and paced the room, looking without seeing, touching without feeling. She wondered where he was going to put the secretaire she had bought for him. Probably over there in the corner, she thought, walking toward the designated space. The current occupant was a round Biedermeier table dotted with several black marble obelisks and other complementary *objets d'art*. Needing to distract herself, she examined several of the pieces.

One held her interest more than the others because it seemed out of place. It wasn't eighteenth or even nineteenth century. It wasn't even really an object. It was a tapestry fragment, a monogram—ER—protected by a gilded frame. The E was gold, the R was red, the link between them the same tasseled cord she had found binding the double M's in *The Garden of Love*, the script the same fancy, flourishing type as she had seen in the fragment Max kept on his desk at La Maison.

"You take your coffee black, yes?"

She turned, the frame still in her hand. He stared at it in a way that made her uncomfortable. Quickly, she returned it to its allotted spot on the table. When she looked at him again, she realized he had changed out of his robe into slacks and a shirt. She was disappointed. She returned to the couch, took the cup Max offered her, sipped slowly, and then put the cup on the table and stared directly at the man seated opposite her.

"Why are you so angry with me?" she said bluntly.

"Why do you think I'm angry?"

She searched his face for clues as to what he was thinking, but his blue eyes remained guarded.

"When I left you at the airport in Brussels," she said, "both of us seemed to have a problem separating from each other. Since you've arrived in New York, however, one of us has had a problem being in the same room with the other. I'd like to know what the problem is!"

"There's no problem, Gaby. I just think we were getting ahead of ourselves, perhaps rushing into something too quickly."

"And I think you're bullshitting me." Her voice was sharp, her stare direct. "I think you found out I followed you to the *béguinage* in Damme and you're furious."

"That's right," he said evenly, without inflection. "I did and I am."

"You told me you were going to Diksmuide. I saw you get into a cab and head the other way. I was curious and so I followed you. I did it without malice and without any motive other than to find out why *you* lied to *me!*"

Even in a simple cotton blouse, loose pants, and sandals, Max thought she looked beautiful. Her eyes were lit with the fire of injustice. Her skin was lightly golden, basted by the sun, scented with the delicate floral she had worn when they were together. Her hair, full and lustrous, flew about her face as she spoke. But as always when he looked at her, it was her lips that hypnotized him. He watched as her upper lip puffed and pouted, then tightened and drew in when she uttered her accusation. He barely heard what those lips said, because his entire being was consumed with trying to resist leaning forward and kissing those lips, tasting them, indulging himself with the luxury of feeling them press against his own lips.

"Are you denying that you lied to me? Or is it that your lie is acceptable, mine is not?"

The tremble in her voice touched him. That she had been unwilling to accept his rudeness without challenge touched him.

"I'm not denying anything, Gaby. You're right. I lied to you, but I had my reasons."

"Am I entitled to know what those reasons are, or haven't I slept with you long enough to be worthy of the truth?"

"I was visiting my aunt," he said, choosing to ignore her sarcasm, knowing he had earned the snipe.

"You told me you had no family."

"I was protecting her."

"From what?"

"Her husband."

"Why would she need protection from her husband?"

"Because if he ever knew she was still alive, he'd kill her."

Gaby was stunned into silence.

"Her husband was a violent man who mistreated her from the very beginning of their marriage. Once, when she was in the early stages of her first pregnancy, he beat her until she miscarried."

Gaby flinched, drawing in her shoulders protectively, involuntarily turning her face away.

"When the Germans invaded Belgium in May 1940, there were many people who eagerly collaborated with the enemy. He was one of them. He couldn't wait to throw his lot in with Hitler's thugs. My aunt, pregnant once again, was terrified. She was half Jewish. She had heard that in exchange for money and the promise of a governmental position, he had been providing the Germans with names and addresses of Jews in the area. She was certain that any day he would turn her over to the Gestapo."

"Did your uncle know she was half Jewish?"

"Yes." Max's face had hardened. "It hadn't bothered him when he was negotiating her dowry or stealing her family heirlooms or bleeding her of her fortune. But she was certain that if he thought for even a moment that her ancestry would taint him or put him in disfavor with the Nazis, he would have had her arrested."

"She must have feared for the life of her child as well as her own."

"Very much so, which is why she ran away. For most of the war, she hid, from him and from the Germans. Afterward, she left the country, hoping that he would believe she had died."

"Did he?"

"He must have because he remarried."

"Then why is she hiding in the *béguinage?* What made her come back to Belgium?"

"Loneliness. A desire to spend her waning years in her own country. I don't know, but that's what she wanted. I helped her arrange entrance to the *béguinage*. I support her, and whenever I can, I visit her."

"I gather her husband retained control of her fortune."

Max paused before answering. His fingers curled into fists, pulsing, clenching and releasing, as if he were trying to squeeze the fury out of himself.

"She left too quickly to take much with her, and then, once she was gone, she couldn't try to get anything back because if she had, he'd know she was alive."

"I hate this story," she said. "I hate knowing that that poor woman had to live her entire life hiding in the shadows. More than that, I hate the idea that her husband is living free and easy."

"Not nearly as much as I do."

The granite in his voice shocked Gaby. She had seen the softest side of him—at La Maison with the children, in bed with her—but now she suspected she had seen the hardest.

"I'm sorry. I shouldn't have intruded."

He forced a smile.

"It's I who should be sorry. You're absolutely correct. I lied to you. I have no right to be upset if you followed me."

Gaby was confused. He was forgiving her, but his voice, his body language, his expression—none offered complete absolution.

She sensed resistance, as if he were still reining his emotions, still maintaining distance. Also, despite the fact that she had a number of questions she wanted to ask—especially about *The Triumph of Chastity*—he seemed intent on terminating the discussion.

Trust. It all came down to trust. No matter what he said, the message he was sending was that she had weakened his ability to trust her. He was willing to tell her certain things, not everything. That made her uncomfortable and even a bit annoyed, as if he were using her in some way, but how could she fault him? Clearly, she didn't feel she could trust him with every last detail of her life. If she did, she would have told him about Brian and Steven and Bernard being her uncle and Didier not being her real name and that her apartment really didn't belong to her. Whatever the reason—fear, self-protection, protection of others, obsessive privacy—neither of them was willing to trust. For now, both continued to hide behind the armor of lies. She guarded her secrets. He guarded his.

Gaby thought about confessing, of showing how deeply she felt about him by revealing the truth about herself, but before she could, the telephone rang.

"Hello. Yes. Yes. Of course. This morning? That's great news! I'll be there. See you soon."

Max hung up the phone and looked at his watch. For several minutes, his thoughts were elsewhere. Gaby waited for him to include her, to say something about the call—it was business, family, an old friend, something—but he said nothing. More secrets. She stood.

"I have to go," Gaby said. "You have things to do and people to see, and so do I."

Max appeared surprised, but when she turned to leave, he followed her to the door. There he took her hand.

"Why are you going?"

Because I wanted you to take me in your arms and tell me you loved me, and instead you made plans to see someone else, probably another woman!

"I think you were right before when you said that perhaps we were rushing into something neither of us was prepared for."

Though she spoke with an air of dignified nonchalance, Max felt her hand tighten in his. He had been aloof. He knew that.

The phone call had upset her. He could see that. She loved him and he appeared to be rejecting her. He knew that, too. Yet knowing, hurting as he was hurting her, loving her, wanting her in his life—none of it mattered until he completed his task.

"I'm involved in some complicated business deals right now," he said, refusing to let go of her hand. "My time is not my own."

"Neither is mine. I have the Montgomery auction to orchestrate."

Gaby pressed the button for the elevator, wishing she could run from him before the tears came.

"I'd like to see you."

The elevator arrived. The door opened. Gaby moved to step inside. Before she could, Max pulled her toward him and kissed her lightly.

"Soon," he said, reluctantly letting her go.

The doors closed, and for the first time since they had met, Gaby and Max had a language problem. As he stood in the mirrored foyer staring at the descending numbers above the brass doors, he knew he meant *soon* to be "in a couple of months," "in the near future," "once I'm finished." Behind the brass doors, however, Gaby's interpretation had a more cynical cast. She had no way of knowing how Max felt about her or what he intended or what he was doing. All she knew was that she felt a barrier between them, a barrier of indifference, of resistance. And then there was the matter of the blonde.

It was no wonder that Gaby translated Max's *soon*, as "never again."

It was hot, nearly ninety degrees. The 10:30 A.M. Concorde from London had just landed. The air-conditioning inside Kennedy Airport was straining. Humidity hung like a wet shower curtain. Yet most of the passengers didn't seem to care. They exited the plane laughing and smiling, leisurely making their way through the Concorde lounge and down to the baggage area. For many, this had been a special flight—an antiques safari arranged by Vincent Prado. Fifty of his most devoted customers and friends, all of whom had flown over to visit Grosvenor House, had stayed on, flying with him to Paris, touring the finer antiques shops there, then traveling outside Paris to several of the antiques stores in the Loire Valley. Vincent had arranged everything, from group rates on round-trip Concorde tickets, to luxurious suites at the finest inns and hotels, to dinners at Michelin three-star restaurants, wine tastings, picnics, cabaret shows. For all fifty, it had been the highlight of the summer. If Vincent's popularity had been soaring before, now it had rocketed into the stratosphere.

With his trademark bravura, Vincent led his entourage down the escalator, chortling, waving his hands like a conscientious guide, pointing the way as if no one had ever been in an airport before. Suited in beige shantung, shirted in loose, pale linen, shod in basketweave leather loafers, he was the picture of summer elegance. Turning the corner into the baggage area, however, he passed a mirror and clucked his tongue disapprovingly. Sweat had formed damp crescents on his underarms. He shook his head, disgusted. Laborers sweated. Men of his station were supposed to remain cool and neat, no matter what.

Fanning himself with his ticket, he grabbed a metal trolley and pushed it toward the moving luggage bay. As he watched the first few pieces going around, he exchanged quips with Pat Buckley and Anne Bass.

"Don't you just love it?" he asked, pointing to the array of Louis Vuitton luggage parading past them. If not for different-colored ribbons tied on handles or attached to name tags, it might have taken hours to sort things out.

Along with the normal assortment of suitcases and duffles, carefully packed boxes and crates circulated, waiting to be lifted off the moving shelf. All around him, eager hands reached out to retrieve paintings and cachepots and candelabra and even small pieces of furniture. Prado watched as one by one the contents of the plane's cargo rolled by. Suddenly, his eye caught what he had been looking for—a wooden box with a bright red sticker. He snatched it off the mechanical ledge, secured it in the basket of the trolley, and headed through the doors toward customs.

Pausing, he studied the inspectors. Never go to someone who looked too bored. If they needed excitement, he didn't want to provide it. Never go to someone with narrowed eyes. They took their jobs very seriously, and odds were they would take his luggage apart just for the sport of it. Vincent hadn't planned on exposing his soiled laundry to his guests as his finale. And never go to agents positioned in the corners. Because their queues filled up last, they stretched out their inspections, taking an inordinate amount of time to complete a very small task. Directly in the center, he spotted a young woman who was just finishing up with someone. She looked efficient, but not too efficient, tough, but not combative. There were two other gentlemen before him, but Vincent pushed his trolley onto her line anyway and waited his turn.

He watched his friends head for various other agents, each of them calling out to him, thanking him, adoring him. Pat Kluge. Jerry Zipkin. Carroll Petrie. Catie Marron. Lee Radziwill. Bill Blass. How fabulous, he thought, to be so revered by this extraordinary assemblage. Throughout the plane ride home, all they had talked about was how clever Vincent was to have arranged such a trip, how precious it was of him to give everyone a gilded pith helmet as a reminder of their special safari, how anxious they were for him to schedule a repeat performance for next year.

He was so caught up in the sound of his own applause, he never noticed the customs agent press a button on a small remote-control unit signaling her supervisor to come out. He was so blinded by the attention being lavished on him by the haut monde, he never noticed an older, craggy-looking man take his place beside her.

"Next!"

Vincent was rattled. He had expected a pleasant, placid young woman. Instead, he was facing a surly man hardened by years behind a customs counter. For a moment, Prado stumbled, pushing his trolley the wrong way, bumping it into the corner of the desk, having to reroute it, finally squeezing it into the proper lane.

"Do you have anything to declare?"

Vincent laughed, an offhanded chuckle meant to point out the absurdity of the man's question.

"You must be joking! With the dollar being as weak as it is, it's more expensive to shop there than it is to shop here." He knew his voice was too loud and a touch on the falsetto side, but he couldn't help it. Something about this didn't feel right.

"Is that a yes or a no?"

"A no. It's a definite no."

"Open your suitcase."

He hoisted one of his Louis Vuittons onto the counter, unlocked and unzipped it, revealing a sloppy pile of rumpled shirts and underwear. Without pause or comment, the inspector reached down into the suitcase and rummaged around. Thoroughly embarrassed, Prado fumbled around in his pocket, found his handkerchief, swabbed his forehead, and then wiped the moisture gathering under his eyes.

"Close it up."

Prado did as he was told, checking to see who had been standing behind him or alongside him, anyone who might have seen his personal disarray.

"Do you want to check the other one?" he asked, more solicitously this time.

"What's in the crate?" Wiggling a thick finger in the air, the inspector motioned for Vincent to put the crate on the counter.

"It's an antique clock," Prado said, quickly searching through his wallet for the bill of sale. "Here. See? It's more than a hundred years old, so there's no duty on it." He went to remove the crate. The man's hand fell on top of his.

The inspector looked him squarely in the eye.

"I know the law," he said.

"Then what's the problem?" Prado's voice had tightened.

"I don't know. You tell me." Reaching beneath the counter, he took out a small crowbar and proceeded to jimmy open the crate.

"Hey! Stop that! You have no right to open my package. It's an antique. I have the papers to prove it."

Vincent's voice had grown shrill. Their altercation had attracted attention. All eyes turned toward his aisle. All activity halted.

"Your papers say this clock was sold to Village Green Antiques in Larchmont, New York. Do you own Village Green Antiques?"

"No. Clive Bennett owns it. But he couldn't go to Europe, so I bought it on his behalf. I was going to ship it to him, but he cabled me saying that he would be unable to pick it up. I brought it home with me. It's as simple as that."

"Really? I don't think so. Come with me."

Vincent felt the sweat pouring down his chest. He wanted to

grab the clock, but the man's thick hands were firmly clamped around it. Trying desperately to maintain control, Vincent followed the heavyset customs officer into a small, glass-walled office. There were several men and an attractive blond woman standing around a wooden table. At the far end of the table, out of sight of the passengers craning to see what was going on, was a familiar face.

"Max! Max Richard!" Prado was so grateful to see a friendly face, he didn't question Max's presence or the fact that he was being surrounded. "Please help me out. Tell this . . . gentleman . . . who I am and that I am entitled to bring antiques into this country without having to suffer his brand of harassment."

"You are entitled to import antiques, Vincent. You're not entitled to smuggle diamonds into this country."

Prado's face drained of all color.

"I don't know what you're talking about."

"What I'm talking about is using antiques as a means of illegally smuggling diamonds."

"Really, Max." Prado forced himself to laugh. It was a self-conscious laugh accompanied by several sideways glances through the glass windows at his cronies, who were too confused to do anything other than stand and gawk. "It's just too, too ridiculous."

Max smiled. "Then you won't mind if I examine the clock, will you."

"Certainly not," Vincent said, unsuccessfully trying to keep his own smile intact.

Max lifted the top slats of wood with the crowbar and then loosened the sides. With the delicate hands of a man familiar with precious objects, he lifted a bulky form covered in a flannel cloth out of the box. Unfolding the cloth, he exposed a neoclassical clock that was heavily gilded, its workings encased in a black onyx orb which was centered inside a series of arches and columns, a spectacular example of late-eighteenth-century craftsmanship.

Max doubted the diamonds had been hidden in the workings. In case customs had decided to inspect it, that would have been the first place they would have looked. Experienced smugglers would know that. He began to tap the arches, the base, and then the columns, listening for odd sounds or hollow cores. He tried to twist one of the columns. It didn't move. He tried another column and then a third and a fourth. None moved. He played with the gilded dome that sheltered the black onyx orb, but that too offered no give. Turning the clock over, he checked for a false bottom or a notch that might have opened a secret compartment. Nothing. For a moment, he was stumped, but then he looked at the four golden eagles perched on top of each corner. Gently, he screwed one to the left. It moved. Very carefully, he continued unscrewing first that eagle, and then the other three. When all the tops were off and he had picked inside the columns, he found four cloth bags containing over half a million dollars in diamonds.

"Arrest him." Max said it quietly, without removing his eyes from Vincent's face. Suddenly, one of the four men standing around the table snapped handcuffs around his wrist. The others drew their weapons in case he resisted.

Vincent's heart stopped. Terror clogged his throat. He should have known. He should have guessed when he got that telegram from Clive Bennett. That traitorous wimp had sold him out, and he had been too busy playing bon vivant tour guide to read between the lines. If he had, he would have shipped the clock to someone else. He wouldn't have tried to bring it in with him. And he wouldn't be standing here now being shown badges and credentials, or listening to a recitation of his rights, or being handcuffed and pushed into a chair.

"Vincent Prado." A tall man with a short crewcut, who had identified himself as an FBI agent before he attached himself to Vincent via metal bracelets, took the chair next to him, his jacket open, his gun and shoulder holster in clear sight. "Well, Mr. Prado, judging by your recent activities, I guess the decorating business isn't as profitable as people seem to think it is."

Prado ignored him. He turned to Max instead.

"What are you doing here?"

"Trying to find out why you're doing what you're doing, Vincent."

"Are you FBI?"

"No. Interpol. But since we have no jurisdiction in the United States, I had to ask my friend to do the honors for us and arrest you."

"For what?"

Though Vincent kept his eyes on Max, the listing of the charges against him came from the other man.

"For smuggling diamonds into the country. For federal tax fraud." He turned to Max. "How's that for a start?"

"Sounds good to me. How about you, Vincent?"

Prado squirmed. How had they found out about him? Had one of his fences squealed? Had someone turned him in? No. They had too much to lose. Bennett? He also had too much to lose. Irina! Yes! It had to be her. She had everything to gain. She did it for revenge. Because he refused to be her toady. Because he refused to do her bidding. She didn't know anything, he was sure of that, but, he recalled, she had questioned him after the Lafitte debacle as to why he insisted upon keeping third-rate dealers like Clive Bennett in the fair. She must have put two and two together somehow and come up with sufficient cause to sic the police on him. Bitch!

"I demand a lawyer."

"Good thinking, Vincent. You're going to need one."

The FBI man handed him a piece of paper and a pencil.

"Why don't you write down your lawyer's name and phone number. I'll have someone call him and he can meet you at my office."

He did as he was told.

"Now," Max said quietly, knowing there was no need to rough up someone like Prado in order to get cooperation, knowing that capture and fear of imprisonment were motivation enough. "We're going to take you downtown, Vincent. On the way, I'd like you to consider your options."

"And what are they, Max?"

"Negotiated immunity based on the quality of whatever information you give us, or a messy trial and a very long prison sentence."

Prado laughed, a nervous trill born of fear that echoed throughout the crowded room.

"It's a hell of choice," he said, feeling sick to his stomach, praying he didn't embarrass himself any further by puking in front of them.

"How did you get involved with all this?" Max asked. "Why did you get involved with all this?"

For the first time that morning, Prado looked embarrassed.

He grew shy, hesitant about explaining his participation. Suddenly, he realized how seedy it would sound to someone like Max, how seedy it sounded to him.

"I was in Monte Carlo about five years ago. I was gambling heavily then. Sometimes I was a winner. That night, I lost track of my losings. I had a running credit line with the casino and by the time they stopped me, I had run up a hundred-thousand-dollar debt. I don't keep that kind of change on me. I guess I panicked. The man sitting next to me struck up a conversation. He had recognized me. I had done the homes of some of his friends. He offered to help. I accepted. He paid my debt, and when I asked him how I could repay him, he asked me if I wanted to be his business partner."

"He's the one who supplies the diamonds?"

Vincent nodded. "He has several dockworkers in both Amsterdam and Antwerp on his payroll. They lift the diamonds before the manifests are checked. He gets the stones and buys the antiques. I arrange where they're to be shipped. And I contact the fences. When I've concluded a sale, I send him his cut."

"Why, Vincent? You're one of the top designers in the city. You make lots of money. You're famous. Why did you need to do this? I don't understand."

"Of course you don't understand! Because you're rolling in money, you snotty, rich bastard! You don't know what it is to be rejected all the time! To be laughed at and shunned. To be thought of as *less than* or *not as good as* or *lower than*."

Prado was up out of his seat, growling like a jungle animal caged for the first time, oblivious to the horrified stares of his friends who could see him through the window.

"I was poor, Latino, and gay. If I wasn't hit on for one reason, I was kicked around for the other. It took me years to dig my way out of *el barrio,* but I did. I put myself through school by juggling four jobs at a time. I swept floors. I ran errands. I washed dishes. I scrubbed toilets. You name it, if it paid, I did it. And when I got out of school, I let every decorator in town who was willing to give me a job stick it up my rear. And when, finally, I was able to scrape together enough money to start my own business, I worked my ass off and sucked up to every Park Avenue broad who came my way. But you know what I discovered? That you straight, uptight, fat-wallet WASPs only tolerate fags like me because we make good party decorations. You don't like us and you don't accept us. You don't accept anything except money. *Big* money. *Mega*-money. *Fuck you* money. Well, someone offered me a chance to grab that kind of money. He offered me a chance at acceptance, a chance to be one of you. Can you understand that, Richard?''

His fist crashed down on the table. His eyes flamed and his body shook as he glared at Max. Max never flinched. He continued as if Prado's harangue had been nothing more than a noisome belch.

''We want a signed confession as well as a list of every pickup and delivery you made. We also want a list of every person connected with this operation. And let me warn you, Prado. We have another witness who has already compiled similar lists. They had better match.'' Saying that, Max waved his hand, dismissing everyone, leaving Vincent to the FBI.

As he was led out of the customs hall, Prado longed to hear shouts of support, words of understanding and forgiveness. But the hall was eerily silent. No one said a thing. Not the customs inspectors, not those passengers standing on line waiting to get finished and go home, not those people who, not more than half an hour before, had been his devoted fans. Everyone was silent. They didn't speak for him. They didn't speak to him. Worse, when he walked by handcuffed to the man with the badge, they turned their heads and looked away.

PART
FOUR

22

It was unusually chilly for the middle of October. Only one week before, Indian summer had brushed the landscape with brilliant swipes of color, but now the sun had lost its golden glow, and a cool wind asserted itself. The sky faded to gray. Summer was gone.

Garrett was delighted. He checked to see if the staff had arranged kindling and logs inside the fireplace. With temperatures dipping into the low forties, having a fire wouldn't seem like part of a stage set. It would be romantic, but appropriate. Then he checked the kitchen. He lifted pot lids, scrutinized the hors d'oeuvres tray, and watched his chef squeeze whipped cream out of a cloth bag into a pastry puff shaped like a swan which would float on a sea of imported raspberries. He went over timing with Harold, his head butler. They discussed the wine, the champagne, the after-dinner drinks. And when there was nothing left to check or discuss, Garrett returned to the living room, inspected the table setting one last time, and then simply waited, wondering whether everything would be to Gaby's liking.

He had planned this dinner down to the last detail, choosing the living room because the dining room was too formal, the parlor too casual. His mother's sitting room was too much his mother, the library too much his father. The living room, with its light aquamarine silk couches and slipper chairs, its crewelwork sofa and throw pillows, its massive Mouhteshan Kashan rug and golden lacquered walls, seemed the perfect blend of civilized intimacy. And for this particular occasion, perfection was what he wanted.

For months, he and Gaby had been working on the Montgomery auction. Garrett had given her an office next to his. There she had set up a command post. First she had delegated responsibility for the cataloguing and estimating of the various lots to the Old Masters department. Then she had single-handedly planned every other phase of what Garrett had come to consider his night of nights. Thanks to her, this auction promised to be the most sensational of the year, perhaps of the decade. There had already been numerous newspaper articles and advertisements, a spot on *20/20*, a piece in *Vanity Fair*, and a preview of the auction scheduled for the November issue of *The Connoisseur*. The hardbound catalogue—complete with the history of Annabel and Philip Montgomery, their collection, and its importance to the world of art—had gone back to press three times, and the auction was still a month away. Reservations for seats in the salesroom—something rarely done—were practically filled and still coming in, an extraordinary feat considering that, the Monday before, the stock market had plummeted more than five hundred points.

So far, everything Gaby had suggested in the way of publicity had worked extremely well, particularly the tour of the major pieces from the collection. For Garrett, the only drawback was that she had requested that he be present at all, or at least most, of the stops on the tour. Her reasoning was twofold: his presence added to the significance of the event, and since she had also planned an invitation-only cocktail party for each of the chosen cities, he was needed to serve as host. Though he had enjoyed the experience, it had kept him out of town and out of touch with Gaby. Tonight, he intended to renew their acquaintance.

He knew he was behaving like a schoolboy, but when he heard the doorbell, he nervously adjusted his bow tie and his jacket, brushing a speck of lint off the satin collar of his tuxedo.

He waited at the top of the stairs, a portrait of complete composure. As she ascended, whatever calm he had mustered failed. She was carved ivory packaged in red silk. Short, tight, strapless, her dress was the ideal wrapping for a precious gift. Her face was delicately pale, her lips daringly red. Her hair was longer than he remembered, but still frothy, still a mane of undisciplined splendor. She smiled. He held out his arms. She slid next to him. As he held her, breathing in her scent of hyacinths and lilacs, he prayed that the evening would go well, that when, finally, he unwrapped this package, the ceremony would be a celebration of betrothal.

"I thought you invited me to a party," she said, in a cheery but confused tone as she peeked into the living room and found it empty except for a table by the far window, a fire raging in the fireplace, and Harold holding a tray with two champagne glasses and an orchid.

"I did. A party of two."

He took her arm and led her inside. Inviting her to sit in the sofa facing the fire, he handed her champagne, put his glass on a table, and took the orchid from the silver tray. With a nod, he dismissed Harold.

"For my lady."

He bowed grandly, presented her with the delicate blossom, and joined her on the sofa. Gaby fumbled with the orchid, unsure about where to put it.

"I seem to have left my lapels at home," she said, laughing, shrugging, holding it up to a naked shoulder.

"Allow me." With experienced fingers, Garrett pinned it to the bodice of her dress, centering it on the shirred fabric that covered the furrow between her breasts. When he finished, he leaned over and kissed the flesh above the flower. "Pity the poor orchid. It must feel unbearably intimidated by you."

Gaby smiled, but his ardor was making her uneasy. To begin with, though clearly he thought it charming to tell her tonight was a party, she felt slightly put out. Thinking he had invited her to the usual Castleton-type gala, she had gone to the thrift shop, bought this dress, and then spent hours fitting it and refurbishing it so it looked new and stylish. Had she known this was going to be dinner à deux, she could have saved both time and money by wearing something she already owned. In each instance, she had little to spare.

Too, she suspected that along with the brandy would come an invitation to spend the night. For months, she had managed to avoid that particular situation. Either Garrett was away—and whether consciously or subconsciously, she had made certain he was away a great deal—or they had spent so many long hours at the office, at the end of the day she was able to beg fatigue. It wasn't that she didn't enjoy Garrett's company or that she didn't care for him. She did. But she couldn't sleep with him again. Max had made that impossible. He had spoiled her. He had introduced her to explosive passion, a condition she had never experienced with Garrett and doubted she ever would. Also, though Max hadn't called her in almost three months and though she was terribly hurt, in the short time they had been together she had fallen in love with him, and until she got over him, it wasn't fair to toy with anyone else's affections.

". . . and then, of course, there's the *après*-auction party my parents have planned. According to my father, it's going to be quite sensational." His eyes had a starry look and his voice jittered with nervous anticipation. "I think that's when he's going to announce his successor."

"What a wonderful night that's going to be, Garrett," she said, resting her hand on his arm, knowing how much it meant to him to wear the Castleton crown. "I can't imagine him selecting anyone else. But if, for a single foolish moment, he even entertained the idea of appointing someone other than you, after watching you auction the Montgomery Collection, there'll be no room for doubt."

"Thank you," he said, lifting her hand to his lips. "Your support is very important to me."

"I'm only stating the facts. You're the best at what you do, and your father knows it."

"How do you know he knows?"

Gaby heard the echo of vulnerability in his voice and smiled reassuringly.

"Because he impressed me as a man with a finely tuned instinct for detecting superior quality. I saw that in his home. I saw that in your mother. I saw that in the party they hosted. And I see that in you." Leaving out Irina was probably conspicuous, but there was no way Gaby could bring herself to speak kindly of Lady Stoddard. "Your father respects . . . no, he reveres excellence. There is no way he will allow anyone but you to sit in his chair."

"You're very astute. You've honed in on the essence of my father. I hope he does as you say, but even if you're wrong about that, you are correct about his devotion to the nonpareil." Garrett's wide forehead wrinkled as a thought interrupted his dialogue. "Speaking of nonpareils, wouldn't it have been marvelous to have been able to present him with *The Marriage of Brussels*? Grouped with *The Courtship* and *The Garden of Love*, it would have made a truly exquisite centerpiece for this auction." He drifted, caught up in a pleasant daydream. "I would have asked him to take the hammer and preside over the sale of the Dinant Love Trilogy. What a fitting farewell performance for a man of my father's preeminence." He shook his head. "If only I could have found it. Think of it! Three of the finest tapestries ever loomed being auctioned off with some of the finest oils ever painted!" He was practically swooning.

Gaby more than understood. Having seen two of the Dinants, she could only imagine the sublimity of *The Marriage of Brussels*, the excitement that would surround its discovery, the overwhelming frenzy that would accompany its appearance on the block.

"What if you had *The Triumph of Chastity*?" As soon as the words left her lips, she regretted them.

Garrett's face blanched.

"Do you know something about that tapestry no one else does?"

She could practically see his heart thumping beneath his pleated silk shirt. How could she have let that slip? Was she that angry with Max? Or that intrigued with the notion of personal accolade?

"No, of course not. I just wondered why no one ever mentions looking for it."

"Because it was destroyed during World War One."

"You say that with such certainty I'm surprised you don't assume *The Marriage of Brussels* met with a similar fate, that it was destroyed during the Second World War."

"There have been sightings, people who seem to know it

exists, rumors that it was owned by a Nazi collaborator and given to the German commandant of the area. No one has seen or heard about *The Triumph of Chastity* in more than seventy years.''

"Seventy years!" Gaby was desperate for a way out of the quagmire she had jumped into. "That's much too long for something that valuable to remain hidden without someone seeing it. You must be right.''

Garrett wasn't listening. He was staring into his champagne glass as if the tiny bubbles floating within held answers to universal questions.

"You know, you may have raised an interesting point.''

Gaby's nerves were jangling.

"I did?''

"Perhaps *The Marriage of Brussels* was destroyed. Perhaps the German who took it burned it for revenge or got rid of it because he feared being caught by the Allies with an art treasure in his possession. Or perhaps he gave it away to someone with no idea of its importance. Who knows?''

"Who knows indeed," Gaby said, wondering if Max knew where *The Marriage of Brussels* was, or *if* it was. He certainly knew exactly where to find *The Triumph of Chastity*. He hadn't mentioned it, but if, as he said, he visited Damme often, he had to be aware of the fact that it hung in that remote chapel. Of course he was! He was probably the one who had put it there. It was obscure enough to be the perfect hiding place. There was a guard at the gate. His aunt lived there.

Suddenly, it occurred to her that perhaps that was what he had been doing these past few months: tracking the last Dinant. It made sense. He had admitted buying *The Meeting, The Battle of the Lion and the Unicorn*, and *The Betrothal*. By owning three—four if she counted *The Triumph*—if he were to find *The Marriage of Brussels*, he would gain incontestible control of the Dinants. In effect, Garrett's two would become devalued. Max could buy them at a noninflated price and then, if he remained true to his word, present them to the Belgian government. Gaby had two problems with that: she didn't know who actually owned *The Triumph of Chastity* or if *The Marriage of Brussels* still existed, and based on her own recent experience, she didn't know whether or not Maximilian Richard was a man of his word.

But what if she found *The Marriage of Brussels*? According to Oncle Bernard, though that possibility was extremely remote, he didn't feel it was time to abandon the search. He had put the word out among his friends, people who had an antiques underground of sorts, that he was looking for the missing Dinant. He had actually received a few leads. Upon further investigation, they had all proved bogus, but the fact that there were any leads at all told Bernard that more people believed the tapestry existed than believed it had been destroyed.

Gaby had spoken to Oncle Bernard once a week since her return from Paris. Her visit had meant a lot to both of them. It had reminded them that they were family and that they had been out of touch for too long. Oncle Bernard was determined not to let that happen again. He called every Sunday. They chatted about their health, the weather, whatever progress he was making with their search, whatever progress she was making with the Montgomery Collection, whatever. . . . When Gaby had told him about Max abruptly exiting her life, he was upset for her. When she had told him about Steven's visit to her apartment, his misinterpretation of the facts, and his stubborn refusal to speak to her about it, he was upset with Steven. When she had told him of her plan to move to Paris after the auction, he had been delighted, but cautious.

"Life has a way of changing our plans," he had said, protecting himself against disappointment, but also trying to prevent his niece from doing anything prematurely.

"But I have nothing here, no one, no reason to stay. Once I fulfill my obligations, I'm free to go."

"I'll tell you what. You'll come for the Christmas holiday. We'll discuss it then."

"I have the most wonderful idea." Garrett's voice insinuated itself on an image of Oncle Bernard's face, rattling Gaby. It took a moment before she separated the illusion from the reality.

"What's that?" she asked, reluctant to let go of Oncle Bernard.

"I'm going to put the two Dinants I have on the block."

"What? Why?"

"Because I'm beginning to believe they're the last two in

existence. To hold onto them until someone finds *The Marriage of Brussels* might be foolish, like keeping a bottle of wine so long it turns into vinegar."

"But you said before you don't know if *The Marriage of Brussels* was destroyed." *And you don't know that* The Triumph of Chastity *is hidden away in a tiny chapel in Belgium.*

"I've spent thousands of dollars and hours searching for it. I also know my beloved sister has been chasing it with her usual bulldog tenacity. Max Richard has made a religion out of the Dinants. And there are dozens more who have dedicated their resources to finding this treasure. Despite all of this attention and activity, no one has come up with it, which leads me to believe the treasure chest is empty."

"But why put them up now?"

"Because the Montgomery Collection is attracting an audience of big money, which is what I want for the Dinants. And because after Black Monday, no one can be certain how long the market for art and art treasures will remain strong. Why not cash in on *The Courtship* and *The Garden of Love* while I can?"

He was right. The economy was precarious. For all intents and purposes *The Marriage of Brussels* was still missing. Everyone believed *The Triumph of Chastity* was missing. Why not put the two available Dinants under the hammer? Besides, she said to herself, with the Dinants going up for auction, there was no question that Max would be there.

"So? What do you think? Can you get out some fast publicity on this?"

Gaby nodded, again shaking off images of one man so she could respond to another.

"I'll give it to the wire services first thing in the morning. That way, it'll appear in newspapers all over the world. Then we'll work up special ads and pamphlets for insertion in the catalogues and for mailing to those with seats already reserved." She paused and then continued. "When we set up the exhibition, I think we should hang the tapestries in a separate area decorated so that the atmosphere is medieval. We should have candelabra and huge floral displays, maybe even an archway of pennants that copy the coats of arms of the lord and lady of the Dinants. We should definitely have a table displaying pictures of the entire series and a card that tells the story of their origin so that visitors can understand and appreciate the inherent romance in *The Courtship* and *The Garden of Love*. And on the day of the auction, I'd like to see bouquets of carnations decorating the front of the saleroom.''

"Why carnations?"

"They're the medieval flower of betrothal, and to me they should be the symbol of the Dinants."

Unable to control his enthusiasm, he hugged her.

"You're the best!"

"Dinner is served."

Garrett released her and looked up at his butler, who stood at attention behind the sofa.

"Harold. Did anyone ever tell you your timing stinks?"

"You have, sir. Many times."

Garrett laughed as he escorted Gaby to the other side of the room. The table was laid with Coalport china, English crystal, and George I silver. A bulbous crystal bowl brimming with pale pink roses basked in the reflection of two tall candles. Smoked salmon garnished with caviar, onions, capers, and chopped egg waited as they took their seats. With practiced ease, Harold spooned a dollop of *crème fraîche* onto the side of the plates, poured a chilled Pouilly-Fumé, and silently retreated, dimming the lights as he went so that only the fire and the flickering of the candles illuminated the room.

When they were alone, Garrett proposed a toast: "To the success of the Montgomery auction! To our success!"

He held out his glass and touched Gaby's. He smiled, and in his eyes she saw love and appreciation and admiration and enormous trust. As she sipped her wine and drank in her surroundings, she couldn't help but regret not being in love with Garrett Castleton, Jr. He cared for her and wasn't ashamed to express his feelings, either in large doses of affection or small, whimsical ways. Like the orchid. Like the glass of champagne his chauffeur had handed her after settling her into Garrett's limousine for the ride from her apartment to the town house. The music—a Bach prelude and fugue from *The Well-Tempered Clavier*—perfuming the air with Baroque elegance. The dinner—more than likely a selection of her favorites. Here was a man who would do anything to please her. Why couldn't she love him?

A young man cleared the table as Harold and an assistant served the entrée—roast duckling with bitter-orange sauce—and changed the wine from white to red. Though they tried to keep the conversation varied, and for most of the meal they did, neither could help returning to the project closest to them.

"I know I've said it before, but I must tell you again what a smashing job you're doing."

"I've enjoyed it."

She smiled and returned to her duck. He trained his eyes on her, studying her, as if deciding what to say next.

"Gaby, I don't mean to introduce any unpleasantness into this evening, but there's something I must know. Why did you leave Castleton's? Was it because you felt your job didn't make use of your talents? that it was beneath you? Would you have stayed if I had offered you Giles Deffand's job?"

Gaby knew there was no way those words could have come from Garrett's mouth unless Irina had fed them into his ear. The way she saw it, she had several choices. She could defend herself by denying the charges. She could laugh and ignore his questions as if they were too ridiculous even to comment on. Or she could tell him the truth.

"Irina fired me."

All color drained from Garrett's face, leaving it frighteningly white, as if someone had just tossed bleach onto his skin.

"What do you mean, she fired you?"

"Months ago she called me into her office and told me that there was an overload of employees. As part of an officewide cutback, my services were no longer required. I was asked to resign, but since I would never have done so without Irina's . . . encouragement, I considered myself fired."

"I'm outraged!" Now Garrett's skin reddened with a mix of embarrassment and anger.

"She claimed that her actions had your stamp of approval."

"Did you believe her?"

"I didn't want to."

"But it sounded reasonable, so a tiny portion of your brain said that, yes, I condoned her actions."

"I suppose."

He shook his head.

"Never. I never knew a thing about it until after I had returned from Europe. She said you quit."

"It doesn't matter, Garrett," she said, reaching across the table to pat his hand. "In a way, it all worked out. I like being a broker. I like being independent."

"But you liked working at Castleton's."

"Yes. Very much."

Suddenly, Garrett's anger grew too large for his chair. He pushed it back and stood, pacing alongside the table.

"She did it to me again," he muttered, his teeth so tightly clenched his jawbones protruded.

Gaby rose and gently held him by the arms.

"What difference does it make?" she said, understanding that there were layers of meaning in his words and a history behind his rage. "So I'm not there on a day-to-day basis. We're working together on the Montgomery Collection. Maybe we'll team up for some other projects. Don't let it bother you."

He nodded, but he didn't speak. He couldn't speak, not until he had exorcised Irina, not until he had chased her malevolent spirit from the room so that he and Gaby could once again be alone.

"Let's have coffee and dessert by the fire," he said, wishing to leave the table, to escape Irina's aura.

Gaby followed him, taking her place on the couch, watching as he added logs to the fire and stoked it until it roared. Behind them, Harold and his helper cleared the table. At Garrett's request, they left. They would return with dessert later. He closed the doors, refilled her wineglass, and sat next to her. For a while, they sat quietly and companionably, Gaby watching the fire dance, Garrett watching Gaby. When he took her wineglass and placed it on the table in front of them, she steeled herself for the question she expected him to ask. She wasn't at all prepared for the question he actually posed.

"I was going to wait until after the Montgomery auction was over before raising this," he said, sliding next to her, taking her hand in his, "but having just learned how easy it is for others to interfere with my plans, I've decided to preempt myself." He lifted her hand to his lips and kissed her fingers. "In case you couldn't tell, I'm madly in love with you, Gabrielle Didier. Not only are you the most beautiful woman I know, but you've added dimension and color and sparkle and fire to my life. I count the minutes I'm away from you because I can't wait until I see you again. And then I count the minutes I'm with you because I can't bear the idea of you leaving. I've thought long and hard about it," he said with a shy grin, "and there seems to be only one solution. Will you marry me?"

Gaby's face registered surprise and confusion. A thousand thoughts fizzed inside her brain. She was flattered that someone like Garrett would want to marry her, upset that she didn't want to marry him. She didn't want to hurt him, but she didn't love him. Or did she? Did she even know what love was? Was she in love with Max? Or was she confusing an emotion with a physical sensation? Was Max simply a better lover? Or had he touched her in other ways as well? How had she felt about Brian? Think, she commanded herself. Think back. Once upon a time. That's what it had been with Brian. A fairy tale. Small-town girl. Boy next door. Local beauty queen. Football hero. Happily ever after. Back then, love had been defined on movie screens and by quizzes in teen magazines. When she married Brian she had based her hopes on dreams. She had no reality then. She was young, inexperienced. But what about now? She wasn't a small-town girl. She wasn't young. She was no longer inexperienced. And if, over the years, disappointment and disillusionment had demanded a new, more complete definition of love—a need to be together with someone spiritually, emotionally, and physically, a need to share her most intimate thoughts and feelings, to be willing to trust in, lean on, laugh with, cry with, and support someone without conditions—in her heart she knew. She liked and admired and respected Garrett, but she didn't love him.

"I didn't expect this," she said, wishing there was another way. She breathed deeply, smiled briefly, and then did what she had to do. "I can't accept your proposal. I'm flattered. No. To be more exact, I'm honored, but I have to say no."

Dejection bathed Garrett's face in a dull, gray light.

"Is there someone else?"

Max flashed before Gaby's eyes.

"No," she said, "there's no one else."

Garrett nodded slowly, his head bobbing heavily, as if that was more devastating than being told he had competition.

"Are you afraid I wouldn't make you happy?"

"I'm afraid *I* wouldn't make *you* happy," she said, hating herself for hurting him.

He thought about pleading his case, but decided against it.

"Maybe I should have waited," he said somewhat absently, as if speaking both to her and to himself. "Maybe you need more time. After all, it's terribly difficult to think about such an important step when you're under pressure."

"Maybe," she said, sensitive to his need to explain her rejection to himself and to avoid further embarrassment.

"More wine?"

He filled her glass and then his own, hiding behind the safe, impenetrable shield of good manners. They drank quietly, each retreating into his own space, each pretending that the thick pall of awkwardness that surrounded them was really a tiny cloud that would soon evaporate. Yet no matter how hard they tried, they couldn't escape the sting of truth. There were no maybes. The question had been asked. And answered. And time wasn't going to make any difference.

CASTLETON'S TO AUCTION THE LAST OF THE DINANTS

October 28, 1987. On December 11, when Castleton's offers the Montgomery Collection of Old Masters for auction, the two known remaining Dinant tapestries will also go on the block. A series of seven tapestries loomed in the late fifteenth century as a gift from a Belgian lord to his lady on the occasion of their marriage, the Dinants have long been famed for their beauty, admired for their craftsmanship, and beloved for the romance that inspired their creation. Of the seven, three—*The Meeting, The Battle of the Lion and the Unicorn*, and *The Betrothal*—have already been auctioned, purchased by anonymous collectors. *The Triumph of Chastity*, the fifth in the series, was believed destroyed during the First World War when the German army raided the town of Dinant. According to Garrett Castleton, Jr., the crowning jewel of the Dinants, *The Marriage of Brussels*—reputed to symbolize both the marriage of the lord and his lady and the joining of Flanders and Walloonia—is also believed to have been destroyed. *The Courtship* and *The Garden of Love*, two of the most romantic of the series, are in the possession of Castleton's. They will be exhibited and sold along with the Montgomery Collection, making this, in the words of Mr. Castleton, "a truly historic occasion."

In Saint-Cloud, Max read the article with mixed emotions. On the one hand, he was delighted that *The Courtship* and *The Garden of Love* were coming up for auction, particularly both in the same place at the same time. It certainly made things easier. On the other hand, publicizing their sale worldwide, trumpeting them as the last two Dinants in existence, and declaring the search for *The Marriage of Brussels* a dead end, could raise a number of complications.

It might prompt whoever was hiding *The Marriage of Brussels* to bring it forward. Either that or to bury it even deeper. It might reroute the energies of those on the trail of the missing Dinant, galvanizing them to unite and perhaps outbid him on what they thought were the last two Dinants. The hoopla generated by the auction might also inspire those who had never taken an interest in the Dinants to seek a piece of history for themselves.

And what about those with a lifelong fascination with the Dinants? Belgian collectors with a patriotic interest. Medieval enthusiasts. Tapestry dealers. Museum curators. Those to whom the Dinants were intensely personal. Certainly, they would all be in the audience at Castleton's.

And if Max's instincts were correct, *he* would be there too.

His eggs were undercooked. The yolks were runny, the whites barely done. If that wasn't bad enough, his coffee was tepid. What could possibly be so difficult about brewing a decent cup of coffee? He was about to push the cup aside when his eyes fixed on the article about the Dinants. His hand jerked, sending the delicate china crashing to the floor. The Marriage of Brussels *is believed to have been destroyed.* How did they know? Did they have proof? Or was this simply another example of American hype? Was this Castleton fellow holding it back as a publicity scam, planning to reveal its existence days before the auction? It didn't matter. He had to know. He had to be there. Two of the Dinants were going up for sale. What if Castleton was bluffing about *The Marriage of Brussels*? What if it still existed and was put on the block? And what if *she* was there?

After all these years, he wondered if he would know her. More important, he wondered if she would know him.

It was late afternoon by the time she got around to reading the newspaper. The sun was setting and the trees outside her small apartment were dappled with spots of fading yellow. She loved Damme, particularly in the autumn, when God's artistry was most evident. With thin, delicate hands, she pushed back her sheer white curtains, wanting to indulge herself with the last moments of the day. She sat in her favorite chair, the big cushy one with the fringed bottom, poured herself another cup of tea, and put her feet up on the slightly worn ottoman. When she saw it, her heartbeat accelerated, pumping faster and faster until she had trouble catching her breath. Quickly, she rose from her chair and closed her curtains, hiding, just as she had done for most of her life.

When would it stop? When would people stop looking for the Dinant tapestries? When would *he* stop looking for her? So far, Max had protected her. But how long could he continue to do so? What if something happened to him? She'd be alone, vulnerable, an easy target. What if word leaked out that *The Triumph of Chastity* still existed? Or what if *The Marriage of Brussels* were found? Was it possible this man Castleton was telling the truth? Had *The Marriage of Brussels* been destroyed? The thought distressed her, but if it were so, then maybe this auction would prove to be a blessing. Maybe the sale of those other two would end it. Maybe then she would feel safe.

To Irina, Garrett's announcement confirmed her ascendancy to the leadership of Castleton International. Weakness. The article exhibited weakness and inefficiency. Obviously, his sources were inept. Clearly, his pipeline hadn't reported the rumor about *The Triumph of Chastity*. And she was certain he had no idea whether or not *The Marriage of Brussels* was destroyed. That was pure rot! He had given up the search. He had decided to play whatever cards he had in his hand to trump up as much excitement as he could for this Montgomery auction, believing that that night was going to be the turning point in their battle for control.

The Montgomery auction! She was beginning to think if she heard one more word about it, she would be ill. Around the office, that was all anyone talked about. Among her friends, it was topic A on their list of things to discuss over lunch. Naturally, her parents had turned into blithering idiots on the subject, carrying on as if it were the Resurrection itself. Even her children had decreed it an evening worth flying in for. The only person who didn't seem to give a damn was Drake. Actually, thinking about it, Drake didn't seem to give a damn about very much these days, including her. When they went out, he was preoccupied. When they spoke on the phone, there were huge silences. When they went to bed, he was listless, ineffectual, practically impotent. Except that one time, two or three weeks ago, when he had been exceptionally vigorous, too much so, in fact. His grip had been viselike—she still had black and blue marks—and his kisses had too much bite in them to be considered loving, or even erotic. Several times, when she had squirmed free of him or had otherwise indicated displeasure, he had balled his hand into a fist, making it clear that if she didn't do as he wanted, he would punch her.

After that, she had decided that perhaps she should reassess her view of Drake Reynolds as a potential mate. Before, she had dismissed his erratic behavior as a side effect of the mourning process. His daughter had died tragically. She had committed suicide, after all. That had to leave scars. But physical abuse was a definite negative. Too, he had been excessively moody. Since she didn't love him, the least she expected in a suitor was that he would amuse her. Lately, there had been little that was amusing about Drake Reynolds. Every now and then Irina wondered why she persisted in continuing this relationship. Then she remembered that he held the key to settling an old score with Chelsea Reynolds.

Thinking about Chelsea reminded Irina she had a job to finish. Having decided that the link between Chelsea and Gabrielle Didier was worth exploring, Irina had launched a campaign to dig into every corner of Chelsea's life. She was certain that somewhere in her background she would find Gabrielle Didier's piece of dirty laundry. When discreet but direct inquiries into

Chelsea's life as Lady Winston Stoddard and Mrs. Roy Patterson had indicated no acquaintanceship with anyone even remotely resembling Gaby, Irina had decided to go further back and had called the alumni office of Skidmore College, requesting copies of their yearbooks for the years 1964 through 1970. They had arrived this morning. Taking her coffee into the library, she decided that this was definitely going to be her lucky day. The article in the paper was the first stroke. These yearbooks were going to be the second. Putting her coffee down on one table, sitting in a huge armchair, and picking up the first book from another table, Irina set to work. Her one regret was that she had never asked Drake if he knew Chelsea's maiden name. If she had, this would have been an easier chore, but if she found what she was looking for, time spent wouldn't matter. The end would have more than justified the means.

Flipping through page after page of black-and-white photographs of young women with bare shoulders and lacquered hair, searching for a pale blonde with a square jaw and light eyes, was beginning to hypnotize Irina. She had to blink often to keep her vision clear and her concentration crisp. Finally, she found it. The class of 1968. Chelsea Harper. White Plains, New York. Like a miner who has suddenly spotted a glimmer of gold amidst the pitch, she started with the A's and slowly, carefully, meticulously studied each and every picture. Her heart thundered inside her chest as she felt herself getting closer and closer to the vein. When she did, she shouted in triumph!

Gabrielle Didier Cocroft. Wadsworth, Ohio.

"Wadsworth, Ohio! Well, well, well. So you're not from France, eh? And how odd that Didier should be both your middle name and your married name. How coincidental!"

Irina cackled with pleasure as she put down the yearbook and picked up the telephone.

"I have a job for you," she said quickly, without preamble. "Gabrielle Didier Cocroft. Wadsworth, Ohio. Graduated Skidmore College in 1968. I want to know everything about her, including the color of her toenail polish and how many cookies she ate after school. And I want to know soon."

She put down the phone and picked up the yearbook. A youthful, innocent Gaby smiled at her.

"You may be riding high right now," Irina said with a

satisfied grin, "but you won't be for long. You see, Madame Didier, your past has just caught up with you."

"Max spoke to you about this a couple of months ago. He said you had agreed to make a very large contribution. Where is it?"

"I've changed my mind. I'm not going to allow you to desecrate my daughter's memory by affixing her name to some sleazy center on Spring Street."

He looked so sincerely offended, it took Chelsea a moment to react. When she did, it was minus all control. She went at him, rushing the couch where he sat. It took all Terry's strength to keep her from clawing Drake's face.

"You don't want to desecrate Belle's memory! You desecrated her life, you fucking slime!"

Drake refused to give her the satisfaction of flinching. Instead, he turned to Terry, his cool as unnerving as it was commendable.

"Either you muzzle her or I shall have to call someone and have her physically removed."

Terry admonished Chelsea with a quick nod. She turned and walked away. Terry set his sights on Drake.

"Three months ago you agreed to fund the Belle Reynolds Center for Abused Children, starting with one million dollars. You signed a paper to that effect. So far, we haven't seen one cent."

"Three months ago, the stock market was booming. In case you've both been living under a rock or," he said, lifting a disapproving eyebrow, "simply spending your days and nights rutting under a blanket, the stock market has taken a rather serious nosedive. I don't have a million dollars to give you."

"You're full of shit!" Chelsea shouted, her anger intensified by the patronizing tone in his voice. "I don't care what happened to your precious portfolio, you have millions stashed away in private bank accounts. Money daddy left you. Money mommy left you. Money you stole. Money that was put away for Belle."

"And how about the money I gave you?" he said, retaliating. "How about the millions I gave you as payment for staying away from my daughter?"

"I'd give you back every red cent if it would bring Belle

back or prevent what you did to your daughter.'' Regret choked her voice. Though her mouth was set in an indignant scowl, her green eyes pooled with a sea of unrelenting guilt.

"I didn't do anything to her," he said, automatically, mechanically.

"This letter says different." Terry waved Belle's letter in front of Drake's face. Chelsea was shocked. She had no idea Terry had brought it with him. "This letter says you abused her. That you impregnated her. That the only way out for her was to kill herself."

"She was sick. Delusional."

"No. You're the one who's sick," Chelsea said. "Recently, I've spent a lot of time talking to Louise. She told me how upset you were when she told you she was going to have a baby. How you couldn't look at her naked body while she was pregnant. How afterwards, you were annoyed that her breasts had increased in size and that her hips had rounded out. You were upset because she didn't have the body of a child anymore. She had become a woman and you don't know how to deal with women, do you, Drake?"

"Easy." Terry had noticed a change in Drake's face. He was becoming enraged.

"Get her off me," Drake said, growling at Terry.

"Get you off me! What a joke. One of the reasons I left you was I could never get you on me."

Drake was up and out of his seat. He started for Chelsea, but Terry stopped him.

"Leave us alone," Terry said, motioning for Chelsea to leave, still holding on to Drake.

Chelsea gladly complied. She left the living room and walked down the hall toward Belle's room. She stopped outside, staring at the closed door. Somehow, she had expected a yellow police tape, the kind they used to cordon off murder scenes. Surely they had to know that this was a murder scene. They had to know that Drake had killed her as surely as if he had put those pills in her mouth, one by one. He had pushed Belle out that window as surely as if his hands had been on her back.

Her hand turned the brass knob slowly. As the space widened, her mind saw the pale yellow walls and carpet. She saw the perfume bottles lined up on the top of the dresser, the hair spray, the brushes, the different-colored ribbons and barrettes. She saw the pictures of Belle's favorite movie stars tucked into the frame of the mirror, her schoolbooks spread out all over her desk. She saw the closet door open, the insides bulging with clothes carelessly hung. She saw Throckmorton curled up next to a fluff of pillows on the chintz armchair. But she refused to see the bed. And she refused to see the window.

Finally, she opened the door. The room wasn't yellow, it was brown. There was no dresser or chintz chair or mirror or bed. There was no Throckmorton, no pillows, no drapes, no curtains. There were bookshelves lining the walls, a desk, a leather wing chair, a Persian area rug, and dark wooden shutters. He had covered the window. He had redecorated the room. He had erased Belle.

Chelsea's knees buckled. Grabbing hold of the nearest wall, she stood in the doorway, looked at the deliberate cancellation of a young girl's existence and wept.

In the living room, Terry had decided to confront Drake.

"I think you should know I've spoken to the DA's office on Chelsea's behalf." That was half true. He had made discreet inquiries among some of his friends downtown. He had told Chelsea that they felt she had a case. Lately, since she had joined Alanon and had begun to deal with her own weaknesses and her own failings, since she was beginning to see the negative effects of blind denial, she was beginning to feel stronger about pointing a finger at Drake Reynolds. "I think the DA can mount enough evidence to warrant an indictment."

"I think your evidence is circumstantial and hearsay at best. Even if this case went to trial, and I doubt that it would, you'd never get a conviction."

"Maybe not, but a trial would sure kick the shit out of your lily-white reputation."

"It wouldn't exactly do Chelsea's name, such as it is, a lot of good either, which, my friend, is the real reason she hasn't gone after me before."

It annoyed Terry that someone as smarmy as Reynolds would know Chelsea that well.

"I don't care what you think. I only care what you do. And

what you haven't done is to uphold your end of a bargain you made with Max Richard.''

"And if I don't?"

"Then no matter what Chelsea does, I'll try you in the media. I'll spread enough rumors and tell enough dirty stories that you'll be off the A party list and persona non grata in the business community in no time.''

"Are you threatening me?"

"In a word, yes."

"I don't respond well to threats."

"Then how about to a little good advice.'' Terry shifted gears, washing his voice of antagonism. "You need help, Drake. Whether you want to admit it to me or Chelsea or anyone else, you repeatedly abused your child. You forced her to have sex with you time and time again. And because you did, she killed herself.''

Drake looked away, but Terry was certain he was listening. Outside, in the hall, Chelsea was listening too.

"The way I see it, you owe her. At the very least, you owe her the promise that you'll get professional help so that you will never, ever abuse another child or beat another woman. And you owe her a fitting memorial, which is what the center would be.''

"She was my daughter and I loved her.'' He said it softly, wistfully, displaying the first hint of honest emotion Terry had seen since entering the apartment. He paused, remembering. Then, in an instant, the gentleness disappeared. Drake's face had become a slate on which was chalked a look of defiance.

"But I don't owe her. Not in the way you mean. Belle was a disturbed child, sick and dependent, just like her mother. She was jealous and possessive. She was also spiteful. I was dating, out a lot of the time. She must have been angry at me and wanted to punish me by saying those awful things.''

"You know what? I'm angry and I want to punish you.'' Chelsea strode into the room. Though her face was stony, her voice was calm. She turned to Terry. "I want to file charges against him.''

Both men responded with complete shock.

"Are you sure?'' Terry asked, thrilled at her decision, but wanting to give her a chance to back down.

"Positive." Her eyes fixed on her ex-husband's face, searing through his skin like a laser.

"You'll be sorry," he said, meeting her stare.

"I'm only sorry I didn't do it sooner."

Drake laughed.

"You won't bring charges against me because of all the ugly little things you know I'm going to say about you."

Chelsea folded her arms and leaned against the wall. She was the picture of self-assurance. Inside, she was trembling, just as she had at her first group meeting, the first time she admitted that her father was an alcoholic, that he had died because he was a drunk, that she had hated him then and hated him now, that she hated herself.

"I don't care what you say about me," she said, gathering the strength she had gained from her support sessions. "I care about seeing that justice is done."

"Right! And what about your precious little image. Don't tell me you don't care about that?"

He was taunting her. Terry was watching her.

"Not anymore."

"Since when?"

"Since I've learned that protecting one's image doesn't work. Image doesn't make good things happen and it doesn't prevent bad things from happening. It's just image. Fake and false and totally unreal."

Terry smiled supportively. Drake was wary.

"You sound like some trendy proselyte."

"Call it what you will. The fact is, I have changed the way I see things." She paused, thought for a moment, and then continued. "Actually, you might say I'm *seeing* for the first time. Before, I wore a blindfold so I wouldn't have to see what I didn't want to see. But that blindfold also prevented me from seeing things I should have seen, things about myself and about others. Things about you and about Belle." Her insides wobbled as she thought about what she should have done and what she might have prevented. She looked at Drake and reaffirmed what she had to do. "These green eyes are wide open now. I don't care what you say. I know what you did. And whether you understand my motives or not, I'm going to do right by Belle. I'm going to take you to court.''

"You're making a mistake," he warned.

"Maybe, but I'm willing to take the chance because if I've learned anything lately, it's that in this life you pay for your mistakes, Drake. One way or the other."

23

Irina was certain that if one more bit of good news came her way she would burst. A few moments before, just as she was about to leave for a family dinner at the town house, Bootsie Cavendish, one of her friends on the January Antiques Fair committee, had called to tell her that, as expected, Vincent Prado had resigned as head of the show. Bootsie was devastated. Irina pretended to be devastated, but actually she was ecstatic. She had been Vincent's co-chairman, his right arm, his confidante, his vice-president. It was only natural that once everyone had had time to adjust to the tragic void created by his departure, they would turn to that one person who could so ably fill the gap, that one person whose standards of excellence were above reproach, that one person whom they could rely upon to continue the noble traditions of the fair—Irina Stoddard! She was so gleeful, she was practically dancing. What a coup! What a triumph! Everything was falling into place.

By the time she arrived, the others were gathered in the living room over cocktails. As she walked in and greeted everyone, she magnanimously decided that even after she was made head of Castleton's, she would allow Garrett to continue living in the town house. She would be big about it. It was only right. She would have so much. He would have nothing.

"You're looking well, Mother," she said, bussing Charlotte on the cheek, marveling at how well the older woman looked in her black dinner dress and diamond brooch. She was about to grouse about how clear and unwrinkled Charlotte's skin was, but then she remembered skin tone was an inherited trait. She forced herself to feel grateful.

"Thank you, dear. So do you."

Charlotte eyed Irina as her daughter made the rounds, barely acknowledging Bentley or her brother, briefly bussing Bentley's wife, Phoebe, holding back a bit with her father, still the little girl waiting for him to make the first move. Despite that, she appeared happier than usual, perky almost. Her dress, a column of navy-blue velvet, flattered her figure and brought out the color of her eyes, as did the bib of sapphires glittering against her chest. Her smile was broad, her laughter a bit on the giddy side. Charlotte and Irina weren't close—not in the way other mothers and daughters were close—so she didn't know whether or not this joviality was the result of a new romance, but in her heart she hoped it was. Irina needed someone to look after her.

"Before you came, dear, we were discussing the festivities for the Montgomery auction," Garrett Sr. said, filling his daughter in as she accepted a glass of wine from Harold and seated herself next to Phoebe. "It's going to be an unforgettable evening."

"I'm certain it will be," Irina said, with too much conviction to suit Garrett Jr.

"It was a veritable stroke of genius to add the Dinants to the Montgomery Collection, don't you think?"

Irina glanced over at her brother, with something that resembled mockery glinting in her eyes.

"A stroke of genius," she repeated, her tone confirming what he thought he saw.

As the others continued their conversation, Garrett Jr. stood off to the side, trying to put his finger on what was wrong with the scene being played out before him. Was it that Irina was too pleasant? Displaying an uncharacteristic enthusiasm for a Castleton event? Was she plotting something? Was his father being overly solicitous to Irina? If so, was it something that should concern Garrett? Something else he should worry about?

Ever since his dinner with Gaby a week before, he had begun to be obsessive about everything, from the biggest problem to the smallest detail. Recognizing that it was probably his way of avoiding dealing with her rejection of his proposal didn't help. His entire life had suddenly become centered around the Montgomery auction. He had come to view it as the beginning and end of all that was important or significant. Its success and his success were inexorably linked. If it failed, it would not only destroy his chances for taking over at Castleton's International, but would squash whatever tiny chance he might still have for winning Gaby's heart.

What troubled him now was the fear that history would repeat itself. In the past, whenever he had thought he had secured a hold on something, Irina had somehow found a way to loosen the moorings and set him hopelessly adrift. Though he didn't want to blame her for Gaby's refusal, neither could he totally eliminate her as a factor. And though he didn't want to make more out of her outward charm and sideward glances than he should, a warning light had clicked on inside his brain. He was on alert.

"Did you invite the Lafittes to the auction?" Bentley had come up next to him, taking advantage of a flurry of conversation about Vincent Prado's arrest and subsequent resignation as head of the antiques fair.

"Yes," Garrett answered, lowering his head so his response could be heard only by his uncle. "Even though I didn't find *The Marriage of Brussels*, offering them a chance to be present when Caravaggio's *The Fortune Teller* is put on the block is even more meaningful. You know it originally belonged to Josette Lafitte's father."

Bentley nodded. "Of course. That painting was the showpiece of the Rosenberg Collection, the one Etienne gave to Peter Wilson instead of to your father, the one that started this whole feud." He smiled quickly. "Funny how sooner or later, things tend to come full circle, isn't it? Have they responded?"

Garrett contained his delight. The last thing he wanted to do was to arouse anyone else's interest and invite questions.

"They'll all be there."

"Marvelous! Here's to the end of ancient hostilities."

The two men toasted each other, happy to share a warm

moment of camaraderie. Once dinner was announced, they followed the others into the dining room.

For this particular evening, an oval table had been positioned in the center of the room, set for six. The linens were gray. The flowers were white. The crystal was uncut Baccarat, the dishes an opulent floral. There were no place cards because in this group, seating was practically automatic: Garrett Sr., Charlotte to his left, the Oudenaarcle tapestry on his right, Garrett Jr. next to his mother, Phoebe, Bentley, and Irina.

Surprisingly, almost eerily, dinner moved along without incident. The Castletons behaved like Everyman's family, talking easily, exchanging ideas, listening to opinions without snide asides or the competitive flare-ups that normally distinguished their gatherings. It was when Garrett Sr. raised the issue of Gabrielle Didier's future with Castleton's that the flush faded and the complexion of the clan returned to its normal shade of green.

"She's such a tremendous asset, I would love to induce her to join our staff on a permanent basis," Garrett Sr. said.

"What a wonderful idea!" Charlotte had liked Gaby. Also, she had not been oblivious to the effect the young woman had had on her son. "Why don't you make her a generous offer?"

Garrett smiled at her, but then his face clouded as he turned toward his sister.

"She'll never come back to Castleton's," he said firmly, keeping his eyes fixed on Irina's face.

"Why not?" Garrett Sr. asked.

Charlotte felt a storm brewing. She thought about changing the subject or interjecting a diversionary tactic, but on second thought she remained silent. A human hand was powerless against a bolt of lightning about to strike.

"Because Irina fired her. And because Gaby knew that the reasons proffered had been false, fabricated to cover up personal reasons."

"And what were those personal reasons, Irina?" Garrett Sr.'s tone had turned demanding.

"I was looking to spare the family needless embarrassment."

She said it quietly, stoically, her excitement camouflaged by an expression of deep concern. After a moment's hesitation, she turned toward her father, a move that put her back toward her brother.

"From the first, there was something about her that didn't sit right with me. I can't explain it, but she seemed, well, a bit off. Garrett was so taken with her, I thought surely I was wrong, but I couldn't shake this feeling that came over me whenever I was with her." She paused, rolling her eyes as if a spirit from beyond had invaded her body. "When the feeling got so strong I couldn't bear it, I followed a hunch and chased her from our midst. I know that sounds bizarre, but now I'm glad I did." She faced the others, her gaze lingering on Garrett Jr. "I hired a private detective to follow up on my hunch. I regret to report that my suspicions have been borne out. Gabrielle Didier is not who she appears to be. The woman is a fraud."

Charlotte and Garrett Sr. looked confused, but upset. Bentley remained cautious, having learned that what Irina said was true and what was actually true were often two different things. Garrett Jr. jumped out of his seat so quickly, he almost toppled it.

"What the hell are you talking about?" he shouted, disregarding the servants, the disapproving looks of his parents.

Irina had been waiting for this moment all night. Actually, she decided, she had been waiting for this moment all her life. Though she wanted to stick the knife into his heart as fast and as savagely as she could, she decided to hold off for just a second longer so she could savor the look of expectant horror etched on his face.

"Gabrielle Didier is really Gaby Cocroft from Wadsworth, Ohio. She never married any Frenchman. She never lived in France. She has no fortune. She has no social connections. But she does have an ex-husband, Brian Thayer, who works for the Wadsworth Match Company, and a son, Steven Thayer, who's a freshman at Brown University. She was born in Wadsworth and grew up there. She was orphaned at twelve and raised by an aunt who owned an antiques store in Wadsworth called Tante Simone. She went to Skidmore College, where her roommate was none other than Chelsea Harper Patterson Stoddard Reynolds. She graduated in 1968, married shortly thereafter, and had a child shortly after that. Three years ago, just after her husband walked out on her, she came to New York. For several months, she worked as a salesclerk at Bergdorf Goodman's. She took a class in antiques at the New School and was subsequently hired by her instructor to work in his shop." She deliberately turned toward her father. "Her employer and benefactor was none other than Armand Lafitte."

"Gaby worked for Etienne's son?"

Though Garrett was still recovering from the shock of Irina's disclosures, he couldn't help noticing the way his mother had phrased that: *Etienne's son.* Also, he realized that his father had not stormed about or vocalized anything that sounded like "any friend of a Lafitte is an enemy of mine." Bentley was right. His parents had softened their stance on the Lafittes. Quickly, he shifted priorities, pushing aside his personal distress over what Irina had said, concentrating instead on feeding his brain other data. Within seconds, he arrived at a conclusion which allowed him to quiet his nerves. Whatever damage this revelation about Gaby had inflicted on his family rank, would be more than erased when Garrett effected a reconciliation between his father and Etienne Lafitte.

"She not only worked for him, but from what I understand, they're still very good friends," Irina continued, prodding, pushing, wondering why her father had not exploded at her news. She had expected him to rant and rave, to ban Garrett from Castleton's forever, to thank her for sparing the family from a fox in the henhouse. Instead, he was just sitting in his seat, scowling, but not screaming, like a stick of dynamite with a fizzled fuse.

"No wonder Castleton's got the Montgomery Collection," Bentley muttered, as if musing about something he hadn't fully thought out.

"What do you mean?" Garrett Jr. and his father both spoke at the same time. Charlotte and Irina remained silent, but they too were curious.

"Since she's both a friend of Armand's and a friend of Garrett's, it follows that if Annabel wanted her collection auctioned off and asked Armand to help arrange it, he gave it to Gaby, and she decided that in spite of, or maybe even because of, the shabby treatment she had received," he said, pointedly nodding toward Irina, "she would offer it to Castleton's."

Now it was Irina's turn to be rattled. Bentley was holding

two wires together and the electric charge they were creating was jolting her insides.

"You're leaving a few things out, Uncle Bentley. What is the connection between Armand and Annabel Montgomery?"

Bentley laughed, jolting Irina further. He knew he had shocked her and grabbed the undivided attention of the others. Frankly, he was enjoying it. It was a rare occasion when Bentley Castleton held center stage.

"Armand Lafitte and Annabel Montgomery have been lovers for more than thirty years."

Irina's heart stopped beating. "That's not true!" It was a lie, an insidious lie!

"Oh, but it is. As a matter of fact, after the auction they're planning to get married."

"You're making this up."

Garrett stared at his sister. Bentley's information was interesting and definitely noteworthy, but nothing to become hysterical about. Irina's face, her demeanor, the sound of her voice—it was a classic panic attack. Why would she panic? Why would she care about Armand Lafitte and Annabel Montgomery? A thought poked at his brain, insisting on being developed and considered. For the moment, however, he allowed it to go only as far as infancy. There he stopped it, waiting for further details which he suspected would be forthcoming.

"I'm not making anything up, my dear niece. I've been a confidante and friend of Annabel Montgomery's since her marriage to Philip. We've played bridge together for years. Trust me, she and Armand are mad for each other. Always have been. Always will be."

"If you're such a good friend, why didn't she give *you* the Montgomery Collection? Why funnel it through Armand? And why did he sneak it into Castleton's via that charlatan Gabrielle Didier?"

"In answer to your first question, everyone at this table knows why she wouldn't come to me about her collection. I'm the irrelevant Castleton, the one who shows up at corporate functions, shakes hands, and then goes home. No one ever thinks of me as being part of the business, because my own family doesn't consider me part of the business."

It was a small but satisfying reward to notice that all except his wife displayed some embarrassment.

"In answer to your second question, I can only hazard a guess. Since the collection also included a host of antique furniture, she probably needed someone to help organize the distribution of all the property. When your lover is an art scholar as well as an antiques dealer, it makes sense to me to take advantage of his expertise."

Each time he referred to Armand as Annabel's lover, Irina's gut wrenched.

"And in answer to your third question, the reason he had to go through Gaby is that, if I remember correctly, Armand Lafitte has been barred from buying or consigning anything to Castleton's."

The bomb sat in the middle of the table, ticking.

"I feel as if I'm in the twilight zone," Garrett Sr. said, angry and confused. "What are you talking about? Who barred Armand?"

"Why, you did, Father," Garrett Jr. said, happily pulling the pin. "Right after the 1986 fair, when Armand caused a ruckus by taking a stand on vetting, Irina told me you had issued a directive that he was never to set foot in Castleton's again. She also told me that you wanted your wishes conveyed to the other auction houses. Naturally, I complied with those wishes. Bentley's quite right. The only way Armand Lafitte could have gotten the Montgomery Collection, or anything else for that matter, into Castleton's was through an intermediary like Gaby."

"I never issued such a directive." Garrett Sr. directed his statement first to his wife, so she would know he had been true to his word and had not further widened the chasm between them and the Lafittes, and then to his daughter along with an expression that demanded an explanation.

Irina was totally befuddled. When and how had she lost control of this evening? Why was she being attacked when it was Garrett who had brought a wooden horse into their camp? Quickly, she commanded herself to regroup.

"I considered it in the best interest of Castleton's to keep vermin like Armand Lafitte away from its doors."

Vermin. Rather harsh, Garrett thought. Her whole attitude was too exaggerated, too laced with vengeance to have been spawned by a single incident at an antiques fair. She sounded more like a woman scorned. Inside, Garrett smiled. So that was it! Irina had once been in love with Armand Lafitte. Obviously, he had rejected her. Knowing Irina, she had been seeking revenge ever since.

"Why say the directive came from me? Why not just advise your brother or myself of your feelings and let us decide?"

"Because *he* never listens to me," she said, pointing a furious finger at Garrett. "The only way I could get him to do what I thought was best was to tell him the orders came from you. If I were accorded even the slightest respect or was permitted even the smallest authority, I wouldn't need to resort to such devious tactics. But my beloved brother seems to think he is the only one whose surname is Castleton, and my darling father seems to think that despite my achievements, my position in the business that bears my name is purely decorative!"

Years of frustration surfaced, erupting with volcanic force, causing Irina to tremble and quake. Unwilling to lose control and sacrifice her dignity, she grabbed onto the table, steadied herself and continued to speak.

"I'm supposed to be part of the decision-making process of Castleton's. At the time, it was my decision that based on his performance at the armory, Armand Lafitte was not someone we should be dealing with. It was my decision that he had proved himself untrustworthy, divisive, and most of all, disloyal to his friends and colleagues, just as his father had been disloyal to you."

"I'm not sure I would have viewed his behavior at the fair in those terms," Garrett Sr. said, "but if you saw it that way, dear, I'll abide by your decision."

Irina wasn't making sense, but because she was so clearly distraught, he opted to let the matter rest. What Armand Lafitte did, whom he loved or married or befriended or betrayed, made no difference to him. For whatever reason, and by whatever means, he had chosen to allow Castleton's to auction off an historic collection. This was no time to split hairs.

Slowly, the others attempted to pick up strands of conversation. The only one who refused even to try was Irina. She had fixed on what Bentley had said about Armand and Annabel. *Lovers for more than thirty years. Mad for each other. Getting married after the auction.* She still couldn't believe it. He had made an even bigger fool of her than she had thought. All the while he was romancing her, he had been involved with Annabel Montgomery. His heart had never been available. He had never cared for her. He had toyed with her. He had used her. And now he was going to use Castleton's.

No! She wouldn't allow it. Months ago she had put a plan into motion that would destroy her brother. The only thing comforting her at this moment was the knowledge that that same plan—with a few adjustments—would destroy Armand, his precious Annabel, and Gaby as well.

Irina never questioned whether or not her plan would work. She had ruined Armand once before. She would, and could, do it again. If his disgrace ruined Annabel Montgomery, all the better. As for Gabrielle Didier, that meddlesome climber, Irina would ruin her once. And for all time.

If this last day of October wasn't the worst day of Gaby's life, it certainly ranked in the top five. Since their dinner, things between her and Garrett had been strained, but civilized. Occasionally, they had even managed to share a laugh and a few moments of warmth, which was probably why his brusqueness that morning seemed so startling. He didn't ask her to come into his office, he commanded her. When she entered, he was standing at the window, his back to the room. Immediately, Gaby divined that the chill she felt had nothing to do with the weather outside and everything to do with the frigid climate inside.

"You wanted to see me?"

He didn't answer. He didn't turn around. For several horrible minutes, he let her stand there and imagine the worst. When he did face her, there was an odd set to his mouth, an unfamiliar vehemence in his eyes.

"You're fired!"

"What?" Suddenly, she couldn't breathe. It was if he had clicked a switch that turned off her oxygen supply.

"I want you out of here by noon today!"

"Why? What happened? What did I do?"

"What did you do?" He laughed, but the sound was hardly that of someone amused. "You lied! About everything! Who you are. What you did before you came here. Your friends. Your relatives. The fact that you have a husband buried, not in a cemetery in France, but in some match company in Ohio. The fact that you are not childless, but have an eighteen-year-old son in college in Rhode Island. For all I know, you haven't spoken a single truth since the day we met.''

Gaby's entire being rocked from his assault. She staggered, as if each of his words were a bullet exploding inside her body and her brain.

"Garrett, let me explain. It's not . . ."

"No. I've heard all I ever want to hear about you. What infuriates me is that I had to hear it from Irina.''

"Irina! I should have known.''

"No!" he shouted, unable to hold back his rage, "I should have known! I should have been told about all of this by you. That would have been the decent thing, don't you think? I trusted you. I relied upon you. I confided in you. I loved you, for God's sake! How could you betray me like this?''

"I didn't mean to,'' Gaby said, wishing she could deny his accusations, knowing she couldn't, knowing that he wasn't listening anyway. "I had to—''

"You had to!" Again, there was that terrible laugh. "Just like you had to turn down my marriage proposal. Was someone twisting your arm? Or threatening you with an excruciating death?'' He was pacing, circling around her like a mountain lion stalking a deer. "And what am I to believe about the Montgomery Collection? Is that a lie also? Did you bring it to me only to pull it away at the last minute?''

"No. It's yours. I consigned it to you because Annabel Montgomery wanted the best exposure for her collection. Castleton's is the best. You're the best.''

"Don't flatter me! And don't con me! You gave me this collection for a reason. I want to know what it is and where Armand Lafitte fits in.''

Gaby felt as if she had walked into a metal snare. One wrong move and the trap would spring.

"Okay. I did have an ulterior motive. I did want to challenge your ban against Armand. He's a good friend. I thought his exile was wrong. I thought that if I told you it was Armand who was responsible for the consignment, you, and by extension the rest of the antiques community, would forgive him and end this ridiculous banishment.''

"And if I didn't, you would have pulled the rug out from under me. Is that correct?"

"No. I don't know. I don't think I would have done that. If you'd only let me explain."

"I don't want to hear anything except the sound of the door closing behind you."

Gaby had barely walked into her apartment when the doorman buzzed to tell her Max Richard was in the lobby and would like to come up. She hadn't seen or spoken to him in months. In fact, she had given up hope of ever seeing him again. For him to appear now, after such a traumatic morning, seemed propitious. Maybe the universal scales were balancing.

The first few minutes were awkward. Each of them was being overly polite, uttering more pleases and thank-yous than would normally be heard in a four-hour conversation. Once both of them were seated, however, Max got to the point of his visit.

"I've heard something unsettling." *Join the club*, Gaby wanted to say. "Something I think you should know. The Caravaggio *Fortune Teller* is a fake."

"What!"

"The painting that's sitting in Castleton's storeroom is a forgery. If it goes up for auction, Castleton's reputation will be ruined. Since I knew your reputation was also on the line, I thought I might spare you."

Gaby shook her head as if trying to free herself of the tangled web she had woven about herself.

"I don't understand. Who told you this? How do you know it's true?"

"I have my sources."

That phrase, his tone of voice, his deliberate vagueness—it all registered, but in the back of her brain, in the subconscious, rather than the part of her mind that was busily racing to figure out her next move. She had to tell Armand. She had to tell Garrett. There was no question about that. Except as to whether or not he would believe her. Why would he? She had lied to him about everything else.

"Who are your sources?"

"Friends. Business associates. I can't tell you their names."

She nodded suspiciously.

"Can you trust them?"

"Implicitly. They don't lie."

Was she reading something into what he said or was it there, the insinuation, the implication that while *they* don't lie, *she* did? Had Irina gotten to him as well? Or had her confrontation with Garrett made her overly sensitive? What did it matter? It was the truth. She was a liar.

Max was uncomfortable. He had planned a different sort of reunion with Gaby, one that he had meant to have after the auction. Unfortunately, circumstance had intervened. He had known that his news would upset her, but she appeared to be suffering, struggling about what to do. Maybe it was because he made her uneasy. He stood.

"I have to go."

"No. Don't."

This was probably one of the most difficult decisions Gaby had ever had to make, but something Garrett had said continued to haunt her. *I loved you and you lied to me.* She didn't know whether or not Max had loved her—if he had, it was fleeting—but she loved him, and for that reason alone he deserved to know the truth from her lips rather than from someone else's.

"I have something to tell you."

She motioned for him to take his seat. He complied, watching her carefully. For a few moments, she sat with her eyes lowered, knitting her fingers together as she measured her words. When she looked up, her eyes told a story of conflict.

"I'm as much of a fake as the Caravaggio."

Max tilted his head quizzically, but he remained silent.

"My name is Gabrielle Didier Cocroft Thayer, and for much too long I've been masquerading as something I'm not. I'm not the widow of a French industrialist. I'm a divorcée with an eighteen-year-old son. I'm not some wealthy socialite. I'm a poor working girl in debt up to my ears. I don't hobnob with people like Chelsea Reynolds or Armand Lafitte because I'm of their ilk. I worked for Armand and roomed with Chelsea in college. And I don't own this apartment. I was house sitting for the owner who was sick and recently died. Right now, I'm looking for a new place to live because I can't even afford the utilities here."

She paused, unable to control the quivering of her lower lip.

"I'm telling you this because I care a great deal for you and I don't want you to think I did anything deliberately to embarrass you or anyone else. I lied because I had to. Because I needed a job and no one would hire me. I had no experience. For sixteen years, I was a housewife and a mother. Suddenly, my husband walked out on me and I was told it was my responsibility to go to work. Too bad the judge didn't tell the marketplace it was their responsibility to hire me. The only way I could get a job was to lie. And so I did."

Her voice was steady and her back was straight, but huge teardrops rolled down her cheeks. Max wanted to take her in his arms and console her, but he couldn't, just as he couldn't tell her that, after Damme, he had run a thorough check on her, that he already knew all about her, that he understood what she had done and why, that he loved her all the more for telling him the truth. The problem was that he couldn't reciprocate in kind. Until his mission was completed, Max's secrets had to remain Max's secrets, especially from Gaby. The coincidence of a major art forgery in the same auction as the Dinants had convinced him that December 11 was a date rife with potential danger. He was probably being watched. The last thing he wanted was for Gaby to get hurt. If they reestablished their romance, she would become a target.

"I can understand the first lie," he said, injecting into his voice an annoying patronizing tinge, "but to perpetuate it, particularly with someone with whom you've been intimate, is the ultimate betrayal." He stood and started for the door. "I was disappointed in you when you followed me to Damme. But that was minor to the way I feel at this moment."

"You don't understand," she said weakly, wondering why neither Max nor Garrett had been able to comprehend the complexity of her predicament. "I needed the money. I needed the job."

"You're right," Max said, exiting before he lost his resolve, forgot his vow of caution, and swept her into his arms. "I don't understand."

The door closed. Gaby simply stared at it. She was numb, incapable of feeling anything other than a gnawing, cavernous void. It was as if there had been a death and she had vented every ounce of emotion she possessed in the course of her mourning. In a way, there had been a death. Gabrielle Didier no longer existed. And it appeared as if the only person who mourned her passing was Gaby Thayer.

Gabrielle Didier had been her shield, her protection, her armor against the sticks and stones of a callous world. Gabrielle Didier had also been her fantasy, her dream come true, her storybook heroine come to life in a land of make-believe. But Gabrielle Didier had just become her bane and a curse upon her friends. Thanks to her, Armand was in more trouble than ever. Annabel's credibility was at stake, as was Garrett's, not to mention the two-hundred-year-old reputation of Castleton's.

Quickly, Gaby wiped her eyes and headed for the telephone. She would feel sorry for herself later. Just then, she had things to do. And to undo.

Fortunately, Garrett had not instructed anyone—the doorman, the receptionist, his secretary—that Gaby was persona non grata. She made it to his office without incident. But when she opened the door and walked in, she closed it quickly, knowing that if she didn't, he would probably be tempted to throw her through it.

"What are you doing here? I thought I told you to get out!"

"You did," she said, accepting his anger. "I came back because I have something important to tell you."

"Another lie? No thanks. I've had my fill of those."

"It's something you have to know. There's a strong possibility that the Caravaggio *Fortune Teller* is a forgery."

Garrett threw his head back and laughed.

"I love it! This little comedy of yours has more acts than one of Shakespeare's plays."

"It's not a comedy. And it's not funny, Garrett. You have to pull the painting from the auction. It's a fake."

"Really! How do you expect me to believe that—or anything you say?"

"Whatever you think of me, and you have every right to think the worst, you have to believe me now. You have to take the Caravaggio out of the Montgomery auction."

"I don't have to do anything, especially on your say-so."

She was willing to absorb his sarcasm. She deserved it. But she had to convince him that what she was telling him was the truth. She wished she could repeat the conversation she had had with Armand. Naturally, he too had been shocked at the notion of a forgery. He reminded her that the Caravaggio had been part of the Rosenberg Collection, part of Annabel's collection for years. It had been authenticated several times. He himself had examined it before the Montgomery Collection had been boxed for delivery to Castleton's. Then again, the painting had been crated and uncrated in several different locations. A switch could have been made at any point on the tour. Gaby thought someone would have noticed. Armand doubted that. Good forgeries were almost impossible to detect during a cursory viewing. An expert analysis was needed, and soon. If only she could convince Garrett.

"What about Max Richard's say-so?" she said, grasping at straws. "He's the one who told me this. Less than an hour ago. Would you take his word?"

Suddenly, Garrett was confused and nervous. He had a great deal of respect for Max Richard. But what did he have to do with this auction, that painting? How would he have known? Why would he have told Gaby? Why was she telling him?

"Who told Max?"

Gaby knew he was going to ask her that. Unfortunately, the only answer she had was the truth.

"I don't know. But he said his sources were reliable."

Garrett felt his face flush with anxiety. He stuffed his hands in his pockets and began to pace. He needed time to think, to decide what to do. Gaby knew what to do.

"There's only one way to find out whether or not the painting is a fake," she said.

"And what's that?"

"Have it examined by a scholar, by someone who would know the difference, someone like Pico Cellini."

"And where did you hear about Cellini? In your antiques class?"

"Look, Garrett. You can stand here and abuse me as much as you want, but after I leave you're still going to be faced with the problem of the Caravaggio. I'm trying to help. For now, let's concentrate on this. You can browbeat me later."

He turned away, toward the window, so she wouldn't see how bewildered he was. Giuseppe "Pico" Cellini was a master at detecting art forgeries. His reputation was international. A man of exceptional talent and artistic instincts, he was credited with restoring Caravaggio's *Judith and Holofernes* and *The Denial of Peter*, as well as authenticating or condemning hundreds of others. It didn't matter where she had heard of him, her suggestion was valid.

"I'll try to reach him."

He pointed to a chair, silently agreeing to let her stay while he attempted to locate Cellini. Garrett's secretary called Rome, Milan, Florence, Venice, Naples, wherever they had a number, wherever they thought Cellini might be. They left messages all over Italy. Finally, one of those messages was returned. Cellini was somewhere in Greece and couldn't be reached. He was expected to return to Rome in a month.

"I don't have a month," Garrett said despondently as he replaced the receiver in its cradle. He looked at Gaby. "Any other suggestions?"

"Yes, but you're not going to like it. Call Armand Lafitte."

"You're absolutely right. I don't like it at all." A few seconds before, Garrett had appeared thoroughly exhausted. At the mention of Armand's name, he was instantly energized, up, out of his chair, bounding around the room like a tornado in a box. "You must think I'm some kind of fool. Either that, or you're so daft you're beyond rational thinking." He shook his head and rolled his eyes as if he were standing in the presence of a certified madwoman. Then his expression changed. His eyes darkened and his mouth tightened into an even, unwavering line. "This is a setup. This whole thing is a setup. There is no fake Caravaggio. You just want me to believe that so that you can get your chum Armand Lafitte in here like some sort of hero. Is that it? He rides in on his white horse, examines the painting, tells me not to worry, that it's authentic, and then rides off into the sunset fully redeemed?" He leaned over, bringing his face close to hers. "You're good. You're very good. But I'm not going to fall for your little scam."

"It's not a scam!" Gaby insisted, rising from her seat. "You've got it all wrong."

"Maybe I do," he said, tapping his lips with his index finger, his eyes illuminated by the fire of a growing rage. "Maybe what it really is, is an attempt on the part of the Lafittes to destroy the Castletons. Why not? They hate us. We hate them. Yes. That sounds right. Armand is Annabel's lover. He's there when the paintings are crated for shipment. He substitutes a forgery, one he's commissioned, in fact. And then he waits. He waits for you to do your part, to come sniveling to me about a fake Caravaggio. I'm supposed to get frantic about my auction and my family's name and honor, and I'm supposed to run to Armand Lafitte for help. He says, yes, it's real. I auction it off. It's a fraud. Castleton's is ruined. And you and your friends spend the rest of your days slapping each other on the back and congratulating yourselves on your success. Well, I'd rather take my chances with whatever is in my storeroom than give any of you the satisfaction of relying on Armand Lafitte. Nice try, but no go. Now, as I said to you once today, get out!''

Gaby could see that further discussion was useless. He was so furious he was deaf to anything but his own distorted opinion.

"I'm going," she said, "but please, Garrett. Get someone, anyone, to examine that painting. Just in case, this once, I'm telling you the truth.''

It was one o'clock in the morning when the telephone rang. Gaby's eyes were closed, but she was dozing more than sleeping. When her hand gripped the receiver, she held it for a second, almost afraid to put it to her ear. It was only when she heard Oncle Bernard's voice calling her name that she responded.

"Gaby! Are you there? Are you all right? Gabrielle?''

"I'm here, Oncle Bernard. A little groggy, but otherwise okay.''

"I know it's late, but I couldn't wait any longer. This is important.''

Gaby's stomach knotted. His voice sounded strange. Quickly, she sat up in bed, rousing herself so that she could give him her full attention. Suddenly, her heart fluttered nervously.

"You're not sick are you?''

"No, no, *chérie*. I'm fine.''

"That's a relief. Well, then, listen, Oncle Bernard. If it's bad news, couldn't we put it off or ignore it altogether?''

"What makes you so sure it's bad news?''

"It's been that kind of day.''

"Today is another day.''

"True." She nodded and smiled. Oncle Bernard should have been either a philosopher or a preacher. He loved spouting esoteric, inspirational phrases. "Okay, what's up?"

"You have to meet me in Geneva as soon as possible."

"What? Why?"

He paused and in that tiny second, Gaby experienced a wave of fear that paralyzed her entire body.

"Because I think I've found the missing Dinant. I think I've located *The Marriage of Brussels*."

24

Gaby and Oncle Bernard practically ran to the small shop on the rue de l'Hotel de Ville in Geneva's Old Town. As they climbed the narrow, winding cobblestone streets, starting at the oldest of them all, the Grand'Rue, Gaby felt her heart pounding with nervous anticipation. Usually, she would have stopped to admire the medieval charm of this ancient section of town. She would have paused outside of number 40, where Jean-Jacques Rousseau had been born, or studied the architecture of the magnificent houses built in the seventeenth century by Italian refugees, which lined the rue de l'Hôtel de Ville. She would have taken the time to look up at the Cathedral of Saint Peter where John Calvin, the sixteenth-century French Huguenot, had preached his sermons of reformation. Today, however, all she wanted was to get to Madame Boussac's antiques shop.

It was a tiny cave, dark, cramped, and so overstocked that even the finest pieces, of which surprisingly there were many, seemed somewhat diminished in value. Here genuine, top-quality antiques sat alongside items that could only be described as junk. Bernard had warned her. Florence Boussac was a soft-hearted woman who often bought from those who needed to sell. Frequently, she paid for second-rate items rather than say no to someone down on his luck or appear to be doling out charity.

"That," Bernard said as the elderly madame went into the basement to fetch the tapestry, "was probably how she came to acquire *The Marriage of Brussels*. Someone in need of immediate cash must have brought it to her, knowing full well that she never turned anyone away."

"Wouldn't she have been able to see how valuable it was?" Gaby asked, keeping her voice down. "Looking around, it's clear that she has a discerning eye, when she chooses to use it."

"That she does."

"Then how come she didn't recognize it?"

"The tapestry is probably in great need of restoration. I only hope you'll be able to recognize it."

"Me, too."

"Eh, voilà!"

Florence Boussac, a woman of approximately seventy-five years, stumbled a bit under the weight of the folded tapestry. Bernard went to help her, taking one end of the ancient piece, asking her to hold the other taut, stretching it out to its full length. Since there wasn't a clear, flat spot in the entire shop, the tapestry bellied and arched depending on what lay beneath it. Bernard nodded. Gaby approached, feeling her body quiver with a mix of excitement and nerves.

Bernard had been correct. The piece required extensive repair. Seams where the loom had changed colors had split. Much of the relay work—the threads which connected various parts of the design—needed to be replaced. In several key spots, the actual armature of the tapestry had been damaged. And more than anything, the piece needed a bath. It needed to be cleansed of centuries of dust and grime so that not only could the beauty of its coloration be revived, but also so that its fibers of cotton, wool, and silk, made brittle by the harshness of central heating, could be softened.

Once Gaby accepted the dilapidated state of the tapestry, accepting that it could and would be restored to its original magnificence, she moved on to studying the design. It was a mystical pictorial with a millefleurs background dotted with several of the small animals representing the forest bestiaries so beloved by medievals: birds, rabbits, goats, sheep, squirrels, and hounds. In the center was a pavilion of blue cloth flecked with golden spirals. Holding open the two side flaps were the lion—symbolizing the strength and courage of the man, as well as the nation of Flanders—and the unicorn—symbolizing both the chastity of the lady and the land of Walloonia. Two flagpoles flanked the pavilion, one flying the standard of the unicorn, a blue ground with three yellow fleurs-de-lis, the other a red standard with a golden lion rampant. Standing inside, holding a single red carnation and examining a box of jewels being held by a young attendant, was a beautiful maiden gowned in gold. Her hair, dark, long to her shoulders, was crowned by a coronet of marguerite daisies.

Other allegorical symbols of the Middle Ages abounded. There were long-lived oak trees, known to be an important symbol of fidelity. There were rose bushes, white for virginity, red for charity and compassion; the many-seeded pomegranates denoting plenitude and hope; the hazelnut tree which was believed to have been endowed with magic powers of unity and immortality; holly to protect against danger; the English bluebell to chase away evil. A stag lurked in the background, because to hunt the stag was to seek faithfulness in love. Turtledoves fluttered above the pavilion, because the turtledove was believed to mate just once in its life. A butterfly hovered over the carnation, because according to the books of beasts, that winged insect signified love. A nightingale flew near the bride; not only did it signal the dawn of a new day, but it was viewed as a watchful guardian. At first, Gaby had to search her memory to understand why a pair of partridges rested beneath a bench just outside the tent. When she recalled their particular symbolism, she smiled. Though they posed innocently, their presence was meant to invite erotic thoughts, since by nature, it was believed, partridges exhibited extreme lustfulness and a great desire to cohabit.

Yet despite all the similarities and all the clues that might have led Gaby to declare this *The Marriage of Brussels*, she knew that many tapestries of the time depicted many of the same scenes and relied upon all of the same symbols. There were, however, certain undeniable scraps of evidence. Banding the top of the pavilion was the inscription: *à mon coeur*, "to my heart," a phrase known to have been inscribed on *The Marriage of Brussels*. Too, there were the crown of field daisies and the standards of the two families. But what clinched it for Gaby were the monograms: not only were the ER and the MM woven onto the collars of a panther and a weasel, respectively, but on a tiny banner flying from the top of the pavilion she noticed an ER and an MM connected by golden cords tied in a bow and known as a *lac d'amour*, a linking of letters by cords to symbolize the loyalty and love a couple had for each other. Gaby was certain. This tapestry depicted the marriage of Edouard de Rosier and his lady, the fair Marguerite of Dinant. This tapestry was *The Marriage of Brussels*.

With as much calm as she could muster, she looked up from the weaving and nodded to Bernard.

"Where did you get this?" he asked Madame Boussac, folding the tapestry as if he wasn't certain as to the level of his interest.

"It was so many years ago, I hardly remember."

She shrugged her shoulders, as if it should have been obvious that she would never have bothered to retain such an insignifcant fact.

"Florence, please. This is me, Bernard. I know you better. You have a memory like a vault. You know the provenance of every piece in this shop." He laughed congenially. "You probably know the provenances of every piece being sold in the Old Town. Who brought it to you?"

Madame Boussac enthroned herself in a red velvet chair. From a nearby table, she retrieved a package of unfiltered cigarettes, lit one up, and dragged deeply on it several times before answering.

"A German. It was after the war. He came to me late one night on the recommendation of a friend. He needed money and he needed it quickly. For passage to Argentina, I think. This was part of a huge lot. I didn't ask any questions. I gave him what I had and said good-bye. I don't know his name. I don't know whether or not he stole the goods he sold me or owned them. And I don't have a provenance on anything." She sucked on the cigarette, inhaling the bitter-smelling smoke, holding it in her lungs and then expelling it in a quick white puff. "Why are you so interested in this particular piece?"

"I'm Bernard's niece," Gaby said, taking a seat near the madame, unobtrusively insinuating herself into the conversation.

"I've been trying to get a new business started as an antiques broker. One of my clients seems to think this is a long-lost family heirloom. He asked me to find it. It would be a boon to my career if I did."

Florence nodded, the skin on her neck, loose and crepey, oscillating like reeds in the wind.

"Why do you think this is his?"

"The initials," Gaby said quickly. "Supposedly, one of his ancestors was Edouard de Rockeville, a Burgundian in the service of Philip the Good. Recently, some documents were found that spoke of a tapestry. Naturally, owning this means a lot to my client."

"How much is a lot?"

Now it was Bernard's turn. Examination of the piece was her province. Negotiation for its purchase was his. Gaby wasn't as adept at bargaining as he was. And she had no money to bargain with. The question was, how much did Madame Boussac want? And how much did Oncle Bernard have?

"Ninety thousand."

The old woman shook her head, grimacing as if his offer was insulting.

"Two hundred and forty," she said.

Bernard laughed, chuckling in that condescending way that dubbed her price absurd.

"It's in terrible shape, Florence. It will cost a minor fortune to repair."

"True, but still." She held her hands out and tilted her head to the side, looking for a moment like a street beggar panhandling for pennies instead of thousands of francs.

Bernard leaned back, affecting a casual, controlled pose. He tapped two fingers against his lips, thinking, stalling, letting the pressure mount. She lit one cigarette from the butt of the other, drawing in the smoke as if it contained the power of prescience, the ability to give her the foresight to know how hard to push, how high they would go.

"One hundred and fifty," Bernard said.

"Not enough," she responded.

"Too much, as far as I'm concerned." He stood and motioned for Gaby to do the same. Without another word, he started for the door.

"One hundred and eighty," she called out before Bernard's hand could turn the knob.

"I'm not authorized to spend more than one hundred and fifty thousand," Gaby said firmly.

"Okay, okay," she said, clearly surrendering. "But I want it in cash."

Bernard smiled as he removed an envelope from a secret pocket in the lining of his vest. He tossed it to Madame Boussac and waited patiently while she counted the Swiss francs. When she finished, she pointed to the tapestry.

"It's always a pleasure dealing with you, Bernard. À bientôt!"

Once they were out in the street, the tapestry safely hidden inside a large suitcase, Gaby asked Bernard about the money.

"It's the least I can do."

"What does that mean?"

He stopped and faced her. His hand gently grazed her cheek.

"It took a while, but I have finally figured out that you have been paying off Simone's hospital bills. She was my sister. She was my responsibility too. You wouldn't take money from me for that, so I'm giving it to you for this."

"But where did you get that kind of money? Did you wipe out your savings?"

"Let's just say that my bankbook doesn't look quite as pretty as it did before."

"Oncle Bernard!" She was upset. I should have thought this out better, she reprimanded herself. I should have arranged for a loan. No. Cancel that. I can't get a loan. According to the banking community, I'm a bad credit risk. I should have called Armand. He would have given me the money. Or Chelsea. She would have loaned it to me. "I can't let you do this."

"Why not? Just consider it an investment. Once it's sold, you'll repay me the principal plus an outrageously high bonus. How about it? Do we have a deal?"

"You bet we do!"

She grinned and hugged him, agreeing, suddenly wondering what she was actually going to do with The Marriage of Brussels. Would she offer it to Garrett to complete his trilogy? Would she offer it to Max so he could add to his collection and eventually donate the series to his country? Would she consign it to an auction house other than Castleton's? Would she sell it privately to a tapestry dealer or another collector, keeping the profits as well as the glory of the discovery for herself? Certainly that last had a definite appeal. She owed Lakewood and now Oncle Bernard a great deal of money. Thanks to the possibility of a Caravaggio fake, the success of the Montgomery auction was in jeopardy. Her business could use the boost that would come from the inherent publicity. Why not use this to her best advantage? Why not squeeze this opportunity for every plus and positive she could? Why not think of herself first? If she didn't plan for her future, who would?

"Why did you come?" Garrett asked, making certain the door to his office was securely locked.

"Because you asked," Armand said simply.

Garrett nodded and then turned, walked to the windows, and shut the blinds, closing out the night.

"Do you know why I asked you here?" He turned and fixed his eyes on Armand's face, watching for the truth in his expression in case what came from his mouth was a lie.

"No, but somehow I don't think it's for tea." Armand lifted his lip in a half smile that spoke of amused curiosity.

Garrett had been certain that this Caravaggio situation was a scam, that Gaby and Armand and Annabel Montgomery had conspired to embarrass him as reparation for barring Armand from Castleton's. But Armand's manner was cool, not combative. His body wasn't tense with anticipation. Garrett was impressed, but should he be convinced? A flush of anger rouged his cheeks. Irina had orchestrated Armand's banishment. If not for her, he wouldn't have to be convinced of anything; he wouldn't have to have this meeting; he wouldn't have to question the Caravaggio or anything related to this auction. But once again, he had allowed himself to be an instrument following the lead of her baton. Once again, he had permitted her to conduct the course of his life.

"*The Fortune Teller* is a fake." He said it quickly, still testing, still hoping to catch Armand off guard.

"What the hell are you talking about?"

The look of horror and outrage on Lafitte's face seemed genuine.

"I would have thought Gaby would have told you."

"Told me what?"

It was interesting that he didn't deny his association with Gaby.

"That Max Richard told her that informants told him that the Caravaggio in the Montgomery Collection is a fake."

"It can't be," Armand said, shaking his head, hoping he appeared befuddled, hoping not to expose Gaby. "I saw that painting in Annabel's apartment. I crated it myself. I . . ." He glared at Garrett. "Wait a minute. What are you trying to pull?"

Garrett held up his hands.

"Nothing. Really. If this is a joke, it's on me, too, old boy, so back off." Armand calmed. Garrett moved behind his desk. "Gaby suggested I call Pico Cellini to verify Max's tip, but Cellini was out of reach. Then she suggested I call you. I told her she was out of her mind. I may be out of my mind relying on you, but I need someone to tell me yea or nay. What do you say, Lafitte? Will you help me?"

"Will you trust me?"

"You're here, aren't you?"

"Bring it out."

For the next hour, while Armand examined the painting, Garret paced his office like an expectant father in a hospital waiting room. He watched as Armand stroked the canvas, checking paint application, stood back to study composition, touched the gilding on the frame, examined the signature. He watched as Armand bent over the large oil, looking for clues, hints, mistakes that would tell him then and there what he wanted to know.

"I don't know," he said. "I need to analyze the paint and the canvas so I can determine the age of the piece. Then I need to check my books on Caravaggio to be certain this is *The Fortune Teller* Annabel owned."

"The one from the Rosenberg Collection," Garrett said quietly.

"Yes," Armand said, looking at the other man squarely. "The one my father consigned to Sotheby's. The collection that started the feud between our two families." He pursed his lips, folded his arms across his chest, and glowered at Garrett. "You think I arranged this to get back at you for a host of past grievances, don't you?"

"It did enter my mind."

"Well, forget it! *The Fortune Teller* belonged to my grandfather. It's also one of the finest paintings the world has ever seen, and anyone who knows me at all knows I'm a man who loves art much too much ever to tamper with it, no matter what the reason.''

Garrett nodded, issuing a smile of conciliation.

''I do know that. I think that's why, in spite of my reservations, I called you. You don't want to desecrate this auction any more than I do.''

''No, I don't. For once, *mon ami*, it appears as if we're both on the same side.''

''True, but will we win the battle? We don't have a lot of time.''

Armand looked at the painting. It looked exactly like the one he had seen. If it was a fake, it was a masterpiece.

''All I can promise is that I'll do my best.''

Garrett extended his hand, bridging a chasm handed down like a legacy from father to son.

''That's good enough for me.''

Northwest of Paris, in the modest suburb of Courbevoie, in a building that looked more like a garage than a place in which precious antique tapestries and carpets were cleaned and restored, Gaby and Oncle Bernard stood on a metal balcony with the foreman of the Chevalier restoration studio and watched as *The Marriage of Brussels* was laid out on a moving ramp that passed between two enormous sets of brushes geared to extract the dust from its fibers. Slowly, transported by metal rollers, it moved up and under the stiff bristles charged with the task of sweeping away centuries of discoloration.

As they observed the dusting, it was explained that in the early nineteen hundreds, the dust from the cleaning of tapestries was sold to fertilizer manufacturers. During the occupation of France, from 1940 to 1945, it was sold to wine dealers who used it to age those bottles of wine which were in favor at the time. Currently, it was donated to the Pasteur Institute to be used in the manufacture of vaccinations against allergies.

''See, already the colors are much brighter,'' the foreman said, pointing to the section of the tapestry coming out from under the brushes. ''After this, we will examine the piece and make up our list of design elements to be restored. Then it will be washed, and then, once it's thoroughly cleaned and we can be certain about the actual colors, it goes into the studio for the needlework.''

"It's not in very good shape," Bernard said.

"The Messieurs Chevalier have instructed me that this takes priority over everything else. I have already arranged for overtime shifts.''

Bernard and the young man went on to discuss timing and delivery. While they spoke, Gaby stared in wonderment as foot by foot of the large, historic piece rolled into a canvas catch. She couldn't believe that she and Bernard had actually found *The Marriage of Brussels*. The chances had been so remote, so slim, and yet, there it was. What would people say? What would Garrett say? What would Max say? She and Oncle Bernard had talked about it briefly, but he was more concerned with restoring the tapestry to its original greatness, and she was still conflicted about what to do—whether the tapestry should be united with *The Courtship* and *The Garden of Love* and auctioned off in a package or sold privately to Max.

Once the last portion of the tapestry was finished, two burly men rolled the oversized basket into an elevator that deposited them on the second floor. Gaby, Bernard, and the foreman followed. As they walked through the room where the needlework was done, Gaby paused. There was something so aesthetically wonderful about this large room with wooden floors, enormous skylights, and rows of women bent over their work. Everywhere Gaby looked, she found color and texture. There were huge baskets filled with scraps of thread. There were cubbies stocked with spools of cotton, woolen, and silk threads, each grouping a rainbow of innumerable tints and hues, each dyed in hopes of matching the rainbows of the past.

Though tapestries were originally woven, restoration was carried out with a needle. The weavings were stretched tight between two large round parallel posts known as *ensouples*, or beams. It was slow, tedious work. If the armature was damaged, which was frequently the case, the first thing that was done was to reweave the warp. Using either wool or cotton, parallel threads filled the empty spaces, anchored by knots onto the existing frame. Once the warp was sound, the weft, or the decor, was completed. With great delicacy, the women who worked the beams, using techniques they learned during their apprenticeships, revived the glories of their predecessors, stitch by stitch.

Reluctantly, Gaby left the workroom and headed beyond it to where *The Marriage of Brussels* was laid out on the floor. Bernard and Chevalier's experts were already on their hands and knees, analyzing what had to be done. They listed separations, missing relays—stitches which join different-color portions—damaged warp, faded or badly worn threads. They turned the piece over and scrutinized the back. Gaby also examined the piece. She found several spots where the front remained intact, but the stitches in the back had thinned to the point of disintegration. Many of the golden threads that drew the lady's gown had frayed. Two of the corners were ripped. And there was an odd six-inch section in the lower hem which appeared to have been slit and restitched, indicating recent—within the last hundred years—handling.

It took hours for the list to be completed, but once it was, *The Marriage of Brussels* was carted into a huge, white, high-ceilinged room outfitted with the most up-to-date, state-of-the-art laundering equipment available. As the tapestry was laid out in a movable crib which was suspended above an enormous pool, Gaby and Bernard were treated to a tour of the computerized bath.

Here, water was treated to be as neutral and soft as possible, carefully weighed so that the pressure on the tapestry didn't destroy fragile fibers. The type of soap, the concentration of soap in the water, the number of times the tapestry would be lowered into the water, the length of time it stayed in the water, how much air would circulate around it—everything was tested and analyzed.

As the computer operator took her place and began to press the buttons that activated the system, something inside Gaby's head clicked also. She watched the crib inch its way closer to the water. Those stitches. That six-inch strip. Why was that bothering her? Why did it seem so strange, so out of place? It was what Garrett had told her in Steamboat Springs. That the owner of the tapestry had given a makeshift deed to the German. Could he have hidden that deed inside the hem?

"Stop!"

Panicked, convinced she was right, she ran toward the control booth, begging the young woman to halt the procedure. A button was pressed. The crib was halted in midflight.

"Raise it up."

The young woman did as she was told.

"I need to check the hem," she called to the foreman. "How do I get to it?"

"There." He pointed to a metal pathway running alongside the interior wall. "On the catwalk."

"What are you doing?" Oncle Bernard shouted, confused and upset by her behavior as he watched Gaby ascend the ladder and step out onto the narrow ledge.

Without answering, she made her way to the far edge of the tapestry, hugging the wall, trying to control an attack of vertigo, swallowing the nausea rising in her throat. Finally, she lowered herself to her knees and, holding on with one hand, bent over the piece, turned it over, and located the strange stitching. Using a key she had pulled from her purse before mounting the ladder, she slit the threads and reached inside. Her hand shook as her fingers closed around a folded piece of paper.

Carefully, she pulled it out and made her way back to the ladder, down and onto the main floor. Bernard was waiting.

"What is it?"

"It's written in German and so I can't make out more than a few words, but I'm convinced that this little slip of paper is going to tell us who owned *The Marriage of Brussels*."

Bernard signaled the controller to start up the machine. Then he returned his attention to his niece. Without saying a word, she handed him the piece of paper.

> This is to certify that I am hereby gifting my friend, Colonel Dichter Bruener, with *The Marriage of Brussels* tapestry and thereby transferring ownership to him. I do solemnly swear that it is authentic, the seventh in a series known as the Dinant tapestries. It is mine to give as it was part of the dowry granted me by my wife's family at the time of our marriage. My wife is now deceased.
> March 19, 1941
> Pieter von Gelder

Bernard's German was rusty, but with the help of a Chevalier staffer, he translated the note. Gaby's face had turned ashen.

"Pieter von Gelder was the only person to respond to the ads."

"What ads?"

"The ones Garrett placed in the European papers asking if anyone knew anything about the Dinants."

"So?"

"So he's alive, and I'll bet he wants this back," she said, holding up the incriminating note. "The Belgians aren't proud of the fact that so many of their own buddied up to the Nazis. They frown on collaborators. Pieter von Gelder is a wealthy man with a solid-citizen reputation. This note could destroy him."

Bernard considered what she said. He took it a step further.

"What if this tapestry didn't really belong to him in the first place?"

"What do you mean?"

"His wife may have died, but that doesn't mean she was without a single living relative."

"If we put it up for sale and a long-lost brother or sister were to show up, would we be liable?"

Bernard shook his head.

"I don't think so. We have this as proof of an exchange of ownership and we have our own bill of sale proving that we paid for it."

A soft whooshing sound attracted Gaby's attention. Gentle sprays were wetting the tapestry. They shut off and the crib dipped the ancient weaving into a bath of mildly soapy water. The crib lifted. The sprays rinsed the soap. The process began again.

"Do you know what we have to do?" she said, suddenly grinning.

"No. What?"

"*Cherchez la femme!*" she exclaimed as if it were so obvious they should have thought of it hours before. "We have to find his wife."

"Gabrielle, my pet, the man says she died."

"I know, but when or where she died doesn't matter. When and where she married Pieter von Gelder does. If we can find their marriage certificate, we'll know her name. If we know her name, we just might be able to find out if she has any descendants.''

"You're a clever girl," Bernard said, hugging her tightly.

"It's in the genes," she said, winking at him, so grateful to him for his trust and his amiable nature.

"I do happen to have some friends in Brussels who might be able to help."

"Honestly?" Gaby's entire being had become infused with excitement. Her face glowed and for the first time in months, she felt hopeful.

"Since von Gelder is a known commodity, it'll be easy to find out his age and determine approximately when he might have married. Then I'll ask them to check the licenses issued in Brussels, Antwerp, Dinant, and maybe one or two other major cities within a span of five years or so. If, however, von Gelder chose a remote little farm town as the site of his wedding, we may never discover the name of his bride."

"I know we decided that you were going to stay here to oversee the restoration of the tapestry and I was going to return to New York to set up its sale, but if you'd like, I'll stay in Paris and you can go to Belgium."

"No, ma petite. You go home. When this is done, I'll fly it to New York personally. As for our detective work, as soon as I know something, you'll know."

But what would that something be? she wondered. Was this search for Frau von Gelder akin to opening Pandora's box? Was Herr von Gelder a threat? Would the publicizing of her role and Bernard's in the unearthing of The Marriage of Brussels put either of them in danger? Take risks, Tante Simone had said. But how great should those risks be?

It took Armand three weeks to complete his analysis of the Caravaggio. On the night of December first, ten days before the auction, Garrett initiated a gathering of the Castleton family for a presentation of Armand's findings. Annabel Montgomery and Gaby were also invited to attend.

They gathered in the private viewing salon of the gallery. Just off Garrett's office, soundproof, windowless, with a private elevator operated by a single key, it was the room in which Armand had been sequestered these past three weeks, the room in which he had conducted his investigation. For this evening's meeting, the Caravaggio in question was poised on a large easel at the front, in the center. Eight chairs had been positioned in a single curved line so that no one's view was obstructed. With Armand standing alongside the painting and Garrett on the opposite side of the room, however, only six chairs were filled: Garrett Sr., Charlotte, Bentley, Annabel, Gaby, and Irina.

"I've called you here because we have a crisis," Garrett said, rejecting politesse and preamble. "About a month ago, it was brought to my attention that *The Fortune Teller*, the painting we intended to use as the centerpiece of our upcoming auction, was a possible forgery."

The senior Castletons audibly gasped. Irina's face tightened into a hard, iron mask, her eyes trained on Armand. Gaby stole a quick glance at Annabel. Armand had told her about the forgery. In what Gaby was coming to recognize as a standard Annabel Montgomery response, her only concern was how the situation would affect Armand. She had presented him with this collection as a prenuptial affirmation of her love, and she was determined that nothing should sully that expression of emotion.

"For several weeks, Armand Lafitte has been studying the work. He says it's a phony."

"Takes one to know one, they always say," Irina mumbled to Bentley, who was patently ignoring his niece.

"On what basis did you reach your conclusion?" Garrett Sr. asked, surprising everyone by not questioning Armand's presence or challenging his credentials.

Armand shot the elder Castleton a grateful smile.

"First of all, let me say that it's an outstanding copy. If the dean of Italian forgers, Icilio Ioni, were still alive, I'd swear this was his handiwork. But he's been dead a long time, so I'm certain it's not his. I'm also certain this is not from the brush of Michelangelo Merisi da Caravaggio. So much so, I'd stake my reputation on that."

"That's so generous of you," Irina sneered, "since you no longer have a reputation of any worth."

Annabel leaned forward so she could eyeball Irina and deliver a message: back off! Gaby shifted in her seat, growing more and more uncomfortable by the minute. Armand remained composed, intent on what he was saying, not what Irina was saying or what others were thinking.

"I performed several tests on the paint, all of which came up positive, but it's an easy matter to mix oil with lead chips to duplicate the chemical structure of paint in the seventeenth century. The gilding on the frame is also of the period, but that too can be faked without difficulty." Armand pointed to the thumb of the young man. "Even the spatula-shaped thumb that distinguished most of the figures in Caravaggio's paintings has been replicated. However, the forger made several mistakes."

Garrett brought out another easel on which Armand placed three poster-sized photographs, one that looked like the painting in front of them and two others that looked identical to each other, but slightly different from the painting.

"This," he said, pointing to the first one, "is a picture of *The Fortune Teller* that hangs in the Musei Capitolini in Rome. This second one hangs in the Louvre. And this one," he said, pointing to the last photograph on the easel, "used to hang in the London apartment of Annabel Montgomery. Now, let's study the evidence," he said in a voice that reminded Gaby of the first time she had seen Armand, lecturing at the New School. "As you can see, the forger copied the composition of Annabel's painting with extraordinary precision. He duplicated every detail, down to the rakish tilt of the young man's hat and the exact number of strands on the feathers in that hat.

"He made certain he used the face of Mario Minnitti, a Roman painter believed to have been the model for several of Caravaggio's works, including the Louvre's *Fortune Teller* and Annabel's, rather than the face we see in the Capitolini version. He re-created a worn paint surface, deliberately wearing it particularly thin on the youth's hand, a fact that's well documented in scholarly books on Caravaggio. But," he said, wishing he had a piece of litmus paper to test whether the silence in the room was respectful or hostile, "everything is not as perfect as it appears to be."

Reaching behind Garrett's desk, he removed several papers from an attaché case, placing one alongside the picture of the Capitolini *Fortune Teller,* placing one next to the Montgomery version, and holding the third one in his hand.

"In 1965, in preparation for a Paris exhibition of Caravaggio, all three examples of *The Fortune Teller* were subjected to intense analysis. Because the first two hung in public places, the results of those examinations were published worldwide. Because this last was privately owned, the documents were sent to the owner, Philip Montgomery, to the Italian minister of culture, to several scholars researching Caravaggio and others of his time, and to a Frenchwoman known to be cataloguing the where-abouts of works done by seventeenth-century artists, Josette Rosenberg Lafitte.''

Charlotte Castleton allowed a smile to dance across her lips at the mention of her old, dear friend, a smile that was not lost on Josette's son or her own.

"For the uninitiated, a pentimento is the emergence of an earlier form in a painting that has been altered or painted over. Today, they're easily found with the use of special X-ray equip-ment. Pentimenti were not unusual in paintings of that long-ago era. Canvas was very expensive. If an artist wasn't happy with the way a painting was evolving, he simply painted over it. If he couldn't afford new canvases, he reused old ones. Also, some artists, and Caravaggio was one, made it a habit to sketch their scenes directly on the support in dark tones that weren't easily hidden.

"This is an X ray of the Capitolini *Fortune Teller*. Look closely and you can see that beneath the youth's sleeve there is a fully drawn face of a woman either asleep or dying. Oddly enough, there were no pentimenti uncovered in the Louvre paint-ing, which probably inspired our forger to paint on a clean canvas. What he didn't know, because it was only printed in limited documents, was that the X rays taken in 1965 of the Montgomery *Fortune Teller* showed that Caravaggio debated about using the model and tilted head of the first painting, but opted instead to use the Minnitti face and a more upright pose.''

He paused, giving his audience time to absorb what he had said. Then, he unfolded the piece of paper he held in his hand.

"This is an X ray of the painting sitting here before you. It was done two weeks ago by one of the curators at the Met. I have signed affidavits attesting to the procedure and its results. The X ray is blank. There is no pentimento hiding on this canvas. It's a fake.''

"I think you're a fake!'' Irina was on her feet. Her body was rigid, but her eyes blazed with hot indignation. "I think you concocted this whole scheme to humiliate my family and to destroy the Castleton name."

Fighting for control, Armand answered her calmly.

"What you *think* is irrelevant compared to what I *know*. This painting is a fraud, and if it's allowed to come under the hammer, Castleton's name will be ruined."

"And if we pull this off the block, I suppose you expect your name to be hailed throughout the art world as some kind of hero."

"I don't expect anything."

Without responding, Irina turned to her brother. "Who told you this might be a fake?"

Garrett hesitated, but the moment he did he knew he had to tell the truth. Irina had guessed. His pause had already provided her with confirmation.

"Gaby."

"Gaby! Oh, that's rich. Gaby Thayer, that model of honesty, of forthrightness. That paragon of integrity and moral fiber!" Irina laughed, filling the room with a harsh, cacophonous sound. "What a fool you are, Garrett. This woman makes an ass out of you, and yet when she comes to you with something as outlandish as a forged Caravaggio, you believe her. I wouldn't believe her if she told me the sky was blue. The woman lied about everything including her name, for God's sake!"

She strode over to Gaby's chair and looked down at her. "Who told you this charming little story? Your fairy godmother?"

"Max Richard." Gaby stood, meeting Irina eye to eye, feigning a confidence she didn't truly feel.

"He knew for a fact that the paintings had been switched?"

"An informant told him."

"Who was the informant?"

"I don't know. He said he had his sources. I believed him."

"I'll bet you believed him when he told you he loved you, too."

Again, she laughed. Gaby wasn't amused. Irina was being cruel, and not just to her. Gaby saw the hurt in Garrett's eyes. He felt betrayed. She didn't blame him. More than anything, she longed to lash out at Irina, but now wasn't the time for personal vendettas.

"It doesn't matter who or what I believed. Armand has given you undeniable proof that Max's informant was correct. The painting is a forgery."

"That much seems clear." Garrett Castleton, Sr., rose and walked behind the desk, taking a seat that afforded him a better view of the players acting before him. "What isn't clear, Irina, my dear, is why you're protesting the evidence."

"Because the facts don't add up. She's his mistress," Irina said, pointing a finger at Annabel as if the elegant Englishwoman were a direct descendant of Hester Prynne. "And she's his tool. The only other corroborating evidence he has is the word of his mother! Really, Father, I don't understand why you don't see it. Together with Etienne Lafitte, these three cooked up this entire scheme as a way of humiliating you while, at the same time, restoring his precious name. It's all too obvious."

"What's obvious is that you still haven't forgiven Armand for dumping you."

Annabel spoke quietly, but her words exploded with nuclear force. Irina spun around like a gyro, her eyes wide and wild.

"What are you talking about?"

"You. Armand. The fact that you and he had a brief affair several years ago. The fact that you wanted desperately to marry him, but he told you he didn't love you. The fact that all of this occurred just weeks before the 1986 January Antiques Fair and that when, at that fair, he and Vincent Prado had their set-to, you took advantage of it by initiating a whisper campaign meant to destroy Armand so that you could get revenge on him for leaving you. That's what I'm talking about."

The silence in the room was palpable. People assumed awkward poses in an effort not to seem as if they were staring. Irina appeared stricken. For several moments, she stood frozen to the spot, unmoving, hardly breathing. She looked to her mother, but Charlotte seemed too confused to be of any real help. She didn't dare look at anyone else. The last thing she wanted to see was the smug satisfaction she knew had to be coloring Garrett's face or the disappointment on her father's.

Though she fought it, her eyes were drawn to Armand. Had he looked at her with even the slightest feeling, had he offered her a hint that perhaps he had loved her as intensely as she had loved him, had he displayed the slightest remorse, she might have dropped the matter. But when she looked at him, he was standing at Annabel's side, his arm resting affectionately on her shoulder.

"I find it admirable that you would want to come to the defense of your lover," Irina said, her voice low and venomous, "but who in polite society could possibly believe a trollop like you?" She smiled like a crocodile baring its teeth. "Everyone in London knows you and Armand got your jollies cuckolding a fine gentlemen like Philip Montgomery, but if you think I'm going to allow you to attack me as a way of deflecting attention away from your attempt to perpetrate this dastardly hoax on my family, you're sadly mistaken. If Armand didn't commission this fraud, who did? Who made the switch? And where is the real Caravaggio?"

Irina folded her arms across her chest, accepting the ensuing turmoil as a victory. Everyone spoke at once, advancing theories, making guesses, offering advice. In the midst of the clatter, Gaby left the room. She knew someone who might hold the answers to those questions. All she had to do was find him.

It took Gaby half an hour to reach Max. She tried calling him in New York, but when she heard his answering machine click on, she immediately dialed London and asked Prudence to track him down.

"Have him return my call as soon as he can," she said. "It's an emergency."

As she paced around Garrett's office, she tried to understand how everything had gotten so fouled up and why all the blame was being focused on Armand. A host of emotions battered at her, but the one that dominated was guilt. Guilt about possibly devastating Garrett's chances at taking over Castleton's and making him look foolish in front of his family. Guilt about putting Armand and his family in a position requiring such strong defense. Guilt about exposing Annabel to needless embarrassment. Guilt about not giving Garrett *The Marriage of Brussels*. Guilt about not telling Max she had found it. She wanted to scream from the weight of it all.

Maybe when Max called she would tell him about the tapestry. Maybe she would offer it to him. Maybe it would be the catalyst that would bring them together again.

"You don't barter for love," Oncle Bernard had told her when she had intoned this same soliloquy in Paris.

"And you can't buy forgiveness," he had said, when she had rationalized that giving Garrett the tapestry might make amends for the pain she had caused him.

"What about repaying a friend, Oncle Bernard," she said to the air. "How do I do that?"

Garrett's private phone rang. Her body jerked from the noise. Quickly, she brought the receiver to her ear.

"Gaby?"

She couldn't believe that the sound of his voice could evoke a smile, especially now, when her entire being was so taut with tension. But it did.

"Thanks for returning my call."

"Prudence said it was an emergency. Are you all right?"

Was that concern she heard? W is it possible he still cared?

"I'm fine. It's Armand who's in trouble."

"What's the matter?"

"Remember that tip you gave me about the Caravaggio?"

"Yes."

"You were right. Garrett had Armand analyze the painting and it's a fake. But Irina's questioning Armand's findings. She's making it seem as if he arranged the whole thing. I thought that since you were the one who first heard about it, you might know who's really behind it."

"I'm afraid I don't."

His voice had changed. She heard him grow distant, retreating from her. She wanted to reach inside the telephone and pull him back. She wanted to retrieve the warmth of moments before, the love they had shared months before, but clearly none of that was possible. *They* weren't possible.

Forget it, she told herself. *This isn't about us. This is about Armand.*

"You don't know, or you won't say?"

"I don't know."

"Max," she said, wiping away the tears that had gathered in her eyes, wishing it was as easy to wipe away the memories that had flooded her mind, "my friend's reputation is on the line. You obviously knew something or you wouldn't have called me.

Who told you about the forgery? Who are your mysterious sources?''

"I can't tell you."

"Again, you can't!" Anger built up inside her like a steel structure, solid and immovable. "I thought you would help me."

"I don't have what you want . . ."

She slammed the phone down too quickly to hear him say, "but I can get it."

Garrett's blood pressure had spiked. His face felt flushed. His temples felt swollen. He could almost feel his blood boiling as it coursed wildly through his body. This was a genuine crisis. Despite Irina's protestations, Armand's analysis clearly proved the Caravaggio was bogus. If it had gone on the block and been sold, sooner or later its fraudulent nature would have been discovered and Castleton's would have been ruined. As it was, announcing that they were pulling the painting from the auction would cause more of a stir than was comfortable. In a business based on authenticity and credibility, one bad apple prompted people to worry that perhaps the rest of the bushel was tainted as well. Unless the real Caravaggio was returned, the Montgomery auction, an occasion they had all counted on to be one of the family's triumphs, was destined to become one of the biggest busts in the history of the salesroom.

Naturally, concern for his own future surfaced. How much of the blame for this scandal would fall on his shoulders? How would this affect him? What would happen to his career? Castleton's reputation? His reputation? Garrett forced himself to suppress his fears. This was not the time for personal reflection. All around him people were speculating and attacking and antagonizing each other. Irina was hurling insults at Armand and Annabel. Armand, ever the gentleman, was permitting Irina to vent her rage at being jilted without any form of counterattack. Bentley, who had never been fond of his niece, had positioned himself physically and vocally alongside his friend Annabel. Charlotte was trying to do the motherly thing and align herself with her daughter, an extremely difficult task. But the sight which touched Garrett most deeply was the sight of his father standing in front of the fake Caravaggio, his face drawn and colorless.

"Stop it!" he shouted, insinuating himself into the center of the fracas. "Instead of wasting precious time accusing each other, why don't we try to figure out how to salvage this situation?"

"Garrett's right," Charlotte said, walking over to her son. "I should think the most important order of business is to find the real Caravaggio."

"Garrett's right," Irina mimicked. "If your darling Garrett had allowed me to review the collection in the first place, we wouldn't be in this fix."

"Meaning what?" Garrett demanded.

"Meaning that this fake was probably part of *her* collection all along," Irina snapped, turning from Garrett to Annabel. "Clearly, Lady Montgomery has the same distorted vision you do, my dear brother. Whether it's a painting or a lover, it seems that neither one of you can tell the difference between true and false."

"But you can," Armand said, his voice low and powerful, rumbling like thunder in a heat storm. "You know all about the subtleties that distinguish masterpieces of art from masterpieces of deception. We discussed it many times, you and I. We discussed how talented art forgers are, how sad it is that they don't use their talent to create something new rather than duplicate something already done. I remember you saying you thought it was a shame that people didn't recognize and appreciate the skill of the better forgers."

"What's the point of all this?" Garrett asked, guessing where Armand was headed, surprised at himself for hoping he was wrong.

"The point is, I'm certain that Irina is the one who commissioned this fraud!"

Every eye turned toward him. He returned the stare of only one.

Irina rocked back on her heels, momentarily dizzy and disoriented, as if her lungs had collapsed from the blow dealt by her one-time lover.

"What are you babbling about?" Quickly, Irina dressed

herself in irate indignation. "How dare you accuse me of such a thing!"

"I dare because you dared to take my name and Annabel's name and, yes, even the Castleton name lightly." Armand's sense of outrage was obvious. "I dare because you stole a valuable piece of art, a painting that belongs to history, not to you!"

"This is not the way," Garrett said, shaking his head. "This could have destroyed Castleton's. This could have brought our house down. This is not the way."

"Stop it!" Irina shouted, ignoring her brother, directing her anger at Armand. "Stop pretending you care about what happens to Castleton's. You're a Lafitte! An enemy! How do we know you weren't the one who commissioned this fraud? Of course! That's it, don't you see?" she said, ranting wildly, looking to her mother, her uncle, and finally her father for confirmation. "He did it so he could end what his father started. He wants to ruin us. Once a traitor, always a traitor."

"That's not true." Garrett spoke quickly, before Armand could utter a single word in his own defense. "At first, I will admit I also thought this scheme had Armand's fingerprints on it, but, Irina, the evidence is pointing directly at you."

"And you love it, don't you?"

"No," he said quietly and with honest sadness, "I don't."

Irina fairly shouted with disbelief. "Oh, please! Don't lie! Don't pretend to care about me just so you can score extra points with Father or impress the others. We've never been close. We've always loathed and distrusted each other. Why pretend anything different? So that you can costume your slimy accusations in a cloak of sympathetic regard? For as long as I can remember you've blamed me for everything that's gone wrong in your life, including Cynthia Hawthorne and Gabrielle Didier. Each time you've made a poor choice, rather than own up to your own incompetence you've tried to shift the blame to me. Why not now?" Irina turned to her father, her hysteria mounting. "He's lying to protect himself. He's probably in cahoots with them. He would do or say anything to make certain you choose him over me."

"There is no choice to be made," Garrett Sr. roared with authority. "No one is taking over anything. I am still in charge of Castleton's International and I want the Caravaggio returned. Do you have it, Irina?''

For a moment, defiance continued to dominate Irina's face. But then her lower lip quivered.

''Yes,'' she whispered meekly.

''Speak up,'' her father demanded.

''Yes,'' she said, more loudly this time. ''I have the real Caravaggio! Yes, I commissioned the forgery!''

The silence was deafening. It was as if her words had sprayed the room with poisonous gas, stunning each person there. Each face registered shock, not so much at the admission as at the fact of what she had done. Each face displayed emotion: Charlotte was both distressed and embarrassed; Bentley was disgusted; Armand and Annabel appeared oddly sympathetic. Garrett was ambivalent. He vacillated between anger and pity, fury and disbelief that she would have gone so far. His father, however, was the picture of rage.

''First you will return that painting,'' he said, in a tone that discouraged debate. ''Then you will clean out your desk. You no longer work for Castleton's. Nor will you ever work for Castleton's again.''

Irina staggered. She grabbed onto the nearest chair and held onto it as if she feared that any second the floor would open and she would fall into an abyss.

''You don't mean that,'' she said, knowing that he never said anything he didn't mean.

''You went too far,'' he said, his voice softer, but no less definite. ''You almost destroyed the only thing that matters to all of us, the only thing that binds us together even in this ragtag package known as a family. You were about to destroy our name. If you had, there would have been nothing for either you or your brother to take over. Nothing!''

Only Charlotte knew how close Garrett was to tears. Only Charlotte knew how deeply he felt Irina's betrayal. Even so, the others looked away or lowered their eyes.

''Thanks to the two of you,'' Irina said bitterly, glaring at Armand and her brother as she started for the door, ''now I have nothing.''

She opened the door and walked through it, her head high, her back straight. Only someone who had seen her face would have known that her spirit had been broken. The door closed behind her, and for several minutes an uneasy silence prevailed.

Finally, Garrett Sr. broke it by asking Armand, "How did you know about this?" He was disturbed by his daughter's actions, but there were still several unanswered questions. "And if you suspected Irina, why didn't you come forward sooner?"

"I didn't put the pieces together until tonight," Armand said. "Quite frankly, before that I was only concerned with the painting and how, if it was a fake, all this would affect Gaby."

"Who did you say told Gabrielle about the painting?" Garrett said, turning to his son.

"Max Richard."

The senior Castleton chuckled, as if he had remembered something so obvious, it was funny.

"What is it now?" Charlotte asked.

"We could have saved a great deal of time if we had simply spoken to Max. If he said it was a fake, it had to be. He's not a man who gives out false information."

"You sound very certain of that," Garrett Jr. said. "Why?"

"Because Max Richard is an intelligence agent for Interpol. If he got a tip, he would have investigated it thoroughly before passing it on."

Gaby, who had missed most of what had gone on, but had returned in time to hear Garrett Sr.'s last remarks, was too stunned to control herself.

"Max Richard is an agent for Interpol?"

"Has been most of his life," Garrett Sr. said casually, unaware of the impact of his words.

Gaby's head reeled. How dare he talk about trust and truth and honesty! How dare he walk out on her because she hadn't been totally up front with him! All the time he was scolding her for her so-called duplicity, he was the ultimate practitioner of duplicity. An Interpol agent! She was furious. With him. With herself. To think that she had felt less than worthy compared to him. To think that she had believed he was the most honest man she had ever met. To think that she had almost given him *The Marriage of Brussels* because he claimed he wanted to give it to the government of Belgium. He had sounded so noble, so altruistic, so philanthropic. For all she knew, he was conning her. For all she knew, he was tracking Pieter von Gelder for Interpol and needed that little piece of paper she had found so he could convict the old man of war crimes. For all she knew, his intentions had never been honorable—about anything.

"If no one minds, I have an announcement to make," she said, noting with pleasure how rapidly the room silenced and all attention was directed at her. "Recently, my uncle and I located the missing Dinant tapestry. We found *The Marriage of Brussels,* and if it's all right with all of you, I'd like to consign it to Castleton's to be auctioned off on the eleventh as part of Garrett's Love Trilogy."

If she had tossed a bushel of live firecrackers into the center of the room, she couldn't have engendered a more explosive response. Everyone swirled around her, asking a thousand questions, too fired up to wait for answers. Garrett forgot himself and took her in his arms, hugging her, holding her, speaking to her as if there were no one else there.

"Thank you," he whispered. "After the way I treated you, I don't deserve this."

She smiled and said, "No one deserves it more."

Secretly, she delighted in knowing that by giving the Dinant to Garrett she was denying Max the one thing he claimed to want most in this world. What she didn't know—what she couldn't know—was that she had just done exactly what Max would have wanted her to do.

25

"It's been a long time," Garrett Sr. said as he opened the door of the town house and faced his old friend.

"Too long, I'd say."

Etienne embraced Garrett without hesitation or embarrassment, hugging the other man tightly, choking back a wave of nostalgia that threatened to overwhelm him. Behind them, Charlotte and Josette enjoyed their own reunion. They cried and laughed and clung to each other as if a few moments of togetherness could erase many years of separateness. When, finally, the exuberant emotions of reconciliation had subsided, Garrett invited everyone to join him for drinks in the library.

Once settled, Garrett rang for Harold, who arrived seconds later with a bucket of champagne, followed by one assistant carrying a tray of glasses, another toting a tray of canapés. When the champagne had been poured, the servants had gone, and everyone had a glass, Garrett raised his and looked directly at Etienne. With moist eyes and a tremulous voice, he proposed a toast: "To a friendship strong enough to outlive our best efforts to kill it."

"Hear, hear!"

The men bivouacked on the sofa nearest the fireplace and attempted to encapsulate almost thirty years by linking their personal history to world history, by using business successes or failures as signposts along the road of change. Josette and Charlotte reknotted their ties in a more feminine way, bonding the way women do by reestablishing a friendly intimacy, inquiring about primary concerns—health, children, friends, dashed hopes, dreams come true.

"I wish I could say you haven't changed," Josette said, smiling at Charlotte, remembering her as a young, willowy blonde, recalling how that had contrasted with her own dark, sultry kind of pulchritude, "but I'm afraid we've both turned into old women."

Charlotte laughed, in tune with Josette's thoughts. She too had noticed how time had diminished the differences between them. Now, with both of them silvered and somewhat stooped, the sameness of age predominated.

"I wish I could have watched your children grow," Josette continued, her face taking on a wistful cast, "and been around to celebrate birthdays and anniversaries. I wish we could have shared these past years instead of having to catch up now."

"I know how you feel," Charlotte said gently. "I can't begin to tell you how many times I needed your ear and craved your friendship, but that's in the past. This is the present, and since we don't know what the future holds, let's be grateful we're all still here and that we found our way back to each other."

"You should be immensely proud of your son, Garrett," Etienne said, touched by the sight of his wife and her best friend embracing each other. "He's endowed with a great deal of courage."

"You mean for him to call Armand and entrust him with something as delicate as authenticating a painting?"

"That, and," he said with a sly grin, "sending Josette and me an invitation to tonight's auction without asking or telling you, without knowing how you would react."

Garrett thought for a moment. He hadn't known about the invitation until after that night in the viewing room. Then, hoping to find his father softened by the afterglow of Armand's daring rescue of Castleton's, Garrett Jr. had announced that he had invited the Lafittes to be his personal guests at the auction and that they had accepted. What Etienne said, however, was true: Garrett could not have known whether his father's reaction would have been positive or negative.

"It's interesting. Over the years, I've attributed many qualities to my children and accused them of having many faults. Amazingly, I never ascribed courage to my son, but you're right. Inviting you without my say-so was probably the bravest thing he's ever done. And the smartest."

Both men laughed, each exhibiting regret over the wasted years and wasted emotion their feud had caused.

"As long as we're exchanging compliments," Garrett said, "allow me to praise your offspring. I was extremely impressed with Armand, not only for his obvious scholarship, but for his tact, his generosity of spirit, and his chivalry." He sipped his champagne slowly, almost shyly. "I'm sure you know it was my daughter who orchestrated this fiasco."

Etienne nodded.

"Somehow I feel it's all my doing. Thinking about it afterward, discussing it with Charlotte, it seems clear that Irina's desperation was born from her need for my approval. Obviously, I was insensitive and blind to those needs. Had I been a better father, had I been more loving and affectionate when she was a child, had I praised her talents and achievements as a young woman, perhaps she would have used more conventional methods of campaigning, perhaps she wouldn't have resorted to something quite so dramatic."

"Those are questions you'll never be able to answer, Garrett, because the time is past. What's important is what you're doing now."

"Nothing." He shrugged. "I'm doing nothing. She's my daughter. Despite the criminal implications, I'm not taking any legal action." He didn't want to say that he had relieved Irina of all her business responsibilities and that he had ordered her never to interfere in the workings of Castleton's. Neither did he want to say that he had drastically changed his will. Or that he would never trust her again. But all of that was true. "Unfortunately, because forgers love to brag about their work, we couldn't be certain who might have caught wind of the story, so when we released it to the press, we took great pains to craft it as if it were just another of the many unsolved art thefts and forgeries already on police blotters. Luckily, the notion of a potential fraud being sidetracked by the brilliant detective work of Armand Lafitte was enough to satisfy the public's lust for cultural skullduggery. As for Irina, she will be present tonight, seated with the family. She's still an angry woman, but hopefully time will soften her.''

Etienne heard the sharp, cutting edge in the father and remembered how fierce Garrett's temper could be. Obviously nature had repeated that trigger-fast fury in the daughter.

''I'm sorry for whatever role my son might have played in her unhappiness. I know she was involved with Armand for a time, but I'm afraid he used other women to try to forget his own unhappiness. There's never been anyone for him other than Annabel.''

''At least with them, all is ending well,'' Garrett said.

''With them and with us.'' Etienne patted his old friend on the shoulder.

Garrett returned Etienne's smile and nodded, but he appeared distracted.

''Is something wrong?''

''Do you ever think about the war? About that bastard who duped us in Antwerp?''

''Sometimes,'' Etienne said quietly, noticing a strange tenseness in Garrett's pose.

''Do you ever wonder what might have happened to him?''

''Of course. For a long time, I checked to see if he was listed as dead or arrested or relocated. I never found anything, and so eventually I stopped looking.''

Garrett nodded. ''Me, too.''

''Unfortunately, men like that often slip through the cracks and get away with their crimes. Why are you bringing this up now?''

Garrett leaned forward and lowered his voice so the women couldn't overhear. ''Do you know Max Richard?''

''Yes. Impressive man.''

''He called me a few days ago to ask if he and several other Interpol agents could use one of the booths above the salesroom as a monitoring station.''

Etienne arched his eyebrows. He hadn't known about Max's affiliation with Interpol. "Who is he looking for?"

"A Belgian who collaborated with the Nazis. Max seems certain he's going to be at the auction tonight."

"Why?" Etienne asked.

Garrett shrugged. "I don't know," he said, noting the anxiety in Etienne's voice, admitting that it matched the disquiet grumbling in the pit of his stomach.

"Does Max anticipate trouble?"

Garrett chuckled, but it was a sound without gaiety, a sound that resonated with echoes of past experience.

"Think back, *mon ami*. It's his job to anticipate trouble."

Etienne looked at Garrett. Just then, he didn't see the septuagenarian before him, he saw the young intelligence officer Garrett used to be, the young man he himself once was. He remembered other times, other places. He remembered missions that succeeded, missions that failed. He knew Garrett was remembering too, because as he raised his glass, the two men exchanged a look that could be understood only by those who had been there before.

"Let's hope Max does his job well," Etienne said.

"Let's hope another one doesn't slip through the cracks," Garrett agreed.

Beneath an archway of pennants—the red coat of arms of Edouard de Rosier alternating with the blue coat of arms of the lady of Dinant—and flanking the red carpet leading to the special exhibition gallery where the Dinant Love Trilogy was on display stood huge black marble urns filled to overflowing with pink and red carnations. At the entrance to the gallery, actors garbed in medieval page costumes handed visitors souvenir booklets which told the story of the Dinants, the poignant love story of the lord of Flanders and the maiden from Walloonia. Just inside, a group of singers, also clothed in medieval finery, warbled madrigals to the accompaniment of a trio of harpists. Though the auction wasn't scheduled to begin until seven-thirty, even now, an hour before, Castleton's was jammed with people in black tie eager to view the famous tapestries, eager to be part of a night everyone expected to be eventful.

Gaby and Bernard wended their way through the crowd

slowly, each, without having to say so to the other, enjoying a special feeling of triumph. Nine days before, at Garrett's insistence, Gaby had given the press a release telling about the discovery of the missing Dinant, detailing the cooperative network of European antiques dealers who had helped Bernard track the tapestry to Madame Boussac's shop in Geneva, the restoration work that was being done on it, and the fact that for the first time in nearly a century, *The Marriage of Brussels* was going to be reunited with *The Courtship* and *The Garden of Love*.

As they entered the gallery, Gaby felt her mouth dry and her heartbeat quicken. Everything she had planned, everything she had hoped for, had happened. The exhibition was glorious. On her left was *The Courtship*. On her right, *The Garden of Love*. And in the center, washed with a soft, sensuous bath of pale yellow light, was *The Marriage of Brussels*. The colors were rich and brilliant. The millefleurs looked dewy fresh. The golden wedding gown glittered. The face of the bride was tinged with a modest blush. And the white silk of the unicorn shimmered as if the threads that had woven it had been kissed by an angel.

"It's breathtaking!"

"That it is," Bernard said, his hand gripping that of his niece. "And so, my darling Gabrielle, are you."

He stretched out his arm, distancing her from him so he could take in the length of her, the beauty of her. Gowned and gloved in delicate, peekaboo black lace, she was a vision of classical loveliness. Her chestnut hair cascaded onto bare shoulders, falling in full, voluminous waves. Her makeup was soft and pale except for the riotous red that rouged her lips and the dusky taupe shadow that dusted her eyes. She wore no jewelry other than diamond stud earrings. Her scent was light. But her aura was powerful.

"This is an important night, *mon chou*," Bernard said, suddenly serious. "It's a turning point for you. All of these people know it was you who delivered that magnificent treasure. You've gained their respect and their admiration, and that is going to lead to that career you want so badly."

"I hope so," Gaby said, "but first, I need the money from tonight's auction. I have to pay back Mrs. Sloane and you, and I have to find a new place to live."

"And you have to make peace with your son."

A gray pall descended over Gaby's face like a veil of mourning. The light drained from her eyes, and her voice echoed the sadness that had been with her for far too long.

"I called him at school. He wouldn't come to the phone. So I wrote him, inviting him to come tonight, telling him how much it would mean to me to have him here with us. I asked him to come to Paris with me over Christmas vacation so that the three of us could recapture some of the wonderful family feeling we used to have. I apologized again for deceiving him and for hurting him even though it was unintentional. I begged him to be fair, to see my side, to remember how much I love him and that never, ever, would I do anything to hurt him." Her eyes puddled and her voice broke. "I never received an answer."

"Monsieur Didier. What a pleasure to see you again." Giles Deffand grabbed Bernard's hand and shook it warmly. They had met two days before when Bernard had arrived from Paris with *The Marriage of Brussels*. "What a night! You must be so proud of Gabrielle."

"That I am," he said, watching her chase her tears with a quick, unobtrusive flick of her finger.

"I hate to bother you, but you have an overseas call. If you'd like, you can take it in my office."

Gaby and Bernard stared at each other. Until now, they hadn't heard anything from Bernard's friends in Belgium. Maybe this was the call they had been waiting for. As Giles led Bernard toward the back elevators, Gaby wondered whether or not their contacts had discovered the identity of Frau von Gelder and whether or not it mattered. The tapestry was set to go on the block in less than four hours. Finding a descendant now would be impossible. It was too late. They would just have to let whatever was going to happen, happen.

At the other side of the gallery, near the entrance to the salesroom, Armand and Annabel acted as unofficial host and hostess. They shook hands and welcomed those who had come to bid on the Montgomery Collection. Naturally, most of the talk was about the Caravaggio. For Armand, there was nothing but the highest praise. Not one personage in the arts walked by without paying homage to his skill and expertise. Not one news reporter or television correspondent passed without requesting an interview. Not one socialite neglected to buss his cheek and beg his presence at an upcoming soirée. Earlier, Armand had even received a telegram from Pico Cellini congratulating him on a job well done. But when his old friends Antony Vinter and John Davenport arrived, Armand's evening was complete.

"You've become quite the celebrity," Vinter said, clapping Armand on the back.

"It's the accent," Davenport added. "Americans are suckers for people who *parler*."

"No. It's Annabel. You've attached yourself to a real star, Lafitte."

"Thank you Tony, darling," Annabel cooed. "I always said you had marvelous taste."

"I heard you two are planning to take that long walk down the aisle."

"Next week," she said with unmistakable glee.

"Could you do us a favor and take a short honeymoon?"

"What are you talking about?" Armand asked, looking first at Davenport and then at Vinter.

Tony cleared his throat dramatically, adopted a sober expression, and then spoke in the reverent tones he felt suited the occasion.

"It is with great pride and personal pleasure that John and I, on behalf of your fellow antiques dealers, invite you to replace Vincent Prado as chairman of the January Antiques Fair."

Annabel's delight was instantaneous. She threw her arms around Armand and giggled like a small girl who had just been granted her fondest wish. Armand held onto her for fear that if he let her go, the dream would fade, he would awaken, and Tony and John would disappear, as would their offer of full redemption.

"So," Davenport said with a huge grin, "are you playing hard to get or what? Will you do it?"

"Of course I'll do it! I'd be happy to do it! I can't wait to do it!"

While the three men discussed timing and availability and committees and exhibitors, Annabel mentally replanned her wedding. It would be in New York instead of at Willowsgate. It would be small and simple, attended by only their nearest and dearest instead of everyone in the immediate world. And, she supposed, skiing in Gstaad would have to wait for another time. But so what. They would have the rest of their lives together, she reasoned blissfully. Besides, in a way, they had been honeymooning for thirty years.

When Tony and John left, Armand drew Annabel to him. It didn't matter that people were milling around them and watching and whispering. He kissed her deeply and lovingly.

"I told you I was nothing without you," he said. "It's only because you're here with me, by my side, that all of this good fortune is coming my way."

"I would argue with you, but I don't ever want you thinking otherwise."

"I have to tell Gaby," he said, parting from his beloved with great reluctance.

"You'll have to wait," Annabel said, pointing toward *The Marriage of Brussels,* where Max Richard and Gaby were engaged in conversation. "She's busy."

She felt his presence seconds before he touched her shoulder. She tensed. Her breathing stopped. Her body seemed to shut down. His flesh touched hers, and suddenly she felt electrified.

"Thank you," he said, unwilling to remove his hand. "I can't tell you how grateful I am that you found that fabulous piece of art."

"Don't thank me," she said, pulling away, frightened by her reaction, angry that he could elicit such a volatile response. "I didn't find it for you."

"I know that," he said, understanding her anger, taken aback by the vehemence of it. "But thanks anyway."

She turned as if she were going to walk away. If she did, within seconds the crowd would swallow her. He grabbed her hand. For a moment, for one single moment, he was certain he felt her tighten her grip as if she didn't want to let him go.

"I wasn't very kind that night in your apartment," he said quietly. "I'd like to apologize."

"You weren't kind and you weren't honest," she said, snapping her hand out of his. "You were patronizing and arrogant and holier than thou without any reason to be, and I resent the hell out of it!"

Gaby controlled the level of her voice, but not easily. She

wanted to shout at him, but the last thing she wanted to do was make a scene. Recognizing that this was only the beginning of what Gaby had to say, Max steered her to a pocket of space on the side of *The Marriage of Brussels*. Though everyone was clamoring for a close-up view of the tapestry, most people gravitated to the center, leaving the sides of the room slightly less crowded.

"What wasn't I honest about?" he asked, wishing they were alone so they could talk this out without bucking hordes of eavesdroppers, knowing that the line "you're beautiful when you're angry" was overused and trite, but believing that in this case it was positively accurate, wanting to take her in his arms and slowly strip away her gloves and slide off her gown and . . .

"You're an undercover agent, Max Richard! A professional liar! A guy who spends his life mucking around in the nether-world! Yet you had the audacity to stand in my apartment and look down your nose at me because I falsified a job application! Damn you!" she said, venting her frustration by poking him. "I did what I did out of desperation and need. You do it for kicks!"

"I don't do it for kicks," Max said, wishing he could explain, knowing he couldn't.

"Then why do you do it? It can't be for the money. You have tons of that. You can't do it for prestige because intelli-gence agents have to keep their identities secret. Is it excitement you want? A thrill a minute? Then try being a woman without any hope of finding a decent job. You want something to keep you on the edge of your seat? Take it from me, 007, that's it!"

"I wish we could start over again."

"From when? From the time we were introduced at the Castleton gala and I thought you were one of the most fascinat-ing men I'd ever met? From that night in Paris when I thought we made love like two people in love? Or would you like to start from that day in Damme when you went to visit your aunt and I committed the ultimate sin by following you?" Tears glittered in her eyes. Her lip quivered, but she fought it, refusing to surren-der to the whirl of emotions eddying inside her. "And speaking of sins. Is it really a violent husband that's keeping your aunt in hiding? Is she an aunt or is she another Interpol operative put there to protect your precious tapestry?"

"What?" Max looked confused, but he wasn't. He knew exactly what she was going to say next.

"I saw *The Triumph of Chastity*. Funny. When you told me about all the other Dinants you own, you neglected to mention that particular one. Was that an oversight? Or just another bald-faced lie?"

"I know it looks bad, but I have my reasons, Gaby. One of these days I'll be able to tell you all about it, but right now I can't."

"I know. Like you couldn't tell me who commissioned the forgery. Like you couldn't tell me who and what you were."

If the man hadn't knocked into her, she might never have noticed. As it was, she saw it only peripherally. A man worked his way through the crowd admiring *The Marriage of Brussels* and slid behind the cord that guarded the tapestry. He touched it, running his hand across it. The guard stopped him. The man looked up. The guard spoke to him. The man went quietly, but Gaby couldn't shake the feeling she had seen him before.

"You know what, Max," she said, refocusing. "Right now, I don't care what your reasons are for doing anything, because right now, I don't care about you. And as for explanations, don't bother. Frankly, I wouldn't believe a thing you said."

With as much dignity as she could summon, she turned and walked away, demanding that her eyes not tear, that the sob erupting in her throat not come out, that her heart break quietly so that no one else would hear.

"Would you like to go to the ladies' room to powder your nose? Or would you like to replay that scene for Joe Papp?" Chelsea took Gaby by the elbow and escorted her out of the exhibition gallery and into the hall.

"I hate him!" Gaby said, allowing herself to break down in front of her friend.

"Sure you do. And I'm a nun. If ever I saw two people more in love than you and Max, I don't remember. Watching the two of you trying to keep your hands off each other was like watching an experiment in defying the law of gravity."

"Very funny."

"It wasn't funny, sweetie. It was hot! Why you didn't just take off for the nearest hotel is beyond me."

"He lied to me."

"You lied to him."

"I didn't lie. I just didn't tell the whole truth," Gaby said, knowing how lame that sounded. "I wasn't sure he'd understand."

"Don't bullshit me, Gaby Thayer. You were into living your lie, and Max was part of it. You were afraid that if you told the truth, the movie would end and you'd be back in the real, everyday world of Wadsworth, Ohio."

"Okay, okay," she said, feeling her head clog with an overload of disturbing thoughts. "So I was playing let's-pretend. He was, too."

"How?"

"I thought he was Max Richard, international construction mogul. A few weeks ago, I found out he's Max Richard, international spy."

Chelsea's eyebrows lifted in surprise.

"Whew! He's even hotter than I thought."

"I'm glad you find this so amusing."

"Don't you?"

"No. I find it upsetting. He's a man trained in deviousness. I thought he was one thing. Now I find out he's something else. He says he has his reasons and that soon he'll explain them to me."

"So?"

"So I don't know what to believe. Do I believe the man I knew in Paris and Switzerland? Or this man?"

"Believe Max."

"But who is Max?"

"I've always found that when a man is naked, you really get to see his true character. Think about how Max was when you were in bed. Was he kind? Was he caring? Loving? Gentle? That's all you need to know. The rest is crap!"

Gaby thought. She remembered. She felt the way it had been between them.

"What do I do now? Chase after him? Beg him to come back to me? What about my pride?"

"Let me tell you what I've learned about pride," Chelsea said with an undercurrent of sadness in her voice. "It's a so what."

"I don't understand."

"Most of the time when you talk about pride, it's false pride.

It's ego. It's fear of being embarrassed or looking like a jerk. In the big picture, that's a so what. It's not worth getting upset about, or aggravated about. Save your tears and your anger and your outrage for important things. Don't waste your emotional energy on pettiness.''

Gaby smiled. ''That sounds like the gospel according to Terry Kirkpatrick.''

Chelsea actually blushed. ''Terry and my support groups.''

''How're you doing?''

''As well as can be expected, considering that next month Drake goes to trial.''

''I'll be there,'' Gaby said, squeezing Chelsea's arm. ''All your friends will be there for you.''

Chelsea laughed.

''All my friends? You'll be there by yourself. But that's okay,'' she said, growing serious again. ''For once in my life, I'm not doing this for show. I'm doing this for Belle.''

''And for yourself.''

Chelsea nodded. ''And for myself. By the way,'' she said, ''have I thanked you for convincing Garrett to go along with our idea for an auction benefiting the Belle Reynolds Center?''

''It wasn't a big deal,'' Gaby said. ''Garrett has a good heart and a big soul. He was happy to put it on the schedule.''

''He's a nice man. Too bad he can't find someone to love him.''

''He will,'' Gaby said, secretly grateful that she and Garrett had revamped their romance into a friendship.

''If I can, anyone can.'' Chelsea had spotted Terry. Her face brightened. Quickly, almost self-consciously, she smoothed her gold crushed-velvet gown over her hips and licked her lips. ''Have we settled the issues of life and liberty? Because if you don't mind, I would like to move on to the pursuit of happiness.''

Gaby laughed. ''Pursue away.''

As Chelsea walked toward Terry, who then led her inside the salesroom, Gaby went to look for her uncle. At the edge of the archway, she ran into him.

''I've been looking all over for you,'' he said, his face flushed.

''Are you all right?''

''I'm fine. And I have news.''

Gaby drew him off to the side.

"Tell me."

"Pieter von Gelder married a young woman named Maguy Montrichard Strauss in Brussels on August 26, 1938. According to the marriage license, her father was Martin Josef Strauss, her mother, Madeleine Montrichard Blume. I had also instructed them to check something else. As far as they can tell, there's no death certificate for anyone named Maguy von Gelder."

It took several minutes for the information to sink in and make sense. When it did, Gaby's eyes widened.

"MM. The monogram on the Dinant tapestries. Maguy Montrichard. Madeleine Montrichard. Marguerite Montrichard." Her euphoria was beyond containment. "It must have become a family tradition for the women to carry the initials MM. How charming. I love it! I don't know what it means or what to do with it or whether it even matters. But I love it!"

Just then, the lights flashed. Trumpets sounded. Over the address system, a voice invited everyone to take his seat. The Montgomery auction was about to begin.

Garrett ascended the steps, took his place behind the podium, and closed his fingers around the mahogany gavel. He breathed deeply and looked out at the assemblage before him. Though the men were all formally attired, creating a sea of black and white, and the women were magnificently gowned and jeweled, producing a landscape of lush color and glitter, he might as well have been facing an endless grassland, a spread of infinite verdancy. Green was the color of the evening. Green, as in money. As in outrageous wealth. Green, as in the eyes of the monster who craves what his neighbor has.

Tonight was his night. Tonight, the ghost of Peter Cecil Wilson would look down on his successor. Tonight, every other auctioneer in the world would look upon him as the crowned king of the salesroom. Tonight, his father would have to look up to him and consider him an equal.

The crowd continued to rustle in their seats. Television cameras were all around, panning the audience, focusing on the curtain behind which was the turntable which would present the items on the block. Sprinkled throughout were emissaries of the finest, most prestigious museums in the world, as well as art collectors of unquestionable repute. There were nouveau riche and *ancienne riche*. There were socialites and scholars, bluebloods and new blood, the interested and the interesting, Europeans, Asians, Americans, Canadians, first-timers, and those inveterate auction junkies who haunted the homes of the hammer.

Garrett tightened his grip on the gavel, knowing it contained the power to hypnotize his audience, to create awesome wonder and enchantment. He looked up into the booths above the floor, lit like NASA control centers. His eyes roamed from one to the other, checking, always checking, making certain that no detail had been overlooked. The tote board was ready. The accountants and computer operators housed in the two booths above and to the right of the podium were ready. His parents, Uncle Bentley, Aunt Phoebe, Irina and her children, the Lafittes and the other honored guests, including Armand, Annabel Montgomery, and Gaby's uncle, Bernard Didier—all those in the private booth facing the podium were ready. And the last booth, the one with a view of the turntable, the podium, and the movements of the audience, the one manned by Max Richard, his fellow Interpol agents, and two men from the FBI, the one with a dozen monitors being fed images from all over the salesroom and adjoining galleries, the one that was searching for Pieter von Gelder—that booth, too, was ready.

So was Garrett. He raised his gavel, and instantly the room silenced. Slowly, his lips curled into an inviting, seductive smile. He leaned forward, pressing closer to the microphone which would carry his voice out over the vast gathering, the microphone that would imprint his voice on television tape to be replayed on the evening news. He had planned his opening sentence carefully. This would be *the* quote, the anthem of the auction, the phrase that would replace, "What, will no one offer more?" in the lexicography of public sales. With these words, he would set the tone, establish the mood, and christen the occasion memorable.

The gavel came down.

"Welcome to history!"

The curtains lifted.

The turntable revolved.

There, hung on a panel of unobtrusive, parchment-pale velvet, was Caravaggio's *The Fortune Teller*.

The applause was deafening.

His ploy had worked. Usually, auctions began with lesser pieces, heightening tension by allowing momentum to build slowly, so that lot by lot, the pace accelerated until the only natural conclusion was a crashing crescendo that translated into a record-breaking price. But this auction was exceptional. Garrett had two pièces de résistance—the Caravaggio and the Dinant Love Trilogy. Why not start with the one and end with the other? Why not, indeed!

"Ladies and gentlemen, the first lot of the evening is *The Fortune Teller*, painted by Michelangelo Merisi da Caravaggio in the late fifteen hundreds, more recently examined and positively authenticated by Monsieur Armand Lafitte." He paused, permitting several seconds of whispering, so that if there was anyone in the room who had not read or heard about the forgery, a kindly neighbor could now inform him or her of the narrowly averted scandal. "I am now opening the bidding at five million dollars."

Again the room exploded with near incendiary excitement. The gauntlet was down. This was a bidding war into which only those to whom money really was no object could plunge.

"Six million two from the man to my left.

"Eight million on the phone.

"Ten million from the gentleman in the rear. Are we having fun yet?"

The audience howled. Up in the private booth, Etienne turned to Garrett Sr.

"I wonder what old PCW would say if he could see what he wrought."

Garrett Sr. watched his son manipulate the crowd, teasing, tickling, casting a spell over them, so that as the prices escalated beyond all rationality, he felt an almost inexpressible respect. Even at his best—and in his day, Garrett Sr. had been good—he knew he had never been this good.

"I think Peter would be proud," was all he could say.

"Fifty-two million five.

"I have fifty-three million from the phone on my right.

"Fifty-four from the telephone on my left.

"Fifty-eight million dollars from the gentleman in the center of the room. Do I hear more?"

A nervous giggle rippled through the room. No hands were raised. Everyone was looking around to see who it was who had placed the last bid, but even a number as grand as fifty-eight million dollars needed only a nod, a blink, a twitch of a finger.

"Fair warning," Garrett Jr. said, holding his gavel high, his face flushed pink with triumph. "I have fifty-eight million dollars on the floor. *Going*," he said, scanning the crowd. "*Going*," he said, knowing that he had pushed this painting to its capacity. "*Gone*! Sold to Mr. Jonathan Thoreau of the Cleveland Museum of Art."

The gavel thundered onto its block. The sound reverberated throughout the huge room like a sonic boom, blending with the raucous shouts and inelegant catcalls of a group who appreciated the ability to spend at stratospheric levels. For several minutes, Garrett allowed the audience to wallow in their own amazement. He had been right. They had all been part of history. During the past several years, two van Goghs, *Sunflowers* and *Irises*, had surpassed all previous records for paintings sold at auction. Tonight, those records had been broken.

Garrett looked up into the private booth at Annabel Montgomery, smiled, and nodded his thanks. Without her, there would have been no auction and no glory. He turned to his father, who offered a simple thumbs-up. Coming from someone else, it might have appeared a brief, insignificant accolade. From Garrett Sr. it was a wreath of gold.

A signal. A button pressed. A revolution of the mechanical turntable and lot number two appeared.

"Ladies and gentleman, showing at the front of the room . . ."

Gaby felt as if someone had just injected her with a massive dose of adrenaline. Her heart pumped at a furious rate. Her face grew hot and feverish. Her body quaked with seismic intensity. Months before, back in London when Gaby had first raised the idea of consigning Annabel's collection to Castleton's, it had been agreed that she was entitled to one percent of the total sale. The Caravaggio alone had set her free. Fifty-eight thousand dollars was more than enough money to pay off Mrs. Sloane and a host of unpaid bills. After that, the only debts outstanding were to Bernard and to the Chevaliers for the restoration work. Since Gaby was the single consignor of *The Marriage of Brussels*, and since Garrett had created an aura of unprecedented acquisitive-ness, it seemed reasonable to assume that her share of the profit from the sale of the Dinants would more than cover both obligations.

Suddenly, life was brighter. The air felt cleaner, lighter, less polluted with dense clouds of worry and despair. For the first time since that night when Brian had staged his exit, Gaby felt she was in control of her own destiny. Yet something was gnawing at her. It was an odd sensation, like the first seconds after anesthesia, when one's skin prickled and one's brain crack-led and one's blood seemed to stop and start, and one's body fought unconsciousness with spurts of awareness.

She looked around, hoping that something or someone would cue her mind. Row upon row. Seat after seat. The faces were celebrated, but not one jogged a thought. Then she looked up. Her eyes traveled from booth to booth, stopping at the one in the back, the one where Max stood hovering over a TV screen.

Max. The Dinants. Frau von Gelder. The monogram in Max's apartment. The one in his chalet at La Maison. Madelaine Montrichard. Maguy Montrichard. Maximilian Richard. Maxi-milian Montrichard. MM! When Max had told her the story of his early childhood, he never mentioned what happened to his parents. When he told her the story of his aunt, he never mentioned what happened to the child. Was he that child? Was the reclusive aunt, the woman he visited in Damme, in fact his mother? And Pieter von Gelder his father? That would explain his obsession with the Dinants. That would explain his secrecy about his visit to Damme. And that would answer her question about descendants with a rightful claim to those precious tapestries.

Quickly making her way upstairs, she wondered whether it was providence that had compelled her to bring the note she had uncovered in the hem of *The Marriage of Brussels*. If Max was the son of Maguy Montrichard—and to Gaby, it appeared certain that he was—he shouldn't be bidding on these tapestries. They belonged to him. Was it possible he didn't know he was con-nected to the original Edouard de Rosier and Marguerite Montrichard? His name was changed. That was curious, too, she thought as she presented identification so she could enter the booth. Why didn't he call himself Max Montrichard? Maybe all of this was coincidence and she was about to make a colossal fool of herself.

When she walked inside, Max was standing in front of a bank of television screens, each one surveying a different section of the salesroom audience. Next to him stood the blonde he had brought to La Côte Basque, looking far too splendid for Gaby's taste in a long, slim black velvet gown. It took Gaby a few seconds to realize she was an Interpol agent. Unfortunately, whether or not she was Max's paramour wasn't quite as easily discerned.

The man who had examined her identification tapped Max on the shoulder and whispered something in his ear. Max turned, confusion engraved on his features. He didn't hesitate. He came right over, but Gaby's antennae told her he would rather have remained in front of those screens. What was he watching for?

"I can see I'm interrupting something," she said quietly. "I'm sorry."

Max placed his hands on her shoulders and stared deep into her eyes.

"I'm not," he said, smiling, his hands gently caressing her shoulders, his magnetism drawing her in, captivating her all over again. "Judging from our conversation earlier, I was afraid you were never going to speak to me again."

She averted her eyes. She didn't want to deal with their personal relationship. This wasn't the place or the time. Besides, suddenly there were questions to be answered. Without looking at him, she opened her evening bag, took out the wrinkled scrap of paper she had taken from the hem of *The Marriage of Brussels,* and handed it to Max. He read it without any change of expression.

"Why are you giving this to me?"

Though his face presented no clue as to his inner reaction, Gaby was certain she heard caution in his voice.

"Because Oncle Bernard and I investigated Pieter von Gelder. And found out that he married a woman named Maguy Montrichard Strauss, a woman I believe is your mother."

"What makes you think that?"

"Circumstantial evidence and a gut feeling."

"What's your evidence?"

"The fabric swatches in your apartment and at La Maison

with the monograms ER and MM. Your name. Your nationality. Your obsession with the Dinant tapestries. Your family background as told to me by you, with the blanks filled in by me." She paused, slightly out of breath, slightly anxious about asking what she was about to ask. "Are you Maximilian Montrichard? Is your mother Maguy?"

"Yes."

"Is . . . ?"

"Max! Come here. Is that him?"

The blonde called and he ran to the screen, leaving Gaby standing in the background, trying to absorb what he had said as well as what was going on inside this booth.

"No." He scrunched his face into a scowl.

Suddenly, the door opened. Max spun around. All talking stopped. Two men reached inside their jackets and rested their hands on visible holsters. A guarded silence permeated the room as everyone watched Garrett Castleton and Etienne Lafitte enter.

"Sorry," Garrett said, immediately sensing the tension their unexpected arrival had aroused. "We just wanted to see what was happening."

"It's okay," Max said, signaling the others to relax. "As a matter of fact, you might be able to help. Do either of you know the Baron Pieter von Gelder?"

"Vaguely," Garrett said.

"I've done business with him several times," Etienne said, clearly surprised. "Is that who you're looking for?"

"Yes." Max's answer was crisp and chilling.

"Is he here?" Garrett asked, joining the crowd huddled in front of the wall of television monitors.

"I think so," Max said, "but so far we haven't been able to spot him."

"Let's have a look," the senior Castleton said.

"Run the tape," Max said to one of the technicians.

A young man with earphones on pressed a button on the complicated control panel. Tape whirred. He pressed another button. The sequence everyone had viewed minutes before was replayed.

"I don't see him," Garrett said.

"Neither do I," Etienne concurred.

"This is it," one of the Interpol agents announced, nodding

toward the front of the salesroom where three large screens were being lowered. "The Dinants are going on the block."

Suddenly, there was a flurry of activity inside the booth. The mood turned anxious and expectant. Everyone took positions which were clearly prearranged. Garrett Castleton and Etienne Lafitte were asked to stand behind the elegant blonde. Max stood where he could oversee everything, including the floor where Garrett was preparing once again to create history.

"Showing on the screens, the Dinant Love Trilogy. The Courtship. The Garden of Love. *And* The Marriage of Brussels. *I'm accepting an opening bid of one million dollars."*

"Keep your eyes on the monitors," Max said to the two older men. "Our cameras are panning the audience. If you even think you see him, say so and we'll freeze the frame."

The men nodded. Gaby moved next to Max.

"Why are you looking for Pieter von Gelder?"

He had almost forgotten she was there.

"I'm sorry. I guess I sort of left you hanging."

"Max. Is he your father? Is this whole thing . . . personal?" she asked delicately, indicating the elaborate equipment, the trained personnel, the intensity of the mood.

Max's face hardened. His blue eyes glinted like sharpened steel.

"Yes, Pieter von Gelder is my father. But he is also a wanted war criminal. He collaborated with the Nazis at the expense of his fellow Belgians and was directly responsible for the deaths of several hundred Jews."

Gaby felt her stomach knot.

"I've been tracking this bastard for years," Max said, squeezing the words through clenched teeth. "And yes, it's personal."

"I have one million seven hundred thousand on my left. Two million from the lady in the rear."

"What makes you so sure you'll find him here tonight?"

Max stared at her. His face reflected a profound, incurable pain. His voice echoed a deep, unshakable shame.

"I know he's here tonight because he's looking to see if my mother is here." He looked out, down onto the floor, as if the hatred in his eyes could seek and destroy his enemy. "And because he's afraid whoever buys those tapestries is going to find this."

He turned back to Gaby and held up the note she had given him.

"Three million five from the gentleman in the corner. Do I hear four? Thank you. Four million from the woman in the center. Do I hear five? Better yet, I hear six million from the telephone on my left. Now we're getting somewhere!"

Gaby felt hypnotized by the note. She gazed at it as if entranced, as if it were transmitting a message only she could receive. Signals. She was getting signals, but they were vague. They didn't make sense. Or did they?

"Max. How extensive has your videotaping been? I mean, were you watching the cocktail hour or did you start the cameras when everyone had come into the salesroom?"

"We've been taping since the doors opened. Why?"

"Could you rerun the tape recorded during the exhibition?"

Without wasting time with superfluous questions, Max shanghaied one of the technicians and told him what Gaby wanted. Within seconds, Gaby and Max were viewing the arrival of the first few guests.

"Could you fast forward it, please?"

"Seven million dollars from the telephone on my left. Seven million five hundred thousand from the gentleman on my right."

The images blurred as the tape raced ahead. Periodically, the young man at the controls stopped it and let it play at normal speed so Gaby could study the picture.

"What are you looking for?" Max asked.

She didn't take her eyes off the screen as she answered.

"It didn't hit me until a moment ago, but while you and I were arguing, someone bumped into me. It was a man. He approached the tapestry and felt around a bit until the guard stopped him. Now I'm thinking maybe he was looking for that note. I'm hoping your camera got a picture of his face."

"Welcome to double digits. I have ten million dollars on the floor. Do I hear ten five? Yes! Thank you, madame."

"Stop!" Gaby put her hand on the technician's shoulder. She had spotted herself and Max. "Let it play."

The three of them watched as the camera replayed their contretemps. Gaby studied the figures surrounding her on the screen, particularly those over her left shoulder, searching for the man who had bumped into her. "There he is," she said, pointing. His face was turned away, deliberately hidden from Max. What was clear, however, was that he had been eavesdropping on their conversation.

"Fifteen million dollars. Isn't love grand?"

Garrett and Etienne moved over to the monitor where Max and Gaby stood. Max was edgy. Gaby couldn't imagine the turmoil that had to be going on inside him. All she knew was she loved him and if there was any way she could spare him the pain he was about to experience, she would.

The man bumped her. The camera watched as he approached the tapestry. Max, Garrett, Etienne, and Gaby watched as the guard walked toward him. Gaby feared that the camera wouldn't change perspective. If it didn't, von Gelder or whoever that man was might just walk away without his face ever appearing on the tape. Just as the guard began to speak to him, a second camera clicked on. The man looked up.

"Stop the tape!" Gaby shouted.

Frozen on celluloid was a man she knew she had seen before. It was the man from Grosvenor House, the one who had been hovering around the Clarkson Galleries booth. She looked at Max. He had turned a ghostly white.

"That's him," Etienne said.

Max said nothing. He just looked. The delft-blue eyes. The round face. They were the only two features they shared, but as far as he was concerned, they were two too many. Silently, Gaby took his hand.

"Twenty-five million dollars. Ladies and gentlemen, I have a bid for twenty-five million dollars from the telephone on my left for the Dinant Love Trilogy. Do I hear more?"

"Is he still in the house?" Max asked, his voice tightly controlled.

"Fair warning."

"Check security!" one of the agents barked into a walkie-talkie.

"Twenty-five million dollars."

"We've gone over the tapes, Max. He's not down on that floor. If he's bidding, he's one of the guys on the phones."

"Going!"

"Alert the guards at the door!"

"Going!"

"Does anyone remember seeing him after the cocktail hour?" Max's nerves were beginning to show.

"I think he's gone," Gaby said quietly, not wanting to verbalize what everyone already knew.

"Gone!"

The hammer came down, demanding everyone's attention.

"The Dinant Love Trilogy. Sold for twenty-five million dollars!"

For a moment, the excitement of the auction charged the atmosphere of the booth. Garrett and Etienne cheered. Gaby applauded. Even several of the agents clapped in appreciation. Only Max remained silent, his eyes glued to a frozen image on a small screen.

It's over! he heard someone say. "It's not over," he said to the face staring back at him from the electronic box. "But it will be, Herr von Gelder. Very soon."

26

For those who had been in the surveillance booth, von Gelder's disappearance cast a pall on the reception following the auction. Max arranged for a team of FBI agents to cover all the major airports in the metropolitan area, as well as Logan Airport in Boston and Dulles Airport in Washington, D.C. He also alerted Interpol headquarters in Saint-Cloud. Within an hour, operatives backed up by sharpshooters were stationed at airports and railway stations in Brussels, Antwerp, Paris, Amsterdam, and London, as well as on the roads leading to von Gelder's estate outside of Antwerp, his apartment in Brussels, and his offices in both cities. For now, Max and Gaby could do little except wait.

In the rear gallery of Castleton's, however, there was a party going on. Across from the Dinants, a buffet table that stretched the length of the room groaned beneath an extravaganza of temptations. Black Beluga caviar. Smoked Scotch salmon. Carpaccio. Blini and red caviar. Crepes. Delicately sauced pastas. Sushi. Shrimp. Clams. Stone crabs. Lobster tails. For those who favored chilled vodka with their caviar, thin glasses poked through mounds of crushed ice like stalagmites. Champagne flowed like rivers after a rain. There were pastries and petit fours, coffee and espresso, four varieties of tea, chocolate truffles, and mints imprinted with the Castleton C.

The only person without a glass in her hand or a celebratory glow in her eyes was the somber, unsmiling Lady Stoddard. Her expression was stony and had been from the moment she had arrived early that evening and had looked to take her place on the receiving line. Since Irina rarely considered the consequences of her behavior, it hadn't occurred to her that there would be a problem. But there was. She couldn't stand next to her father or Garrett. They were still too furious with her for her to feel comfortable in their presence. There was little question as to where her mother's loyalties lay, so that eliminated Charlotte. Standing beside Armand or Annabel Montgomery was an impossibility. She could barely cope with the knowledge that they were a couple. Seeing them together, hearing them accept congratulations on their upcoming wedding or Armand's appointment as chairman of the January Antiques Fair—it was simply too painful to contemplate.

That left Uncle Bentley. Whether either of them liked it or not, Irina had declared him her anchor. In an uncharacteristic display of chivalry, he had actually risen to the task, remaining fast by her side despite her incessant under-the-breath grousing about the family and what they had done to her and how she didn't deserve this kind of treatment and why they should have been more understanding about what had motivated her to take such drastic measures.

"She's the one everyone should be stoning," Irina said, pointing to Gaby, who was off in a corner deep in conversation with Max Richard. "The woman was caught in a web of a thousand lies, any one of which could have precipitated a scandal. Did my father bat an eye? No! Did he raise even the mildest protest? No! Did he bother to thank me for saving Castleton's from the disgrace of having a phony of her magnitude on their employment rolls? No!"

With a practiced harumph, Irina drew herself up into an indignant pose. Though at the moment she appeared laughable and somewhat pathetic, Bentley surprised himself by admiring her ability to manipulate situations until they favored her. Mental gymnastics. Character quirk. Tragic flaw. Whatever, it indicated a unique strength. Given similar circumstances, he doubted he would be able to conjure up that kind of toughness. He could never subject himself to this brand of humiliation, for instance. Then again, she didn't think she was being humiliated. She thought she was being victimized. And as Bentley had observed over the years, the protective cover of an eternal victim was like an iron carapace—impenetrable.

"Look at him!" Irina sniffed in her brother's direction, holding her hand in front of her face as if to shield herself from a bad odor. "Prancing around like a horse's ass. You'd think *he* did something extraordinary. If *I* hadn't created such a stir with that forgery, do you really think the Caravaggio would have sold for that outrageous price?"

Bentley sipped his scotch and nodded. She had a point. The preauction furor surrounding the forgery had dusted this particular painting with a must-have patina. Fifty-eight million dollars! The Cleveland Museum of Art wasn't paying for canvas and paint. They were paying for drawing power, the ability to attract both the curious tourist and the generous benefactor.

"As for my parents, well! Any minute now, Father is going to announce his successor. I should be the one named. I am the firstborn and, therefore, the rightful heir to his throne. But will he give it to me? No! Frankly, I don't understand it."

"Perhaps it's because Garrett is far more qualified for the post," Bentley said.

Irina squared off with him.

"Qualified, my eye! Why? Because his pants zip in the front? I should have known you'd take his side. You always take the side of the one who signs the checks!"

"I'm going to ignore that, Irina," Bentley said tightly.

Irina let loose a cruel snickering laugh.

"That's so like you. Backing away. Running away with your tail tucked between your legs. If you don't like what I said, why don't you say so?" She was deliberately baiting him, growing even more upset when he refused to take the bait and continued to sip his scotch. "Well? Don't you care what I think?"

"Not very much."

"Why not?" She put her hands on her hips and tilted her head in a pose of aristocratic challenge.

"Because I don't like you very much."

"As if you've never made that clear," she said, manipulating, maneuvering, making certain that she was the victim. "You've never liked me. Why!"

"Why?" Bentley handed his empty glass to a passing waiter, and with great aplomb said, "Because you're a bitch!" and walked away.

"Will they catch him?" Gaby asked Max, wishing there was something she could do or say that would alleviate his distress, knowing there was nothing.

"Sooner or later."

He was distracted. His mind was racing. There must be something he had overlooked.

"Max, did you buy the tapestries?"

"I had someone bid for me with instructions to buy at whatever price." His jaw tightened. His voice rumbled. "The last person in this world who was going to possess my mother's dowry was Pieter von Gelder."

"Now you own all seven. I'm glad." She smiled, hoping to lighten his mood. She waited for a response. There was none. Again, silence fell like a thin curtain, keeping them separate but not completely apart.

"What were we talking about when he bumped into you?" Suddenly, his eyes were dark.

"I'm not sure."

"Think!" His insistence frightened her.

Counting on her ability to recall details, she retraced their conversation. As she got to the part he was asking about, she shivered. No wonder he sounded so concerned.

"We were talking about *The Triumph of Chastity*. Actually, I was talking about it. I said I saw it in Damme." She felt her heart stop. "You're afraid he's gone after your mother."

"He's clever, and right now he's not sure whether or not he's been tailed. Rather than take a chance, I think he'll lie low for a few days, but yes, I believe Damme is his ultimate destination. He has to get to her. Aside from the damaging testimony she could give at a war crimes trial, they never divorced but he remarried. Twice! If we can't get him for anything else, she's living proof he's a bigamist."

"When are you leaving?" Gaby said.

"Right now." He pulled her toward him and kissed her with

a ferocity that both excited and alarmed her. "Thank you for all you've done. I love you."

With that, he bolted for the door. She wanted to run after him, to help him, to find out if he meant what he said, but she knew she shouldn't. Interpol would help him. As for whether or not he loved her or had simply added that as an addendum to his thank-you—she wouldn't know that until Pieter von Gelder was captured.

When Garrett Castleton approached the microphone, it took a few moments for the crowd to quiet. Bernard found Gaby and stood beside her, sensing that Max's exit had left her shaken, also sensing that, just then, she didn't care to discuss any of the reasons why. Across the gallery from them, Garrett Jr. felt as if a thousand needles were sticking in his skin. His nerves crackled like a fuse about to short out. Though he thought he knew what his father was about to say, he knew his father well enough never to take anything for granted. Nearby, Armand and Annabel, still buoyed by the monstrous success of the auction, stood arm in arm, anticipating the senior Castleton's announcement with sincere pleasure. Since Armand's involvement with the Caravaggio, he and Garrett Jr. had established a peaceful, respectful rapport. In fact, Tony Vinter had told Annabel that Garrett had informed the National Antique and Art Association of Armand's unselfish assistance before the press had gotten wind of it. Though no one could say for sure, Annabel believed that Garrett's recommendation had gone a long way toward assuring unanimous approval of Armand's appointment as head of the fair.

Chelsea and Terry Kirkpatrick stood in the second row, behind the Lafittes. It didn't escape Chelsea's notice that the Castletons were gathered to her left in front of the podium, while Irina stood to the right, all by herself. Belle's death, Louise's influence, the infusion of strength from her support groups, the growing love between her and Terry—a number of new and potent ingredients had been sprinkled into Chelsea's life. Some of her philosophies had changed. Many of her habits had been altered. But no matter how much she mellowed, the essence of Chelsea remained. Irina had lied and cheated and contrived and had been arrogant enough to believe she would get away with all of it. She didn't. And Chelsea couldn't have been happier.

"Ladies and gentlemen. Earlier this evening, my son welcomed you to history. I think his choice of introduction was extremely apt."

The audience thundered its approval of the conduct of the auction by clapping and shouting *bravo!*, applauding not only Garrett Jr.'s performance, but the extraordinary amount of money bid as well.

"In keeping with his theme, I have chosen this time to announce my retirement as chairman of the board of Castleton's International. I'm sure it comes as no surprise to any of you that I have chosen my son to succeed me."

Again, the crowd expressed its approval, this time demanding that the younger Castleton make his way to the podium. The father embraced the son, and the roar grew louder.

"Having watched him work over the years, I have complete confidence in his ability to run Castleton's in accordance with our centuries-old standard of excellence." He paused and, in a rare display of public affection, put his arm around Garrett's shoulder. "Having watched him work tonight, I have no qualms about saying that I was filled with pride and that, to me, he is the best auctioneer in the world today."

As Castleton *père* and *fils* enjoyed the tumultuous applause, Josette hugged her friend Charlotte, who unashamedly dabbed a lace handkerchief at her eyes.

"Before I officially turn the reins over to Garrett, I have one more act I'd like to perform as chairman of Castleton's."

An expectant buzz filled the room. Irina's back stiffened. Her heart fluttered. She knew he wouldn't banish her completely. She knew his own ego was too bloated to bear the fallout that would occur if anyone found out what she had done. What better way to cover up a potential disaster than to make her head of Castleton's New York?

"Since Garrett will now be headquartered in London, his position as president of Castleton's New York needs to be filled. It's a post that requires a willingness to work hard and the ability to make whatever is done look easy. It's a job that demands a business eye and a creative soul. Again, I'm sure my choice will come as a surprise to no one, except perhaps the person I've selected—Gabrielle Didier!"

The response was instantaneous, the sound so deafening that

Gaby felt as if she were in a closed tunnel with hundreds of cannons exploding around her. She heard Garrett Sr. invite her to join him. She heard Oncle Bernard shout congratulations in her ear. She heard her name being chanted by the crowd. But she was still too shocked to move. It was only when she felt Armand's hand on her arm and heard him say, "You earned this. You should be very proud of yourself," that the trance lifted. She was proud of herself. And by God, she *had* earned it!

She kissed Oncle Bernard, Armand, and Annabel and then, accompanied by another burst of affectionate applause, walked to the front and joined the two Castletons. As the senior Garrett lifted the hands of his son and his choice for the plum job of president of Castleton's New York, Irina, in a fit of high dudgeon, turned to leave. As she passed Chelsea, her face as white as Carrara marble and just as hard, Chelsea said, "Once a loser, always a loser." Her only response was a sibilant hiss.

After thanking a horde of well-wishers and accepting the congratulations of just about every guest present, Gaby gratefully followed Garrett Sr. to his office for a private toast.

"I'm really overwhelmed," she said, sitting on a couch facing him, allowing herself to relax for the first time all evening. "I never expected this."

"I know, but you do deserve it. Without your input and your talent, this New York branch would never have achieved the high level of success it has."

She smiled. It felt so good to be patted on the back and told that her efforts had been noticed and appreciated. She felt so rewarded, so intensely proud of what she had achieved. Though she knew that Armand had already arranged a small celebratory party for her, she also knew that by choice and by chance, the two people she most wanted to share this with weren't here— Steven and Max.

"By the way," she said softly, suddenly deciding that she should return Garrett's surprise with one of her own, "you really should take the two Meissen figurines from the apartment and put them together with the two you have in your library. They're a set and should be displayed as such."

Garrett burst into laughter, chuckling heartily as if she had just told him one of the funniest jokes he had ever heard.

"So," he said, still grinning, "you knew about me."

She nodded with benign smugness. "When I first saw the women representing the continents of Europe and America, I thought they looked familiar, but I couldn't be sure. When I returned home to my apartment and noticed the two Meissen figurines in the bedroom, the women representing Africa and Asia, I knew. I checked the markings and the colors, and then I remembered that the rare set of four had been sold at Christie's in the late seventies."

"Just so you don't think you're the only clever one," he said, still smiling, "I knew all along who my tenant was."

Now it was Gaby's turn to be shocked. "You knew I was a phony, yet you didn't say anything, even when you knew your son wanted to marry me. Why?"

"First of all, because I know that quite often people aren't who they seem to be. Second, no matter who you said you were, you were doing an outstanding job for Castleton's. And third, I thought you were the best thing that had ever happened to Garrett. Not only are you beautiful and charming and talented, but you're full of spunk and spit. It couldn't have been easy pretending to be a wealthy socialite when in reality you were five paces away from the poorhouse. I admire your tenacity, your bravery, and your determination to turn your dreams into reality. My only regret is that my son was not the man of those dreams."

He sipped his champagne calmly, as if they had been chatting about nothing more urgent than whether or not graffiti was an art form or a form of vandalism. Gaby was having a more difficult time absorbing the revelations of the past few moments. He could have destroyed her with the information he had. Yet he had chosen not to. Perhaps because he didn't want his own secrets revealed.

She hesitated, wondering whether or not she had the right to ask the next question. "Have you been with Madame Duvall all this time?"

Garrett tilted his glass and studied the bubbles, admiring the persistence of the carbonation.

"Kate entered my life during a time when, to be honest, I was bored. Though the term 'midlife crisis' hadn't been coined then, it would probably have been an apt description. I longed for some kind of excitement, and Kate provided it. She was young and beautiful and exceptionally gifted. Our relationship began when a friend took me to a showing of her art. I was unbelievably impressed. I offered to recommend her to friends of mine in London so that she could gain Continental exposure. As they say, one thing led to another and we plunged into an affair. It became apparent very quickly, however, that I was not cut out to be a rakish Don Juan. As fast as our affair began, it ended.''

''Then why keep the apartment?'' Gaby asked.

''Several reasons. First of all, I genuinely liked Kate and wanted to give her whatever advantages I could. Also, because of her, I came to understand what a wonderful marriage I had, and for that I was very grateful.''

''Then the clothes I cleaned out from the apartment weren't yours.''

He shook his head.

''I hadn't seen Kate in many years. I do know that she had many lovers. Who they were and how long they stayed was none of my concern. I simply paid the maintenance on the co-op.''

''Were you afraid she would leak the story of your involvement?''

Garrett nodded.

''I'm sure you understand what news like this would do to Charlotte and the rest of my family?''

Gaby held up her hand to stop him from continuing.

''Please,'' she said, thinking of how she had felt when Irina had exposed her deception in front of the Castletons, of the embarrassment Armand had suffered at Prado's hands, of the pain on Max's face when he had told her that Pieter von Gelder was his father. She lifted her champagne glass and looked directly into his eyes. ''Here's to keeping things that are better left unsaid, unsaid.'' *Things better left unsaid.*

It hit her suddenly, but with such force she almost dropped her glass. She hadn't mentioned exactly *where* she had seen *The Triumph of Chastity.* Damme wasn't a very big place, but the *béguinage* was slightly outside of town, hidden away in a small wood. It was conceivable that because von Gelder didn't know exactly where Maguy was, she could be spirited out of the *béguinage* before he found her. Where was Max headed? she wondered. Was he going to Antwerp? Directly to Damme? Brussels? Her brain flooded with a barrage of thoughts. Von Gelder had not only eavesdropped on their conversation, but he had seen Max. He had heard Gaby question whether or not the woman was his mother. He had heard her blurt out that Max Richard worked for Interpol. Was it possible he was not going to go after Maguy until he had eliminated Max? Gaby was frantic. This was not her milieu. She didn't know how to think things like this through. All she had to go on were her instincts, and they told her to get to Damme as quickly as she could.

"Garrett," she said, rising abruptly. "I need a favor."

"Anything you wish."

"I need an advance on my salary, enough for a ticket on the Concorde to Paris tomorrow morning and a connecting flight to Brussels, as well as a little extra for expenses. I also need the use of your phone so I can send a telegram."

"If you give me fifteen minutes, I'll get the cash from my private safe. While I'm gone, feel free to use the phone." He started to leave, but before he did, he asked, "Are you all right? If you're in any trouble, tell me what it is and I'll try to help."

"Someone I care about is in trouble."

He nodded. "Max Richard is a lucky man." With that, he closed the door behind him, leaving her alone.

She ran to the phone and arranged for an urgent telegram to be sent to Max via Prudence.

LET'S START OVER AGAIN. ON THE FARM WHERE IT ALL BEGAN.

TAKE CARE
YOUR MOM.
GABY.

It was late by the time she arrived in Brussels. Trying to behave normally, yet aware of the possibility that she was being watched, she rented a flashy red Porsche and drove out of the airport heading south. On the flight over she had studied a road map of Belgium, memorizing her route. Working on the assumption that there was no such thing as being too careful, she got on the main highway, drove south for about twenty minutes, checking her rearview mirror constantly for a tail. Deciding she had none, she got off the highway and then got on again, this time going north, and drove directly to Bruges. Once there, she registered at the Duc de Bourgogne, brought her clothes up to her room, and came back down again. Leaving on foot, she walked into the center of town to the railway station, where she rented another car, one less noticeable than the red Porsche.

Driving slowly, not wishing to attract anyone's attention so late at night, she headed for the *béguinage* in Damme. Relying on her memory, she found it, drove past, and parked in a darkened spot several blocks away. She approached the gate with tremendous trepidation, unsure as to how she would handle a rejection.

"Good evening," she said in French to the guard, who had spoken to her in Flemish. "I'm here to see Maguy Montrichard. It's an emergency. Please let me in."

He didn't answer, so she repeated herself in English. He might not have understood French. It was also possible that he was a Flamard with a resentment of those who spoke French. Whatever his predilection, she had to make him understand.

"I can't," he said in a very official voice.

"Please," she begged. "Something's happened to her son, Max. I must see her."

The man heard Max's name and opened the gate immediately. Gaby ran to Maguy's door. The house was dark. Rapping lightly, not wanting to frighten her, she waited before pounding more loudly. A light switched on. A few seconds passed and then the door opened a crack.

"Who is it? What do you want?"

"You don't know me," Gaby whispered, "but I'm a friend of Max's. He sent me to take you away from here."

Two large brown eyes peered through the slit between the door and the portal. They were intelligent, sophisticated eyes that had seen too much to accept things at face value.

"How do I know you're telling me the truth? Why did Max send you? Why must I leave?"

"He sent me because Pieter von Gelder knows you're alive. He knows you're here in Damme, and Max thinks he's going to come after you."

Gaby couldn't see the woman's mouth, but she heard the quick, frightened intake of breath.

"Where is Max now?"

"He's following von Gelder."

"Why are you doing this? Pieter is a dangerous man."

"I love Max." She said it simply, but evidently Maguy heard something in her voice that prompted her to unlatch the chain that held the door.

"Come in."

At first sight, Maguy Montrichard von Gelder was an older woman with salt-and-pepper hair, dressed in a yellow bathrobe tied tightly around a tiny waist. When Gaby looked again, she saw the dark eyes and bowed lips and heart-shaped face she had seen in the picture at La Maison. She thought of her own mother and how she might have looked had she lived to be Maguy's age. The memory of Delphine tugged at Gaby, making her realize that no matter how much time elapsed, one never stopped mourning loved ones who died too soon.

"Tell me what happened."

Maguy wasn't asking, she was demanding. Gaby complied, telling her everything, but doing it quickly. When she had finished, she pleaded with Maguy to get dressed so that they could take *The Triumph of Chastity* and get out of Damme before von Gelder had a chance to find her.

"You still haven't told me anything to assure me I should place my life in your trust. Pieter is not only dangerous, he's clever. How do I know you're not working for him?"

"You have to believe me," Gaby said.

"No, I don't. You have to prove yourself to me."

Gaby wracked her brain to think of something that she could have heard only from Max.

"I'm taking you to the Glucksmann farm. We're going to hide in the bomb shelter where Max was born and you and he hid during the war."

Maguy's jaw tightened. Her expression didn't change, but Gaby could almost feel the rush of memories that had insinuated themselves on her mind.

"I'll be ready in five minutes."

Twenty minutes later, with *The Triumph of Chastity* safely hidden in the trunk of the car, they were on the road to Oostkamp. On the way, they spoke, but haltingly. Maguy needed to know Pieter von Gelder's suspected whereabouts and his postwar activities. Gaby told her what little she knew.

When they arrived at the farm, it was three in the morning. Nonetheless, Berthe was outside waiting for them. Maguy had insisted upon calling ahead so that her old friend wouldn't be needlessly frightened by their arrival. In the time it had taken to drive to Oostkamp, Berthe had roused the other adults in the household and fixed up the bomb shelter. As Gaby followed Berthe and Jan, the only remaining brother, out to the subterranean safe house, she tried to imagine what it must have been like living beneath the ground, suspecting every sound, believing that each time the wind rustled it signaled the approach of an enemy. She thought of her mother and Simone and Bernard and what it must have been like for them trying to survive the war. She thought too of her father and how frightened he must have been, a young boy who'd barely tasted life being shipped off to a strange land to kill or be killed. As she often did, she thanked God that, so far, her son had been spared the horror of having to participate in such acts of carnage.

Holding a kerosene lantern, Berthe led them down an old wooden staircase into a musty darkness. She placed the lamp on a table, turned up the wick, and went about lighting several other lanterns. Soon, pockets of luminosity squeezed between the shadows, intruding on the pitch until the entire area was lightened with a yellow wash. The walls were concrete, but the floor was wooden, covered with a worn but serviceable rug. There were a couch, several chairs, a couple of tables, and a huge basket covered by a cloth which, Gaby guessed, was filled with food. At the far end, Gaby could see a curtain pulled to the side. Behind it were several mattresses, two of which were dressed with clean sheets and blankets. It was primitive, but considering its purpose, luxurious. In fact, it surprised Gaby how quickly she settled herself and how normal it felt talking with Berthe and Jan about Pieter von Gelder.

For most of the time, Gaby sat quietly and listened as the others tried to reconcile the man von Gelder had been and the man he had become.

"What was he like when you met him?" Gaby asked, curious as to what had attracted Maguy to him in the first place.

Maguy's face grew contemplative as she tried to remember the youthful Pieter and why she had married him.

"I was nineteen, in my second year at the university. I was studying art history and, as part of my curriculum, I was apprenticed to a curator at the Royal Museum of Fine Arts. Frequently,

I was sent out to assess art collections. One such visit was to Baron Pieter von Gelder's estate outside of Antwerp. Pieter was eight years older than I, very handsome and very soigné." Maguy sighed and then scowled, as if remembering something good or appealing about her husband was dishonorable and, under the circumstances, utterly distasteful. "He pursued me with such amorousness, he swept me off my feet. I was young and naive. I saw his intense attention as flattering. I interpreted his possessiveness as passion, his arrogance as confidence. Even after we were married, I continued to avoid the signals. I had been a virgin, with practically no sexual experience. I accepted his aggressiveness in bed as masculine. He hurt me, but I thought that was the way it was."

"When did you know something was wrong?" Gaby asked, thinking about how much she had accepted out of innocence, how much she had thought was *just the way it was*.

"After two quick miscarriages, I became pregnant again. Despite my doctor's warnings to be careful until after the first trimester had passed, Pieter's demands for my body continued to be frequent and vigorous. Most of the time, I submitted, but on the rare occasions when I didn't, when I felt too ill or tired to please him, he beat me. One night, just after I had started my fourth month, just when I thought I had passed the critical time and would actually carry the child to term, he beat me so badly I miscarried."

Gaby winced. She knew how desperately she had wanted a child. She could only imagine how she would have felt losing that child.

"Why did you stay?"

Maguy considered the question.

"I don't know. I suppose I thought I had no choice. It was the Depression. There were so few jobs. My family had no money. I only got to attend the university because both my parents were professors there. I was educated, but in those days it didn't mean very much. Where was I to go? What would I have done? And who would have cared? I was married to a baron. To have left would have made me appear ungrateful at best, stupid at worst."

Gaby nodded, a wry, sympathetic smile grazing her lips.

Times change, she thought, but not as fast as people wanted to believe.

"What finally made you decide to leave? Were you afraid he would do something to cause you to miscarry?"

Maguy laughed, but it was a bitter, angry sound.

"I was afraid he'd cause my death. When he married me, he knew that although my ancestors were Catholic, my grandmother had married a Jew and both of my parents were Jewish. At the time, it seemed irrelevant, but once the Nazis began to spread their bigotry, he began to focus on my Jewishness. He taunted me with anti-Semitic comments. He berated Berthe and Jacob."

She looked at her friend with apology, as if she still believed Berthe had suffered because of her. Gaby looked confused.

"Jacob and I worked for him," Berthe said, seeing that an explanation was in order. "Jacob was the overseer on his land. I was his cook. He was a tyrannical employer, and Jacob and I hated every moment of our service there. If we hadn't needed the money to support the rest of our family and this farm, we would have left. In a way, I'm glad we didn't. If we had, I never would have met Maguy."

The two women reached across the rough-hewn table between them and clasped hands as if repledging their friendship. Gaby thought of Chelsea and how grateful she was that, despite differences and distance and the passage of time, their friendship had survived.

"Around the time when it appeared certain that the Germans were going to invade Belgium," Maguy continued, "we noticed that suddenly nearby farms were abandoned. Shopkeepers disappeared. Families vanished. All of them were Jewish. We began to hear terrible rumors. Horrible accusations. People were whispering about Pieter, saying he was providing the Germans with names and addresses of Jews in exchange for money." The lines in her face tightened. Her large eyes welled with unshed tears. "I began to listen whenever he and his Nazi friends had meetings. Several times, I overheard him bargaining for a position in the new Belgian government. I overheard him discussing various ways to transport people out of Antwerp. I overheard him bartering some of his art as well as most of the artworks I had contributed to the marriage. I decided I had to take action. Since I knew I couldn't do it alone, and since I would never have left my friends behind, I confided my intentions to Berthe and Jacob. By working together, we escaped, but we managed to salvage only some of my dowry. I took money and provisions and whatever we could carry that I thought I might be able to sell in the black market to keep the three of us alive, but I had to leave *The Marriage of Brussels* behind. I had planned to take it, but when the Belgian army surrendered, we knew our days were numbered. He would have turned us all in. We had no time to save anything except ourselves. Though I wanted to take the tapestry with us, nothing was important enough to risk our lives and the life of my baby.''

"How did you live? I mean, Max told me about all of you living here," Gaby said, indicating the bomb shelter, "but what did you do after that? Have you been hiding from him all this time?"

"Yes and no. After the war, I lived here for a little while longer, but then we heard that Pieter was asking about me, looking for me. He knew I had overheard conversations he didn't want repeated. He also knew that, given the chance to testify against him, I'd tell them every last thing I could remember.''

"Did you testify?"

"I wanted to, but I didn't have any solid proof to back up my story. It would have been my word against his. He was a baron, a powerful man. I was a runaway wife. What if I couldn't convince the court of his guilt? What if he went free? I didn't want to endanger my friends any more than I already had, and I certainly didn't want to put my son's life in jeopardy. I decided to leave the country and try to start a new life in France. I spoke the language, and Berthe had some relatives there who were willing to put me up until I got established. The only heartache was that because I had no papers and had to sneak out of Belgium, I had to leave Max behind. My plan was to have Berthe bring him to me when I was settled and earning enough money to support the two of us.''

"What did you do?"

She laughed, obviously recalling something humorous. "I changed my name to Maguy Richard, created a résumé for myself, and was lucky enough to get a job in the Louvre.'' Her eyes misted. "I was also lucky enough to meet and fall in love with a very wonderful man, Roger Bertain.''

"Did you marry him?"

"I couldn't. I was still married to Pieter. If I had instituted divorce proceedings, he would have known I was still alive."

"Did Roger know about Pieter and Max?"

"Not for a long time. I gave him one ridiculous reason after another as to why I couldn't marry him, but always I avoided telling him the truth. I think I was ashamed."

"Of what?"

"Of so many things. Of marrying someone like Pieter. Of stealing from him, running away from him, hiding from him, not standing up to him. Of leaving my son behind while I went to make a life for myself."

Gaby felt her heart swell. Tears of empathy pooled in her eyes.

"Do you have any regrets?" she asked, a nervous flutter upsetting her stomach.

Maguy never hesitated.

"None. I'm a fatalist. I believe everything happens for a purpose, that it's all part of a universal scheme. How can I regret marrying Pieter when he gave me Max? I wasn't happy leaving Belgium, but I met Roger in France. I lived with him until he died four years ago, and I don't regret a second of it. Though Max spent most of his childhood here with Berthe and Jan and Jacob, he spent a great deal of time with Roger and me. He knew he had a mother."

"How did he learn about the Dinants?"

Again, Maguy smiled, as if remembering something sweet.

"When he was a small boy, I used to tell him the story of Edouard de Rosier and Marguerite Montrichard. I told him about his ancestors and how they had married and intermarried and dispersed all over Europe. I told him about that horrible time in the First World War when the Germans razed Dinant. My mother's family had the tapestries hidden in a secret room in the basement of their house. When the Germans came, the family ran, each taking one of the precious tapestries with them. My grandmother took my mother and *The Triumph of Chastity*. My grandfather took *The Marriage of Brussels*. When I got married, those two were part of my dowry. The others were believed lost."

"But Max bought them."

Maguy nodded, her face glowing with pride.

"He knew what the Dinant tapestries meant to me and what they meant to him. They're his heritage. They're who he is."

"Did he know about his father?"

Maguy's face grew dark.

"Not from me. I didn't want him to bear that burden. I didn't want him to know what Pieter had done or why I had left. I told him his father died in the war."

"Who told him the truth?"

"I did," Berthe interjected proudly, still convinced she had done the right thing. "When he was eighteen, he went to enlist and was asked for his birth certificate. He didn't have it, so he went to the hall of records for a duplicate. It was then he learned that his father was not the fictional man Maguy had told him about, but Baron Pieter von Gelder. Naturally, because Pieter was a very visible man in Antwerp and Brussels, Max knew of him. Von Gelder was a successful businessman, a well-respected citizen, a nobleman. Why, he asked me, had his mother lied?"

Berthe sighed, as if it was just as difficult explaining Maguy's motives to Gaby as it had been explaining them to Max.

"At first, I tried inventing a story that would satisfy his curiosity. I had known the evil that was Pieter von Gelder, and I suppose that until that moment I had agreed with Maguy's decision to spare her son the pain of who his father really was. Unfortunately, I'm not very creative. Max knew I was lying. He insisted that he was entitled to know the truth. He said if I loved him, I would tell him. And because I do love him and because I thought it might be easier for me to tell him than for Maguy, I did."

"How did he react?" Gaby asked, somewhat rhetorically. She knew how sensitive Max was. She also knew the agony of being confronted with a horrible, unavoidable, unacceptable truth. Suddenly, she was a twelve-year-old girl hearing about an accident. She was a woman hearing that her husband didn't love her anymore, that her beloved aunt was going to die, that her son didn't want to see or speak to her. No. She didn't have to wait for Berthe's answer. She knew how Max had reacted.

"He was angry," Berthe said. "But his anger was confused. Instead of directing his fury at his father, he accused me of making it all up as a way of covering for Maguy. Remarkably, he refused to believe that the man who had sired him was capable of such contemptible acts. He began to rant and rave about Maguy, dredging up all the resentments he must have harbored as a small boy about her moving away. That's when I got angry. I gave him names, dates, details. I told him about how Pieter had beaten his mother, how he had caused her to miscarry and almost abort him with his violence. I told him how Pieter had condemned neighbors to death in exchange for a few francs, how willing he was to sacrifice women and children and innocent men and, yes, even his wife, for power and position. I'll never forget the look on his face." Berthe's eyes moistened as she relived that sad day. "He ran out of my home and for several years refused to return."

Gaby looked from Berthe to Maguy, who said, "Max didn't believe Berthe because he didn't want to. He was young. The truth was devastating. He hadn't heard it from me. It was just too difficult." She shook her head, displaying a deep vein of remorse that might have lessened over the years, but had not disappeared. "Though he denied the truth for a long time, I know that all the while, his heart told him I would never have lied to him without reason."

"What turned him around?"

"Immediately after he completed his tour of duty in Burundi, he was recruited by Interpol. I suppose that having access to files such as theirs was simply too great a temptation. He made inquiries and studied case records, probably in the hope of disproving Berthe's story. Instead, he found reports of rumors and insinuations and accusations. Too many to dismiss. When he questioned his superiors, they verified what Berthe had told him, adding that in the years immediately following the war, the Belgian government had tried to build a case against Pieter as a collaborator but had been stymied by a lack of tangible proof. They had hearsay and recollections and suspicions, but nothing definite, nothing to positively link him with the Nazis. They shelved the matter. Max didn't. He came to see me and we had it out. He yelled and vented his rage. I listened and begged his forgiveness. He commanded me to tell him everything I had kept secret. And so I opened the doors I had closed so many years before, letting out all the evil I had tried so hard to keep hidden." Her eyes narrowed. She laced her fingers together, clasping them as if in desperate prayer. "He cried," she said, her own voice breaking. "At first his tears were hot and angry, but then they grew sad, dropping onto his cheeks like so many lost moments. I held him then as I had when he was small and we cried together, he for things he never had, I for things I never should have done. After that, Pieter von Gelder became Max's personal crusade. For over twenty years, he's been obsessed with the notion of making his father pay, but with all his cleverness and all his resources, he was unable to find what he needed." Maguy paused, stared at Gaby, and smiled warmly, gratefully. "Until you found it for him."

"Suddenly, I'm not sure if that was good or bad," Gaby said, her voice betraying her efforts to keep her fears for Max to herself.

Maguy leaned over and squeezed Gaby's hand.

"I know what you're thinking, my dear, but he'll be all right. And yes, finding that deed was a good thing. My son needs to bring Pieter to justice and for more than his war crimes. He wants to extract payment for what Pieter did to me, what he took from me. He wants payment for what he did to Berthe and Jan and to the others. More than that, I think he needs to avenge what Pieter did to him. After all, Pieter deprived Max not only of a father, but of a name as well."

Maguy's voice was weak, but her emotions were strong, rising to the surface, causing her to shiver. Gaby went to the back of the room and brought back a blanket.

"Why don't you rest?" she said, tucking the handmade quilt around Maguy's frail body.

"I am sleepy," she said. "How about you? Will you be all right?" She reached up and touched Gaby's cheek. It was a simple gesture, but the way it was done, hearing her speak in French, it provoked a powerful bolt of *déjà vu*, memories of snuggling with Delphine, memories of being comforted by Tante Simone.

"I'll be fine," Gaby said, wondering where Max was, wondering if he was safe, praying for all their sakes that he was. "We'll all be fine."

By the time Prudence had tracked Max down, he had left Brussels and had headed to Antwerp. It took a few moments to decipher Gaby's message, but when he did, he smiled. He knew exactly what she had done and where she had gone. He also knew he had been right to let down his guard and to fall in love with her. Much as he wanted to think about Gaby and what life with her might be like, Prudence read him another telegram, this one from an Interpol agent in Düsseldorf. Von Gelder had been spotted disembarking an SAS flight from Denmark that afternoon. By checking passenger lists and piecing together his itinerary, Interpol surmised that von Gelder had taken a train to Philadelphia, where he had boarded a plane for Miami. He must have stayed there overnight, taken a plane from Miami to Copenhagen, from Copenhagen to Düsseldorf. A tail had followed him to a house in a suburb called Neuss. Four men were posted outside that house. So far, he had remained inside. The assumption was he intended to spend the night.

Max called the Interpol office in Düsseldorf, gave the bureau chief there his number, and instructed them to call him the instant von Gelder made any move. The call came at three in the morning. Taking an educated guess as to where he was headed, Max estimated that he had at least six hours before von Gelder arrived in Damme. Max would be there in an hour and a half. And then he would wait.

Everything looked right. The gate was closed and locked. The guard in the sentry kiosk was busy reading a newspaper. Two nuns walked through the chilly square, their hands tucked inside their sleeves, their heads bowed against the wind. Once or twice, an elderly woman opened the door of her house and aired out a small rug, beating it with a stick to release the dust that clung to its fibers. A man with a woolen cap and navy peacoat raked the frosty gardens in front of the chapel.

Everything looked right, but the guard in the sentry house was an Interpol agent. So were the nuns who patrolled the square, their hands clasped around loaded pistols. So was the gardener whose pockets were filled with bullets. So were the people in the houses that bordered the square. Today, no one in this peaceful community of Damme was who he or she appeared to be.

Pieter von Gelder drove up to the gates shortly after noon. When he spoke to the guard, he was polite but insistent, requesting that he be admitted so he could visit his wife, Maguy

Montrichard. For the purpose of verisimilitude, the guard hassled von Gelder for several minutes. He claimed to have no knowledge of a husband. Von Gelder said they were estranged, but he was there on a matter concerning their son. Again, the guard questioned him. Again, he invented answers. Finally, when both men felt they had successfully completed their lunge and parry, the gates opened. As von Gelder walked toward the small apartment in the rear of the quadrangle, his pace unhurried and supremely confident, the guard buzzed Max.

When Max opened the door and von Gelder looked him straight in the eye and said, "Hello, son," he didn't know whether to be astounded or impressed. He stepped aside and watched as the tall, balding man with the delft-blue eyes walked in and surveyed the room.

"Where's your mother?" he said bluntly.

"Far away from here," Max answered, sizing up his opponent, knowing that von Gelder was doing the same.

"I thought she was dead, you know. I thought the Germans had come and taken her away."

"Why would they have done a terrible thing like that to the wife of such a good friend to the Third Reich?" Max's sarcasm filled the air.

"She was Jewish."

Max nodded as if to say, Oh, well, then, it all makes sense. "She was pregnant," he said.

"I didn't know that at the time. However, knowing you by reputation, I must say I'm glad she did escape. You're quite a credit."

He was cool. Max had to admit the man was cool. He must have known that Max wasn't alone. He must have known that it was only a matter of minutes before someone was going to burst through a door brandishing a gun. He must have known that Max was dying to attack him and to extract from him the pound of flesh he felt he and Maguy were owed. Yet he remained in control.

"Look," Max said, "we're not here to catch up on old times. You're here because my mother presents a problem for you. I'm here because you present a problem for me."

"And what problem is that?" Casually, as if they were

discussing the weather, he perched on the arm of a chair and crossed his arms in front of his chest.

"As an agent for Interpol acting on behalf of the Belgian government, I'm obliged to bring you in to the authorities so you can be tried for the crime of collaboration with the enemy during a time of war." Max, determined to appear equally nonchalant and unruffled, circled the chair, speaking in a deliberate monotone. "As the son of a woman you brutalized and intended to sentence to death in a gas chamber in exchange for a high-level governmental post, I want to reach into my pocket, take out the knife I keep just for occasions such as these, and slit your fucking throat. I'm not supposed to do that without provocation. That's my problem."

Von Gelder cocked his head and narrowed his eyes. He studied Max for a long moment and then laughed.

"You have another problem, dear boy, and that's one of proof. You have none. You have nothing that will stand up in court."

"But I do." Moving at a deliberately measured pace, yet exhibiting great relish, he reached into his pocket and withdrew the wrinkled piece of paper that sealed von Gelder's fate. He unfolded it with excruciating slowness, turning it so von Gelder could study the handwriting. "*This* will stand up in court."

Von Gelder didn't flinch. "It's a fraud," he said. "That's not my signature."

"My mother will swear that it is."

"Your mother is a fugitive, a thieving bitch who deserted her husband and her country by sneaking off into the night with things that didn't belong to her."

"*The Marriage of Brussels* didn't belong to you," Max countered heatedly, trying to rein his temper. "Many of the paintings you gave the Nazis didn't belong to you. The people you turned over to the Nazi death camps didn't belong to you!"

Von Gelder ignored Max's outburst, brushing it off as if Max was no more significant than a gnat.

"I'm surprised you're doing this, Max. I could ruin your reputation. After all, don't they say the apple doesn't fall far from the tree? If I'm so despicable, that doesn't speak well for you."

"You don't speak for me at all," Max rejoined. "My mother

is the only parent I ever knew, and she's a gem. *She's* the tree from which this apple fell."

Suddenly, he felt odd, just like when he had been a little boy and he had defended his mother against the taunts of neighborhood bullies who teased him about Maguy living with Roger without benefit of marriage. He felt the lump in his throat, and just as he had those many years before, he forced himself to swallow it. He was determined not to embarrass himself or Maguy by simpering or backing away from a challenge.

He reached into his pocket and pressed a button. Within seconds, Paul van der Hamme, senior Belgian agent, who had worked with Max on this case for years, appeared from the kitchen. Three other agents came through the front door. Von Gelder's expression never changed. His eyes bored through Max like a laser, threatening to reach his soul and burn it with a hellish fury. Though Max's insides tumbled and twisted with cyclonic force, he stood firm.

When he spoke, his voice was steady. "It is with a mixture of extreme joy and extreme pain, great pride and great humiliation, that I say something I've wanted to say for years. You're under arrest."

As the handcuffs snapped around von Gelder's wrist and van der Hamme was about to take him away, he turned, looked at Max, and laughed.

"When you hear someone say 'like father, like son,' think of me, won't you?"

Max stood in the doorway of his mother's home, listening to the laughter, hearing the echo of triumph in that laugh, the madness and the overriding tones of remorseless evil.

"It's over," he said aloud to no one but himself. "It's over."

But, he thought, as he locked the door and slowly headed for his car, would it ever really be over? Would he ever forget the malevolence of the man whose seed had created him? Would he ever forget the hatred he had felt when he discovered the truth of his parentage? More than that, would he forever remember the sound of von Gelder's voice as he cursed him with the words *like father, like son*?

* * *

Gaby was still a bit dazed. Everything had happened in such a rush. Max had come to the farm, but before she could have a private moment with him, he had been gobbled up by his mother and Berthe and Jan and their children and grandchildren and everyone else living on the Glucksmann compound. They bombarded him with endless questions about von Gelder's capture, demanding that he tell the story again and again. Throughout it all, he was Max, patient to a fault, repeating himself a dozen times without ever allowing an edge to sharpen his tongue or dampen his mood.

Maguy clung to him, proud one moment, shaky the next. It was hard for her to believe that she was finally free to walk the land of her birth without fear. She talked about moving to Brussels, about going to the opera and the ballet, about visiting Dinant and old friends who still lived in Antwerp. Gaby saw how pale she grew when Max interrupted her and reminded all of them that von Gelder still had to stand trial and that, until he was behind bars, they should remain on guard. Clearly, though Max despised his father, he respected his cleverness too much ever to take him lightly.

It seemed like hours before Max was able to break away. When he did, he took Gaby by the hand and walked with her into the naked fields. The dirt was frozen beneath their feet, but as is typical of the low countries, even in December, the wind felt damp. Gaby tried to remember how this land had looked when they had driven through it months before, when it had been green and lush with vegetation, brilliantly hued with the colors of summer's harvest. It was difficult coaxing such a warm image on such a cold day, but Gaby recalled every detail, every nuance, every shade of crop and clothing. It had been a day spent with Max, and each of those precious days was not simply stored in her memory, but etched on her mind.

When they had walked beyond the reach of even the strongest voice, Max turned and took Gaby in his arms. His hands slid around her back and drew her close. His mouth pressed against hers, his lips warm and welcoming. They embraced eagerly, luxuriating in the feel of each other, the nearness of each other. Like an animal from the wild caged and then unleashed, sensations held at bay during their separation coursed through their bodies and electrified their former intimacy. They felt now what they had felt then, a desperate need to touch and to hold and to love each other. Yet, what had happened then happened again. Circumstance pushed a wedge between them. Max had to take Maguy to Brussels and find her an apartment. He had to prepare her and himself for von Gelder's trial. He had to tender his resignation from Interpol and close out his files.

"And when all that's done, I'm going to come to New York to get you."

After a few more hours together, Max drove Gaby to the airport so that she could fly to Paris and, from there, home. As she watched the monitor at the front of the Concorde register MACH 1, informing the passengers that they had reached the speed of sound, she wondered if Max's return would be as swift. A part of her wondered if he would return at all. He hadn't told her he loved her. He hadn't proposed. He hadn't taken any vows. He hadn't done anything except reaffirm the strong hold he had on her emotions. Like this supersonic jet, her heart soared when she was in his arms. He spoke and the sky dressed itself in its most brilliant blue. He smiled and the sun donned a crown of the shiniest gold. He touched her and the earth changed into a paradisiacal land of contentment and peace.

What if he didn't come to New York?

Gaby stared out the window and considered that thought. She sighed. Out of the corner of her eye, she caught a filmy reflection of herself in the glass. It wasn't a full-blown portrait like one would get from a mirror. Rather, it was a sketch, a misty outline of a woman in midflight. Just then, at that moment in time, at that juncture in her life, that was precisely how Gaby felt—as if she were in midflight, halfway between where she had been and where she was going.

She had a new job with new responsibilities and, she supposed, new problems. She loved Max, but she wasn't willing to sacrifice her life to be a part of his. If he came to New York and they built a life together, it would be wonderful. If he didn't, she would survive.

She smiled. *I have come a long way.*

Three years before, she couldn't have said that. Three years before, she had been a dependent person, someone who relied upon the largesse of another, someone who had no individual status, no individual assets, and little individuality. Circumstance had necessitated the creation of a persona. Had the persona begotten a person?

Gaby recalled that time—was it only a year ago?—when Garrett had invited her to the Castleton gala and she was telling Armand how frightened she was about going and possibly making a fool of herself.

"I'm not sure I know where the real me ends and the pretend me begins," she had said.

"Perhaps they're one and the same," he had answered.

The loudspeaker crackled. A steward announced that the airplane had begun its descent. As Gaby buckled her seat belt and looked down over the city she now called home, she thought, perhaps Armand was right. Perhaps Gabrielle Didier and Gaby Thayer had finally become one and the same.

27

January 1988

Christmas had been strange. Wonderful in its way—being back in Paris and back with Oncle Bernard—but unsettling, as all transitions are unsettling. For each step forward, there was a tug back, for each push, a pull. Thanks to the colossal success of the Montgomery auction, Gaby had paid off her debts and was now, for the first time in years, solvent. More than that, she was independent. She didn't have to rely on anyone other than herself. She had a healthy bank account, a credit rating, her own American Express card, and the respect of the financial community, which had once deemed her unbankable. Yet as positive as the changes in her circumstances were, her new position negated her plans with Oncle Bernard. Realizing that a move to France was impossible, Gaby had spent the entire week of her visit trying to convince him to move to New York. They had grown so close over the past year that the thought of being thousands of miles apart disturbed her. Without him, she felt alone, adrift, alienated from one of life's basics. With him, she felt part of a family, part of an emotional unit that provided security and shelter and support. With him, she was able to accept the fact that she had been orphaned, that Tante Simone was dead, and that her only child had rejected her, refusing her calls and returning her Christmas gift unopened.

Bernard thought about her offer—after all, he too had grown accustomed to the fond familiarity that had recently marked their relationship—but in the end, both of them knew, just as Simone had known back when Delphine and Bill had died, he wasn't the type to be uprooted. Reluctantly, but realistically acceding to life's demands, they had agreed to compromise. They would continue their weekly telephone calls. Bernard promised to fly to London if and when she was there on business and, if he was up to it, to fly to New York for a stay in the spring. Gaby promised to spend next Christmas with him in Paris, and both of them vowed to spend one more August in Antibes.

When Gaby returned home, her melancholia was cut short by the pressures of her new job. In less than three weeks, the January Antiques Fair would open, and Castleton's would host three of its biggest auctions: one for important French furniture, one for important English furniture, and one for magnificent jewelry. Within a very short time, she had to assure the success of those sales as well as ensure her own success within Castleton's. Quickly, she promoted Edwin Rathbone, Castleton's expert on English furniture, to the post of head auctioneer. He was a man with exquisite taste and flair, a dry British wit, and the ability to wave the gavel and create magic. It didn't hurt that he was also the favored choice among those in the New York office to replace Garrett. She promoted Giles Deffand to the position of assistant to the president, filling Deffand's post with her old friend Beezie Zarlov. She increased the size of the publicity department, staffed it with talented Madison Avenue imports, and instructed them to come up with an advertising campaign that would give Castleton's an exciting high-gloss image, as well as a public relations program designed to upgrade Castleton's prestige. She revamped the schedule to allow charity functions and cause-auctions. She formed a committee to oversee and improve the quality and range of courses offered to the public. And, as Giles's first major job in his new capacity, she asked him to investigate the feasibility of increasing the number of annex auctions.

"Now what?" Gaby said, studying her reflection with the

same critical eye she was using to adjudge her work. "Do I panic or do I have confidence in what I've done?"

After her return from Belgium, she had spent two weeks closeted with Garrett Jr. as he shifted the reins of the New York branch over to her. Their relationship had also shifted, but in reverse, returning to the warm, respectful, comfortable friendship it had been before. But despite the ease with which they worked, she knew that whether they had been friends or lovers, he was now chairman of the board. He was her boss and she was accountable. Tonight, she would hear what Garrett and the entire Castleton clan thought of her efforts thus far.

"Trust your instincts. They got you this far," she told herself as she fluffed her hair, wishing she could arrange her life as easily as one arranged a coiffure.

It was true that most of her instincts had been extremely reliable. Most, but not all. She had believed Max when he had said he would come to New York and they would rekindle their relationship. Yet it had been weeks and she hadn't heard from him. She had believed Oncle Bernard when he had said that Steven would come around, that his anger would abate and he would see that he had viewed her life through eyes tainted green with Brian's jealousy. She had believed that once the ponderous burden of debt had been removed, life would be a continuum of blissful contentment. Certainly, her situation had improved. She was happy in her work, pleased with her progress, and hopeful about her future, but none of that filled the immense void inside her heart. How could it? She was a mother with no son, a woman in love, with no man to love her in return.

The week before, she had presided over her first official function. Castleton's had hosted an auction to benefit the Belle Reynolds Center for Abused Children. Gaby had been more than pleased with the results, but for her, and for Chelsea, it was a bittersweet evening. Though they had raised enough money to assure a decent start for the center, it was the poignant reminder of the reason for that center that had struck Gaby the hardest. Belle had killed herself because she had seen no other avenue of escape. She had tried to tell others of her torment. She had hinted. She had offered clues. She had asked for help. But she was a child, and so no one listened. No one paid attention. The night of the auction, everyone paid attention, especially when the turntable slowly revealed Belle's last painting.

It was a portrait of pain, a half-drawn girl huddled in the corner of a huge canvas, no features on her face other than a mouth opened and ready to cry, no clothes on her body other than a blouse ripped from the shoulder down. Attacking her from all sides was a riot of aggressive, abstract shapes and bold, belligerent color. Dribbled paint. Careless forms. Angry masses of black. Splotches of red bleeding into the white space surrounding the cowering girl. It was a hostile world, a world deaf to her cries, blind to her private agony. The first time Gaby saw it, she wept. When the name of the buyer was revealed, she wept again. Louise Reynolds had bought her daughter's last will and testament.

Though she knew the situations weren't similar, she couldn't help but think about Steven. Had she really listened to him? Had she really paid attention to his needs? His wants? Or was her interest superficial, there only when it didn't interfere with her needs and her wants? Had she been so involved in her own problems that she hadn't considered the effect her life was having on his? The questions weren't new. She had asked them over and over again, but that night, thinking about Belle, she had asked them in a different voice, a voice shrill with fear and urgency. What would she do if something happened to Steven? How would she feel? That night, she had come home and started a campaign to reunite herself with her son. She wrote him several letters and phoned his dorm every single night, hoping to wear him down if nothing else. So far, he hadn't responded. It didn't matter. Sooner or later, he'd have to give in because she wasn't giving up.

Gaby blinked away her tears, reminding herself that tonight was a joyous occasion, a night for laughter and celebration. This was the night of the Castleton gala, the night she made her social debut as president of Castleton's New York. She refreshed her makeup and then turned, glancing over her shoulder at the extravagant design of her gown. She had seen it in the window of Ungaro's boutique in Paris and knew she had to have it. It was a lush, rich satin, the color of South Seas coral. Strapless, tucked and shirred tight around her body, flaring at the bottom, poufed at the back, it was a dress sewn with magical thread. She who wore it felt instantly beautiful, immediately elegant, irrefutably secure. Gaby remembered trying it on, falling in love with it, picturing herself making a grand entrance in it. Then she had looked at the price. She had visibly blanched. Oncle Bernard had told her to think of it as a reward for a job well done. When that didn't convince her, he reminded her of her position, of who she was and how important this night was to her career. He told her to consider it a business expense. It wasn't the most romantic argument he had ever advanced, but it was effective.

Thinking about Oncle Bernard prompted Gaby to look at the clock. She had arranged for a limousine to pick him up at his hotel. He should have been here ten minutes ago. Just as she started for the phone to call his hotel, the doorbell rang.

"Thank God," she said as she opened the door and stepped aside, expecting Bernard to walk past her into the foyer. "I thought you'd never get here."

"I told you she'd be thrilled to see us."

Gaby's mouth dropped. There were two tall, handsome, tuxedoed men standing in her entry, but Oncle Bernard wasn't one of them. Max was one. Steven was the other. Max was beaming, clearly pleased with himself. Steven was not quite as sure about the impact of their surprise.

"You look incredibly gorgeous," Max said, leaning over to kiss her cheek, allowing his lips to linger for an extra second before he pulled away. "Don't you think so, Steven?"

"You really do look great, Mom."

Gaby couldn't stop staring. She had a thousand questions, but her tongue had ceased to function.

"Come," Max said, taking her hand, tugging slightly to get her to follow.

"I . . ."

"We know, we know. You have a party to go to. In fact, in case you haven't guessed, we're here to escort you, Madame President, but first . . ." He settled her on a couch, inviting Steven to sit on one side, taking a seat on her other side for himself. "Your son has something to say."

Steven glanced at Max and then looked at his mother.

"I have a lot of apologizing to do," he said. "I acted like a spoiled brat, Mom, and I'm sorry."

He paused. Gaby noticed that he looked to Max again for encouragement. Max nodded. Steven continued.

"I was angry when you and Dad split up. Real angry. My whole world had changed and I guess I blamed you without thinking it through. You were my Mom, the one who always made everything better, yet it seemed that the one time I wanted you to make everything all right, you refused. I hated you for that."

Gaby winced, but she didn't protest.

"For whatever reason, I needed Dad's approval more than yours. I guess that's why I sided with him. I believed whatever he said and doubted everything you said. You said you were broke. He said you weren't. He was taking care of me, so I just assumed he was taking care of you. He told me Mr. Lafitte was your lover. When you told me Mr. Lafitte was a friend, I didn't believe you because I didn't want to believe you. When I came here that day, him being here confirmed that I was right and Dad was right and you were a liar. I shut you out. I never gave you a chance to explain. I never even tried to understand. Until Max helped me to see your side of it."

Gaby looked at Max with questions in her eyes.

"Let's just say that Steven and I had a long talk about mothers and sons."

"Where did you have this talk?" Gaby asked. "And when?"

"Max came to see me at school." Steven smiled. Gaby could see he had remembered something funny and wanted to laugh, but wasn't sure it was appropriate. "I was as rude to him as I was to you, but this guy is real persistent. He hounded me until I either spoke to him or adopted him."

"Would you mind repeating some of the conversation?" Gaby said, stifling a smile as well as the urge to hug Max for bringing Steven to her.

Steven lowered his eyes for a moment, measuring his words, recalling Max's words.

"Max told me about his mother, Maguy, and how life had given her a raw deal and how she had done what she had to do to protect her son and herself. He told me how angry he had been when his mother had gone off to France without him. He said he would tell himself that he hated her and hated her lover, Roger, and that he never wanted to see her again. But whenever he did see her, he knew in his heart that he had lied to himself, that he loved her very, very much.'' Steven bit his lip, fighting back the swell of emotions that threatened to overwhelm him. ''He said that it was only when he got older that he understood the sacrifices she had made on his behalf and that her life hadn't been dictated by her own personal choice. Max talked to me about you and what you had had to do. He told me how hard you had worked and how difficult it had been for you coming to New York alone, owing all that money, having no one to go to.'' He shook his head and then bowed it, wiping his eyes, unable to dam his tears. ''I should have stood by you,'' he said. ''I should have been there for you. God knows, you were always there for me.''

Gaby couldn't stand it anymore. She opened her arms, and when she closed them around her very grown-up son, she thought she would explode from the rush of feelings inside her.

''Thank you,'' she whispered to Max, proffering a wobbly smile.

''Okay, Steven,'' Max said, affectionately clapping the young man on his back. ''You're cutting into my time now. Remember? We had a deal. You had your say. Now I get to have mine. Right?''

Steven wiped his eyes, took a deep breath, and sat at attention.

''Right,'' he said.

Max took Gaby's hand.

''Since tonight seems to be a night for honesty, let me state from the start that I love you. I've loved you from the instant I laid eyes on you, exactly one year ago tonight. I confess I haven't always been the perfect suitor, but my behavior has never been a reflection of my true feelings.''

He raised her hand to his lips and kissed her fingers.

''I know how hurt you must have been when your marriage broke up, how frightened and hostile you must have been. I sensed it. What's more, I understood it. Probably because your anger and your insecurity so closely matched my own. After Catherine died, I swore I'd never allow anyone in my heart again. It was too painful, I told myself. Too much of a risk. No matter how wonderful romance seems at the beginning, when the end comes, if it comes, it hurts, and I wasn't willing to hurt again. I locked myself into a cage where I thought I'd be safe.

I hadn't realized how lonely it was in that cage until I met you."

Suddenly, Max rose from the couch and went to the front door. He opened it and bent down to get something. When he returned, he knelt in front of Gaby and, with great ceremony, presented her with a bouquet of roses and pink carnations.

"In the tradition of my ancestors, Edouard de Rosier and Marguerite Montrichard, and with the approval of your son, Steven, may I ask if you, Gabrielle Didier Cocroft Thayer, would do me the honor of becoming my bride? I can't offer you a guarantee of a happily-ever-after, but I can promise to love you and to try my best to please you."

Gaby clutched the flowers in her hands and tried to steady her emotions. It felt so odd to have Max propose in front of her son. It felt odder still to think of Brian at a time like this. But perhaps it was right that she did. Then, when she had accepted his proposal, she had agreed to give herself to a man. She had kept that agreement, giving of herself until she had nothing left to give. With Max, it would be different because she was different, he was different. With him, she wouldn't be living his life, she would be part of his life, sharing her life with him.

As for guarantees of a happily-ever-after, Max was right. There were none. Besides, they were beyond that. They weren't young innocents blinded by storybook illusion. She and Max had already experienced the harsher side of life's reality. They had tasted the sour fruit of disappointment and heartbreak. They had known love and they had known death and they had known failure and they had known success. They had suffered and they had triumphed, but more important, they had come through the pain with enough of a need to love to be willing to take the risk of loving again.

Following medieval custom, Gaby pulled a single carnation from the bouquet and handed it to Max.

"Yes," she said, in a voice that was loud and clear, strong and very sure. "Yes, I'll marry you! Yes, I'll be your bride! Yes, I love you!"

Gently, tenderly, Max took her face in his hands, and with their eyes opened so they could see the love each had for the other, they plighted their troth with a kiss.

Steven joined their embrace, and as a warm flush of happiness engulfed her, Gaby decided she didn't need guarantees. The fullness in her heart told her she and Max would find their own happily-ever-after. Because they weren't starting their new life together with once upon a time.

ABOUT THE AUTHOR

DORIS MORTMAN has worked in advertising and magazines. Her previous two novels, *Circles* and *First Born,* were both *New York Times* bestsellers. She lives in New Jersey, is the mother of two, and is currently at work on her fourth novel.

THE WORLD OF
Doris Mortman

They come to a world of endless dreams and glitter, hoping to become a part of the rich, the elite, and leave behind their ordinary lives. And though quick acceptance is not easily achieved, these women are determined, talented, and beautiful. They are the women of Doris Mortman's world. Like the intriguing Gaby Cocroft of RIGHTFULLY MINE, striving for success is what these fascinating heroines do best. Read Doris Mortman's other two *New York Times* bestsellers, CIRCLES and FIRST BORN and share their wonderful secrets.

CIRCLES

Jennifer Cranshaw had everything: beauty, intelligence, a happy marriage and a successful career. On the brink of the biggest triumph of her career, Jennifer will, in one bold move, single-handedly attempt to salvage the fashion magazine *Jolie* from its own destructive forces . . .

Jennifer Cranshaw's office resembled a Broadway rehearsal hall. Long-limbed models were everywhere: slouched against walls, sitting cross-legged on the floor, doing exercises in the corner, or lounging in the doorway drinking coffee from Styrofoam cups. All attention was centered on Jennifer, who was patiently instructing a tall redhead in denim overalls and a T-shirt.

Jennifer removed her burgundy mohair jacket and dropped it on the nearest chair. Placing her left hand on the gentle curve of her hip, she shifted her weight, lowered her right shoulder, assumed a theatrical pose, and threw back her head. Then, with the grace of a dancer, she glided across the floor, her slender legs peeking through a slit in her skirt. Her trim body swayed provocatively, moving in time to an imaginary beat, her mauve silk blouse rippling as she walked. When she had reached her desk and resumed her normal posture, she was greeted by a spurt of enthusiastic applause.

It was three days before the *Jolie* party—a grand celebration of the magazine's fortieth anniversary—and Jennifer was making her final selections for the fashion show she was staging as part of the evening's festivities. Her present concern was Coral Trent. The young model was obviously nervous. After explaining once again the movement she had just demonstrated, Jennifer left Coral in the care of *Jolie*'s models' editor so she could zero in on the others. She switched on a disco tape and, directing each woman with hand signals, indicated stops and turns and do-it-agains with long, expressive fingers.

In a few days, twelve hundred people would descend on Cloud 9, New York's famous see-and-be-seen disco, to honor the magazine. As promotion director, Jennifer was in charge of monitoring every detail from the spectacular fashion retrospective, to coordinating guest lists, hiring entertainment, supervising menus, and insuring ample press coverage. As other projects piled up on her desk, temporarily ignored, she tried to balance her anxiety with her genuine anticipation of the event. Jennifer took pride in the fact that she had never missed a deadline. She was determined to maintain that record.

Three leggy blondes strode across the room in time to the music, hoping to attract her attention with the hip gyrations and bumpy dance steps of the fifties. Jennifer encouraged them to continue while she located her countdown sheet and scanned it for last-minute chores.

"Meet with caterer: 3 P.M." She jotted "hors d'oeuvres" next to his name, reminding herself to check on the current price of caviar. Brad Helms, *Jolie's* publisher, had insisted on caviar and champagne, but with an already overstretched promotion budget and a worrisome decline in ad revenues, Jennifer had decided to exercise caution first and worry about Brad later.

"Call florist!" Jennifer motioned for the three young hopefuls to take a break, signaling for a round-faced brunette named Uta to settle herself in Jennifer's large bergère desk chair as she dialed Vincent Matteo, the floral darling of the Park Avenue set and the man she had commissioned, with a small amount of trepidation, to do the flower arrangements for the party.

Mimi Holden, Jennifer's secretary, arrived carrying a wicker tray stocked with an assortment of eyelashes and black eye pencils. Tucking the phone in the crook of her neck, Jennifer took a tweezers and gripped a stiff eyelash between the metal tips. Like a well-trained operating room nurse, Mimi slapped a small tube of adhesive into Jennifer's free hand, watching carefully as Jennifer spread a wiggly white line on the edge of the lash, then slid it onto the model's eyelid, centering it, gently pressing it to the soft skin, fitting it to the natural lash line.

While she waited for Vincent, she cautioned herself against impatience. Her initial encounter with the florist had been just shy of combative. She suggested and he demanded. She mentioned price. He dismissed it. She wanted a contract. He preferred the honor system. Jennifer had prevailed, but it had required delicate handling to effect a tentative friendship.

She had the second eyelash trapped in the tweezers when his high-pitched voice attacked her ear.

"Jennifer Cranshaw?"

"Yes, the very same." She spread the gooey white paste along the fringe and wiped the excess off with her finger. "From *Jolie* magazine. You're doing a job for us this Thursday?"

"Jennifer. Of course. Forgive me. I'm glad you called. I don't know how to tell you this, but the big glass beakers for the lilies are out."

The second lash was in place. Jennifer stood back, squinting to be sure they were even, and counted to ten.

"Out? Why?" She selected a pitch black kohl pencil from the tray.

"Because they're tacky."

"Tacky? A month ago they were *the* most outrageous things you'd ever seen."

"I had a dream."

"You had a *what*?" Jennifer paused for a second to absorb what he had said, and then continued drawing thick black lines in a semicircle beneath Uta's lids.

"A dream, darling. I saw lilies in baskets. There they were, floating before me. Bunches and bunches of fabulous lilies in the most marvelous baskets. The colors were simply divine, and the effect, well, my dear, it was nothing short of drop dead! I knew then that the beakers were wrong, wrong, wrong."

"Did you?" Her voice reverberated with controlled anger.

"Glass is, well, too obvious. Baskets are warm. Subtle. Sort of cozy, don't you think?"

"Vincent, this is not a picnic. This is an elegant evening hosted by a major fashion magazine."

She could hear him sniveling.

"Vincent, are you listening to me?"

"You're treating me like a child, Jennifer."

"You're whining like a child," she said, struggling to keep the phone steady while she applied the lower lashes. "We agreed on huge glass beakers overflowing with prize lilies, and that's what I want."

"But I don't like it anymore."

"But I do!" Jennifer took a deep breath, standing back to admire her handiwork and restraining an urge to shout at the man on the other end of the phone. "I know you're trying to give us the best job possible, and I appreciate the fact that you've explored other avenues, but your first instinct was lilies under glass. It was brilliant! Why tamper with genius?"

After a few minutes' deliberation, Vincent agreed. "Glass beakers it shall be."

Mimi responded to the frustrated look on Jennifer's face with a sympathetic laugh.

"That man will be the death of me. If his work weren't so extraordinary, I'd kick him out on his diamond-studded ear!"

"You pays your money and you takes your choice," Mimi said, replacing the cap on the eyelash adhesive.

Jennifer nodded and continued to experiment with a short, asymmetrical wig she had placed on Uta's head.

"Voilà!" She helped the model to her feet and presented her dramatically to everyone in the room.

The girl had been magically transformed into an exact duplicate of Peggy Moffett, the doll-faced model with the Sasson hairdo who had helped rocket Rudi Gernreich to fame during the late sixties. As Mimi watched Jennifer lead the young woman over to the window where Hilary West, the models' editor, was auditioning newcomers, she marveled at Jennifer's unbridled energy. She was gesturing excitedly, making large sweeps with her arms, pausing only to readjust the wig. The sun was getting stronger, and Mimi noticed the way the light played with Jennifer, spotlighting her own brightness. Jennifer's hair was a flurry of titian waves, brown kissed with coppery strands that glinted in the sun with a reddish henna'd glow.

Even now, Mimi thought, with all that was going on, Jennifer appeared to tower over everyone else by comparison. A dynamo in a petite package, Jennifer had the fervor of a top-ten coach. Where her penchant for excellence intimidated others, it inspired Mimi. They had only worked together for two years, but Mimi considered Jennifer a friend and an idol. If anyone could pull off this circus on Thursday night, Jennifer Sheldon Cranshaw could. What's more, Mimi knew she would do it with tremendous style!

Jennifer returned to her desk and eased herself into the wide-bottomed chair, trying to avoid the sharp twinge stinging her lower back. Mimi handed her a cup of coffee and then some advertising proofs. Jennifer studied the ads, and marked her corrections in the margins.

"When you drop these off in the Art Department," she said, checking her countdown sheet again, "would you ask Patrick Graham to come in? I think I need help."

As Mimi headed for the door, a photographer and his assistant weaved their way toward Jennifer.

"Albert, you're so late, I was sure you had found a better job." There was more tease than temper in her voice.

"What could be better than working for you?" Albert handed his camera bags to his assistant. "But enough chitchat. How about a few snaps of the eminent Mrs. Cranshaw at work?"

"You have enough of me," Jennifer said. "Concentrate on the staff, the models, and whatever editors you can find. Also, make sure you get a couple of shots of my secretary. That poor girl has run herself ragged, and I'd like to see her get some recognition."

Albert grabbed his Nikon, spoke to his assistant in Italian, and then went to work. As Jennifer looked on, the two men stalked the room, shutters clicking. Only one of the cameras was loaded, and even Jennifer didn't know who was holding the loaded camera. Every once in a while, they switched and then switched back again. That way, they eliminated posing and posturing, framing people in natural, unaffected pictures. It was, she supposed, what made Albert's work so magical.

"What can I do?" Patrick Graham, *Jolie*'s art director, had taken a seat near Jennifer, a cigarette dangling from his mouth.

"You can play Bert Parks. I'm having trouble choosing the last few models, and I've decided to take advantage of your outstanding judgment."

Pat screwed his boyish face into a skeptical grimace.

"How many models do you need, and what are you looking for?"

"Seven and lots of expression. No blank faces or limp bodies. I booked all the big names months ago. Yasmine, Brinkley, Chin, Cleveland, Iman, and I don't even remember who else. But I need thirty altogether. These girls are from the runway agencies. Strictly shows. No magazine experience and no TV. They're good, but I want the best of the lot."

"Isn't Hilary handling this?"

"She is, but it's a big job, time is running out, and I'd feel better if you'd help."

"Your every wish is my command." Pat put out his cigarette and went to the opposite end of the room where Hilary stood surrounded by eager mannequins.

"Jennifer?" The photographer was coming toward her. "Your secretary seems to be a bit camera shy. She refuses to have her picture taken. I can't understand it, since she is one foxy-looking lady, but Giancarlo and I have wasted two rolls of film on the back of her head already. What gives?"

Jennifer looked for Mimi, but she was nowhere to be found.

"I don't know. I told her we might use some of these shots for a feature in an upcoming *Jolie*. I thought she'd get a kick out of having her parents see her in the magazine. If she's uptight, though, let it go. You'll catch her at the party."

Albert saluted and went back to work. Jennifer picked up the morning newspaper and began to check for press coverage on the party. She found a small blurb in *Women's Wear Daily*, circled it with a red grease pencil, and turned to *Fashion Report*.

FR was the Gideon of ladies' fashion, the indispensable trade paper for the nation's fourth largest industry. Manufacturers of everything from thread to furs looked to the *Report* for design trends, market swings, buying patterns, technical innovations, and inside information on their competitors. Retailers scoured the pages for sources producing merchandise that might prove appealing to their clientele. Designers sought inspiration as well as recognition for their current lines. Display directors searched for unique ways of decorating windows and interiors. And everyone read the fiscal reports. No one, whether chain store or specialty shop, couture designer or schlock house, could afford not to read it.

Usually, Jennifer studied the paper thoroughly, but today she flipped immediately to the gossip section. She scanned a few articles, hoping to catch a plug for the party. It disturbed her that there wasn't one. Just as she was making a note to call her contact at the *Report* and request something in the next edition, her phone rang.

"Mrs. Cranshaw? This is Mr. Helms's secretary. He'd like you to come to his office immediately."

The other woman's voice was grave and insistent. Something was seriously wrong. Brad rarely called unscheduled meetings, and he wasn't the type to invent a crisis.

"I'll be right there!" Jennifer practically ran out of her office.

Despite her success at *Jolie,* Jennifer's private world is about to be struck a shocking blow that sends her reeling, and soon the woman with everything must account for the price she paid to have it all. Set against the glamorous world of the New York magazine industry, CIRCLES welcomed a stunning new voice to the world of fiction.

FIRST BORN

In her spectacular second novel, Doris Mortman tells the story of four magnificent women—all head-strong, all beautiful, all linked by a long-buried secret. Cissie, bold in business, but betrayed by love . . . Frankie, America's hottest model, yet constantly under the thumb of her domineering mother . . . Becca, determined to destroy everything that is precious to a half-sister who doesn't know Becca exists . . . and the fiery and irresistible Jinx . . .

"Frances Rebecca Elliot! Where have you been?"

Jinx burst through the front door and nearly collided with her mother.

"I called you at the hotel and they said you hadn't been there all day. I was afraid they had recruited you for the night shift and you'd have to miss my Christmas Eve party."

Jinx had forgotten all about her mother's plans. As she looked into the dining room, she saw the table pushed up against the wall, chafing dishes separated by holly sprigs and tall white candles. Kate Elliot loved holidays and celebrated them all with equal fervor—religious or national. Two weeks ago, the family had hosted a Chanukah party for half the neighborhood.

"It's been so long since we've all been together, what with you and Heather at school and Dad's hectic schedule. I've made turkey and sweet potatoes and . . . well, tonight is sort of a Thanksgiving rerun." She laughed, a full-hearted chuckle that let the world know she was aware how silly her holiday fetish appeared—and that she didn't care.

"Don't get crazy, Mom, but I'm not going to be able to stay." Jinx gave her mother a quick kiss and started for her room. Kate's silence stopped Jinx at the door. "I have a date," she said slowly, wishing her mother didn't look so crushed.

"Anyone I know?" Kate asked.

Jinx's mouth spread into a wide, excited grin. "It's Harrison Kipling! You know, Kipling of Kipling Hotels and Resorts." Kate's face was without expression. "Kipling. As in my boss. The man who owns the Kipling Oasis."

"Then tonight is a business meeting." Kate made no effort to temper her sarcasm.

"I hope not." Jinx answered her mother with the same biting tone.

"I wasn't aware that you had ever met Mr. Kipling."

"I met him today."

Infatuation had attached itself to Jinx like fairy dust, blushing her cheeks, sparkling her eyes, warming her smile. Kate Elliot felt a small ache grip the dark recesses of her soul.

"Where did you meet him?" Kate insisted that her lips form a smile.

"It's a long story which I'd love to tell you, but I have to jump into a shower and get dressed. His car is picking me up in an hour." She started to turn, but Kate caught her arm.

"You don't have to tell me the whole saga. Just the highlights."

Jinx told her mother about Kip's runaway horse, the breakfast, the ranch—everything except the fact that her heart had not stopped racing since the moment Kip had opened his eyes and looked at her for the first time.

"And you've been at his house all day? It's almost six o'clock."

"We talked and talked and talked. It was endless. I told him my ideas for improving some of the services at the Oasis as well as ways to update and improve his other resorts. He listened to everything," she said, picturing his face, the little lines around his eyes, the way his upper lip lifted unevenly when he smiled. "At least I think he listened."

Kate heard the hope in her daughter's voice. She saw the dreamy veil over her eyes. "Go take your shower," she said with a forced smile. "You don't want to be late."

As Kate watched Jinx race into the bathroom, her long

hair flying behind her, she felt the palms of her hands go moist and wiped them on her apron. Harrison Kipling wasn't the first older man in Jinx's life, but, Kate thought with frustrated resignation, if he was anything like Dell Talbott, she hoped he would be the last.

The Oasis was a sprawling luxury resort located on Phoenix's north side. A large stone entrance with a brass gate opened onto a palm-lined roadway that led up to the two main buildings. They were twin structures, each three stories high, built around open courtyards and connected by a gracefully arched arcade. In all Kipling hotels, both architecture and interior design reflected local tastes and styles. The Oasis was a blend of Spanish and Indian. It was Kipling's belief that since it was an innkeeper's job to make visitors feel at home, the inn had to be a part of, not stand apart from, the city it served.

Inside each main house was a sundry shop, a front desk, a travel desk, and a gift shop. Both had handmade tile floors and twenty-foot ceilings in the lobby. Both were constructed so that each room had its own balcony overlooking the courtyard. And both were heavily staffed with congenial people eager to please. One contained a massive convention complex, while the other catered solely to vacationers.

For amusement, the Oasis had twelve tennis courts, a stable, a riding rink as well as mountain trails for experienced equestrians, a small movie theater, three swimming pools, and a championship golf course, site of the annual PGA Sun Valley Classic. There was a small exercise room, a beauty salon, a barber shop, and five top-quality restaurants on the premises: the Mesquite, a poolside snack shop that featured salads and sandwiches; the Saguaro, a coffee shop with a large menu for those who wanted inexpensive meals and quick service; the Cottonwood, a hotel dining room for those on the American plan; and two gourmet restaurants—the Palm, a glass-walled gazebo just off the arcade, and Paloverde, a rooftop nightclub that overlooked the city and boasted the finest food in Phoenix.

Tonight, on Christmas Eve, the stark decor of Paloverde was softened by huge terra-cotta pots overflowing with white poinsettias. Tiny votive candles flickered gaily from one end of the room to the other. Bunches of red-ribboned mistletoe hung from chandeliers and doorways. Each table had at its center an arrangement of holly branches and pine. And ceiling-high ficus trees were strung with tiny white lights that blinked in concert with the stars, creating a magical setting for a young woman falling in love.

Jinx sat across from Kip. Their table, cornered between two expansive picture windows, made her feel as if they were floating. This was not the first time Jinx had dined at Paloverde, but tonight everything seemed special. The food had never tasted so good. The service had never been so attentive. The wine had never been so perfect. The room had never looked so glamorous.

"This has been a wonderful day, Frances Rebecca Jinx Elliot." Kip clinked his champagne glass to hers, and sipped slowly, watching her.

Throughout dinner, he had tried to keep himself from staring. Jinx was beautiful, and she excited him in a way that no other woman ever had, including Elizabeth. His wife had been as pretty, but in a delicate, ladylike way. She had been a pale blonde, petite, with a keen intellect and a droll sense of humor. But Elizabeth had been a shy beauty, embarrassed by compliments, ill-at-ease with too much attention. Kip used to think that in another era, she might have taken comfort behind the protective flutter of a lace fan.

Jinx wore her womanhood blatantly. Tonight, her black silk dress was mini length and decidedly spare. A dainty slip top formed a low V that tantalized Kip with hints of a strong, firm bosom, rounded and youthful. The high hemline accentuated long, slender legs that gleamed beneath sheer black hose. Her hair was a mass of springy, untamed curls. She wore no jewelry. Her scent was fresh. And her makeup was so artfully applied that it appeared as if she wore nothing except the berry-red lipstick that stained her mouth.

What appealed to Kip most was that she was so obviously unaware of her impact on him. Each time she leaned forward and her breasts pressed against her dress, he was tempted to think she was teasing him. Then he would look into those lavender eyes and see the innocent uncertainty, and he would know that only he was thinking about sex.

He was fighting it, but the nearness of this young woman made him feel as if he had inhaled a ray of sunshine. He felt like laughing even when nothing funny had been said. He felt like smiling even when she was discussing something serious. Still, Jinx was not yet twenty and he was over forty. She was his employee. He was her boss. No. He would not take advantage of her, but oh, how he would love to make love to her.

"Would you like some more champagne?" he asked, hoping the huskiness of his voice didn't betray his thoughts.

"No, thanks," Jinx said, wondering why she felt like blushing. "Not right now."

"Then how about teaching an old dog some new tricks on the dance floor?" He stood and extended his hand to her. "I warn you. My feet are extremely independent. They go where they want, when they want. I have absolutely no control over them."

He led her out of the restaurant, up the circular stairway to the nightclub. The dance floor was crowded with elegantly dressed guests and locals gyrating to a medley of Motown favorites. The captain led them to a table on the upper tier next to a window. Kip whispered something into the man's ear and within seconds, a waiter was popping open a new bottle of champagne.

Suddenly, the roof opened, revealing an enormous skylight. Oohs and aahs and a smattering of applause greeted Paloverde's newest contrivance. Instead of a ceiling, they were being treated to a glimpse of infinity.

Jinx turned to Kip, who was smiling like a delighted child.

"Do you like it?" he asked. "I saw this at a restaurant in Paris and loved it so much, I've had it installed in several of my southern hotels. What do you think?"

"If you'll pardon the pun," Jinx said, "I think it's heavenly!"

Kip laughed, pleased by her approval.

The band shifted to a slower tune and Kip invited Jinx onto the dance floor. The minute he took her in his arms, something electric passed between them. Without words or signals and without hesitation, Jinx slid next to him as if she belonged there, her head nestled close to his, her hand resting on the back of his neck. Kip encircled her waist, holding her so closely she could feel how uneven his breathing had become.

She, too, felt the current. His cologne filled her nose, swirling around her brain like an aphrodisiac. Her nerve endings pulsed with excitement, her muscles felt weak and unsure. All around the room, people stared at the striking young woman and the handsome older man, but Jinx was oblivious. The evening had become a fairy tale, and she was completely swept up in it, suspended in the timelessness of romance.

When the music changed tempo again, she wanted to stop it, to keep it soft and slow. Kip's sheepish grin told her he, too, was reluctant to let go. But the music grew louder, wilder, hotter, Jinx began to move with it, letting her body slither and slide. Kip thought she looked like a young filly—all lean and limber, her hair flying around her face, her hands raised above her head, her legs pumping in time to the beat. He didn't even try to keep up with her, but instead watched appreciatively, clapping his hands, thoroughly mesmerized by her performance.

As she twirled around, his imagination placed her next to him on a bed sheeted in creamy satin to match her complexion. He watched his fingers stroke the silken strands of her hair and touch the ivory coolness of her skin. He imagined her moving beneath him the way she was moving before him—without inhibition, without restraint. They were in a nightclub, yet watching her dance with such primitive abandon, under the open sky, he felt as if he were witnessing a tribal ritual celebrating a young girl's passage into womanhood.

When the music stopped, Jinx was momentarily disoriented and then embarrassed, as if she had just snapped out of a trance and had found herself standing naked in the middle of the street.

"I guess I got a little carried away."

"Nonsense! You were fabulous!"

On impulse, he pulled her to him and kissed her. His lips

tasted the softness of her mouth and for that brief instant, he forgot that they were standing in the center of the dance floor; he forgot that there were people watching them; he forgot that he had vowed never to get involved again. Then, there, it was only the two of them and the world was perfect.

The band began to play and reality crashed through.

"I'm taking you home now."

He was so abrupt, Jinx was certain she had offended him. Should she have apologized for dancing the way she had? Should she have kissed him differently? Should she have kissed him at all? Before she had time to say anything, he had taken her by the arm and was leading her toward the door.

"Let's go." His tone was parental and demanding. By instinct, Jinx obeyed, but long after he left her at her door, she wondered what had caused his sudden change of mood.

Spanning twenty tumultuous years, and moving from the glittering world of Paris high-fashion to the headquarters of a luxury hotel conglomerate, from the set of a prime-time TV sizzler to a major Senate race, Doris Mortman's FIRST BORN unfolds the lives of these four fascinating women in a novel the *Associated Press* hailed as, "Filled with romance, intrigue and suspense. It shouldn't be missed."

At the heart of Doris Mortman's novels are her women— Jennifer, Jinx, Gaby, and others—contemporary women, facing contemporary issues. Women challenged to balance their private and professional lives and find in themselves the strength to overcome their greatest fears. Discover Doris Mortman's world . . . for her world is yours.

CIRCLES and **FIRST BORN**
are available wherever Bantam paperbacks
are sold!

DON'T MISS
THESE CURRENT
Bantam Bestsellers

☐	28390	**THE AMATEUR** Robert Littell	$4.95
☐	28525	**THE DEBRIEFING** Robert Littell	$4.95
☐	28362	**COREY LANE** Norman Zollinger	$4.50
☐	27636	**PASSAGE TO QUIVIRA** Norman Zollinger	$4.50
☐	27759	**RIDER TO CIBOLA** Norman Zollinger	$3.95
☐	27814	**THIS FAR FROM PARADISE** Philip Shelby	$4.95
☐	27811	**DOCTORS** Erich Segal	$5.95
☐	28179	**TREVAYNE** Robert Ludlum	$5.95
☐	27807	**PARTNERS** John Martel	$4.95
☐	28058	**EVA LUNA** Isabel Allende	$4.95
☐	27597	**THE BONFIRE OF THE VANITIES** Tom Wolfe	$5.95
☐	27510	**THE BUTCHER'S THEATER** Jonathan Kellerman	$4.95
☐	27800	**THE ICARUS AGENDA** Robert Ludlum	$5.95
☐	27891	**PEOPLE LIKE US** Dominick Dunne	$4.95
☐	27953	**TO BE THE BEST** Barbara Taylor Bradford	$5.95
☐	26892	**THE GREAT SANTINI** Pat Conroy	$4.95
☐	26574	**SACRED SINS** Nora Roberts	$3.95

Buy them at your local bookstore or use this page to order.

Bantam Books, Dept. FB, 414 East Golf Road, Des Plaines, IL 60016

Please send me the items I have checked above. I am enclosing $_____
(please add $2.00 to cover postage and handling). Send check or money
order, no cash or C.O.D.s please.

Mr/Ms _____

Address _____

City/State _____ Zip _____

Please allow four to six weeks for delivery.   FB–4/90
Prices and availability subject to change without notice.